Catherine Cookson was born in East Jarrow on Tyneside and the place of her birth provides the background she so vividly creates in many of her novels. Although acclaimed as a regional writer – her novel THE ROUND TOWER won the Winifred Holtby Award for the best regional novel of 1968 – her readership spreads throughout the world. Her work has been translated into seventeen languages and her worldwide sales figures are over 85 million copies, over 40 million in English paperback alone.

Mrs Cookson was born the illegitimate daughter of a poverty-stricken woman, Kate, whom she believed to be her older sister. Catherine began work in service but eventually moved south to Hastings where she met and married a local grammar school master. At the age of forty she began writing with great success about the lives of the working class people of the North-East with whom she had grown up, including her intriguing autobiography, OUR KATE. Her many bestselling novels have established her as one of the most popular of contemporary women novelists.

Mrs Cookson now lives in Northumberland.

CATHERINE COOKSON

· KATIE · MULHOLLAND

Futura

A Futura Book

ISBN 0 7088 4425 1

Printed and bound in Great Britain by
Cox & Wyman Ltd, Reading

Futura Publications
A Division of
Macdonald & Co (Publishers) Ltd
Orbit House
1 New Fetter Lane
London EC4A 1AR
A member of Maxwell Macmillan Pergamon Publishing Corporation

To My Ain Folk

Acknowledgements

I would like to offer my grateful thanks to my husband who first suggested that I should write a story with Palmer's shipyard for a background. And to Mr. Adrian Palmer, who answered my request for information on his family background by spontaneously lending me books and giving me an unbiased opinion of his great-grandfather, Sir Charles Mark Palmer, who was the founder of Palmer's shipyard in Jarrow.

And to Mr. R. G. Wilson who spent many hours in many northern libraries delving for information covering the past hundred years in the North, and who transferred this information to me in so clear and so precise a manner.

Also to Miss Millie Petersen, who so unselfishly offered for my use material she had gathered over a number of years, together with cuttings and photographs passed on to her by her uncle, one-time photographer on the *Shields Daily Gazette*.

And lastly, but by no means least, to my secretary, Mrs. Muriel Johnson, for her hard work and unceasing efforts on my behalf.

However, I must explain that the story, as all my stories are wont to do, decided which line it intended to take, and from the beginning it dictated that this was to be the story of a woman's life, and the shipyard and the mines and the two towns but a backcloth for that theme. Yet without all the information so kindly gathered for me by the aforementioned I could not have written the life of Katie Mulholland.

CATHERINE COOKSON

LORETO,
HASTINGS,
March 1966.

Contents

BOOK I

Katie
1860

1

"I don't like marriage, Mama."

"You don't know what you're saying, child."

"I do, Mama, and I don't want to go back. I'm not going back."

Agnes Rosier shut out her reflection in the mirror by closing her eyes tightly. She also shut out the face of her seventeen-year-old daughter, her plain, nondescript daughter.

Only three months ago she had sat on this very seat and looked at herself in this mirror and said "Thank God". She had said it reverently, as befitted a good churchwoman. She had thanked Him for getting her daughter settled, the daughter she had imagined she was to be saddled with for the rest of her life. But the Almighty, who always answered her prayers, had arranged for Mr. Arnold Noble to come visiting in the vicinity. Mr. Arnold Noble was a man in his prime, a widower with two children. What caused the gentleman to become enamoured of her daughter, or which part of her had captivated Mr. Noble, Agnes Rosier did not question. Had she done so, she would immediately have ruled out her face and her manners, for neither the one nor the other had any claim to charm. There were plain women, she knew, whose features had a certain attractiveness, but not her daughter's. How this had come about was beyond her, for she herself was a handsome woman; and the proof of this lay in the fact that she had passed her benefits on to her eldest son, and a portion to her second son. Theresa took after her father, at least outwardly; whom she took after inwardly they had yet to discover, for whoever heard of a mineowner's daughter going to a Chartist meeting. They had thought they had heard the last of Chartists in 1855 when that madman O'Connor had died; but there was an element trying to revive itself in Newcastle and their own daughter had attended a meeting and dared to voice her views at the dining table. That any girl of seventeen should talk back to her father was unheard of, but that she should bring into the open a matter that was like a gaping wound in his side was so monstrous that she had feared on that particular occasion that Mr. Rosier would collapse. And if this wasn't enough, her own brother had espied her, three miles away on the fells, talking to groups of evicted miners from the village, trouble-makers, men who were more like savages and brutes than human beings. At the sight of his sister degrading herself Bernard's rage had been almost as great as his father's. To use his own words he had thrown her into the carriage. Mr. Rosier had confined his daughter to her room for a fortnight, and she, her mother, had had to bear the brunt of his tongue. What, he had demanded, had she bred him, a viper? A viper indeed. Then the Lord had provided Mr. Noble, to release them from their impossible predicament.

She herself had been in a constant state of nerves until the moment when the ceremony was over, and immediately the couple had left on their honeymoon she had drunk three glasses of champagne, one after the other—a thing she had never done in her life before. Following this, she had proceeded to enjoy the reception and could remember very little after two o'clock in the morning, only that everyone voted the occasion an outstanding success.

And now here was her daughter back home, on a visit presumably to attend the engagement ball of her eldest brother, and daring to tell her that she was not going to return to Mr. Noble.

She opened her eyes and looked through the mirror at the face that was staring at her. It was a thin face, thin cheeks, thin lips, thin eyebrows, thin light brown hair pulled so tightly back from her brow that it looked painful. But the main feature of her daughter's face was her thin nose. It poked itself outwards; it was a Rosier nose, a feature that she had always been ashamed of. Her husband bore this affliction, as his father had before him. His father had changed their name from Rosenberg to Rosier, but he could do nothing about his stamp of heritage.

She didn't like her daughter's face; she didn't like any part

4

of her daughter, and the thought of having her in the household again brought her swivelling round to confront her angrily.

"Now listen to me, Theresa. You are a married woman with responsibilities and you must face up to them."

"I've told you, Mama, I don't like . . ."

Agnes Rosier now held up her hand, and through the narrow aperture of her lips she hissed, "Would it surprise you to learn that few women do?"

They stared at each other. Then Agnes Rosier, composing herself and moistening her lips, asked, "Is it the children?"

"No; I like the children."

"Does . . . does he keep you short of anything? I understood he was of a generous nature?"

"He is."

Agnes looked down at her hands, lying one on top of the other on her taffeta petticoats. She did not want to ask the question, because she knew the answer; but if she did not ask it her daughter would tell her in any case, and she objected, as much as her husband did, to the free flow of words that emanated without let or hindrance from this child of theirs. It was much better to appear in control of the situation, and so she asked, "What is it you don't like about marriage?" She lowered her lids again as she waited for the answer. It came brief and terse, startling her, even although she had been aware of its substance.

"Intimacy."

"Theresa!" Agnes had her eyes wide open now. "We went into this a month ago. I gave you my advice. I . . . I told you to . . ." She could not go on and at the same time look at her daughter, so she swivelled round to the dressing-table again and began sorting some jewellery on a silver tray as if looking for a particular object, adding as she did so, ". . . to let Mr. Noble have his way, just . . . just be submissive, do nothing whatever. I . . . I told you." She glanced now through the mirror at the pale face behind her. "One gets used to it; you . . . you think of other things while it's going on."

"I'll never get used to it. I hate it, loathe it; I can't think of other things. I'm not putting up with it."

"Theresa!" Agnes was now on her feet. "Stop this nonsense once and for all. Where do you think you will go if you leave Mr. Noble's house?"

5

"I . . . I can come back here, I suppose, can't I?"

"No."

"You mean you wouldn't let me come home?"

"It isn't what I would do, it's your father. Under no consideration would he allow you to leave Mr. Noble."

"What if I leave him without his consideration? What if I just leave him? I've a hundred pounds a year of my own."

"Don't be ridiculous, child. How could you live on a hundred pounds a year after the life you've been accustomed to. Anyway, you're under age."

"You seem to forget, Mama, that I'm a married woman; I no longer come under the jurisdiction of Papa."

Agnes drew herself up to her full height, all of five foot eight. She held her hands stiffly by her sides, the fists clenched. "Do you want to bring disgrace on us? You'll set the whole county afire if you do this. And at this particular time, this crucial time . . . Theresa." She took in a long slow breath of air, then, bending slightly towards her daughter, her manner changing, she begged, "Please . . . please do nothing until after the wedding. Promise me, for if anything should happen to stop Bernard's marriage it will be the end of your father; he's relying on this liaison. In fact our whole future depends on our being joined to the Talfords. I . . . I told you weeks ago how things stood financially. Your father is a very worried man at the moment, so I beg you, if you are set on doing something drastic like this, wait. For my sake, wait."

For the first time since she entered the room Theresa took her eyes from her mother and, looking down, she said, "I'll do nothing until after the engagement party, but I can't promise to wait until they are married."

As Agnes Rosier stared at her daughter's bowed head there came to her a strange thought. Her daughter didn't look like a woman at all, there was nothing feminine in this creature before her. What, as Mr. Rosier had said, had she bred him?

With her four flounced petticoats making a sound like retreating waves on sand, she went swiftly towards the clothes closet, saying, "Leave me and send Stockwell in; I want to finish dressing . . . But, Theresa"—she swung sharply round again—"you won't leave the grounds, will you? I mean . . . Well, you know what I mean." Her voice was harsh. "No going into Jarrow, or Felling . . . Remember."

To this demand Theresa made no answer; she simply bowed her head and went out of the room.

6

She kept her head down as she went along the wide corridor that opened out into the gallery, and she did not raise it until she almost bumped into the first chambermaid.

Florrie Green was coming from a side passage that communicated, by a door, with the servants' staircase. She had a big wooden slop-bucket in her hand and "Pardon, mi . . . ma'am", she exclaimed, accompanying her words with a slight dipping of her buttocks. There was no deference in the action; it was merely a habit. Nobody was very deferential to Miss Theresa, or Mrs. Noble as she now was. Well, it was as Mr. Kennard said, she didn't keep her place. She spoke to you as if she was just like you, and it wasn't right.

Theresa paused on top of the wide oak stairway and looked down into the hall where Mrs. Davis, the housekeeper, was bustling about, and Kennard, the butler, was supervising two of the maids, directing how they should move a long oak chest, but never putting his hand on it to assist them. She descended to the middle landing, where the stairs turned at right angles into the hall. She paused a moment looking to the left of her across the hall and into the drawing-room. John Swan, the second coachman, and Albert Nash, the under-gardener, crossed her line of vision, one at each end of a long sofa. They were rearranging the furniture in the drawing-room, making it and the dining-room, adjoining and divided only by a portable partition, into a room large enough for the guests to stroll in and to eat and drink casually from well-laden tables lining the walls. Her mother had brought this idea of eating from London. It was, she said, called a buffet supper. The dancing would take place in the hall, and the musicians would be seated on a raised dais at the back; the gallery wasn't wide enough to accommodate them and allow for the passage of guests. This fact about the construction of the house had always irked her mother, as had these stairs, which she would have had circular. . . . One could never sweep down stairs that had a sharp bend; to do justice to a gown and a fine carriage one needed a circular staircase.

This cynical thought seemed to speed Theresa down the remaining stairs and into the hall. Walking quickly across it, and not looking at Kennard, but thanking him merely with a slight movement of her head when he opened the stained-glass door into the vestibule for her, she hurried through this large, tiled and chilly entrance and out into the sunshine. Still hurrying, almost at a tripping run now, she went down the five broad stone steps on to the drive.

The drive was wide and could take three coaches abreast. It was bordered directly in front by an ornamental privet hedge, not high enough to obscure the view of the gardens beyond. Yet the view was checkered by the contorted mass of sculptured trees. To the right of the house was the main drive; to the left, well to the left, was a high, ivy-covered wall, with an arch which led to the walks. Through this she now went. But she did not take any of the paths into the pleasure gardens, she walked by the wall which now became the back of the stables and courtyard. Beyond these the wall continued, covered with a mass of roses and clematis, and the scent of the roses was heavy in the hot morning air. She did not stop and bend towards their fragrance, as her mother would have done; she had no use for flowers. She did not like the garden; you cannot grow to love a prison, no matter how beautiful or sweet-smelling.

The wall ended where a copse began. It stopped abruptly, the sharp ends of the sandstone sticking out here and there from the creeper. It was as if the builders had suddenly run out of material. She continued through the copse and into a green pasture that ran steeply uphill, and not until she reached its summit did she stop. And then she turned and looked over the way she had come. She stared at the scene before her for fully five minutes; than slowly she sat down on the ground.

From where she sat she could see the whole of the back of the house, the stable yard, the courtyard, and the servants' quarters, where the male servants slept; the women had their rooms in the attics in the east wing. The house, like the wall, was made of stone, except for the ornamental pieces at the front which were picked out in red brick. Theresa had always considered it an ugly house, impressive but ugly. It was not large, as country houses went, and from the time she had first become conscious of her home she had never liked it; but now she had the urge to hold out her arms to it and say, "Take me back. Please, take me back."

She had looked on her marriage as a way of escape from the narrowness and hypocrisy of her family, and their friends; escape from her plainness and the pain it had caused. She had wondered during the last few weeks if she would have possessed the awareness to gauge her mother's real feelings for her and what went on behind her smiling face, and of those of the women who came to the house accompanied by loud, hearty-voiced men, if it hadn't been for Ainsley. Likely, as she grew older, she would have come to judge for herself, but she doubted whether she would have come to her present way of thinking at her age without the tutoring and guidance of her governess.

Ainsley had been a forcing house, like the one over there near the greenhouses where Mr. Wisden, the head gardener, performed miracles on plants with a stove-pipe. Ainsley had been her stove-pipe, and she thanked God for her. Yet, perhaps, without Ainsley she might have suffered this marriage. . . . No, no, never. The thing that she couldn't tolerate in this marriage had nothing to do with the mind. . . . But hadn't it? "Think of other things while it's going on," her mother had said. It seemed to her that without the mind this thing in itself would be nothing, or at least something that was over so quickly it was nothing more than a purge. She plucked at the grass, then raised her head and looked towards the house again and tried to recapture the times she and Ainsley had sat on this very spot, laughing at it and all that went on inside, from the kitchen to the drawing-room. The jealousies, the pettiness, the striving for place, the pomp. Ainsley had taught her to see things as they really were.

She had been five years old when Ainsley came into her life. She could remember the day when she first saw the tall, thin woman and realised that Ainsley was plain-looking. That was before she became aware that she herself was saddled with the same complaint. Ainsley was thirty when she came to Greenwall Manor. She was forty-two when she left it, on the day following their secret, exciting visit to the meeting on the Newcastle Town Moor, when the cavalry came and rode into the thousands of people, and they had run with the rest and almost been trampled to death. It was there they had been seen by Mr. Careless, a magistrate and friend of her father's.

Ainsley had been turned out in disgrace and without a reference. For who could give a reference to a governess who had corrupted a young mind? That's what her mother had said. Her father had said much more and his language had been much stronger, for had not the woman made him a laughing-stock by inveigling his daughter to attend Chartist

9

meetings, and making her an open sympathiser with the rebel and scum in his own pit?

Ainsley had refuted nothing her employer had accused her of, and she had dared to stand up to him and say that she was proud she had enabled one of his family to think for herself, and that he, too, should be proud that he had one intelligent person among the dunderheads in his household.

She had known what it was to die when she saw Ainsley being driven away from the door. She hadn't been allowed any word with her; she was locked in her room, but she had hammered on the window and Ainsley had lifted her joined hands towards her. They said, "Be strong. Be strong." She had tried to be strong, but it was difficult without Ainsley's support. She had begun by proposing setting up a weekly class in the village to teach the miners to read and write. When her mother had recovered sufficiently she had said, "Child, do you think a miner would go down a mine if he could read and write correctly? Do you want your father's business to collapse? Do you want us to starve? Never let such a proposal come to your father's ears, it could cause him to have a seizure."

Then Mr. Noble came on the scene.

Theresa now experienced a sickness in the pit of her stomach; her whole body shrank inwardly, for even sitting on this hilltop she could actually feel his hands on her. He always wanted to touch her; wherever they met, even at the dining-table, his hand would come out and touch her. But there was one thing that puzzled, even amazed, her about Mr. Noble. It was the fact that he cared for her. Perhaps caring wasn't the right word, but innately she knew she held an attraction for him. Was it just her extreme youth? It certainly wasn't her looks, or her charm, or even her conversation, for she found she couldn't talk to this fat, greasy-looking man, who had stubble all round his face if he didn't shave twice a day, and whose lower lip was soft and moist and whose head was going bald, and whose stomach, without the support of his belt, bulged.

She was on her feet again, looking about her, diverting her thoughts from her husband. There, far away to the left, she could see the headings of her father's mine; and farther away still, where the land fell into the valley, another heading. That was the dead head of the Jarrow mine which had been closed down. To the side of it was the silver thread of the river Don hurrying towards the Tyne—the busy, bustling Tyne.

She had not been along the banks of the Tyne more than half a dozen times in her life, but these brief visits had filled her with excitement. There was so much to see, for what had once been a mining village no bigger than the village attached to her father's mine was fast becoming a town. Already the old salt-pans were going, as were the coke ovens that spread along the river bank and whose waste heat had kept the salt-pans working. A paper mill was now flourishing on the river bank, as also were three chemical works.

Then there was the main industry on the river, the industry that made her wish at times she had been born a boy. This was Palmer's Shipyard. She knew quite a bit about the Palmer brothers and their shipyard—at least her father's opinion of them, for the Palmer brothers were like a thorn in his flesh, yet a thorn that he wanted to drive deeper, for he wanted, above all things, to be close to the Palmers, to be attached to them in such a way that whatever profits their new and thriving concern would make he would have a share in them. It was primarily because of this that her brother Bernard was marrying Ann Talford.

The Talfords were very rich. They had a house three times the size of Greenwall; also James Talford had his fingers in all kinds of pies, including boat building, and he was a personal friend of the Palmers. She understood from things that had been let drop, mostly from her brother Rodger, that James Talford didn't like her father and had opposed this match with his only child. But, as Rodger said, Mr. Talford had found himself thawed by two weapons, both used against him with effect. The first was he loved his daughter and would do anything to further her happiness; the second was the tenacity of her suitor.

For three years Bernard had wooed Ann, and in so doing had apparently become a reformed character, for once there had been loud whispers about his escapades, and not only with regard to gambling; but now her brother was supposedly a steady, sober man of twenty-six, and James Talford, a strict churchman, could no longer put forward any arguments against the marriage.

Today was Friday and on Tuesday the engagement ball was to be held, and in four months' time, early in October, the wedding would take place. Could she suffer Mr. Noble for another four months? Theresa shook her head slowly. Not unless she locked herself away at night. And she couldn't do that either, for there were the servants; and whereas the servants in her old home did not exactly like her, the servants in her new home took no more notice of her than if she was one of her husband's hounds. Were she to ask for a key to a room, they would, she knew, merely refer her to Mr. Noble.

Yet it wasn't true that all the servants here didn't like her; there were two who did, three in fact. There was Mrs. Davis, the housekeeper; Katie Mulholland, the scullery-maid; and Tatman, the head coachman. They liked her, and she liked them. But of the three, she liked Katie Mulholland best. Katie had been the only other young thing in the house that one could look at, and like looking at. It was strange the pleasure she had always got from looking at Katie Mulholland.

As if her thinking had drawn the substance of it from out of the house, she now saw the unmistakably thin figure of Katie Mulholland staggering from the side door of the kitchen with a large wooden bucket in each hand. The door led to the attic stairs down which it was one of Katie's daily chores to carry the maids' slops. She watched the figure crossing the yard. Then she was lost to her sight for a moment until she emerged through the arch in the long wall. She watched her staggering to the bottom of the kitchen garden; then she saw her tipping up her buckets into the trough that led down to the cesspit. Her nose wrinkled and she closed her eyes for a moment. "The indignities that were heaped upon human beings." Those were Ainsley's words, but they were her own sentiments.

She now heard, from the far end of the drive, the sound of hooves and she looked away from the small scullery-maid to see her father's coach racing up the drive. She wondered what had brought him back at this time in the morning. Trouble at the mine? More than likely; there was always trouble at the mine.

2

George Daniel Rosier was a small man, at least two inches
shorter than his wife. He had a swarthy dark complexion,
thin grizzled hair, round eyes which could be likened to jet
beads, and then his main feature, his nose, a large bony protrusion dominating his face. Physically he had no presence,
but he made himself felt by his temper and his tongue, and
both were feared by every member of his household, except
perhaps his eldest son and his only daughter. He leapt
straight out of the carriage and up the steps, pushing his butler to one side and crying, "Get Mr. Bernard. And now!"

He stormed across the hall towards the library door, but
with the knob in his hand he turned round and cried to Kennard, "Where is he?"

"I think he's in his room, sir."

"In his room!" The nose jerked itself upwards in disdain,
taking the rest of the face with it, as he thrust open the door.

The library was a long, high room, lined with books from
floor to ceiling, and never in the thirty years that George Rosier had lived in this house had he disturbed one of them. At
the end of the room were four tall windows which faced the
drive, and in front of the middle two was a large bog-oak
desk, covered with a disarray of papers and letters. To the
right, in the middle of one long wall, was a huge fireplace,
and although the day was warm, even hot outside, a wood
fire was burning in the iron basket.

George Rosier stood glaring down at the fire for a moment; then he turned his back to it, put his hand under his
coat tails and flapped them angrily upwards and, marching to
the table, scattered papers here and there until he found what
he was looking for. He was reading the letter when the door
opened and his son, Bernard, entered.

Bernard Rosier was tall—taller than his mother by five
inches. His complexion was dark, as were his eyes; his face
and body, like his mother's, were inclined to heaviness, yet

13

his lips and nostrils were thin. Altogether he looked a handsome man, a gloweringly handsome man.

"Where the hell 've you been?"

"In my room." The reply was cool, and there was no trace of annoyance on Bernard's face at his father's tone.

"At this time in the morning? It's no wonder we're in the devil of a mess."

"I was at the works until seven o'clock last night."

"That's no reason to sleep abed till eleven in the morning."

"I wasn't abed. Nor was I abed at seven o'clock this morning. I've been exercising Falstaff, after which I had a rub down."

"You and your rubbing down. This is no time for riding or rubbing down. Rubbing down at eleven in the morning." He snorted. "It's a time for action. Those buggers are going on strike again."

"Well, you knew that yesterday."

"Don't stand there being so bloody cool—of course I knew that yesterday. At least I expected it. But I thought I'd put a spoke in their wheel and the fear of God into them. I told Brown to set the word around there was a boatload of Irish coming in, but that Fogerty and Ramshaw have started spouting again. If we can't keep to the schedule Palmer'll drop us; he'll just transport our coal when he's slack. He's already too big for his boots. God, if only I was on that board." He stumped one stubby fist into the palm of his hand, while his son surveyed him calmly for a moment, before saying, "You should have bought the shares when you had the opportunity."

"Don't say that. I've warned you, don't you say that to me again." George Rosier turned a purple countenance upon his son. "I've told you before. Eight years ago I was in no position to buy shares of any kind. I was just keeping my head above water, literally so, the water in the mine. . . . Anyway"—he flung round and glared into the fire—"who on earth would have thought a hare-brained scheme of iron ships driven by steam would have proved successful? The steam had failed before, the price it entailed was prohibitive; the whole combination seemed fantastic, except as an experiment."

Bernard Rosier wiped the tiny beads of perspiration from his upper lip as he stared at his father's back. Who would have thought? Now he wanted to say, "Don't say that to me again." He was sick of hearing that phrase repeated and repeated over the years. He knew what he would have done if he'd had any say eight years ago; he would have borrowed money and bought shares in the hare-brained scheme; hundreds and hundreds of them, thousands and thousands of them. Even if his common or business sense hadn't told him he was on to a good thing, his gambling instincts, he felt sure, would have guided him.

He was a youth of eighteen, eight years ago, when on a June day in 1852 he had stood with his father in Palmer's Yard and watched the launching of the *John Bowes*; and many besides his father thought it was money being thrown to the wind on nothing more than an expensive experiment, for up to this time sailing vessels were the cheapest form of transport. But they were to be proved wrong. On her first voyage the *John Bowes* carried six hundred and fifty tons of coal to London, discharged it and was back on the Tyne in five days. What she had done in five days would have taken two sailing colliers close on a month to accomplish. Palmer was set fair.

Now, eight years and many ships and a great growth of the town later, there was talk of turning Palmer's into a limited liability company, and before that happened Bernard Rosier knew that his father would be in that company or die in the attempt. And he might just do that, for it would not surprise him should his father collapse during one of his spasms of rage and so end it. But he really wasn't concerned about what happened to his father. The old man, as he thought of him, irritated him beyond endurance. But he must bide his time until October, and with his marriage would come money and, what was of equal importance, influence. For had not his future father-in-law been a life-long friend of Charles Palmer's father, and was he not now mentor to the said Charles Palmer? Oh, give him a year at the outside and the boardroom of Palmer's would be open to him. And not only the boardroom, but all the other concerns that Charles Mark Palmer had an interest in.

At this point in his thinking the door opened and his brother, Rodger, entered. Rodger was a young man of twenty, of medium height, with fair brown hair and eyes to match. His expression was gentle, yet alive. If his sister had been born with his features she would have grown up to be pretty, and if he had taken on hers he would have been dubbed a keen, attractive-looking man. "I'm sorry," he said, "I didn't know you were using the library."

"Come in, come in. Don't stand there waverin'." His father made a wide sweeping gesture with his hand which held the letter. Then as his younger son came slowly forward he thrust the letter towards Bernard, saying, "Look at that, an inspection . . . an inspector coming."

Bernard Rosier read the letter, then handed it back to his father, saying, "We only wanted this. You can't get into number-two working unless you swim, and if they stop work, as they've threatened, it'll be the middle gallery next."

"It won't, it won't!" George Rosier tugged at the ends of his coat to meet in front of his chest. "I'll see them in hell first; I'll see them gnawing their arms off, as they nearly did two years back, before they get the better of me. I'll do as we all did then; I'll bring in the labour. And this time, if I bring it in, it'll stay . . . every man-jack will stay, and my loyal workers can rot watching them feed and sleeping in their houses . . . Thankless lot of scum." He flung the letter from him, aiming at the desk. It missed and fluttered down to the floor. Rodger picked it up and laid it gently on the top of the pile of papers; then, turning and looking at his father and brother, he said in a quiet, almost apologetic tone, "Wouldn't it be easier in the long run if you all got your heads together and tried to rectify the damage done by the Percy Main flooding?"

"Don't talk bloody nonsense, Rodger. Why should I pay out hard cash, even if I had it to spare, on helping to keep the water down in other buggers' mines when they never show their nebs outside of London, at least not in this direction. No, they sit tight and enjoy life. I'm about the only bloody fool in this county squatting on my mine shaft, up to my chin in debt, worry, and danger. Yes, an' I say danger, for that mob down there are half maniacs. If I had my way I would chain them up. The Bishop of Durham knew what he was doing when he manacled them to the mangers. Look." He turned and pointed to Bernard. "Go down and tell Bunting that he's got to get rid of Ramshaw and Fogerty. I don't care how he does it—I'll leave that to him. He's got to earn his money somehow. It's about time he did. . . ." He stopped abruptly, pressed his hand on the top of his stomach, bent forward, then gave a mighty belch of wind. "I'm . . .

I'm going to Newcastle to see Bullard; I want a draught for this." He patted his stomach again. "Nearly driving me mad. Now do as I say." He thrust his finger towards Bernard; then, turning abruptly from his sons, he marched out of the room.

The brothers looked at each other. Then Bernard, again wiping the moisture from his upper lip, walked to the window and said, "How would you like it every day?"

"I wouldn't."

"You're lucky."

"Yes, I suppose I am. In fact, I know I am." Rodger's eyes roamed up and down the long rows of books, and again he repeated, "Yes, I'm lucky," but to himself this time.

Rodger had just come down on vacation from Oxford. How he had ever got to Oxford was still a surprise to him. When he thought of his father and brother, and he often did, their whole life spent in extracting money from the mine, he wondered how he had escaped. He wondered why they had allowed him to escape from the commercialism, from the degradation of thrusting men and boys into the bowels of the earth, literally to drag out the coal by hand, then to deprive them, by trickery—and this was openly done through the master weighman, such as Mark Bunting—of a portion of their small earnings which at best were not sufficient to support a way of life that it was generally supposed God had willed they should have.

Apparently God had willed that his parents could live no other way but in this house, with its farm and thirty acres of grounds, its twenty servants, not counting the lodge-keeper and farmhands. Yet, with all this, he knew that his parents were not entirely satisfied with their way of life. It wasn't luxurious enough, at least for his mother, nor held enough prestige for his father.

His father had built the miners' cottages in the village, and he ran the grocery shop, and most of the wages that he paid his men came back to him through the shop. You could say he owned the village, but that wasn't enough. His father wanted power and Bernard wanted power. They were social climbers of the first water, and, in a way, that was the reason they had allowed him to go to Oxford. A son, and brother, who could be dubbed a scholar would be an asset in this commercial-ridden district. It would also be something to be scornful about, even though the scorn could be seen merely as a thin cover for the pride of an association with learning.

Oh yes, Rodger knew why he had been allowed to go to Oxford. He wasn't a strong-willed young man like his brother, but he was a discerning one, and he knew on which side his bread was buttered.

"I've got a new hunter."

"What?" Rodger turned, screwing his eyes up against the light to look at his brother.

"I said I've got a new hunter, a chestnut."

Rodger shook his head slowly and smiled to himself. They hadn't any money, they were up to their eyes, didn't know where to turn, but Bernard had got a new hunter.

"Come and see her?"

Without saying anything more Bernard walked down the long room, and Rodger followed him. They crossed the hall towards a passage that ran to the far right of the stairs, and at the end of it Bernard, going first, stepped through a doorway, straight into the courtyard and Katie Mulholland.

As the girl went sprawling on the rough cobble-stones and the two buckets of kitchen slops she was carrying spewed about her, Bernard let out a series of oaths, ending with, "Blind, blasted fool of a girl!" He glared down at his bespattered breeches and the still figure lying at his feet, the hem of her print skirt around the back of her knees exposing her thin white-hosed calves. One arm was stretched out, the hand still gripping the handle of a bucket; the other hand, pressed against the stones, was cupping her face.

Katie Mulholland remained motionless, not daring to lift her head. It was as if God had rended the heavens and was towering over her. And indeed it could have been, for was it not Mr. Bernard who was speaking, and, without looking, she knew that she had messed up his breeches. Anything could befall her for this, anything. It had all happened because she had got such a gliff, for who would think Mr. Bernard would come through the side door at this time of day. He had come so fast he had knocked her over . . . Eeh no! She'd better not say he had knocked her over; she had slipped.

"Come along, get up. It's all right." She was pulled upwards, and through her stretched fingers she peered at Mr. Rodger. Mr. Rodger was smiling. He looked her up and down and said, "You are in a mess. Go and get yourself cleaned up. What's your name again?"

"Katie, sir." She remembered to bob.

"Well, go and have a wash under the pump, Katie, and get that stuff off you." He wrinkled his nose.

"Yes, sir." Slowly she drew her hand from her face and glanced to where Bernard was now entering the stables across the yard. Perhaps . . . perhaps she wouldn't get it in the neck if she could get it cleaned up before Cook saw her. She bobbed again and said, "Thank you, sir," gave a dive to the left and then to the right, retrieving the buckets, turned and ran across the courtyard and round the corner to the pump, and there, pumping like mad, she filled the buckets with water, brought them back to the yard and sprayed the contents, with a quite expert fling, over the cobbles. This done, she quickly picked up the soggy crusts, bacon skins and bones and other refuse scattered around her, then ran down the length of the courtyard, through the archway in the wall and emptied the depleted contents of the buckets in a pig-swill trough. Within seconds she was back at the pump splashing her face and hands and rubbing down the front of her dress. She had taken off her coarse apron—she could put a clean one on and wash this one later. There—she looked down at herself—that wasn't so bad. If only Cook hadn't missed her. The next minute she was in the kitchen pushing the empty buckets under the wooden sink, making sure that one of them was directly under the bunghole.

Out of the corner of her eye she looked towards Cook who was standing at the far end of the long white table which ran down the centre of the enormous kitchen. Apparently she hadn't heard the commotion. She was in a good temper the day. Katie sighed, then, seating herself on a cracket that was placed opposite a sawn-off wooden barrel filled with potatoes, she began her daily task of peeling them.

Katie had started in the Rosier kitchen when she was eleven. She was now fifteen and the dirtiest, longest and most dreary tasks were still hers. She didn't especially mind, except when Dotty Black, the kitchen-maid, got the scraps to take home. After all, she told herself, she was earning a shilling a week and was, moreover, the favourite of Mrs. Davis, the housekeeper.

The cook's voice, coming at her now, startled her. "Haven't you got that lot done yet?"

"Nearly, Cook."

"You done the turnips?"

"Yes, Cook, an' I cut some with the star cutter and some with the three-cornered one."

"This'll drive me mad." Cook now placed a frill around a mayonnaise of turbot done in aspic; then, carrying the dish to a long narrow table that was attached to the length of one wall, she said, "You'd think they'd pick something easier with all I've got facin' me, and only four days to do it in. You'd think they'd give me extra down here, but no, no, take what little I've got to help upstairs. I'm not standin' it much longer."

Katie, besides listening attentively to the cook's yammering, slanted her eyes to the colourful array of dishes on the long board. They were having cold upstairs the day, for lunch anyway, but there wouldn't be anything left of that lot, not after it went to the housekeeper's room and Mr. Kennard and Miss Stockwell had a go at it. But from the dinner the night there should be some over. The first course was soup, and then there was whitebait, and next there was boiled capon and tongue, and stuffed vegetable marrow and four other vegetables; they would finish up with a choice of three puddings—one was a fruit salad. She felt sure that Mrs. Davis would save her some of the scraps if she could, to take home with her. She remembered suddenly that tomorrow was wage-day, and that on Sunday afternoon she could take her month's wages home.

Oh, how she wanted to go home; she wanted to see her ma and da, and her granda and their Joe and Lizzie, and to tell them everything, all about the preparation for Mr. Bernard's engagement ball; about the people who had been invited; about the food, the beautiful food; about the chickens, ducks and geese that were hanging up in the cold room; about the pigs that had been killed, and the smoked hams that had been brought in from the wood room; about the gallons of cream being made and the hundreds of eggs that were coming to the kitchen daily; and then there was that great crate of cheeses that had been sent all the way from London. And she wanted to tell them about falling with the slop buckets in the yard and splashing Mr. Bernard's breeches. Eeh, she had been scared out of her wits. But now she could laugh at it, and when she was home and she told them how it had happened she would make them all laugh; she could always make them laugh. Her granda would laugh loudest of all because he had no respect for the gentry; her granda was awful in that way.

"Come on, come on. Don't spend all day sittin' there on your backside."

Katie's head jerked towards the cook as she said, "Nearly finished, Cook. Just two more."

"You've taken your time. Now get those pots scoured." She pointed to the side of the hearth where were standing, one on top of the other, three piles of copper cooking pots. "And I said scoured, mind—and put more sand in than salt. I want them bright."

And so for Katie the day went on, a succession of dreary tasks, each one more depressing than the last, until some time after nine she had finished and she took her candle and went to bed.

In the winter they were allowed two candles a week, in the summer one, and although Katie never used all her candles, for she was almost walking in her sleep by the time she reached the attic, there was no chance of taking the ends home because they had to be given in before she could get a new one. She was sorry about this because the ends would have been a great help, especially in the long winter nights and her da wanting to read and teach some of the men their letters the same way as he had been taught by Mr. Burns, the preacher.

But, anyway, nothing mattered at the moment but the fact that it was wage-day the morrow and on Sunday she was going home. She crossed her two index fingers to placate the gods, and a spurt of joy rushed through her, lighting up her face and giving to her body the urge to leap into the air.

* * *

On Saturday morning George Rosier, sitting behind the long desk in the library, looked down at the leather bag that was spewing sovereigns. This monthly occasion always brought on a peculiar pain behind his ribs. The fact that in the course of a year he was doing each member of his staff out of a month's wages did not ease his pain. He considered it was bad enough when he had to pay his miners, although he admitted that some of them, just some of them, earned it. But, in this particular case, to hand out money to people, particularly females, whom he not only housed but clothed and fed, made his bile rise.

He thrust his hand out and pulled on a thick, twisted and

tasseled red bell-pull. The next moment Kennard opened the door and stood waiting, and when his master said "Right!" he inclined his head over his shoulder, then entered the room, followed by Mrs. Davis, Jane Stockwell, Frank Tatman, the first coachman and James Wisden, the head gardener.

Mary Davis advanced with her sedate walk to the desk. She made a slight dip with her knees, then waited. She watched her master separate a gold sovereign and a half a sovereign from the pile on the table, add to it a florin and push these towards her, saying, "One pound twelve shillings." She watched her master sorting money into small piles. And these he began pushing towards her, consulting a list in his hand as he did so, and barking, "Fanny Croft, sixteen shillings. Daisy Studd, twelve shillings. Florrie Green, fourteen shillings. Mary Ann Hopkins, seven shillings. Delia Miller, one pound. Dorothy Black, eight shillings. Ivy Walker, eight shillings. Betty Taggart, eight shillings. Kate McManus, four shillings. Katie Mulholland, four shillings. . . . There." He pushed the list of names towards her. "Get their marks. By the way . . ." His big nose jerked and his face puckered, and now he stabbed his finger towards the last name and, looking at Mrs. Davis, said, "This one, Mulholland. Can she write?"

"Yes, sir."

"And read?"

"Yes, sir."

"Who taught her?" He was looking at Mrs. Davis under his lids now, and she hesitated for a long moment before saying, "Her father, I think."

He considered her while he thought: Big Mulholland, reading and writing. He'd have to remember that. That's how trouble started. He now made an impatient movement with his hand, and Mrs. Davis gathered the money on to a salver that was lying ready on the desk, and picking up the paper and making an almost imperceivable bob she turned away and made room for Jane Stockwell.

One at a time, the household staff stepped forward to receive their payment.

When the men had left the room Patrick Kennard stepped up to the desk, and his master pushed towards him two golden sovereigns. It was fitting, at least to Mr. Kennard, that he should receive his wages apart from the rest of the staff, and no one should know what he earned. His master looked at him as he made his mark and he wondered at the incongruity of the situation where the chief member of his staff could only identify himself by two crossed lines whereas the least of his staff could sign her name.

When George Rosier was alone again he looked at the sum total of what he had paid out. It amounted to sixteen pounds eight shillings. Sixteen pounds eight shillings, to which was added their keep, and their clothing. And this wasn't counting the farm-hands, or the lodge. Yet it was a mere flea-bite to the overall expenses of the house. And where was it all coming from?

And then those blasted savages down there threatening to strike because of unfair treatment by the keeker who had fined them for short corves. Why had he to have this trouble? A few miles away in the Felling pit they had nothing like this. It was true what a magistrate had said recently: the natural place for the Jarrow and Hebburn toughs was underground, and they should be kept there; for most of them were just evolving from the slime. And, by God, he was right.

3

Katie was ready to go. She had clean clothes on right to her shift, and at the neck of her best print frock was the brooch that had belonged to her grandmother, and sitting straight on the top of her thick shining hair was the hat with the daisies on that Mrs. Davis had given her last year.

She smoothed down the front of her dress that fell to the top of her boots; then her eyes stayed for a moment on her hands. They were red and swollen, the nails worn down to the flesh, but they were as clean as a floor scrubbing-brush and hot soda water could get them.

She gave a last look at her corner of the attic to see that she had left everything tidy, in case Mrs. Davis had a walk round. Then she went downstairs to the housekeeper's room, knocked on the door and went in.

The housekeeper was not wearing her cap at this moment, and she looked funny to Katie without it. Her greying hair was drawn back from her forehead, her round face with its high colour had a criss-cross of faint lines covering it, but her body was slim and trim and youngish-looking. She drew Katie to her with an outstretched hand, saying, "Oh, you look nice and tidy, Katie." She did not say, "You look beautiful"; it wouldn't have done. There were times when it pained her to look at this lovely child, especially when she had been younger and she'd seen her dropping with fatigue late at night. She touched the brooch at Katie's neck saying, "That sets you off, Katie. You look grand."

Katie smiled at Mrs. Davis, the delicate mould of her lips stretching to show her even teeth.

Mrs. Davis's fingers moved upwards to Katie's cheek. Its texture was as smooth as satin and its colour was like thick cream with a blush on it. But it was the child's eyes that made the whole face what it was; there was something rare about them. She had never seen another pair of eyes in a human head like them. It wasn't because they were green or heavy-lashed, there was something more. There was a kind of starriness about them, a dewy starriness. And then her hair topping it all, its dark chestnut waves throwing out gold gleams here and there. Her figure, too, was getting to be noticeable. As yet it was too thin, but her bust had developed even in the last month. She put her finger gently in the centre of it, saying, "You've got your money safe, Katie?"

"Yes, Mrs. Davis." Katie nodded her head. "I've pinned it in me bag."

"That's right. Well, now, I've got one or two things here." She went to a chest of drawers and took out several small flattish packages, and when Katie lifted up her dress and top petticoat Mrs. Davis inserted them one after the other in the two side pockets attached to the inside of her under petticoat. "These," she said, holding two packages up to Katie, "are a little tea and sugar. It's my own, out of my allowance."

"Oh yes, Mrs. Davis, I know, I know." Katie was quick to assure her benefactor that she did not for a moment think the stuff was cribbed from the staff's allowance.

"And this is a little bit of ham and tongue left from my supper last night; and this is my pudding from today; and these are some pieces of capons."

The capons, Katie noticed, was the largest packet of all. Cook had grumbled last night because so little had come out

24

of the housekeeper's room, and there was the reason. Merriment rose in her when she thought that through the ingenuity of Mrs. Davis she herself had got one up on the cook.

"There now, you're all ready." The housekeeper touched Katie's cheek again. "Give my kind regards to your mother and tell her I said you were doing splendidly and are a very good girl."

"Oh . . . oh thanks, Mrs. Davis. Thanks. I will, I will. An' thank you for all the things." She whispered the last words.

Mrs. Davis jerked her head sideways as one confederate to another. Then, pressing her towards the door, she said, "And you'll be back by six?"

"Yes, Mrs. Davis."

"That's a good girl. Don't depend upon meeting a trap or any of the carts to give you a lift, mind; set out in time."

"I will, Mrs. Davis. Goodbye and thank you. Thank you very much."

"Goodbye, child. . . ."

The day was hot, the sky blue and high. After she had passed through the wicket gate at the end of the grounds she ran along the rough track until she began to sweat; then for a time she walked, hitching once or twice because she felt happy. Once she laughed out aloud, then clapped her hands over her mouth and shook her head.

The track widened to a rough road and was going steeply uphill now, and when she reached the summit she stopped. She always stopped at this point for a minute because she could see for miles about her, even more than you could from the hill behind the house. To the right and left of her lay wide expanses of grassland and fells, and in the far distance was a dark huddled blur—that was Jarrow. And there was the river. She could just make out the slim outlines of the masts of the ships, and the funnels too, big round chimneys stuck in the middle of the boats.

Now she was running again, and she continued to run, until she caught a glimpse of the first row of whitewashed cottages and she knew that she would be home within three minutes.

There were eight rows of cottages in the village, each containing twenty dwellings of two rooms each. The Mulhollands' house was number twelve in the first row, and the first row faced the moor. There was only a twelve-foot width of powdery roadway, which turned into a quagmire in wet weather, between the doorway and the wide-open grassy slopes.

The situations of the first and last rows of cottages were enviable ones in the summer. In the winter they bore the brunt of the open blast from the fells. And the row where the Mulhollands lived in particular took the full force of the flood-water that came down from the hills. But today there was no flood-water, there was only sunshine, and dust, and a strong smell from the middens.

Catherine Mulholland was waiting at the door for her daughter. She resisted the urge to run towards her. She didn't want the neighbours to talk. They did enough of that, always showing surprise that Katie should continue to return every other Sunday from the big house where she was living in luxury to a pit cottage. Of course this came from them who had daughters in the rope works, or, worse still, scraping cinders from the pans or tips. And she could understand this. Oh yes, she could understand this envy, for hadn't she felt the same towards the more fortunate at the time when Katie, from the age of seven, had gathered cinders until her fingers ran blood.

"Oh, hello, Ma."

"Hello, me bairn." Catherine moved back into the framework of the door; then opened her arms and Katie went into them and hugged her mother round the waist. And after a moment, while they stood still together, she lifted her head and looked at her mother; then turned her eyes and glanced through the half-opened door into the room, to where she could see the outline of men, and hear the buzz of conversation.

Her mother's head came down to her and she whispered, "It's Mr. Ramshaw and Mr. Fogerty."

The smile slipped from Katie's face and, her eyes stretching, she said one word, "Trouble?" and watched her mother nod once. Then she asked in an apprehensive whisper, "Are they out?"

"Not yet, but I think they're comin'." Her voice very low, she explained quickly. "Your dad was due for thirty shillings and he only got twenty-one, and for a fortnight's work. They said his corves were short. But he's not come off so badly as the others. It's been a bad patch all round. Mr. Ramshaw was off two days bad. They said he wasn't bad. That was Bunting again. He couldn't have earned more than four shillings if he'd been there, but they fined him twelve. They've all had it one way or the other this last few weeks. It can't go on." She shook her head slowly as Katie stared at her. Then she whispered again, "They won't be long; they're goin' to the chapel in a few minutes. But come on, see your da."

She drew her daughter around the door and into the room, and there three men and a boy faced her. All were smiling at her. Rodney Mulholland, a tall man of thirty-nine with big, deep-sunken eyes, hollow cheeks and brown hair, stepped towards her, saying, "Hello, me lass." He placed his hands tenderly on her shoulders and she looked at him and said, "Hello, Da." Katie knew she took after her da. Her da was a fine man; stern, but fine. But today his face looked old, and tired.

"How are you keepin'?"

"Fine, Da."

"Good. Good." He took his hands from her shoulders and they gazed at each other for a moment longer. Then she turned to her brother and said, "Hello, Joe."

Joe was a year younger than herself, thin like his father and with the same colouring. She noticed that his face was whiter than usual and he too looked tired. Then her father was saying to her, "You know Mr. Fogerty and Mr. Ramshaw."

"Yes." She nodded at each man in turn, smiling broadly.

"Hello, Katie," they said one after the other. Then Mr. Fogerty, a small, thick-set man, with an Irish lilt to his voice, said, "You get bonnier every day, Katie."

Katie did not reply but drooped her head and shook it from side to side.

"You're right there, Dennis," said Ramshaw, nodding towards his friend.

"Enough of that. Enough of that." It was her father speaking, his tone jocular yet with a reprimand in it. "We don't want her head turned." Then, lifting her chin upwards with his bony fingers, he said, "I won't be more than half an hour; I want to hear you read." His look held admiration.

"Yes, Da. All right."

"We'll away then." Rodney Mulholland jerked his head towards his two companions, and after making their farewells they left the house.

Immediately the door had closed Katie said, "I've brought some bits, Ma."

"Have you, lass?" Catherine stood by the little table looking at her daughter, and Katie, turning her back on her brother, lifted up the front of her skirt and petticoat and brought the little packages from their hiding-place. "There's nearly two ounces of tea, Ma."

"Oh!" Catherine held the small package on her hand and gazed at it as if looking at gold dust. And at sixpence an ounce at the company's shop—the Tommy-shop, as it was called—it was to her like gold dust.

"And that's sugar; and that's ham; and there's some chicken; and Mrs. Davis saved her puddin'. I think she was thinking of Joe and Lizzie." She turned and smiled warmly at her brother, then said, "Where's Lizzie and Granda; has he taken her out?"

Her mother shook her head. "Lizzie's in the room," she said. "It's better so with company." She nodded at Katie; then added, "Your Granda's gone out after larks . . ." She bowed her head swiftly and pressed her teeth into her bottom lip, saying, "I'm sorry, lass; I needn't have told you that. But, you see, he's got to do somethin', and it makes him feel a bit independent like. Besides, it helps out in a stew. I'm sorry." She put her hand on Katie's shoulder now and pressed it sympathetically. She knew that her daughter adored her grandfather but could never understand or get used to him trapping the birds, and she had never eaten them, no kind of bird, not even a sparrow. At that time when her belly had been swollen and rumbling with wind and emptiness she had tried, but had been violently sick, so she had never pressed her again. "He won't be long," she said now. "He thought he'd be back for you comin'. Perhaps he's walked too far; his stump has been playin' him up lately."

Katie turned from her mother and looked at her brother and asked gently, "You feeling bad, Joe?"

Joe, seated on a cracket to the side of the hearth, an open fireplace, shook his head, then smiled at her and said. "No, just tired. I'm at Boldon now."

Katie's face stretched. "You mean they sent you there and you've got to walk all that way?"

"Aye." He nodded. "It isn't so bad goin', it's comin' back. You're so tired."

"Will you be there for the winter?"

"I don't know. You've got to go where they send you, its in the bond."

28

Aye, it was in the bond. The words her son had spoken seemed to check Catherine Mulholland's hands as she undid the little packages. Bond, bond, that crucifying bit of paper that her husband and son had to put their name to, that all men had to put their names to before they could get work, before they could eat. Her poor lad had been down the pit from when he was ten years old. She had nightmares, even now, about him sitting in the darkness for ten hours at a stretch. It had been twelve, even longer at times, and for twelve shillings a fortnight.

Joe was the only boy she had reared out of five sons. Her heart had seemed to break with each loss, but now she was glad they were gone, for they were in heaven, and warm, and happy. She had given birth to eight children altogether but had only managed to rear three, and she wished to God she had only reared two. But there, there, she mustn't say that. It was God's will she should have Lizzie.

"Ma." Katie had come to her side. "Do you think I should speak to Mrs. Davis to speak to Mr. Kennard, and for him to see Mr. Wisden, the head gardener, you know? He was asking for another boy; I heard Cook on about it."

Before Catherine could answer Joe said, "No, I'll not go, so that's it, not for three bob a week. So don't. Next year I'll be gettin' eight shillings and in a couple years' time I'll be up the face with me da. I'll be getting as much as him. I'm not goin' to waste the three years I've done and go and start in a garden for three bob. Besides, I know nowt about gardens, and don't want to." As Katie lowered her head he said quickly, "But thanks all the same, Katie." The brother and sister looked at each other and smiled. They had always been close, never fighting, even when they were small. But this family never fought; they laughed together, and cried together, but they didn't fight. They took their family grievances to God. It might be a different matter outside of the house when the men had to fight for their livelihood, and against the militia, and the police, and the knockers. But inside all was harmony.

"Can I bring Lizzie out now, Ma?"

"Aye, yes." Catherine nodded, and Katie went across the stone-flagged kitchen to a door which led into the other room.

On a pallet beneath the tiny window sat a woman . . . or a girl. It all depended upon how you appraised her. Lizzie

Mulholland was eighteen years old; she was of medium height, and no matter how little she ate she put on weight. To those outside the house she was known as Mulholland's idiot; to her family, she was slightly wrong in the head; but to Katie in particular she was like a crippled bird, and evoked the same tenderness.

Lizzie would sit for hours without moving, and if she wasn't taken to the water closet regularly she would do her business where she sat. Yet she couldn't always be depended upon to sit where she was put, for there were odd times when, as if obeying a beckoning finger, she would rise suddenly and leave the house if not detained, and once outside she would walk and walk. Once she was missing for nearly a day and had been found by a carrier outside Newcastle. He had recognized her and brought her home, and she had not been scolded but welcomed as if she was a member of the family on whom they all depended. But these sudden infrequent spurts of energy made vigilance necessary where she was concerned. Her talk was such as would be expected from a child of two, and now, on the sight of her sister, her flat face stretched into a shapeless smile and she muttered, "Katie." And when Katie went and stood by her side and said, "Hello, Lizzie," Lizzie placed her big head on the slender breast. It was an action of endearment that she kept for Katie alone; she never did it to her mother, or father, grandfather, or brother.

It was the act of Lizzie leaning on her breast that suddenly reminded Katie of what was secreted there, and, turning her head swiftly towards the open door, while she gave her hand to Lizzie and pulled her to her feet, she cried, "Ma! Ma! What's come over me. You know what I forgot? . . . Me pay." She swiftly undid the two buttons of her dress, unloosed the tape that tied her bodice, then thrust her hand inside the neck of her chemise and unpinned the calico bag. Her breath was coming quickly and she gabbled now, "You wouldn't believe it. That's all I've thought of for days, getting me wages, and I couldn't get home quick enough, but since I come in the door I haven't thought a thing about it. Would you believe it?"

She bent her slender body towards Catherine and pressed the calico bag into her hands, and Catherine slowly took the four shillings out, looked at them, then swiftly she opened her arms and drew her daughter to her, and as swiftly she pushed her away again. Unclenching her fist and holding out her palm with the money in it, she said in a voice that was cracking slightly, "You must have a shilling back every month."

"A shilling, Ma! No, no, I don't want a shilling." Katie's voice was high and she shook her head from side to side. "The threepence will do. Mrs. Davis has got a half a crown saved up for me, now; I don't want a shilling." She pushed her mother's hand away, and so quickly that the money spilled on to the floor, and immediately she was on her hands and knees picking it up. One of the shillings had rolled into a mud-filled crevice between two of the stones, and when she dug her finger in to get the coin she disturbed the earth and a strong obnoxious smell rose to her and filled her nostrils. The smell in the house was always worse in the summer when the water from the middens seeped under the foundations and oozed upwards. In the winter the rain dispersed it more quickly.

When the four coins were retrieved they all laughed. Katie now opening the back door, stood under the lean-to and rinsed her fingers in the wooden tub of water that stood on a bench attached to the wall.

She looked towards the cottage opposite, and over the yard walls she saw the head of Betty Monkton standing at her door. Betty called out to her, "Oh, hello, Katie," and she called back, "Hello, Betty," before turning indoors again.

At one time she had played with Betty, but it was a long, long time ago, and now she felt different and far removed from Betty, for Betty worked in the rope works and her father drank and her mother was feckless. Besides, they didn't go to chapel or church. Katie knew she was wrong in looking down on Betty Monkton, but she couldn't help it; it was because her own family was respectable and looked up to, even with their Lizzie being wrong in the head. It made her feel different. And then, hadn't she a fine job at the Manor?

She had just seated herself when the clip-clop of her granda's foot and crutch came to her from the yard and she jumped up and ran to the back door in time to see the old man hastily putting a small sack under the bench.

"Aw, there you are, me bonny lass." With an expertness born of eleven years' practice, he almost jumped over the step, and, pushing his crutch against the wall, he enfolded his granddaughter in his arms.

"Aw, hinny; it seems years. Let me look at you." Balancing on one leg, he held her away from him now, his hands on her shoulders. "Eeh, you're growin'; I can see it more every time you come home. But you're not putting much fat on you." His voice ended on a high inflexion, and he tapped his fist gently against her chin. "With all the grand feeding you tell us you get you've got little to show for it."

"Aw, Granda." She smiled widely at him. "How you keepin'?"

"Fine, fine. Never felt fitter in me life. Come on, let's sit down and hear your crack." He pulled his crutch to him and moved into the room, and his daughter brought a wooden, high-backed chair from against the wall and placed it in the circle at the other side of Katie.

Now Katie looked from one to the other. Then, resting her eyes on her mother, she asked, "I won't wait for me da then."

Before Catherine could reply William Finley put in, "I wouldn't count on him for the next hour." He looked over Katie's head towards his daughter. "There's blokes makin' for the chapel, some comin' over the hills. There'll likely be a lot of talk afore the Sunday school starts."

Catherine looked away from her father for a moment. She wished they hadn't to use the chapel. Yet if they were seen talking outside, especially to Mr. Ramshaw and Fogerty, they'd be suspected of starting trouble. She always had a fear on her of them on top starting the evictions again. They had threatened to pull down the chapel next time; and it wouldn't take much pulling down, being little more than a lean-to against the end of the far block of cottages. The men had had to fight to be allowed to erect it and use it. It was awful; they had to fight for everything. Yet they didn't want to fight, they wanted to discuss and negotiate, but the masters weren't for that. They wanted to keep the men under, stamp them as trouble-makers and blame the unions for agitating them. . . . But enough of worry; Katie was here, her wonderful little lass, and she was going to hear her news.

"Well," Katie began, casting her soft gaze from one to the other, "the house is all upside down; you never saw anything like it. They've cleaned right from the top to the bottom, and all new satin curtains in the drawing-room and dining-room and gallery windows."

"What colour?" Catherine put in, leaning towards her.

At this Katie blinked. She had never been in the drawing-room or dining-room, and only glimpsed the curtains as a distant gleam of colour through the half-open green-baize door when she took the water up to Mary Ann Hopkins. But after a moment's hesitation she said, "Blue—a bird blue, you know, bright. And they're thick and padded. And they've washed the stair carpet. It was out on the lawn, yards and yards of it. And they've cleaned the hall from top to bottom. And on Friday they moved the furniture out, 'cos that's where they'll dance—you know, to the band." She now nodded her head to Joe, and Joe, his thin face full of interest, nodded back to her. "And you should see the food. All kinds. Oh, you should see what's in the storeroom already. And Mrs. Davis starts the morrow mornin' making the fancies. She's marvellous at the trifles and fancies. She makes meringues . . . O-o-h!" Katie now worked her jaws and smacked her lips. "Talk about meltin' in your mouth, Ma, they're wonderful. An' she's arranging all the flowers in between the dishes. She's got a wonderful hand with decorations." She moved her head slowly to emphasise this statement, and her grandfather asked, "You seen the tables set afore, Katie?" She stared back at him. If she were to admit she hadn't actually seen a table set the telling of this tale would lose some of its magic. So she told a little lie. She nodded it first, then she added, "Just a peep . . . once."

Following this, she went on to give a long description of the cook and her culinary prowess, omitting her pettiness and carping ways. Then she spoke in glowing terms of her mistress—whom she could go months without even glimpsing, her mistress who had been to London to buy a dress for the ball. And she described the dress. It was green and made of taffeta and could stand by itself. Oh, it was beautiful. And it had rosettes and leaves sewn all over it in lovely patterns. Katie's description of the dress was pretty accurate, seeing that it had come through Jane Stockwell discussing it with Mrs. Davis, overheard by Daisy Studd, who passed it on to the clientele of the kitchen.

Then she came to Miss Theresa. She described her unobtrusive arrival, saying that nobody would have known she was in the house if Mr. Kennard hadn't mentioned it. She described her plain way of dresssing, which was even plainer than before she married; and turning to her mother now, she ended, "She doesn't look happy, Ma, she looks sad-like, the way she walks and hangs her head. Afore she was married, when Miss Ainsley was there, I've seen her running and laughin'. They used to go along by the wall a lot up on to the hill, but she's sad now. I like Miss Theresa, Ma."

"I know you do, Katie," said Catherine, and she didn't wonder why the seventeen-year-old girl looked sad, married to a man old enough to be her grandfather.

And now Katie came to the incident in the courtyard. She was adept at turning a joke against herself, and when she finished they were all laughing uproariously, even Lizzie, although she didn't know what she was laughing at.

Now Joe asked, "Was his clothes all messed?"

"Yes, they were splashed round his gaiters."

"Did you get wrong?" Joe asked.

"No. Nobody saw, thank goodness, only Mr. Rodger. He was with him. He picked me up." She turned her head now and looked at her mother. "Mr. Rodger's nice, Ma. He's like Miss Theresa; kind like, you know." Catherine nodded, and Katie went on, "He laughed . . . Eeh! I don't know what would have happened if he hadn't been there. Mr. Bernard would likely have raised the yard an' had Cook out, and then . . . oh, dear me." She dropped her head to one side and closed her eyes for a moment before finishing. "She would have hung me up on the spit and left me there all night; I'm sure she would." Again they all laughed.

And so it went on until Rodney Mulholland returned, and then the atmosphere took on a more serious note.

Rodney now sat beside his daughter, as he did every other Sunday, and heard her read passages from the Bible, and during this Grandfather Finley sat nearer to the fire although the day was hot, and Lizzie continued to stare at her sister, and Joe slept.

When his father had come in Joe had given up his cracket and gone to the dim corner of the room where stood his parents' bed, a similar erection to the smaller ones in the other room, and sat on the edge of it; and after a while he had dropped sideways and fallen fast asleep. And his father had not awakened him today and reprimanded him and bid him join in the lesson, but had gently lifted his feet up on to the bed, after placing an old rag between them and the patchwork cover.

Katie's reading was slow and she stumbled on the big words and her father made her repeat them, as when she came to atonement.

"Who shall offer it before the Lord, and make an . . ."

"Split it into three, a-tone-ment, atonement."

Katie nodded and repeated "A-tone-ment"; then read, "Make an a-tone-ment for her; and she shall be cleansed from the issue of her blood. This is the law for her that hath borne a male or a female. And if she be not able to bring a lamb, then she shall bring two . . ."

"Tur-tles."

"Tur-tles, or two young pigeons; the one for the burnt offering, and the other for a sin offering; and the priest shall make an a-tone-ment for her, and she shall be clean."

Katie didn't understand a word of what she was reading, but it was nice to read.

*　　*　　*

She was ready to go. She had, after some protest, allowed her mother to put six pennies into her calico bag; she had stoutly refused to take a shilling, although with a shilling she would have been much nearer to getting the lace collar and the white cotton gloves that she craved for from the pedlar on his next visit to the back door of the house.

The procedure was as always. She kissed Lizzie on the cheek and stood still for a moment while her sister rested her head against her, then she patted her and said. "Be a good girl, Lizzie; I'll see you in a fortnight's time." And Lizzie stared at her, and the colour of her eyes changed, indicating that somewhere beyond the dim regions of the stunted brain there was an awareness that understood loss.

Next Katie stood in front of Joe. She put out her hand and touched his shoulder, and he did the same to her. "Try to get more sleep," she said.

"Aye," he said. "Ta-rah, Katie."

"Ta-rah, Joe," she said. Then lifting her arms she put them round her father's neck and kissed him on the cheek, and he held her tightly for a moment. Then it was her mother's turn. Her mother did not embrace her until she was actually at the door, and then she, too, held her tightly; after which she traced her fingers gently aound her face, straightened her hat, then said, "Be a good lass, and please Mrs. Davis."

"I will, Ma. Yes, I will. Ta-rah."

"Ta-rah," they all said, all except her granda, for he always accompanied her on the first mile of her return journey.

At the end of the row of cottages she turned and waved, and they waved back, and when she and her granda were on the moor making for the road, just before they dropped from sight, she turned again and waved vigorously; then she and her granda were alone.

For William Finley this was the peak of his granddaughter's visit, when, side by side, they walked together over the fells. Rain, snow, or shine he had set her on her journey every other Sunday since she had been at the house. Down the shallow valley he hobbled, and up the other side to the high ground, where she would leave him and from where he could watch her progress for almost a mile.

William was not a God-fearing man like his son-in-law; he did not hold with chapel, or church, but there was scarcely a day went by that he didn't thank God for giving him his granddaughter; he thanked Him for the light and joy she had brought into the fast fleeing years of his life, years that would have been corroded with bitterness, because of his infirmity, had she not been there to prove to him that God tempered the wind to the shorn lamb. He had lost his leg in an accident at the Hebburn pit. It was just after they had started to use the Davy safety lamp. Instead of as an asset to their work the men of the pit had viewed this new and much-praised acquisition with the same feeling they viewed the men who had introduced it into their working life, for the owners looked upon the safety lamp as if it was Aladdin's very own, and after its inception they took even less safety precautions in the mine than they had done before. The very necessary ventilation shafts were not sunk; why go to such expense when they had this wonderful lamp? And so the danger of bad air that was ever present, the increasing invasions of water, resulted in explosions. Thirty-one men had died in the accident where William had lost his leg. And from that time he had suffered from nightmares, nightmares in which he was suffocating among mangled bodies and blood. He never saw the mangled bodies or blood, he only felt them, for the nightmare always placed him in total and absolute blackness. . . . But in the daytime there had always been the child, his only daughter's laughing, gay, talkative, lovely child.

They were now approaching the top of the hill, where she would leave her granda. He was puffing a bit and she said to him, "You shouldn't come this far."

"You get me a pair of eyes that can see through the hill and I won't." He jerked his head at her.

"But it's all right now, not like in the winter in the dark." She always ran like a hare the last mile or so of her journey in the winter.

On top of the hill the old man lowered himself down on to the grass, and she sat down beside him, then she undid the front of her bodice, took out her bag again, and, taking three pennies from it, she pushed them in his hand, only to have him say, "No, no, I'll not. I'll not."

"Go on, Granda; get some baccy."

"No, lass, no." He thrust her hand away. "Workin' for a month for threepence."

"I don't, I don't." Her voice was high and indignant. "I get four shillings."

"Aye." Now his face looked stern. "You get four shillings and it goes to support me."

Her eyes stretched, her mouth fell open; then her lips came together and she swallowed as if in indignation and said loudly, "Don't be a silly-billy, Granda. What put that into your head? I'd always given me ma me money."

"Aye, aye." His head was moving slowly now. "I suppose so." Then, turning towards her, he ended, "But I'm not takin' it."

"You are so. There it is." She put the coppers on the ground. "And if you don't pick them up they'll stay there till they take root." She was smiling gently at him and he was looking at her from under his eyebrows. It was at this point they both became aware of the approach of footsteps. They turned simultaneously and looked down the hill, staring for a moment into the distance, where a man was approaching. Then William, screwing his body around, looked directly ahead and said under his breath, "It's Buntin'."

Katie looking ahead now said, "I'll get off, Granda."

"No, sit tight till he's passed; let him get his distance."

Mark Bunting, the master weighman for the owners, or the keeker as he was called by the men, was the man who checked the corves of coal hewed by the miners; he was the man who had the power to cut a man's wages by as much as half if the seven-hundredweight basket the miner sent up from the black bowels of the earth should show a deficiency of two or three pounds. Often when this happened all the coal in that basket was made free to the owner. The same procedure was followed when there was a small quantity of stone among the coal. No account was taken for the men having to get the coal out, even by the light of a candle. The keekers worked on a commission basis; the more corves they found faulty and could pass as free to the owners the more money they themselves made.

Mark Bunting was a man of medium height, thick-set with dark bushy brows over deep-set eyes. His face was full and his lips thin. Like most keekers he was a lonely man, working between the devil and the deep sea, between the men who hated him and the owners who despised him. Bunting lived half a mile from the village, not in a stinking two-roomed cottage but in a good solid house with two rooms up and two down. It was provided by the Rosiers and it had a garden in which a dog was chained. Mark Bunting needed protection; he needed warning of approaching visitors. There was a blue mark running from the rim of his cap down to the top of his left cheekbone, which was proof that he had not always been on his guard. It was not an uncommon thing for keekers to be found in ditches with their heads split open.

"Fine day." He came to a stop about a yard from where William sat.

It was some seconds before the old man, without glancing at him, said, "It'll do."

Katie, lifting her eyes slowly upwards and over her granda's head, looked at this man about whom she had heard so much yet had never seen. She saw that he was very well put-on, and he looked entirely apart from the men in the village in that he was wearing a cravat and a fancy waistcoat. There was a pattern about him that reminded her of her master, and his sons, but she did not include his voice in that pattern, for it was rough-sounding. In the brief space of time that she looked at the man there came over her a feeling that she couldn't understand, only that it was in a way a betrayal of her own kind, for why should she feel sorry for a keeker.

Bunting's eyes were covering her face when William lifted his head sharply and glared up at him, and the man, turning abruptly, walked away from them.

William didn't speak until Bunting was well out of hearing, then he said under his breath, "Bide your time; you don't want to come up with that 'un."

No, she didn't. The way he had looked at her had frightened her a bit. Perhaps he frightened the men in the same way, by just looking at them, because although he was thick he wasn't very big.

Silently now they watched the figure become smaller, and when the head disappeared from view William pulled himself up, tucked his crutch under his arm and said, "Well now, you'd better be away."

"Yes, Granda." She dusted some dry grass from her skirt; then raising her face to his she kissed him, while putting one arm around his neck and the other hand in his pocket and dropping in the three pennies, and before he could protest further she was running down the slope. At the bottom she turned and called, "Ta-rah, Granda," and he called back, "Ta-rah, me bairn."

At intervals along the road she turned and waved; and then came the bend and after one last wave she could see him no longer.

It had been a lovely day, a wonderful day. She felt so happy she could sing. Suddenly she whirled around, and her scraping feet sent up a cloud of dust from the road, while the skirt of her print dress swirled into a balloon about her legs. Then she was running and laughing. She was daft, daft, but she was happy, and the ball was on Tuesday. The excitement of the event brought a fluttering in her chest. Perhaps she would see them dancing. Mrs. Davis had let her and Dotty peep through the landing door once, but they hadn't seen much from there, just the occasional figure floating past the bottom of the stairs. But even that had been wonderful. Oh, on her next day off she would have something to tell them at home, wouldn't she?

She began to run again. Then suddenly she stopped and her step became sedate, while her eyes stared to the far end of the road and the approaching figure. Even at this long distance she knew it was the keeker coming back from his walk. As the distance lessened between them her limbs began to tremble. Dotty had told her that she had once seen the devil and that she got such a fright her face came out in spots and she hadn't been able to get rid of them since. And it was true; her face was covered in spots.

Mark Bunting now took on all the appearance of the devil, and when he stopped dead in front of her she thought her knees were going to give way, and she put her hand to her face.

"Where are you off to?"

"The . . . the house."

"Rosier's?"

She nodded.

"What do you do there?"

"I'm scullery-maid."

He stared at her, wondering the while why he had stopped; he didn't like women. Fortunately for him they were not a necessity in his life. "What's your name?" he said.

"Katie . . . Katie Mulholland."

Big Mulholland's girl. "That your grandfather back there?"

"Aye. Yes."

He hadn't taken his unblinking stare from her face. He saw that she was frightened of him and this fact gave him a sense of pleasure and he prolonged the interview.

"What do they pay you?"

"A shilling a week."

"Huh!" His head went up and he made a sound like a laugh, yet it wasn't a laugh. "You get off every Sunday?"

"No." She shook her head and backed a step from him as she said, "Every other." Then she added quickly, "I'm due in; I'll be late." She took another two steps back.

Her fear amused him; he had the desire to pretend to spring on her. He was further amused by the thought that she would do it in her bloomers if he did. It came to him, as he watched her turn swiftly round and move from him at the point of a run, that she hadn't addressed him as sir. A girl of her standing should have; he wasn't a man of the village. He felt piqued that even her fear hadn't prompted her to use the term sir. He watched her for a full minute before going on his way.

When Katie left the track and entered the grounds by the wicket gate she was still running, but once inside the grounds she came to a halt and pressed her two hands to her chest as she gasped for breath. Eeh, he had frightened her; the way he had looked at her. . . . Yet it was funny she couldn't help feeling sorry for him. But she'd better not let her da or granda hear her say that.

She was still panting when she reached the rise that overlooked the house and saw Miss Theresa sitting there. She had a book in her hand but she wasn't reading.

Katie gave a slight bob and went to pass her, when Miss Theresa spoke. "You've been home, Katie?"

"Yes, Miss . . . Miss Theresa." Somehow she couldn't call her ma'am.

"How are your folks?"

"Oh, they're fine, Miss Theresa."

"And you enjoyed yourself?"

"Oh yes." The smile reached to Katie's ears. "It's been lovely."

"Come and sit down a moment and tell me all about it." She moved on the grass as if making room for her, and Katie looked down on her, her mouth falling into a gape, and she said, "What, miss?" as if she hadn't heard. But she had heard all right. Miss Theresa was funny. Just imagine what they would say back at the house if they saw her sitting there. It was as the others said, she didn't really act like a lady. But that didn't stop her from liking Miss Theresa the best of the lot.

"Thank you, Miss Theresa, but . . . but I'm due in and Mrs. Davis will be waitin'."

"Yes, yes." Theresa looked up at her and moved her head slowly. "But I'm glad you've had an enjoyable day, Katie," she said.

"Thank you, Miss Theresa."

Katie turned and walked slowly away now, down towards the copse. She wished she could have done what Miss Theresa had asked because she sounded lonely. But there, Miss Theresa couldn't be lonely. She was with her family, and in this lovely house and garden, besides which she had a great big house of her own—better than this one, they said.

It was odd, Katie thought, as she neared the yard, but in the last half an hour she had met two people and she had thought they were lonely. Likely they weren't at all; it was just her and her fancies. She was daft.

Back on the grassy slope, Theresa sat, her legs straight out before her, her hands lying limply in her lap. She was think-ing of Katie, and Katie would have been surprised, even amazed, had she known of the times since she had come into the household that Miss Theresa had thought about her. From the first Theresa had been fascinated by the young girl's face. She thought the feeling was an artistic quality she possessed that could appraise beauty, that could be stirred and excited by it. Once, when they had been talking about money, Miss Ainsley had said, "Now take a child like Katie Mulholland, educate her, clothe her and what would you

41

have? Someone who would doubtless be acclaimed from here to Rome. Yet what will happen to her? She will marry a miner, have two or three children before she's twenty, and by the time she's thirty there'll be no semblance left of the beautiful girl. Whereas if she had money she could cosset and pamper that beauty and at thirty she would just be in her prime. Never despise money, Theresa," Miss Ainsley had ended.

Oh, if she could only go to Ainsley, but Ainsley was now in London, instilling wisdom into two young ladies.

What was she to do following Tuesday? Write to her husband and tell him she wasn't coming back, or do what her mother asked and put up with it until after the wedding? She closed her eyes and saw vividly what it was she would have to put up with, and it came to her with clarity that never, as long as she should live, could she bear to be a partner in this with any man. Turning her body slowly round, she lay on the grass and buried her face in the crook of her arm.

4

The ball was well under way, and there was a pause in the running, rushing and scurrying. All the guests had arrived, all had eaten and some were now dancing, and the house was filled with the echo of the music.

This side of the façade of the flower-bedecked rooms the staff were breathing more easily, some even daring to relax; and Cook was one of the latter. She was sitting in the rocking-chair to the side of the open spit fire, fortifying herself with a strong cup of tea laced with gin. She was extremely tired but was experiencing a sense of deep satisfaction, for, as she had just remarked to Dotty: say it, as she herself would, for nobody else was likely to, she had done more than her duty this past week. More had been asked of her than should have been asked of any human being. But had she faltered? Not a step. And now her legs were killing her.

Katie's legs too were very tired and every other part of her body, especially her arms. She had been on her feet from half-past five, and now all she wanted to do was to drop her head forward on to the table and go to sleep. She slid off the end of the wooden form, lifted her plate and said to Dotty, "I think I'll swill me face under the pump, that'll bring me to."

"Before you do any swillin' you see to them boilers."

"Yes, Cook, I'll do them right away." And she did them right away.

The last of the twilight was fading and it was very warm when she went outside, but cooler than in the kitchen, and she breathed deeply for a few moments before walking across the yard to the pump. The aspect of the courtyard was changed tonight, for the wide entrance was blocked with carriages. She would have loved to squeeze in between them and look towards the drive and the front door where all the lights were hanging, but she was afraid of running into the grooms. At present the grooms and coachmen were all in Mr. Tatman's harness room where beer and food was set for them, but if one of them should come out and catch you on your own they would rumple you, so Dotty said.

She pumped the water, then quickly held her face towards it, being careful that she didn't get her cap wet or the front of her dress. . . . There, that felt better. She looked up into the sky. It would soon be black dark and then the house would look lovely. She wished she could go along the wall and up the hill and look at it from there. But she would never dare, not only because she would be frightened of the dark, but because some of the guests went into the garden, and things went on, Dotty said. But Dotty told lies; her mother had told her to take everything Dotty said with a pinch of salt.

She finished drying her face on the underside of her coarse apron; then she walked back to the kitchen.

Florrie Green, the head chambermaid, was in the kitchen now and she had apparently caught Cook's interest enough to cause her to put her feet down and sit up straight. "Frumpish the mother is," Florrie was saying. "Little and dumpy, and no style at all. Well, I was surprised. An' you know what? She's an honourable, and Mr. Kennard says she's one sister who's a lady, and another who's a countess. Well! To look at her"— she bent down now and put her face close to Cook's—"you would think a pedlar had dressed her."

"No!"

"Aye, you would."

"How's the daughter dressed—Miss Ann?" Cook asked now.

"Not bad." Florrie adjusted the bib of her fancy apron. "Pink she's in; it suits her complexion. She's pretty in a way, but she's the kind that'll fade early." She accompanied her pronouncement with a telling movement of her head. Then she went on quickly, "But the father now, he looks somethin'. He's tall and thin, and his hair's dead white. He's got a sort of . . . a presence. You know what I mean, Cook?"

The cook now wagged her head slowly, signifying her complete understanding of class; then, bringing it close to Florrie's, she said in a low voice, "It's funny them not staying in the house, isn't it? All going back to Shields."

"You're not the only one who thinks that, Cook."

"Who they staying with?" Cook asked now, and Florrie replied, "The Palmers; old family friends. They're here; husband and wife. Uppish-lookin' . . . I bet Miss Ann's disappointed." She pushed the cook in her flabby chest with the flat of her hand. "She's right over the hoop for him; you should see her lookin' at him."

"You've seen them together then?"

"Uh-huh! I was taking the dishes from Fanny at the side door and they were dancin'."

As the chambermaid went to leave the kitchen Cook screwed her body round in the chair and called to her, "You never said what the missus looks like?"

Florrie turned, saying, "Outshines the lot of 'em, if you ask me. Her frock looks wonderful, an' you can see she's pleased as punch; everythin' goin' smoothly an' that. But there's one damper on the proceedin's." She flapped her hand towards the cook. "Miss Theresa. Coo, she looks as if she's lost a sixpence and found a threepenny bit. She was never very pleasant at any time, was she, but her face the night, Lordy me! I saw her dancin' round with Mr. Rodger; I don't suppose anybody else would ask her. An' she's got a frock on . . . well." She closed her eyes and made a deep sweep with her head. "I'm tellin' you, I wouldn't swap it for me Sunday one."

"No!"

"It's a fact, Cook. And it isn't like as if she mightn't be able to buy one, for the old fellow was potty over her, wasn't he? An' her with a face'd turn milk sour. But God, there's no countin' for taste, I say that every day in the week—there's no countin' for taste."

"You're right there, Florrie. You're right there."

The final word had been said on the matter, and Florrie went out and Cook settled herself again, only to turn her gimlet eyes on the girls seated at the table and shout, "An' don't you two sit there as if you're finished. You, Dotty, can clear up the dishes and get the pans ready for the porridge; an' you, Katie, get on with your floor."

Katie stared through her tired eyes at the cook. She had somehow thought that the floor would have a miss the night, seeing that people would be tramping back and forward on it until the small hours of the morning. Her thoughts must have shown in her face, for the cook, her voice even higher now, cried, "An' don't you look at me like that unless you want your ears boxed."

Katie immediately sidled from the form and went and got her bucket, and she had just started on the floor in the corner next to the ovens when Mrs. Davis came hurrying into the kitchen. Seeing the cook sitting with her feet up, she said, "It's all right, it's all right, take a minute when you can; I just wanted to tell you how pleased everybody seemed with the dishes. I've heard a number of favourable remarks."

To this the cook inclined her head and gave Mrs. Davis a tight smile, then said, "Well, I did me best as always. Nobody can say I don't do me best."

"Yes, you always do your best, Delia." Now Mrs. Davis turned her head to the dim corner to where Katie was kneeling, and without stopping to think she said, "Oh, that's going to be a waste of time, Katie, with all the tramping back and . . ." Her voice trailed away as she realised that in a way she was infringing on Cook's domain, and so, looking at Cook again, she added in a pleasant, and apologetic tone, "It'll be dirty again by two o'clock, Delia."

"Well, you would have somethin' to say if I made her scrub it after that hour, wouldn't you?" Cook had put her feet down and was sitting bolt upright in her chair.

"Yes, I think I would, Delia. But this being a special occasion I should have thought the floor could have been left for one night."

"And have you find fault the morrow?"

Mrs. Davis immediately became the dignified housekeeper. "If I gave an order that a thing wasn't to be done, Cook, I wouldn't be so foolish as to find fault the following day because my order had been carried out; besides, you'll need

Katie in a very short while to see to the side dishes and the big plate that will be coming from the tables. Mr. Kennard and I will see to the sets and the silver in the pantry, but the rest can be washed here."

The cook and the housekeeper looked at each other squarely in the eye. Then Mrs. Davis turned slowly about and left the kitchen, and the cook repeated to herself, "Mr. Kennard and I will see to the plate in the pantry." There was no doubt but they would. She glanced towards Katie, who had moved to a fresh patch of stone floor, but she didn't countermand her order. If the dishes were to be washed, then she would wash them when she had finished the floor.

* * *

It was now two o'clock. The music from the orchestra could still be heard in the kitchen. Cook held her candle in one hand while she supported herself against the table with the other. She was dead on her feet, she told herself. "You two ready?" She spoke over her shoulder, and Dotty was the first to say, "Aye, Cook." She, too, held a candlestick in her hand.

"Katie."

Katie came running out of the pot room, saying, "Yes, Cook, I'm comin'. I've just banked the fires down. I'll just wash me hands."

"Come on this minute, girl. Don't try me any more, I've had enough for one day."

Katie grabbed up her candle from the mantelpiece, lit it from the glowing embers of the fire, then followed Dotty, who followed the cook. In procession, they went out of the kitchen, along the long corridor that led to the butler's pantry and the housekeeper's room, and through the door that led to the back staircase.

They had just reached the first landing when the green baize door connecting with the gallery was pushed open and Mrs. Davis came through, and with her a loud swell of music. Closing the door behind her, she said in a thick whisper, "Oh, I was just coming down. . . . Would you like to have a peep?"

This was the moment Katie had been waiting for, but the work of a long day and a longer night had swamped her interest; all she wanted to do now was to reach the attic and throw herself down on her bed; she doubted if she would be able to take her things off. She knew a sense of relief when she heard Cook say in a stilted tone, "Thank you all the same, Mrs. Davis, but I'm done up. All I want is me bed."

As she finished speaking she raised her candle just the slightest and peered at the housekeeper, at her flushed face and bright eyes, which told her that Mrs. Davis had drained a number of not quite empty bottles already and would doubtless drain a few more before she went to sleep.

She was about to move on when Mrs. Davis said, "But you would, wouldn't you?" She was bending towards the two girls.

Dotty Black stared at Mrs. Davis dully. She knew on which side her bread was buttered. The housekeeper might have power in the house, but she was in the kitchen under Cook, and she didn't intend to get on the wrong side of her and have a life like Katie Mulholland, and so she said, "I'm tired, Mrs. Davis."

Mrs. Davis straightened her back and her lips took on a set line, and her eyes stayed on Dotty some seconds before she looked towards Katie and asked, "Well, you, Katie; you would love to have a peep, wouldn't you?"

Katie peered up at her benefactress in the dim light. She always wanted to please Mrs. Davis—she had promised her mother she would—and she knew now that if she refused her invitation she wouldn't please her. Mrs. Davis seemed bent on showing off the scene in the hall as if it was a personal triumph of her own. Katie sensed this, as the housekeeper's wine-laden breath wafted over her; and so, while knowing that tomorrow in the kitchen she would suffer the consequences of her choice, she said, "Thank you, Mrs. Davis, I'd like to."

"I knew you would." Mrs. Davis, not quite herself, put out her hand and caught at Katie's, saying, "Put your candle down and nip it."

Katie did as she was bidden, and as she was taken through the green baize door she was aware that Cook and Dotty were standing still, their faces dark with disapproval, watching her.

Mrs. Davis now led her along the short passage to where it opened out into a corner of the gallery, and there she brought her to a halt, whispering, "We'll wait here a minute until they start dancin' again."

Katie stood blinking in the light from the chandelier hanging over the hall and from the four lamps hanging along the length of the gallery. After the dimness of the kitchen, and latterly the stairs, the light was dazzling. And then there was the smell—scenty, warm, like the smell from the flower garden late at night.

"There, they've started." Mrs. Davis glanced about her, then, saying to Katie "Stay still", she went along the gallery until she came to the last of the big windows and there she stopped, looked around her again, then beckoned Katie towards her.

Slightly more awake now with the excitement, Katie scurried across the strange ground of soft carpet, past the wide passage that led to the bedrooms; then, hugging the wall, she went swiftly past the four long windows and came to where Mrs. Davis was standing pointing.

There was an open balustrade edging the gallery, and through it, from where they were standing, Katie could only see a quarter of the hall below and the odd dancing couples. One, two, three steps forward, one, two, three steps back, then the men bowing and the ladies dipping; then twirling round and again one, two, three steps forward, and one, two, three steps back. She glanced up at Mrs. Davis and found that Mrs. Davis was looking at her.

"Aren't they lovely, Katie?"

"Oh yes, Mrs. Davis. Oh yes." She was gazing down on the dancers again before she finished speaking. Oh, if only her ma and da and their Joe could see them. But somewhere at the back of her mind, even as she thought this, she got the impression that her da and Joe might not have viewed the scene through hers, or her mother's, eyes.

How long she stood entranced she didn't know, but she almost jumped from the ground when Mrs. Davis caught her arm tightly and pulled her backwards, then stood looking in the direction of the main passage as she whispered low, "Someone's coming."

The next minute Katie found herself gripped by the collar of her frock and thrust between the long curtains of the gallery window.

"Sit on the sill," Mrs. Davis hissed at her, and Katie, always quick in emergencies, hoisted herself up on to the broad padded window-sill, and there she knelt stiffly, waiting.

It seemed dark in here after the light of the landing; yet,

glancing through the window without moving her head, she saw that a moon was riding high behind fluffed clouds. She was also aware that Mrs. Davis was still standing in front of the curtains. Then she heard a voice, which she recognised instantly as belonging to Mr. Rodger. She heard him say, "Oh, there you are, Mrs. Davis; I was just going to look for you. It's Miss Theresa; she's feeling upset. It must have been something she ate that has disagreed with her. I wonder if you've got a minute to look in on her."

When Mrs. Davis's voice came to her she knew that she was no longer outside the curtain but along the gallery. She heard her make some answer but she couldn't make out what was said. Following this there was just the music again, soft now, muted.

After waiting for some minutes she sat back on her heels, careful not to touch the curtains. She wished Mrs. Davis would hurry and get her out of this. The tiredness was over-powering her again, and sitting on her haunches was a strain, yet she was afraid to alter her position in case she touched the curtains. She knew if she had been one of the parlour-maids, or a chamber-maid, she could have walked across the gallery to the green baize door and it wouldn't have mat-tered very much if she had met one of the guests, or even a member of the household, because she would have been dressed for inside the house. But the way she was, with her dirty frock and apron, and crumpled cap, she knew she was no fit person to be in this part of the house at any time, but especially tonight.

Minutes passed, which seemed like hours, and Mrs. Davis did not return. Daringly now, she inserted a finger between the curtains and squinted along the gallery. It was empty, and they were still dancing down below. . . . Slowly she let her-self down from the sill and, creeping close to the panelled wall between the windows, she had almost reached the last one when the music stopped. At the same moment she heard a door open along the corridor and from the direction of the stairs came voices, and she must cross in front of the stairs to get to the passage that led to the green baize door. For just one second she pressed herself against the panelling, and then, with the quickness of a lizard, she was behind the cur-tain and on to the sill of the last window.

On her hands and knees now, she remained motionless, and her breathing almost stopped when she heard her master's voice. He must have been only a foot or two away from the curtains; it was as if he was shouting in her ear. He was talking in a hearty, laughing way to someone. Then came other voices, ladies' voices and a lot of rustling sounds as they walked up and down the gallery. After an eternity when she found she couldn't remain on her hands and knees any longer she held her breath as she slowly let herself down on to her side; and there she lay with her head on her arm not daring to move.

The sill was not long enough to take her stretched-out length, but it was broad enough to allow her to bend her knees without them touching the curtains. She told herself that when the music started again they would all go downstairs, then she would fly out and get away. But when the music did start there remained the sound of voices, and the one on which she concentrated her attention was the loud boisterous voice of her master. It went on and on until it became mixed up with the music. The music was slow now and lovely, and soothing; becoming softer and softer, it gradually faded away altogether and she was asleep. . . .

It was about ten minutes later that the gallery emptied and Mrs. Davis hurried to the end window, only to find that Katie wasn't on the sill. She drew a deep breath of relief. Katie was quick, bright; she had taken the opportunity to slip away when all was quiet.

Half an hour later the ball came to an end and the guests came upstairs for their cloaks and the hall rang to the sound of goodbyes and congratulations to the happy couple, not forgetting the master and mistress of the house who had put on such a splendid show for them. The last of the guests to leave were the Talfords. James Talford shook George Rosier's hand, saying courteously, "I only hope I do them as much justice at our little affair next month as you have done them tonight."

"Oh, I have no doubt but that you will excel anything that I have attempted, no doubt at all," said George Rosier heartily, beaming up at the tall man. And he hadn't any doubt.

Agnes Rosier was now embracing Mrs. Talford as if they were devoted sisters, and when she came to say goodbye to her future daughter-in-law she hovered over the blushing girl as if she was finding it hard to restrain her affection for her, and then with a gracious gesture of her hand she passed her

50

over to her son, and Bernard accompanied his future wife down the steps to the carriage. Once there, however, he was quick to turn aside to assist her mother into her seat and bow gravely to her father before bending over his fiancée's hand and raising it to his lips.

Not until the carriage had disappeared round the curve in the drive did he enter the house again. He walked slowly through the vestibule, crossed the hall and looked to where his father and Rodger were standing talking. Then he turned his gaze to his mother where she was standing in the doorway of the small parlour, and as he went towards her his father and brother joined him.

Once inside the room, and the door closed, they all stood looking at each other. It was Agnes who spoke first. "Well," she said, looking directly at Bernard, "what do you think?"

"You mean, how it went?"

She inclined her head impatiently.

"Oh, excellently."

"You think they were impressed?"

"Who can tell? He's as close as a clam."

"You're right there." George Rosier walked to the mantel-piece and rested his hand on it, and, looking down into the almost dead fire, said, "You never can tell with types like him, the holy Joes, but I think he was impressed all right. Nothing was too ostentatious, everything just as it should be. Don't you think so?" He had now turned his head sharply and addressed his younger son.

Rodger undid the second pearl button of his waistcoat as he replied, "I thought everything went marvellously, and the food was superb." He would have never dared say what he was thinking; that if tonight's show hadn't been ostentatious he wondered to what extreme they would go to put on something they did consider ostentatious.

"Good; good." George Rosier returned his gaze to the fire, and Agnes said, "I must remember to tell Mrs. Davis to congratulate the cook tomorrow. . . . Ah, well!" She heaved a deep sigh. "We can do no more at present, so if you'll excuse me I'll retire."

Her husband made no comment on this, not even casting his glance towards her, but her sons went to her and, one after the other, kissed her on the cheek; then Rodger opened the door for her. But before she had actually passed through it George Rosier turned from the fireplace and asked, "What happened to Theresa? Where did she get to half the night? And she wasn't there at the end."

Agnes turned her head and, looking over her shoulder towards him, said, "I don't know what happened to her"; her tone implying, "Nor do I care."

"She felt sick and had to go to her room," Rodger put in. And now both his parents turned and looked at him, and, glancing from one to the other, he said, "It must have been something she ate, the lobster perhaps; it never did agree with her."

Agnes continued to look at Rodger for a moment, but she made no comment, and when she turned away he watched her walking across the hall to the stairs, her dress spreading like a peacock's tail behind her.

"Well, I'm off too. Good-night, Father. Good-night, Bernard." Rodger nodded to each in turn, and they both answered, "Good-night."

The father and son left together now, there was silence between them until Bernard, stroking the hair on his cheekbones with his spread finger and thumb, said, "He was more affable than I expected."

"Yes, I suppose you could say that; in fact I found him surprisingly civil. But don't you take anything for granted. Be wary. And mind"—George Rosier now turned fully around and faced his son, and, wagging his finger at him he said darkly, "Keep your nose clean. You understand?"

Bernard moved slowly away. His father's expression was distasteful and it angered him, for he understood its implication only too well.

"God, I'm tired, and that's putting it mildly. You coming?"

"In a moment or so."

George Rosier turned to go, then stopped and asked, "What do you make of Palmer?"

"I don't really know except that he's playing the father figure already and he's too young for it."

"He's too young for nothing. He's as wily as a cartload of monkeys. Did you notice they went off early? You would have thought they'd have waited for Ann and her people, seeing they're friends of theirs and are giving them hospitality for the night. You didn't talk big to him, did you?" When Bernard looked at him he added, "Well, I wouldn't put it past you, even sober." And on this show of confidence he marched out and into the hall, where he stood for a short while watching the men quenching the candelabra, and putting out the lamps.

Back in the parlour, Bernard brought his staring gaze from the door; then, dragging a chair towards the hearth, he dropped into it and, bending forward, poked the fire and threw on a log. As he sat back he shivered. He'd had very little inside him since yesterday to keep him warm; for having been cautioned by his father to take his wine in moderation when in the company of the Talfords, he had gone even further and hardly drunk anything at all. But now the time for moderation had passed. He leant towards the bell-rope, but, remembering that there would be no one in the kitchen at this hour, he rose from his chair, went to the door, pulled it open and called softly across the hall to Kennard.

The butler left his two assistants and came to the room door, saying, "Yes, sir?"

"Bring me a tray and bottle."

"A wine, sir?"

"No, brandy."

"Very well, sir."

A few minutes later Kennard returned to the room and, placing a small table near Bernard's side, he put down the tray holding a bottle of brandy and a glass.

"Pull them off." Bernard nodded to his feet, and Kennard, standing in front of him, lifted one foot after the other on to his bent knees and gently eased off the soft leather boots.

Bernard now said, "You needn't wait up, I may be some time. I'll put out the lamp."

"Thank you, sir." Kennard walked with his stately step towards the door, giving no sign, at least in his posture, of his utter weariness.

Bernard poured himself a large measure of brandy, placed his feet on the top of a tapestry stool and lay back with the glass in his hand. He swirled the liquid around the glass once or twice before putting it to his lips; then he contemplated the now glowing log on the hearth as he let his mind travel into the future.

She'd be like clay in his hands, and through her he'd win the approval of her father; he had no doubt in his mind but that he could achieve this. Yet he was aware that he would have to be cautious; all the while he would have to be cautious. He did not really know what she would prove to be

53

like behind the four-poster curtains, and he doubted very much if she'd be entertaining in that way, for already she was much too pliable. He knew that he would soon sicken of her adoration, in fact it tired him already, but the price he would have to pay for what she would bring to him would be in proving to her that his ardour was sincere. He did not minimise the fact to himself that this pose would be hard to sustain.

He favoured two kinds of women; one that could turn love-making into a wrestling match, and, at the other end of the scale, the clever intelligent woman who could spar with her tongue. His future wife belonged to neither of these categories. His mind now dwelling on a lady of the first kind, that attracted him, his body moved restlessly in the chair. He hadn't visited her for over a month, but, by God, he would rectify that within the next twelve hours, come what may.

He refilled his glass and set to wondering how long James Talford had before him. He was much older than his wife—nearing seventy, he would say; he had married late. He hoped he would not leave his demise too late. The bulk of his money would be left to his wife. Well, that wouldn't matter; she was just an older edition of her daughter. He would enjoy managing them both. She was attracted to him too. He knew this; he had always appealed to older women.

When the clock struck four he was finishing his fifth glass of brandy. Slowly now he rose from the chair and, taking from the mantelpiece a candlestick that held a new waxen candle, he lit it from the embers of the fire, blew out the lamp and went from the room.

His gait was not unsteady; except once when his stockinged feet slipped on the highly polished surface of the hall floor, and he laughed to himself as his hand went out and gripped the huge round knob of the balustrade. Slowly now he mounted the stairs and, having reached the gallery, he was about to cross it when he was brought to a dead stop by the sight of a leg being thrust out between the folds of the window curtains. Another leg followed. They were white-stockinged right up above the knees. Then the curtains parted and he saw a pale face peering out. It was there for a second; then both the face and the legs disappeared as quick as a flash of lightning.

Slowly now he approached the window; slowly he parted the curtains and, raising the candle high, looked down on to the crouched figure and staring face of a young girl. The buttons of her dress were open and showing the top of her calico shift, and this was rising and falling rapidly over her sweating flesh.

As he continued to stare down into her face that was now without movement, her body odour came to him. It was neither an unpleasant smell nor a pleasant scent; it was what some women gave off more than others. He had always been sharp to detect this odour, and it had in the past played tricks with him. He put his hand out and, placing it on her shoulder, brought her from the sill, and as she stood on her feet staring up at him through the candle-light the tremors from her body passed through his own.

Slowly, and still staring down at her, he turned her about and pressed her along the gallery. Almost opposite the stairs was a table with a lamp on it. This lamp was kept burning at low ebb all during the night. It augmented the solitary candlelight and showed the way more clearly down the broad passage to the bedrooms.

When Katie realized that she wasn't being pushed towards the far passage that held the green baize door her body stiffened, and at this the pressure on her shoulder tightened and she was pushed rapidly forward. The next minute she was standing in a big bedroom. As yet there was no power in her to protest; she was dazed with sleep and petrified with fear. All the muscles of her body felt stiff and out of her control; even when she watched, out of the corner of her eye, Mr. Bernard place the candle on the table near the four-poster bed, it was as if her eyes were stuck in her head and she could only move them with an effort.

Then as her terror heightened to an intensity that brought her muscles into play and her mouth open to scream Bernard's hand came tightly over her stretched face; his other hand, gripping a handful of her clothes about her chest, heaved her, with one lift, into the centre of the big feather bed.

For a moment he held her there with only one hand, and that across her mouth. It kept her head and shoulders deep in the bed, but her limbs flayed wildly, until a weight dropped on her body and hell opened and engulfed her. The hell she had read about in the Bible, the hell Mr. Burns talked about in the chapel, the hell into which sinners were thrust for their everlasting life. Her body was being rent in two; she was screaming but could make no sound. Then for some seconds she was aware of nothing, nothing at all, no pain, no fear, no terror. But all too quickly this passed and she was crying through every pore in her body. Her eyes were gushing water, her pores oozing her tears through sweat. The weight rolled off her and she lay sunk deep in the centre of the soft downy coverlet, limp and drained of life, her crying soundless.

After a time, and of a sudden, his hand came on her again, this time giving her a great push that thrust her to the edge of the bed. But before she could fall to the floor he had stayed her; he remembered just in time that she might even yet cry out and rouse Rodger next door. He raised himself up and looked at her sprawling, part-naked limbs with distaste. Then his eyes travelled to her hand which was clutching the bedclothes; it was red and smeared, the nails broken and the cuticles encased with dirt, black dirt. He heaved himself up and away from her and on to the floor. Gripping her shoulders again, he pulled her to her feet; then, jerking her head up, he stared down into her twisted, wet, terrified face and, lifting his forefinger, he wagged it at her.

He had taken her without the slightest endearment, not even bothering to caress her limbs, which courtesy he bestowed on the meanest of his women. He had taken her with less feeling than a dog would a bitch, and he hadn't deigned to open his mouth to her from beginning to end. But the wagging finger spoke volumes and she understood his meaning.

Now he was again pushing her towards the door, but before he opened it he once more wagged his finger cautioningly before her face; quietly he turned the knob and glanced into the corridor, then pulled her forward and thrust her from him.

Her hand pressed tightly over her mouth, her feet dragging, but soundless, on the thick carpet, she stumbled along the passage towards the gallery. Once there she turned to the left and groped her way to the dimmer passage until she felt the green baize door.

When she had been pushed from the room Katie's head had been bent, and she had kept it so; yet even if she had raised her head her terror was blinding her so much it is doubtful whether she would have noticed the woman standing in the gallery near the head of the stairs.

Theresa had been sick again and had gone to the toilet room for a potion and she was returning, a bottle in her hand, when she heard a door click open and saw a head come poking out, which she recognised as Bernard's; then before her amazed gaze she watched Katie Mulholland come stumbling down the corridor, her body crumpled, her hand across her mouth, and apparently in great distress.

The only reason her brother hadn't seen her, she concluded, was that she was standing in the shadow of the pedestal that held the bust of her grandfather. She had also, from the moment she heard the door open, remained still. Now she was still no longer. A rage that was deaf to reason and decorum, even the decorum required of a sister to a brother, flooded her, and on its wave she was swept to Bernard's door, and without even knocking she thrust it open and entered the room, taking him unawares and catching him in a very undignified position as he completed his undressing.

"What the hell!" He turned towards her, not bothering to cover his nakedness, at least not for a moment. Then, pulling a dressing-gown towards him, he strode towards her where she stood with her back to the door and hissed at her, "What the hell do you want coming in like that!"

"You're a fiend."

"What!" All the muscles in his face moved upwards, almost closing his eyes as he peered at her in the dimness. For a moment he was unable to understand her rage. It didn't dawn on him that she was here on behalf of his late visitor; sisters minded their own business, that was part of a woman's duty. But Theresa, although still his sister, was no part of the household now; she had nothing whatever to do with what went on inside it. Never having had any affection for her, he had always considered her utterly lacking in feminine appeal. He had even voiced the opinion to Rodger that the best place for her would be a convent. He had at one time likened Ainsley to a jocular Mother Superior and Theresa as her doting novice. . . . He bent towards her now and whispered hoarsely, "What's the matter with you? What are you talking about?"

"You know what I'm talking about." She thrust her face so close to his that their noses were almost touching. "You're a fiend. That child . . . Katie Mulholland, she'll be another Maggie Pratt, I suppose, pushed out and into the poor house, and someone else blamed."

"Shut your mouth!" He was glaring at her now, his rage equal to her own. "You mind your own business."

"Yes, I'll mind my own business. I'll make Katie Mulholland my business. I'm warning you, if anything happens to her she'll be my business."

He gripped her by the shoulder, his finger-nails digging into her flesh, and she growled at him, "Take your hands off me at once!"

"You'll mind your own business, do you hear? Promise me. Promise me." His breath was on her face.

With a twist of her body and thrusting at him with her two hands, she freed herself and, grabbing the door-handle, she said under her breath, "I'll promise you nothing; I'll just warn you, and also at the same time remind you that that child has parents, and menfolk, which Maggie Pratt hadn't."

His hand came out to make a grab at her again and she said quickly, "You put a finger on me and I'll raise the house. One last word. I'm leaving tomorrow, or today rather, but I'll be back." With this she pulled open the door and went out. Her body was still shivering with her anger.

Back in her own room she sat down on the side of the high bed, her feet resting on a foot-stool, and rocked herself. That poor child, that poor child. Yet in this particular moment she was not seeing Katie Mulholland under the hands of her brother but herself on her wedding night.

Then Katie, in all her utter dejection, was before her eyes once more, as Maggie Pratt had been three years ago. She was supposed to know nothing about Maggie Pratt. Maggie had been second chambermaid. She was an orphan, plump and pretty. She was sixteen, she became pregnant, and she had named the man as Bernard. Bernard had denied it indignantly, and Maggie was sent packing. With no home to go to, no reference, she ended up in the poor house, and there she was yet, and there she would remain until her child was of an age when it could work and earn its own living.

But that it should happen to Katie Mulholland, that beautiful, beautiful girl . . . child. How old was she? Fourteen, fifteen at the most. How had this come about? What was Mrs. Davis up to? She suddenly stopped the rocking movement. She had an impelling urge to go to the housekeeper's room and demand to know what she was doing, not to see that the junior staff were safely in their rooms before she retired; that was part of her duty, an essential part which had been emphasised by her mother since the Maggie Pratt affair. But what good would that do now? It was done, and only time would show if there were to be consequences.

* * *

Katie, sitting on the edge of her pallet, was also thinking about Mrs. Davis. She had not been to bed, and she hadn't taken off any of her clothes. She had a fear on her; it was new, different. She didn't know much about fear, except of the dark, and Cook going for her, but this fear was strange, making her sick, for all of a sudden she was afraid of her body. She wished she could throw it off, get outside it and take on the body that was hers yesterday, but the strange fear told her that that body would never be hers again. She wanted to fly home to her ma and get rid of the fear by telling her what had happened; but she couldn't tell her ma without her da knowing, and her da mustn't know about this. Her da was quiet and even-tempered, except at times, and at these times, which she had witnessed only twice in her life, he forgot himself and shouted and threw things. The last time she had seen him like that was when the cavalry charged the men in the village and the police and mine officials turned the Monktons and the Hepburns and a lot more families into the road, and threw their furniture after them, breaking it in the process. It was on that day that her da had attacked two policemen and one had hit him on the head and left him senseless in the ditch. The other attackers weren't so fortunate; they had been taken and locked up and brought before the magistrates. Five of the men had been banned from the pit and had taken to the road with their families. . . . So, if she told her ma about this and her da got to know he . . . he could do things that would make him lose his job . . . but she'd have to tell somebody; she'd have to tell somebody . . . Mrs. Davis? Yes, she would tell Mrs. Davis, because if he came after her again she would scream this time; she would even scream at the sight of him.

As she rose from her bed Dotty turned over in her sleep and her loud snores were checked by a succession of snorts. In the faint light of the dawn she looked awful with her spotty face, wide gaping mouth, and tangled hair, but Katie envied her.

Her body was shaking and the tears were raining from her

59

chin as she groped her way down the dark stairs and along the short passage and down the three steps and through the door that led to the landing and Mrs. Davis's room, and she had her hand actually raised to knock when she heard a voice. It came from within the room and it was a man's voice, and although it was speaking very low she recognised it. Then there was a movement on the other side of the door. One minute she was gaping at the door, the next she was flying up the steps again, and she just reached the foot of the attic stairs when she heard the passage door being opened gently. Halfway up the stairs she stopped and, pressing herself against the wall, she stood rigid, looking downwards to where a man had paused on the landing below and now stood buttoning up his trousers. He was wearing only his undervest and carried his coat over his arm. With a quick movement he swung the coat behind his back and thrust his arms into it; then, taking a few noiseless steps forward, he dropped from her view.

Katie was now experiencing another feeling, shame mixed with revulsion, and added to it was a strong element of surprise. The surprise kept her lips apart. Her Mrs. Davis, the woman whom her mother said was a natural lady and as good as any she served, was up to things with Mr. Kennard. In this moment it was made clear to her why Cook dared to sit in her presence, why she dared to speak as she did; why Mr. Kennard rarely came into the kitchen and, when he did, never spoke to the cook.

She could never tell Mrs. Davis now. She could never tell anybody, but she was resolved that if Mr. Bernard came near her again she would scream, and fight, and kick. She would know what it was all about next time. She would never let it happen again. She stopped crying and, lifting up her dress and taking the rag pinned to her petticoat, she rubbed it round her face, then softly blew her nose. She'd better get washed. She wouldn't go to the pump because somebody might see her, and it was still very early. No, she'd go down into the boiler room and lock the door and wash herself. Yes, she'd wash herself all over with hot, hot water. Scrub herself all over until she got rid of the feeling.

"What is it, lass?"

"Nothing, Ma."

"But, child, you've been like this on your last few days off."

Catherine had brought Katie into the bedroom and they were sitting on the side of the low bed looking at each other. Catherine put out her hand and stroked the soft hair from Katie's brow. "And you're so white and peaked-lookin'."

"It's the cold, Ma. I couldn't get rid of it; me eyes and nose were runnin' all the time."

"But that's weeks ago, child, as far back as the ball. Is . . . is the other all right?"

Now Catherine bent towards her, and Katie, lowering her lids, said under her breath, "It hasn't come yet, Ma." She didn't say it hadn't come the last two months either.

"Aw, that's it." Catherine straightened herself up and pulled her chin into her neck, saying knowingly, "There's nothin' that makes you feel more off colour than that. And you were never really regular; that's it. Oh, I've been worried about you, but I never gave that a thought. But that's it," she repeated. "An' we've all missed your chatter. Meself, I just live for your Sunday." Again she was leaning forward, and gathering Katie's hands between her own she shook them gently, saying, "Once that gets goin' you'll be your old self. And you know"—she dropped her voice—"I forget you're growing up, you're no longer a child. You're just on sixteen. I can't believe it; it seems but yesterday since I had you on me knee."

Katie's head drooped over her swelling throat. In another minute she would be on her mother's knee again, her head buried in her neck while she poured out this dreadful fear that was filling her and told her of the sickness that was always assailing her, and her absolute horror of the future. She pulled herself from the bed, saying, "It's nearly time, Ma; I'd better be going."

"Yes, lass." As Catherine followed her to the bedroom door her brow puckered, and her face showing once more a look of bewilderment, she said, "The wedding will soon be on you, an' you've never told us anything about it."

"I've been so busy, Ma, and Cook keeps at me. . . ."

In the kitchen she picked up her cloak and put on her straw hat, then tied a band round it and under her chin, for the day was windy and wet; then she stood watching her da put on his coat and tie his muffler. And when he was ready she went to the side of the fireplace, to her granda. William's face looked yellow and drawn; the hollow cheeks were sucked in, as were his lips. He put his arms about her, saying, "I'm sorry, me bairn. This is the first time I've never set you along the road." There were tears in his eyes and she kissed his stubbly chin. Then, patting his hands, she whispered brokenly, "Get better soon, Granda. . . . Soon." She stood looking at him, nodding her head, while his eyes held her face as if drawing each feature into himself.

And now she was kissing Lizzie, and Lizzie, as always, laid her head against her. But she did not speak to Lizzie, telling her to be a good girl, as she usually did. Then she turned to where Joe sat, and as usual they touched shoulders, but today he did not immediately relinquish his hold but mumbled under his breath, "Watch that cold, Katie."

"Aye, Joe, I will."

At the door, as she bent to kiss her daughter, Catherine thought, She looks like Jimmy did afore the fever got him—all her other children had died with the fever. She pressed her tightly to her; then, again looking down into her face, she said, "Now if you feel bad you go and tell Mrs. Davis. Promise me?"

Katie did not look at her mother as she said, "Yes, Ma."

Now putting his hand on his wife's shoulder and pulling her back into the room, Rodney said, "Keep in, woman; you'll get soaked." And Catherine, looking at the tall square figure of her man, at his threadbare coat, said softly, "Put a sack over your shoulders," to which he replied, "I can do without a sack on a Sunday, lass."

Pressing Katie before him, they moved out into the road, and immediately the mud came over the uppers of their boots. But once clear of the road and on the fells the ground, though slippery in parts, was hard. They hurried, their heads down against the driving rain, and now and again, when a heavy gust met them, Rodney's hand would go around her shoulders and support her, and, apart from the question "All right, lass?" and her nodded reply, they had nothing to say until after they reached the top of the hill, where on that glorious Sunday many lifetimes ago she had sat with her granda and the sun had shone, and the sky was high, and her heart was light. On her half-days since, the sun had never shone.

Both breathing hard, they stood for a moment squinting through the rain that was falling like a great grey sloping curtain across the land below them. Then, bending towards her, his eyes blinking, his face streaming, Rodney said, quietly, "What is it, lass? I feel somethin' troublin' you."

She forced herself to look back into his eyes. She loved her da, but in some corner of her mind she was a little afraid of him. She had been brought up under her mother's idea of her father's moral code, with sayings such as "Your da wouldn't stand for that", "Your da's not afraid of the truth", "Tell the truth and shame the devil", "Straight as a die, your da is". But she could at least answer part in truth and say, "I'm tired, Da."

"Aw, lass." He passed a wet hand over her streaking face; then, cupping her chin, he said, "If it's too much, leave. You'd be better in another job. There's piles of things openin' up in Jarrow, chemical works and such; there might be work of some sort in them for you. Leave, lass."

"I'll think about it, Da."

"Before you come home again I'll prepare your ma so she won't be disappointed. She lays so much stock on Mrs. Davis."

"I know, Da. Thanks, Da."

"Now go on, on your way."

"You go home, Da, don't wait."

"Just for a little while."

"No, please. You're soakin', and you can't see far anyway. Go on, Da."

"I will when you get to the bottom of the hill. Go on."

She turned away from him and went on her way.

She made herself hurry as much as she could against the wind until she knew she was out of her father's sight, and then her step became slow and dragging. Already her cloak was soaked through and she could feel the water seeping through her dress on to her back, but she didn't mind; she wouldn't mind about anything if only the jollop had worked.

She had taken so much senna and salts that she felt she had no inside left, but it hadn't helped. What was she going to do? Oh, dear God, what was she going to do? Dotty was noticing things about her being sick in the mornings. There'd come a time when she'd have to tell Mrs. Davis, and then her mother must know. But she wasn't now really afraid of telling Mrs. Davis, or her mother; it was her father she was afraid of knowing, not because of what he would do to her but of him coming up to the house. She was terrified of him coming up to the house. If he were to hurt anybody . . . if he were to hurt HIM he would be put in the house of correction. Then what would her ma do, and her granda, and Lizzie? They would be turned out of the cottage, and nobody would dare take them in. She had seen people thrown out on to the fells for much less than what her da would do to Mr. Bernard. She couldn't bear to think what would happen to her family if her da did anything, and all through her; she would die first.

The dark figure loomed in front of her before she was aware of his approach. It was Mr. Bunting. She had met him every time on her day off since that sunny Sunday. She wasn't afraid of him any longer, because, with the exception of one thing, she wasn't afraid of anything any longer.

Mark Bunting had his dog with him. It was a big dog, a cross between a collie and a labrador. It came to her feet and sniffed round her ankles; it had done that twice before. Bunting, looking down at her, his eyes moving round her face, did not give her any greeting but said, "He's taken with you. That doesn't often happen with him." Then, his gaze narrowing, he said, "You all right? You look under the weather."

"I've had a cold."

"The same one as you had last time?" He ended this on the sound like a laugh, and she nodded at him, saying, "It hangs on."

He now let his eyes roam over her, but her cloak told him nothing. One thing he was certain of, she wasn't the same girl he had met some weeks ago. The sparkle had gone out of her face. In an odd kind of way he was interested in her. Nor, apparently, was he the only one who had an interest in the Mulhollands. He was still wondering why young Rosier had called him into the office and pumped him about Big Mulholland. It looked, by what he said, as if he was wanting something on him to get rid of him. Yet Rosier hadn't known until he told him that Mulholland was thick with Fogerty and Ramshaw, the troublemakers, and so, in the first place, it couldn't have been about that. But once he did know it he had harped on about it. . . . Now why would he want to get rid of Big Mulholland, for Mulholland was an excellent worker. He himself had put the manacles on him once or twice by docking his corves, but that was a different kettle of fish. He wouldn't want to get rid of him. There were many others he would like to see go before Mulholland. He could send up half as much coal again as most of them.

He said now, "Is it hard work up there?"

"Yes."

"Do you still like it?"

She paused before saying, "Yes." And now she added, "I've got to go; I'm wet through."

As he had given her no greeting he gave her no farewell, but he smiled his queer smile as she turned away, and he stood watching her for a moment before hitting out with his stick at a bramble, then striding on again. . . .

When Katie entered the kitchen, Cook was sitting at the table drinking from a mug of steaming tea. She turned her head and looked at Katie for a long moment before saying, and not unkindly, "I'd get them things off, you must be wringin'."

"Yes, I am, Cook."

"Hang them in the boiler room."

Katie went into the warm steamy room and took off her dripping straw hat and her cloak; and when she re-entered the kitchen, Cook, still in kindly tones, said, "You must be wet to the skin; I'd go up and put your other frock on. But first fetch the teapot."

Katie went to the hob and, lifting the big earthenware teapot, brought it to the table; and there Cook, looking at her with a slanting gaze, said, "Pour yourself a cup out."

"Oh ta, Cook, ta."

"Sit yourself down while you're drinkin' it." She nodded to the form and Katie sat down. But Cook's unusual kindness and the hot tea began to undermine her, and slowly great tears whirled from her eyes and rolled down her face and dropped off the end of her chin.

Cook, turning fully round to her now, said, "What's the matter?"

"I don't feel very well, Cook."

It was a full minute before Cook, nodding towards her, said, "Well, you wouldn't, would you?"

Without looking at what she was doing Katie pushed the mug to the corner of the table while her eyes remained fixed on the cook's face. Cook knew. She knew!

She jumped up from the form, ran out of the kitchen, along the corridor, through the door, up the back stairs, past the green baize door and up the rest of the stairs to her room, and there, flinging herself on her bed, she sobbed unrestrainedly.

It was fully a quarter of an hour later when Dotty came into the room, and, shaking her by the shoulder, said, "Come on, you're wanted."

Katie turned on her side and looked at Dotty, and she saw that Dotty also knew. She felt that Dotty had known for some time. She looked at Dotty's spotty plain face. She had always been sorry about Dotty's spots and the way she looked, but she wished now from the bottom of her heart that she could change places with her, be her altogether, although she wouldn't wash her face in the chamber-pot every morning like Dotty did because the cook had told her it was good for the complexion. But at this moment she would have willingly been her in every other way.

When Katie sat up, Dotty, giving a hitch to her skirt, placed herself on the mattress beside her and, putting her face close to hers, whispered, "Who was it?"

Not a muscle of Katie's face moved as she stared back like a petrified rabbit into the kitchen-maid's face, until Dotty said, "Was it Billy? He's always pokin' me; he's tried it on more than once. He caught me one night and I knocked him into the midden. You should have heard him swear."

Katie sprang up from the pallet now, tore off her dress, pulled the dry one from the hook, and she was buttoning it up before Dotty spoke again. And then quite patiently she said, "Aw, well, if you won't tell, you won't; but it's one of 'em isn't it? There'll be high jinks when Mr. Kennard gets goin' . . . You'd better come on, Mrs. Davis is in no good mood."

When Dotty left the room Katie's head sank on to her chest. This was only the beginning. Would she be able to stand what was to come, or should she do what she thought of doing last week, jump into the water-filled quarry on the road to the mine? . . .

She had been standing before Mrs. Davis for ten minutes and Mrs. Davis had been talking all the while, quietly if somewhat stiffly; and now, seeming to lose patience, she said harshly, "Katie! You've got to answer me. I'm asking you again, are you sick every morning?"

Katie drew a great long breath into her body, and as she let it out there went with it her resistance. She would have to tell, at least some part of it, and so she said, "Yes, Mrs. Davis."

Mrs. Davis now closed her eyes, bowed her head for a moment and wiped her mouth with a small white handkerchief; then, looking at Katie again, she said, "How long is it since you saw anything?"

"Over two months, nearly three, Mrs. Davis."

"Are you going to have a baby, Katie?"

It was some time before she could bring herself to answer this, and then she could only do it by bowing her head.

"Oh, Katie, Katie!" There was utter despair in the house-keeper's voice. "How could you let this come about, you above all people? I trusted you more than anyone else in the house. Do you hear me, Katie? Before anyone else. Who is it, Katie?"

A full minute elapsed and Mrs. Davis said again, "Come along, Katie; you know you'll have to tell me in the end, so you might as well do it now, because I'll find out. Who is it? Is it Billy?"

"No, no," she answered Mrs. Davis, emphatically now. Billy, the garden boy, with his great loose lip and grinning face—she would hardly speak to him, let alone allow him to touch her. She had never let anyone touch her, and when she came to think about it there was only Billy who had tried. No other man attempted to lay a hand on her until . . .

Mrs. Davis stared at the young, slim, pathetic figure before her. Dear, dear Lord, how had this come about? Who? Who? She felt responsible for the child. Hadn't she been the means of getting her the position? Her mind asking when this had taken place, she was presented with a picture of Katie the day following the ball. She had not been herself. Her face was red and swollen and Cook had reported that she had been sick twice, doubtless with stuffing herself. But it was from that morning that she had noticed the difference in her. . . . It must have happened the night of the ball, and it must have been the first time, for whoever had done this to

67

her it hadn't been to her liking. Poor, poor child. But who? Who? Mrs. Davis tried to recall the events of the night of the ball, but they were hazy in her mind, she had been very tired. Moreover, although she drew a veil over it, she knew that she had taken more wine than she should have done. But, as she told herself the following morning when she was suffering from a bad headache and an irritable temper, so had everyone else.

Vaguely she remembered taking Katie to the gallery. She also had a vague memory of hiding her behind the curtain, then returning to see if she was still there. She wondered now if, in her bemused state, she had gone to the wrong curtain. Anyway, there had only been three male servants in the house that night, and she couldn't for a moment suspect Frank Tapman, the father of two daughters of Katie's own age, and certainly not John Swan, a God-fearing good man. That only left Patrick. Her whole being rejected the idea that Kennard would perpetrate such an act with a young girl, little more than a child. No, she knew Patrick. Who better. Then someone in the house? . . . Oh no. No. She must never think that. But it had happened before, hadn't it? Yes, but this had been his engagement ball; she would not think that of Mr. Bernard. She had no liking for him, but after all he was a gentleman and had his code and . . . and he would certainly have done nothing like that with his fiancée hardly out of his sight. . . . Mr. Rodger? Again, no. Mr. Rodger *was* a gentleman. There was no doubt in her mind about that. Well, it only left the master. Nonsense. The word was loud in her head. The master, be what he may, rough-mouthed, uncouth at times, he was a man of honour. . . . Billy Denison. It must be him—unless, that is, it was someone from her village. She had been home on the Sunday and the ball was on the Tuesday. Yet she had seen her in the intervening time, and if she had looked like she had done on the morning following the ball she would have remarked on it to herself. No, it was Billy Denison. And that was why the child was so vehement in her answer when Billy's name was mentioned.

"I'll have Billy brought in and then we'll see, Katie."

"Oh no, Mrs. Davis." Katie was daring to grip Mrs. Davis's arm. "It wasn't him, it wasn't him. I wouldn't . . . I mean, I wouldn't let him touch me; I don't like Billy, he's dirty." She squared her lips from her teeth and the action alone fully convinced Mrs. Davis, in spite of her reasoning, that whoever the man was it wasn't Billy Denison.

Mrs. Davis bowed her head. She felt utterly deflated, terribly sad, and not a little afraid. The mistress would have to be told. She remembered what happened the last time on an occasion like this. But that time was different. Then there had been accusations against the son of the house. Her voice now flat, she said, "The mistress will have to be told, Katie."

"Oh no, please, Mrs. Davis." Katie's head was back and bobbing as if on a string. "I can just leave. Nobody else need know. I can just leave."

"Your mother or father will be bound to come to the house, Katie. More likely it will be your father."

On this thought Mrs. Davis realized that she was more afraid of Rodney Mulholland visiting the house than she was of imparting this obnoxious news to her mistress. Rodney Mulholland was a righteous man, and righteous men could be terrible in their anger. She had been brought up by a righteous man; she knew all about righteous men. Her life would be different today if it hadn't been for the fear of that particular righteous man.

But, apart from whatever action Rodney Mulholland would take, there was Catherine. She would have another mouth to feed, two shortly . . . and on the pittance that Rodney worked for. . . . She could let the child stay on for another few weeks, say until after the wedding. But then there was more than a possibility that Catherine would become aware of what was wrong with her daughter. She was surprised that she hadn't already done so. But would she ever dream that her Katie, her beautiful, good little Katie, was in this predicament? And the term remained as it had been, for the child was good; this thing had surely happened to her against her will. But the point she must consider at the moment was that if either of her parents should come to the house and demand to see the master or mistress then she herself would be in the soup, for the mistress would demand to know why she hadn't been told about this before. . . . There was nothing for it but she must tell Madam, and it was a foregone conclusion what the result would be. Katie would be sent packing.

* * *

Katie was sent packing. Two days later she left the house carrying her belongings in a bundle that was no bigger than the one she had arrived with five years earlier. But she didn't go home alone. It was Mrs. Davis's half-day and she took her in the carrier's cart.

They arrived at two-thirty in the afternoon, and Mrs. Davis left the house an hour later, and she had to let herself out because Catherine was too stunned to move.

Catherine sat looking at Katie, who was sitting on the cracket by the fire, her body almost doubled in two, and by her side with his arm around her shoulder sat William. He, too, had been stunned, but now a feeling of rage was ousting the stupor. It boiled in him, stiffening his muscles and pushing his jaw-bones outwards. He took his arm from about her, but not before he had patted her. Then, pulling himself from his seat, he grabbed at his crutch and stamped across the room to the door.

Only now did Catherine rouse herself, saying, "Da! Don't . . . don't go out; you're not fit. Stay where you are . . . please." But William paid no heed and the door banged behind him.

And now Catherine stood looking at her daughter, and all the while she shook her head; then, moving slowly towards her and seating herself in the chair her father had just vacated, she pulled Katie round to face her, and she had to press her body upwards before she could look into her face. It was no longer beautiful, and in this moment it was so contorted with sorrow that she couldn't find it in her even to harshen her tone as she asked, "But why, lass?" Not "Who was it?" but "Why?".

Katie, looking into her mother's face for the first time, shook her head and muttered, "It wasn't me, Ma."

"Not you? What do you mean?"

"I . . . I didn't want . . . I mean, I would never have. He . . ." She dropped her head and could go no further, but Catherine finished for her. "He forced you?" And to this Katie gave a small nod.

And now Catherine asked, "Who, child?"

For answer she received silence, and no matter how she

talked, or how she coaxed, she couldn't get her daughter to say who had done this thing.

Then Rodney came in at half-past six. He came in with William, who had walked all the way to the pit-head to meet him and to try, in his own thoughtful way, to lighten the shock. But by the look on Rodney's face he hadn't succeeded.

He came in the back way, as he always did when coming from the pit, but tonight he did not take his black, damp, coal-impregnated coat off and bang it against the wall underneath the lean-to. He did not even drop his can on to the shelf outside the back door, but he entered the kitchen as he had left the pit, and inside the door he stopped and looked at his daughter.

Katie was sitting at the far side of the table, not eating, just sitting, and she no longer needed to wonder how her ma would go about telling him, for she saw immediately that he knew. He looked taller than usual, older, terrible. His eyes were no longer the nice grey colour but seemed to be shining red out of his black face. He approached the table slowly, the can still in his hand.

Catherine, at the stove where she was stirring a stew in a black pot, did not turn round. After the first sight of her husband's face she could not bear to look at him, and as her father came in and sat slowly in his chair she thanked him in her heart for taking this burden from her. She went on stirring the pot, and all the while Rodney stood at the table staring down into his daughter's face.

All along the road he just wouldn't believe it. He had wanted to strike William when he told him this thing about his beloved child, whom at times he had thought he would never rear because she was so good, so beautiful. Never a Sunday went past that he didn't kneel in the chapel and thank his God for the gift of her; for her gaiety, her joy, her kindly nature, her beauty. And now she had come to this. He stared at her until her head drooped deep into her chest, but he didn't speak to her. His feelings were beyond words. Slowly, he turned away and walked into the bedroom, and William, quickly putting out his hand, touched Catherine and indicated the door with a jerk of his head.

Catherine took the pot off the fire and placed it on the hob. Then, rubbing her hands on her coarse apron, she went into the bedroom and closed the door. And there they stood looking at each other until he said simply, "Who?"

71

"I don't know."

"You've asked her?"

Catherine lowered her head on to her breast and swung it from side to side as she said, "Until I'm tired. All afternoon I've been at her. She wouldn't tell Mrs. Davis—Mrs. Davis brought her home."

Rodney looked away from Catherine towards the little window. He could see the sun going down behind the roofs of the cottages opposite. It was a calm, quiet, October night, a night when after a wash and a bite to eat he would have taken a walk in the long twilight and become refreshed in mind and spirit. But now the darkness had enveloped his spirit. It was a darkness blacker than the bowels of the mine when a man was entombed behind a fall. He said slowly, "That's what has been wrong with her all these weeks." He turned his eyes back to her. "She didn't mention anything to you?" The words came from between his gritted teeth.

"No. No." Her voice became high for a moment; then it dropped to a whisper again as she added, "How could I have kept it from you?"

Thrusting his body round as if pressing it against a force, he turned his back on her and demanded, "Why am I pestered like this? Four of them taken, Lizzie as she is, and now this. A shame before God. Brought down to the level of the middens."

"Rodney!" She went to him and put her hand gently on his shoulder, and she gazed at his stiff black profile as she said, "She must have been taken against her will. Mrs. Davis said as much. She came in here and had a word with me. She said she had grieved since the day following the ball; she had grieved long before there were any consequences."

Rodney did not look at her as he asked, "Hadn't she any idea at all?"

"Only the gardener's boy, Billy Denison, but she said that Katie had denied flatly that it was him, and she's denied it to me an' all."

Turning now, his step heavy but unhurried, Rodney went into the kitchen and, facing Katie again, he said to her, "Will you give me his name, or have I to go up to the house?"

She looked up into his face, her eyes wide and dry. They were burning as if they had been sprayed with hot sand. If she said Mr. Bernard he would stalk up to the house, but he would never get inside. They wouldn't let him into the real part of the house. And should he wait for Mr. Bernard and waylay him and hit him, what then? He would, as she had known all along, be sent to prison. If she could only be silent and keep on being silent . . . She could as long as they didn't blame Billy Denison. Although she didn't like Billy, she wouldn't want to get him into trouble through her. They might send him packing too, and he was from the orphanage.

"Very well," Rodney answered her silence. Then, still with the unhurried step that spoke more clearly of his anger than any bustle could have done, he stripped himself to his small clothes, washed himself in the tub of water that Catherine had got ready to the side of the fireplace, changed into the only pair of decent trousers and coat that he possessed, and without bite or sup after his twelve-hour shift, and without speaking another word to anyone, he left the house.

He must have reached the road leading off the fells by the time the lie came into Katie's mind, the lie that, with her agile, imaginative brain, she should have thought of much earlier if she hadn't been half demented with worry about the very thing that was taking place now, what her da would do when he found out. She sprang from her seat, making both Catherine and William start; then she was out of the front door, rushing by the cottages, past Mrs. Weir and Mrs. Bailey, who were talking at their front doors about the trouble that had come on young Katie and the Mulhollands; for anybody with half an eye could see the way the wind blew with the housekeeper bringing her home, then big Rodney going along there looking like that. And they didn't need two guesses as to where he was making for. She ran unheeding past three girls coming home from the rope factory who knew nothing yet about the scandal, and who half paused and greeted her almost in a voice, saying, "Why, hello, Katie. What's fetched you yhem?" and she flew past the men who were playing quoits at the top of the end cottages.

She caught sight of Rodney as he dropped on to the road from the heathered bank, and she cried, "Da! Da! Wait, Da."

Rodney turned and waited, and when she was standing before him, gasping for breath, unsteady on her feet, he put a hand to her shoulder and stayed her.

Her words interspersed with gasps, she looked up at him and cried, "Don't go, Da. Don't go. I'll tell you. 'Cos . . . 'cos it wouldn't be any use you goin'." She bowed her head; then after a moment, during which he waited without speaking, she went on, "It was the night of the ball. It was dark, late. I . . . I was tired. I . . . I went into the yard to get the air so's I wouldn't feel so sleepy. It was warm and I went through the arch and along the path by the wall for a little way, and . . ." The lie now stuck in her throat, but her da's voice eased it out as he said, "Aye, go on."

"Well. Well, somebody caught hold of me. They put their hand over me mouth." That was true enough, anyway. "And . . . and I couldn't do anything. It . . . it was then. . . ." Her voice trailed away, and after a space he said, "You didn't see him, his face?"

"No, Da. No."

As he stared down on her bent head he remembered the moon had been shining on the night of the ball because Catherine had remarked it would be lovely up there. The moon shining and it being nice and warm, the guests would likely be strolling in the garden. He said, now, "The moon was shining, Katie, remember?"

Her head jerked, and she looked up at him uner her eyelids staring at him for a moment before saying, "It was dark, where . . . where he pulled me into the bushes."

"Tell me one thing, and tell me truly, for you're bound to know. Was it one of the staff?"

"No. No, Da." She could tell the truth about this, and she was wise to the fact that her da would know that she knew the difference between the clothes of a servant and those of the gentry. Moreover, as she had found, there was a distinct smell about all gentry—not only a soap-and-water smell but the smell of pomades on their hair and such.

Rodney turned his gaze from her and looked into the blue misted night light falling over the fells. There had been a hundred guests at the ball; half of them would have been men. If he went up to the house now he would have to say, "My daughter was taken by one of your guests," and they would laugh at this. "Send round the three counties," they would say, "to find out which man had had a tousle with a maid behind a bush in the garden, a place where she didn't ought to be on that particular night. What was she doing in the garden, anyway, if she didn't want trouble?"

The hopelessness of the situation pressed his anger down and there came into its place a feeling of compassion. When his arms went out and drew her gently to him, the dam of terror inside her was released, and there, in the growing dusk on the fell, her crying reached a height of hysteria, until Rodney, lifting her, carried her up the bank and sat down on the heather and cradled her as he hadn't done since she was a child, and rocked her until he brought a measure of comfort to her.

6

George Rosier pulled himself up straight as the carriage entered the drive. He tugged at his green satin waistcoat, patted his protruding stomach and smiled to himself. It had been a very good day. He'd had a fine lunch with James Talford, but, what was more important, there had been present at that lunch Mr. Charles Palmer. It had been stimulating just to be in Palmer's company. . . . There was enthusiasm, drive and the Midas touch if ever he saw it. Palmer was no age yet, only thirty-eight, and the yard had only been going nine years, but he was coining money, making it hand over fist; not only was he building ships but he was making the materials on the spot to build the ships. Jarrow was booming. He had turned it from a village into a literal iron and steel goldmine. The thought that thrilled his breast now was that he, too, would soon have access to this particular mine. He had prepared the way over the last few years. Young Palmer knew what was in his mind, but he was no fool. If, as was likely to happen, the concern which was growing too fast for Palmer and his brother to handle was turned into a limited company, then he intended to be of that company, and young Palmer could make the going easier and would do so if he got his finger in another mine. He had already more fingers down mines in the county and about than he had on both of his hands, but he wouldn't mind having another down the Rosier mine. Oh, he was no fool was Charles Palmer, this fast-rising star, who was cunningly making a name as a philanthropist. We could all be philanthropists if we could dig gold out of steel.

But in the end it all boiled down to the number of shares one could buy, and this was where Talford came in. Talford himself was too old to take an active part in a company like Palmer's, but he had the wherewithal to make it possible for both him and Bernard to accomplish this—an active part. He had the vision of himself running the shipyard. And why not?

So buoyant did he feel that his small body almost bounced out of the carriage and up the steps to the house. Kennard was waiting at the open door, and although the lamps were burning at each side of the door he held another at head height to illuminate the steps; then he ushered his master through the lobby and into the hall and there relieved him of his hat and coat, before saying, "The family are in the library, sir."

George Rosier glanced at his butler, at the man who had valeted him for the last twenty years. There was little they didn't know about each other, and the inflexion in Kennard's voice told him that his words meant more than they said.

"Mrs. Noble arrived this morning, sir." Kennard did not make the mistake of still calling his master's daughter Miss Theresa.

"Yes. Well?" He stared at Kennard. He was surprised to learn that Theresa had arrived; she wasn't due until next week. If . . . if there were any more bees in her bonnet about leaving Noble and coming home he would soon scatter them for her.

"Mr. Bernard is also in the library, sir. They have been closeted for some time," Kennard's voice dropped to a discreet whisper as he added, "I went to attend the fire, sir; I found the door locked."

George Rosier's face puckered, his eyes narrowed to slits, and he gazed at Kennard for a moment longer before turning briskly away and marching towards the library door. The bees in her bonnet must be working, and Agnes and Bernard must be trying to cope.

He turned the handle of the door, and when it didn't respond to his touch he said loudly, "What's this?"

The next moment the door was opened and there stood Agnes, her face under its coating of powder and rouge looking like dirty dough. He glanced beyond her to his son and daughter, then in his usual bustling manner he charged into the room.

Bernard was standing with his back to the middle window and Theresa was sitting to the side of the fireplace. His son's face, he noticed immediately, was not pale but almost purple.

Of the three, his daughter looked most composed. He hadn't seen her for some weeks; she looked different, older, a woman, and yet that was not the proper description for his daughter. Always being devoid of womanly attraction, he did not imagine her marriage to old Noble would have improved matters in that direction. But there was a change in her.

"What's this?" He stalked to the centre of the room and cast his eyes from one to the other; then when he received no answer he bellowed, "What's this, I say? Locked doors in my own house. What next!"

"George." Agnes Rosier moved slowly towards her husband, and when she was close to him she said in a strangely quiet voice, "Sit down, George."

"What the hell's this? I'm not sitting down. Come on, spit it out. What's the matter? You're acting like a lot of bloody amateur players."

Her husband's swearing and obscenities no longer affected Agnes Rosier. The first time he had levelled a mouthful at her, shortly after their marriage, she had swooned, and immediately he had made sure she wouldn't do it again by swearing even more roundly as he slapped her face on both sides. But she did close her eyes before she said, "Theresa is determined to make trouble."

"Trouble! What about?" He looked towards his daughter, and Theresa, rising to her feet, looked towards Bernard and said, "You'd better ask him, Papa."

Now George Rosier turned towards his son and demanded, "Well?" Whereupon Bernard, taking one step from the window and bending his body in the direction of his sister, growled through his teeth, "She's mad. She should be locked up, certified."

"And I have no doubt but that you'd try it. You'd try anything, wouldn't you, to shut me up. Well, you won't." Now she swung round to her father and went on, "Do you know that the Mulhollands have been turned out of their house under the pretext that Mr. Mulholland is an agitator."

"What the hell has that got to do with you, girl?" George Rosier moved towards the back of a chair and, gripping the knobs at the top bent his head over it and peered at her.

"Did you give the order that put them out, Papa?"

Slowly he straightened up and looked towards Bernard. No, he hadn't given the order. He didn't know what this was all about, but he'd damned soon find out. Returning his atten-

77

tion to Theresa again, he said, "That's neither here nor there. Anyway, what have the Mulhollands to do with you?"

"Nothing, Papa, except that Katie Mulholland was your scullery-maid, and she was dismissed last week because she was going to have a baby. But she hasn't, up till now, said who gave her that baby because it's likely she was frightened of the very thing that has just happened—of her father being dismissed from the mine and the family turned out to live on the fells."

George Rosier was experiencing a feeling as if a cold hand had been pushed inside his shirt and was gripping his flesh. He wanted to look towards his son but kept his eyes on his daughter and said grimly, "Go on."

And Theresa went on. Her voice sounding thin and cold and coming through lips that scarcely moved, she said, "It was on the night of the ball, the ball that was celebrating his engagement to Ann Talford, that he took Katie Mulholland into his room. . . . I . . . I was crossing the landing turned four in the morning; I was feeling unwell and had been for a draught, when I saw him pushing the child out into the corridor. She was crying and in great distress. I immediately went into his room and told him that if anything should happen to that child he wouldn't get away with it this time, it wouldn't be another case of . . . of Maggie Pratt."

Now George Rosier was looking at his son, and Bernard, his whole body quivering visibly with his rage, cried, "I tell you she's mad. Her mind's gone." But before his father could make any reply to this Theresa put in, "As I've said already, you'll have to prove that, but I wonder what the Talford's will make of my state of my mind when I tell them the pretty story. . . ."

"What did you say?" George Rosier sprang round to her, and again he cried, "What did I hear you say?" This was followed by a silence that trembled on the outburst of a terrible rage.

At one time Theresa would have been intimidated by her father's voice alone, but now neither his voice nor his ferocious attitude had the slightest effect on her. It was as her father had recognized, she had changed. Six months of marriage had brought her slumbering, shrewd, unfeminine, dominant personality to the surface. She had just passed her eighteenth birthday and she was as mature as she would ever be, and more so than many a woman four times her age. She knew she would never like men—perhaps with one exception, her brother Rodger. The knowledge that she preferred women's company and that their figures and faces gave her pleasure did not frighten her. She knew now why she had always been attracted by Katie Mulholland, why she liked looking down on the kitchen quarters from the hill.

She said, in a clear, unswerving tone, "If something isn't done for Katie Mulholland in way of reparation, and good reparation, then I intend to inform the Talfords."

"You devil! You bloody little devil!" As George Rosier's hand went out to grab his daughter, Agnes cried, "George! George!" And now he turned on his wife, crying, "You think I'm going to be defied by a slip of a girl just because she's got a wedding-ring on her finger? Do you know what this could mean?"

"I know well enough, George." Agnes's voice was low and trembling, and she added, "And unless you want the whole household to be aware of the situation I would speak a little quieter. And it will be less tiring in the end. You've just come into the fray; we've been battling for hours." She cast a quick glance towards Bernard, then went on, "And we can't make her see sense."

"See sense!" George Rosier was glaring at his daughter. "I'll make you see sense, madam, if I've got to take a horse-whip to you. Now get to your room and I'll see you stay there until your husband comes to fetch you, and I'll see that he does that double quick."

Theresa rose to her feet. Her face was flushed but her voice was still cool. "I'm not afraid of your threats, Papa. If you'd look at things calmly you'd see the solution doesn't lie in locking me up . . . even if you could. I could write a letter to the Talfords any time within the next fortnight, and even if I was prevented from doing it during that time I could do it later . . . after the wedding." She now turned her eyes towards her brother and the hate between them seemed to vibrate in the tense atmosphere. Then, turning to her father again, she said, "The damage is done, but I'm going to see that you supply the means whereby Katie Mulholland doesn't suffer by your son's action for the rest of her life. I will keep my tongue quiet if you'll agree to settle a thousand pounds on her and see that her child, whether male or female, is educated."

George Rosier stared at the girl as if she was indeed mad.

He stared at her for fully a minute in absolute silence; then with the palm of his hand he beat his brow in a slow, regular motion. A thousand pounds, she said. A thousand pounds! And to educate the child, and by doing so own up to the fact it was a Rosier. Why was he standing here doing nothing? Why didn't he pick up the long steel ruler from the desk and beat her with it? His hand dropped to his side and he stared at the grey-clad figure before him. She wasn't even dressed as a young woman should be dressed. You could almost see the shape of her limbs through her straight skirt. It was indecently short, well above her ankles. She hadn't the figure of a woman, she was more like a youth . . . a man. Yes, she had the character and disposition of a man. As if he was attacking a man, he gripped her fiercely by the shoulders and dragged her towards the door. But there Agnes's hands pulled him to a halt, and, her voice hoarse, she whispered, "You don't want the household to know about this; have sense. Not even Kennard; not a whisper, it would be fatal. Go up with her; lock her in but don't mishandle her. They can imagine it's because she's left Mr. Noble."

Agnes was speaking as if Theresa was no longer present, or at best as if she was someone who didn't matter; yet she did matter, and nobody was more aware of this than herself.

Reluctantly George Rosier released his daughter. His stomach was moving up and down as if worked by bellows. He drew in a succession of short, sharp breaths; then, bending forward, he opened the door, waited until she had passed him, then followed her closely up the stairs.

Back in the library, Agnes Rosier covered her face with her hands; then, drawing them slowly down her cheeks she looked at her son, who was now standing rigidly gripping the high mantelshelf, and she muttered tensely, "Bernard! Bernard! You must have been mad."

"Shut up, Mother." He turned his body half towards her. "What do you know about it? There'll be enough when he comes in. . . . Look, go on, leave me alone; I can fight this out with him in a way I can't when you're here."

He watched her turn her stately, overdressed figure around like a ship on still waters and walk out of the room. When the door closed on her he began to beat his fist on the sharp edge of the marble mantelpiece, and he was still beating when his father re-entered the room.

George Rosier didn't demand of his son, "Is this true?" but

going up to him and clamping his hand on his arm he pulled him round and, facing him squarely, growled, "You know what you are? You're a bloody, stupid maniac, nothing more, nothing less. You couldn't wait to go into town to ease yourself, you had to revert to the kitchen again. Your tastes favour the kitchen, don't they?" His grip tightened and he shook the arm he held. "And it's a hell of a pickle this time, a hell of a pickle. You bloody fool! Do you realise that this could put the kobosh on everything? It just could, it just could, me boy. Just think of old Talford being confronted with a story like this and coming to find proof, and it here to his hand, with your own sister being able to substantiate all she says through the Mulholland slut. . . . Well, should that happen—get this into that big head of yours—you're on your own; for, as you well know, the mine, working under the present conditions, is not even paying its way, and it's no longer able to support you and your gaming debts . . . and your women. I'm hard put to it to keep this place and all its commitments going . . . so if you've never bothered thinking before start now. But don't start thinking in lump sums of a thousand pounds. As for signing a paper to the effect that you'll educate the brat, you might as well go straight away and tell Talford the lot. Another thing I've just thought of." He stabbed his finger into Bernard's chest. "It's a certainty that Mulholland's got no inkling yet as to who interfered with his daughter. It's as that mad bitch said." Her jerked his head towards the ceiling. "The girl's kept mum to keep him in his job, but I'd be wary. I've known Mulholland since he was a boy. He's the quiet type and they're the most dangerous sort when they're aroused. . . . By the way"—he narrowed his eyes now—"who gave him the push?"

His lips stiff, Bernard said, "I did. He was agitating; he's been seen with Ramshaw's lot."

"You were very high-handed, weren't you? He's been seen with Ramshaw's lot for years, but you didn't give him the push and turn him out of his cottage before. . . . You did it because you thought that he would move on, take the whole family with him, didn't you?"

Bernard returned his father's stare without blinking, and when his father said again, "You bloody fool!" his teeth grated against each other, and the muscles of his stomach tensed.

Of a sudden George Rosier dropped into a deep leather

chair near the fire and, resting his elbow on the arm, supported his head with his hand. After a moment, and in a more moderate tone, he said, "Well, what are you going to do?"

Bernard Rosier walked to the window and stood staring out into the darkness. Then after a time he returned to the fire and, looking down into it, asked, "Can I have a hundred pounds?"

"What are you going to do?"

"I'll . . . I'll tell you later if I bring it off. Can I have a hundred? At least fifty tonight and fifty ready to hand."

"I hope you know what you're doing this time."

"I know what I'm doing."

"Who's it with?"

"I'll tell you later. I'll be back in a couple of hours. If it works, everything will be settled, as will that cow up there." He threw his head back and gazed towards the ceiling for a moment.

George Rosier now rose from his chair, and unlocking a section of a panel near the fireplace, disclosing behind it a cupboard, he took a leather bag from a number lying there, and, carrying it to the desk, emptied the contents on to the table, counted out fifty sovereigns and pushed them to one side.

When Bernard had picked up the money and placed it in his wallet he walked down the length of the room and would have left without further words had not his father stopped him, saying, "Whatever it is, make it foolproof; it's your future." And to this Bernard answered bitterly, "Do you think I need to be reminded." He then collected his hat and cloak from the vestibule, together with a walking-stick, and went out into the night. He did not call for the coachman, nor yet take the trap, nor yet his horse. There was a short-cut over the fells to Bunting's house, which was only half a mile from the mine, and the more unobtrusive his visit the better.

*　　*　　*

At half-past nine the same evening Agnes Rosier visited her daughter to tell her that Katie Mulholland was going to be married to Mr. Bunting, the master-weighman at the mine, and she was a lucky girl to get a four-roomed house with a garden, together with a man like Mr. Bunting who could earn a lot of money if he tried.

The fact that Bunting had agreed to Bernard Rosier's plan was sufficient for Agnes Rosier to consider the matter closed. Pregnant girls with the alternative of the workhouse or sleeping in the open on the fells had very little choice.

7

Mark Bunting walked through the village on his way to the lower fell. He could have avoided it, but he didn't choose to do so. He was dressed in knee-breeches and leggings and wore a dark-green cloth coat that reached to below his hips. He was also wearing a white neckerchief tied in the form of a cravat. On his head was a hard high bowler, and in his hand a thick hawthorn stick.

It was early dusk and there were children playing in the roadway and women at the doors. Some of the children stopped their play and stared at him; all the women stared at him, and with hate in their eyes. One of them even spat in his direction; another, on his approach, went in and banged her door just as he was passing it.

Women were fools, he thought; they endangered their own and their men's livelihoods by showing their spleen. But their attitude had little or no effect on him—in fact he relished it in a way; it gave him a further sense of power. When one woman said in a loud voice, apparently speaking to her neighbour, "We does like copyin' our betters, doesn't we?" he knew she was referring to his mode of dress, and he felt complimented.

Although he hadn't been the means of Mulholland being stood off—Brown, the under-manager, had seen to that—he knew he was being blamed for it, but it didn't trouble him. He had been blamed for so much that he now set out to earn as much blame as possible. Blame usually meant money in his pocket.

When he left the road and took to the fells he saw the

shanty, or what looked like a shanty, when he was some distance away. When he got nearer he saw it was an erection made with two tables, one standing on blocks of wood with a chest of drawers for one wall and a cupboard affair for another. The third wall consisted of the backs of two chairs and the top of one table; two sides of the shelter were draped with bracken and pieces of material.

To the side of the erection a fire was burning in a square of stones; and he saw a woman bending over the fire, a pan in her hand. To her side there was a jumble of pots and pans and crockery. He saw Mulholland kneeling in front of the shelter bending over someone lying on a pallet, and beyond him more figures were huddled.

When Mulholland twisted round on his approach and sprang to his feet Bunting stopped. He knew it was always well to keep a distance between himself and men who had been evicted. He spoke immediately, saying in a conciliatory tone, "This wasn't my doing, Mulholland. I'll have you know that right away."

"What do you want here?"

"I want a word with you."

It was on the point of Rodney's tongue to say, "Get yourself away," when Catherine spoke. She just said his name, but it was so full of pleading that he remained silent. Straightening his shoulders, he walked a few yards from the shelter and Bunting followed him. When he stopped, Bunting came closer to him, but still not within arm's reach. He said again, "You mustn't hold it against me for this; I had nothing to do with it, it was Brown. And even if I'd had anything on you I wouldn't have used it under the circumstances."

"What do you mean?" Rodney's voice was a growl.

"Well"—Bunting dropped his head to the side and looked towards the ground—"your daughter's condition; not to speak of the other handicaps you have in your family."

Rodney forced himself to remain silent. His teeth clamped tight together, he waited. He couldn't imagine this man's actions being motivated by anything but greed, and so when his proposal came he was stunned into absolute silence.

"I wonder . . . I wonder if you'd consider me marrying your girl?"

The shock on Rodney lasted for some seconds; and then it was thrust aside by the thought, It was him. It was him. William had said he had seen him on the road Sunday after Sunday when she was going back to the house. He could have been sneaking around the night of the ball, keeking at the gentry. The voice that erupted from him was a cross between a roar and a yell. "You! You!" He would have been on Bunting within the next second had not Catherine's voice again checked him; and not only her voice but Katie's too. Katie's cry was even higher than her mother's. "No, Da, no! Not him. It wasn't him. Never."

It was something that Katie put into the word never that brought Rodney back to himself.

Bunting lowered his hawthorn stick. You see, it was as he had always told himself; they would be on you whether you were guilty or not. In an offended tone, he said, "I have never been near your girl, Mulholland. I have passed the time of day with her on the road on an occasional Sunday, that's all. I made the proposal out of good faith. I need a woman in the house; my mother has been dead for years. I'm offering her a home that even you should see is necessary at the present time. Moreover, I can promise that you'll be reinstated."

They all stood in silence for a moment; then Rodney, after moving one lip tightly over the other, said, "Thank you . . . Mr. Bunting"—he laid stress on the mister—"but I can see to me daughter."

For answer Bunting slanted his eyes towards the shelter and said, "I'll leave you to think it over. I'll come tomorrow night."

As he went to turn away Rodney said, "I wouldn't trouble; the answer'll be the same."

Bunting now turned and looked to where Katie was standing close to her mother's side, but he did not allow his eyes to rest on her, his gaze was directed fully at Catherine and it said, "You'll suffer this too."

Catherine watched him walk away. If it had been anyone else but him she would have gone down on her knees to him, but not to Bunting. She couldn't bear the thought of her daughter being under the protection of this hated man, as great as her need was. Anyone who attached himself to Bunting was shunned by the whole village. But at the same time Catherine wondered how long they could last out living like this. They were all right as regards to food, for the neighbours had been kindness itself. Each day they collected enough to feed them, but it was more than their livelihood was worth to offer them shelter. Anyone in the village found harbouring those who had been evicted as troublemakers at the mine shared the same fate as those they were endeavouring to help. But her Rodney hadn't been a troublemaker; this was all some plot which she couldn't fathom. She put out her hand and pushed Katie towards the shelter, then went to her husband and, looking into his face, whispered, her voice laden with regret, "If it had been anybody else but him."

He bowed his head before her gaze, and in his heart he repeated her words, "If it had been anyone else but him." His daughter needed shelter, and his father-in-law needed shelter because the old man was in a bad way. If it hadn't been for William he would have moved to a fresh town; traveling the road couldn't be any worse than up here on the wind-swept fells and the bad weather on them. But he wouldn't put William in the poor house; the old man had a horror of dying in the poor house.

From under his lowered gaze he saw Catherine's joined hands trembling, and he put his own out to steady them, saying, "There's always a chance I'll get set on at Palmer's. I'm going in the morrow again; they're setting men on all the time." He didn't add that it was hard for a black-listed man to get a job anywhere, for she knew that, but he went on, "The place is like a gigantic hive now, you wouldn't believe it. They've got four blast-furnaces goin' an' rolling mills, and boiler shops, and engine shops. You wouldn't recognise it now. You'll see, I'll get a start in one or the other of the shops."

"But they'd want experienced men, wouldn't they?" Her voice was very small.

"No, no; there's a thousand and one jobs that doesn't need experience. I've as much experience as the Irish, I'd say, and the place is alive with them."

"But . . . but would there be any chance of gettin' shelter? You said last week they were sleeping twelve to a room in some of the tenements. It wouldn't be any use getting a job if you couldn't get shelter."

He closed his eyes and bowed his head and said helplessly, "One thing at a time, Catherine, one thing at a time. Let me get a start first."

* * *

Her mind overwhelmed with despair, her body shivering with the cold, Katie lay curled up between her mother and

Lizzie. All night she had lain like this, listening to the breathing of the others, to the hard cutting cough of her granda, to the moaning of her father. She knew when they were awake and when they were asleep; only Lizzie slept undisturbed. Even Joe, who could sleep on his feet, told her at intervals, by the small sound he made in his throat, that he was awake. Now that he had the chance to sleep—he had been dismissed three days ago—he couldn't take advantage of it.

Sometime, long before the dawn broke, she heard her da get up; then her ma moved from her side. The day had begun, the endless day of just lying or sitting. No one talked much any more.

It was early in the evening of this day that Katie put on her cloak and said to Catherine, "I'm goin' over to see Betty."

Catherine stared at her. The Monktons, knowing the risk, had offered to give shelter to her father and Katie, but both had steadfastly refused to go. Now she imagined that Katie, feeling frozen to the bone as they all were, was about to seek the warmth of four walls for a short while before the night set in.

"All right, lass. Stay as long as you like," she said, after which she added quickly, "You'd better get back afore dark though, hadn't you." Then as she stared into the white peaked face the real reason for Katie seeking shelter at the Monktons came to her. She didn't want to be here if Bunting kept his word and came back tonight. That was it. . . .

But Bunting didn't keep his word and come to the shanty that evening, nor did he come the next night; nor yet the next; nor the one after that, on which particular night Katie again went to visit Betty Monkton.

It was the eighth morning after Bunting's visit, when things had reached the point of desperation for them all, with the exception of Lizzie, that Rodney rose just after four o'clock and made his way to Jarrow, to be at Palmer's Shipyard when the gates opened at six o'clock. A man had said that was the time to be there when there was a liklihood of jumping into someone's boots, a sick man's boots, because no man stayed away from work unless he was sick, and desperately so.

And it was later the same morning when the wind was driving the rain into the shelter that Katie, having taken off the dress in which she had slept, put on the only other one she had; then, washing her face and hands in the dead-cold water from the stream, she pulled on her cloak and set her straw hat straight on her head.

William, watching her from his pallet, asked feebly, "Where you goin', lass? Have . . . have you heard of a job?"

She was kneeling, searching in her bundle for a handkerchief, a new handkerchief, the one Mrs. Davis had given her on her sixteenth birthday, which was only a few days before she was sent home, and, still on her knees, she moved toward him and, bending down and kissing his sunken cheek, she said, "Yes, Grandpa, I'm going after a job."

Catherine, coming to the opening of the shelter, stared down at her, then exclaimed, "What did you say? Where you goin', lass?" She pushed Lizzie under cover as she spoke; she had just returned from making her clean. She took her some distance from the dwelling each morning for this purpose.

Katie moved past her mother and a few steps away from the shelter, and Catherine went with her, and again she asked, "Where are you goin', lass?" Then added, as her father had done, "You've heard of something? A job or something?"

"You could look at it that way, Ma." Katie's lips were trembling, and now she clutched at Catherine's hand and stared beseechingly into her face as she muttered, "Don't be upset, don't, but I . . . I'm going to marry Mr. Bunting."

Catherine drew in a sharp breath that cut off her words; then she gulped twice before crying, "No, lass! No! It would drive your da mad. No! No!"

"I promised; it's all arranged. That's where I went the other night, an' the night he was to come here . . . I told him then."

"But . . . but it's only a week ago, lass."

"I know, I know. They can do these things quick by licence, he said . . . He said leave it to him and . . . and he's promised you'll have a house by the morrow."

"Aw, lass." Catherine moved her head in slow wide sweeps, never taking her eyes from Katie's face.

"I've . . . I've got to do this, Ma, 'cos . . . 'cos Granda'll die if he's out here much longer, an' you an' all and . . . and then the baby comin'."

"But your da, child."

Katie now hung her head and said softly, "It was because

of me he was stood off and you were turned out. They did it because . . ." She stopped and bit on her lip and Catherine said quickly, "No, lass, no. It was nothing to do with you; it was because he had been holding meetings with Fred Ramshaw and Mr. Fogerty, and they're known to be strong union men going from pit to pit stirring up—at least Fogerty does."

"No, Ma, no. It wasn't because of that; it was because of me."

Catherine stood contemplating her daughter. For a space of time, during which her mind took in and rapidly sorted what Katie had said, she continued to stare at her, and then, putting her fingers tentatively to her lips, she whispered, "They know up at the house, the master and them, who it was?"

Katie lowered her head as Catherine exclaimed, "Oh, dear God! And you, you know who it was?"

Katie's chin jerked up and she whispered rapidly, "Yes, Ma, yes: Mr. Bernard. But don't tell me da ever. He would make trouble. You saw him at Mr. Bunting; he . . . he would kill somebody."

"Aye, yes." Catherine knew that her daughter spoke the truth. Her God-fearing, quiet husband was quite capable of killing the man who had brought his daughter to this pass. But she need have no fear; he wouldn't get to know anything from her.

"So you see, Ma"—Katie's lips were trembling so hard the words spurted unevenly out of her mouth—"by . . . doing this . . . me da, me da an' all of you will be all right. He'll . . . have his job, for good."

"Oh, Katie! Oh, child!"

"Bye-bye, Ma. Tell me da not to come. Don't let him come, Ma. Stop him; 'cos once it's done, it's done. An' . . . an tell him I want to have the baby properly; tell him that."

As her hand trailed away, Catherine grabbed at it, saying, "But the village. Nobody will speak to you any more, lass."

Now Catherine saw her daughter straightening her stooped shoulders, she watched her head go up, and it wasn't her Katie but someone much older who said, "It doesn't matter to me now what anybody says and who speaks to me and who doesn't; all that matters is that you and them"—she inclined her head slightly towards the shelter—"are all right. Bye-bye, Ma." Bending swiftly forward, she kissed Catherine, and

Catherine clutched her tightly, crying, "No, lass, no," until Katie, tearing herself away, ran from her, her hands covering her mouth to stop the moaning sounds.

* * *

It was in great trepidation that Catherine waited for Rodney to return. But it wasn't until half-past six, when the last vestige of light was going, that she saw the dim outline of him hurrying over the fells towards her. And when he came up close to her she saw that his face was dirty, and bright and happy; more so than she had seen it for years. His hand came on to her shoulder as he said, "I've got a start, lass. I've been at it all day. An' we've got a place . . . of sorts. It's not what I would want, but in this case beggars can't be choosers. An' we'll soon get out of it; it'll just be for the meantime."

His words were gabbled; the excitement was filling him so much that he did not for the moment take in her pitiful expression, but, turning his head to the side, he shouted towards the shelter, "I've got set on, William, in the rolling mills." He expected an answer to come back immediately to him saying something like, "Thanks be to God, lad!" But William didn't answer him, nor yet did Joe make his appearance. He brought his eyes back to Catherine, and, putting his face close to hers, asked, "What is it? Something's happened." Then, looking wildly round him, he added, "Katie!"

"She's gone, Rod."

"Gone? Where's she gone? What do you mean, woman?"

She now took hold of his arms and she felt the hard knots of the muscles as she gripped them and said slowly, "What she's done she's done for us, remember that. Do you hear? Remember, what she's done she's done for us." Her voice had risen. It was loud, like a cry echoing across the fells, and he pulled himself away quickly from her, saying, "What's she done? Where is she?"

She kept her eyes tight on him as she said, quickly now, "She married Bunting this mornin'."

She had feared his reaction. All day she had steeled herself against this moment, imaging herself hanging on to him, trying to hold him down to keep him away from Bunting until he saw reason, but she hadn't prepared herself for what was happening now. Her man seemed to be shrinking before her eyes. She watched his body slump; she watched him turn from her and cover his face with his hands, much as her father had done when he had heard the news. He was acting like a man from whom the spirit had been whipped. He had got work; he had got them shelter; but the light had gone out of his life.

8

If Katie could have been sustained by the fact that her marrying Mark Bunting had provided her family with food, warmth and shelter, she might have felt that there was a purpose in her suffering. But the morning after a surprising night —surprising because this man, who was now her husband and whom she already feared, had not touched her—Joe came to the door and, gazing at her as if she was an utter stranger, told her that they were going into Jarrow to live. In a kind of cottage, was the way he described their new home, off Walter Street, No. 3, The Row. Their da, he said, had got started in Palmer's Shipyard.

On this news she'd had the childish desire to take Joe by the hand and fly with him to this new home in Jarrow. It was only the sure knowledge that Bunting . . . her husband . . . would come and bring her back that stopped her.

She did not ask Joe into the house, for already she'd had her orders on that score—no visitors. Bunting had sat most of last evening opposite to her at the other side of the blazing fire and given her her instructions. He wasn't having her family here or her going there, and it wasn't likely they'd have any visitors from the village. He'd buy the food, as he had always done, and dish it out to her every day. And she'd have to be careful; if there was any waste she'd have him to reckon with. Moreover, there was to be no saving of bits and pieces to be sneaked out. If the cooking was done properly the food would be eaten and nothing left over. Did she understand? She had moved her head, and on this he had taken his hawthorn stick, which was never far from his side, and poked it, not too gently, in the middle of her stomach, saying, "You've got a tongue in your head."

Later, shaking like a leaf in a gale, she had preceded him up the steep stairs, and on the tiny landing he had pushed one of the two doors open, and thumbing inwards, had said, "You're in there, until I need you."

By the light of a stub of tallow candle she saw a little room holding a single bed and a chest of drawers. Her relief at finding herself alone was so great that her shivering increased until her whole body appeared to be affected by ague.

And so the pattern went on for three weeks. She would rise early in the morning, make up the fire, heat his water to wash in the big black kail pot, make his breakfast of porridge and potato cakes fried in dripping; then when he was gone she would start her business of cleaning the house. She would have loved this task under other circumstances, for to her it was a lovely house, with a big kitchen holding two tables: one for eating off, one for cooking on. At one side of the fire was a small wooden settle, at the other a straight-back wooden chair with a padded seat. There was a long delf rack in the kitchen with good crockery on it. In the parlour there was a horsehair couch and two chairs, all worn but comfortable still. There was a round table in the middle of the room on a spindle leg, and under the good-sized window was an oak blanket chest. The stone floor was almost covered with hand-made clippie rugs.

The first time she saw the parlour she imagined a roaring fire in the grate and her ma and da sitting in the armchairs, and her granda on the couch, and their Joe and Lizzie and herself on the mat in front of the fire.

At the end of the first week the longing to see her people was so intense that she got as far as putting her cloak on and going to the door, but there she stopped. He had come in early last night, around five. It was now nearly two o'clock; she wouldn't be able to walk there and back before five o'clock. If she had known where Walter Street was she might have taken a chance. As it was, she thought better of it and contented herself with sitting mending his clothes.

It was on this day that she made the further acquaintance of Roy.

The dog had shown an interest in her from the beginning; it hadn't growled when she took its food down to the kennel. Bunting had said nothing to her about what attitude she should take to his dog, so as soon as the thought came to her she ran down the garden and undid the chain, and holding on

92

to his collar brought him into the house. He acted in such a queer, mad way at first, tearing round and round the room, sniffing here and there, that if she could have laughed she would have. After a while, his curiosity satisfied, he came to her where she sat and put his front paws on her knee, and she put her arms around him and cried.

But then came the day when Mark Bunting hastily swallowed his dinner and was out of the house around half-past twelve instead of one o'clock. The yearning to see her people had been almost unbearable for days, and so, donning her cloak and tying her straw hat on with the band of ribbon, she locked the door, put the key underneath the wash-house table, patted the dog, telling him she was sorry he would have to remain on his chain all day, then she set off at a good pace to walk the three and a half miles into Jarrow.

It was years since she had been in Jarrow and she remembered it as a busy place with rows of white cottages and streets branching off containing bigger houses, two-storey houses. Now it was a bewildering place. The cottages were still there but grimy-looking; and there was a maze of streets and houses all around. The main road was packed with carts: dray carts with barrels piled high on them, coal carts, coke carts, fruit carts.

Going up one of the streets she saw two women filling buckets from a tap in the middle of the road and she asked them the way to Walter Street, and they told her.

When she found Walter Street and the row of cottages behind it she was appalled by the dirt and the stench. She had to go down a bank to get to the little row of cottages, and she slithered in mud right to the very door.

When she knocked on No. 3 it was opened by her mother. They looked at each other for a moment; then fell into each other's arms, Catherine crying, "Oh, me bairn, me bairn!" and Katie repeating brokenly, "Oh, Ma, Ma!" Then Catherine, pressing her daughter from her, turned her head into the dim depths of the room behind and cried, "Da! She's come."

Katie, guided by Catherine, stepped down into the room. Then in the dim light she saw her granda lying on a raised wooden platform to the side of the fire, and she rushed to him and was enfolded in his arms, and his tears wet her face, but he said not a word.

When he had lain himself back on the bed Katie looked at

him and her heart sank. He wasn't better. Having shelter hadn't helped him. He looked bad, so bad. She touched his cheek and said, "Oh, Granda," and still he didn't speak, only held tightly on to her hand.

Now of her own accord Lizzie came to her side and she spoke Katie's name, saying it softly, and when Katie got up from the bed she put her arms around her and brought her head down to Katie's shoulder and laid it there.

After a moment Catherine gently drew Lizzie from Katie's arms, and, taking her to a chair, said, "There now. There now." She was touched and slightly amazed that this daughter had the sense in her to feel Katie's absence.

Going to the fire in the black wall, she said between her catching breath, "I'll . . . I'll make a pot of tea," and, turning and looking at Katie again, she added, "Get your things off, hinny, and sit down."

"I . . . I can't stay long, Ma. Perhaps half an hour; I've got to be back afore five."

"Oh!" Catherine turned to the fire again. Then William spoke for the first time. "How are you, child?" he said.

"All right, Granda."

And now quite bluntly he asked, "And how does he treat you?"

She paused before answering. How did he treat her? How he treated his dog, giving her orders and expecting them to be obeyed without question. Only he didn't sit staring at his dog as he sat staring at her for hour after hour until she felt she would scream. Once she got up and said she was going to bed and he had ordered her to sit down again. She always made sure now that she had something to occupy her hands in the evening so she wouldn't look at him looking at her. Yet he had never touched her. She was still sleeping in the little room by herself. She couldn't understand it. Although she was petrified of the moment when he would come near her, she still couldn't understand why, as yet, he hadn't.

Catherine now asked, "Is the house comfortable?"

"Oh yes, Ma." There was even a touch of enthusiasm in her voice. "It's a nice house, and warm . . ." She wished she hadn't said that because this place wasn't warm, it was chilling to the bone. She now glanced about the room. It was dreadful. The walls were running with water; the bricks of the floor were oozing water. It was dark and damp and terrible.

As if Catherine read her thoughts, she said, "Houses here

are impossible to get. This is bad, but we're on our own. You should see them up the streets; they're packed closer than hens in a cree. And the beds are never aired; as one gets out another gets in. The night shifts sleep through the day and there are strange men and women in one room. It's awful. And the middens—they've got to be seen to be believed. The smell would knock you down. You might think this is bad, lass"—she shook her head—"but it's nothin'. And they're asking three shilling a week for a room; they can get any price now. We were lucky to get this. It was a Mr. Hetherington who got it for us; he's the one who got your da set on. He knew your Granda Mulholland years ago. As a lad he worked under him. It was a stroke of luck in a thousand your da meetin' him. He knows your da; he knows he's no trouble-maker at the pit or anywhere else."

Katie watched her mother moving around the dim, smelling room, talking as if to herself most of the time. The smell that pervaded the room was a filthy smell like sitting in the closet. She wanted to get into the air and breathe deeply. Oh, if she could only take them all back to the house; if only Mr. Bunting—she thought of him as either Mr. Bunting or he—if only he was different, a bit kind; if only she could talk to him. . . . She missed talking, although she hadn't wanted to talk very much since the night of the ball. Somehow now she felt inclined to talk, but not about the things she used to talk about, such as the Rosier family and Mrs. Davis, and the staff, and food. She didn't know what she wanted to talk about now; she only knew that she needed to speak to some-one and hear them reply.

She had a cup of tea but would eat nothing, and then it was time to go, and she felt she'd hardly got in. She kissed and hugged her granda to her; she kissed and held Lizzie; and when she was at the door she mentioned Joe for the first time. "Where is he, Ma?" she said. "Our Joe."

"Oh!" Catherine smiled weakly. "Didn't I tell you? He's been set on; he's in the boiler shop. And the way he describes it, it's marvellous. And he's tickled to death working in the daylight. He'll never go down below again, never. He's a run-ner to one of the men with hot rivets and things, you know. Oh, he likes it. So you see, lass"—she spread her hands— "we're all right if only we could get out of this."

"Will you come again, lass?" Catherine asked tentatively now, and Katie nodded her head. Then she put her arms around her mother and they kissed and held tight for a moment; but when it was over she didn't immediately walk away, for there was a question she wanted to ask. She looked down as she said, "How's me da?"

"Not bad, lass. He was upset, but he's getting over it. I know one thing; he's dying to see you. You . . . you couldn't come one night?"

Katie turned her eyes towards the bank again and said, "No, Ma, I couldn't come at night."

"He'd walk you nearly all the way back."

"I couldn't, Ma."

"All right, lass." Catherine patted her arm, and again she kissed her; then she watched her mount the slimy bank. And when she turned at the end of the street she waved to her.

It wasn't four o'clock yet but the winter twilight was already beginning, and the effect of night coming fast was helped by the smoke belching from the great chimneys of the steel works. When Katie reached the main road she found it blocked with stationary traffic. Men sat high on their carts or stood at their horses' heads and shouted to each other. She walked quickly up the uneven pavement, past a row of shops all showing, to her mind, wonderful things: food, clothes, boots, butcher's meat, pig meat. She would have liked to stand and gaze in one window after the other, but she knew she mustn't waste a minute. Further along the pavement she came to the reason for the blockade. Two drunken women were sprawled in the middle of the road, fighting. Their hair was hanging down their backs, their clothes were rent and muddy, and as they tore at each other they were encouraged by a large group of onlookers while, a policeman tried to disentangle them, getting no assistance from any bystanders.

The sight of the fighting disgusted her—not that she hadn't seen drunken women before. But her mother never touched beer or gin, nor did her father. Her granda did, but only when there was a copper to spare.

The whole town seemed crowded with people, and it was not four o'clock. What it would be like when the shipyard and the chemical works let the men out she couldn't imagine.

When she reached the outskirts of the town and the open land stretched for miles before her, with the river winding through it, she breathed deeply and told herself she would die if she had to live in Jarrow and that hovel; she needed fresh country air.

The thought brought her to a stop and she clutched the neck of her cloak; she didn't need fresh country air. Given the choice she would run back to that evil-smelling room this minute.

As she skirted the village she was confronted on the narrow trail by a number of men coming off the second shift. She knew most of them; they all knew her. Some of their glances were scornful, some pitying, but no man spoke to her.

It was dark when she reached the house. She had run most of the last part of the journey. She was still running when she reached the wash-house, but when her hand went out to pick up the key her fingers remained stiff and bent; it was gone. Her eyes moved wildly about. If he were in the candle would be lit. She went slowly towards the house door and turned the handle, and when she entered the room she saw him in the light from the fire, sitting on the settee just as he had come from the pit. His eyes were waiting for her, and the look in them caused her whole body to go cold. She walked slowly forward, taking off her cape as she did so, and she passed him and was pulling off her hat and going towards the scullery to bring in the wooden tub for him to bathe in when he barked at her, saying, "You did it then?"

She turned and peered at him outlined against the firelight, and she gulped twice before she dared to protest, "I had to go; they're my folks."

"Are they, begod!" He was on his feet now, coming towards her. "Well, I'll tell you something which you seem to have forgotten, Mrs. Bunting." He stressed his name. "You happen to be a married woman now." He put four stiff fingers out and pushed her in the chest, causing her to stumble backwards. "You think because he's got work away from the pit you can take a high hand now, don't you? Well, let me tell you Mr. Rosier's arm is long and it's linked with Palmer's and a word from me and your da'll be out in the gutter again. Now remember that, the next time you want to take a walk . . . Get goin'; I'm waiting for the water. I've been waiting for the last half-hour."

While she scurried back and forward filling the bath, first with cold water, then adding the boiling water from the kale pot, he stripped himself of his clothes. He stripped himself naked as he had done since the first day she got the bath ready for him, not leaving his small clothes on as her father did, and other miners, when there were women and bairns about. While he washed she always kept her eyes lowered from him. She couldn't understand this attitude of his any more than she could understand him letting her sleep alone. She would have understood it better if he hadn't let her sleep alone.

When he sat down in the bath, his knees level with his chin and the water barely covering his thighs, she went forward and, stooping low, picked up the flannel out of the water, keeping her gaze fixed tightly on it the while; then, going behind him, she washed his back. Following this, she scooped some hot water from the pot into the wooden bucket; then going to the back door, where stood a barrel that caught the rainwater from the roof, she half filled another bucket, returned to the kitchen, and with it she cooled the hot water in the other bucket. Then, lifting it up, she stood waiting.

And Mark Bunting kept her waiting. His movements were slower now, leisurely. After a time he got to his knees and, bending forward slightly, held on to the sides of the tub while Katie poured the warm water over him. It was a refinement to his toilet that he had thought of only recently.

He always changed his clothes after the bath, and Katie now took his pit suit and underwear into the yard and banged them against the wall, getting rid of as much dust as possible. When she returned to the kitchen he was almost dressed and he barked at her again, "You could have left that till after, couldn't you? Where's the meal?"

The small protesting voice within her was quite silent now, and, scurrying still, she set the table. It was cold meat left over from dinner-time. He measured out for her three slices of bread, a small two-inch square of meat, a dob of dripping, and a mug of tea. He put no sugar in her tea but some in his own.

When the meal was over and she had washed the dishes she took her seat by the fireside and began to sew. She was turning in the frayed ends of his working trousers. She could hardly see what she was doing, for there was only one candle alight, and if she moved nearer to it it would mean moving nearer to him.

Mark Bunting now lit a spill from the candle and applied it to his wooden pipe—he did not smoke a clay pipe as the ordinary men did—and when the pipe was going well he lay back in his chair, his stockinged feet resting on the raised stone hearth, and surveyed his wife.

If Bunting had been other than he was, this scene could have held happiness for him, even having married Katie for a price, as he had done. She would have repaid the smallest kindnesses shown to her a thousandfold if he could have found it in his heart to be kind. If he had been kind she would have liked him, because he wasn't an unattractive-looking man. Being Katie, with a bountiful amount of sympathy and affection in her nature, she would have stood up for him in spite of what was said about him, if he had only been kind. And who knew but that the kindness would have grown into love, for kindness, like witchcraft, caused things to happen.

But there was a strong unnatural twist in Mark Bunting's make-up. How else could he have stood for years the scorn of his fellow men and found pleasure in their suffering, especially when the suffering was instigated by himself? With workmen, however, he knew exactly where he stood, what the result of his actions towards them would be, but in the present situation his position wasn't at all clear and he was in a quandary. He pulled hard on his pipe now as he looked at Katie: at the mass of gleaming hair, the tendrils hanging across her pale face; at her big eyes—the eyes that told him all her feelings—lowered over the sewing; at the small swelling bulge of her stomach; and he wondered where he stood. He didn't know but that young Rosier wasn't finished with her; he had been vague the night he called here, asking simply if he wanted to earn a hundred pounds. When he had replied with a laugh, "Show me the man who doesn't, sir," he had been told, "If you'll marry the Mulholland girl there'll be fifty when you ask her and fifty when it's done . . . she's to have a child." He had stared into the lean, handsome face which he hated more than that of any other man in the mine, and he had considered the proposal for a full moment, during which his thinking hadn't been concerned with the Mulholland girl but with the fact that this business could mean an assured income for years ahead. And even when he had given his answer he had not allowed himself to appear eager, but had said, slowly, "All right, sir; it's a deal," and all Rosier had said after that was, "Go to the Reverend Pinkerton. Tell him you want a special licence. Explain the situation, without my name of course; make it urgent. I'll see to the cost."

And that was all. It might be that when the child was born he would see to its upbringing if it was a boy. As for her—

well, if you fancied women she was a one to fancy. Rosier likely wasn't done with her. He had only seen him once since his marriage into the Talford family and then he had looked straight through him. But that was part of the game; he didn't mind being treated like scum as long as he was paid for it; he was treated like scum most of the time and not paid for it.

As he stared at her he wondered why he had no desire to take her to bed. She was his wife, he could, and Rosier couldn't do much about it, could he? It would be like eating your cake and having it. He had often thought if he had a woman in the house he would feel different, but he didn't. The thought of having her in bed stirred him not at all, but there were other ways in which she could afford him satisfaction, only he'd have to hold his hand about them until the child came and he knew Master Rosier's reactions. It wouldn't do to get on the wrong side of him; because it wasn't only the source of revenue for years ahead that could be jeopardized, there was also his job, and this house, of which he was very proud, that went with it. He would hold his hand. There was no hurry; he was a patient man.

He startled her by saying, "Have you seen about a mid-wife?"

Her eyes wide, she said, "No."

"Then you'd better, hadn't you? They get full up. A very busy time the spring is . . . for babies. Mrs. Morgan in the village, she's one, isn't she?"

She dropped her head before saying, "She wouldn't come."

He was sitting bolt upright in his chair now. "Who said she wouldn't come? You've asked her?"

"No . . . but a village woman wouldn't come to the house; you know she wouldn't." She felt a certain strength flow into her after having dared to say that to him, and something of this seemed to get across to him, for he got to his feet and, standing over her and digging his thick finger into the hollow of her shoulder, he said, "Go the morrow and ask her. She'll come. If she's sensible she'll come."

Again, in spite of his prodding finger, she forced herself to speak what was in her mind. Although her voice was little more than a whisper, she said, "I'd rather have me Ma."

She was nearly knocked from the chair with the flat of his hand on the back of her head. "You're not havin' your mother here. I'm not having any of your scum inside these four walls, get that! At no time. Do you hear me?"

She snapped off the thread from the trousers with trembling fingers; then she folded them up and laid them by the side of the fireplace where he always left his clothes so that they would be warm to put on. Following this, she proceeded to set the table for his supper, and when this was done she stood between the kitchen and the scullery door and said, "I'm going to bed, I'm tired."

"Like hell you are! If you go on walks that make you tired that's your look-out. Sit yourself down there." He pointed to a chair. "You'll go when I'm ready and not afore."

So she sat until nearly ten o'clock, and only the thought of having to light one more candle drew him up the stairs, and she followed him, thinking all the while that tonight he would push her into his room. But he didn't.

9

Katie's baby was born towards the end of April, in the first minutes of a Thursday morning, and it was a girl.

She lay exhausted after the long fifteen hours of labour while Mrs. Morgan cleaned her up and washed her and saw to the child. Then the midwife, sitting on a chair by the bedside, dozed until the dawn should break and she could see her way home.

The sun was shining in through the little window when she stood, her shawl over her head, ready to go. She looked down on Katie with the child in her arms and said, "You can be proud of your bairn; she's a beauty, lass. What you goner call it?"

"Sarah," said Katie.

Hearing a door bang downstairs, Mrs. Morgan went and looked out of the window and, coming back, she said, "He's gone." Then after a pause, during which her head drooped to one side, she asked, "Why in the name of God did you marry that one?"

Looking all eyes, Katie said quietly, "Because of them, Mrs. Morgan, me ma an' da and them. I couldn't stand to see them freezing to death out there. And he said he'd get me da set on straightway and give them a house.

"And then your da went and got set on in Jarrow. Aw, lass, all for nowt. . . . Is it hisen?"

"Oh, no, Mrs. Morgan, no."

"Well, you can say thank God for that, an' all."

"Mrs. Morgan." Katie eased herself upwards on the straw pillow. "Could . . . could you get word to me ma and tell her I've had it, and tell her not to come afore Tuesday. That's the best day. It's No. 3, The Row. . . ."

"Oh, I know where she lives, lass, an' I'll get our Micky to go as soon as I get back. . . . But don't you think she'd better come up and see you ordinary like?"

"No, Mrs. Morgan. It's no use asking, an' I'm afraid for me da's new job."

"Aw, to hell flames with him, he can't do anything in Palmer's; he's got no say there. Did he say he could get your da the push if your ma came?"

Katie closed her eyes, then said, "As much."

"The stinking bugger! Somebody'll do for him one of these days, an' I hope it'll be soon. And you won't be the only one that's relieved, lass. But there you are; don't worry your head at the moment." She patted her kindly. "I'll be back in a little while; you're all right for the time being."

"Thanks, Mrs. Morgan, thanks." She put out her hand and touched the thick rough hand of the old woman, but she withheld her tears until Mrs. Morgan had gone down the stairs. Then they flowed so fast that they dropped on to the child's face and rolled down its cheeks like dewdrops.

* * *

The child was nearly a month old before Mark Bunting got the chance of a private word with its father.

Bernard Rosier wasn't seen so much at the mine now, and for two reasons. First, because he was living in Newcastle, in a house that had been a wedding present to his bride from her father; the second was because his interests had apparently widened. It was said that his father-in-law had a slice in Palmer's Shipyard and Mr. Bernard was moving in that direction to take a bite.

On this particular morning Bunting saw him going into the works office apparently looking for Brown, the under-manager. The office was separate from the one where the clerks were housed, and Bunting, knowing that Brown was below ground, saw this as a good opportunity to speak of the matter that was foremost in his mind.

Bernard Rosier turned, on his entry, and stared at him; then when Bunting took off his cap but made no effort to speak he said in a cutting tone, "Well?"

Bunting moistened his thin lips and, his hands remaining stationary on the rim of his cap, muttered in an undertone, "I was thinking, sir, perhaps you'd like to know, the baby came nearly four week ago. It's a girl. I—I just thought as you'd like to know."

As Bunting watched the blood flood up into Bernard Rosier's face he knew immediately he was on the wrong track. His eyes were unblinking as Rosier came and stood close to him and he watched him sift the words through his teeth as he said, "Now look here, my man; you were paid for what you did, and well paid, and that's the end as far as I'm concerned. If you think you're going to bleed me over this matter you'd better stop and consider. . . . Get it into your head you've had all you're going to get. . . . And don't say that you can talk; you can do all the damn well talking you like and who'll believe you? And even if they did, it's no longer of any importance." He paused here for a number of seconds before adding, "If you want to find another job just bring up this subject again. Do you understand me?" His head moved just the slightest bit towards the keeker, and after a moment of silence he picked his hat up from the desk, then gave Bunting one last long, hard look and walked out.

*   *   *

There was a cold black fury in Bunting as he hurried towards his home at the end of the day. He saw himself in a situation that he had been over and over again during the hours since he had met Rosier. He was saddled for life with a woman in the house, and a squawking kid—Rosier's squawking kid. And for what? A hundred pounds. If he had stood out he would have paid him five hundred. Aye, he would, five hundred. He saw now that Rosier had that night been in the tightest corner of his life. What the real reason was for wanting her married off he didn't know and he couldn't guess at it. Certain, it wasn't the fact that that little loose bitch would give him away, because if that had been her intention she could have done it afore, or she could have got money out of him to keep her family. But he'd know the ins and outs before he'd finished with her. But here he was, saddled with the pair of them. He would have to feed and clothe them for the rest of their lives. At least her he would. The thought brought the sweat pouring out of him. He didn't take into account that she washed and cooked and cleaned for him; he had done that for himself for years and found it no hardship.

By God, he had been taken for a monkey, hadn't he? All these months he had held his hand because he didn't know where she stood with Rosier, but now he knew all right, and he need hold his hand no longer. No, by Christ alive, he needn't!

He almost put his foot through the door as he entered the house, and Katie turned a startled face on him from the fire-place. He stood for a moment glaring at her, and then to-wards the child lying in a basket near the window which was open from the bottom. The window gave him something to start on. "Close that blasted window. What's the good of hav-ing a fire on and letting the heat out, you bloody fool?"

He had never sworn at her before; and now he didn't only swear but from him flowed a torrent of obscene abuse. As she filled the bath and poured the clean water over him every action of hers brought a vile stream from him. She was at first stunned by it; then as it continued without ceasing, through the meal and after, it came to her that something had happened, something that had released the real Mark Bunt-ing, for the objectionable, hard, unfeeling man she had lived with since she had married was a nice person compared with this fiendish individual.

To every filthy word he threw at her she said nothing; nor did she retaliate when he almost pushed her on her back as she carried the tub from the kitchen; but when his foot came out to kick at the child's basket she checked it with a scream that startled herself. "Don't you dare do that!"

He turned round and stared at her. Then a twisted smile spread over his face as he said, "I'm glad you've got some spunk; it'll give me all the more pleasure to knock it out of you."

Not waiting now for him to give her the order when she could go to bed, she lifted the basket with the child in it and carried it up the stairs, and she had just taken off her things and put on her coarse calico nightdress when the door burst open.

"Come on," he said.

"What!" She stammered on the word.

"You heard what I said. Come on."

When she made no move he thrust out his hand to grab her, but she crouched against the wall. Then slowly, her eyes riveted on his face. She sidled past him. On the landing she stood transfixed for a moment; then, like someone in a trance, she moved before him into his bedroom.

After banging the door behind him he advanced on her and, grabbing the collar of her nightdress, wrenched it from top to bottom with a twist of his hand and, saying "You won't be needing this any more", tore it from her back.

And this was only the beginning of Mark Bunting showing his hand.

* * *

It was fourteen nights later. Katie thought of them as nights, for so she had totalled them up. Each evening, like a prisoner approaching the rack, she wondered if she would be able to suffer what was before her. Not the least of her feelings was humiliation. The indignities he heaped upon her crushed her spirit so low that in the agonising, wakeful stillness of the night, when she was afraid to move in case of waking him again, she would tell herself that in the morning she would take the child and go to her mother, but in the light of day she was always deterred by the thought of him following her and what would happen when her father and him came face to face. But she knew that when her ma came on one of her secret visits she would tell her; at least she would tell her that she would have to get away from here, if not all the reasons why. Then she would think that were she to go he could put the police on to her and claim the child. Perhaps it didn't matter that it wasn't his; he had taken on the responsibility of it, so he could claim it. There were so many things that seemed to block her way of escape. If only her ma would come. She hadn't been for the past fortnight; afore that she had been every week. . . .

Then came the beautiful June evening. If she had stood at the door she would have heard the birds singing, she would have seen the rabbits scampering on the moors and a hare sitting in startled surprise at finding himself only a few yards from the gate; but she was busy preparing the meal, and making it as tasty as possible so as to give him no loophole to find fault.

He came in as he had done over the last fortnight, his brows meeting, his mouth tight. Then followed the usual procedure. He tore off his clothes, he got into the bath, he washed his front and she washed his back.

Came the moment when she was about to get the water to rinse him. He had been spitting obscenities at her, just single words, and it was at the precise second when she had filled the bucket half full of boiling water from the kale pot that the child began to cry. It let out a sharp wail, a hungry wail. Katie turned from the stove, the bucket in her hand, to hear Bunting curse and to see him scooping up a ladle full of black-scummed water with the evident intent of throwing it on the child who lay in the corner only a couple of arm-lengths from him; and as she had stopped him from using his foot on the basket with a scream, now she screamed again, "Don't! Don't do that!" At the same time, without pausing to think, she threw the water over him.

His scream ascended high above hers; it rent the house. She was knocked flying backwards, and, the settle breaking her fall, she cowered trembling in the corner of it, utterly petrified at what she had done, and done unintentionally.

She watched him dancing like a mad dervish, screaming all the while. Then to the screams were added deep groans, while the fingers of his hands, like those of a blind man, hovered over his neck and shoulders. After a time his screaming stopped and there was only his moaning filling the strange silence. He turned towards her, staring at her; his face looked inhuman, twisted, like a stone gargoyle. The next minute the silence was broken by his loud screaming curses. She was still crouched on the settle and her breathing almost stopped as she watched him scattering his clothes and riving his leather belt from out of the loops of his trousers. Before the buckled end of the belt came down on her she screamed, and she continued to scream as he flayed her round the room. Her own warm sticky blood ran from her fingers, and she thrust them into her wide open mouth as she screamed. When she felt the clothes being torn from her back she clung on to the end of the settle, and when he dragged her forward the settle came with her. And then he was belabouring her again, but she wasn't screaming so hard now. She had almost stopped screaming when the hammering came on the door. Before she fainted she imagined she saw Joe and heard his voice shouting.

When she slowly came to her senses she actually saw Joe's face abover hers; it was streaming with tears and he was moaning as if he, too, had been almost beaten to death. She tried to speak but found she couldn't. Her body seemed to be torn in all directions with pain, and then she thought of the child and pushed at Joe and rolled on her side, looking towards the basket. When, after a moment, she pointed, Joe whispered, "It's all right; it's all right." He now helped her to prop herself up against the overturned settle; and there she sat, her eyes glazed and her breath coming in painful jerks.

Slowly her wits returned to her, and now she muttered faintly, "Where . . . where's he?"

Joe pointed upwards, then whispered, "His back is all scalded. He said you did it."

"Joe."

"Aye, Katie."

"Get . . . get me cloak. It's on the door . . . in the scullery." She lifted one trembling red hand and pointed.

When Joe returned with her cloak she was on her hands and knees pulling herself upwards. Her clothes were hanging in blood-soaked ribbons from her back, and when she stood on her feet the room swam about her and she had to clutch at Joe to steady herself. Her vision clearing, she now whispered urgently, "Can . . . can you carry her?"

He nodded; and quickly gathering the child up and supporting it on one arm only, he put the other around her waist and led her through the open door.

The main bedroom window faced east and their road from the house lay westwards. As they stumbled on they heard no voice behind them, but before they approached the village Katie could go no farther and she dropped down by the side of the road, and it was only Joe saying "Come on, Katie, try and carry on a bit farther; he could catch us up yet" that got her to her feet again.

When they came in sight of the village there were the men playing quoits, and one turned and looked at the young boy carrying a baby and leading the stumbling girl, and when he made an exclamation in a loud voice the men, almost as one, hurried towards them.

It was Jimmie Morgan, the husband of the midwife, who reached them first, and softly he said, "Why, lass, what's happened thee?" Yet he had no need to ask. Her face and hair were blood-splattered, her neck was bare and a gash along her shoulder-blade was oozing blood still. Through her open cloak they could see her torn, blood-stained clothes.

"Come, lass," said Jimmie Morgan, "the wife'll attend thee," and with the help of another man he carried her the rest of the distance. . . .

It was Jimmie Morgan himself who went into Jarrow and brought Rodney. Catherine couldn't leave William who was dying, and there was Lizzie to see to. It was the message that William wanted to see Katie before he went that had brought Joe to the house.

It was close on nine o'clock when Rodney entered the room. When, in the light of the tallow candle, Katie saw the tall, commanding figure of her da she wanted to throw out her arms to him, but she could move neither hand nor foot. Rodney, kneeling down by the bed and touching her cheek gently, said pityingly, "Lass," and she whimpered, "Oh, Da." He did not ask her any questions; he just continued to stare at her, his eyes moving over her face. It was nearly eight months since he had seen her, and she had changed almost beyond recognition. Her eyes were still the same shape, still the same colour, but they were no longer his Katie's eyes. Her mouth was still the same shape, but it was a trembling, pathetic mouth he was looking at; and the cheeks that had been round were now hollow.

He was aroused from his scrutiny by Mrs. Morgan saying, "Take a look." With this, she pulled down the single blanket, and Rodney, leaning over, saw the distorted mess of open wounds, weals, and discoloured, darkening flesh.

Mrs. Morgan's voice now came to him as if from the far end of a pit drive, saying, "I've done the best I can, but she should see a doctor."

"Aye." He got to his feet, his eyes still held by the sight of his daughter's back, and he said, "I'll get her there. In a little while I'll get her there." Then turning abruptly, he left the room. And his departure brought Katie to life, and against the pain that racked her she forced out her arms towards him, crying, "Da! Da! don't. Take me home. Da . . . Da!"

Through the open door she heard Mr. Morgan say, "I'll come along of you," and her da replying, "No, no. I'll do this on me own. Thanks, Jimmie, but I'll do this on me own." His voice dropped on the last words and they seemed like weights pressing her back on to thhe bed.

Mrs. Morgan pushed the damp hair from her face, saying soothingly, "There, lass, don't fret yourself; it's got to be done. He wouldn't be your da if he let this pass, an' if he didn't do it there's others who would. The place is up in arms. They've been waitin' for something like this for a long time."

Although it was impossible for her to think clearly, there was in the back of her mind a deep sense of futility for all she had done over the past months to avoid this moment when her da and Bunting should meet. It wouldn't, she felt now, have been half as bad as if he had met . . . the other one, because he wasn't hated like Bunting was.

* * *

It was an hour later when Rodney returned. Katie heard his voice in the other room and she pulled herself up on her elbow and waited for the door to open. When he came in her eyes searched him for evidence of what he had done, but his clothes looked tidy. It wasn't until her eyes dropped to his hands, with the knuckles broken and running blood, that she whimpered, "Oh, Da! Da!"

"There now." He did not touch her but dropped on to his hunkers before her and repeated, "There now. Everything's all right. Don't worry any more. You're going home."

Mr. Morgan's voice came from the doorway, saying, "We'll rig up a sling and the lads will give a hand."

Rodney turned and looked at Jimmie Morgan, then moved his hand in acceptance, and looking at Katie again, he said, "Don't worry any more. I'm telling you, you'll never go back. Don't worry any more."

Half an hour later they lifted Katie into the canvas sling, a replica of those they used to get injured men from the pit bottom, and, Rodney and Mr. Morgan at the front and Mr. Morgan's two sons at the back, they carried her into Jarrow.

And they broke their journey to take her to a doctor in the town, because doctors didn't come out in the night for people who lived in places like No. 3, The Row, and when he had seen to her and asked a number of questions they took her home.

* * *

It was about five o'clock the following day that the police came to the house. There were three of them, two dressed in uniform and a man in a black cloth coat and hard hat. Catherine opened the door to them, and her heart almost stopped at the sight of the uniformed men. "Is your husband in?" the man in the ordinary clothes asked.

"No, he's at work."

The police knew that Rodney was at work, but they had no intention of arresting him among a crowd of workmen. They didn't look for trouble—not the kind of trouble the Jarrow shipyard men could stir up; they experienced enough of that during the strikes. "We'll come in and wait," the man said, and the three of them walked into the room.

Katie raised herself on the pallet which was lying near the fireplace. She pressed her joined hands into her breast and stared at the men, her mouth wide open. And she looked from them to her mother as Catherine, her voice trembling, said, "What do you want with him?"

There was a long pause before the man in the ordinary clothes said, "He's wanted for the murder of the keeper at the Rosier pit, a man called Bunting. He was found in the ditch this morning with his head split open. He'd also been beaten up and scalded. Nice sight," he said bitterly.

"What! What!" Catherine held her face between her two hands. "My . . . my husband never did that, not him. He hit him, yes; he hit him because . . . look." She flung her arm wide in the direction of Katie. "If you saw what he did to my lass—she's his wife—any father would do the same. But kill him? No! No!"

"Well, he'll have the chance to prove that he didn't do it. But nevertheless the man is dead."

"But who said my man did it? There are others who want rid of him, and my man would never use an implement to anybody. His hands, aye, but nothing else. There's the whole

110

village lives near to him; it could have been any one of them."

"But as things stand the evidence points to your man, missis. You see, the doctor who attended to your girl last night took her name down as Mrs. Bunting, and it so happened that he's the colliery doctor an' all, and it didn't take much to put two and two together when he saw the body this mornin'."

At this point Katie gave a moan and lost consciousness and she didn't regain it until she heard her father's voice raised, high, crying, "I didn't kill the man. I wanted to but I didn't. Look, I hit him with me fists—look at me knuckles; but I used no bar on him, an' I left him glaring at me. He was alive, more alive when I left him than he left my lass. I didn't kill him, I tell you."

And then he went out with the men and there was no sound in the kitchen until Catherine let out a shuddering cry, and, flinging herself on the floor, beat the bricks with her fists.

10

It was a week later and Rodney was awaiting trial in Durham Prison. Bunting had been buried. A clerk from the mine had come and asked Katie if she had any wishes concerning the funeral, and when she had turned her head to one side he had apologised and said he had been sent; it was a matter of form. Then another man had come, a Mr. Brown, and asked her if she had any money to pay the funeral expenses, and she had rounded on him and cried, "No, no. Where would I get money?" He had then said that it was known that her husband hadn't been without money; he had been a careful man. Did she know where he kept his money? Again she had said no, except that he carried it around with him. "You can get into trouble for withholding it," he had said darkly, "for although you are his widow I doubt whether you would be entitled to it under the circumstances."

It was following this man's visit that Katie's mind was forced to move along practical lines. As she said to herself, somebody would have to do something, and soon, because her mother was so overwrought at what had come upon her that she seemed incapable of thinking for herself, let alone for the family. There she had sat, as she was doing now, day after day and far into the night, staring at the wall, rousing herself only when a strange voice was heard at the door. Her mother couldn't cope any more.

Joe was earning six shillings a week, but that only paid the rent and bought firing; there was nothing left to live on. She herself was in no fit state as yet to look for work, and even if she had been her mother was quite incapable at the moment of seeing to her granda, who was still lingering on, and the child, and Lizzie.

Besides all this, her mind was numbed with agony concerning her father, and to the pain was added the weight of her conscience, for was not his plight due entirely to her? If she had never married Bunting he wouldn't be in jail at this moment. She was to blame for it all. But no, no, not all. The child was not her blame; she would never take that blame on herself. She looked towards it now lying on a blanket in a low wooden tub, and a separate part of her, untouched by the misery of the moment, seemed to leap towards it and enfold it. She had never imagined she would feel like this about the child. She had hated it all the time she was carrying it, but now her love for it seemed to swell her body every time she looked at it.

But Sarah was now whimpering; she was hungry because Katie was hungry, she wasn't making enough milk to feed it. There was no food in the house for any of them, and Joe would be coming in at six, and Joe must eat. If he was to work he must eat. And then there was her granda. As she now washed the old man's face with a flannel and made him tidy and answered the thanks in his eyes by gently patting his cheek because his speech had gone, she thought that soon there'd be another funeral, but this one would be a workhouse one. Her poor granda; he had always dreaded the workhouse. But he wouldn't know anything about it; he'd be dead before they took him there.

As she went into the kitchen with the dish of water there came back to her the man's query, "Have you any money for the funeral?" and immediately following it three words flashed through her mind. They seemed to come out of no-where; they had no real connection with anything she had been thinking. The words were . . . a hundred pounds, and what brought a tremor to her body was that it didn't seem to be herself who was saying them, but . . . *him*. A hundred pounds. A hundred pounds. The sum went over and over again in her mind and she was hearing it said in Bunting's voice. Vaguely, very vaguely, she remembered hearing him say this. But the more she groped in her mind to bring the memory to the fore the more vague it became. If he had said anything about a hundred pounds to her she would have re-membered, as she did everything he had done to her up to the night of the beating. Things that she considered worse than the beating she remembered.

It was as she threw the water on to the spare ground out-side that a door opened in her mind and she heard his voice coming through it, clearer now, and accompanied by the swishing of the buckled belt, "A hundred pounds," it was say-ing. But now there were two more words added. "For you," the voice said. "A hundred pounds for you!"

And so it went on all that day, the words kept coming and going in her mind, and that night as she lay awake thinking of her da shut away in prison, perhaps never to come out again, they broke through again, loud now, yelling, "A hun-dred pounds for you! A hundred pounds for you!"

At one point she thought she was going mad, or funny like Lizzie, because she couldn't stop the words from repeating and repeating themselves. And then as she lay wide-eyed and hungry she began to think about what the man had said about it being known that Bunting had money, and Mrs. Morgan too had said he should have money. Everybody in the village knew he had money hoarded away, she said, and all out of his cheating the men. . . . Well, if he had, where had he hoarded it? She had cleaned every inch of the house and she had never come across anything that looked like a hidey hole. Yet if he had money he must have hidden it somewhere. . . .

It wasn't until the next day when she climbed the six-foot ladder that gave entry to the roof space where Joe had his bed that light dawned on her.

Every Saturday afternoon Bunting had sent her to Batley's farm two miles away for half a dozen eggs and some vegeta-bles. Immediately dinner was over he would hand her the money and tell her to get going; whether it was rain, hail or shine he would order her out. Even when she had to carry the baby all that way—she would never have left it with him. Why did he want her out of the way like that every week if not to have a space of time in which to hide his money? And what better place to hide it than in the roof? She had never thought of going up there because the hatch was eight feet above the landing. . . .

The following day was Sunday, and early in the morning she said to Joe, "I'm goin' out for an hour or so. Will you see to them?"

"Where you goin'?" Joe whispered, and she whispered back, "I'm goin' to the house to get some of me thinngs."

"But you won't be able to get in; it'll be locked up."

"There's a way. I know how to open the scullery window."

"Won't you get wrong if you're caught?"

"I can't see how. Me things are there; I'm goin' for them."

When she was about to leave the house he came to the front door with her, and, his voice very low, he said, "Why don't you have a look round and see if there's anything about. You know what I mean?"

She nodded at him and they looked at each other in full understanding. And then he said, "But you're not fit, you're not up to that trek; you shouldn't try." To which she answered, "The air'll do me good."

But even before she left Jarrow she didn't see how she was going to complete the journey. For the past week she had just moved slowly around the room, but now she was finding the movement of her muscles, particularly her back muscles, excruciating. Moreover, as she put it to herself, she felt bad right through.

The morning was bright and warm; the larks were soaring like winged notes from their ground cover into the heavens. She had always loved the larks and was horrified at their destruction. But this morning she did not even look upwards, for out here in the open the enormity of the trouble that had come upon them seemed enlarged. It seemed to spread away from her on all sides, filling space, filling her life right down to the end; she could see no easing from the feeling that was in her now.

When she saw the village away to her left she was surprised that she had got this far. She kept well clear of the village, for she didn't want to meet any of them in case she would say, "Why don't you get them to own up—the ones who did it, Mr. Morgan's sons and the rest? But the Morgans had been kind to her and she had no proof, only another jumbled memory of men talking in the Morgans' kitchen, and later, after her da had gone to Bunting, of men and women, silent men and women, coming and looking at her back.

As she approached the house a fear settled on her, a fear of entering it, of him still being there. It was no use telling herself he was dead and buried.

She entered the back garden by sitting on the low stone wall and lifting her legs over, one after the other. Then she was standing outside the wash-house door. She stood quietly listening for a moment. Who knew but someone might be about; a house that had had a murder always attracted sight-seers. She went into the wash-house and looked for the key. Perhaps it had been put back in its hiding-place; but no, it wasn't there.

She sat down for a moment on an upturned tub; then, real-ising that it was the tub in which he had bathed, she sprang up and, pulling her skirts about her, leaned against the half-open door, looking at it. If contact with the tub frightened her, how would the inside of the house affect her? Before her thinking would drive her down the road again she went round to the scullery window, and, lifting her skirt and taking from the pocket in her petticoat an old knife, she inserted the blade between the window and the latch.

The process of climbing through the little window racked her body, and as there was no support on the other side she had to fall to the floor on her hands and pull her legs after her. When she was through she lay panting for a moment, looking round at the familiar scene. Then, rising slowly, she closed the window and made towards the kitchen door. It took a great effort of will to open the door, and having done so her body jerked and her eyes closed simultaneously before she looked into the room. It was no longer familiar. The set-tle was pushed against the wall and in front of it stood three broken chairs. On the delf rack, piled together as if someone had swept them up, was the crockery, all smashed, and the mantelpiece was stripped of its pewter mugs and brass can-dlesticks. But they were nowhere to be seen; someone had likely taken them. As she looked at the devastation she whim-pered, "Oh, Da! Da!" Slowly she crossed the room to the stairs. But at the foot of them she remained standing; she couldn't go up there, she couldn't. The sweat was pouring down her face now, and she glanced behind her. She could feel him; he was still here. Only the thought of No. 3, The Row full of hungry bellies impelled her forward.

When she stood on the landing she had to open the bedroom door to be able to see the hatch, and immediately she knew she could never reach it from a chair. The only thing to do was to bring the chest of drawers out of the little room and climb upon them.

After taking out the three drawers from the chest she pulled it through the doorway; then with trembling limbs she mounted it and, putting both hands up, she pressed against the hatchway and, to her surprise, it moved easily. With her head through the aperture she looked around her. The roof space was lit by a tiny window, but little light came through because of the grime on it.

It took something of an effort to pull herself up and on to the floor, and when she was standing upright she gazed about her. The floor was boarded and there was nothing on it except a wicker basket and a wooden box lying close to the sloping roof.

When she pulled up the close-fitting lid of the basket she saw it held clothes, women's clothes—his mother's clothes likely. They were all tumbled together as if someone had already been sorting them. She forced herself to pull the garments out one after the other. They smelt musty and dirty, but there was no money lying among them. In the long wooden box there was a gun and two boxes of small shot, but no money.

Where? Where? If he'd hidden it anywhere it would be up here; it must be up here. The chimney breast ran up through the floor, then through the roof. She examined every brick but couldn't feel a loose one. That left only the floor. On her hands and knees now she tried each board to see if it was loose. But no; they were all firmly held by nails. Wearily she sat down on the long black box, her back bent because of the roof. She had looked everywhere, searched every corner; there was nothing more she could do. If he'd had money he had hidden it well, and it would lie hidden until in the far future the house would be pulled down, and then somebody would find it; somebody who didn't need it like she did the day.

When she got wearily to her feet she stood shaking her

head, her eyes cast down, and like this there came over her a strange feeling, an excited feeling, a sort of nice feeling that had no connection with the horror she had experienced during the past weeks. She felt for a moment as if she was back, up there, in the house, going happily about her work, eating well, sleeping well, with the knowledge of the forth-coming pleasure of going home on her day off always looming before her. The feeling made her grab the iron handle of the box and drag it aside. Before she came to laugh at the existence of a God, she thought that He must have instructed one of His angels to reveal Bunting's secret by way of repayment for what she had endured; but she never really could work out what made her suddenly heave the box aside.

Now she was looking at a floorboard with a gap in it, just a little gap that wouldn't have been noticed unless someone was looking for it. Inserting her little finger-nail she lifted up the loose board, and there below her, on a piece of wood supported between the beams, lay four bags and a little black, leather-bound book.

Like someone mesmerised, she picked up one of the bags and, undoing the loop of string that tied its neck, she looked down on to the gleaming gold coins, sovereigns. The same in the next bag, and the other two: all full of sovereigns. And the little black book. She opened it, but the writing was so small and the light so bad that she couldn't read it.

She stood up, her hands holding each side of her face. All that money, all that gold. She was overcome by a panic feeling. What if someone came? It would be no use saying she was just after her clothes if they saw the chest on the landing. Like lightning now she swooped up one bag after the other and, putting two in each side of her petticoat to balance her, together with the little book, she replaced the board, left the box as she had found it, then went to the hole and let herself down to the top of the chest, pulled the hatch into place, and dropped to the floor. Five minutes later, the chest back in the bedroom, she went stealthily down the stairs.

Now, as if the devil was after her, and he could have been from the feeling that filled the house, she let herself out of the back door—there was no time to make the difficult journey through the narrow window. Running now, she got over the low wall, and not until she was well away from the house did she slow to a walk. And it was just as well, for, in the distance, around a rise in the fells she saw coming towards her, from the direction of the road, three girls. They were Haggie's rope-work girls, from Wallsend. Haggie's Angels they were called. You could always tell them by their clogs and thick serge skirts and woollen shawls. Their fearlessness of man or beast was personified by their coarse prattle. They were laughing and larking on as they walked, one of them pushing at another while she gripped her own waist to ease the ache of her mirth. Catching sight of Katie, they came in a straight line towards her, their faces still broad with their laughter, and when they were abreast one of them said, "Can we get to the hoose where the morder was done this way?"

Katie stared at them. Her instinct was to fly from them, but that would make them think she was wrong in the head, perhaps even suspicious of her, and they might talk. One thing led to another; it always started that way. She made herself say as calmly as possible, "It's about five minutes' walk. That's the straight way." She pointed back towards the road they had left, and, their faces still laughing, they said one after the other, "Ta." She could still hear them laughing when she was a good distance from them, and as she hurried on she thought, The dog'll go for them . . . Roy. She stopped. She hadn't thought of Roy. Poor Roy. One thing was sure: he hadn't been there else he would have raised the place. Somebody must have taken him. It came to her that she must have been in a bad way altogether these past days not to have thought of the poor beast.

When she entered the town again she forced herself not to scurry. With every step she took she was conscious of the bags knocking against her legs. It being Sunday, the town was quiet. The good God-fearing people were returning from church, the men in their broad cloth and tight-fitting trousers and shining boots, the women in their best dresses of grey, dark blue or black. You could almost tell which church they had been to from their dress. The women going to the Church of England nearly always were bonneted; the women who went to the Catholic church nearly always wore shawls. But then what could you expect, for the Catholics were mostly drunken Irish. In her own chapel just some of the women managed a bonnet, and then it was nothing as elaborate as those worn by the Church of England women. Her mother had pointed all this out to her, yet she had told her that farther away up in Newcastle, and farther still in the

Midlands, the Methodists had fine chapels and the women nearly all wore bonnets.

But there were those in this town who didn't go near a church or a chapel. The men were now filling the public-houses, and the women were making the Sunday dinner, and between times standing on their front steps talking to their neighbours while their children scampered in the muck and running filth of the road.

It was among most of this latter type that she had to pass before she came to The Row, and there was many an eye turned on her and many a whisper that came to her ears, such as "You don't get a hammerin' for nowt, not if he doesn't booze, you don't. He must've twigged summat." When she pushed open the door and entered the dim room she was on the point of collapse.

Catherine was sitting at the table. There was no sign of a dinner of any sort in preparation. Lizzie was sitting on the pallet that was Katie's bed, and Joe was walking the narrow distance between the walls shaking the child up and down to try to stop its crying.

They all looked towards her. Then Catherine, for the first time in days, showed interest in what was going on around her. She got to her feet and asked dully, "Where've you been, lass? Why did you leave us?"

Katie didn't answer, but, going to Joe, she took the child from him and, sitting down, bared her breast to it. Then after drawing in a number of quick deep breaths she looked up at Joe, whose eyes were waiting full of enquiry, and she said softly, "Put the bolt in the door, will you, Joe, and pull the curtain."

She hitched the cracket on which she was sitting nearer the table, and, supporting the child with one arm, she pulled the four bags and the book from her petticoat and laid them in front of her. Then she said to Joe, "Open them."

Joe spilled a bag on to the table, then stood gaping at the sovereigns. And Catherine stood staring at them. Then, looking at her daughter, she whispered, "In the name of God, lass, what have you done now?"

It was the word "now" that pierced Katie, telling her that deep in her heart her mother held her responsible for all that had happened. She swallowed in her throat, then said, "He had money hidden up in the roof. I went and got it."

"You shouldn't have done that, lass. It's bad money, evil money. Any money he had would be evil money."

"But, Ma, listen. Listen." It was Joe now tugging at her arm, bringing her round to face him. "We need it, an' Katie's got a right to it. Who better after what she's been through? Don't be daft, Ma."

"No matter what way you look at it, it's bad money."

"It'll help me da, Ma." Katie was looking up at Catherine. "We . . . we can buy a man to speak for him like they do for the miners."

"Aye. Aye." Joe was excited. "That's it, Katie." He put his two hands on the table and leant towards her. "The miners have got one—solicitor he's called. Aye, yes! How much is there?"

"I don't know," she said. "Count it."

Joe counted the coins from the four bags, and when he was finished he looked at Katie and said, in awe-filled tones, "Two hundred and twenty-seven pounds." And again, "Two hundred and twenty-seven pounds." Then, gazing at his mother, he added, "We'll never be hungry again, Ma."

"Be quiet!" said Catherine harshly. "Can you only think of your stomach."

Joe bowed his head and murmured, "I know, Ma, I know."

Catherine, now looking down at Katie, said, "Where are you going to keep it? And when you start spendin' people will twig, an' you'll be had up."

That was a point. Katie stroked the soft hair from her daughter's brow. Sovereigns were few and far between among the poor. If she went round here breaking into sovereigns and no man in the house to bring even half a one in, of course people would twig. She would have to go farther afield to do her spending, and be careful at that. As to where she would hide the money, she had already thought of that on her way home. "I've figured that out," she said now. "I'm going to sew them all on to me shift."

"Sew them on to your shift? Carry them round with you?" said Catherine. "But the weight, lass."

"It'll be spread over. I'll make a sort of little pocket for each one and just take them out as we need them. I can wear me other shift near me skin for washin'."

"Aye. Yes." Catherine was nodding now, and it brought a little lightness to Katie's mind to see that her mother had come out of her trance-like state.

All afternoon they sat, the three of them, Joe cutting out inch squares from pieces of old calico, and Katie and Catherine sewing three sides of them to the garment, slipping in a coin, then securing it with a stitch or two.

They had come to the last twenty sovereigns when Joe said, "If you're going to see a solicitor hadn't you better keep some money out, Katie—say ten pounds or so. They cost a lot."

Just as she was about to answer Catherine said, "Where will you say you got the money from . . . golden sovereigns?"

The question stumped Katie. Then after a moment she said, "I—I could say I got it from a friend."

"Lass, folks like us don't have friends who throw golden sovereigns around."

"Well"—Katie shook her head impatiently now—"I'll think of something, Ma, when the time comes."

"What'll I do with the bags and the book?" asked Joe, holding them out in his hands.

"Burn them," said Katie. "But wait a minute. . . . Here, let me see the book."

She now opened the book, and going and standing near the window she drew the curtain just the slightest and looked at the column of figures which filled the first page. The entries always followed the same pattern, and the dates went back for years. They started on a January day in 1850, and opposite this date was the sum of three pounds. The second entry was in June 1850, and the amount stated was four pounds. As she turned the pages she saw that as the years came more up-to-date the entries followed closer together, there being frequently two in the same month. Then an entry made last year brought her attention fixedly on it. The date of this entry was the day following that on which she had gone to him and said she would marry him. The entry was for fifty pounds; and something else was added to this entry, two letters, B.R. The next entry in the book was also for fifty pounds, and it was made on the same day on which she had married Mark Bunting, and again this entry was followed by the letters B.R.

"A hundred pounds for you" . . . B.R. He must have given him a hundred pounds to marry her. She lifted her eyes and looked at her mother, and then at Joe. She wanted to say to them, "But why? Why?" If she hadn't let on up till then, wasn't it pretty plain to him that she was going to keep her mouth shut? So why had he paid Mark Bunting a hundred pounds to marry her?

"What is it?" said Catherine.

"Nothing," said Katie. Going to the fire and pushing the book into the dull embers, she moved it about until it caught fire, then motioned to Joe to follow suit with the bags.

*   *   *

It was the following day that Katie learned why Bernard Rosier had paid Bunting to marry her. At the same time it was made possible for her to spend a sovereign when she liked, and these two things were brought about through a visitor to the house.

The visitor was Miss Theresa, and she came to the door surrounded by a horde of children. When Katie heard the noise outside she opened the door and a girl said, "She was lookin' for you, missis."

There stood Miss Theresa, surrounded by barefooted, ragged, dirty children. An ordinary woman coming to this quarter would have aroused no curiosity, but even children could recognise gentry when on the rare occasions they happened to meet.

"May I come in, Katie?"

Katie turned her head round and looked into the awful room. Her shame was deep. She would like to have said, "No, Miss Theresa," but what could she do but pull the door wider and allow the quietly dressed, tall young woman to enter. Then she closed the door and pushed the bolt in in case the children might be curious and open it.

"Ma." Katie looked towards the seat where her mother sat and said, "This is Miss Theresa from the House."

Catherine got slowly to her feet. She did not bob or curtsy, she merely inclined her head. This was a member of the household that had brought disgrace on her girl; she owed them nothing, only hate, and she had been taught not to hate.

Theresa willed herself not to look round the room, at the shocking conditions under which this family was living, but one thing she couldn't do was close her nostrils to the smell that pervaded the whole place. She moved towards Catherine and, looking her straight in the face she said softly, "I'm

122

deeply sorry, Mrs. Mulholland, for what has come upon you. I . . . I wonder if I could be of any help?"

"I would welcome help from any direction, ma'am," said Catherine quietly. Following this, an embarrassing silence fell on them, until it was broken by a noise from the corner of the room, a noise which startled Theresa. Lizzie had pumped. She looked in the direction and saw sitting in the dimness a great fat lump of a girl.

"That's . . . that's Lizzie," said Katie apologetically under her breath. "She's . . . she's not quite right in the head."

There was pain in Theresa's eyes as she brought them back to Katie.

"Won't you sit down?" said Katie now, pulling a stool forward, and Theresa, thanking her, sat down. But she was no sooner seated than she was startled again by another noise coming from beyond a door facing her, and as Catherine turned away without excusing herself and went through the door Katie again explained, "That's me granda; he's . . . he's had a stroke."

"Oh, Katie." Theresa began to twist her hands together. "I feel that all this has come upon you through me. I've suffered agonies of mind since I heard about this happening, because I feel that . . . that I'm to blame; not because of . . . of that." She pointed to the child lying in the tub. "That began it all, but if . . . if I had only left it there and let you work out things for yourself, as I'm sure you would have done with the help of your parents, you wouldn't have been in this terrible trouble today. But I did what I thought was for the best. Believe me, believe me, Katie."

Katie looked back into the thin, troubled, pale face and said, "I don't quite understand what you are on about, Miss Theresa. I don't see how you had anything to do with it."

"I had, Katie, and you'll hate me for it when I tell you. You see, it was me who forced Bernard's hand. I told him and my parents that if reparation wasn't made to you I would tell his fiancée. It was then, and then only, he thought up the scheme of getting Mr. Bunting to marry you. . . . You see?"

Yes. Although bewildered by this information, Katie saw in part; what she didn't see was how Miss Theresa knew it was Mr. Bernard, and she said so.

"How did you find out, Miss Theresa, about. . . ?" She

123

moved her hand towards the child, which did away with the necessity of using Bernard Rosier's name.

"I . . . I saw him push you from the room the night of the ball, and witnessed your great distress."

"Oh!" Katie bowed her head and Theresa went on, "I was greatly concerned for you."

"Thank you, Miss Theresa."

The silence fell on them again, and in it the smell seemed to have become intensified, and Theresa, taking a handkerchief from her beaded bag, dabbed gently at her nose, and then said softly, "I'm in much the same position as you yourself are, Katie, in that I'm poor." God forgive her. The same position as this child, for she still looked a child, in spite of her swollen, milk-filled breasts. There were grades of poverty, and she was in the presence of the lowest.

"What do you mean, Miss Theresa?" Katie's face held concern now for her visitor.

"Well, I have left my husband, Katie. You know I should never have married him; it was my parents' doing. I . . . I was to have a baby but I lost it."

"Oh, Miss Theresa, I'm sorry."

"Don't be sorry for me, Katie; I didn't want the baby. I'm really very fortunate. I see that now. I . . . I have a small income and it's been accumulating over the years; it's been enough to buy me a little house on the outskirts of Westhoe village in Shields. And Miss Ainsley's going to join me at the end of the year. We're to start a little school."

Miss Theresa a school-marm! Brought up in that big house with everything she wanted, and now she was going to be a school-marm, and seemed to relish the idea. Life was funny, very funny.

Theresa was now bending towards her, her hands joined on her knees as she said, "I wonder, Katie, when . . . when your trouble is over, whether you will come and live with us. You . . . you can bring the child." She wanted to add "Not as a servant"; she wanted to go further and say, "I will teach you all I know. There is time yet for you to be not only a beautiful woman but a cultured one." She had a picture of a life that appeared to her like paradise spent in the company of Ainsley and Katie, but the figure of Katie loomed much larger than Ainsley within the frame.

"Oh, thank you, Miss Theresa, but . . . but I don't know how things are goin', an' I'll have to see because me mother

124

isn't well at all now. She can't manage like she used to. And there's Lizzie." She motioned her head towards the corner. "But it's very kind of you, Miss Theresa, very kind of you. I'll . . . I'll think of it."

Although Katie said she would think about the offer, which if it had been made a year ago she would have considered came straight from God, she now had no intention of accepting it. Already she knew what she was going to do. Whatever happened to her father—and the thought of what might happen to him made her shudder—she had plans for the family, plans that would take them out of this hovel. She went on quickly now, "It all depends on what happens to me . . . me da. Miss Theresa . . ." She bent forward. "Do you know of a solicitor man that would speak for him? I . . . I've got a little money, I could pay him."

Theresa knew of many solicitors; her husband's solicitors, her father's solicitors, solicitors who were friends of the family, but would they be impartial and speak for such a man as this girl's father who had murdered a keeper at the mine? Anyway, it would need a barrister to defend him. She thought for a moment, then said, "There's a firm in Shields by the name of Chapel and Hewitt; I remember my father mentioning them. You could try them. I think their business is in King Street."

"Thanks, Miss Theresa, I will. I'll go down straight away." As if she had appeared rude she added, "Well, I mean later."

"I hired a trap to fetch me here, Katie; would you care to drive back with me? I could take you right to the door."

"Oh, thanks, Miss Theresa, yes. Yes. Would you wait till I put me other frock on?"

"Certainly, Katie, certainly."

In the room, as she changed her dress, Katie whispered to her mother, who was sitting on the foot of William's bed, what she was about to do. "This'll solve it," she whispered. "If they see me drivin' up in the trap with her they'll think she's given me the money. If anybody asks where I got it, I can say I got it from a friend, and they'll think it's her."

Catherine nodded her head. "Yes. Aye," she said.

"You'll see to the child, Ma?" asked Katie, anxiously now.

"Yes, don't worry. But . . . but I'm not comin' out there again; tell her anythin', but I'm not comin' out there again."

"It's all right, Ma." Katie put her hand on her mother's head and stroked her hair for a moment; then bending over

William she patted his cheek and smiled into his dim eyes. "Everything's going to be all right, Granda," she said. "Everything's going to be all right; Miss Theresa's come an' she's going to help us. She's takin' me down now to get a solicitor man to speak for me da. Everything's going to be all right, Granda, don't you fret." And she believed what she said; since she had found the money she had found hope.

11

They sat in the court like reluctant visitors to a strange world, and just as fearful. Katie sat on one side of Catherine and Joe on the other, and each gripped one of her hands.

Rodney was sitting between two policemen. He looked grey, thin and gaunt. His eyes had sunk deep into his head and it seemed to Katie that she hadn't seen him for twenty years, so changed was he; yet he held himself straight. In contrast, his guards looked thick and solid; their bodies seemed to be pressing out of their uniforms. They represented to her the impregnable wall of the law, a wall at which the barrister who had talked, and talked, and talked, seemed to be beating his head in vain. She had felt the inevitableness of the whole proceedings from the beginning, although he had done his utmost—and she felt sure he had done his utmost, but mainly because he thought she was under the patronage of Miss Theresa. Miss Theresa was a Rosier, and the name told. She had let it be known to the solicitor the first time she had seen him that Miss Theresa had recommended him to her, had even brought her along. She knew that this recommendation would make a difference to his fee, that he would sting her because he thought Miss Theresa was paying, but that didn't matter; nothing mattered except that the man up there would convince the judge of her da's innocence. And he had tried—oh yes, he had tried—but he hadn't touched the old man in the wig sitting on the high bench, and now the old man was about to speak to the jury.

Mr. Justice Dowry was tired; added to this, his gout was troubling him, and he was hungry. He had no patience with the case in hand and had been further irritated by the defending counsel, talking the way he did. A valuable man had been lost to the industry, and so he began to speak pointedly to the jury. Passing lightly over the facts presented by the defence counsel, he dwelt on that of the prosecution.

"As you have heard," he continued, nodding three times slowly towards the jury, "the deceased made an offer of marriage to the daughter of the accused who was with child, and not to him. Let that point be remembered, gentlemen. The daughter of the accused bears this out: the child was not the deceased's, yet this man married her and gave her a home.

"On the night of the events which you are considering the deceased comes back from his work; tired, no doubt, as all men connected with mines are tired at the end of the day. He takes his bath. What followed, we are given to understand, is that he splashed some water from the bath towards the child, probably in play; but we are told the action was not in play. However, this is a point that can't be proved. His wife evidently thought that the action was malicious and she retaliated with something equally, if not more malicious. Repeating her own words, she tipped the hot water over him. From the condition of the deceased's back when examined by the doctor we have his asurance that the water must have been more than just hot, it must have been boiling. . . . What happens when a man gets scalded? He is almost demented with pain. Isn't it understandable that when the deceased was suffering the agony of his bare neck and bare back being scalded he should be beside himself, and the reflex action would be to grab the first thing that came to hand and belabour the person who had scalded him?

"It is not for the moment to be thought that if the deceased had been in his right senses he would have used his belt on his wife to the extent he did. We are not disputing the fact that she was beaten cruelly. Dr. Bullard, who examined her, has been emphatic about this. But I would stress the point here that, given the opportunity when once again in his right mind, I have no doubt but that the deceased would have been extremely sorry for his actions, but he wasn't given the opportunity. What followed you have already heard. The deceased's wife made her way to the village with her brother who had called at the house. A man, James Morgan, goes into Jarrow and brings her father. From there we take up the accused's account. He saw the condition his daughter was in and he was filled with rage. He went to the deceased's house and fought with him. He said he fought with him. You must remember that the deceased had been badly scalded and would still be suffering from shock; would he be in any condition to fight? But we have the accused's word that he made a stand. We also have the accused's word that he beat him round the room with his fists, then left him lying on the floor. . . . Alive, he said. You know the rest, gentlemen of the jury. The deceased was found not far from his house, lying in a ditch; his head was split open and near him lay an iron poker. Remember there was no poker of any kind to be found on the deceased's hearth when the police searched, so we can but understand he was beaten to death with his own poker. That is the case, gentlemen. It is up to you to bring in a verdict."

Among the jury were the managers of three mines; they were out for five hours. When they returned, their spokesman gave a verdict of guilty and Rodney bowed his head deep into his chest. Catherine, after one look at him, collapsed, and Joe put his arms about her, crying, "Ma! Ma!" But Katie looked at her da. Her da was going to die . . . *her da was going to die,* and it was all her fault. "Oh no, you can't! You can't!" She had turned and was screaming at the judge. "He's good; he reads the Bible, he does. You can't! He didn't do it, he didn't! It's wicked, it is. Don't to it! Don't do it!"

Before Mr. Justice Dowry passed sentence the man's family had to be removed from the court.

12

It was on a beautiful soft day in early August that the cart came to the little village of Hilton, lying between Bishop Auckland and Barnard Castle. It was a four-wheeled flat cart driven by an old shaggy-haired horse. The cart was covered by a canvas canopy supported by four poles. It had the appearance of a square covered wagon.

The cart passed through the village and stopped on the outskirts; it wasn't always wise to come too near the houses.

Some people got nasty and turned their dogs loose; they always thought you wanted something for nothing, but Katie was always quick to hold her hand out with money in it before she asked for anything. They had taken three weeks over the journey from Jarrow. They had travelled by the coast road to Sunderland, then on to Seaham Harbour; from there they had cut inland, by-passing Durham and coming to Bishop Auckland. And now Joe was restless, wondering when Katie was going to stop.

Between blowing on the fire and wafting the sticks with his cap he whispered, "When are we going to settle, Katie? We're getting farther away from the towns; I'll never find work around here, 'cos it's wilder than any part we've come across yet."

"There's no hurry for you to find work, you know that," Katie whispered back. Then, leaning nearer to him, she said, "Did you notice the stone cottage standin' back from the road about a mile before we came to the village?"

"Where the blacksmith's shop had been? Aye, I did; but it was tumbled down."

"The main thing is it was empty. We could repair it. It might be let cheap. I've been thinkin' I'll take a walk back in the mornin' and have a look round."

Joe screwed his face up as he looked at her and asked, "You'd be content to stay out here in the wilds?"

"Yes, yes. Wouldn't you? Isn't it different from Jarrow and the filth and the smell?"

"There's new houses going up there all the time; we could have got a better one. . . ."

"Don't be silly!" Katie's voice sounded harsh, adult. "What would have happened if I'd rented a new house and us not supposed to have any money, and after the under-manager comin' again and asking how I'd been left, and him saying he was sure there was money somewhere? He said they had searched the house; you know he did."

"Aye, I know. I'm sorry, but . . . but Katie, I wouldn't like to settle out here."

"We'll settle where we can, Joe. She wants peace; she'll never find it back there." Katie rose from her knees and went to the cart, to where her mother was sitting with the child in her lap. "Come on, Ma; give her to me and get down and stretch your legs."

Obediently Catherine handed Katie the child, and as obediently she stepped down on to the grass and began to walk slowly about.

Katie, the child in her arms, said to Lizzie, "Come on, now, and you'll soon have a drink," and Lizzie sidled off the tail end of the cart, smiled widely at Katie and rolled towards the fire.

Joe unharnessed the horse and staked him by a long rope to allow him to feed—not that the animal would have strayed far, he was too old and tired; also, he was content with his new owners.

Katie sat on the grass feeding the child, while with her free hand she fed the fire with bits of dry twig from a sack which they kept slung under the cart to be used when they couldn't find wood or when it was raining; and like this she waited for the kettle to boil, every now and again glancing round to see that her mother was still with them.

She had thought that once she had got Catherine away from Jarrow and the quay corner she would recover her balance, but as yet there was no sign of it. For days after her da had been hanged her mother would walk through Jarrow without a covering to her head or a coat and would stand at the quay corner in front of the little white cottages at the point where the River Don ran into the Tyne. She would stand looking across the expanse of the Jarrow Slacks, the great mud-flat that twice a day was covered by the tide flowing in from the North Sea and swelling the river.

Dotted here and there on the mud-flat high black posts were standing. So many enterprising people, like Simon Templer, had had ideas of what could be done with the Jarrow Slacks, and the posts had been the beginning of one idea that never reached fruition. Over a foot square and ranging from eight feet high above the mud line, they looked ominous; and they were, for on one of them about thirty years earlier a man had been gibbeted. His name was William Jobling; he was a miner and on strike, and when out for a walk with a mate he stopped for a drink at an inn on the South Shields road, and it should transpire that a magistrate named Mr. Fairless happened to be passing by on his pony. The two men dared to argue with the magistrate and Jobling's friend hit out at him, giving him a blow from which he later died. Jobling's friend Armstrong disappeared from the scene, but the authorities had Jobling and they hanged him for the murder of the magistrate. The execution took place in public, and later the man's body was covered with pitch and gibbeted on one of the posts in Jarrow Slacks. This event had taken place during Catherine's lifetime. She was a child at the time, but she well remembered seeing the dangling, putrefying body, which the soldiers guarded until the stench became too much for them. The penalty for removing the body was death, but it was eventually removed, supposedly, by Jobling's mates. And it was to that place where she had stood as a young girl, looking towards the horror, that Catherine returned daily. It was as if she could see Rodney, who had no burial place, hanging from the black post out there.

At first Katie didn't know where her mother went. It was a woman from the white cottages overlooking the Slacks who came and told her. From then onwards part of Katie's daily routine was to try to keep Catherine away from the scene, and if she should escape her vigilance to go and fetch her back.

The life had gone out of Catherine. She was a being now without a will, except the will to die. Even this mustn't have been strong enough, else she would have taken measures to end her life.

And so Katie had thought up the idea of the cart to get them all away. But there was more than one reason why she wanted to leave Jarrow. There was Miss Theresa. Miss Theresa was wanting to help her, but somehow she didn't want her help. She wanted no help from the Rosiers, no one of them, for it was they who had put her where she was today; put them all where they were, even her da. Moreover, she was embarrassed by Miss Theresa, for she treated her as if she were the same as herself. So she had bought the cart and horse in Gateshead, and one morning at four o'clock she had loaded them all with household goods, even Lizzie, and set off to walk the four miles to the cart and horse. And now it had brought them this far.

The following morning Katie, taking the child with her and leaving Joe with whispered orders to watch her mother, made her way back to the village and there enquired as to who owned the stone cottage with the broken roof farther down the road.

"Oh," said a little fat woman who was feeding her hens at the bottom of a garden, "that belongs to the Misses Chapman. Never been lived in for years, gone to rack and ruin." And on Katie asking her where she could find the Misses

Chapman she was told, "In the Dower House. Not in the big house, that was their cousin's, Mr. Arnold Chapman; the ladies preferred the smaller house." She pointed across the open moorland to where in the distance stood a pair of iron gates. "Go inside them," said the little woman, "and to the right of the lodge. You won't find anyone in the lodge because Alice Worsley sees to the Misses Chapman and her man does the garden and such, but if you go right up to the house they will see you. They are nice ladies, the Misses Chapman; they've done a lot for the village in their time, and their father and grandfather afore them."

After thanking the woman Katie hitched the child up in her arms and went towards the gates, then through them to the house.

The pleasure the sight of the long, low, white creeper-covered house gave her brought something like a smile to her, but it was only an inward feeling, she showed no expression of it on her face; the face that had smiled and laughed so readily now looked like a piece of alabaster, and, in repose, just as set. As she neared the house out of the open door came a tall, middle-aged lady with a garden basket on her arm. She paused for a moment and stared across the terrace down at Katie and the child, then called cheerfully, "Are you looking for Alice?"

"No, ma'am; I'm . . . I'm looking for Miss Chapman."

"Oh." The lady came forward to the top of the steps. "I'm Miss Chapman."

"Good morning, ma'am." Katie dipped her knee.

"Good morning."

"I've . . . I've come to see if you would think of letting me your cottage?"

"Our cottage? But the lodge is taken. I have . . ."

"I mean the one down the road."

"Oh, that! But it isn't habitable, the roof's rotting and no one has lived in it for years."

"I'd be very much obliged, ma'am, if you'd rent it us."

"Is your husband with you?"

Katie lowered her lids for a moment, then said, "No, ma'am; he's . . . he's dead. It's my family I have with me, my . . . my mother, who is sick, and my sister and my brother."

"How . . . how did you get this far? Have you come from the town by trap?"

"No, ma'am; we've come from Tyneside, from Jarrow. We've got a cart."

Ann Chapman stared at the thin young girl with the beautiful sad face and remarkable eyes. Then she came slowly down the shallow steps and stood within a yard of Katie, and on closer inspection she remarked to herself, Dear, dear, such an unusual face, and come all this way from the coast on a cart. She said now, "I don't think you'd be able to live in the cottage, it'll need so much repair."

"We could do that, ma'am. My brother is very handy; he's very good with wood. He can make stools, and chairs, and things."

As Miss Chapman stood considering, there came round the side of the house another lady, not so tall as this one but younger and prettier. Miss Chapman turned to her and said, "Rose, dear, this young woman, who is a widow, is wanting us to let her and her family have Putman's cottage, but I'm saying it isn't habitable. Yet she thinks they could do the repairs themselves."

Miss Rose Chapman came and stood near her sister, and she looked at Katie for a moment, then at the baby in her arms, but she didn't speak and Miss Ann went on, "They came from the coast, the Tyne. They've come by cart. It's a long journey, don't you think, Rose, to come by cart?"

"Yes. Yes." Rose's voice was low and unemotional. She turned her eyes to her sister then back to Katie and said, "How old is your baby?"

"Just over five months, ma'am."

"May I look at it?"

"Yes, yes, of course, ma'am." Katie pulled the shawl back from the child's head and showed its sleeping face to the two women. Miss Rose now moved two steps nearer to Katie, and she stared down at the child for a full minute without speaking; then, looking over her shoulder towards her sister, she said, "It's a beautiful child, isn't it, Ann?"

"Yes, yes, Rose; it's a beautiful child. You take great care of it." Miss Ann nodded towards Katie. "It's so very clean."

"Thank you, ma'am."

"What do you call it?" Miss Rose addressed Katie stiffly.

"Sarah, ma'am."

Now Miss Rose turned round, her back towards Katie, and looking at her sister she said quietly, "I think they might be able to repair the cottage, Ann. Perhaps Worsley could give them a hand."

Miss Ann looked hard at Miss Rose, then she inclined her head forward and smiled and said, "Yes, dear, perhaps that could be arranged."

Katie closed her eyes, swallowed and said with deep gratitude, "Thank you, ma'am. Thank you, indeed. An' we'll be able to pay the rent. You needn't fear about the rent, we'll be able to pay it."

"Oh, the rent." Miss Ann's head went up. "We couldn't charge you very much rent for it, not in the state it is in at present. . . . You said you had a brother; how old is he?"

"Just turned fifteen, ma'am."

"Well, then, perhaps we could come to an arrangement. Perhaps he could help Worsley, our gardener and handyman. We had a boy from the village but he has gone into the town. The town is attracting so many of them these days. Yes, I think we could come to some arrangement."

Katie now bent her knee, first towards Miss Ann, then to Miss Rose, but as she turned to go she hesitated and said, "Will the key be there, ma'am?"

"Oh, the key." Miss Ann laughed, a high amused laugh. "I'm afraid there's no key; you'll find it open. My cousin's coachman used to live there, but my cousin is away so much abroad that he doesn't keep many staff now. I think there are bits of furniture in the house too. I've never been near it for years."

"Thank you, ma'am. Thank you ever so." Again Katie bent her knee to each, then hurried away, her heart lighter than it had been for many a long day. They would have a house; Joe would have a job. They might be able to keep a few hens and have a garden, and when her mother got better, which she would do in this peaceful atmosphere, she would be able to look after the child and Lizzie, and then she herself would find work at one of the big houses round about.

The black curtain that shrouded their existence was lifting. She could see their life moving into quiet, peaceful lanes. There would always be a sadness on them, for no life would be long enough to make them forget what had happened, but through time they wouldn't feel it as acutely as they did now.

The very air of this place was like a balm, and those two ladies were like angels. Katie looked down at her child and whispered aloud to it, "Yes, like angels they are."

*   *   *

As the days turned into weeks and the weeks into months Katie became filled with a sense of security. There was now some colour in her cheeks, and twice recently she had laughed at the antics of the child as she crawled about the floor.

The cottage was a daily source of wonder to her. She couldn't understand how such beautiful furniture had been left to rot. There were two chests of drawers, a carved settle, a black oak chest, and a corresponding refectory table, two real beds and many other smaller items, among which were two sets of heavy brass candlesticks. All the pieces, Katie realized from their quality, must have come from the big house, for she had glimpsed similar ones in the Rosier place.

Joe had mended the roof carefully, plastering the broken tiles, then fixing them back into place. Together they had whitewashed the stone walls inside and out, scrubbed the mould off the furniture, then polished it with wax. When all was complete they had laid the three bright rugs that Miss Ann had given them in the living-room, and it was home—a home that Katie had never imagined possessing.

But as time went on she shut her mind to the fact that of the three thinking people in the household she was the only one that was finding any form of satisfaction in their new surroundings. During the day Joe went up to the house and worked in the garden and did odd jobs, for which he received three shillings a week and the cottage free; added to this he brought vegetables home daily. In his spare time he whittled at things. He made a cradle on rockers for Sarah. He cut and hand-polished pieces of oak and made rough platters with them, and all the while he worked he sat quietly, as if he were brooding.

Then there was her mother. Catherine occasionally helped with the chores, but for most of her time she sat staring ahead, staring straight back into the past. She didn't speak more than half a dozen words a day. Katie told herself she was better, much better, since they had settled here; but she wished she would talk more, move about more, for then there might be a chance of getting out to work. There were several big houses within walking distance of the cottage, and she was sure she could get daily work if she tried. Miss Ann would recommend her; she knew she would. Her shift was very much lighter than it had been when they first sewed the sovereigns on to it; she had a little over a hundred pounds left. The solicitor's bill had been seventy-five guineas, and there had been her granda's funeral to pay for. She had seen that he was put away decently, and she had bought the horse and cart. Besides which they had all to be fed for weeks. The way they were living now she reckoned the money would last them just over three years, but what then? What if her mother didn't improve? It would be years before she could leave the child on her own. . . . Added to this there was the ever-present burden of Lizzie.

But then, she kept telling herself, three years was a long time, and before then something nice would happen. In this place only nice things could happen. She supposed it was because of Miss Ann and Miss Rose; she still thought of them as angels, Miss Rose particularly. There was hardly a day went by that Miss Rose didn't call in on them; at least not on them, but on the child. She had a great liking for Sarah, and Sarah for her. Sarah always gurgled happily when held in Miss Rose's arms. She had said to Miss Rose only yesterday, "She's taken a great fancy to you, ma'am." And Miss Rose had looked at her and smiled that half-shy, half-sad smile of hers as she asked, "You really think so?" And Katie had answered, "I do indeed, ma'am."

Katie found she always wanted to be nice to Miss Rose, because Miss Rose, like herself, had known sorrow, only a different kind of sorrow. She had heard her story from Alice. Miss Rose's affianced husband had been killed in the Crimean War and she had never been the same since. She had been very gay at one time, Miss Rose had, so Alice said, but now, to use Alice's own words, Miss Rose's heart was buried with Mr. Francis and she would die an old maid, like Miss Ann. But then Miss Ann had never been bespoken, and, as they said, what you never had you never miss. But it was different for Miss Rose.

On Sarah's first birthday Miss Rose and Miss Ann came to the cottage. They carried between them a large hamper, and Miss Rose carried a long cardboard box in the crook of one arm. In the box was a beautifully dressed doll and in the hamper was a great quantity of baby clothes which, explained Miss Ann, had been packed away in the attic, and only yesterday Miss Rose had remembered them, and did Katie think she'd be able to alter them to fit Sarah?

The tears came into Katie's eyes at the kindness of these two ladies.

There were such good people in the world. There were bad, oh yes, yes; but, on the other hand, there were many more good people. She looked at Miss Rose clasping Sarah, and Sarah clasping the doll, and she sent a prayer of thanksgiving to God for guiding her to the Misses Chapman.

This took place in the morning. When Joe came in at six o'clock he started on his tea; then, pushing his plate away before he had finished, he walked to the door and from there beckoned Katie outside. The evening was soft, the air was filled with the smell of wallflowers and lilac, the birds were singing, and Joe said, "Katie, I want to go back."

She looked down at him—for Joe hadn't grown much—into his thin face, into his kindly eyes, and she shook her head at him before saying, "Oh no, Joe."

"I can't stand it here, Katie; it's getting on me nerves. I was rude to Mr. Worsley the day."

Again she said, "Oh no, Joe." But now she had her hand to her face.

Joe bowed his head. "I couldn't help it, Katie, 'cos I keep thinkin' all the time of Jarrow and the shipyard. I was happy there. I wouldn't go back to the pits, but I felt I'd found me place like in the shipyard. Those few weeks in the boiler shop were the happiest I've known in me life . . . Look, Katie, I'll go back on me own an' find lodgin's. I'll go to Mr. Hetherington. He'll get me lodgin's; I know he will. He was sorry I left; he said everybody didn't take to it like I did, they just work 'cos they had to. He'll set me on if he can." He now looked up at Katie and added, "It isn't as if you hadn't anything to get by on—I wouldn't go if you hadn't; but I can't stick it here." He flung one arm out indicating the open land and the abundant greenery. "It drives me mad all this, it's so quiet."

"Aw, Joe." She bit hard on her lip but she couldn't stop the tears running down her cheeks. "I thought we were settled. It won't be the same if you go. Me ma . . . well, you know what she's like now, hardly a word. I haven't a soul to say a word to me all day, except when the ladies come along. Oh, Joe, it'll be awful without you, and I won't be able to get a place because of Lizzie and the child."

"I'm sorry, Katie." He caught hold of her hand. "I don't want to leave you, honest I don't, but I'll go daft here I, will."

There was a movement behind them and they both turned to see Catherine standing in the doorway. She was looking straight at Joe, and speaking directly to him she said, "Did you say you were goin' back, Joe?"

He made a small movement with his head, "Aye, Ma."

"Well, I'm goin' with you; this is no place for me."

"Ma, Ma, you can't. What'll we go back to? The Row?" Katie's voice was harsh now. She had taken control of the household; she had done her best; she had got them this lovely little house amid peace and quiet; they ate well, and slept soundly; when they awoke in the morning it was to fresh air, not to a filthy stench; and yet her mother wanted to go back, and Joe wanted to go back. Suddenly all words of protest dried up in her and, bowing her head and pushing past her mother, she went indoors and into her little room, and there she threw herself on to her bed and sobbed.

* * *

The Misses Chapman appeared in a state of great distress when Katie told them of their coming departure, but she made it plain that she didn't want to leave, but her mother and brother did, so she must go with them. While she was speaking she had watched the colour drain from Miss Rose's face; then she watched Miss Ann go to her sister and put her arms about her and say, "There, there, Rose. There, there, we'll see to it." That had been yesterday, and now here were the two sisters sitting in the cottage making a startling proposal to her.

They wanted to adopt Sarah.

Katie stared at them dumbfounded for a moment. Then, stooping instinctively and gathering up the child from the cradle as if to protect it from an onslaught, she shook her head vigorously, saying, "No! No! Oh no, I couldn't ever. Thank you all the same, but no."

Miss Ann was speaking now, gently. "Have you a home to take her to, Katie?"

"No, but we'll soon find one; if not in Jarrow, in Shields. There's plenty of houses in Shields."

"I know this has come in the form of a shock to you, but I

think on reflection you might reconsider. You see, we can offer Sarah great advantages. She would be well educated; she'll never know want of any kind; moreover, she'll be loved. It isn't as if you will be letting her go to someone who didn't really want her. Miss Rose, as you have seen, loves the child, Katie, and you have said yourself that the child is greatly attached to her. We'll . . . we'll go now and leave you time to think it over, and please, please think carefully, Katie."

The two ladies turned towards the door. Then Miss Rose, coming back, put out her hand and touched Katie's arm, saying softly, "I know what I'm asking of you, but I . . . I love her so. I've . . . I've seen other babies, but not one that has touched me as she has done, and I promise you I'll spend my life seeing to her needs."

Katie said nothing. The chill had already settled on her heart, and it grew colder when the door had closed on the visitors and she looked from Joe to her mother. It was a long time before either of them spoke; then Joe said, "You've got to think what's best for her, Katie; you'll never get a chance like this again. And . . . and when you get back and you want to go to work you'll have to put her out to be minded." As he finished speaking he glanced quickly at his mother with an apologetic look in his eyes. Katie, too, looked at her mother. She knew what would happen once they got back to Jarrow. There would be journeys to the quay corner; there'd be Lizzie to see to . . . besides the child. There'd be no chance of her going out to work, and when the money was gone from the shift they'd have to depend on Joe. She knew it wasn't fair to Joe, but she couldn't give up her child, she couldn't. If she had been asked when she was carrying it would she give it away she would have said, without hesitation, yes, but not now . . . "It'll have a fine education and want for nothing; moreover, it will be loved." That's what Miss Rose had said. Well, it would never have more love than she could give it. But there was no hope in her to give it an education of any sort, or to promise it would never want for food or warmth. She could only promise it it would be brought up in the smoke, dirt and grime of Jarrow or Shields.

Joe said now, very quietly, "You might get married again, Katie, and have another one. She . . . Miss Rose, I mean . . . there's no chance for her; she's thirty, if she's a day."

For the first time in her life Katie rounded on her brother,

139

crying, "Shut up! Shut up! You know nothing about it, an' I won't marry again." On this she turned from her mother's staring eyes and Joe's bent head and Lizzie's laughing, gaping face and went into the bedroom, and there, sitting on the edge of her bed, she held the child closely to her, rocking it backwards and forwards. Then, stopping the movement abruptly, she looked down into the child's face and Sarah laughed up at her with eyes just like her own.

Almost daily since the child was born she had searched its face for some feature that might identify it as a Rosier. Although it had looked like herself from the first day, she knew that children had a habit of changing; but Sarah resembled herself more closely as time went on, at least the self she once was. This had comforted her, except at times when she thought that perhaps her daughter would grow up to be a Rosier inside, a particular Rosier. Yet the nature of her child, seen so far, showed only a reflection of her own inward character—again as it had once been, laughing, free. . . . She couldn't let her go, she couldn't. She was rocking the child once more when the door opened and Catherine came in.

Katie stared at her mother and saw that the dazed look had lifted almost entirely from her face. She kept her eyes on her while she seated herself on the other side of the bed, and when she started to speak she thought, with not a little resentment, She can talk all right when she likes. She's likely been all right inside all the time; she just doesn't want to bother any more, for now Catherine was saying in a quiet, persuasive tone, "It's the best thing, lass. What chance is she going to have back there? And remember, many of them never see five. Get a bout of fever, typhoid an' such, an' they're gone, if they've not already been took with whooping-cough or diphtheria. Don't I know. There's little chance for youngsters back there. But with them"—she gave a lift of her head—"she'd have every chance. She'd have all the things I dreamed about givin' you."

"Would you have let me go, Ma?" There was a deep note of bitterness in Katie's voice, and Catherine looked away for a moment before she replied, "Aye, I would. It wouldn't have been easy, but I would. Given a chance like you have, I would."

Although she sounded sincere, Katie couldn't believe her mother, yet it was at this moment, she knew, that the decision was made; the child had already gone from her. She

140

knew that should she take it back to what Jarrow had to offer and anything should happen to it, what she had suffered through Bernard Rosier, Mark Bunting, and the death of her father would be a pinprick compared to the mountain of remorse that would weigh on her for being the cause of depriving her child of a better chance in life, perhaps of life itself, for, as her mother said, many of them died before five.

Suddenly she began to cry, loud uncontrolled crying, unlike any crying she had done before; not even when the hour came for her da to be hanged had she cried like this. It was like an avalanche of sorrow pouring from her body, getting stronger with its flow.

Joe came into the room and took the child from her, and Catherine held her in her arms, but her mother's affection now brought her no comfort, only a strange, growing resentment; for no matter how the Misses Chapman had pleaded, and no matter how Joe had backed them up, it would have made no difference if her mother had, as she had done for months past, kept quiet. But it was as if she was saying to her, you owe me something. I'd have your da here the day but for you. You've caused all this, so do this one thing that is not only good for the bairn but will simplify matters back there, and ease our plight.

And it was in this moment, too, that she realised that her mother had never liked the child. She had never touched it unless she'd had to. It was a child of sin, unintentional, but nevertheless sin.

The thing was settled; she had lost her Sarah.

BOOK II

Andree
1865

1

At ten minutes to five on a January morning in 1865 Joe closed the door of No. 14, Crane Street behind him and walked up through Temple Town in South Shields. The air cut at his throat like a knife; the black darkness seemed filled with ice and all pressing on him. He could feel it on his skin; it was as if he wasn't wearing two coats, a shirt and a singlet; and he might not have hobnailed boots on, for his feet were already stiff with the cold. But he had the comfort of knowing that before an hour was out he would be sweating.

As he neared the corner of a street, a few yards from the low wall that bordered the river, two small hopping figures came out of the darkness and joined him, saying, "You, Joe?" and got for a reply, "Who else, you think—the devil?"

"Coo! Joe, it's a freezer, ain't it?"

"Aye, Ted, 'snifter all right . . . You awake yet, kidder?"

The twelve-year-old boy, towards whom Joe had turned his head, gave a shudder and through chattering teeth replied, "I'm gonna try for the docks next week; this mornin' march is too much of a bloody good thing."

"Oh you get used to it, man; you've only been on it a few months. An' I'm tellin' you, Bob, there's no chance in the docks, else I'd be there meself. . . . But no, I wouldn't." Joe pushed out his chin. "It's Palmer's for me, even with the trek. Not that I like it, mind, but I'd rather do it in the mornin' than at night, comin' home dead beat. Aw, man, I could fall asleep on me feet."

"Me an' all," said Ted.

"It would be all right if they would pick us up or summat an' take us there," said Bob.

Joe put his head back and let out a bellow of a laugh. It was a deep, manly laugh, and at nineteen Joe was a man. Although he was still small, below medium height, he was broadly made and his voice was deep and pleasant. He said now, "Let's do a sprint," and began to run up the long road by the new Tyne dock wall, past the stables where they heard the horses champing at their bits, and past the dock gates, without much bustle yet. The bustle here wouldn't start for another hour; at about the same time it would start in Palmer's Shipyard three miles away. After a while they stopped for want of breath and Joe asked, "Is that better?"

"Aye," said Ted.

"How about you, Bob?"

"I'm warmer," said Bob, "but I wish I was there."

"Now don't keep yarpin' on." As a man of years, Joe admonished the young boy. "You'll have somethin' to grumble about if you're out shortly. Then you'll have plenty of time to lie in an' all; but remember, it's better to walk on a full belly than sleep on an empty one."

"Do you think there'll be a strike, Joe?"

"It's lookin' like it. If Andrew Gourlay doesn't get his way there will be. It's a nine-hour day or nowt. The only thing we've all got to do is to stand together." He addressed the boys as if they were staple men of industry.

"Me da says when men stop spittin' we'll get a nine-hour day," said Bob now.

"Your da's wrong then," said Joe. "It'll come. It could be here now if they'd all hang together and not have so many bloomin' little craftsmen's unions, all going at each other's throats." Following this piece of wisdom there was silence between the three of them, until Joe said, "Come on; let's do another sprint."

"But we'll only have to stand and wait for the gates to open if we get there too soon."

With a gentle cuff along the ear, together with a "Come on, Dismal Dan", Joe urged the boys forward, and again they were running. They passed the Jarrow Slacks and made across the fields, cutting off the quay corner, and so entered Jarrow.

Joe never went round by the quay corner if he could help it; it reminded him too much of his mother and the times he had to go and fetch her home. From the very week they had come back she had started going to the quay corner again

146

and standing staring out at the gibbet pole. Katie had become worn out with trailing after her, and so it had been part of his day's work to take the road to the quay corner when he left the shipyard, and there nearly always, and in all weathers, he would find her, just standing staring.

It was on a black day such as this one tended to be that she had caught pneumonia, and within a fortnight she was gone. At times he was weighed with a sense of guilt concerning her—he had been very fond of his mother—but he couldn't help but admit to himself that life was much easier without her. There was only Lizzie now, she was a problem all right, but Katie saw to her. But here again his conscience worked overtime when he wondered how long Lizzie was likely to last. She was so fat and swollen up she could hardly walk now, and she had taken to crying out aloud and making weird wailing sounds. He didn't envy Katie stuck with her all day.

When they came on to the main road the half-past-five buzzer sounded. It was like a trumpet in their ears, and Joe remarked, "We've made good time this mornin'."

A flat cart trundled by them, its presence made visible by a swinging lamp near the driver. On the cart itself sat a number of men, their legs dangling over the side, their bodies making a darker pattern of blackness. When Ted suggested they should hang on the back Joe answered quickly, "Don't be daft; you'll get the whip or a kick in the teeth."

"I wish I could take the cart," said Bob now; "but I'm not payin' fourpence a day. It's robbery. A third of me wages for a ride there and back to Shields!"

"Well, from where he comes it's a good four miles, and he's got to get back there."

"He takes night-shift chaps back," said Bob. "He's coinin' money."

"I went in the steamer to Tynemouth on Saturda'," said Ted; "there and back for fourpence, half-price. Eeh, it were grand."

"You're barmy," said Bob. "Wait till Blaydon time comes, an' you won't have a penny put by for the races, like last year."

"Aw, give over, man, an' shut your clapper. By that time I'll have a rise. Mr. Palmer hissel told me tother day that he was goin' to double me wages 'cos I'm a good lad. 'Ted', he said, pattin' me on the heid, 'they don't come like you every

147

day. Without men like you the *Defence* would never have been finished. Nor would the last troopship's keel've been laid. It takes men like you, lad, to build a battleship in three months'."

At this point Ted found himself flying into the roadway from a push of Joe's big hand; then they were all laughing.

A little farther on and they were just three small dots in a mass of moving blackness, men coming from all districts of the town converging on the shipyard. The clatter of their boots was like the sound of an army marching out of step.

Joe and the boys took up their position some yards from the gates in the middle of the dense mass. They stamped their feet and blew on their hands, and the ten minutes they had to wait before the gates were opened seemed longer than the whole journey from Shields.

Then the great iron gates were pulled back and the black human mass surged in and spread itself. Like streams of tar running over a great surface they flowed in all directions: to the boiler shops, the engine shops, the puddling mills, the blast furnaces, the carpenters' shops, the fitting-out shops, the dry dock.

Presently, Joe bade goodbye to the two small boys, who were making for the dry dock; he himself, in the midst of a smaller flow of men, crossed over a railway siding where stood wagons filled with stone which had been brought there by the company's own boats from the Yorkshire mines. This stone held the ore which would eventually be known as Cleveland iron. They passed the great blast furnaces. Here was the heart of the concern; here was where the stone, after being roasted, gave up its ore. It was here that it was fed into the blast furnace, together with coke and limestone, two essential additions, necessary to complete the manufacture of the iron, or pigs, as the iron bars were called. There was a special ore imported from Spain and Africa; again in the company's own boats. This was a sulphur- and phosphorus-free ore which did not need to be roasted as did the Cleveland ore.

The knowledge of the making of iron was known to every man in the yard. They were iron men, steel men; they talked of hardly anything else, for only by iron and steel could they eat. Once a man had worked in Palmer's for some years he felt he would be no good for anything else; nor did he want to be. There were men who had started with the yard in its infancy and who spoke of its creator with the respect that men give to a general. As they said, "the old man" not only conceived the ships, he gave them ribs, bones and guts; then dressed them fully and fine ready for the water. Anything that left Palmer's, they said, could sail to the limits of the globe. But this was the talk of the older men. The younger ones didn't eulogize so. They were more apt to ask questions.

Along their way now, near the rolling mills, there lay great lengths of iron. They lay on bogies and would finally find their way to the boiler shop.

Joe had been working for three years in the boiler shop under Mr. Hetherington, and he knew he was fortunate, for he could not have found a better man to serve his time with; for Mr. Hetherington not only supervised the making of boilers—hearts for ships, he called them—but he talked, ate, and slept boilers, and was said to be able to tell with his eyes shut whether he was touching Cleveland iron of number one, two, or three quality, or simply number four forge, the stuff that was made into wrought iron. Nor did he have to see the brand of Jarrow or Tyneside stamped on the pigs to distinguish between the grades.

Apart from feeling himself lucky he was working under Mr. Hetherington, Joe also felt proud that he held a special place in Mr. Hetherington's esteem. He had been to Mr. Hetherington's house a number of times, and only yesterday, when Mr. and Mrs. Hetherington were passing through Shields to get the steamer across the water for a Sunday jaunt with their daughter Mary, they had called in.

Joe now entered the great boiler shop that would, to an outsider, have appeared like a large enclosed space which had experienced an earthquake. It looked a place of utter disorder, a place of contorted iron, jibs, cranes, cylinders, all seeming to be mixed up together. Joe made his way to the far end of the shop, took off his outer coat, pulled off his muffler and stuffed it in his pocket. Then, picking up his black tea can from his bench, he prised off the lid, sniffed at the stale grouts, and wrinkled his nose. Then, reaching out to his coat, he put his hand in the pocket to make sure he had brought his tea—he had forgotten it one day last week. He pulled out the small twisted piece of paper that held a spoonful of tea, jerked his head at it as a man might do who knew himself to be the possessor of something special, then pushed it back into the pocket. As he did so a voice came to him above the din that was already filling the shop, saying, "Hello there, lad."

"Oh, hello, Mr. Hetherington." Joe smiled broadly at the prematurely aged man facing him.

"Nippy this mornin'?"

"Aye, it is, Mr. Hetherington."

"Well, let's get started; standin' jabberin' won't get anything off the stocks."

"No, it won't, Mr. Hetherington." Joe was moving forward to pick up his hammer when Mr. Hetherington, coming to his side, said quietly, "Joe, at break I'd like a word with you."

Joe narrowed his eyes at Mr. Hetherington, and there was a note of apprehension in his voice as he said, "Aye, Mr. Hetherington. Have I done owt wrong?"

"Oh no, lad, no." Mr. Hetherington put his hand on his shoulder. "It's a private word I want with you, just a private word."

"Oh aye, Mr. Hetherington, all right." Joe still felt a young lad when talking to Mr. Hetherington.

From then until eight o'clock, when the shop stopped for a short while to enable the men to have a drink and a snack, which came under the heading of breakfast, Joe kept on thinking about what private word Mr. Hetherington could want to say to him.

He was seated with his can lid full of tea on his knee and a shive of thick bread in his hand when Mr. Hetherington came and seated himself by his side, and looking straight at him he said, "I'm comin' to the point, lad, without goin' round the houses. You see, it's like this. After callin' on you yesterday the missus and I got talkin'; in fact she's never stopped talkin' about it since. It's about your sister."

"Katie?"

"Aye, it concerns her; but it's about the other one an' all. Have you ever thought of putting her away, Joe?"

Joe looked down into the lidful of tea, and it was a moment before he spoke. "I've thought about it a lot, Mr. Hetherington. But . . . but Katie won't. You see, she promised me ma. Me ma went on terrible at the last about Lizzie, and she made Katie promise. . . ."

"Aw." Mr. Hetherington threw his head from one side to the other. "These death-bed promises make me sick. The peo-

150

ple who are crippled for life through death-bed promises.
. . . Look, lad." He brought his face close to Joe's. "Your
sister Katie is wastin' her life. She's a bonny lass, I've never
seen a bonnier. The wife's never stopped, I tell you, since
yesterday. She says it's a sin afore God to have that lovely
lass cooped up there at the top of that awful house with that
lass. It would be no company for an old 'un but a young
fine lass like that . . ."

"I know, Mr. Hetherington." Joe still had his head down.
"I've been at her time and time again, but she won't."

"How long has she been lookin' after her?"

"Oh, since me mother died last year. And afore that. You
see, she would get a place—she's had three in Westhoe—but
then me mother would take to her roaming, you know, and it
was then Lizzie would start to howl and the woman below
started to complain; mind you, aye, they're very good, the
rest—oh aye, they're very good. An' that's why we stay there.
I could get a little place farther into the town, away from the
waterfront, more respectable like, but the neighbours might
kick up, whereas the present ones . . . well, they understand."

"How many families are livin' in the house?"

"Three asides us."

"Sup your tea up; time's getting on." Mr. Hetherington
watched Joe empty the can lid then fill it again before he
said, "It isn't fair on either of you. Say you wanted to get
married, what's going to happen to the pair of them then?"

"Aw, Mr. Hetherington," Joe smiled. "It'll be a long time
afore that happens to me; I'll always look after them."

"You're talkin' through the fat of your neck, lad. It'll hit
you one of these days an' you'll want to marry afore you
know where you are. And there's no lass in her right senses
. . . I'm not meanin' to be nasty, I'm just using common-
sense, Joe, but I maintain there's no lass in her right senses
who'll take you on if you have to support the two of them.
Anyway, you'd never make enough because afore you knew
where you were you'd have a family of your own. . . . Aw"
—he raised his hand palm outwards towards Joe—"don't
contradict me on that; you're a man and you'll want to
marry."

"I don't want to contradict you, Mr. Hetherington; only if
it came to the push I know the road I'd have to take."

"Well, as you say, it'll be up to you, lad. An' I hope you don't think I'm interferin'. But the wife kept on talkin'. . . . By the way, has Katie got a lad of any sort?"

"No." Joe shook his head. "She wouldn't have a lad from round there, not among those sorts, foreigners, sailors, an' the like."

"But they're not all foreigners and sailors; there's decent fellows about, an' some good fishin' families down there, an' I can't see them closin' their eyes to one that looks like her."

"Oh, they haven't. She used to be followed time and again, but you know, Mr. Hetherington . . ." Joe cast his eyes towards his boots. "She not taken with men of any kind; she had a bellyful for the short time she was married. I told you."

"Aye, aye, lad, I suppose she had. But nature has a way of covering things up. It's some years gone now an' it isn't natural for a lass like her, a woman—for that's what she is—to be on her own and without friends."

"Oh, she isn't entirely without friends, Mr. Hetherington. Miss Theresa—you know, the daughter of the house where she used to work—she's always popping in. She's got a little school in Westhoe. She lends Katie books; Katie's a great reader."

"Aye, she might be. And it's a great thing in itself to be able to read, but that's not goin' to satisfy her all her life."

They remained silent for some minutes until Joe, trying to turn the conversation, said, "What do you think about the movement, Mr. Hetherington?"

"What do I think about it?" Mr. Hetherington took a bite out of a meat sandwich. "I think it's comin' to a head, lad."

"You think there'll be a strike?"

"It's as near as damn it, but none of us wants it."

"Have they put the petition to the old man?"

"Aye, but things are different now." Mr. Hetherington put his head back and looked up at the tangle of gear attached to the grimy roof. "They've changed; the whole place has changed since it went over into a company. I've seen the day when you could go to the old man an' talk to him. Aye, even me. Many's the time he's stopped by me side an' said, 'What do you think, John? Is it an improvement?' He was always out for improvement, makin' things better and better."

"Well, he still is, isn't he?"

"Aye, yes, but at a price. He hasn't got the hundred per

cent backin' of the men he used to have in the old days. You can't get at him, or any of them up top for that matter; they're workin' from London now instead of inside the works here, although the bloody place is so full of offices and staff now we'll soon have to move the blast furnaces."

Joe laughed at this but continued to look at Mr. Hetherington—he liked to listen to the older man talking—and Mr. Hetherington went on, "See what they've done to the puddlers. Given them a ten per cent cut, and the whole country has accepted it like sheep—that is, all but North Staffordshire. They're standin' firm and they've come out."

"Do you think wor puddlers'll support them, Mr. Hetherington?"

"No, lad, I don't. There's too many unions, too many heads of unions, too many bosses, too many under-bosses. It's every man jack for himself, or his own little band, instead of them all joining up together. After all, we're all steel men. But God knows we don't want any strikes; I've seen enough of them in me time." On this Mr. Hetherington rose to his feet, saying, "Well now, here we go, lad. Let's see those rivets flyin'."

And all day Joe helped the rivets to fly until the buzzer went at half-past five. He had entered the boiler shop in the dark and he left it in the dark. But that didn't trouble him; he had seen the daylight through the grimed windows of the shop, and at dinner-time he had sat on the river bank where the skeleton ribs of a ship were rising from the keel, and with his mates he had talked ships, talked "Palmer's" with as much pride in the firm as if he was one of the shareholders getting his ten per cent.

Palmer's men might fight, and argue, and talk against the bosses, even against the old man himself, but they were Palmer's men, and underneath it all, proud of the title.

2

It was March and the strike had come about. The steelmasters of the country were determined to break trade unionism,

153

and so on March 11, 1865, seventy thousand men all over the country were locked out. Palmer's men were particularly bitter about this because earlier they had been presented with an ultimatum. There would be no lock-out in the yard, they were told, if they did not support the Staffordshire men by contributions in any form. The leaders of the various unions had reluctantly agreed to this, because the struggle for a livelihood was hard enough as it was now, but in a lock-out there were the wives and bairns to think about. Moreover, scab labour could be imported from other parts of the country, but mostly from Ireland, and when that started hell was let loose. It had been let loose before through the same cause. The Jarrow men became a fierce, battling, frightening horde when treated unjustly. They were aware of this; they knew themselves, and it wasn't only the low drunken types among them who gave scope to their battling tendencies. Quite a good percentage of the workmen were property owners under Charles Mark Palmer's factory building society scheme. When in work, even for as little as twenty shillings a week, they felt responsible men; they and the town were going places. The overall general feeling had been that old man Palmer was not only pushing the ships out of the yard, he was also pushing the town on. Wasn't the building society proof of this? And also the Mechanics Institute he had built for them last year? The town was growing. Subsidiary firms were prospering, streets and streets of houses were springing up like mushrooms. They had actually brought the mains water into the town from Shields, and some of the new houses had their own taps in the yard. Moreover, the sewage was being seen to; the gutters were no longer running with filth. Things were moving in Jarrow; they didn't want a lock-out.

But the lock-out had come; their earthly God, whose name was Charles Mark Palmer, who had promised them that if they played square with him he would play square with them, had joined up with the other steelmasters. Many excuses were given for his action, one being similar to that which had brought the Staffordshire men out: a depression in trade. This alone made the men angry, for the yard was full of work, with a troopship for the Admiralty in the stocks.

But anyway they were out, and such was the fibre of the men that within a fortnight, when Mr. Palmer would have re-started them again, they became stubborn and refused to go back, and now because of Andrew Gourlay and his demand for a nine-hour day. Only one or two unions could afford to pay the men strike pay, for the rest there was nothing. This meant families living, or existing, on tick, or help from their more fortunate neighbours, who might be in work at one or other of the new factories.

For the first week of the strike things had been normal for Katie and Joe. Katie had Joe's pay to work on and she made it spread out into the middle of the second week, at least with regard to food. But the rent hadn't been paid.

She sat now looking at Joe across the small refectory table that had once graced the little cottage in the country. She drummed her fingers on the edge of the polished wood and watched their movement as she said, "Well, there's nothing for it, I'll just have to break into it."

Joe ran his hand through his sandy-coloured hair and, twisting round in his chair, looked out of the window on to the jumble of rooftops and chimneys. The roofs were grey slate, and the chimneys, though made of red brick, were black. Nearly all of them were spouting forth smoke, and this moved upwards to form a cloud under the already lowering sky. The wind had dropped and within a few minutes it would likely rain. He was glad he had got in before he got wet; you always seemed much more hungry when you were wet. He had just finished a meal that Katie had ready for him; it had been tasty enough, for she was a grand cook, but there hadn't been enough of it. Now they were really on their beam ends and she was saying she would have to break into the last sovereign. Times had been hard before, but they had never touched the sovereign; they were both of the opinion that if they kept that one sovereign intact they were all right. But now they had to face up to the fact that whereas they could economise on food and pull their belts well in they could do nothing about the rent man. Owe two weeks around this quarter and you were put on the street. It was anything but a savoury neighbourhood, but the rooms and houses were always snapped up, and for a purpose Joe's mind wouldn't allow him to go into. Although Joe no longer went regularly to chapel, his early training under his father was still with him, and there was only stern condemnation in him for the dirty, low-living bitches who changed their rooms frequently to keep one jump ahead of the police. He had his strong suspicions about the two occupants on the ground floor of this actual house, but they had made no advances to him, and they didn't complain about Lizzie, so he did not question how they made their living. He said now, "It'll likely be over next week, and then we can put it together again."

"What if it isn't, Joe?"

"We haven't got to think like that."

"Look, I could get a daily place the morrow, you know I could, if you'd stay in and look after her."

He got abruptly to his feet and walked to the fireplace, where some salt-soaked damp wood was smouldering, and he took the poker and turned it over before saying, "Aw, Katie, don't let's go into it again. I can't, lass. I've told you. I'd go stark starin' mad being stuck up here with her all day." The poker still in his hand, he turned round and faced her. "I don't know how you stick it, I don't really. You know, some time ago, in fact the day after they first called here, Mr. Hetherington said . . . Well . . ." He made an impatient movement with the poker. "He said she should be put away."

Katie slowly put her elbow on the table and supported her face on her hand before she said in a tired way, "She's not going into the workhouse, Joe."

"But as I said"—he was moving towards her now—"she won't know; she doesn't know where she is."

Katie's face jerked from her hand and she stared at him, her tone low and harsh now. "Get it into your head, Joe," she said, "she does know; she's not just a lump of puddin'. She might look like it, and act like it, but she's not. I can tell by the look in her eyes when I go near her she's not. After she's been left alone for hours an' I come back her face changes."

"You just think that."

"I don't, I don't, I know." Her voice had risen to a shout; but now she clapped her hand over her mouth and, bowing her head, finished quietly, "I'm not puttin' her away, Joe."

"Well, where's it going to end?" Joe's voice was rough now. "You could give your whole life to her; it could go on and on. It isn't fair."

"No, no, I know it isn't; it isn't fair to you."

They were looking at each other, and he said quickly, "I wasn't talkin' about meself. I haven't got her all day."

"Well, don't worry about me, Joe, I'm all right. As long as you're all right I'm all right." There was a pause, and then she smiled, and it was a replica of the smile that he remembered was hers as a young girl, and he thought, Mr. Hetherington's right; she's a beautiful lass . . . a beautiful woman.

"Where did you get to this mornin'? Nothing doing?" she said now as if to change the subject.

"No, not a thing. You know"—he turned from her and walked to the fireplace again—"you wouldn't believe it, but they treat you like mad dogs. I mean in the docks here. You go in just to ask if there's any chance, and it must be something about you that shows the fellows you're after a job, 'cos they're givin' you the full of their mouths an' tellin' you to bugger off or what they'll do to you. I . . . I felt like hittin' one at the mill dam this mornin', an Irish bloke he was. I did say to him, 'If you were back in your tatie fields there'd be more jobs for them that have a right to them.' I thought him an' his pals was goin' to brain me, but a ganger came up. Then I went along the pier. Coo, that's a walk! They're still mucking about at the end, an' you know what one chap said to me? I'd better clear off if I didn't want to go down with the ballast. I tell you, when there's a strike on anywhere t'others are like tigers."

He now went to the window, and from there he said, "Charlie Roche is talkin' of walkin' to Seaham Harbour. He's got a cousin there who's set up on his own. Blacksmith shop and carpentry next door; the whole family are in it. They make chairs an' things. He said they can always do with a hand or two, an' they'd likely be able to stretch a point when it's only for a short time. He wants me to go along of him. He said he wouldn't go on his own, not walkin' all that way; he wants company. He said one thing is certain, we'd come back with as much grub as we could carry. They've got pigs and things, and there's always umpteen hams hangin' up." He smiled at her. "Me mouth's waterin' already."

"How long would it take you?" she asked.

"Aw well, going at it hard we could do it in a day there and a day back, an' if we could put in a few days' work we'd get a few shillings; enough to pay the week's rent. An' I could bring enough back to feed us. It would help things along, don't you reckin?"

"Yes." She nodded.

"You wouldn't be afraid to stay here on your own?"

She closed her eyes and smiled derisively. "Don't be silly," she said.

"Do you think I should go?"

"Yes, yes, of course. An' there's a chance you might strike

157

something on your way." And as she looked at him she added to herself, "And it will take you away from here, away from her for a time."

She had never fully understood Joe's antipathy towards Lizzie. Unlike herself, he had no compassion for his sister; she had only to look at the misshapen form and her heart became moved with pity. Yet there were times when she wished her dead. Yet she didn't really want her to die, for when Lizzie went there'd be no one to mother. Lizzie was her child now, the baby she still cried about at night.

She said to Joe, "Go and tell him you'll go along with him. And look . . ." She went to the mantelpiece and taking the last of Mark Bunting's hoard from a little box she handed it to Joe, saying, "Get it changed and take five shillings with you."

"No! No, I'll do no such thing." He waved her hand aside.

"Well, look"—her voice was harsh again—"you're not goin' on the road with nothin' in your pocket; you don't know what happens; you might have to come straight back if there's nothing doin'. An' you'll want a bite to eat. Anyway, if you don't spend it you can bring it back. . . . Now you're not going unless you take it."

"Aye, well." He nodded briskly at her as if she was forcing him to do something mean and underhand. "You can take it from me, you'll get it back whole. I'm not going on a trip."

She was smiling as she said now, "Make it a trip; you might as well be killed for a sheep as a lamb. An' don't worry about us. Everything at this end'll be all right; I'll see to that."

He dropped his head shyly before her. Then, going out of the room, he took his hat and coat off a nail on the wall on the tiny landing where there was just room enough to turn round between the two walls, that held two doors, and the little table, on which stood a wooden bucket and a wash-bowl. Then he went down the steep dark stairs that led to a similar landing; down another flight that opened into a small dark square hall with doors at either side, and into the greasy street, where, through the steady falling rain, there loomed the river and the masts of ships lying at the buoys.

Upstairs, Katie went into the bedroom where Lizzie was sitting propped up in a low bed, and, pulling the bedclothes aside, she took her two hands and tugged her to her feet, then wrapped the patched quilt around her. Katie herself was now five feet six inches tall with a finely shaped figure, but without the bulbous hips seen on so many women, yet compared with Lizzie's bulk she looked a thin slip of a girl, for Lizzie's glandular disease had made her into a living balloon. Katie guided her waddling form into the kitchen and sat her down on a broad cracket with her back against the wall near the fire—there wasn't a chair big enough to hold her—and she patted her bulging cheek with her fingers and said, "All right?" And Lizzie looked at her and blinked and moved the muscles of her face into greater contortion.

Katie always kept Lizzie in bed when Joe was about, but she reckoned that once he got talking about the journey to Charlie Roche it would be an hour or so before he was back, and she sensed that the only pleasure her sister could experience was to be in her presence, so whenever she could she brought her into the kitchen.

She now went to the chest of drawers and her eyes moved over a number of books lying there. She had read them all many times over—that was, all except *The Stones of Venice;* she had only read it once. She couldn't get interested in painters and buildings. But Miss Theresa said you had to read such a book again and again before you could appreciate it. She knew she was very lucky to possess this book, where under the name of John Ruskin was that of Rodger Philip Rosier. Miss Theresa had given it to her after Mr. Rodger had died, and she treasured it because it had belonged to Mr. Rodger, but as a book she couldn't like it. She wondered again why Mr. Rodger had to die; why couldn't it have been the other one, why couldn't he have got smallpox? That any gentry should die of smallpox had been a surprise in itself.

She picked up another book; it was *Vanity Fayre*. She liked Mr. Thackeray's books, they had a story in them.

Going to the fireplace, she pulled her chair as close to it as possible and, in a position such that the light would fall on the paper, began to read. But she only read for a short time, and then, as she had done often of late, she allowed the book to drop into her lap and she turned and looked about her as if expecting to see something different, something that might surprise her about this room that had become an enclosed world to her. She knew that she should consider herself fortunate that it was decently furnished. THEY—she always thought of the Misses Chapman as THEY—had insisted that she take the entire contents of the cottage with her when she left. THEY had also wanted to pay her for the transaction of signing her daughter to them. She knew they had been amazed when she refused to take their money. But she was glad now she had brought the furniture—all except the beds —for she would never have bought the like of it round here, even if she'd had the money, for they were craftsmen's pieces and she kept them shining. Miss Theresa always remarked on this.

Miss Theresa. Katie now brought her eyes to the window and the blue velvet curtains that hung there. Miss Theresa had brought them the last time she had called. She had apologised for them being faded at the edge but had pointed out they could be cut down. Miss Theresa was kind. She was always bringing little things, but she wished she wouldn't; more and more she wished she wouldn't. She couldn't forget she was a Rosier, although she'd said openly that she hated her brother. But there was something more, somehow she didn't like her the way she used to do; she didn't really know why, except that she thought Miss Theresa was a bit dominating, always telling her what to do, and how to do it, yet at the same time treating her as if there was no difference between them. It was odd, disturbing.

*　　*　　*

Joe left the house at eight o'clock the next morning. His face wearing an expression of excitement, he looked as if he were actually going on a holiday. Yet again he asked Katie if she would be all right, and in answer he received a push from her. Then self-consciously he kissed her on the cheek and, turning hastily away, ran down the stairs, the sound of his hobnailed boots reverberating through the house.

Katie stood in the middle of the kitchen for a moment looking about her. She was going to miss Joe. No matter what she said, she was going to miss him. But there, she told herself, she must get on if she wanted to get to the market this morning.

Her "getting on" took the same pattern it did every day: getting Lizzie up, changing her, washing her, then draping her in a gigantic napkin. This done, she tackled the bed. It was always wet, and she was lucky if this was all she had to cope with. After making the bed up with rough dry pieces of twill she took the dirty pieces in the wooden bucket down the two flights of stairs to the yard and there, in the communal wash-house, she washed them, without soap, in cold water and hung them on the line. She was always thankful for a fine day when she hadn't to try to dry them completely indoors. She next filled the bucket with cold water and humped it back upstairs. This done, she did Joe's room, which was on the other side of the landing. It was only large enough to hold a six-foot pallet bed and a wooden box. Next, she tackled the kitchen, first of all stripping her own bed, which, just being a raised wooden platform, acted as a settee during the day; then once more she polished the furniture, after which she scooped the drips of tallow from one of the brass candlesticks, trimmed the wick of the small piece of candle left in the socket, then carefully gathering up the nodules of tallow she put them in an iron pan together with other tallow scrapings and small ends of candle to be melted down for further use.

The room put to rights, she now got herself ready to go to the market. She took off her coarse apron and rough working skirt and put on a grey serge one. It was of fine quality and edged with a dust fringe at the bottom. This, together with her three-quarter-length coat, had also come from Miss Theresa; the coat was a plum colour and heavily braided, and if anything more was needed to bring out the beauty of her complexion it was this. Her bonnet had been given to her by her last mistress. According to the present fashion it was now out of date; the trimmings were mostly on the brim, the crown being quite plain. When she was ready she took a bass bag from the cupboard and her purse from the top drawer of the smaller chest. She opened it and after looking at the money within she decided against leaving any of it in the house. You never knew; anybody could break in. Meggie Proctor from down below had stopped her last week and told her there had been a robbery only three doors down; they had got over the roof and through the attic window.

She now went to Lizzie, who was sitting on the cracket, and, bending her knees, she brought her face level with her sister's and slowly she said, "I'm going to the market, Lizzie, for the groceries. You'll be a good girl?"

Lizzie's hand came out and touched her, and from her shapeless mouth came a sound that only Katie could interpret as "Yes, Katie".

Although there was no longer any necessity to tie Lizzie up she always did this, just in case the old urge should revive itself and set her on the move; not that she would get far, but once out on the landing she might fall down the stairs. And so taking a piece of rope she put it round her waist, then tied it firmly to the table leg.

When she reached the foot of the second flight of stairs she saw the tenants from the bottom rooms standing on the step talking. One was Meggie Proctor, whom Katie always addressed as Miss Proctor, the other was a Mrs. Wilson. Katie had never seen Mr. Wilson, nor had anyone else. Both women were in their early thirties and looked dirty and unkempt, but they were warmheartedly pleasant to Katie. "You're out shoppin'?" said Meggie Proctor.

"Yes, Miss Proctor. Goin' to the market."

"Aw, lass, I wish you wouldn't call me Miss Proctor." Meggie's mouth stretched wide and she laughed. "You're the only one that does; it makes me feel funny. . . . She's always called me Miss Proctor since she come here." Meggie addressed her neighbour, and Jinny Wilson, laughing too, said, "Aye, weel, she was brought up proper; you get that way o' talkin' when you're in good service. Me mother was in good service for years."

"By, she looks grand, doesn't she?" Meggie stood back and surveyed Katie. "I wish I could go out shoppin' in clothes like them. You're lucky to have a friend like that Mrs. Noble."

"Yes, yes, I am," Katie squeezed between them. You could keep nothing hidden living in a house like this, living in a district like this; everybody knew everything about you. They all knew, for instance, that she had been married to a keeker, and her father had murdered him and got himself hanged for it, that it had turned her mother's brain, and also that her sister was barmy.

Perhaps it was this knowledge, together with Katie's own reserved manner, that set her apart from her neighbours. Then there was her looks, those big, misty, sad-looking eyes. Meggie had once said to her, "If I had your peepers they wouldn't look sad on me, an' I'd be livin' in clover."

She knew the two women were watching her as she went down the street. And not only them; there were others at their doors. There was a high wind blowing and she had to hold on to her bonnet as she turned into Thames Street and cut up by Comical Corner, and she paused for a moment by the steps leading down to the river. There was a sculler boat tied to a ring in the wall and some small children were jumping from the bottom slime-covered step on to one of its two plank seats. She wondered that they didn't slip and drown themselves. But then they were used to the water; they lived as close to it as the rats that infested the houses round about. She went on past the Cut, or the Mill Dam as it was now known, then on down the hill into the Market Place. The Market Place was a large open square, grassy in parts, with the Town Hall, supported on its arched columns, dominating it. It wasn't full market day and there weren't many people about—some women sitting by their high skips of taties, some pedlars with tapes and ribbons and such, and at the far side a number of stalls. It was towards these she made her way.

She knew exactly what she was going to buy: a quarter-stone of potatoes, some pot stuff to make broth, a scrag end of mutton, a quarter-stone of oatmeal, a half-stone of flour and some yeast, some pigs' fat, two ounces of tea, some bacon ends, half a pound of black treacle if it was still tuppence, and a quarter-stone of salt, also at tuppence if they wouldn't split it and let her have a pennorth. She could get everything but the flour and yeast in the market, and these she would collect from Tennants on her way home.

To save her arms she got the lightest things first. The tea was the cheapest brand and the two ounces cost her sixpence, but the stall hawker was yelling its merits. She opened her purse and handed him a shilling, and when he had given her the tea and a sixpence change she placed it in her purse and put it back in the bass bag. She next went to the bacon stall, and, her searching eyes coming to rest on some scraps, she pointed to them and asked for a pound.

"That lot throopence hapenny, lass," the man said.

"Thank you." She nodded and put her hand into the bag for her purse. Then, her two hands tearing the bag open, she let out a yell that made the stallholder jump and those nearby turn and gape at her.

"Me purse! Me purse! It's gone. Oh, my God, it's gone!" She looked wildly around her, her arm outstretched, the bass bag dangling from her hand. "It's all I've got, every penny," she appealed to two women and a man who were standing staring at her.

"You should have kept it in your hand." The stallholder came round to her. "A daft place to leave a purse, in your bag."

"It's all I've got." She stared at him, her eyes stretched wide; her voice was still high but it held a choking sound now. She brought her clenched fist to her mouth, and one of the men said, "How much was in it, lass?"

"Fifteen shillings. No, fourteen and six. I've just bought the tea." She held out the small package in her hand.

"Let's see if you've dropped it on the way. Walk back to the tea stall," said one of them.

Like somebody drunk, and accompanied by the two women and the man, Katie walked back to the tea stall, searching the litter-strewn grass as they went. But there was no sign of the black purse. Back at the bacon stall once more, Katie looked at the man. Her bacon pieces were all wrapped and lying on a board, and he looked at them and said, "I'm sorry, lass, but you should've been on the look-out for your money; it's happenin' every day. Transport the buggers, that's what I say, not just send them along the line. Transport them when they're copped . . . Here!" He pushed the package of scraps towards her, and she took it and muttered, "Ta. Thank you."

The two women and the man moved away muttering; people were going about their business, the little incident was over; there were many such in a day. The stallholder said, "You go and tell the police, hinny. They might catch him some time later and he might have yours on him. On the other hand, it could be a woman who snipped it. Some of the bitches' fingers work like greased lightnin'."

Like someone in a deep trance Katie slowly moved away. She knew there was a policeman standing outside the Town Hall but she didn't go towards him; she was afraid of policemen, the polis always meant trouble. She was still walking slowly when she reached the house.

Meggie opened her door as she was passing and said, "I brought your sheets in, Katie; it was startin' to drizzle." Then, bending forward, she said, "You taken bad?"

Katie shook her head. "Me purse was stolen in the market."

"God Almighty! Much in it?"

"All I had, and the rent."

"Christ! The buggers want crucifyin'. Why don't they go

up Westhoe and do their pickin' there? It's like the other night. One of my . . ." She blinked. "A friend of mine, he was fleeced, pulled up an alley near the Anchor and every ha'penny cleared off him; an' got a bashin' in the bargain. Oh, if I could only lay me hands on the sods at it. . . . But I'm sorry, lass. . . . You stranded?"

Katie moved her head slowly downwards, then said, "I'll have to go out and get some work. You won't mind if she cries?" She jerked her head upwards, and Meggie said, "Not me. She would scream the hoose doon for all I care, and the same goes for Jinny. But Ma Robson up above she'll open her mouth. But don't you worry, lass." She pushed gently. "If she opens it too far I'll stick me foot in it for you." Katie made no reply to this, but turning blindly away she went up the stairs.

Lizzie's eyes were waiting for her as she opened the door but on this occasion she took no notice of her. Letting the bass bag fall to the floor, she pulled off her bonnet and, sitting down at the table, dropped her head on to her arms and gave way to a paroxysm of weeping.

*　　*　　*

Three days later Katie had reached the end of her tether and was in a state of panic. Between them Meggie Proctor and Jinny Wilson had lent her half a crown with which to meet the rent, and yesterday Meggie Proctor had lent her another shilling, out of which she had got a quarter-stone of flour and yeast, and a bucket of coal to bake the bread. But now the fire was dead and they had just eaten the last of the bread—at least Lizzie had. Lizzie's appetite was insatiable, and when she was hungry she cried. She was crying now. All she herself had had to eat over the past three days was a third of the bacon scraps and a small amount of bread and weak tea. She looked at Lizzie looking at her, the tears lying in puddles on her puffed cheeks. Joe was right; she should have let her go to the guardians. At least she would have been fed, and warm. But if she were to go now to the guardians and ask for them both to be taken in, even temporarily, they would come and take the furniture, and then there'd be no home any more, for Joe or any of them.

If only Joe would come. But it wasn't likely he'd be back; a day each way and two or three days there, was what he said, and this was only the fourth day. If only Mrs. Robson hadn't complained about Lizzie's crying and threatened to bring the polis she could have got a job. Lizzie would just have had to put up with being left all day; there were worse things that could happen to her that she didn't know about. She wondered if she knew what was happening to her now, except that she was hungry. Joe was likely right in all he said.

She could have got set on in four different places today, but not part-time. Two of the places were cookhouses, and each wanted her there at six in the morning till six at night. She would have got six shillings a week and her food. Either would have been splendid if only she could have taken it. But she was terrified at coming back home and finding that Mrs. Robson had carried out her threat and brought the authorities in. The next step from this would be they'd contact the landlord, and then she and Lizzie would find themselves in the street, with the furniture around them. She had seen so many people in the street sitting helplessly amid their furniture that she had a horror of it happening to them.

There came a tap at the door and when she opened it there stood Meggie Proctor. She was dressed ready for outdoors; she looked different to what she did in the mornings. She had on a bright skirt and blouse, and a blue woollen shawl over her head. She said to Katie, "I don't know if it'd be up your street, but the Anchor's wantin' help in the evenin'. I was just talkin' to a . . . a friend of mine, and he said the barmaid's gone down with the fever and Jimmy Wild is looking for help. He'll set you on in the evenin' 'cos that's when they're busiest. That . . . that's if you fancy it."

"It doesn't matter what I fancy, Meggie," said Katie frankly. "I'll take anything. I'm at me wits' end."

"I wish I could help you more, lass."

"You've done all you can and I'm grateful. Believe me, I don't know where I'd have been if it hadn't been for you and Mrs. Wilson."

Now Meggie leaned forward and, peering closely into Katie's face and her voice very low, she said, "I'm surprised you haven't got a friend."

"A friend?" Katie narrowed her eyes as she repeated the word.

"Aye." Meggie pushed her now in the breast with her forefinger. "With your looks it would be as easy as slippin' off the docks. Lass, I'd never have an empty belly if I had your face."

Katie felt her stomach pulling itself tight, as if away from physical contact, but she showed no offence and said simply, "I couldn't, Meggie."

"Aw well, you know your own know best, lass, but hunger's a long whip. Anyway, you go along to Bullard. He'll likely snap you up, 'cos you'll thicken his custom if anything will. I must be off now. Ta-ra."

"Ta-ra, Meggie. And thanks."

Katie stood with her back to the closed door. The Anchor was only a few streets away. It was a notorious public-house, notorious for many things. One of its activities had gained it the name of the "whore market".

If only Joe was here. But he wasn't here, and there wasn't a bite or sup in the house, and no warmth, and she was down to her last half-candle. She came from the door as if released by a spring, pulled Lizzie to her feet, guided her into the room and got her into bed, and again she tied her by the waist, this time attaching the end of the rope to the leg of the bed. Then, going back into the kitchen, she took the iron shelf out of the oven—it still retained some heat—and taking it into the bedroom she pushed it under the clothes beneath Lizzie's feet, hoping that the warmth would send her to sleep and ease her crying. She could hardly see her face in the dim light of the room, but, bending close to her, she said, "I won't be long, Lizzie. Be a good girl." For a minute longer she stood and stroked the lank hair back from the bulging brow; then, going into the kitchen, she rapidly donned her outdoor things and went out of the house.

She hated to be out on the streets after dark. Although some streets were lit by the new gas lamps there were alleys and dark corners where things were known to happen.

The noise from the Anchor greeted her long before she reached it, and she paused outside the double doors before pushing one open and half stepping inside. And then she could go no further. Through the light of the oil lamps she saw a seething mass of people, mostly men, and mostly sailors. Two faces turned towards her with lifting eyebrows and drooling lips, and when two pair of arms came out to her she sprang back, pulling the door with her, and, dashing to the end of the building, she hid round the corner. Here she stood panting. She couldn't go in there. . . . Yet, perhaps her duties might keep her behind the counter. She could ask him. She'd have to ask him.

She moved along the wall to where there was a side door, and from behind this, too, there issued the sound of men's laughter. This was still the bar, likely the best end. She must find a door to the house. But there was no light farther on. She was about to grope her way along the wall beyond the door when it opened and a huge figure stepped into the yard. The next moment a hand was placed on her shoulder and she was swung round, and in the light from the doorway she looked up into an enormous bearded face. The eyes looking out of it were moving over her, the expression in them like that of the two men in the bar. She watched the red lips in the fair beard part, and a deep voice which she knew immediately was not English, said, "Ah-haa!"

She stammered, "Please . . . I . . . I want to see the barman. I'm after a job. . . . Please." She tried to pull herself away from the man, but his hold on her tightened and, bringing his face down to hers, he said in precise clipped English, "A job is it? Oh, min skjoun, I could give you a job. Ah yes." His head went back and he laughed.

"Look, give over, you. Let me go."

Still peering at her, he said, "Stop trembling. You frightened? Why do you come here if you're frightened?"

"Please, I . . . I just want to go. I want to go home."

"You want to go home?" He was laughing at her again, his face seeming to expand to twice its size. "All right, min skjoun, we will go home. Ah yes, how pleased I'll be to go home with you."

"No, no!"

"Aha! Yes. Yes."

At this moment the door was pulled wide open and another man appeared. He, too, was a sailor and spoke in a foreign tongue, and the bearded man answered in the same tongue, and when the second man emerged into the yard Katie found herself pulled from the wall and pushed forward. And now the bearded man called over his shoulder to the other man, who shouted back apparently in reply. Then they were in the street.

"Which way?" He still had his arm about her, gripping her firmly and forcing her to walk, but when they reached the flare lights outside the pie and pea shop he stopped and peered at her again, saying now, "Why do you tremble all the time? Why go to the Anchor if you tremble?"

"I . . . I went for work; they . . . I heard they wanted a barmaid."

Again his head went back and the street rang with his laughter, of which the passers-by took no notice. A drunken Swede laughing with a woman in the streets at night was nothing new. "You a barmaid in the Anchor! Ah!" He grabbed her face in his big hand and pressed her jaws in as he said, "You'd be eaten alive. Do you want to be eaten alive? . . . No, no." He answered himself. "You're frightened of being eaten alive. Why did you want to be barmaid in the Anchor? There are other works you could do."

"My . . . my sister is sick. I've got to look after her; I can't go out durin' the day."

"No one else to look after your sister? No parents?"

She shook her head.

"You married?"

Again she shook her head.

"You live by yourself?"

"With . . . with my brother."

"Why does your brother not work for you then?"

"He's on strike. He's away lookin' for work. . . ."

Before she had closed her mouth on her words she knew she had made a mistake, and he lost not a minute in making use of it. With a nod of his head he said, "So. So he's away. Well, we go home then?"

"No!" Her voice was harsh now. "No, no, I tell you. No!"

He did not seem to take any heed of her protest but went on, "What do you want money so badly for you go to the Anchor?"

When she didn't answer he brought his face down close to hers and said on a surprised note, "You sulten . . . hungry?"

She closed her eyes for a moment but still didn't speak; and when she opened them she did not look into his face but at the top brass button of his uniform, and some section of her mind registered the fact that he was a captain. This seemed to explain the way he talked, for although a foreigner he used his words like the gentry did.

"My God! That's right, isn't it? You're hungry. Come, come." He now took her by the hand as if she was a child and pulled her through the doorway of the pie and pea shop, and there, in a voice that seemed to shake the ramshackle place, he cried, "Pies! Half a dozen. Hot. No, one dozen; I could eat half a dozen myself. And peas, two pints."

"Where's your can?" said the man.

"Can?"

"Aye, sir, yer can't carry peas in a bit paper."

"That one there, I'll buy it."

"It'll cost you fowerpence, sir."

"Fourpence it is. And fill it to the brim."

The man beside the counter now wrapped up the pork pies in a piece of newspaper, and when he pushed the parcel across the counter the captain, picking it up, thrust it into Katie's arms.

As she held it against her breast she could feel the heat of the pies through the paper and she had a desire to grab one out and thrust it into her mouth. She also had the desire to take to her heels and fly; and she saw her chance as he was paying the man. Once outside the door she could be away up one of the dark alleys and safe, and the pies with her.

She was backing to the door when he turned round, and like someone chastising a child about to do a mischief he turned his chin to the side, while his eyes remained on her and gave that telling exclamation of "Ah-haa!" Then, thrusting his hand back towards the counter and the man, he received his change and without looking at it thrust it in his pocket. Then his hand groped towards the can; he picked it up and came towards her, and after looking at her hard for a second said, from deep in his throat, "We go home now, eh?"

He held her with one hand and carried the can of peas with the other, and like this they went through the warren of dimly lit streets and past the black alleyways until they reached the end of Crane Street, and here, pulling him to a halt and her voice full of pleading, she said, "Please, please don't come any farther."

"You don't want me to come to your home?"

"No."

"You're lying. You want me to come."

"I don't, I don't, I tell you." She was hissing at him now. "I just want you to leave me alone. Don't you understand? Just leave me alone. You can have the pies . . . here." She thrust them at him. But he ignored her action and said, "I don't believe you. But, look, we're on the waterfront and near the Middle Gates. There'll be one of your polis men there.

Shout. Go on, shout, and they'll come and order me off. . . . Go on."

She stood breathing deeply and peering at him. She had thought of that herself. She had thought, if I shout the polis'll come. But as afraid as she was of this great bearded man, she was more afraid of the polis. It was when she thought of being afraid of him that she realized she was only afraid of him because of what they would say in the house, her taking a man up there, and what Joe would say if he found out.

She said lamely, "We . . . we could walk and eat these as we went." She patted the bundle of pies.

"But I don't want to walk, I want to go to your home. I want to know where you live. . . . Besides, it would be very uncomfortable eating peas while we walked." He gave a small laugh now. "Come," he said. "This is your street?"

When she didn't answer he took her arm again, and like someone under escort she walked up the street with her head bowed.

There were people about, but they took no notice of her or her companion. Again, what was unusual about a sea captain walking this street with a woman?

Before she opened the door softly she paused and was about to say to him, "Be quiet," but she felt that if she did he would let out his big laugh and raise the house.

As soon as they entered the hall Lizzie's wailing came to her, and she hurried forward up the dark stairs; and when he stumbled after her she put her hand out to steady him, and he gripped it and held it until they came to the top landing. And there she whispered, "Stand still; you . . . you might knock the bucket over." As she groped for her key in her coat pocket he said, "What is that noise?" She didn't answer but unlocked the door, and when she opened it it came to her that here was another chance of escape, she could bolt the door in his face. Yes, and have him bellow the house down. From the little she knew of him she could well imagine him doing just that.

She groped her way towards the table, put the pies on it, then moved cautiously towards the mantelpiece and instinctively her hand found the candlestick. There was no glimmer left in the fire to light the candle, so, going back to the landing, she whispered, "I haven't a light."

Without a word he handed her a bulky box, and taking a match from it she struck it on the rough underside of the candlestick; then she lit the candle, shielding its flame for a moment with her hand. Now, turning abruptly, she walked back into the room.

He was standing in the centre of the room near the table when, looking towards the door from where the noise came, he said, "Your sister, is she a baby?"

"No. You . . . you can sit down; I'll . . , I'll have to see to her for a moment."

"You do. Do that; the night's young." He turned from her and looked slowly around the room.

"I'll have to take the candle," she said.

He was looking at her again. "That's the only candle you have?"

"Yes."

"Go ahead."

She picked up the candle. Then, pointing towards the pies that had now spread themselves out of the paper, she said, "I'll . . . I'll take her one of these." Under his penetrating gaze she picked up a pie and went into the bedroom.

"There, there," she said to Lizzie. "Don't cry. Aw, don't cry any more. Eat this, it's a pie."

Lizzie's face moved into a smile; she opened her mouth and in two bites the pie had disappeared, and her eyes, looking into Katie's, said she wanted more.

"Later. You'll have another later."

As she straightened up from over the bed she was aware that the door had opened, and half turning her head she saw him standing looking at them. She wanted to place herself in front of Lizzie to shield her from his sight, but it was too late. Lizzie didn't see him, or if she did she took no notice, and Katie, pushing the pillows into position behind her back and putting the patched quilt over the enormous bulging stomach, said, "There now. Be a good girl. I'll be back in a moment." She walked past the man and into the room, and it was a full minute before he came and joined her.

"Is she a mongol?"

"A what?"

"A mongol?"

Katie did not know what he meant by a mongol. She said, "She was born like that; she's always been like a child."

"And you, you look after her?" He was standing straight now, his face unsmiling. "Since when?"

"Since my mother died. And before that. The past few

172

years or so." She looked down at the pies now, and, his gaze following hers, he said breezily, "Well, let us eat."

She brought two plates and some cutlery from the cupboard, and she had just started to eat when he said, "Bread. I like bread with peas."

She had her mouth full of pie and she had to swallow three times before she could say, "There's no bread." There was a rough defiant note in her voice, and her expression was bitter as she stared at him through the candlelight and added, "I wouldn't have gone to the Anchor for the job if . . . if I'd had bread to spare."

He put down the spoon that was hovering over his plate, and leant against the chair rails. Pushing his elbows well back until his hands were resting on his stomach, he slowly drew in his bearded chin tight against the high collar of his jacket, and like this he surveyed her from across the table. He was looking into a face the like he had never seen before in any port, and he was not even seeing her clearly, for the illumination from the tallow candle was limited. Her eyes were the largest, the strangest, most arresting he had ever beheld. He had come upon something here he couldn't as yet understand. Why wasn't there any man about the place . . . about her? What were they up to in this land of frozen faces, faces which didn't know how to laugh; this land of mean, calculating minds? He didn't like the English. He had never liked the English. All brothers under the skin, so the saying went; but how did you know you were an Englishman's brother? You could never get under the Englishman's skin. But this woman, this woman without a man, this woman with a face of . . . what? Not an angel. No. No. What kind of a face was it? A strange face, a beautiful face. Yes, yes, but something more. A good face. Yes, a good face. A lonely lost face. Why hadn't it brought a man to her? There must be a man; somewhere there must be a man who owned her. It was against all nature that, looking as she did, she should be alone. He slowly brought himself from the back of the chair, and leaning forward, his elbows one each side of his plate, he asked quietly, "You have a man? The truth now. You have a man?"

She raised her eyes from the plate and said with a calmness that puzzled him, "I have no man. Nor do I want one."

"No!" There was that jocular, cynical tone in this voice again, but hers was hard as she replied briefly, "No."

Not moving his position, he said, "Pity, great pity, you feel like that, because . . . I have a surprise for you . . . you've got one." He now dug his thumb into the middle of his waistcoat. "I am your MAN."

She had been chewing on a mouthful of peas and one stuck in her throat and brought on a spasm of coughing. She rose from the table and stood aside, her head bent, one hand pressing against her chest. She had her back to him, and when she heard his chair scraping on the wooden floor she turned swiftly, still coughing, and the next minute she found herself pressed against him. One big hand on her buttocks, the other under her armpit, he arched her stiff body into his. Her eyes staring into the face within an inch of hers, at the full red mouth through the mass of fair hair, she watched the lips move and say again, "I'm your man . . . yes?"

She was trembling from head to foot, more than she had done when he first grabbed her. There was no pore in her body that wasn't open, pouring sweat. Yet it wasn't with fear —at least not the kind of fear she had previously experienced; the fear that Bernard Rosier had brought into her body; the cold, cold fear that Mark Bunting had filled every hour of her waking days with, and most of her nights. Nor was the fear that was possessing her now created by this great blond man, this utter stranger. The fear was of herself, her feelings, of the very fact that she wasn't afraid of him.

When he kissed her her whole face seemed lost in a tangle of hair. The kiss lasted a long time, and the strange fear in her mounted again. After the first moment of it she no longer resisted it; she did not return it, but she did not resist it. When he withdrew his face from hers he did not look at her, but his eyes flashed around the room and alighted on the raised pallet in the dim corner. Still with his arms about her, he now drew her towards it, circling the dark bulk of a chair in the progress. When they were standing near the bed her body became stiff again and unyielding. He felt the change in her immediately and, one hand going swiftly around the back of her knees, he lifted her upwards as if she was a child and the next minute she was lying on her back on the bed and he was beside her, and when his arms went about her the trembling of her body increased. He became still against her for a moment, silent and still, and then he said, "Don't tremble; I won't hurt you."

And he didn't.

*   *   *

She was actually laughing. She couldn't remember the last time she had laughed like this. As a child she had felt full of joy and laughter, but she imagined that that was a natural part of childhood; all children could laugh and feel joy until life got at them. But now, with her arms laden with packages of food, more food than she had ever seen in her life at one time, except up at the House, she was walking beside the burly captain, who had a sack of coal perched on his shoulder which he supported with one hand, while under the other arm he carried a bundle of candles, and she was laughing.

Just over an hour ago she had wanted to go to sleep, drop into a soft beautiful sleep, but he had pulled her to her feet and said one word, "Food." And she had repeated dazedly, "Food." And then shaking her by the shoulder, he had laughed and cried, "Wake up, wake up, min elskling. Yes, food and coal; I'm going to warm you inside and out." He had gripped her face in his hands, pressing her mouth outwards. She had explained that it was too late, at least for coal; the shops were open till ten, some after, but not the coal depots.

But he had opened the coal depot. Knocking on the man's door, he had demanded him to fill the sack with coal. And now here she was, like an excited child, hurrying by his side. What had come over her? For a moment she thought of Joe, then dismissed him. Joe wouldn't be back the night. Something had happened to her, something strange and beautiful, and she wanted to hang on to it. She would have to face Joe, likely tell Joe, but that was tomorrow; there was still tonight. . . .

The fire was blazing, the cupboard was full, she had eaten the best meal she'd had for many a long day. She'd had a piece of steak half an inch thick, a lump of black pudding and two fried eggs. Between them they had finished a crusty loaf and half a pound of butter, and now they were sitting on her bed which he had pulled right up to the fire, drinking cups of steaming tea, with whisky in his. Lizzie was asleep on a full stomach; the grate was full of burning coal; and she felt at rest within herself as she had never done in her life before.

She was pressed close to him, held there by his arm, and

175

every time she turned her face towards him his eyes were waiting for her. She liked his eyes. She could see them clearly now in the light of the six candles he had lit all at once. She had wanted to stop him lighting more than two, but she didn't; this was a night apart, a strange night, a night that would never happen to her again. She knew she was doing what the bad women did, and she knew that her mother and father, and her granda, would be turning in their graves, but she didn't feel any great sense of sin because God and sin and chapel-going had fled her life the day they put a rope around her father's neck.

Her head now resting against his shoulder, she asked softly, "What do they call your ship?"

"The Orn. It means eagle in your language."

"Is it a big ship?"

"So—so, big enough to carry timber . . . and odds and ends." He raised his eyebrows.

"Do you come into the dock often?"

A deep rumbling chuckle went through his body and into hers, and, putting his head down to try and see into her face, he said, "Do you want me to come into the dock often?"

"No, no." She tried to pull away from him now, but he held her tight and she muttered, "I didn't mean I . . ."

"There. There. It's all right. I understand you to mean whatever you didn't mean." He chuckled quietly as he pressed her hard against him, then said, "Half the year we come to the Tyne, from April to October. Some of our men come over on the last ship and stay here all winter. They get ships plying along the coast." He laughed heartily as if at a joke; then, stroking his beard with his hand, he asked, "How old are you?"

"Nearly twenty-one," she said softly. Then, glancing up at him, she said, "And you, how old are you?"

"Ah!" He closed his eyes and moved his big head from side to side. "Too old. Too old."

"Thirty?" She knew she was being kind to him.

"Huh!" His head jerked backwards. "You think I look thirty? That is good. Ah, good." After a space of time, during which he held her face turned upwards to him and stared into her eyes, he said, "I am thirty-seven years old. But to-night I am twenty-seven. No, twenty-three, and life is just beginning." There followed another silence before he said, "We have been together three hours—no, three hours and a half, and I don't know how they call you."

"Katie Mulholland." She never called herself by her married name.

"Kaa-tee Mulholland. It is a full mouth of a name. Kaa-tee Mulholland."

"And your name?"

"Andree Fraenkel."

"Ann-dree. It's like Andrew in English." She laughed and said, "I'll call you Andy."

"Andy!" He put his head on one side. "That is like what my . . ." He broke off, swung her around until she was resting with her back against his chest, then said, "Andy it is." After this he remained quiet for a time, his arms tight about her, his bearded chin resting on the top of her head.

In the strange warm silence, as she lay staring into the fire like someone entranced, there were forced into her mind thoughts of tomorrow, of who might see him leave; Meggie Proctor, Jinny Wilson, or Mrs. Robson. She was afraid of Mrs. Robson seeing him go. Perhaps he would go early before anybody was up; he'd have to get back to his ship. She brought the niggling worry to the surface by asking, "When do you sail?"

"Sail?" He seemed to drag his thoughts from some distant place. "Ah, not for some three days. She is having repairs and her bottom is needing a scrape. Three whole days, Kaatee."

She hadn't time now to feel fright or apprehension at the thought of him being around the place for three days, because his hands were loosening the buttons of her bodice and she did not stay them.

It was when her breast was exposed above the line of her shift that his eyes came to rest on the zig-zag red weal standing out from the warm cream flesh. His eyes now asked her a question, but she did not speak. Then slowly he moved his finger from the end of the weal and followed its course, his hand mounting to her shoulder. Now, half hitching himself up, he swivelled her round towards the candlelight. She felt his hands undoing the hook of her skirt; then, with a quick jerking movement, her shift was tugged up from within the bands of her petticoat and thrust forward over her head. Following this, there was silence again.

177

Slowly now she turned towards him and she saw the red gap of his mouth open and his tongue waver in it before he asked in an undertone, "Who did this?"

"Oh." She drooped her head and swung it back and forward before saying, "Oh, it's a long story."

"Who did it?" His voice was louder now and roughly his hand jerked her chin up.

"My . . . my husband."

"Your husband?"

She moved her head once, then said, "My father killed him for it. . . . No, no." Again her head was shaking. "He didn't, it was the others; but he beat him and he was found dead later and they hanged him, my father."

He was staring at her, his eyes wide, his mouth open, his cheeks pushed upwards with incredulity. He began to speak rapidly now, in his own language, but when he finished it was in her own tongue and he said, "Almighty God, you have been flayed."

Turning her slowly round again, he once more examined the network of red ridges, some pronounced, some faint, that covered her back. When he turned her to face him he said simply, "Tell me. From the beginning. Tell me." Then he pulled up the coverlet and put it gently round her shoulders and pressed her towards him again.

So, sitting cradled in the arms of this strange man, a man whom a few hours ago she hadn't known was alive but whom she felt she knew better than anyone in her life before, even her parents, her grandfather, or Joe, she talked, and as she did so she unwound herself back to the time before the night of the ball.

She told him everything, right from the beginning; from the day she had started as scullery-maid to the Rosiers right up to the day when they hanged her father. And she finished with meeting the Misses Chapman and giving them her child. The only thing she didn't tell him was the name of the man who had given her the child.

And as he listened Andree Fraenkel realized, with disquieting certainty, that he had reached a cross-road in his life. He had felt the pull of her when he had grabbed at her and looked into her face for the first time. But with the telling of her story he knew that a woman had been washed up to him the like he had dreamed of from when he was a boy. For good or bad he was ensnared—possibly for bad, for to keep and hold her would mean the eventual breaking up of his home in his own country, if not the end of his career; at least with the big ships.

3

For two and a half days Katie lived between a joy that she likened to heaven on earth and an apprehensive feeling that she likened to all hell being let loose as she waited Joe's return. For three nights the captain had stayed with her, and most of the two days, leaving her only to look over his ship. But today he was sailing. He had to be aboard before eleven o'clock tonight and she was praying earnestly within herself that he'd be gone before Joe got back.

It was to happen that he and Joe were to meet; but before he met Joe he was to meet Miss Theresa.

He was sitting in the armchair; his big feet, encased in a pair of bright red soft leather slippers, were sticking upwards on the fender. He had his two hands joined behind his head, which swivelled slowly back and forwards as his eyes followed Katie about the room.

"Kaa-tee."

"Yes, Andy?"

"You happy?"

For answer she came to his side and stood looking down at him; she did not touch him, nor he her, but she said, "If I'm not it doesn't matter, because I want to remain in this state all me life."

"It's not three days, do you realize that, not three days since we met?"

"Well, as I told you, I think I knew within the first three minutes. That's why I couldn't stop shaking."

His fingers now snapped apart, his head and body came up like a released spring and he was on his feet with his arms about her, holding her close. His face above hers, he stared down at her as he asked, "What are you going to do with yourself all the time?"

"Oh, the usual. Lookin' after the house, and Joe and Liz-

179

zie. But it won't be the same. . . ." She smiled softly at him. "Nothing in me life will ever be the same again."

"It'll be a full two weeks before I'm back." He didn't say, "You won't have anybody else in the meantime?" He would not insult her; he hadn't linked himself with any waterside trollop.

"I'll be here," she said softly. "I'll always be here, and waitin'. . . . What time are you leaving? I mean . . . I mean from here."

"I should be aboard by five to see things under way; but if I can slip ashore for a while later, I'll be back."

Their lips were pressed close when there came the sound of footsteps on the wooden stairs, and Katie, pulling herself away from his arms, turned and stared towards the door. Then she took in a deep breath of relief when there came a tap on it. After glancing at him she went and opened the door, but slightly, and there stood Miss Theresa.

"Good afternoon, Katie."

"Oh! Good afternoon, Miss Theresa."

When she didn't stand aside and allow her visitor to enter the room, Miss Theresa looked at her for a moment in silence, then said, "I've brought you some books . . . and this." She held out a parcel towards Katie, and as she did so her eyes lifted from her face, over her shoulder, and to a great bearded man standing with his back to the fireplace. Her eyes darting back to Katie, she looked at her with her mouth slightly agape. Then, when Katie, her head erect but her eyes cast downwards now, moved aside, she went slowly into the room and stood near the table.

"This . . . this is a friend of mine, Miss Theresa, Captain Fraenkel." Katie pronounced it Frenkell. Then, looking at Andree, she said softly, "This is Mrs. Noble."

Andree, his hands now hanging by his sides, bowed slightly from the shoulders. It was a courtly gesture and Theresa recognized it as such; she recognized it as the action of a gentleman. After staring into the big vivid blue eyes for a moment her own dropped sharply away, but not before they had traversed his broad chest, only partly covered by a white shirt, his belted trousers and slippered feet. The awful truth deprived her of speech.

From shaking fingers Theresa dropped the books on to the table, then the parcel, and turning her back slowly on the man she confronted Katie, her eyes wide and accusing.

Through her thin lips she now said, "I would like a word with you in private, Katie." And on this she went towards the door, and Katie, after casting a glance at Andree, a helpless one this time, followed her on to the landing and to the head of the stairs, where Theresa had taken her stand.

"Katie! What . . . what have you done?" Theresa's words were accusing, bitter, and they came through her clenched teeth. She was trembling as if consumed with rage.

"He's a friend, Miss Theresa." Katie's chin was up.

"A friend? How long has he been a friend? Answer me."

Katie blinked her eyes, then brought her head forward as if to see Miss Theresa better, and in a voice that was almost calm and held a touch of dignity she said, "I'm a woman, Miss Theresa, I'm no longer a child; and I'm me own mistress, I can do what I like."

"And with whom you like, I suppose."

Again Katie screwed up her face as she looked at the woman opposite. She had been prepared for Miss Theresa being shocked, but she couldn't understand her anger. It was like, like . . . She couldn't find words to translate Miss Theresa's attitude so that she could understand it.

"Joe. What has he to say about this?"

"It's not Joe's business, it's mine, Miss Theresa. I . . . I don't want to seem ungrateful. I've always been grateful because you've been so kind to me, but . . . but what I do with me life is, as I said, my business." Now she bent towards Theresa again and, her voice dropping to a soft whisper, she said, "And, I'm happy. I'm happier than I've been in me life afore. He's a good man."

"A good man!" Miss Theresa's lips moved away from her teeth as if she had tasted something vile. "A sailor from the docks—because that's what he is, isn't he? And a foreigner, and twice your age, I would say." Now, her voice and face matching each other in viciousness, she cried, "Don't you know that they have women in every port they touch, filthy women, diseased women?"

Following this, they stared at each other in the gloom; then Theresa, her voice filled with pleading, her manner changing utterly, beseeched, "Send him away, Katie. Go on in now and send him away. Please, please. I . . . I can't bear to think of you with him. I've . . . I've always been kind to you—you said yourself I have—well, do this for me. Go on and send him away . . . now."

181

Katie moved back from Theresa. The funny feeling that she'd had a number of times when Miss Theresa had come near her was emphasised in her now, and she said to her, "No, I won't, not now or at any time. And although I thank you for your kindness in the past, I'd . . . I'd thank you now to leave me alone."

To her amazement Katie now saw Miss Theresa's face crumpling and the tears stream from her eyes. The next minute she was watching her running down the stairs. Slowly she turned towards the door, and when she opened it there was Andree standing not a foot away. As she looked at him he nodded at her and said, "Come, come." He put his arm gently round her shoulders and led her towards the fire where, seating her in the chair, he dropped down on his hunkers before her and, taking her hand in his, said, "I've done you a service; you're well rid of that one."

"But she's been so kind to me."

"Kind? Huh! Unnatural women are always kind to women."

"Unnatural women?"

"Yes, yes, she's no woman, she's a man under the skin. I recognized it, even before she looked at you. I have a cousin who's the same. It is a trick of nature."

"Miss Theresa? No!" Katie shuddered, and he drew her hands to his breast, saying, "Not that I blame her for loving you; no one could help loving you, and it will remain a mystery to me to the end of my days that I found you alone."

"Aw, Andy." She leant her face forward and rubbed her cheek against his beard, and he fondled her and kissed her and spoke long sentences to her in his own tongue, but when he wanted to make love to her she protested softly, saying, "No, no, our Joe might come in. He might come in; you never know."

"Do you think he will come today?"

"I don't know. He might."

"I hope he does; I would like to meet him."

She closed her eyes and said to herself, God forbid. . . .

They were sitting having a meal when Joe made his appearance. Andree was laughing loudly about something she had said. In the last few days it seemed she had recaptured her art of telling a tale, and so she didn't hear the footsteps until they reached the landing. By the time the door opened she had screwed round in her chair and was facing him.

In the framework of the door Joe stood, one elbow bent, his fist gripping the end of a small canvas sack that was hanging over his shoulder. He looked dusty and tired, and in this moment his face had a mild, childlike look of bewilderment on it.

Katie sidled up from her seat that was set close to Andree's. He, too, rose with her and stood looking at the short young fellow in the doorway, and he waited for him to speak.

And Joe spoke. With a sudden twist of his wrist he flung the canvas bag to the corner of the room where it hit the wall with a soft plop, and, moving towards them, but looking only at the man and taking in, as Theresa had done, his attire, right down to the red slippers—mostly the red slippers, for they indicated something that shot the words from him—he said, "What in hell's name are you doin' here?"

Katie, pushing herself in between them now and with her face close to Joe's, said, "I can explain, Joe, I can explain. Now look. Don't lose your temper, just listen an' hear me out. This is Captain Fraenkel."

"What's he doin' here?" Joe, his body as stiff as a ramrod, his fists clenched by his side, was glaring up over her head towards the big bearded fellow.

"I'm a friend of your sister's. I am pleased to meet you." Andree took a step to the side.

"Friend be buggered. Now get yourself to hell out of this. She wants no friends among Swedes; she can pick her friends from among English blokes, and not from the riff-raff of the boats, either."

"Joe, listen to me." She clutched at his arm, only to have him pull it away from her grasp. But she went on, "You're mistaken; just listen. Andy, he's a captain, a captain of a big ship. . . ."

"It wouldn't matter to me if he was captain of the *Terror*, he's a foreigner, and no good at that, else he wouldn't have taken you down."

"Joe, Joe, he didn't! It wasn't like that at all. I lost me purse an' . . . an' he helped me."

Joe turned his eyes from her and his gaze dropped to the red slippers again, and he looked at them for a time before he moved across the floor towards her bed, and there he looked at Andree's boots standing at the foot of it, and at his coat lying across it. Swinging round now, he barked, "Get out! Do you hear? Get out!"

"What if I don't go!" Andree's voice was calm-sounding.

"Then I'll bloody well make you, as big as you are." Joe seemed to spring from where he stood to the centre of the hearth, and in a split second he had picked up the poker and had raised it in his hand, and as Katie let out a scream she saw Andree's arm flash upwards and the next minute the poker dropped like a matchstick to the floor, and so hard was Andree gripping Joe's wrist, and so high was he pulling it upwards, that Joe was almost standing on his toes. Then, as if flicking off a speck of dust, Andree flung him aside. It was a disdainful action. He now went to the bed, and, sitting down on it, pulled on his boots, then stood up and got into his jacket, following which he went to the chiffonier and took his cap from it. This done, he came slowly to Katie where she was standing, her head bowed, her joined hands pressed into her neck, and said grimly, "I'll be back before I sail. Talk to him, tell him how things are . . . I'll be back." He put his hand out and lifted her head up to him, and they looked deeply at each other. Then he turned and went towards the door, but before he reached it Joe shouted at him, "This is my house, I pay the rent, an' if you show your nose on these stairs again I'll put the polis on to you. Get that?"

"Det er det samme for meg," said Andree. "Do that. But I'll be back."

The door had hardly closed on him before Joe, picking up the red slippers, pelted them towards it. Then, with his fists and teeth clenched, he glared at her and she looked at him sadly, pityingly, until, his hands suddenly coming out, gripped the front of her dress. And at this action her whole manner changed. With a swift movement she thrust him from her, crying, "Don't you start that, our Joe! You're not dealing with a child, an' you remember that. There's nobody gonna knock me about again. No, by God!"

From a distance now he glared at her. Then, his voice bitter, he said, "No, you're not a child. I've learned that all right in the last few minutes. It's a whore I've got to deal with now."

"Joe! I'm not, I'm not!" Her protest was loud.

"He slept here, didn't he? Don't deny it. Didn't he?"

"Yes, he did." She reared herself up. "An' he'll sleep here again."

184

"By God, he won't, not while I'm payin' the rent. Now look here. . . ." He came towards her, his forefinger thrust out stiffly. "You can make your choice; it's either him or me. I'm not runnin' any house for whoring. Now you've got it. You give him the go-by, and right now, an' we'll try to live this down; if not, you're on your own."

"Joe, Joe, listen to me." She put out her joined hands towards him. "I'll tell you how it happened; just listen to me, will you? I went down to the market an' I lost me purse. . . ."

Joe interrupted her with a harsh mirthless laugh. "You lost your purse. You who could look after two hundred and forty-seven pounds. You lost your purse."

"I did, Joe, I did. You can ask Meggie Proctor an Jinny Wilson downstairs; they lent me the money atween them to pay the rent. I was at me wits' end. I went to the Anchor to get a job and it was there I met him."

"The Anchor!" His head was back now, and again he made the mirthless sound. "Well, you went to the right place to start, didn't you? You mean to tell me you didn't know what goes on in the Anchor? It's not called the whore market for nothing. You mean to say you didn't know?"

"I only knew I was hungry," she said bitterly, "an' Lizzie was cryin' because she was hungry. I had no heat an' only half a candle. Besides, I'd had nothin' for nearly three days but a drink of tea and a bit bread."

"You could have gone to Miss Theresa."

Now her voice was loud and harsh. "Well, I didn't go to Miss Theresa. An' I wouldn't go to Miss Theresa. An' I'm glad I didn't."

He stared at her in silence for a long long while, and then his voice, quieter now, but his words terrible-sounding to her, said, "You're bad, our Katie. Right at bottom you're bad. There was the bairn, an' then off your own bat you go to Buntin'. Nobody made you go to him, an' because you went me da was hanged and me mother went out of her mind, an' now you're gone on the streets. You're bad . . . you're bad." He repeated the last two words in a dazed fashion as if he had just become aware of the truth of his assertion, and she cried at him, "Joe, don't say that. I'm not, I'm not bad. What happened to me years gone I couldn't help."

Again they were staring at each other in silence. And then he answered her last remark, saying, "Perhaps not, perhaps not all the other things, but this one you can. This is your test piece. Send him packin', an' I'll believe you."

Another silence. And Katie, closing the gap between them, came to a stop quite close to him and said, "No, Joe, I'll never send him out of me life. He's in it for as long as he wants."

"That's it then. Aye, well, that's it then. Now we know where we stand. . . . An' her?" He nodded towards the bedroom. "He's goin' to take on her an' all?"

"I'll see to her."

"By God, an' you'll have to. You'll have to work overtime. Bloody well double time." He now let out a spate of obscenities.

She had never heard him talk like this before in her life. She knew he likely did in the shipyard, but he had never used bad language in the house. Neither of them had been brought up to it, but now he was acting like any man out of the docks. And yet, to his mind, wasn't she acting like any low woman from the docks? Yes, she could see that his attitude was justified, but she could do nothing about it.

Clutching at anything that might act as a stumbling-block, he now said, "This is me furniture in here."

"Your furniture?" She wagged her head, then said quickly, "Aw, no, Joe. No, it isn't yours. Miss Chapman gave it me in exchange for the child. They'd have given me the moon to carry away, but you'll remember I wouldn't take anythin' except the furniture because I knew we would want it when we got this end. . . . No, Joe, the furniture isn't yours, an' don't you try to take it from me, Joe, I'm warnin' you. It's all I've got."

He stepped back from her now, his jaws champing, and, groping at the handle of the door, he said, "Well, you think you've made your choice, but I'll let you sleep on it. I'll come back the morrow and see if you've come to your senses."

When the door banged she stood staring at it, her heart beating fast and aching painfully; then slowly she dropped into a chair and, burying her face in her hands, she cried, "Aw, Joe! Joe." Over and over again she repeated his name, "Joe . . . Joe." What would she do with her days? Without Joe to look after, what would she do? There'd be nobody coming in, nobody to get meals for, except Lizzie and herself. . . . Except when Andy was here. . . . Oh, Andy, Andy.

Her body rocked now back and forward. What had come

over her that within three days she could leave Joe without a home because of this man, this strange man? But she couldn't help herself, she couldn't. Nor did she want to; there was no question of choice between him and Joe. If Andy went out of her life now the pain of his loss would be unbearable. All that she had gone through before would be as nothing compared with it. She would give up or sacrifice anything to keep this strange man.

* * *

She had waited through the long twilight and now the darkness had set in and he hadn't come, and she was sick to the soul. She had gone to the head of the stairs countless times. She had wanted to go down to the street door and wait there, but she couldn't face the look in Meggie Proctor's and Jinny Wilson's eyes. As yet she had not encountered Mrs. Robson from the first floor.

On that first day after Andy had left the house she gone down to the yard to empty the slops and they had been waiting for her, Meggie and Jinny. They had come out of their doors together and they had looked at her and smiled. It would have been less disturbing if they had ignored her, or been scornful of her, but their smiles had said, "We're all lasses together. Fishgate whores or Dock Dollies, we're all lasses together." It was Jinny Wilson who had jerked her head at her and said, "Ye've started off well, lass. Keep it up. No need to borrow any more now." She had wanted to defend herself against the insinuation, but she couldn't. What defence had she?

When she heard the quick heavy tread on the lower flight of stairs she went to the door and leant against it for a second, faint with relief. Then she was in his arms, and he was leading her back into the room. And there she clung to him and he pressed her close, and after a moment he said, "He's gone, then?"

She moved her cheek against his and he said, "I'm sorry. . . . Would he have stayed if you had promised. . . .?"

Again she moved her head; and now he raised her face to his and, with great solemnity, said, "You have not made a mistake, Kaa-tee, I'm for you. We have talked over all this. We know, so you go on knowing you haven't made a mistake. . . . And now"—he drew in a deep breath—"I have

187

not more than five minutes; I must get back, and quick. I would have been here sooner but I was held up with the dock authorities, so what I must say will be terse, short. We sail to Stavanger, unload our coal there, and if there is a cargo ready for us we should be back under three weeks. However, if I've got to take her on to Bergen it could be another week or more before I return; it all depends on the weather and the charters. Now, in the meanwhile you must live, so here is five pounds, and if for any reason I should be delayed beyond a month I will get money to you. Never fear. I will get money to you. . . . Take it, take it." He closed her fingers over the sovereigns.

Up to this very moment she hadn't felt a whore, or a bad woman, because all she had taken from him was something to eat, and coal, and candles; but now the exchange had been made, the price had been paid, and it was as Meggie Proctor had said—Fishgate whores or Dock Dollies. No, no, she wasn't one of them, she wasn't. She flung herself against him and her crying shuddered his body, and he began to talk rapidly to her in his own tongue. After a moment his mouth sought hers and he kissed her with a hard, intense passion which she returned. Then, pressing her from him, he looked at her. His blue eyes, seeming to have darkened, now searched her face, moving from one feature to another, before they came to rest on her hair, and his hands moved up and touched it for a moment. Pulling a strand loose from the coil on the back of her head, he whipped out a knife from his coat pocket and, bending the strand into a loop, he cut off about three inches from it. Then he rolled it around his finger before putting it into his top pocket. And now, taking her face between his hands, he muttered thickly, "Know I will be back, Kaa-tee. Know that." Then, again touching her lips, but softly, he said, "Don't come. Just stay there."

It was some time before she moved. It was Lizzie's whimpering that stirred her, and as she looked wearily towards the bedroom door her gaze was caught by the sight of the hessian sack that Joe had brought in. It was lying between the wall and the chiffonier. She hadn't noticed it before, she had forgotten that he had thrown it there. Now she moved slowly across the room and picked it up, and when mechanically she toppled its contents on to the table she saw a hand of smoked bacon and a ring of black pudding.

Odd, the things that happened, and when they happened.

She had a cupboard full of food now and there was a hand of smoked bacon and a black pudding, and if Joe had brought them three days ago she would never have met Andy. . . . A hand of smoked bacon and a black pudding.

*　　*　　*

At twelve o'clock the next day Joe walked down the stairs and into the street. He looked white and was shaking inwardly. He had got his answer from Katie. As he walked to Tyne Dock and through it, and up the long road past East Jarrow, he told himself over and over that he just couldn't believe it. He was hurt and shaken to the core, but his most intense feeling was that of being slighted. He kept muttering to himself, "She's mucky, filthy, putrid. She is. She is."

He went up the bank that led into Jarrow, along past the rows of whitewashed cottages with the women sitting on the steps and the men standing idly at the corners. The whole town was dead; it looked as if everybody was waiting for a hearse to pass. Some of the shops were closed, and those that were open looked empty; only the pubs had customers, and these were from the factories that cluttered round the feet of Palmer's and managed to thrive independently.

But he wasn't bothered about the strike at this minute; he had nobody to care for but himself now and he felt lost, thrown off, tossed aside. Aye, that's what she had done, tossed him aside. And he'd worked for years to keep the house going, giving up every penny to her. He couldn't have done more. And just because she was hungry she had gone and done that. But what staggered him most of all was that she was brazen with it, for she said she wouldn't give him up. She couldn't see she was making a mug of herself; these kinds of chaps didn't wait to be given up, they just went and never came back. Well, it would be no use her coming crawling to him when her eyes were opened. No, by God! He would give her his answer, that he would.

He felt the urge to cry, and he cut down a side street where they were building houses. The builders were still working; the houses were popping up as quick as corks from bottles on New Year's Eve, because the contractors knew that Palmer's would flourish again; whoever sank, Palmer's would swim.

He passed a patch of open ground where a gang of men

were playing quoits, and another were surrounding a couple of cocks; then into a district that looked clean and superior compared to the part of the town through which he had just passed. He went up a back lane where every few feet of yard wall had two wooden hatches let in; one denoting a coalhouse beyond, the other indicating the new innovation of the dry midden. When he came to the eighth door he lifted the latch and walked up the narrow yard and knocked on the kitchen door.

Mrs. Hetherington answered his knock and said cheerily, "Oh, there you are, Joe. You've got back."

"Yes, Mrs. Hetherington."

"Come in; come in, lad."

Joe went into the kitchen, and there looked at Mr. Hetherington where he sat cobbling a pair of boots on an iron last which he held between his knees.

"Hello, lad," said Mr. Hetherington. "How did it go? You made it up?"

Joe stood rubbing his hand hard across his mouth. Then, looking from the dumpy little woman to her tall, thin husband, he bowed his head and said, "It wasn't quite right what I told you about me an' her just havin' words, Mr. Hetherington. It's worse than that. I . . . I can't go back 'cos she's gone on the streets."

4

Almost a month to the day Andree returned to the Tyne. Katie knew of his coming before he docked; she heard of it through Meggie. Meggie had come knocking at the door late last night and woken her up. She said that a friend who was on one of Palmer's colliers plying between Peterhead and Sunderland had sighted the *Orn* when they were about thirty miles off shore from Aberdeen. She was making good headway and had the wind with her, and if she was lucky she should come in on the tide, which was around five in the morning. But if she couldn't make it owing to the weather, she should surely be in later in the day. Then Meggie had added, "Do you think he'll turn up?"

Katie had swallowed and said, "I think so, Meggie." And when she was alone she stood with her back to the door, her hands pressed against it. She would as soon have doubted the dawn breaking as him not turning up.

And now it was morning. Half-past seven and she was ready and waiting. She had made the fire up high and it was burning brightly, the table was set, and she had on her new dress—at least new to her. And as she looked down at it she thought that if Miss Theresa knew to what use her last gift was being put she would burst into flames. The thought had the power to make her laugh inside. She had never laughed outright since Andree had gone.

During the first terrible week of loneliness she had cried most of the time. At one period she nearly went looking for Joe; she knew she would find him with the Hetheringtons. She hadn't intended to ask him to come and live in the house again, only to come and see her now and then, not to cut himself right off from her; but remembering Joe's face when they had parted she knew it would be useless, because Joe had a great deal of her da in him; he might not go to church but he was still a churchman inside.

The second week she had taken to talking to Lizzie, talking as if she was getting answers. But she had stopped that; you could lose your mind that way. . . .

She had to make the fire up three times more before Andree arrived, and when she heard his tread mounting to the landing she could not leave the centre of the room and go to the door.

He did not knock but turned the handle and pushed the door wide and stood there. He had a big canvas bag hanging from one hand and he dropped it to the floor, then moved forward slowly, like she had seen him moving towards her in her dreams. His eyes spraying their blue light over her, he came now, and she couldn't move a muscle to welcome him until she was in his arms.

Not only her mouth but the whole of her body became lost in his, and when the first moment of swaying, rough, painful ecstasy was over he pressed her from him and looked at her and whispered, "Oh, Kaa-tee, Kaa-tee." Then, moving his head slowly, he said, "I didn't dream it, but my memory

191

wasn't vivid enough. You are more beautiful than I remember." She fell against him again, crying, "Oh, Andy, Andy. Oh, I've missed you. Oh, how I've missed you. I've worried every day. And when the wind was high last night I was terrified lest it took you on to the Black Middens."

He stroked her hair gently and leant his cheek on it and said quietly, "Never be afraid of the wind. As long as it blows it'll blow me to you. . . ."

It was an hour later and they had loved and talked and loved again, and now, dishevelled but still unable to lose contact with each other, they were standing close at the table and Andree was undoing the canvas bag.

She had never seen so many beautiful things all at once in her life—at least things that were beautiful to her—and not least of them was a seven-pound jar of strawberry jam. Food to her came under the heading of beauty; anything as necessary as food was beautiful. He spilled on to the table now a whole ham, a pickled tongue, a box of ginger encased in lumps of sugar, another box filled with strange-looking candy. Then there was the cloth. Two rolls of cloth, one of fine green gaberdine and the other of cream silk. She held a length of this latter in her hand and the rough skin of her fingers caught at its fineness. She gazed up at him and said, "Oh, it's beautiful, Andy. Beautiful, real silk."

"For your nightgown and shift."

Her eyes stretched wide and her mouth gaped open before she said, "Use this for a nightgown and shift?"

"Of course."

"It's too good."

"Too good for you?" He pulled her to him. "Spun gold wouldn't be too good for your nightgown and shift."

"Aw, Andy. . . ."

Two hours farther on, when they were sitting on the mattress that was now spread before the fire, she said, "How long this time?"

"Two days, perhaps three."

"Oh, no. Only two days. Oh, Andy." She lowered her head slowly on to his shoulder and he asked, "Are you very lonely by yourself with just . . . ?" He motioned his head towards the bedroom door, and she said, "I'm lonely all the time you're not here."

"I've got a plan." He put his finger beneath her chin and tilted her face towards him. "I'm thinking about leaving my company. . . . This—this Palmer company in Jarrow, they have steam boiler ships that don't have to wait for wind and weather; they just fly ahead. They can do the crossing in half the time. This company get a lot of their ore from Bilbao in Spain. It is a long way off, but it will be quicker in their steamships although the distance is twice as far, I have been talking to a friend of mine. He knows the owner, this Mr. Palmer, and he is going to place a word for me."

"Oh, Andy." She smiled softly at him. "That would mean you always docking here; you wouldn't have to go back to Sweden every time."

He traced his finger around every feature of her face before he said softly, "There is something I have to tell you, but it will keep." Then he added quickly, "Don't look worried; there's nothing to worry about. I just want to tell you about my home. It isn't in Sweden, it's in Norway. Although I'm Swedish by birth, I've always lived in Norway."

"Tell me now—please, Andy, tell me now." Her request was urgent, fear traced, and she held his hand to her breast.

During the weeks that had separated them she had thought about his home and dreaded the ties she imagined were there, a mother and father, a wife and family? No! No! He mustn't have a wife and family. Sisters and brothers, mother and father, but not a wife and family. "Tell me, Andy," she said again.

Andree now turned from her and, pulling his knees up, he leaned his elbows on them, and his forearms and joined hands made a bridge between his legs, and over this he bent his broad chest and stared into the fire. And he remained silent for so long that Katie, putting out a tentative finger, touched his shoulder and said softly, "I'm sorry. It doesn't matter."

"Yes, it matters." He turned to her again. "It matters, Kaa-tee, and I think perhaps now is the time to tell it . . . but I'll do it in my own way, it'll make it easier." He gave her cheek a gentle tap, then said, "Look. My coat, hand it," and she turned from him and, getting to her knees, reached towards the back of the chair and, lifting his coat down, gave it to him.

Andree now proceeded to empty the inside of three pockets. Out of one he took a bulky wallet; from another a fine leather case; and from the third a small book with a brass lock on it. Taking a key from the same pocket, he undid the lock and opened the book and, tapping it with his finger, he said, "Diary."

"Diary?"

"Yes, what I write personal in. . . ."

"Yes, yes, I know."

He smiled now and patted her cheek again, saying, "I forget. I forget you know these things, that you can read."

She moved her head slightly as she smiled softly at him. She noticed something about him at this moment that she had encountered once before; his English became more precise, more stilted when he was upset or agitated. That time with Joe he had talked clipped like he was doing now. The thought that what he was about to tell her was agitating him strengthened the apprehension in her and the smile slid from her face, and she waited.

"Look first." He was pointing to a small map in the back of the book. "Can you see? The print is very faint, but there, that tiny dot there, it is called Karlstad. There I was born. My father was Norwegian and my mother was Swedish. Sweden and Norway, you see, are close like your Scotland and England, you understand?" She nodded, and he went on, "My father's father was English, my mother's father was Norwegian. My English grandfather lived in Norway from when he was a young man, and from the age of seven I lived with him. That's why I speak English so well." He stated this seriously. Then he went on, "You see, we are a large family, eleven—eleven brothers and sisters—so my parents let my brother Jon and me go and live with my grandparents, and life was wonderful." He smiled broadly now and pulled at his beard. "They lived in a little house between Bergen and the top end of Hardanger Fjord, and all around us was water. Water, water everywhere you looked. And great mountains of rock with their feet in the water; and in the spring, blossom. Water, rock and blossom . . . Ahh!" He sighed and closed his eyes. "I went to sea when I was fourteen. I sailed out of Bergen on a spring night with the moon and the wind filling the sails, and that was my first marriage. That night the sea and I were joined for life."

First marriage. A chill came on her, and not even the hard pressure of his fingers could warm her now.

"Seven years later I was first mate on that same ship, and there came the day when we returned to Bergen and almost the whole town was on the quay, for we had been away for two years. We had been right across the North Atlantic Ocean, south to the West Indies, then right round to Montevideo in Uruguay. And here we were, safely back. We hadn't lost a man and we had a rich cargo. There was a ball given that night in the Radhus . . . Town Hall, you know." He nodded at her, and she nodded back. "And there I met a young lady. I had never seen a woman for many months, and this young lady had a fair skin and pretty hair and she seemed to like to dance with me. I did not know then who she was, she was only a pretty girl, but next day I found out when my brother Jon, who also went to sea, and whose boat happened to be in, teased me for being the choice of Miss Peterson at the ball.

"My grandparents were all oohs and ahs and laughter, for was not Peterson Papa one big hell of a man, as you say. Why, he owned great slabs of the town. Well, that, thought I, was the last I would see of Miss Peterson. But no, I was invited to her home and—well . . ." He lifted his big shoulders and spread his hands before Katie. "I was young, I was very flattered, and yes, yes, I was in love. . . . In love. It is a strange thing to be in love. You don't love when you are in love. You can't because you are in a state of madness. Youth and those two long years at sea, and flattery, and the man-urges that were burning me up, took me to the church as if I had all my sails trimmed to a following wind."

He now stopped and brought his face close to hers and, tracing his fingers under her eyes, said softly, "Don't look like that, Kaa-tee. There is nothing to worry about, I tell you, nothing."

He straightened up again, and, his voice taking on a louder note, he went on, "Within months I was a captain and had my own ship. Oh, Kaa-tee, it was a very good thing to be married to the daughter of an influential man." He nodded his head slowly at her. "I was at sea when my first child was born; it was a girl-child, and I did not see her until she was seven months old. I was at home for five weeks with her, and, of course, she did not know me. She cried when I lifted her up . . . screamed. I was always a big hairy thing. I was at sea when my second child was born; I saw her when she was a month old. My first child still screamed when I lifted her up. When I had been married for four years I became master of a bigger vessel—oh, a fine vessel. My father-in-law had a large thumb in the shipping pie, you understand." She nodded again, her eyes fixed, unblinking, on him. "On my first trip in the new ship I was gone for two years. When I returned I had a sixteen-month-old son, and my eldest child still screamed at the sight of me." He smiled widely now. "I think it was this, my child not knowing me, that made me express the wish to change ships yet again, to trade back and forward to England say, in order to be home more often and get to know my children. Strangely, my wish met with opposition, and mostly from my wife. She, it appeared, was perfectly satisfied with the situation as it was. She . . . she lived for her children, whom she spoilt, and her house, which her father had bought her." Again he shrugged. "A master's money is not small, but it is not big—not big enough to provide for ten rooms and a family. Yet, as big as this house was, it was no place for a great clumsy sailor who walked on the floors with his feet." He thumbed towards his waggling toes, then laughed, and said, "I mean with his boots on. Well, away I went again, but this time I returned two days before my fourth child was born. It was another girl. When I held her in my arms I caused a great upheaval in the family because I said I was finished with the big sail. I was going to get a ship that didn't like to wander so far. At least this last child would know me from the beginning.

"After a long fight I got my ship, but in a company in which my father-in-law had no thumb because he would not countenance this great drop in social prestige. But now I was home for nearly half the year when the sea was frozen. Not that I didn't work. Oh, I worked; there was plenty to do. But very soon I wished I wasn't at home at all, for my wife, at the age of thirty, decided she was going to have no more children. She developed a malaise; it was so bad that her mother must come and look after her. Then it was decided that this arrangement could not go on, and so it was just a matter of time before my wife takes up residence in her old home, and of course the family go too." Again he spread his hands. "I am made very welcome. I have two rooms set apart for me all to myself. There is a side door to them so my big feet won't dirty the hall floors which are polished every day. I talk with my children, who are always very polite to me— even my eldest, who is now nearly sixteen and thinks I am a very funny man, I make her laugh. Look, here is a picture of her." He undid the leather case and took out a number of small thin square boards and, passing one to Katie, he said, "That is she."

Katie looked down at the delicate water-colour portrait of a young girl, but, strangely, she stared at it without pain. There was pain in her, but it was for him she felt the pain. She had always had an acute awareness of loneliness in people. Look how she had felt for Miss Theresa, and even for . . . Mark Bunting, but she had never sensed it in Andy until this moment. And now she saw that the loneliness in him was a big, wide, deep thing, eating at him. She looked at the portraits of the children one after the other, at the boy's face the longest; then, raising her eyes, she said, "He looks like you."

"Yes, he does. And I called him after me, Nils."

She screwed up her face. "Nils? But I thought your name was Andree."

He laughed now. "Andree Fraenkel are what you call surnames and I was always called by the first one, Andree, so I let it go. I do not like Nils anyway."

She smiled a little and shook her head, saying, "That's funny. It's like calling somebody here Smith or Brown or"—her smile widened a little—"Mulholland."

"Mulholland." He brought her hand to his face and rubbed it down his beard. "It is a mouthful, Mulholland." Then, picking up a square of board, he said, "These are my grandparents."

"Oh, they look nice."

"Yes, they are nice; they are good people."

He had not shown her a portrait of his wife, nor did she ask about her, but after he had returned the squares to the leather case he looked towards the fire and said, "Well, Kaatee, what do you think of me now? I have a wife and four children in Norway, and I love you. And I say I cannot live without you. What do you think of me now?"

She did not pause for a second but, thrusting out her arm, she pulled him to her as she said, "The same as I did afore, only more so, more so. It's funny, but"—she rocked herself a little in his arms—"I've . . . I've imagined that if you told me what you just have I would be jealous, burnt up, but I'm not. It's strange, I'm not."

"Oh, Kaa-tee, Kaa-tee." He went to kiss her, then stopped and, turning round and grabbing at his wallet, said, "This thing must be settled once and for all. For days and days I have thought. I am responsible for you now; more so because

197

it is through me your brother went. My pay on the little bucket is not as big as I used to get on the great ships—fourteen pounds a month—but I make it up with what I carry on the side." He gave her a knowing little smile. "From men to monkeys. But what I made hasn't really mattered up to now because my wife expects nothing from me. Because she refused to take money from me her conscience is eased, and I leave it like that, so what I am going to do is to arrange that you have a half-pay note."

"No, no, Andy. No."

"Yes, yes, Kaa-tee. Yes."

"But you won't be able to leave me anything; me not being your . . ."

"These things can be arranged; I'll see to it before I sail again."

She gazed at him. It was as if in some magic way he had made her secure for the rest of her days. The nagging feeling of want that was never far from her mind slid away. His half-pay note, something coming in regularly. Oh, oh, she didn't deserve him, she didn't. She fell against him and they remained still, their cheeks together, their bodies joined, staring into the fire. Then, quite suddenly and for no reason that she could explain, she asked, "Is it a beautiful house you have in Norway?" It was quite some time before he answered, "Yes. Yes, it's a beautiful house, Kaa-tee," and his answer saddened her.

5

The six months that followed was a period of fulfilment and was perhaps the happiest in Katie's life. Except for a nagging guilty feeling concerning Joe, and the feeling of panic she would get if Andree's boat was late, she was at peace, and happy. Her bust developed, her hips lost their flatness, and her mind was groping and opening to knowledge as it never had done before, not even from the books Theresa had lent her, for she was seeing different places, going jaunts, as Andree called them. She did not think it odd that it was a stranger to this land that had to show her the city of Newcastle for the first time. She saw Newcastle as a place of excitement, bustle and grandeur, with its Assembly Rooms and, of all things, a row of baths where people could go and wash. But, above all, what attracted her most in Newcastle was the wonderful theatre, and she had actually been and seen a play there. They were building a theatre in Shields but it wasn't finished yet.

All she had known about Newcastle before this visit was that it was the city that kept the rest of the towns on the Tyne poor, taxing them for the use of their own river, refusing them independence, and after her visit she could, in a way, understand the attitude of the city to the towns that crowded the river, because she saw them as servants to a master. But one servant, Shields, spat when the name of Newcastle was mentioned, for had not the vessels bound for the mouth of the Tyne to go all the way up to Newcastle to check in at the quayside so that the Newcastle Corporation could have its toll. The Shields men hated the Newcastle men. But part of that particular strife had ended in August when Shields, after a long, bitter fight, had been created a separate port, and Andree said it was a fine step forward.

Andree's life was linked closely with the Tyne now, for at the beginning of the winter he had left the Norwegian company and signed on, not with Palmers who hadn't a vacancy yet, but with a firm who were running boats to Harwich and London, but by sail, which made his comings and goings still subject to wind and weather.

When next his boat docked for any considerable time he was going to take her all the way to see Alnwick Castle, and they might have to put up for the night in an inn. He loved showing her strange places. He had even said that one day he would take her to France. Oh, he was wonderful, wonderful. The thought of his kindness brought tears welling into her eyes, especially his kindness towards Lizzie. Not even her mother or father had treated Lizzie like he did. He had brought her a doll, of all things, from one of his trips. It was a clouty doll, dressed in scarlet and green. He had said he thought Lizzie would like it, but she had thought, Poor Lizzie won't know it's there. But a strange thing had happened. After the doll had lain near her stomach for a day Lizzie had picked it up, and now she nursed it continuously. And another thing he had done concerning Lizzie; he had insisted that someone should be brought in to see to her when they went out. He said he didn't like the thought of her being tied up; he said he understood it was necessary sometimes but not for long stretches. Once he'd had to chain a man in the bilges because he had gone mad, and seeing Lizzie tied up reminded him of it. And so she got Meggie Proctor to come and give an eye to Lizzie, and he had made it worth her while. There had been one time when he had put off their jaunt because Meggie was bottled and incapable of even climbing the stairs.

But this period of harmony for Katie came to an end the night Meggie Proctor had visitors.

Meggie had got into the habit of popping up to the top floor whenever she was hungry, or short of a copper, and this would happen when there were few boats in the docks—at least boats with white crews, for, as Meggie openly said, she wouldn't let an Arab or a nigger within a mile of her.

At first Katie had resented Meggie's visits, and for obvious reasons, but you couldn't resent a person like Meggie for long, and now at times she even welcomed her, for Meggie was a bit of company, and she could make you laugh. Also, Meggie was tactful in her way, because she never came near the top floor when the captain was home.

The regular visits of the captain had placed Katie in a class apart, not only in the estimation of the other occupants of the house but of the whole of Crane Street, for, as they all agreed, it was a set thing, the Swede was standing by her, not here the day and gone the morrow, leaving the belly big and the heart with sorrow, like the majority of them did.

Katie was unaware in what esteem her neighbours held her; she only knew that they spoke civil to her and gave her the time of day, and no one had poured the slops out of the window on her, as they had done on Meggie Proctor and Jinny Wilson in the street opposite, which backed on to this one. Most of the women in that street were respectably married, with the men coming home each night from the docks; it was these and their like who never missed a chance of drenching a whore. She would have died, she told herself, if this had happened to her, for it would have put the label on her; which was why, although she welcomed Meggie into her kitchen, she would never, if she could help it, walk down the street with her.

She was, this particular evening, sitting sewing and she was being extravagant. She had two candles lit because she didn't want to strain her eyes too much and make them red. She had discovered a little shop that dealt in good-class ladies' second-hand dresses, and yesterday she had bought one and was now altering it.

She stopped sewing for a moment and lifted her moccasined feet up on to the fender and, dropping her head back, she looked at the clock, which was another present from Andree. It was wonderful to have a clock in the house and not have to rely solely on the sun or the one o'clock time gun going off from the ballast hill across the water in North Shields. She wondered now where Andree was, if he had reached Harwich. If the weather had held for him he would have done it in four days; that could mean he would be in at the beginning of the week, and home for Christmas. Their first Christmas together. She did not wonder if he would regret this first Christmas away from his family; she knew whom he wanted to spend his time with; there was not the smallest shred of doubt in her mind with regard to it. She only hoped he docked at Shields this trip. The last twice there hadn't been much time to see to anything, for his ship hadn't docked in the Tyne at all. It being rough weather, he had docked in Sunderland the first time, then at Hartlepool, the water being deeper in both places and not so much chance of the ship going on the Black Middens, or the hard sands, outside of Shields harbour. She was afraid even of hearing any mention of the Black Middens, for it was only a few years ago that thirty-three sailing vessels sheltering from a storm had been dashed to pieces on these sands.

But Andree said that, with the new innovation of the dredging to clear the channels and the new piers of the North and South Towns forming a safe harbour at the mouth of the river, Shields would soon be a first-rate port. She didn't know about it becoming a first-rate port; the only thing that concerned her was that Andree's ship should go safely in and out, and not have to go to Sunderland or Hartlepool, because that meant he could spend less time with her.

She folded up the dress and put the kettle on the fire, which was low now, and she decided not to make it up again but to go to bed. What was there to sit up for? Besides which, she never wasted coal . . . or food. Although she loved food and always had done, she kept her fare very meagre except when Andree was home, and this had enabled her to save a few shillings each week out of the pound that she was allotted.

She took some hot thin gruel in to Lizzie and made her comfortable. Lizzie's condition was changing and puzzling Katie; she was not eating so much but her body was expanding noticeably. She wondered if she should get a doctor, but asked herself what could a doctor do only physic her. Anyway, she decided to leave the matter until Andree came back. He always seemed to know the right way to tackle anything. . . .

It was half an hour later, as she lay in bed on the point of sleep, that there came to her the sound of muffled laughter and footsteps on the stairs. The laughter roused her, and as she recognized Meggie's voice she thought to herself, "She's got a load on by the sound of her. I hope she's not coming here." But a few minutes later it was evident that Meggie was coming to visit her, as there came a knock on the door and Meggie called softly, "Katie, Katie. Open up a minute. Katie. Come on, open up; I want a word with ye."

This was not the first time that Meggie had paid her a visit when she was drunk, and from experience she knew it would be no use telling her to go away. She shook the sleep from her, pulled herself up out of the bed, and groping her way towards the table, picked up the candlestick, took the candle out and lit it in the dying embers of the fire; then, sticking it back into the socket, she went towards the door.

As she undid the bolt the door was pushed quickly forward, almost overbalancing her, and Meggie stumbled into the room. She was, Katie saw, very drunk, and Meggie could be very nasty when in drink, so she said to her quietly, "Aw, Meggie, I was . . ."

Before she could say "abed" Meggie had thrown her arm backwards and cried, "Come on. Come on in." Then, turning to Katie, she said, "I've brought me friends. You're not the only bugger who's got friends with money, Katie Mulholland, you're not the only bugger. Come in. Come on in." She now waved to the two dim figures on the landing, and one of them came forward and into the light cast by the candle which Katie still held in her hand. He was a town man, she saw instantly, by his dress; also that he was of the class. He was a man in his middle years, portly, with a red face and a little beard under his chin.

As the man's eyes swept over her she bent sideways and

made a grab at her skirt lying with her clothes across a chair, and as she held it in front of her she lifted the candle higher and cried to the man, "Get out! Get out, I tell you!"

"Now look here, Katie Mulholland, divn't get on your high horse; ye're no better than ye should be, so don't put on airs. We're all lasses together in this hoose. . . . Come on you in." She again waved towards the landing, and a man came out of the darkness and through the doorway, and when he stepped forward the light from the candle fell on to his face.

The very last time Katie had seen this man it had been in the light of a candle. In the five years that had elapsed Bernard Rosier had changed; he had become fatter, and his face redder, but there was no mistaking him. As their eyes met in recognition Katie felt the blood draining from her body. One minute, such was the shock she felt she would collapse under it; the next minute there was tearing through her a wave of rage and she heard herself screaming, "You! You, get out! Get out of my house!"

His eyes were narrowed, his face was smiling, one corner of his clean-shaven mouth was lifted upward, but nothing of him moved except his head, and that slowly began to lower itself while his eyes still remained on her. Under his smiling gaze her rage seemed to lift her from the ground. One second she was still holding the candlestick, the next it was hurtling through the air. At some point, the candle leaving it made an arch of light, and before it fell to the ground she saw that she had not missed in her aim. There was a loud cry and the dark room became full of curses, mingled with Meggie's screeching.

When a match was struck and held aloft she saw Bernard Rosier leaning against the doorway, his face covered with blood that was running from a gash above his eye. There was another voice from the landing now which Katie dimly recognized as Mrs. Robson's. She had a candle in her hand and she held it high above the three figures crowded in the doorway.

"What's all this?" she was saying. "What's all this? It sounds like murder. What are you about? I'll get the polis."

"It's her! It's her!" Meggie was screaming now. "She hit him with the candlestick. He's my friend. We just come up to see her. She's mad."

"Trollops, the lot of you. Get down, out of here. Get down to your own place, Meggie Proctor, or I'll have the polis called in, I'm tellin' you. Decent people can't sleep in their beds."

"Look at his face. Look at his face. It wasn't us, it was her. My God! Look what she's done to his face." Meggie was now pointing to Bernard Rosier, and he, with his blood-covered hand pressed against the cut over his eye, was staring across the room to where Katie, her back to the table, held in her hand the other brass candlestick, and in a position from where it could come flying at him at any moment.

"Come on, B. Come on, let's get out of here." The older man had to pull Bernard Rosier from the room, and on the landing he said, "Let me have that candle," and Mrs. Robson answered, "Get out! Find your way down as you found your way up." The man swore at her; then, pressing Bernard Rosier before them, they groped their way after Meggie, who was still screaming virulently.

Mrs. Robson now stepped into the room and, coming to Katie, she took the candlestick from her hand, picked up the candle from the floor and lit it from her own, and placing it on the table she said, grimly, "I don't blame you for this, so I won't do anything about it. I heard her bringin' them up an' yappin' on my landin'. But if I thought you had asked them up I'd tell your Swede, 'cos I like fair do's. I don't like to see a man made a monkey out of."

On this, the woman who had always complained about Lizzie's crying turned abruptly and went out and closed the door behind her.

Katie, groping towards a chair, sat down. One hand was still holding the skirt over her breast. The feeling of rage was gone, and in its place was fear. It was the same kind of fear that she had experienced that night in his room. On that night he hadn't opened his mouth, nor had he tonight; and as on that occasion his silence had spoken louder than any words, so had his visit tonight. As she remembered the look in his eyes when the other man had pulled him around and through the doorway she began to whimper, very like Lizzie did, and then to say over and over again, "Oh, Andy, Andy." She said his name louder and louder, as if the incantation would ward off some evil, some evil that she knew was about to befall her.

It was three hours later when she went to bed and she was still telling herself that she was no longer a child, she was twenty-one years old; she was a woman, and she had Andree behind her now. But it was of little use. The feeling of evil Rosier had left in the room was filling the air and she was breathing it in. . . .

The following day every movement on the stairs brought her to a quivering standstill. She rose early before the house was astir, and, making three journeys to the back yard in the dark, brought up a good supply of water. She had got this task over early because she didn't want to come face to face with Meggie.

The day passed and no one knocked on her door, and when at last she allowed herself to go to bed the main thought in her mind was whatever he's going to do he's not going to bring the polis. But this thought didn't lessen her apprehension, and the following morning it was increased if anything.

When in the afternoon she had to go out to get in some food, she found herself tiptoeing down the stairs, and she almost ran there and back to the shop; so that, on reaching the landing, there was a stitch in her side and her breath was coming quickly. As she unlocked the door she gazed around the room amazed that she should find her furniture still intact. Dropping the bass bag on to the table, she now hurried across the room and looked in on Lizzie, where she sat with the doll on her stomach, her eyes fixed on it, and she leant against the stanchion of the door, opening her mouth wide and taking in great gulps of air.

Going back into the kitchen, she sat down before unpacking the groceries. She'd have to pull herself together; she couldn't go on like this. If only she had someone to talk to, someone to tell her fears to. If only Joe was here. She could have told Joe the whole story, whereas she'd only be able to tell Andy part of it. But there, if Joe had been here Meggie would never have brought her friends upstairs. The whole thing would never have happened. What was coming upon her? Was it the Bible retribution because, as Joe had said, she was bad . . . *No! No!* Whatever came upon her wouldn't be because she was bad, because she wasn't bad. If living with Andy was bad, then there was nothing good in the world. She wasn't bad. She wasn't. She wasn't like them downstairs. Yet because she lived in this house, and this quarter, and had Andy, she had their stamp on her. It wasn't fair. It wasn't fair. . . . "Stop it!" She had spoken aloud, and still aloud she said, "Pull yourself together, woman."

She got up and unpacked the groceries, but in the middle of doing this she turned and looked towards the door. She hadn't bolted it. Moving swiftly towards it she shot the bolt in, then stood for a moment biting her lip before she returned to the table to finish her unpacking.

6

It was five o'clock on Christmas Eve and Andy hadn't come, and he wouldn't come now because the tide was going down.

Last week she had bought one or two baubles in the market to hang around the chimneypiece. There was a fancy paper doll in red and blue, there was a coloured paper chain and a paper clown dangling from a spring, but she did not hang them up. What was the use? There was no joy in her, nothing she did seemed able to move the fear that weighed on her. She had sat before the fire until it lost its heat, and she was preparing for bed when she heard the quick heavy tread on the stairs. Her hands cupping her face, she stood gazing towards the door, and when the handle turned and the voice came to her, saying "Kaa-tee, there. Kaa-tee", she stumbled towards it, and after fumbling at the bolt opened it and fell into his arms, and to his astonishment she burst into tears.

"Kaa-tee! Kaa-tee! Oh, my Kaa-tee, what is it? Wait. Wait, wait a moment." He pressed her from him. Then, stepping back on to the landing, he pulled in his bag and lifted another tall package gently into the room, and, hastily closing the door, went to her where she was standing now, her back to the table, her face bowed in her hands, and again she was in his arms and he was saying, "Kaa-tee, tell me what is the matter. Why are you like this?"

She tried to speak, but her crying choked her words and he stood bewildered, stroking her hair, looking round the room the while as if searching for an answer to her distress. And then his eyes came to rest on the bedroom door and he thought he had found it, and the pressure of his arms increased as he said, "Lizzie?" Then again, "Lizzie?" But when her head moved against his neck he again looked about him; then, pressing her from him, he demanded sternly, "Tell me. Listen to me, Kaa-tee. Tell me what has happened to cause this. . . . Them?" He now thumbed the floor, and again she shook her head.

"What then? Come, you must tell me. Your brother?"

"No, no." She forced the words out. "I'm . . . I'm sorry, Andy. It . . . it was like this." She put out her hand and, gripping his, moved towards the fireplace and the high-backed wooden chair, and when he had sat down he took her on his knee and she put her arms about him and laid her head against his neck and told him what had happened. And when she finished speaking and he made no comment she raised her face and looked at him, but he was staring into the fire and it was a second or so before he brought his gaze to hers, and then he said, "This man's name. You have told me everything but his name."

"I can't, Andy. No, no, I can't. I'm . . . I'm frightened. I don't want any more trouble; I've had enough, Andy, I've had enough."

"But can't you see, Kaa-tee." He now gripped her shoulder. "You're having trouble all the time, and you're living in fear of more trouble. Let me put a stop to it. Tell me who it is."

"No, Andy." She pulled herself away from him and to her feet. "I'll never do that, never."

He was sitting on the edge of the chair now with his beard thrust out to her. "I can find out; there are ways and means. I can go to the house where it all started and work back from there."

"It won't help you. Please, Andy, please." She turned to him, her hands joined on her breast. "Just let it go now. But I had to tell you because . . . because I've been so worried, I thought he would send the polis."

"God Almighty!" He sprang to his feet. "I can't go away and leave you and think of you worrying like this waiting for a polis man to come through the door every minute."

She smiled. "Oh, Andy, you're not in the house yet and talkin' of going away. I'm sorry, I'm sorry." Her arms were around his neck again. "I should have kept it to myself. Come on, nothing matters now, nothing, nothing, nothing." She made her smile wider. "How long have you got?"

He didn't answer for some seconds, just gazed at her face;

and then he said, "Three or four days—perhaps more, because they won't load on the holiday."

"Oh, good. Good. So let's forget it. Let's forget about everything."

"Yes, let's forget it, as you say, Kaa-tee, let's forget it." He kissed her hard now, after which he cried, "See what I've brought you", and going across the room he picked up the large package that was standing against the wall and brought it to the table, on which he put it down gently and said, "Guess what I have here?"

She stood close to his side and looked at the tall parcel, and she smiled as she shook her head. "I can't. I haven't an idea."

"Wait, wait." Rapidly now he pulled off the string and the paper and lifted into the middle of the table a glass lamp. Then he looked at her face, at the light and pleasure spreading over the tear-stains.

"Oh, Andy, Andy, how beautiful." She put out her hand and stroked the pale, pink-tinted oil bowl of the tall lamp, then traced her fingers down the slender blue stem to the scalloped base. "Where . . . where did you get it?"

"Here"—his big blond head was bouncing up and down—"in Shields."

"Here?" She sounded incredulous.

"You should have had it two trips ago. Candles! What do people want candles for these days when there are oil lamps and gas coming in? So when I saw Orm's little lamp—Orm, he is my bo'sun—it was so tiny, like so . . ." He measured about two inches between his finger and thumb. "Like this one in every detail. It was swinging from the end of his bunk." He wagged his forefinger. "Swing, swing, swing. 'Where did you get that?' I said to Orm. 'In Shields, sir,' he said. 'I know a family there who all work in the glass-works. The father is very clever.' 'Do you think he could make a big one like yours?' I asked him, and he said 'Ja', he was sure, but I would have to wait for it; just at spare times his master let him create something for himself. . . . And there it is."

"Oh, thank you, darlin', thank you, thank you." She was enfolding him again, and when he saw the tears in her eyes once more he cried, "But she's no good without oil and there is only a little in her. Come, we'll go out shopping. But first my bag."

Now, bringing his sailor's bag on to the mat before the

fire, he pulled out his gifts and handed them to her: coffee, butter, tea. He held the tea aloft, saying, "You have tasted nothing like this. China . . . A-ah!" He smacked his tongue against the roof of his mouth and they both laughed as he ended, "It's nearly as good as gin. And mocha . . . Coffee; oh, it's good, first thing in the morning after much drink." Again they were laughing. Then he handed her up a ham, a whole ham, and candies, three boxes of them, and last, from the bottom of the bag, he tumbled a length of woollen material, and as he pushed it into her hands his face stretched into a wide grin as he said, "For bloomers, warm bloomers."

"Oh, Andy! Andy." She was on her knees, half laughing, half crying as she hugged the piece of material to her breast and rocked herself back and forward, and as she gazed at him she kept repeating his name.

Lastly he put his hand into the inner pocket of his jacket and brought out a small, hard, black case and, handing it to her, said, "Yule-tide gift to my Kaa-tee."

When she opened the box she saw lying on a bed of red velvet a fine gold chain with a heart-shaped locket on the end. She raised her mist-filled eyes towards him, unable for the moment to say anything. Then she opened the locket, and there, gazing back at her, was a miniature portrait of himself. The other side of the locket was blank and, pointing to it, he said, "Your likeness—that is for your likeness, I will have you painted."

The locket cupped in her two hands, she stared at him. Then her body crumpled up against him and again she was sobbing unrestrainedly, and this time it seemed as if she would never stop.

* * *

Andree sailed the day before New Year's Eve. He went on the morning tide. It was bitterly cold and there was a light breeze blowing, and after seeing to Lizzie she had hurried along the river bank, and there in the early light she had seen his ship, guided by a little tugboat, making down-river for the opening in the piers. Long after it had passed from her sight, she had stood until, the cold penetrating to her bones, she turned slowly about.

She did not make her way straight home but went towards King Street, cutting through the market-place, which was thronged, even at this early hour, with shoppers storing in food for the New Year festivities. She noticed that beyond the Town Hall the windmill rearing high up above the houses in the corner of the square stood out starkly against the low grey sky. This was a sure sign of bad weather, and she prayed that it would hold off until Andy got well out into deep water. She made her way between a herd of sheep and horse-drawn carts laden with everything from potatoes to squealing pigs, past the women who sold their vegetables from deep wicker baskets, past the rows of stalls, taking care to avoid the women hawkers with their wares slung on their backs who almost pushed you over to make you buy, and so she came to King Street and the chemist's.

She had seen in the *Shields Gazette* last Saturday an advertisement which said that the chemist had a cure for dropsy, and that's what Andy said was wrong with Lizzie, she was swelling with water. When he was home the trip before last they had gone across to North Shields to a chemist there. This journey had been the result of another advertisement in the *Gazette,* but the medicine for which Andy had paid two shillings a bottle had no effect on Lizzie, except to make her sleep.

The chemist in King Street only charged her ninepence for the medicine and told her it might take up to three months' treatment before she saw any noticeable change in the patient.

On her return journey she skirted the market-place and took a short cut home, and when she came down the steep hill of Thames Street into Lower Thames Street, which ran parallel to the river, she collided with two children, a boy of about six and a little girl of about four years old. The boy was holding the child's hand, and neither had a coat on. The child was wearing a dirty serge frock and her feet, like her brother's, were bare, and on the small heels of both children and on the backs of their hands were smears of blood from the keens and chaps that were splitting the skin.

That was one thing she'd never had to suffer from, bare feet. Joe for a time had gone barefooted, but her granda had seen that that had never happened to her, for he'd had a knack of making a rough kind of shoe out of old boot tops. He would sit and knead the leather between his tallow-coated hands for hours at a time, until it was pliable.

"Wait," she said to the boy as they went to pass her, and

210

opening her purse she brought out a shilling. "You've got a ma?" she asked.

"Aye, missus." The boy moved his head slowly.

"Your da, is he working?"

"Aye, missus; he's at sea."

She knew what that meant; she had learned from Andy that it wasn't only miners, and shipyard men, and the farm labourers who worked for a mere pittance; the sailor's wage was not only desperately low but his food and the conditions under which he worked were horrifying. She said now, "Have you any brothers and sisters?"

"We've got nine, missus. We had ten, but Jimmy he got buried last week. He was older than Bess here . . . next to me."

She bent right down now until her face was on a level with his. She wanted to take her handkerchief and wipe his running nose. His hair was black, but white-streaked with nits. There, too, she had been lucky, for her mother had fought a constant war against body lice, bugs, and dickies in their heads. As she gazed pitifully at the children she realized that in an odd way her early years had been good. She said, "I live at No. 14, Crane Street. Do you know where Crane Street is?"

"Aye, missus; along there opposite the river."

"Well, do you think you could come every Saturday morning and I'll see what I've got for you."

He looked at the shilling in his hand, then looked up into her face and said solemnly, "Aye, missus. Aye, I will."

"Take that to your mother now."

"Aye, missus. Ta, missus."

They moved on, their feet making no sound on the filth-strewn road.

Once in the house she slowly took off her things, looked into the room to see that Lizzie was all right, then, coming to the fire, she poked it and drew her chair close to it; and she sat for a long time staring into the flames, thinking of Andree, wishing him clear of the sandbars. After a while she began to think of the two children and the blood running out of their hands and feet, and from thoughts of them her mind went to Sarah. It was the first time for many a long day that she had allowed herself to dwell on her child. She would be five years old now. Was she bonny? Oh yes, she would be bonny. She'd be talking too, talking differently from what she herself did, talking like Miss Ann and Miss Rose . . . like Miss Theresa. Through the years there had been, deep down, a bitterness in her and a feeling of resentment against her mother and Joe for persuading her to part with her child, but mostly against her mother; but since she had known Andree the feeling had lessened. She would always regret having given up her child, yet in a way she was glad she had given her a chance of a new way of life. Here her lot would have been that of a child of the riverside; perhaps not like those two children she had seen a short while ago, for she would have kept her child clean, spotlessly clean, but she could not have done anything about her environment, because Lizzie dictated their environment. She heard a voice saying in her head, "I would like to see her. Just for a moment, and hear her speak." The voice brought her to her feet. No! No! She must never do that; she must never try to see her, because once she saw her she would never know peace again.

What she must do was to have another child. She was surprised that she hadn't fallen before now. She would love to have a child by Andy. . . . Oh, and the company it would be when he was away. And not only one: two, three, as many as time would allow. She couldn't have too much of anything that was Andy's. She didn't question that she had no claim on him to keep them; as long as Andy lived he would see to her and all that was hers, of this she felt sure.

* * *

On New Year's Eve it snowed heavily and the whiteness turned the drab, smoked-blackened view from her window into a pretty picture. Everything outside looked bright and lighter, but inside the house, inside her heart, everything was dull and heavy. She felt more lonely today than she had done since Joe left the house. She had hoped that, it being New Year's Eve, the first New Year's Eve they had been separated since they were children, he would let bygones be bygones and pop in.

There was preparation and bustle for the New Year all about her. The house was noisy. She had heard Meggie's voice from down below shouting, and calling, a number of times. She had not seen Meggie since that awful night, nor did she want to. There had been two fights in the street today so far; she had watched one of them from the little window

212

in Joe's room that faced the street. It was between two women. Women fighting were always more ferocious than men, she thought. Men struck out with their closed fists, but women tore with their clawed hands, kicked and bit. Before it was over she had returned to the kitchen. She heard the yelling of the second fight, but she did not go across the landing and into the room to see what it was all about. Fighting sickened her.

Then, in the early evening, she had no time to think of her loneliness because Lizzie had one of her wailing fits, and she could do nothing to quieten her. Lizzie sat, as upright as she could, making this wailing noise, and after some time Katie became apprehensive of the effect on Mrs. Robson. She kept listening for her neighbour's step on the stairs. Mrs. Robson had spoken kindly to her after the business with Meggie that night, but she hadn't seen her since. She was a woman who kept herself to herself, but on New Year's Eve she wasn't likely to put up with Lizzie's wailing without making some protest. In desperation she put her arms about Lizzie and rocked her, saying, "There, there. Give over, Lizzie. Give over." But Lizzie, her loose mouth wide open, took no heed of Katie's plea and continued to emit this weird, penetrating, animal-sounding wail.

It was around half-past six that the thing she feared came about. It began as a sort of distant confabulation, and when it died away she thought that Mrs. Robson had gone down to consult with Meggie Proctor and Jinny Wilson as to what should be done about the awful noise up above. But then she could hardly have reached the ground floor when the knock came on the door. Katie paused before going to open it, and when she did she had her hand to her throat. It was an apprehensive gesture, but her expression of apprehension changed to complete bewilderment when she was confronted by two young women whom she had never seen in her life before. From the light of the lamp she could see their faces plainly and those of the two men standing behind them. One minute, as she stared at them, there was silence; the next, the room was filled with such a hullabaloo she wondered if she had gone crazy, because this wasn't like a New Year's call of any kind. Besides, they were utter strangers. The girls had pushed her aside and dashed into the room and were racing around yelling and shouting, and the men after them. It was as if the four had been released by the same spring, and as she stood, holding her head and yelling at them, screaming at them, there came a sound of quick, hard footsteps on the stairs, and in the doorway appeared two policemen, and Katie turned to them as if to rescuers and cried, "Get them out! Get them out!" and the two policemen got them out. They pushed them on to the stairs, where one policeman remained with them and the other came back into the room and said to her, "Get your coat." He nodded towards the back of the half-open door.

"What?" She swallowed deeply, bringing her head forward with the effort. Then she put her fingers to the side of her mouth and after staring at him in stupefaction for a moment she said quietly, "But I needn't go, I've done nothing. They forced themselves. . . ."

"Come along," he said, "I know all about it." As he put his hand out to touch her she sprang back and cried angrily. "What do you mean, you know all about it? You know about what? I've never seen those people in my life afore, not until a minute or so ago."

He moved a slow step towards her, saying, "Now look here, lass, I don't want to handle you, but if I have to I will. I'm givin' you a choice; get your coat or I'll take you as you are." Again she was holding her head in her hands, and her voice almost a whimper, she said, "But you can't, you can't, I've done nothin'." She moved her hand in a slow sweep towards the bedroom door. "Listen. That's me sister. She's sick, very sick, I can't leave her."

"Somebody'll see to her. Come on."

"No." Her voice was again loud. Then she repeated, "No!" But even as she yelled her defiance at him and told herself it was all a mistake, it would soon be cleared up, her whole body was swamped with fear.

When he came at her, after whipping her cloak from the back of the door, she beat him off with her first and struck at him until her arm was twisted behind her back and her body bent double, and like this she was thrust out of the door and down the stairs, and some part of her mind noticed that all the other doors in the house were closed.

She stopped crying out when she reached the street, but when she came to the end of it she clutched at a lamp-post with one hand, and in a loud voice appealed to three men standing within the range of light. "I've done nothin'," she cried out. "I've done nothin'. Help me. Help me. I tell you

I've done nothing'." Her arm was wrenched almost from its socket and she cried out again, but in agony from the pain this time. When they reached the police station in Chapter Row she was pushed into a room where the two young girls were sitting on a form. There was no sign of the men.

Once the policeman had released his hold on her she staggered towards the girls and, bending over them, she beseeched them, "Tell them, will you tell them, I've done nothing? Tell them I don't know you. Do I?"

The eldest girl, who had a thin face capped by tattered fair hair, looked up at her coldly, and her answer was, "Shut thy gob."

Katie slowly straightened her body and stared down into the upraised faces, into the cold, narrowed eyes. Then she swung round to where the two policemen were talking to another one behind the counter, and the policeman who had handled her was saying, "We got the tip-off . . . procuring. That'll be the charge, procuring. The fellows got away but the lasses will testify."

The policeman behind the counter put his head to one side and looked at Katie over the shoulder of the man who had been speaking. He looked her up and down and then he looked back at the policeman, and, bending forward, he whispered something in his ear, and to this the policeman said, "Oh no. It's her all right. We've had our eye on her for sometime. Starts by being kind to a family you know." He nodded, then cast his eyes back to Katie. "The old game. Saw her at it just this mornin'. Gave a shilling to a bairn. We talked to him after. She told him to go round every Satada mornin'. She had asked him how many there were in the family. . . . Same old game."

The man behind the counter had continued to look at Katie all the time the policeman had been talking. Then, taking his eyes from her, he wrote something in a book before saying, "Well, we're nearly full up here, and by mornin' comes we'll be pushing out at the seams; you'd better take her along to the Cross."

"What about the two lasses?" asked the policeman who had brought them in. "There's nothing really on them. They said she invited them to the house for a bite and then she produced these fellows."

"Have you got their names and addresses?"

"Aye," said the policeman. "And I know them."

215

"Then let them go; we'll get them when we want them. Here." He beckoned towards the two girls with a lift of his head, and when they stood at the counter he stared at them hard before saying, "Get yourselves off home, and let this be a lesson to you."

They nodded at him. Then, turning around, they went out without looking in Katie's direction.

"Please, please." Now she was at the counter gripping its edge and bending towards the man behind it, imploring him to listen to her. "Please, it's all a mistake, I tell you. I've done nothing. It's . . . it's a put-up job, it is. Will you listen to me."

"Now! Now! You'd better be careful what you're sayin', put-up job." The man pushed out his chest and patted each side of it with a thick, short hand. "Put up by who? What would anybody go to that trouble for? You've been caught red-handed, so face up to it."

"I tell you, I tell you . . ." She stopped suddenly and, her voice dropping, she looked wildly about her and muttered, "I must have help. I must have help."

"Have you any relations around?"

"Only a brother in Jarrow."

"What's his name?"

"Joseph Mulholland."

"Address?"

She lowered her head; then shook it, saying, "I . . . I don't rightly know. He lives with people called Hetherington, somewhere off Ormonde Street. It's, it's Mayhew Street, I think. Mayhew Street. . . . Please. . . ." She put her hand out across the counter towards him.

"He'll be notified." He now looked at the other policeman and, jerking his head, said, "Get going." And they got going. They stood, one on each side of her, and like that they walked her out of the room and into the crowded street and through the crowded town towards the Market Place, which only that morning she had crossed on her way to the chemist's. And they took her to the Town Hall where there were four, dark, damp cells, and in one they locked her up and she started to scream. She screamed for an hour until a woman came and slapped her hard across the mouth, and then she became quiet.

It was the third day of January 1866. The magistrate took his seat at ten o'clock in the morning and noted that the first case he had to deal with was of one Mrs. Bunting, commonly known as Katie Mulholland. Her offence: procuring young females for improper purposes. He made a motion with his head to the clerk of the court, who made a motion with his head to the usher, and Katie Mulholland was brought in.

The magistrate glanced at the prisoner and his eyes were returning to the paper before him when they switched back to the woman in the box. Her face was beautiful, tragic, the eyes holding a wild stare. The clothes, although rumpled and dirty, were not of the usual quality and type associated with a . . . He looked down at the paper again . . . procuress. He looked at her long and hard, and he continued to look at her long and hard before he said, "You are charged, Catherine Bunting, with the offence of enticing two young females to your house, there to use them for improper purposes for your own gain. Do you plead guilty or not guilty?"

"Not guilty."

"Speak up."

"Not guilty."

The magistrate continued to stare at the prisoner while he sat back in his chair and let the case take its course. He listened to the policeman's evidence of how he had watched the house in No. 14 Crane Street for some time. It was frequented by foreigners, mostly from the ships.

When the prisoner was asked, she admitted to being visited by a Swedish captain. When she was asked how often, she couldn't give any definite reply. Then came the two girls, the main witnesses. The magistrate saw them as low, ignorant, slovenly types, who could be easily led into this sensual and shameful life. One of the girls said she had worked in the pipe facory since she was eight years old, the other worked in the whiting factory. She had been there since she was seven. They both said they earned enough money to keep them, and, as one said, she had no need to whore for it. She was strongly chastised for using this word in court and she begged the magistrate's pardon. They both swore that they had never solicited men. One of the girls said she often went into Saint Hilda's Church and that she was a good girl. This was the one who explained that they had met the prisoner that day in the market and she had invited them around to her house for a sup of something and a bite, it being New Year's Eve; and they'd hardly set foot in the door when she brought the two men from the bedroom, and these men had set about them. When this particular girl had begun to describe what the men had tried to do the magistrate silenced them, saying that the court understood fully what the men had intended to do.

And then the prisoner was standing before him again. She was crying and talking rapidly in a hysterical fashion, shouting about lies and the whole thing being planned. The magistrate found himself listening to her, and he knew that he would have discounted the evidence of the two girls if it hadn't been for that of the policeman and the fact that the woman herself admitted to receiving foreign sailors into her house, although she had only admitted to one man.

When the prisoner became silent and stood staring at him in a most disconcerting fashion, he leant over the bench and asked of the clerk if she had any relations, and when told she had a brother but he was not in court, nor had he been seen, the magistrate nodded his head. A man would not like to recognise a sister who had gone the way of this one.

It was noteworthy that if the case had been the last one of the day the sentence passed on Catherine Bunting would have been twelve months; as it was, she got off lightly. "I sentence you to three months," said the magistrate, "in the house of correction, and during that time I hope you will come to see the error of your ways."

*　　*　　*

It was almost a fortnight later when Andree came up the stairs and, turning the handle of the door and finding it locked, called, "Open up there, Kaa-tee. Open up."

When silence greeted him he took his fist and banged on a panel, and when there was still no reply he looked towards the little table on the landing where had always stood the wooden bucket and the wash-basin. It was no longer there, not the wash-basin or the wooden bucket or the table.

"Kaa-tee! Kaa-tee!" After banging on the door again he looked down the stairs, and there at the foot stood Mrs. Robson, and with her head well back she called up to him, "It's no use doing that, she's not there any more." He left his bag where it was on the landing and slowly went down the stairs, and when he had almost reached the bottom he stopped and, hanging over her, said, "What did you say?"

Mrs. Robson was a thin, tight-faced little woman and her voice had a tight sound too, but there was a kindly note in it as she replied, "Just what I told you. She's not there any more; they took her away."

Now he was standing in front of her, his hairy face close to hers, so close that she leant back to get away from it—she didn't like hairy men. "Look . . ." She cast her eyes down the next flight of stairs. "Come in a minute."

He followed her into the room, and the first thing his bewildered gaze alighted on, amidst a clutter of oddments on a dresser, was the glass lamp he had bought Katie at Christmas. His head down, his beard tight against his breast he stared at it; then, pointing a finger towards it, he turned to her and said, "How did you come by that?"

"Well"—she closed her eyes while at the same time raising her eyebrows—"if I hadn't taken it the others would have nabbed it. I took as much as I could 'cos I knew you'd be back. I wasn't pinching anythin'; I don't want her stuff. You can have them any minute you like. I only hope you manage to get the rest back as easy. They're down below; both of them had their whack."

"Look. Look." His voice came from deep within his body. "Tell me, where is she? Kaa-tee."

"She's in prison, doing three months."

She watched him take off his hat and lift the hair from his brow before she said, "They said in the court that she was keeping a bad house."

"A bad house?" His face was screwed up, his clear blue eyes lost behind his narrowed lids.

"Aye, that's what they said. You were mentioned—not by name, just as . . . well, as sort of her having foreign sailors."

"You me . . . an . . ." He drew the words out, then repeated, "You me . . . an she has gone to prison because of

219

me?" He stuck one finger in the middle of his blue cloth coat.

"Well, no, not you alone . . ." Mrs. Robson folded her arms across her chest, and before she could go on he barked at her, "What do you mean, not me alone? You would say Kaa-tee . . .?"

"Now don't get all worked up, I'm not sayin' nowt. I'm just tellin' you what they said in court. But I can give you me opinion, if you want that."

"Your opinion?" He was staring at her, but not seeing her; at the moment he seemed only capable of listening to her words, then repeating them. They had locked his Kaa-tee up for keeping a bad house, and he was part of that bad house. But his Kaa-tee keeping a bad house? God Almighty! His Kaa-tee with the white light all about her. He never looked at her but he saw her through a white light, the white light of pure love, something which few men experienced but which he had with Kaa-tee. He heard the woman say, "Now take your hands off me and don't get rough, 'cos it won't work."

He shook his head and loosened his grip on Mrs. Robson's shoulder; and, standing back from her, he said, "I'm sorry; I have been shocked. . . ." Then: "Lizzie. What about Lizzie?"

"They took her to the workhouse. An' the best place, I should say. Sit yourself down." She pointed to a wooden chair against the scrubbed white table. Then she sat down opposite to him and, leaning across the table, whispered, "If you want to know what I think, the whole thing was a frame-up."

He stared at her and repeated her words, but only in his mind now, and waited for her to go on. "You see, it was like this. I heard a bit of a kerfuffle on the stairs, an' since that night when that Meggie brought her pals up here I've had me ears skinned; besides which I was out to catch them young brats that goes round the doors knockin' at the rappers. Three months they can get if they're caught. Not that the slops don't want something better to do than go hounding bits of bairns for a bit of a game. . . ."

When he made an uneasy movement she said, "Aye, well, I'm comin' to it; just give me a minute. I was just sayin' about them rappin'. Well, there I was, standin' behind the door 'cos I'd heard the creepin' on the stairs, you see, and then they stood on me landin' there and started to jabber, low like, so I put me ear to the keyhole, but I couldn't hear what they were sayin', except for one thing. An' I heard this twice.

The same thing. It was, 'Five minutes he give us.' That's what I heard. An' I heard it twice, as I said, an' it didn't make sense, not till after. Then I heard them go upstairs, quiet like at first, and then I heard her, Katie Mulholland, comin' out of the bedroom where that lass had been wailin' all the afternoon. Shockin' it was; I was for goin' up. If it hadn't been New Year's Eve an' her on her own, like, I would have gone an' played hell, but I didn't. An' I heard her comin' across the floor, and then all hell was let loose. I'm tellin' you you'd think somebody was bein' murdered. Well, I was goin' to open the door . . . well, I had it open, but I shut it right quick when I heard some more comin' up the stairs. I didn't know then they were the slops. Then I heard Katie scream. God, did she scream! The Lizzie one had nothin' on her that night. She screamed blue murder. An' then they all came downstairs, and she was screaming all the way. . . ."

He put his hand out and stopped her flow, and after a moment, during which his lips were drawn in and lost behind the mass of fair hair, he asked, "Did you know the people who went upstairs, the . . . the men?"

"No, I didn't see hilt nor hair of them, not even the day in court when she was brought up; but the lasses were there, an' I can tell you for nowt they're as much good as a six weeks' unsmoked haddock."

"The names?" he said.

"I don't rightly know their names, except they're known as Sue and Bridget. I heard that outside the court. But I can tell you who'll know all about them. Him that runs the Anchor, he'll know about them or I'm very much mistaken . . . Look," she said, "will I make you a cup of tea? I've got some tea."

"Thank you." He rose slowly to his feet. "Thank you, but no." Then, looking around the room, his eyes picked out the chiffonier with Katie's china on it, and her books, and he said, "The rest of the things are down below, you say?"

"Aye, atween the two of 'em. But it's not much use takin' them, is it, 'cos you can't get them in upstairs."

He turned and faced her fully and, his eyes narrowing again, he said, and in a tone that he hadn't used before, for it held a deep threat, "It will all go back where it belongs, Mrs. Robson, or else they will answer to me. If there's a spoon missing they will answer to me." His tone changing again, he said, "But I thank you, I thank you for what you did. And

221

I'll tell you this also. I'll have Kaa-tee out of that place quicker than the wind can fill a sail." On this he turned from her and, going out of the room and up the stairs, picked up his bag, and when he came to the bottom floor he rested the bag against the outer door and, returning to the hallway, banged first on one door and then on the other, and yelled in a loud voice, "I'm coming back for Kaa-tee's things. Do you hear me in there? I'll be back." He waited a moment, and when the door did not open and no voice answered he picked up his bag again and marched down the street to the docks and his ship.

* * *

But Andree was to find that he couldn't get Katie out of that place quicker than the wind would fill a sail. For two days he went round the town gathering information. He started with the police station, but found it was like beating his head against a stone wall, a stone wall of prejudice. He was a foreigner; the woman he was enquiring about was not his wife, just a woman who had been put away for keeping a bad house. At the end of the second day he returned to the back room of the Anchor and Jimmy Wild. It was on midnight and the bar had just closed, and Andree sat in the dirty, low room sipping a mug of hot rum.

There wasn't much about Shields and its people that Jimmy Wild didn't know, nor yet about the inhabitants of the village of Westhoe, or that of Harton. He had seen men press-ganged from this street; he had seen a man murdered just outside the door there; he had seen men knife each other, and women who had come into his bar laughing together tearing the scalps off each other when they eventually left. He knew practically everybody in his vicinity by sight, but he had never seen Katie Mulholland, and he said this again.

"One thing's certain, Captain; she wasn't in the racket. If she'd been . . . well, you know yersel she'd have made her way here; they all start from here. Whether they go up or down, this is the startin' place around these quarters. Let's face it, I know, I know. But your lass . . . well, I've never set eyes on her. An' you know somethin' else? I'd never heard her name mentioned until the case came up. . . . No, a bit afore that, when Meggie Proctor took those two swells round

222

to her place. It was the next day I heard about the rumpus, an' it was then I heard the name of Katie Mulholland for the first time. She had hit one of the blokes with a bottle, or a candlestick or somethin', and split his head open."

Andree now strained his neck upwards and, gripping his glass, said, "Those men. That's it. You knew those men; those two?"

"No, Captain, no. One of them I'd seen twice afore with Meggie Proctor, the other one I've never clapped eyes on until that night, and then only for a minute when they came in and picked her up."

"What were they like? Come on, describe them."

"I can't, Captain. . . . Well, what can you remember of strangers through the fug that's in here at nights? . . . Only one thing sure I can tell you, that is they were gentry; and perhaps another, and that is there's something fishy about the whole business. It's like a put-up job from start to finish. Everybody round about says the same thing. The coppers had got a backhander from somebody, and they're not the blokes to risk their good jobs at eighteen bob a week for no small fry. It's somebody of importance that's at the back of this. That's the local opinion, an' it's never far out. . . ."

It was around two o'clock when he returned to his ship, but not to sleep. At half-past ten tomorrow he'd be going out on the tide, he'd have to do something before then; find someone to carry on the probing; someone who wouldn't be afraid of . . . the gentry. Someone like an investigator or solicitor . . . a solicitor, yes; the one Katie went to, that was it. He knew the office in King Street, she had pointed it out to him. She said he had got a barrister to speak well for her father.

This decided, he trimmed the lamp afresh and wrote a letter to her. It began: "Oh, Kaa-tee, Kaa-tee, my darling Kaa-tee." Then went on to tell her of his love and his faith, and his determination to clear her name and to get her out of that place as soon as possible. He addressed the letter to Her Majesty's Prison, Durham.

It was eight o'clock when he left the ship again. He posted the letter; then, going to the house in Crane Street, he went upstairs and knocked on Mrs. Robson's door, and when, bleary-eyed, she opened it he said abruptly, "I've had no luck, and I sail today. Will you go and visit her at the times they allow?" When he saw her hesitation he added quickly, "I will pay for your travel, and there's half a sovereign for every time you visit her. What about it?"

"All right, all right, I'll go, and mind, not that I'm doing it for the money alone. . . ."

"Thank you. I have written to her. But you tell her that I'm doing everything to clear her. . . . You will, won't you?"

"Aye, I'll do that. But I don't see much use in raising her hopes."

He pushed one and a half sovereigns into her hand, saying, "One to pay the travel and you, and spend the half on food for her."

"Aye, aye, I'll do that, 'cos it's lean fare they get in there. What about upstairs?" She jerked her head.

"I've seen to that. I've paid the rent for four weeks in advance. Here is the key." He handed it to her. "Tell them"— he looked downwards—"that if everything isn't returned by the time I get back again there'll be some broken pates flying around this house. You understand?"

"Aye, I understand."

"I must go now." He paused. "Thank you for your help; you will not lose by it."

She returned his nod but gave him no farewell, and he went down the stairs, and as he passed through the hall he beat his fist once on Meggie Proctor's door; it was a warning. Then he marched out of the house.

When he reached King Street and the office of Chapel & Hewitt he saw by his watch it was five minutes past nine. Without pausing he pushed the door open, went along a dark passage and up some stairs and to a door which again read "Chapel & Hewitt, Solicitors". After knocking he was bidden to enter, and when he opened the door he saw sitting on a high stool, at a high desk, with a ledger before him, a tall, thin man of middle age. On the sight of him the man slid to his feet and, coming forward, said, "Yes, sir, what can I do for you, sir?"

"Are you Mr. Chapel or Mr. Hewitt?"

The man smiled, a soft deprecating smile, saying, "Neither, sir. Mr. Chapel is deceased. I'm Mr. Hewitt's chief clerk."

"Is he in?"

"Yes, sir. Do you wish to see him?"

"Yes, I wish to see him."

"Will you take a seat, sir, and I will ascertain whether he is available."

Andree waved the seat away, and the clerk hurried now towards the door of another room, and after knocking he entered. It was perhaps three minutes before he returned and, holding the door open, said, "Mr. Hewitt will see you now, sir."

Arnold Hewitt was a good judge of character—it was a necessary qualification of his profession; and as he looked at the big, fair-haired man, whom he dubbed, even before he had opened his mouth, as a Swede or Norwegian, he saw that his client, if he was to be so, was a man of purpose, a man who would waste no words and a man who would likely pay well for deeds.

Almost immediately Andree confirmed the solicitor's summing up of his character by saying, "I haven't much time to waste; I sail in just over an hour back to Norway. I want you to do some work for me."

"Yes, if it is within my capacity, sir, and such work as I am used to undertaking, I will oblige. Kindly take a seat and tell me what your business is."

Andree again ignored the offer of a seat and began: "Just this . . ." There followed, in clipped, rapid but good English, Katie's story as Andree knew it. He commenced at the beginning—at least at the beginning of this last affair when Meggie Proctor had brought the two men upstairs—and as he talked the solicitor listened attentively with the main part of his mind, but there was a section that was telling him that this was a strange, a very strange coincidence, for he had been in court on the day that this girl, this Katie Mulholland, had been put away for three months for importuning, and not only had he felt that the woman was innocent but also he'd had a strong suspicion that there was some jiggery-pokery going on. How had the two men, the two vital witnesses, to his mind, in the case, been allowed to escape? These men that the prisoner, it was understood, had housed, and for whom she had procured the two girls. And then there was the telling point of who those girls were. They came from a family that stank, a family whose name was a byword in the low quarters: but all that this implied had gone by the board on the evidence of the policemen. . . . And this man sitting before him now was the foreign sailor who had been mentioned in the case. And there was something stranger still in his mind with regard to this woman: it was not the first time he had come across her. She had paid a tidy bill five or six years ago for the defence of her father, but the whole case was a foregone conclusion, the jury being made up of picked pit officials. They had used the Mulholland man as a scarecrow to keep the miners quiet. He remembered at the time that the girl had been befriended by the Rosiers. It was Rosier's daughter who had brought her along here, that was why he had taken on the case. And now here was this Katie Mulholland being befriended yet again, but by a burly sea captain this time and a foreigner into the bargain. It was an interesting state of affairs.

Of course he would work for him, he would do all he could. He was speaking aloud now. "Just leave it with me, Captain Fraenkel. I will make all the enquiries I can, but you must understand I can't promise you any magic results. She has been sent to prison for three months. Magistrates don't like to think they have made mistakes, you understand?"

"But you will do something. Find out why this has happened; above all, find out who the men were who Meggie Proctor brought to the house that night, frighten it out of her, anything so that my . . . Miss Mulholland will be freed. And I know this much now, she won't be free until I learn the name of one of those men. This is the second time he has harmed her, and it's worse than the first. . . ."

"Wait, wait." The solicitor lifted his hand. "You mean she knew who the man was whom this Proctor woman brought to the house? She had seen him before?"

"Yes."

"And she never told you his name?"

"No. Would I be asking you now?"

"But it is strange that she did not tell you his name, after telling you so much. . . ."

"Not at all. She was afraid of what I might do to him. He, this man, he gave her a child when she was but a child herself. As I understand it, he was the cause of her marrying the man, Bunting, who was killed by her father because of his treatment of her."

"Yes, yes, I know all about that, Captain."

Andree drew his chin in, then, leaning forward over the desk, he said softly, "Well now, sir, you've seen her, so you'll know she's not capable of doing what she has been impris-

226

oned for. She's a fine woman, a wonderful woman, and she has suffered much. This last is beyond her endurance, and I am afraid of what it will do to her; so you see how important it is that you move quickly."

"I will do all I can, Captain. Leave it to me. How long do you expect to be away?"

"Ten days, a fortnight. A fortnight at the most."

"I may have some news for you when you return."

Andree drew in a sharp breath and repeated, "May have? I want news!"

"Yes, of course. And I can assure you we'll do our utmost for you." He stood up and extended his hand. Andree took it, then made for the door, and Mr. Hewitt accompanied him, and again assured him that he would give the matter his special attention.

As Mr. Hewitt returned to his office he beckoned his clerk to follow him, and once he was behind his desk he looked at the tall man standing at the other side, and it was with some pride in his voice that he said, "You remember the Mulholland woman who was put away for three months for procuring?"

"Yes, sir."

"He wants us to work on it. He is the foreign sailor who was mentioned in the case. You remember I said I thought there was some jiggery-pokery going on in that business, for if ever a woman proclaimed her innocence from the dock she did. You remember I said that?"

"Yes, sir, I remember distinctly."

"He seems a man of substance, Kenny. An educated man. Not all ships' captains are educated."

"I agree with you, sir. Are you going to take the case, sir?"

"Yes, Kenny. Yes. Yes, I've promised to do what I can. Not that I can see us getting her out of Durham before her time's up, but we may be able to clear up one or two matters that are of as much interest to me from one angle as to the captain from another. Did you know that this Mulholland girl had a baby when she was very young, and that she was visited by this child's father a few weeks ago, and that she hit him with an implement, splitting his brow open. And don't you think it strange, Kenny, that the incident of procuring should follow? Who, Kenny, could bribe the police? Not a poor man."

227

"No, sir. Definitely not a poor man."

"Someone of importance. A name behind them. Money. Gentry, Kenny, don't you think?"

"Yes, sir! Gentry."

"The captain would like to know this gentleman's name, and, Kenny, so would we."

"Yes, sir. Yes, sir. Indeed we would like to know his name."

"So that is what we will work on, Kenny, unearthing this very mysterious gentleman who resented so much being hit on the head with a candlestick."

The conversation between Arnold Hewitt and his chief clerk was serious; there was no hint of humour in it. It was only that the solicitor and his clerk were in the habit of discussing cases in this fashion.

8

It was in the middle of March when Andree brought his ship into the Tyne yet once again, and the usual berthing procedure was hardly finished before he stepped from her deck and on to the quay and hurried towards King Street.

Mr. Hewitt was awaiting him. He had word that Captain Fraenkel's ship was in, and he wasn't looking forward to another meeting with the blond giant, whose eyes would look at him with the coldness of frozen sea-water when he had to tell him how little progress he had made with his case.

He was standing on his feet to greet the captain, and he shook him warmly by the hand, and when Andree said the one word with which he usually opened these proceedings, "Well?" he raised his shoulder slightly and spread out his hands, then said hastily, "I'm sorry, Captain, I'm sorry. And I'm sorry for my own sake, too, because I hate to be baffled. But I'm afraid I must admit that I've come up against a blank wall on all sides. I've learned nothing. . . . Well, I won't say nothing exactly, but what I have gleaned has led us to just another blind alley, I'm afraid."

"Well, what did you learn?" Andree's voice had a bitter edge to it.

"That one of the men, the particular man who visited Miss Mulholland that night, was not of the town. He left it on horseback."

"Did you find out where he stabled his horse?"

"Yes, but nothing further, except perhaps . . . that he was gentry. And that places an armour plate against the wall, if you follow what I mean."

"I follow what you mean," said Andree grimly. "About the other. Did you arrange that I could see her?"

Mr. Hewitt lowered his head. "I'm afraid not, Captain. I feel very sore about this, but they would make no concessions. . . . If . . ." Mr. Hewitt now examined his fingernails, then drummed the pads of his fingers on the desk before going on, "If you had any claim on her—I mean legal—then it would have been a different matter, but as it is . . ."

"Did you find out if her brother had been to visit her?"

"We investigated that part of it, and I'm sorry to say that he hasn't."

"God Almighty!" Andree leant his elbow on the desk and dropped his head to his hand.

"And I have a little further news that might add to her distress. Her sister has passed away."

Andree's head jerked upwards. "Lizzie? Dead?"

"I'm afraid so, Captain. About a week ago."

"She is buried, then?"

"Yes."

"Where?"

Now Mr. Hewitt lifted his gaze from Andree's face and looked at his hands again before he said, "In the common grave. You see, I had no instructions."

Andree lowered his head on to his hand again and said, "No, of course not; you had no instructions." After a moment he rose, saying abruptly, "I will call in again before I leave. Good-day to you."

"Good-day, Captain."

Andree now made his way to Crane Street, and going swiftly up the stairs he knocked on Mrs. Robson's door. She, too, appeared to be waiting for him, for she opened the door immediately.

"It's you," she said. "Well, she's all right. I saw her, but she doesn't speak much; she's very quiet like."

"How does she look?"

Mrs. Robson cast her eyes downwards, then folded her arms across her stomach and moved her body back and forward two or three times before she said, "Well, what would you expect in a place like that? She doesn't look robust. She's peaked, thin; she's lost weight. She looks all eyes. They were big afore, they're like saucers in her face now."

It was a while before he said, "You took her some food?"

"Yes, but I couldn't give it to her. I had to give it to one of them wardresses. It seemed a waste to me, for I don't suppose she'll ever see the skin of a sausage."

"Did she get my letters? Did you ask her?"

"Aye, I did, but . . . but, you know, she never answered me, she just looked at me; stared like, funny like. She didn't even nod. I thought she hadn't heard me, but she could through the grid, an' so I asked her again, but she still just stared. Anyway, the time's running out fast now, it's only a couple of weeks off. Sometimes if they behave themselves they let them out a day or so early, so they tell me."

"There'll be one more time to go," he said as he handed her the money, and as she took it from him she said, "Aye, there'll be one more time, an' I'll be glad when it's finished. It's no picnic to go there; it gives me the willies."

He turned abruptly from her and went up the stairs, and outside the door he stopped and picked up the *Gazette*, then let himself into the house.

The room looked dim and it smelt damp. The furniture that had been brought back was set higgledy-piggledy around the place. He walked slowly to the bedroom, and as he looked at the wooden base of the bed he said to himself, "Poor Lizzie. But it is better this way, much better." His nose wrinkled slightly as he closed the door, for the human smell of Lizzie still pervaded the room.

In the kitchen again he stood looking around him. With Lizzie gone there would be no need for her to stay in this house, in this vicinity at all. Yet she would have to have some place to come back to, somewhere familiar. Would that be a good thing? Or wouldn't it be better to make a clean break altogether? But that would take arranging. He would want to consult with her as to where she wanted to live. Anyway, he would have this place whitewashed and scrubbed and papered, and everything shining for her coming back. He

230

would leave that to Hewitt—he would engage someone—but the place must be ready for her.

He sat down on a chair that was standing in isolation on the bare wooden floor and he said aloud, "Kaa-tee! Oh, Kaa-tee!" As he spoke he twisted the paper, that was still in his hands, until it split. What would this have done to her? He had no illusions about prisons, and he did not comfort himself with the thought that women would not be dealt with so harshly as men. The women they engaged to look after female prisoners were coarse dregs of humanity, sometimes lower than their charges, and it was clear to him that any air of refinement or difference, say beauty, such as Katie's, would be bound to bring the worst out in them, and all this, added to the rest, would leave its mark. He looked down towards his hands and smoothed the twisted paper as if he was smoothing her hair back, smoothing the beautiful skin, her face, the soft warm suppleness of her breasts and hips. As he stroked the paper into flatness over his knees he shook his head.

They'd had a great deal of amusement out of the weekly paper. He it was who had arranged that the *Gazette* be delivered to her every Saturday. Not only had he liked to read it when he came in, but the daily Telegraph sheet which they supplied and delivered free he considered a further source of interest for her.

She used to say to him that she got their money's worth of laughs out of the advertisements alone. Although she had read them over and over again she would laugh till the tears rolled down her face when he would read them aloud, giving a special intonation to certain words and interposing his own language here and there. "Come to the Albert House, 11 and 12 Market Street. Patronised by THE NOBILITY and GENTRY . . . Printed pine pattern all over Barege Long Shawls reduced from 22s. 6d. to 16s. 9d."

"South Shields Races. To be run for over South Shields Sands on Whit Monday . . . Bra! Bra! I shall enter *Orn*."

"Sailing to Hull. Great reduction of fares. First-class steamer *Neptune* leaves the North shore for Hull, every Saturday, two hours before high water. Fares: Best Cabin 4s.; second ditto 2s; Steward's fee, Best Cabin 1s. Do you hear? Horer De? Steward's fee only a shilling!" Oh, she had laughed and laughed. Would she ever laugh again?"

Andree found that he was reading the advertisements once more. "Old established family wine and spirit vaults. Old Highlander Inn, 11 King Street, South Shields. The best and cheapest in the trade."

Then almost below this was the advertisement that he could rhyme off without looking at it. It was printed in the shape of a wine glass and headed "The Tree of Dissipation".

THE
sin of
drunkenness
expels reason,
drowns memory,
diminishes strength,
distempers the body,
defaces beauty, corrupts the
blood, inflames the liver, weakens
the brain, turns men into walking
hospitals, causes internal, external, and
incurable wounds, is a witch to the senses, a
devil to the soul, a thief to the pocket,
the beggar's companion, a wife's woe,
and children's sorrow—makes man
become a beast and self-murderer,
who drinks to others' good
health, and robs himself
of his own!!
The
root of
all evil is
DRUNKENNESS!!!

He had always taken a drink after reading this one. His eyes moved wearily over the paper, until the name Crane Street caught his attention and he read: "For sale: Nos. 12, 13 and 14 Crane Street. These desirable, three-floor houses in close proximity to the docks for sale. Apply Tollet, Estate Agents, Fowler Street." Three times he read this before he looked around the room. What would happen when the houses were sold? What happened in England when houses were sold? Did they let the tenants stay on? He supposed so; there would be no reason for turning them out. They might raise the rent; but that didn't matter much, he would see to that. He looked at the advertisement again. Nos. 12, 13 and 14 Crane Street to be sold. If he had been at home in Norway and his wife had read these words she would have looked up immediately and said, "I wonder how much they're asking for them." And likely as not she would have added, "I wonder if Father's seen it." And he would have had to bite on his tongue to stop himself from saying, "Aw, Kristin, don't talk foolish. It's likely one of his; are not nearly all the advertisements his?" And she would have answered, "Why are you so bitter against my father?" To this he would have said what he had said to her before, "I'm bitter because he has grown rich doing nothing. He buys a house, repairs it, then sells it for twice its value."

The last time he had said words to that effect she had accused him of being jealous of her father's power. "You," she had said, "are a big man, but you have no power, only over your little boat. And you and she are at the mercy of a bigger power, the sea, so you are always small inside. Whereas, my father, who is not half your size, and whom you despise, he has power; he is a great power in the town because he owns almost a third of it. You have never given him credit for what he has accomplished. You forget that when he was a young man he started with one house, just one, and now because of his industry he is a great man, a powerful one. When you have power such as he you are afraid of no one, men large or small."

It was on that occasion he had said, "You should not have married; you should have stayed with your father."

He rose to his feet but he still stared at the paper. His father-in-law had become powerful in his town because he owned property, and he had started with one house. Unless you had power of some kind you got nowhere, you were nothing, you were trampled on. And you could not have power unless you had money. He had power, of a kind, but over his ship, over men, but he was only enabled to have this power through someone else's money. He had not enough money of his own to give Katie power, which for her would mean security, freedom from the malice of—unknown men. If she had come from a family of substance none of the things that had happened to her would have happened. Katie lacked security because she lacked power; she lacked power because she lacked money. How could he make enough money to bring power and substance to a woman like Katie, a woman who was badly in need of protection? When she came out of that place she would be in need of something more than his love, something that was going to stand by her when he was far from her.

He crumpled the paper between his hands. His father-in-law had started with one house, why not Katie? Why not indeed! *Why not!* . . . This much he could do for her. . . .

Fifteen minutes later he was standing in the agent's office.

Oh! they said. Yes, they were very desirable houses, 12, 13 and 14 Crane Street, but they were being sold as a lot, not separately.

"How much?" he asked.

Well, they were very desirable properties and they were going very cheap, three hundred and fifty pounds, and would bring in an overall rent of thirty-five shillings a week.

"You'll be hearing from me," he said.

As he walked towards King Street and the solicitor's office he took stock of his own capital. He had not three hundred and fifty pounds. All he possessed of his own was about two hundred, but his name was good.

Mr. Hewitt was surprised to see the captain again so soon, and when he learned of what he intended to do he said he would advise caution. "Property is at a low ebb, Captain," he said.

"Offer them three hundred," said Andree.

"What!"

"I said offer them three hundred."

"But Tollets are rather tough customers."

"So am I, Mr. Hewitt. I know all about the buying and selling of property. Have you heard the name of Petersen of Bergen? He is a Dane, but he's one of the richest, if not the richest in that city. He buys and sells property every day of his life. I happen to be connected with him; I know how these things should be done. Offer them three hundred. Tell them I am wavering between those particular houses and some, say, in . . . Find out where there are other empty ones and mention their names. I will call back this afternoon. I would like this business settled before I sail in two days' time."

"Ah! Captain Fraenkel."

"Never mind! Ah! Captain Fraenkel. In this at least I want you to move. Do as I say, Mr. Hewitt. Good-day to you."

* * *

Two days later, about an hour before Andree sailed, he signed a temporary notice of purchase to buy Nos. 12, 13 and 14 Crane Street for the sum of three hundred and fifteen pounds, and the name he signed on the paper, after laying a deposit of thirty-five guineas, was the name of Mrs. Catherine Bunting, known as Katie Mulholland. It was at his insistence that the signature was written thus. Also Mr. Hewitt was given strict instructions as to what he was to do with the agreement, or a copy of the same, whether fufilled or temporary, on the first Wednesday in April, the day when Mrs. Bunting would be free.

9

On the morning of Katie's release the sun was shining though the air was bitterly cold, and here and there, as if they had strayed from the pack on its way farther north, a snowflake glided down.

The big woman with the huge breasts looked at Katie as if she was loth to let her go, as indeed she was. She had not found such an outlet for her sadistic tendencies for many a long day, but do what she might she couldn't rouse this one to the kind of retaliation that might lengthen her sentence. Purposely now she led her down the stone corridor and through the sacking room where Jinny Fulton and her crowd were gathered, plying their needles. She led the way between stacks of hessian and piles of sail canvas, and almost to the foot of Jinny Fulton herself, and when Jinny cried out "Aw! Here comes Lady Go-Lightly to say goodbye to us poor creatures" she did not reprimand her. She only slanted her gaze towards her and twisted her lips into the semblance of a smile, which smile told Jinny that she had her permission to go ahead, and she went ahead. She thrust her arm out and drove the long curved steel needle she held in her hand through Katie's skirt and into her calf. Because of her petticoats only the point penetrated, but Katie screamed out and Jinny Fulton, putting her head back, roared; then, gathering a dobble of spit into her mouth and taking direct aim, she fouled Katie's skirt. The wardress stopped and, without reprimanding the prisoner who had committed the offence, said to Katie, "Wipe that off. You don't want to go out like that, do you?"

Katie had nothing with which to wipe off the filth from her skirt except her fingers; so, bending her knee, she rubbed the skirt against the stone floor, and this brought a howl of laughter from Jinny Fulton and those nearest to her. But all the women in the bag room didn't laugh. There were those that looked at the Mulholland girl with pity, and one here and there with admiration, for they knew that they couldn't have stood what she'd had to stand without doing murder.

"Tickle your Swede for me." This, followed by a mouthful of obscenities, seemed to push Katie through the door and along another passage and into a room where a woman sat behind a table. This granite-faced individual turned a book towards her, and after she had signed her name, which action seemed an offence to this woman as it stood out against a line of crosses, she was waved away.

It was as she stood at the wooden door and watched the tormentor of her mind and body slowly putting the key into the lock of the small inset door that she thought that her legs would collapse beneath her, that she would never have strength to step through the little door in the gate and into the world again.

But she was almost pushed into it because the door banged so quickly on her heels that it grazed the leather of her shoe. And then she was standing on the rough pavement of Stone Street, blinking. The light and everything out here was different. Her vision seemed blurred against this new light. She started to draw in great draughts of air but seemed powerless to move one foot in front of the other. The road, with its stone houses opposite the prison, was comparatively empty except for two carriages standing on the other side, and some distance apart from each other. Her mind took in the figure of a man leaving the farthest carriage; then from the one nearest to her she saw a woman alight and come running towards her.

It was the sight of Miss Theresa that seemed to give power to her legs, and she turned and walked quickly away from the black door.

"Katie! Katie! Wait, please." Theresa had gripped her arm and pulled her to a halt.

"Oh, Katie!" The two words were a condemnation of all

236

sin, and to them Katie answered in a strange voice, quite unlike her own, "Leave me alone."

"I can't, I can't. Come back with me. I have a room ready for you. Miss Ainsley will welcome you. You must break away from this degradation; look what it has brought you to." She cast her eyes swiftly up the high wall behind her.

"Will you leave me alone?" Still the strange way of speaking, slow, thick, quiet.

"No, no, I won't. I won't let you go back to that man. He has been the cause of your down . . ."

"Be quiet!" Now her voice changed; it was still thick but strong and harsh. "Don't you speak a word against him. Don't you, I'm tellin' you, for he's the only good thing that has happened to me. D'you hear? D'you hear?"

"Don't say that, Katie, don't. I can't bear it. I can't bear the thought of that awful . . ."

"Will you be quiet, Miss Theresa, else I'll say something I'll be sorry for later."

"No, I won't be quiet, Katie. I'll never rest until you give up this way of life. Look what it's brought you to. And not even a coat on your back. And just think where you'll end: filthy houses, foreign sailors."

Katie stared into the thin white face before her, and then with a seeming effort she lifted the top part of her body upwards and, her voice now coming low and bitter, she said, "The filthiest house, the worst sailors you could gather from any port, couldn't hold a candle to your brother, Miss Theresa."

Theresa stared back at her. Then, her chin moving downwards but her eyes still on Katie, she said, "What are you saying, Katie? My brother? You mean Bernard?"

"I mean Bernard, Miss Theresa."

"You mean Bernard has had something to do with . . . ?" Theresa again raised her eyes to the high stone wall. Then, looking at Katie, she moved her head quickly, saying, "No, no, Katie; you're mistaken."

"Your brother put me in there, Miss Theresa."

"No, no, Katie . . . I can't believe it. I won't believe it. How could he?"

Katie closed her eyes, then said, "Because I split his head open with a candlestick. I'm . . . I'm no prostitute, Miss Theresa. Never have been, nor ever will be. I live with a man

237

because I love him. One man, a sailor, a sea captain, a good man. But your brother and another man forced their way into my house with a woman who is a prostitute, and they wouldn't go out, and he would have come at me again and the same thing would have happened as before—I saw it in his face—and so I struck him with a candlestick. And from that day until New Year's Eve, when they came and took me away, I lived in dread of what he would do."

"It can't be, it can't be, Katie. In the court, you remember, those two girls, they said . . ."

"They said what they were told to say. I had never seen them in me life before, nor the men with them, but in the court that day I saw one of your brother's henchmen, Crabtree, from the mine. He was another keeker. And then in there . . ." She moved her head slowly backwards. "He even had them paid in there. There were letters come for me an' I never got them. There was food sent in, but I never saw it. If purgatory and hell is anything like that"—again she moved her head backwards—"I'm going to see that I never get there."

"Oh, Katie, Katie, what are you saying?" Now Theresa had one hand pressed against her cheek.

"I'm saying the truth. And now you can ask why, if I knew this, I didn't say it in court. Well, without asking I'll tell you. It was because . . . because I didn't want another murder done. If my man knew the name of the one who had done this to me he would have cut him up in slices." Katie's mouth was squared now away from her teeth, and she bent forward and repeated under her breath, "Cut him up in slices, Miss Theresa. Before this happened he begged me for his name but I wouldn't say; Miss Theresa, you take a message to your brother and tell him, just one more move like this and I let things take their rightful course. And it won't be through a court of law, where there's no justice for God nor man. Tell him that."

"Wait, Katie, wait." As Katie went to move away Theresa grabbed her arm; then, turning sideways, she looked at the tall man who was standing at the other side of Katie now, and she demanded autocratically, "What do you want?"

"I wish to speak to Mrs. Bunting, ma'am."

"Get yourself away."

"I'm sorry, ma'am; I'm here on business. I am clerk to Mr. Hewitt, solicitor, of Chapel & Hewitt. Would you read this letter, ma'am?" He was now addressing Katie, and he brought his body into a slight bow as he placed the letter in her hands.

Katie stared at the letter and at the man, then at the letter again. She knew the writing. It was Andy's, and slowly she ripped open the envelope and read, "My Kaa-tee. My Kaa-tee. The house is ready for you; I have seen to it. But first go with the clerk, Mr. Kenny, to Mr. Hewitt, who will explain things to you. My heart is so full I cannot make words flow, but when we meet again I will tell you all. You are my life, my Kaa-tee, even more than ever now. Know that I live for you. Take heart. Andree."

Her red swollen hands were trembling so much that she couldn't fold the letter in two and return it to the envelope. She looked at the tall man with the kindly expression and she said, "I am ready."

"Katie, I beseech you."

Katie, now looking straight into Theresa's distressed face, said quietly, "Give my message to your brother, Miss Theresa. Good-bye." Then, walking by the man's side, she crossed the road to the farther carriage. After assisting her inside, Mr. Kenny spoke to the driver, then took his seat opposite to her, and they set out for Shields. And all during the journey, during which Mr. Kenny tried hard not to keep staring into the beautiful, sad, sad face before him, his mind was in a turmoil of excitement. Rosier, then, was the man they had been looking for all this time. Mr. Bernard Rosier. Well, well. He knew quite a lot about Mr. Bernard Rosier, for Mr. Hewitt had handled transactions concerning his wife. She had been a Talford and very, very well connected. He had a memory for these things and knew that the now Mrs. Bernard Rosier had a cousin in Parliament—on the Tory side, of course. Moreover, she had a cousin who was one of the ladies-in-waiting to Her Majesty the Queen. But he also knew other things about Mr. Bernard Rosier. He remembered that he had been a bit of a rake in his early youth but had apparently settled down before his marriage and after, until his father died, when there were rumours of his wild ways coming to the fore again. He now owned racehorses and was a gambler, and from what he had heard only a few minutes ago he was also a trollop trailer, as many of his kind were, but apparently he was less discreet than most, and vindictive—ah, yes, cruelly vindictive.

Mr. Kenny had a strong desire at this point in his thinking to see Mr. Bernard Rosier get his just deserts over this affair of the woman sitting opposite, but he knew that he never would, at least not legally, because the name of Rosier was too important roundabout. He knew that Mr. Hewitt would confirm this, and strongly. Mr. Hewitt would never act as the stick to stir the midden in front of the Rosier mansion, but it was a pity—oh, a great pity. And on this point, too, Mr. Kenny thought his employer would concur with him.

Mr. Kenny was a reserved man, a man who could keep secrets—a necessary attribute to being a solicitor's clerk—but he was also a man who had a way with clients. It was part of his duty to put them at their ease, but now he found great difficulty in opening a conversation with the woman opposite. He felt that her past experience, her many past experiences, had put her beyond small-talk and generalities. Whatever he had to say to her must have point. He said, "Captain Fraenkel desired Mr. Hewitt to have your apartments redecorated. Mr. Hewitt left the matter in my hands. I have followed the captain's suggestions as near as possible; I hope the result will please you."

Katie moved her head twice before saying, softly, "I am sure it will." She had the desire to finish her words on the "huh!" of a laugh, for the transition from back there to this man with his smooth, ingratiating manner seemed unreal. Back there was real, but he wasn't. Yet he came from Andy.

Andy. She tried to recall his face, but his image went into a great pale, hairy blur. That's what had happened to her lately. At night when she tried to conjure him up, willed him to be real, the result was muzziness. But Andy was real, he was real and good. He was the only thing in her life that she could trust. She was going to ask him to take her away, as far from this area as possible, for there was nothing here to hold her any longer, only bitter memories. If she asked him he would do it. . . .

When, the long drive at an end, the carriage entered the Market Place she could not keep her eyes turned from the Cross where they had taken her that night and the woman had slapped her in the mouth. Did she but know it then, the woman had been kind. All she had done was strike her for screaming. She was to find that there were a thousand and one other ways to terrify a human being. To have someone stand looking at you unblinking for an unendurable space of time until you ate the beetle-strewn filth that was called food; and when your stomach revolted and you were sick, to leave you with it all over your clothes and not allow you any water for hours and hours. Oh yes, the woman who had hit her in the mouth had been kind.

Mr. Hewitt rose to his feet to greet her, and took her by the hand, and in a most courteous fashion he asked his clerk if it would be possible to get Mrs. Bunting a cup of tea, and Mr. Kenny replied, "Surely, surely."

Half an hour later, again in the carriage, and again in the company of Mr. Kenny, Katie was driven from the solicitor's office to No. 14 Crane Street. The street was comparatively empty and there was no one at the door when they arrived, and when they came to Mrs. Robson's door it was closed. But no one went past Mrs. Robson's door without her knowing. With Mr. Kenny behind her she mounted the stairs to her house. And there on the landing she saw the wooden table and bowl and bucket, but with a difference, for the table was standing on a rush mat, which covered the whole square of the landing.

Mr. Kenny, now bowing slightly towards her, handed her the key and she opened the door and stepped into her home, and slowly she looked around her, and Mr. Kenny also looked around him. He was very proud of his handiwork.

"Do you like it, Mrs. Bunting?"

"Yes, yes. Thank you. It's lovely." Katie looked from the white-washed ceiling to the wallpaper which had little bunches of pink flowers all over it. She looked at the table. It was highly polished, as were the chiffonier, the chest and the chairs. And lastly she looked at the bright burning fire.

Her eyes were moist as she turned towards Mr. Kenny and said, "You've been very kind."

"Oh, ma'am, it's nothing. It's been a pleasure." He had his hands joined in front of him and he bowed his head several times over them as he spoke. "I hope I can continue to be of service to you. Anything you would like to know you have only to call on us. As you know, ma'am, Mr. Hewitt emphasised this."

"Yes, yes, he was very kind to me. I . . . I can't quite take it all in yet."

"No, no, I can understand that, but you will have grown used to your new position by the time the captain returns, which should be, we estimate, in about four days' time."

"Yes." For the first time the skin of her cheeks moved into what might have been the semblance of a smile.

Mr. Kenny now pointed to the cupboard and said, "The captain gave me a list of the food he thought you would need. I hope you find it adequate for the time being."

"Thank you; I'm sure I will." Katie followed his gaze to the cupboard. Then she looked at him again, and after a moment of silence between them he said, "Now I must take my leave, but believe me, Mrs. Bunting, we will always be at your service, any time."

"Thank you, Mr. Kenny."

"Thank you, ma'am." He held out his hand and she took it; then, with seeming reluctance, he made his departure.

Katie sat down in the chair near the table. She hadn't been in the bedroom yet. She would need to get her breath before she could go in there. She looked at the long envelope she still held in her hand and she muttered aloud, "Oh, Andy! Andy!" What he had done for her should have made her grateful, but for weeks now the main thought in her mind had been that once she got out she would get Andy to take her and Lizzie away—away from this dreadful place, the Tyne, this place that her mother had loved, and Joe still loved; this place they had condemned her to because of their love. . . . And now, inadvertently, Andy had condemned her to it for a further period, for he had bought her three houses. This room where she was sitting, all this house, and the other two down the street were hers. She just couldn't take that in, not as yet; it was too much. Her, an owner of property. But inside this envelope was a copy of the transaction. Andy had done this for her. Yet at the moment it was bringing no grateful response from her. She seemed dead inside; the only thing she was still alive to was fear. There was terror in the depths of her, and she felt it would always be there as long as she stayed in the vicinity of Greenwall Manor and Bernard Rosier.

And her fear must have spoken aloud from her face, for Mr. Hewitt had seen it. He had said the captain was a very discerning and wise man. He believed that the surest way to climb above fear was on the back of power, and the only way to acquire power was through gold; and one of the quickest ways to get gold these days was to buy and sell property.

But would the acquisition of property obligate Big Bess? She could almost feel the wardress standing in front of her, her great bust touching the front of her dress, saying, "You're frightened, aren't you? What you frightened of?"; then making a swift movement with her hand and digging her nails under her chin, saying the while, "Keep your head up. Keep your head up, an' open your peepers. What you frightened of?"

She looked down at the long envelope on the table. Power! If she'd had power she would never have been subjected to Big Bess; if she'd had power somebody would have found out that those two policemen and the girls were lying. If she had been a child of people of power Bernard Rosier would never have dragged her into his bed; she would never have married Bunting; and her father would never have died. . . . But if she'd had power in any form she would never have met Andy. Somewhere, somehow, there was a reason for all she had suffered. . . . Perhaps it was a kind of payment for Andy. And Andy had given her power. As Mr. Hewitt said, Andy was wise; he always knew what she needed. If she was to remain in this town—and it seemed that God, or whoever ruled destinies, willed that she should—then she wouldn't live like a rat . . . a mouse was a better description, a mouse in a hole, a frightened mouse.

There was a side of her that hated her fear, hated being afraid, but had never been strong enough to tackle it, but now a weapon had been put into her hands. She lifted up the envelope and ran her fingers along it, and again she said, "Oh, Andy! Andy!" And now there came a great swelling into her chest and she knew what this meant; it meant that all the unshed tears of weeks that had damned themselves up were striving to bust forth and drown her in a paroxysm of grief under which she might well lie for hours, even days. But it mustn't come yet; there was something she had to do first. Before she even ate anything she wanted to be clean. She would go down and get some water; she would get lots of water and heat it and wash herself. She needed to be clean as much as she did the morning after the ball.

She stood on the stairhead hesitant to pass the doors down below, hesitant to meet the curious gazes, wondering what they would say. Did it matter? No! Not any more. Mrs. Robson had been kind in coming to see her and she would thank her, but she guessed that she had been thanked in a more substantial way by Andy. She guessed that without payment Mrs. Robson would never have come all the way to Durham, but nevertheless she would thank her.

She made three journeys up and down the stairs, but the doors remained closed. Later, after she had washed herself from head to toe, her hair included, she began to wonder why Mrs. Robson, who she could hear moving down below, had not come out to give her a word. She just wondered, but it didn't really matter, for the dam of her emotions was breaking down.

* * *

It was some days before it was brought home to Katie why Mrs. Robson had not visited her. You don't visit the landlord. The tenants of Nos. 12, 13 and 14 Crane Street had been issued with new rent books, and had been told that their landlord was now Mrs. Bunting, known as Miss Mulholland. This occurrence had been a nine-days wonder in the street.

Katie Mulholland was now a landlord, she was one of . . . THEM. From someone who had done time, and was to be pitied, even scorned and shunned, she had now leaped the chasm to the other side, where lived the nobs, gentry . . . and landlords. You had to watch your p's and q's when landlords were about; you had to keep your nose clean when landlords were about. Half a word and you found yourself out on the street. That was landlords for you. But when you had one living at the top of the house—well, it wasn't playing the game. Landlords had no right to live in the same houses as their tenants. But poor people couldn't do much, could they? You couldn't do much against . . . THEM.

So it was that "Katie Mulholland's houses" and power came into being.

BOOK III

Theresa
1880

1

Joe heard the knocker-up starting at the end of the long street. He had been awake with the cold for some time, and he eased himself gently from his wife's back so as not to waken her and, getting swiftly out of bed, he pulled on his socks and trousers, then groped his way quietly out of the room and down the narrow passage into the kitchen, where he lit the lamp, got the fire going and brewed a pot of tea.

The table was set for his breakfast, with two mugs standing apart. These he filled with tea, and, lifting one up, he took a gulp at the scalding liquid. There was neither milk nor sugar in it; only at tea-time did they have milk or sugar in the tea —one or the other, never both. He now took the other mug of tea to his wife. Shaking her gently by the shoulder, he said, "Come on, Mary; have a sup tea."

"O-o-h!" She turned on to her back, then pulled herself upwards, keeping the clothes under her chin. "It's worse," she said.

"Aye. There was ice on the water in the back."

"Will you go in and look at them, and see that they're covered up?"

"Aye . . . aye. I'll see to them."

He now went out of the bedroom, and two steps across the narrow passage took him into another bedroom. It was black dark, but he groped his way knowingly to the first bed where his daughters, Lucy and Bridget, were lying, their bodies curled into each other, and tentatively he touched a shoulder, then tucked the bedclothes around them. Now, moving around the foot of the bed, he groped his way to his son's bed, and when his hands touched the cocoon-wrapped body

247

in the middle of it he smiled to himself, then made his way out of the room and to the kitchen again.

The shrill wail of the half-past five buzzer made him hurry into his coat. He went into the bedroom again and, bending over Mary, he touched her shoulder and said, "I'm away, lass." And to this she replied, "Aye, all right." Another pat and he went out of the room, leaving the house and joining the mass of dark shapes all making their way to the shipyard.

As he often did, even first thing in the morning, he reflected he had a lot to be thankful for—a good wife, three bonny bairns, and a steady job. He usually closed his mind to the shame of Katie; he had never met her since the day she had thrown him aside for the Swede, nor did he want to meet her. To the rest of Jarrow she might be the kind Mrs. Fraenkel, who had started a soup kitchen and presented boots to the poor bairns, as she'd be doing any day now Christmas was coming on, but to him she was still his sister Katie who had brought shame on the family.

His mouth was set in a grim line as he entered the boiler shop, and it remained so all day. It even grew tighter when, around four o'clock, a tall, dark young man in grey overalls, with his face and hands looking startlingly clean, came and stood by his side as he rammed home the rivets joining two curved steel plates; and when the young man bent and shouted something to him he pretended he couldn't hear him above the din. He also pretended he was unaware of John Hetherington's approach and couldn't hear him either when he shouted, "Mr. Rosier says that's a neat job, Joe."

Neat job! What the hell did he know about it. Whipper-snapper. He wasn't against them up top, in fact he'd go all the way for old man Palmer, but this one—well, this one was different.

He saw the young man again that evening when he was leaving the yard with his father-in-law. They watched him hurrying across the road, the tails of his broadcloth coat flying, and when he disappeared beyond the pale light of the gas lamp John Hetherington chuckled and said, "An' I don't have to guess twice what's putting wings to his feet. Aw, but he's a nice young fellow that, one of the best. There won't be much to worry about Palmer's yard in the future if there's fellows like him at the top."

"There might be a lot to worry about if he's anything like his father." The words were out before Joe could stop them,

and John, jerking his head at him, said, "Ah, now, Joe, that's
unfair. It's not always like father like son, an' you well know
it. Admittedly, from all I hear, his father's no good; but,
from all I know from experience, there's a lot of good in the
son. I know men, Joe, from top an' from the bottom. I've
been workin' with them for over fifty years an' I've never
met a more civil one than young Mr. Daniel. An' I've always
thought it strange, Joe, that you've never had a good word
for him when he's come round the shop. You must realise
that he's learnin' the business, an' that's the way to do it—
spend some time in each shop. He could have gone to Oxford, so I understand; but no, he wants to learn about ships,
so he does it the hard way, an' the right way. He'll likely be
managing a yard one day, an' he'll know what he's managin'.
An' you know what I heard? He's only gettin' two pounds a
week during his trainin'. Only two pounds, mind."

"He'll doubtless make up for it later."

"Aw, don't use that tone, Joe. What have you got against
the fellow, eh? Tell me, what have you got against him?"

"Nowt, nowt."

"He's just a young lad, an ordinary young lad; he can't
help being born under a different set of blankets. Did you see
him runnin' like mad to the station there? That's 'cos he's
dashin' to get ready to go to a dinner to meet a lass he's
sweet on."

Joe turned his gaze full on his father-in-law, and there was
a twisted smile on his lips as he said, "You are funny, you
know, John."

"Funny!" John, too, was laughing now. "Why should I be
funny 'cos I take an interest in him? I'm happy when people
are happy. Young Mr. Rosier has his eye on a bonny lass
who's stayin' at the Charltons, an' I'm happy for him."

"How d'you know this?"

"Aw, Betty told me all about it at the week-end. Didn't
Lucy say anythin' about the company?"

"No, an' I didn't ask her."

Joe had John's niece Betty to thank for getting Lucy, his
thirteen-year-old daughter, into service at the Charltons. He
had been pleased that his daughter would be under Betty's
care, because Betty was a staid woman in her forties; but
there was one thing he had stood firm about, his Lucy wasn't
sleeping in. Nobody, except Mary, could understand why he
wouldn't let Lucy sleep in, because going daily meant her

catching the carrier's cart at seven o'clock in the morning and riding the two miles to the house, which lay in the country, and not getting back until seven o'clock at night. But no daughter of his was sleeping in; he'd had a sister once who slept in. And then John had asked, What had he against a Rosier? But then he didn't know the ins and outs of that part of the story.

John now said, musingly, "An' I understand that the young lady's a real bonny piece."

"Do you think they'll ask you to the weddin', John?"

Again they were laughing; and then Joe said, "Are you comin' in for a minute?"

"No, no. Do you want me to get me head in me hands from her mother for keepin' the tea waitin'. You should have more sense than to ask, lad."

"Good-night then. See you the morrow."

"Good-night, lad. Aye, see you the morrow."

Later that same evening, when they were all sitting round the fire after their meal, and there had come a pause in Lucy's chattering, Mary, raising her eyes from her sewing, without which she never sat down in the evening, now looked at her son and asked, "Anything excitin' happened at the works, Tommy?"

And Tommy, his stockinged feet on the fender, his toes wagging at the soothing warmth from the fire, nodded his head and said, "Aye, a woman died."

"Died?" Joe turned his head and looked down on his son. "How?"

"I don't know. She just took bad and they carried her out an' then they sent for her man."

"Was she old?" asked Mary quietly.

"Oh aye, she was old." He nodded again. "Nearly as old as you."

On this Joe put his head back and laughed; then he put his hand out towards Mary and said, "There, old woman."

Mary was trying not to laugh as she looked at her son. "Do you think me that old?" she asked, and he, grinning back, answered, "Well, you know what I mean, Ma; she wasn't young like."

"Don't make it worse, lad." Joe gently cuffed his son's head, then said, "About the woman. She died straightaway?"

"Aye, that's what they said. They said it was the lead; she was working in the paint shop. One of the other women said

250

she had been bad a long time, she had been covered over with great red lumps and she was always faintin' like."

It was a few minutes after this that Mary rose quietly from the group and went out of the room, to be followed shortly by Joe. He found her standing in the cold bedroom. There was no light and he could just make out the dark blur of her against the street lamp on the other side of the road. "What is it?" he asked quietly.

When he was near to her she turned and said, "Get him out of that, Joe; it's nearly as bad as the lead works. He'll get it on his chest, and he'll never get rid of it. Can't you get him a start in the yard?"

"Not for three days a week, lass. An' any road, it's too heavy for him in there as yet: But I'll see what I can do later, when he's finished with school. Now don't worry. Come on, it's freezin' in here; you'll get your death." He put his arm around her shoulders and she leant against him for a moment as she whispered, "I'm frightened. I'm always frightened that he'll catch somethin'."

"We're in God's hands."

"Aye, yes, I keep tellin' meself that, but it doesn't help much."

"Now, now, Mary."

They moved out into the passage together, but before they reached the kitchen he took his arm away from her, and as they entered the room Lucy was saying in ecstatic tones, "Oh, she's lovely! Beautiful! An' her aunties dote on her, an' they're nice an' all. I like Miss Rose better than I do Miss Ann, though."

"What do they call her?" It was Bridget speaking. "I mean the one that's knockin' on for that Mr. Rosier."

"Oh, they call her Sara. Not Sarah—you know, like Sarah Coffin down the street; no, Sa-ra."

Joe had stopped just within the door, his eye on his daughter. There was a sound like an explosion in his head and he was immediately lifted backwards into a garden where two women were always trotting about, and whenever the young one got the chance she would talk to him, and always about his sister's lovely baby.

"What's the matter?" Mary, who had seated herself again, looked at her husband, and Joe, with a slight shaking movement of his head, muttered, "Nowt. Nowt." Then, coming and taking his seat by the fire, he looked at Lucy and said,

"You were talkin' about the visitors. What did you say they called them?"

"Miss Rose an' Miss Ann, and Miss Sara."

"Are they as old as your mother an' all, Miss Rose and Miss Ann?" He made himself smile, and they all laughed; and then Lucy said, "Oh, Da, they're older than me ma, much, really old. But you should see how they go about, like linties. Miss Ann's ever so spry, an' she's as straight as a ram-rod, but Miss Rose is delicate like."

"And they've got their niece with them, you say?"

"Aye, Da. Miss Sa-ra, I was tellin' Bridget here, not Sarah; they don't speak it like that, they say Sa-ra."

"Is she old an' all?"

"Oh, Da!" Lucy pushed him with the flat of her hand. "No, an' she's lovely. Oh, she is lovely. She's got great big eyes, the biggest I've ever seen, like saucers."

Joe, bending forward to push a live cinder under the grate, closed his own eyes. Eyes like saucers. God in heaven! No, no, it couldn't be. This couldn't happen. He straightened up and after a moment he said quietly, "What's their second name?"

"Chapman. Chapman, Da."

Joe had to force some spittle down his throat before he could ask, "What are they there for? Is it an engagement do or somethin'?"

"No, Da." She laughed at his ignorance. "They wouldn't have an engagement party at the Charltons, they would have it in their own house."

"Where do they live?" asked Joe now.

"In a place called Dorset. It was there that Mr. Rosier met Miss Sara. He was down stayin' with relations of his mother's and he bumped into her, and it turned out that they both knew the Charltons 'cos at one time they had lived outside Bishop Auckland—I mean the Chapmans had. Mr. Rosier's a great friend of young Master Wills. An' that's how it started, Auntie Betty says. This is the second time the Chapmans have been here in the last year, but Miss Sara's been about half a dozen times; she's supposed to be visitin' Miss Alice, they're best friends. Eeh, it's a laugh, 'cos Mr. Rosier and her are off out on their own every minute they can. Aunt Betty says the master and mistress are pushing it 'cos they think the Miss Chapmans are two old goats." Lucy hunched her shoulders and giggled, and Tommy and Bridget giggled with her.

"Aunt Betty says it's a marvel Miss Sara's allowed to come on her own 'cos the Miss Chapman's have a Mr. Spencer all lined up for her; he's a minister with money, not like them round here." Again she giggled, but glanced at her father apprehensively. She knew she had to be careful when talking about the clergy, her da was funny about things like that. She went on in a less excited tone now: "Aunt Betty says Mr. Rosier works in the yard and is ever so nice. She says they're not on top like they used to be, the Rosiers, because at one time they had a pit, but the old man, his father, is a bit of a terror with drink an' that. But he's all right, young Mr. Rosier. . . ."

Joe, with a big intake of breath, rose abruptly to his feet and went out of the room, and Mary's eyes followed him.

Lucy, after a quick glance at her mother, stopped her prattle until Mary, getting up, said quietly, "Go on. Go on, it's all right." Then she too left the circle.

When she entered the bedroom it was she who now asked, "What is it?"

It was a minute or so before Joe answered. "That family she's talkin' about, the Miss Chapmans, don't you remember?"

"Remember what?"

"Well, I told you, didn't I, years ago, about our Katie's bairn and the people who adopted it. They were called Miss Chapman—Miss Ann and Miss Rose. An' the bairn was called Sarah."

"Well, isn't that funny, now!"

"Funny? There's nothin' funny about it, woman." His voice was low and harsh. "If it happens it'll be a sin unto God, and it mustn't happen."

"But, Joe, what . . . what are you talkin' about?"

"Use your mind, woman. I told you about our Katie an' who the father was, didn't I? Old Rosier. Me ma told me. I told you it all."

There was a silence between them now as they peered at each other through the deep gloom; then Mary let out a small sound and she followed it with, "Oh no! No, Joe! Oh, no! They're practically brother and sister."

When he turned from her and walked to the window she said to him softly, "You'll have to do somethin'. You'll either have to go an' see him—Mr. Rosier—or your Katie."

Quickly he turned again and muttered thickly, "I'm not goin' to our Katie's, nor am I goin' to him."

"Well, what are you going to do, Joe? You can't let this slide, you know you can't; it's a sin afore God, and nature. What you goin' to do?"

Joe didn't know what he was going to do. But, as he had said, he certainly was not going to see their Katie, nor yet was he going to speak to young Rosier. That would be a fine thing, wouldn't it, to go to a man and tell him he was courting his half-sister. My God! Oh, their Katie! The things she had done, having the bairn, marryin' Bunting, and that alone had caused his father's death—and he carried the shame on him yet. And then there was her spurning of him. Not till the day he died would he forgive her for that. He had thought the world of her and had been willing to work the skin off his hands for her, and what had she done? Brought home a man as soon as she was left alone for a day or so, and she had openly, brazenly, made her choice. And Mary thought he should go and see her. She didn't really understand how he felt. You couldn't expect her to. But one thing was certain: whatever was to be done about this business it would be done without him clapping eyes on her. He never wanted to see her again as long as he lived.

2

In the fourteen years that had passed since the day Katie became the owner of 12, 13 and 14 Crane Street many changes had taken place in her life, and also in the town. The latter had spread itself far beyond the confines of the river. An 1827 map had shown wide stretches of open land between the town and the parishes of Westoe and Harton owned by a certain Mr. Cookson, who in 1837 began the manufacture of sheet glass, but with the years Shields had encroached upon this land until now Westoe village, although clinging tenaciously to its aristocratic bearing, was no longer a separate entity but a suburb of Shields.

It was said that the better part of Shields was full of wor-thy people, but once a man wanted prestige he moved to Westoe or Harton. Here were to be found the owners of shipyards, foundaries, glass-works, breweries, coal-mines, quarries, pipe factories, soap factories, candle factories, pottery factories, bankers and property owners.

The really big houses stood back from the roads guarded by their high stone walls and stiff shrubberies, and titles weren't unknown in this quarter. The not so ostentatious but still grand houses were in rows or terraces, each house being of a different design, some being taller than others, some having porticoes over their front doors, and most having gardens with hedges to screen their lower windows from the public gaze, from the strollers who came in from Shields, to walk under the trees and gape at their betters, or watch the gentry riding in their carriages.

Trees lined the roads, from which they were separated by white wooden railings, inlet at intervals to make a carriageway to the gates or doors of the superior dwellings.

Here and there you would find a small house called a cottage, which might have six to eight rooms. In 1880 Katie Mulholland, known now to some as Mrs. Fraenkel, had bought six so-called cottages and had recently purchased a much larger domain in which she was considering taking up residence. Not that Mrs. Fraenkel wanted to move into the heart of the élite, for she had been happy in her present home in Ogle Terrace for the past eight years; and Ogle Terrace, one of the best of the residential quarters in South Shields, had proved test enough to a woman who had made her money by buying tenement houses that lined the river; houses that were known by her name, Katie Mulholland's houses. And by the conduct of the occupants of her houses she had further gained an appendage to her name which was nothing to be proud of, but against which she was powerless to defend herself, for did she not live on the money she received in rents? Moreover, as was whispered in some parlours, did she not live openly with a Swede, and, whisper softly, had she not been in prison through running one of her houses as a place of infamy.

But for all those whispers Katie Mulholland was now a power in the town, albeit a self-effacing power, but nevertheless a power to be reckoned with, through her rent man.

Her entry into Ogle Terrace eight years ago had caused a stir. Not even the fact that a permanent member of her household was a Rosier brought recognition; no one in the immediate vicinity called on her, nor did they speak to her when they passed her in the street when alone or walking arm in arm with that outlandish-looking man. Yet there were those who called frequently who were of some standing in the town. One was Mr. Hewitt, the solicitor. Of course his visits could be connected with business, for no one ever saw his wife call. Then Mr. Kenny, his chief clerk; he was never away from the door. And there was Doctor Leonard; he called twice a week, sometimes three times, but, as the charitable said, he went to visit Miss Rosier. Yet it was strange, wasn't it, that the visitors to Mrs. Fraenkel's house should all be male ones. The only women who ever were seen going in and out were Betty Monkton, the cook housemaid, and Mrs. Bucks, the daily woman, and at intervals Miss Rosier; but she only went for short drives and was rarely seen outside the house.

That was another mystery. Why should Miss Rosier, the daughter of Daniel Rosier, who at one time owned the Beulah mine, be living with a woman as notorious as Katie Mulholland, a one-time procuress. Of course it was known that Miss Rosier—who wouldn't be called Mrs. Noble—was odd, hadn't she left her husband? But, all the same, that didn't stop her from being a lady. The situation was past understanding. . . .

At times Katie herself thought it was past understanding how she had come to be living with Miss Theresa, or, what was more correct, how Miss Theresa came to be living with her. Yet it had all come about so slowly, so simply, quite differently from the way Betty Monkton had come to live with her. That had all happened in the space of an hour, and she had done it off her own bat, with no promptings from Andree.

On a bleak raw day she was getting into a cab outside Mr. Hewitt's office when she saw a woman staring at her; the face was familiar, and with a shock Katie realized that the poorly-clad half-starved-looking creature was Betty Monkton, her one-time playmate. When she smiled at Betty, Betty smiled back, saying in awesome tones, "Katie, it's you. Why, lass, I'd never have known you."

To get into the cab and drive away after this would have been like a slap in the face to the woman, but Katie wanted to get home, and if she dismissed this cab it meant crossing the market square to get another, and she hated the market square; for even after fourteen years the sight of the market square brought a terror into her stomach. So she said, "I'm glad to see you, Betty. . . . Look, come home and have a cup of tea with me."

It took Betty a few seconds to take in the invitation, and once in the cab she became silent. It was only after being warmed with a meal that Katie learnt of her plight. Her mother had died and her father had taken another wife who didn't want Betty in the house. There had followed years of changing lodgings, intermittent work and illness.

Katie hadn't at that time lived in Ogle Terrace, but her home was in a respectable quarter of the town. It was a six-roomed terrace house topped by a large attic and to Betty Monkton it appeared like a palace. When she rose to take her leave, Katie had said to her, "I'm looking for someone to do the work, Betty; I go out quite a bit. I . . . I buy property."

"Aye, aye, I heard something about it, Katie." Betty had kept her eyes cast down as she spoke, and Katie said quickly, but quietly, "I don't know what you've heard, Betty, but that's all I do. I buy property, and let it, and I live here with Captain Fraenkel."

"Just the one bloke, Katie?" Betty had asked tentatively.

"Just the one bloke, Betty. There's only ever been him, and that's how it'll always be. If you want the job it's yours."

"Aw, Katie. Aye. Oh, an' thanks, lass. Thanks. You won't regret it. I promise you I'll work me fingers to the bone for you just for a decent roof like this."

And Betty was as good as her word. It became one of Katie's tasks to try to lighten her work, but all Betty wanted to do was to show her endless appreciation by making things comfortable for Katie and her man. . . .

It wasn't until Katie moved to Ogle Terrace that Theresa came to live with her, but she had appeared on her horizon again some time before this.

It happened that one day, about a year after Betty had taken up her post in the house in Bentley Terrace, she answered a knock on the door, then went to the parlour where Katie, or ma'am, as she had to keep reminding herself to call her mistress, especially when the captain was about, was sitting with the captain drinking their after-dinner coffee, and she said, "There's a lady at the door, ma'am, called Miss Ainsley and she says she'd like a word with you."

Miss Ainsley. A name from the past. The smile had slipped from Katie's face and, bending towards Andree, she had whispered quickly, "I only knew one Miss Ainsley. If she's the same, she was governess to Miss Theresa. . . . You know?"

"Oh!" Andree's bushy brows moved upwards and he turned to Betty, saying, "Well, show the lady in, Betty. Show her in."

Miss Ainsley came in. She was a woman now in her sixties, but she could have been eighty. Katie would never have recognised Miss Ainsley from how she remembered her, nor would Miss Ainsley have recognised Katie Mulholland from her memory of the beautiful, bright-eyed, lively girl. The woman before her was still beautiful, but her eyes were no longer bright and dancing, they had a permanent sadness behind their level gaze; and the demeanour of this woman was sedate, even lady-like, which was surprising. Only her voice, when she made her greeting, indicated her upbringing.

After Miss Ainsley had taken a seat and refused a cup of coffee, and definitely a glass of wine, she explained the purpose of her visit. "Would Mrs. . . . ?" She hesitated on the name until prompted by Andree saying, "Fraenkel, Mrs. Fraenkel." Then she went on, would Mrs. Fraenkel be so good as to come and see Theresa, who has been very ill for many months now and who, the doctor said, hadn't long to live? Theresa had expressed a wish to see her.

Katie had looked at Andree, then back to Miss Ainsley. She didn't want to go and see Miss Theresa, even if she were dying, nor did she want to come into contact with any one of the Rosiers, for such contact would undoubtedly renew the nightmares that had subsided, the nightmares that had been filled with Bernard Rosier's face, interspersed with those of Big Bess, Bunting and her father. No, she was sorry, but she didn't want to see Miss Theresa. She had been about to say this when Andree had asked, "What is the matter with her?" and Miss Ainsley had replied, "She has bronchial trouble, and a very weak heart. She had pneumonia last year when she was in a low state. It was the strain of running the school; it was too much."

"You still keep your school going?" Andree asked.

"No, no longer," Miss Ainsley replied. "I . . . I had a fall some years ago, and then when Theresa took ill everything became difficult."

Andree had nodded at her, then looked at Katie, and she, after gazing at him, waiting for him to prompt her and not receiving any help, said softly but pointedly to him, "I'll go if you'll come with me."

"Of course I'll come with you." Andree turned to Miss Ainsley and added, "That will be all right, won't it?" And Miss Ainsley swallowed deeply before she replied, "Of course."

And so the following day Katie, accompanied by Andree, and a basket of fruit, took a cab to the little house on the fringe of Westoe, and there they were both appalled by the bareness and cheerlessness of the interior. Andree had waited downstairs, in a room that had been used as a schoolroom, while Miss Ainsley took Katie upstairs to the living quarters, which were hardly more cheerful than those downstairs, and had ushered her into a small bedroom, saying, "Theresa, dear, here is someone to see you."

Since Miss Ainsley's visit the previous evening Katie had been filled with embarrassment and apprehension at the thought of this visit, but after the first glimpse of the thin, emaciated figure lying propped up in the bed her embarrassment fled. She even forgot for the moment that this woman was connected with the Rosier family. Going slowly forward, she spoke as the old Katie would have done, saying, "Hello, Miss Theresa. I'm very sorry you're ill."

"Hello, Katie." The words were broken by short, sharp breaths. "It's . . . it's so good of you . . . to come."

"Take a seat, Mrs. Fraenkel." Miss Ainsley pushed a chair near to the bed, and Katie sat down, and for a moment she was lost for words. Nor did Theresa speak immediately, but when she did she said, "You're looking very well, Katie."

"Thank you, Miss Theresa."

Another silence, a shrieking silence, until Theresa said softly, "Are you happy, Katie?"

"Yes. Yes, very happy, Miss Theresa." Katie kept her eyes full on Theresa as she said this, and Theresa moved her head slowly twice before saying, "Yes, I can see you are. Ainsley tells me"—she took in two or three short breaths—"that you are still with . . . with your friend."

"You mean Captain Fraenkel, Miss Theresa?"

"Yes, Katie. Captain Fraenkel . . . Ainsley likes him. She . . . she says she found him . . . very charming."

There was gratitude in Katie's eyes and a soft smile on her

lips when, after a moment, she said, "Thank you, Miss Theresa."

"I'm glad you're happy, Katie. . . . Can you believe that?"

Katie continued to look full at Theresa as she said, "Yes, yes, I can."

Theresa now began to pull at the edges of a small handkerchief she held in her hand as she said, "Ainsley tells me you have a beautiful home, Katie."

"It's comfortable, Miss Theresa."

"And . . . and I understand you have become prosperous?"

"You could say that, too, Miss Theresa."

Now Theresa pressed her head back into the pillows and gazed up at the ceiling before she said wistfully, "Life . . . life is very odd, Katie. You know, I . . . I remember Ainsley and I once having a discussion about you that . . . that bears this out."

"Discussion about me?" There was surprise in Katie's voice, for even at this stage of her life she couldn't imagine the daughter of the Manor bothering herself to talk about the scullery-maid with her governess.

"Yes, we were sitting on the hill behind the house, you know, discussing chance and circumstance, among other things, and Ainsley said that . . . that if you had money together with your beauty you . . . you would conquer the world, or words to that effect. . . . And now you are doing just that, Katie. In spite of all the terrible things that have happened to you, you are conquering the world. . . ."

"Oh! Miss Theresa, that's far-fetched; an' . . . an', if you don't mind, I'd rather not talk about the past in any way. It's . . . it's better left alone."

"All right, I won't, if . . . if you don't wish me to, Katie."

As Theresa now began to fight for breath Katie said softly, "I've distressed you, Miss Theresa. I'm sorry."

"Oh, no. No. It's just . . . just my chest. You couldn't distress me, Katie; you would never distress anyone. I . . . I know that, not willingly. . . . That's why I asked Ainsley to go to you. I felt I just wanted to . . . to see you once again. You don't mind?"

"No, Miss Theresa. No, not at all." There were tears in Katie's throat now, forming a hard block, and she was endeavouring to keep them from her eyes, so she stood up and said, "I'll be going, Miss Theresa. I mustn't tire you or Miss

Ainsley will be after me, but . . . but I'll come in again if you'd like me to." And to this Theresa said simply, "Please do, Katie."

And that's how it had begun. No one expected Miss Theresa, least of all herself, to last more than a few weeks at the most, and during those weeks Katie became a regular visitor, sometimes accompanied by Andree, and she never came empty-handed. She always brought with her a basket of delicacies, mostly cooked by herself.

Whether it was the good food, or the new interest in her life, Theresa did not pass away, but as the time went on she grew a little stronger, until one day, some months later, she was downstairs when Katie called. And on this particular day she met the captain for the second time, and they stared at each other for a space before he, bowing to her, said simply, "Ma'am." And she, returning his greeting with a dip of her chin, said, "Captain . . . Captain Fraenkel." After which they shook hands. And such is the strangeness and contrariness of human nature that these two, whose interest in life was pointed in the same direction, became firm friends and were to hold each other in deep respect until one of them died.

But there would be weeks on end when Theresa couldn't leave her room. Then one day Miss Ainsley was found dead in bed. A policeman came and informed Katie of this, and she drove immediately to the house, there to find Theresa fighting for breath against the shock that had come upon her. So what could she do? Leave her there unattended in the house with a dead woman?

When Katie brought Theresa into her home she had no intention whatever that it was to be a permanent arrangement, and she said so to Andree when, three days later, he came home from his short trip to the Thames—he was now running coal to London for Palmer's—and he agreed with her heartily. Of course it would just be a temporary arrangement.

Theresa's presence in the house had a stultifying effect on Katie when Andree was at home. When she found herself laughing loudly with him, which she did with no one else, she would check her mirth, knowing that Theresa could hear them from upstairs.

But Theresa's presence had no such effect on Andree. He breezed in on her and laughed at and even teased her, and at times talked to her as he never did to Katie. He talked to her on matters that made headlines in the papers, both world-wide and local: on Disraeli, on the Colonies, on what she thought of John Broughton being made Mayor of Shields for the second time; what she thought of a public library being opened, and the new hospital called the Ingham Infirmary; and wasn't it a marvellous thing that they had elected a school board in Shields; and he agreed with her that even a child of the lowest people should be taught to read and write. On and on Andree and Theresa would talk, and Katie would sometimes sit and listen, but more often she would be busying herself with the particular meal that she knew Andree liked and seeing that Betty hadn't forgotten anything from the table.

Then one night Andree said to her, "You know, my mind has been easier during these last few months than it has been for years. I can get into my bunk and go to sleep now knowing that there is someone with you."

"But," she had protested, "I've got Betty with me!" and to this he had said, "Betty is a good woman, but she's an untutored creature and you'll never learn anything from Betty."

It was then he told her of an idea that had been working in his mind, an idea that would make Theresa feel less under an obligation, and which would accomplish something he had always desired for his Kaa-tee, an education. He would ask Theresa to tutor her.

But what, asked Katie, would she learn? She could read and write; she could reckon like a ready-reckoner; she was a good cook . . . he himself had said so. She could look after a house; she could sew.

In between stating each of her homely accomplishments he had kissed her gently, and to each he had said, "Who better? Who better?" And then he had told her what she could learn. She could learn all Theresa knew, for Theresa was a highly intelligent woman. And also, he ended, "It'll bring me joy, Kaa-tee, to know that you are learned."

And that was how Theresa became a permanent member of Katie's household; and that was how Katie's education came about. That was why Katie Mulholland, who was known to have kept a bad house, who had been in prison, who had begun life as a scullery-maid, and whose father was hanged for murdering her husband, puzzled people when she spoke, even as a lady did, grammatically and without any trace of dialect, merely the inflexion of the Northerner betraying her. That was why Katie Mulholland could play the piano, speak French moderately, could paint on glass, and do tapestry.

And not once did Andree recall his first opinion of Theresa. Never did he say, "She's a man under the skin"; he knew that she loved Katie, but he also knew that Katie was solely his. Theresa's love he now accepted as a compliment to his taste. . . .

The new arrangement also filled a need in Katie. Over the years there had been not the slightest sign of her having another child, and so Theresa, who needed care and attention, became a substitute for Lizzie, for Sarah, for the children that didn't come. She would tell herself at times that her home was complete, she had a family; she had Andree; she had Theresa; and not least she had Betty; Betty in the kitchen with whom she often sat before the fire late at night, when Andree was away, talking of the old days. Betty made her laugh. Betty was full of the old sayings, of which Theresa knew nothing, and which were a foreign language to Andree. She had, she thought, the best of all worlds. . . . But not quite.

Never once from the moment he had left her fourteen years ago had she set eyes on Joe, and at times there would come into her body an ache to see him, because Joe was her real family, blood family. He was her only flesh left. She did not think of her daughter in this case—she tried not to think of her daughter at any time now.

She still missed Andree just as much now when he was away on his trips as she had done in the early days. Sometimes, if he came in on the late tide, he would walk home and surprise her; that is, if he came into the Quay at Jarrow. But if he docked at Sunderland he slept on board during the night and came down by train in the morning.

It was Andree who had given her everything she had in life. She did not know exactly what her own bank balance was, it fluctuated; she only knew that during the last fourteen years seventy odd houses had passed through her hands. Some she had bought and sold within a short time, and always at a profit; others were bringing in steady rents.

She was known as a wealthy woman, and she knew she could carry herself in almost any company, thanks to Theresa. But all this was a veneer, for she also knew that just below the surface she was still the product of her early environment. She was still the child who had emptied slops into the wooden buckets in the maid's rooms and carried them down the long stairs and by the green wall to the midden; she was still the girl who had suffered at the hands of Bernard Rosier and Mark Bunting; she was still the woman who had been in prison; and she knew that if she lived to be a hundred she would always be, inside, what her early years had made her. The rest was a façade, a pleasing façade that gave pleasure to Andree and which protected her with a thin armour against the power of men.

This particular evening she had been to Jarrow, to a church hall where once a year, near Christmas, she distributed money and clothing to the barefoot children. The occasion always saddened her, and made her feel strangely alone. And so when she returned home and saw Andree's big bulky form and grizzled head at the door she sprang over the threshold and into his arms, crying, "Oh, how wonderful! When did you get in? I didn't expect you until tomorrow. Oh, I wouldn't have . . ." Her words were cut off by his kiss, and with his arm about her he said softly, "Come in here a moment, I have a visitor."

"A visitor?" She screwed her eyes up at him, and he nodded as he drew her into the little breakfast room to the right of the hall. Once inside the room he shut the door; then, putting his hand up to her hat, he said, "Come on, take your things off quick."

"But why? Who is it?"

"My . . . my brother."

She was laying her hat on a chair and her hand became still, and with her body slightly twisted away from him she turned her head slowly towards him, saying, "Your brother?"

"Yes."

"But why? After all . . ."

"I'll tell you later. Now I just want you to meet him."

"Was he here when you arrived?"

"No. No, he was waiting for me in the yard. He, too, is a captain. . . . Let me look at you." He held her by the shoulder at arms' length; then, his eyes roving over her, he said, "Yes, yes, he'll see; he'll see the reason."

"Oh! Andy, let me go and make myself tidy."

"Tidy!" He flapped his hand before her face. "You're beautiful—why do you want to be tidy?" He leaned towards her now and gently touched her lips with his.

"Andy, I feel, I feel . . ." She pulled him back as he drew her towards the door. "I feel awkward . . . afraid."

"Afraid? Nonsense! He's the one who'll be awkward; he's a bachelor, a rover. Come."

The man who stood up when they entered the room did not resemble Andree in any way, except in height; he was tall but he was thin, and his fairness was not the stark fairness of Andree; his face was round and almost clean-shaven except for a little hair on his chin. He had deep-set eyes, a big nose and a full mouth. Although his face was straight, even stern, when he first looked at her, Katie's immediate impression of him was that he was kindly.

"This is Kaa-tee, Jon." He led her forward by the hand, then said, "My brother, Kaa-tee."

They shook hands and the man said, "Pleased to make your acquaintance, ma'arm." His voice had a thick sound; his English was not as Andree spoke it. He stared at Katie, his eyes not flinching from her. They seemed to bore right into her, asking a question.

"How do you do?" Katie said, and then the three stood awkwardly for a moment until Andree, with his deep bellow, cried, "We must have a drink. Come on. Betty's got the meal ready."

"She has?" Katie turned and smiled at Andree, glad that she could find something to speak about. "Oh, that's good." Then she added, "Have . . . have you been up to Theresa?"

"Yes, and I took Jon up. He likes her." With his doubled-up fist he punched his brother in the arm, and Jon said something rapidly in his own tongue, to which Andree replied; and then they both laughed before Andree, turning to Katie, said, "I'm sorry. No more foreign chatter; he can speak English. He was just saying to me that he would marry her if she could speak his tongue."

"Nor. Nor." Jon shook his head, and, his face serious, he turned to Katie and said again, "Nor. Nor."

Katie smiled and looked at Andree. Andree seemed excited about something. He generally acted like this when something was disturbing him. It was one of his odd ways. When he didn't want her to be troubled he would, as her granda used to say, act the goat.

The suspicion that there was something unusual afoot deepened as the meal proceeded. Andree had usually a large appetite and would often take a second and third helping of the main course, but tonight he waved all offers of second helpings aside. Another thing she noticed was that he gave his brother very little chance to talk to her. At times she would find Jon's eyes on her, their expression keen and pene-trating, but he would always look away when she returned his gaze.

She was surprised when, almost immediately after the meal, Jon said he would have to be leaving, and she was equally surprised when Andree offered no argument for him to stay.

She did not know whether she liked Andree's brother or not. He was a disturbing factor coming out of Andree's past, the past that she had thought dead. Not for years had he mentioned his wife or family, or his home in Norway, and never had he mentioned his brother and sisters from that night when he had explained his background to her and showed her the photographs. It was as if he had buried them all before he left that far country. But now one was resur-rected, and why? That was the question she was asking her-self as she stood in the hall and said goodbye to Jon.

When he politely shook her hand and thanked her for her hospitality, she said simply, "Will you come and see us again?" And after a moment, during which he flashed his eyes towards Andree, he made a motion with his head before replying, "Yes, I would like zat. When I am in zis port I will come and see you again." And now he smiled at her. It was the first time he had smiled at her, and she smiled back at him. And then he went to the door and Andree went with him, and when they began to speak in their mother tongue she walked back into the parlour.

A few minutes later Andree joined her. He came in slowly, no laughter in his face now. He came straight to her, put his arms about her and hugged her to him once—he did not kiss her—then, taking her by the hand, he went to the couch that stood at right angles to the open brick fireplace and, sitting down, drew her down beside him.

"What is it?" she asked. The anxiety was in her voice, and he turned his head slowly and said, "Now, Kaa-tee, this mustn't worry you. I tell you this mustn't worry you, but I'm going home tomorrow."

He had said he was going home. For fourteen years she had been his home—not this port or this house, or the other places they had lived in, but she had been his home, his country. He had said so. She made a small movement with her hand; her lips fell apart but she couldn't speak.

"My . . . my wife is ill, really ill this time, she . . . she has asked to see me, she asked Jon to come and ask me to go back . . . just to see her. . . . Don't! Don't look like that, Kaa-tee; it means nothing. I would never live with her again. You know. Aah!" He screwed up his face and the point of his beard stuck out. "Do I have to tell you? No. No, I don't. After all these years. No. In all your bones and flesh you know there is only you. But . . . but she is ill, dying, and wants to see me. For what purpose, after all these years, I don't know. But people are funny. I always say that people are funny. Jon says he really thinks she is dying, but Kristin has thought she was dying many times before; yet if she is really very ill and I don't go and she dies, I—well, I'm funny too, I would have it on my mind. But, Kaa-tee, there's no need for you to worry, because I will be back. What am I without you, eh? How could I live without you? You know all that. Come. Come." He patted her face, first one cheek then the other. "Say something. You know what I say is right. We cannot exist one from the other, so why do you worry? Kaa-tee, Kaa-tee." His voice now dropped deep in his throat.

"Andy, I'm . . . I'm frightened. I . . . I can't help it, I'm frightened."

"Why? Why?" He now pulled her into his arms and pressed her tightly to him, and she muttered into his neck, "You'll never be able to realize what you mean to me. . . . You can't understand. . . ."

She now felt herself being pushed almost violently from him. "I don't understand. . . . Don't talk like a stupid woman, because you're not a stupid woman, so don't talk like one. I do understand. I also understand my own feelings." He now thumped his chest. "Why do I not take long voyages, me who loves the sea, the deep sea? Why do I scuttle up and down this dirty river? . . . I do not understand? Oh, Kaa-tee."

"I'm sorry, Andy." She shook her head slowly. "But . . . but I can't help it. I . . . I'm afraid. You're all I have in the world, all I want in the world; I'm afraid of losing you."

She said this simply, and quietly, and when his hand came on to her hair and stroked it gently as he gazed into her eyes she whispered, "How are you going to get there?"

"In Jon's ship."

"But what about yours?"

"I will fix that tomorrow morning. I have never asked the Palmer company for any favours since I started with them and I've never missed a trip in thirteen years. They will put someone on in the meantime; if they don't . . ." His big shoulders moved upwards. "There are other companies. But I don't worry; they will be amenable. In any case, whether or no, I go to Norway tomorrow, Kaa-tee."

"And you don't know when you'll be back?"

"As soon as possible . . . as soon as possible. When I get there and see how things are, if I am not returning immediately I will send a letter by the first boat that's leaving for this part."

One minute she was seeing him, the next minute he was blurred by a mist of tears. She closed her eyes tightly but the tears welled from her lids, and when her face was smothered against him she saw herself on the black picture of her mind, alone, entirely alone. Andree was going back to Norway to his real family. It would be too fantastic to imagine that he hadn't over the years had that lonely longing, that emptiness that spoke of the yearning for family, and his need would have been greater than hers, for he was of a large family . . . and there were four children of his flesh.

And now he was going to his family. But, as he had said, she should know him, she should know that he couldn't exist without her. . . . Would he say it yet again when once he was reunited with his family? The picture in her mind showed him surrounded by four beautiful children—she had forgotten for the moment that they would be grown up now. She only knew that she was frightened of him meeting his children, meeting his wife. She couldn't throw off the feeling, and in this moment there seemed a link between Joe's rejection of her all those years ago and Andy's going now. She wanted to cry to him, "Don't go. Don't leave me. I can't bear it." But she didn't, for she knew that he had definitely made up his mind to go, and when he made up his mind to do something he did it. Had he not made his mind up to live with her?

268

3

Theresa was resting on a couch set at an angle to the fire. To the right of her was the window, with a border of snow mounting against the bottom pane. It had been snowing for two days and all the outside world was white. She stared towards the window while her hands rested on the top of an open book on her lap, and she wondered if Katie had gone out. It was twenty past ten, and if she was going to do a reading she nearly always came up around ten o'clock.

Katie, she realized, was very worried over Andree, and she had reason to be, for anything could happen when he saw his wife and family again. . . . He might never return. . . . Did she want that to happen? Oh no! No! Never. Many times, before she had really known him, she had wished him dead, but life did queer things to you. After fitting you out with the wrong interior it fought you with your inner values, your inner codes, the values and codes that really belonged to another sex. The only right thing it did that you could thank it for was having given you the power to hide your pain, at least most of the time. But she was in no pain now, not mentally; her life was so pleasant, so calm, so beautiful at times that she became fearful that she might not die before it changed. Yet from where she was placed now she couldn't see it changing much, she would always be with Katie. Now she had the power to hold herself in check and not demand anything, not even ask for a minute of her time; she would always be with her. . . . And Andree? She had thought she would be with him too, right to the end, but now she wasn't so sure. It came to her as no surprise the gap that would be in her life if Andree were not to come back, because between her and this huge, grey, bearded Norwegian had grown a kind of rapport; it was a feeling that was deep and strong and had grown through silences and things left unsaid rather than said. Never had she thought she would like any man; never, even in her most reasonable and objective moments, did she imagine herself coming to like Katie's man; but in the depths

269

of her dual nature she realized that if she could have loved a man it would have been a man such as Andree Fraenkel.

Andree she had found an intelligent man and surprisingly well-read for a sailor. Looking back, she saw that she had been brought near to him almost in one leap when he suggested that she should instruct Katie. She came to learn that it was almost an obsession with him that Katie should talk and act like a lady.

At one time she had been pleased that he was only in the house a day or so each week, but this feeling had also passed, for she now looked forward to his coming home nearly as much as Katie did. . . . Not quite, and not, of course, in the same way. But when she heard his hearty laugh from the hall below she always felt herself smiling, and her eyes turning towards the door.

Life was strange. You set a course for it, and when one day you found it had taken the opposite direction you accepted its diversities and said simply, "So be it."

Would Katie be able to say simply "So be it" if Andree didn't come back? No; she would pine and die—that is, if she didn't do something desperate straightaway, for this thing that existed between her and Andree was of an immensity that would be beyond the understanding of most people. But she herself had no need to fathom the reason why a man of the world, as Andree was, should leave his wife and family, his apparently wealthy wife, and cleave to a girl who had known nothing all her life but the humilating dregs of labour.

And now he had gone back to visit his wife. It was too early for word from him yet, for only three days has passed, but already it was as if the house had gone into mourning for his loss.

There was a step on the stairs, but it was only Betty. She came into the room carrying a scuttle of coal, and such were the times and the easy-goingness of the house that she spoke before she was spoken to. "By, miss, we soon won't be able to get out the front door. Mr. Kenny says there's drifts waist high round the market, an' it's not made any better by them shovellin' it off the roads."

"Mr. Kenny is here, Betty?"

"Aye, miss." Betty dumped three big lumps of coal on the hearth of the glowing fire. "He's with . . . the missus in the study."

"He usually comes on a Saturday morning." Theresa spoke as if to herself, but Betty replied in a confidential manner as she twisted round from the hearth towards the couch, "He's come about the new house. Goin' there, I mean. Won't it be grand livin' in Westoe. Eeh, by!" She shook her head. "Wonderful, Ka—the missus says it's a fine house with a big hallway as big as wor—our dining-room is now, an' she says she'll get a new range in the kitchen for me. . . . An' what d'you think?" She moved forward on her knees. "She says there's a room just off the kitchen and that she'll have it fitted up like a sittin' room for me 'cos I'll be like a housekeeper. What do you think of that, eh?"

Theresa smiled kindly. "Oh, that'll be fine for you, Betty."

"As for you, Miss Theresa . . . Aw, your room's right on the ground floor and leadin' out into the garden."

Theresa's face became straight. She understood that there was nothing settled about the house yet, whether they would move there or not, but apparently she had been mistaken. She felt a little piqued that Betty should know more than she did.

Betty, with the quickness of her kind, sensed this and, raising her eyebrows and putting her hand over her mouth, she said, "Eh, me mouth's like a pithead, I shouldn't have said a word. The missus was gonna surprise you like. She'll want to knock me inta the middle of next week when she knows. Don't let on Miss Theresa. Don't let on, eh?"

Theresa now smiled conspiratorially at Betty and said, "All right, Betty, I won't."

As Betty went down the stairs she shook her head as she said to herself, "Eeh! Ye have to be so bloomin' careful." But it would never do for Miss Theresa to think that Katie confided in her. It would upset Miss Theresa, and she didn't want that because she was a nice lady, and poorly.

It was almost half an hour later when Katie came up to Theresa's room. Her face was white and her eyes looked tired as if she hadn't slept much. She sat down near the fire and poked it before she said, "I'm sorry I haven't been up before, but Mr. Kenny came."

"On Friday?" said Theresa. "It isn't his usual time."

"No, he came about the house." Now Katie turned towards Theresa, saying, "I don't know what to do. I told him so. I've told him I'm going to leave it for a while. I . . . I didn't tell him why, of course."

"Of course," said Theresa; but she added, "It'll be all right; he'll be back for Christmas."

"Christmas is less than three weeks away."

"Well, he'll be here before then, you'll see."

Katie gave a small smile and impulsively put her hand out and patted Theresa's; and Theresa didn't clutch at it and hold it to her as she wanted to, she just said, "Let's do some reading . . . that's if you're not going out."

"No, I'm not going out until after lunch."

"Good. I thought we might start on the third volume of Lord Chesterfield's *Letters*; there are fewer French translations in this one, but . . ."

"That's something to be thankful for."

"Oh, Katie." Theresa was smiling tolerantly. "You know that the letters have helped you considerably. I . . . I thought you'd like to do a translation so I've started on page twenty-nine. He's explaining the different kinds of governments." She handed the book to Katie at the open page, and Katie, after looking at it for a while, took in a deep breath and began to read:

> *"Letter Two hundred and twenty-eight*
> London, June 11 O.S. 1750.

My dear Friend,
    The President Montesquieu (whom you will be acquainted with at Paris), after having laid down in his book *L'Esprit de Lois* the nature and principles of the three different kinds of government, viz. the democratical, the monarchical, and the despotic, treats of the education necessary for each respective form. His chapter upon the education proper for the monarchical I thought worth transcribing and sending to you. You will observe that the monarchy which he has in his eye is France."

Katie drew in another breath, and looking towards Theresa said, "Do you want me to try it in French or write the transcription?"

"French, of course."

"It looks so difficult, there are so many big words."

"Go on with you." Theresa flicked her hand upwards; her voice was that of the teacher.

And so Katie began the French version, and when she hesitated Theresa said, "Go on, go on, that's excellent. Your French is as good as mine."

"Oh, nonsense." Katie shook her head; then, putting her hand flat on the book, she appealed to Theresa, saying, "Let's leave it this morning, it's such an effort to concentrate. I . . . I want to talk, Theresa."

"All right." Theresa put out her hand and took the book from Katie's lap. "Talk all you want, my dear."

Katie turned from Theresa and looked into the fire. She felt tired, so tired, but she must talk, pour out all her fears. She had walked the floor in the middle of the night, and had gone to the kitchen around five and made herself some tea. She was still there at half-past six when Betty came downstairs and exclaimed in surprise, "Aw, Katie, lass, what is it? What's troublin' you?" And to her surprise Katie found she couldn't tell her. She could talk to Betty about the old days, she could laugh and joke with her, but she found she couldn't tell her that she feared her man would not come back. Yet, strangely, she could say this to Theresa.

"I've got a feeling on me, Theresa," she said, "that I'll never see him again; that I'll get a letter to say she needs him, his family needs him and he's decided to spend the rest of his days in his own country."

"Katie, look at me." Theresa's voice was sharp, and when Katie turned her head round she said, "You know Andree better than I do, much better, yet you can doubt him. I don't think for a moment that anything or anyone can keep him away from you. . . . You know"—she smiled sadly—"you don't know your own value, Katie, you never have; you don't know how you affect people." She didn't go on to say, "You don't know how you affect me, how you have always affected me"; she kept it general by adding, "Look at Betty, for instance, and Kenny, and Mr. Hewitt. Even take Albert Weir, with his cab always at your disposal—to the inconvenience of other people no doubt. Once people know you, Katie, they don't leave you unless they must. . . . Don't you realize that?"

"That's nice of you, Theresa. But you've just explained it . . . unless they must. She's his wife, and if she's ill and asks him to stay, even for a while, I feel he will. And once he gets a taste of the life he was used to amongst his own people —well, the pull will be too strong. . . . and then there'll be

273

the chance of being master of a big ship again because he really hates these little coal tramps, I know he does. I know, because of the way he laughs at them. And on top of all this there'll be his children. They, if nothing else, will hold him. It'll be too much."

"Not for Andree, Katie. Anyway, his children will no longer be children. Now listen to me." She bent farther forward and was about to put her hand on Katie's when Betty's heavy tread came to them from the landing. The next moment there was a knock on the door, and Betty came in holding out a letter, saying, "The postie's just come."

Before Betty was halfway across the room Katie had risen and taken the letter from her, but when she saw the envelope the light left her face, and, saying "Thanks, Betty", she stood scanning the unfamiliar writing.

"Not from Andree?"

She shook her head at Theresa. "No."

Almost casually she slit the envelope open and, unfolding the single sheet of paper, began to read, and when she was halfway through the letter and her hand moved unconsciously upwards and pressed across her mouth Theresa brought her feet from the couch and said, "Katie! Katie! What is it?"

Katie didn't answer until she had finished the letter, and then she seemed to have to drag her eyes from it to look at Theresa. And now she stared at her for a long moment until Theresa, getting to her feet, came to her and said, "What is it? You're sure it isn't from Andree?"

"Yes. . . . No, it isn't from Andree."

"What is it, then? Sit down."

"No, Theresa, I'm all right."

"Why do you look like that, Katie?" Theresa brought her brows together, and Katie could have answered at this point, "Because you're a Rosier."

"Is . . . is it something bad, bad news?"

"No, no." She shook her head. "It's one of those letters I —I used to receive years ago, you remember, accusing . . . accusing me of making money the bad way."

"Oh, Katie, look. Take it to the police. . . . Let me see it."

"No, no, Theresa." Katie pressed the letter in between her breasts. "I'll ignore it. . . . It's best that way." Then, without pausing for breath, she went on, "No, I won't, I'll . . . I'll

take it to Mr. Hewitt. But say nothing about it, Theresa, if
. . . I mean, when Andy comes back. Don't mention it, it'll
only make him angry."

"No, of course I won't."

"I'll . . . I'll go now to Mr. Hewitt. I'll see you later,
Theresa, at lunch. Goodbye."

"Goodbye, Katie."

Katie went quickly down the stairs, across the hall and into
a small room next to the morning room that she used as an
office, and there, spreading the letter on her desk, she read it
again, and her eyes seemed to lift each childishly rounded
word from the page. The letter began, "Dear Mrs. Fraenkel,
I am Joe's wife and I think there is something you should
know. I have tried to get him to see you but he won't, so I
think I should tell you. You see my daughter, Lucy, works
for the Charltons of Biddle Hall and knows the visitors who
come there, and she mentioned the Miss Chapmans, whose
names are Ann and Rose, and a young lady who was with
them called Sara, which we think is short for Sarah, and Joe
did not take much notice of her talking about these people
until she said that the young lady was courting young Mr.
Rosier, him that is in the yard learning the business, and then
Joe puts two and two together and he says that if these are
the same Miss Chapmans as had your baby then Mr. Rosier
is her half-brother and it shouldn't happen. I told him to
come to you but he is stubborn, but it is a sin before God
and I thought you had better know. Nobody knows here,
only me and Joe, and that's how it will be, but I felt I had to
write to you, and I think he wanted me to although he never
said. I am sorry to have to tell you this."

The letter ended quaintly, "I am, your obedient servant,
Mary Mulholland."

At one time there wasn't a day went by that she didn't
think of her child and that her arms didn't ache to hold her,
but she could never see her growing up. As time went on she
had to make herself visualise a child of six, seven, eight, nine,
ten. Gradually there had come periods when she wouldn't
think of her for days, or even weeks, and if she looked back
it was to tell herself that she was grateful for the pleasant
lines along which her life was now running. She felt she was
being compensated in full for all she had gone through. . . .
The black time was past and would never return. Never
could she be hurt like that again; nor could she be frightened

275

like that again, intimidated, made weak, even cringing. That part of her life was gone never to be resurrected. And now this.

Again and again she read the letter, telling herself each time that it couldn't be possible; it just couldn't be possible that the Rosiers were coming into her life again, bringing a trail of sorrow across it. Her daughter would be nineteen and a half now. How old was his son?

She herself was three months gone when Rosier married. His boy would be just turned nineteen. . . . How had they come to meet? How? How?

She beat her mouth with her clenched fist. What a silly question. Why had she never thought of this happening before?

For the simple reason she never knew he had a son.

She got to her feet and held her two clenched fists tightly against her cheeks and she moved her head desperately as she whispered, "One chance in a million!"

But when she came to consider, the odds weren't as great. This kind of thing must happen often. How many half-brothers and sisters married without knowing it? . . . But not hers, her daughter, and to a Rosier. . . . No! No! She had cried aloud, and now she brought her fingers across her open mouth and glanced towards the door in case her voice had attracted Betty. What must she do? If only Andy was here. But, oh! She shook her head. Thank God he wasn't, for he still didn't know who had fathered her child, who it was who had vented his spleen on her; and if it lay with her he would never know, because his wrath would be even worse than her father's. No, she had now to be thankful that he was away. . . . And there was another one who mustn't know about this, and that was Theresa. Every time Bernard Rosier had touched her life Theresa had picked up the cudgels for her, and the result had been disastrous. Besides which, Theresa was in no fit state to be worried; something like this could give her heart such a shock that she could die from it.

What must she do? It was evident that Joe would never have anything to do with her. Joe was hard, like granite.

Mr. Hewitt? She would go, as she had said to Theresa, to Mr. Hewitt; he would advise her, he always had.

Mr. Hewitt looked at her from across the desk after he had read the letter, and words seem to fail him. He felt increasingly concerned and perturbed about the whole situation. He had a keen sense of devotion to Miss Mulholland, a devotion that was no longer confused by having to handle the business of the Rosier family. Mr. Bernard had severed all business connections with the firm after the death of his father.

Looking back now, Mr. Hewitt was not sorry about losing the Rosier business, for he didn't relish the idea of representing a man like Bernard Rosier in any form; and by what he had since learned the account wouldn't have been worth much, for the family had gone rapidly downhill. Rosier, he understood, was now entirely dependent on the wife's allowance, while she, it was said, had forfeited her fortune on her father's death in favour of her son, and tied the money up so securely that her husband couldn't put his hands on it. All this apparently had transpired after Rosier had had a visit from his sister, Mrs. Noble, shortly after she had learned of Miss Mulholland's wrongful imprisonment. Her visit had, unfortunately—or fortunately—however one looked at it, been badly timed, as when she had demanded to see her brother he had been entertaining three gentlemen friends, and one, who had extra good hearing, was vastly entertained by what came to him when he pressed his ear to the communicating door. The county had laughed about Ann Rosier's reactions to her husband's misdeeds, but some had applauded secretly, for they knew this last item that had come to her knowledge was but the straw that broke the camel's back.

Ah yes, Mr. Hewitt was glad that he was no longer concerned with the Rosier family. But now, it appeared, he would have to contact the man, and about such a delicate, delicate matter. He didn't like it. He didn't like it.

"What am I to do?"

"Well . . ." Mr. Hewitt passed his hands over his balding head, blinked his eyes, adjusted his spectacles again and said, "Well, we have here, Mrs. Fraenkel, a very delicate situation to say the least." He stopped speaking and nodded at her—a small nod that gave emphasis to the fact he had just stated. "I . . . I had better give it some serious thought before I write to him . . . to Mr. Rosier senior." He moved his head slowly from side to side. "He'll have to be made aware of the facts." He paused while looking at her strained, troubled face, before going on, "By what you have told me, the young Mr. Rosier is still a minor, and, of course, he himself will have to be approached; but let us hope he is a sensible young man and will see the impossibility of the situation."

"It—I mean the matter—should be given your attention without delay, don't you think, Mr. Hewitt?"

"Ah, yes. Yes, Mrs. Fraenkel. But, as I've said, it's a very delicate matter and needs some thought. But I will send a letter to Mr. Rosier today, yet I must, as I said, think carefully of the wording." He smiled at her. "You can leave it to me to do the best in my power to ease the situation."

"I know I can, Mr. Hewitt. Oh, I know I can." She stared at him for a moment in silence across the desk, and then said, "As I was coming here this morning I , . . I wondered what I would have done without you all these years. The captain"—she always referred to Andree as the captain when speaking to her solicitor—"the captain set me up, but I doubt if the business would ever have been the success it is without you. I feel sure it wouldn't; I would have had those three houses and nothing more."

"Tut, tut!" Mr. Hewitt got to his feet and came round the desk, taking off his spectacles the while and wiping them again. "Tut, tut, Mrs. Fraenkel. Nothing of the sort. You have a business head on you; you have, as the saying goes, a nose for property. Even at the beginning, when you didn't know a thing about it, you had this acumen. I remember saying so to Kenny the day you came in about the property near St. Mary's, down in Jarrow Docks. That must have been at the end of 1866. It was a real bargain, that property; must have paid for itself three times over during the years."

"You are very good, Mr. Hewitt, so very good." She held out her hand to him, and he took it in both of his and shook it gently, and then asked, "The captain, will he be home for Christmas?"

Her lids fluttered just the slightest as she said, "I hope so." She did not explain that Andree was not on the usual trip but had gone to Norway; there would be plenty of time to tell him about this matter if Andy didn't come back. In an endeavour to keep everything normal she said, "Will we be seeing you over the holidays, Mr. Hewitt?"

"Yes, Mrs. Fraenkel, I'd be happy to call in."

"For dinner one evening, Mr. Hewitt?"

"Thank you. Yes, yes, indeed."

"Can we leave the date until later?"

"Of course, of course."

"Goodbye, Mr. Hewitt, and thank you. . . . You'll . . . you'll let me know as soon as you get a reply."

"As soon as ever I get a reply you shall know. I shall send Kenny to you immediately."

"You are very good. Goodbye, Mr. Hewitt."

He opened the door for her. "Goodbye, Mrs. Fraenkel. Goodbye."

In the outer office Kenny was waiting for her.

Kenny was an old man now, older than his years. His hair was a bleached white, sparse on top with a thick fringe around his neck and hanging over his collar. His long face was deeply lined and there was a perpetual drip on the end of his nose, at which he dabbed with a handkerchief while he talked.

"Mrs. Fraenkel." He opened the outer door for her.

"Thank you, Mr. Kenny."

"It's a pleasure, Mrs. Fraenkel. You're looking very well, if I may say so."

If Mr. Kenny saw Katie four times in a day he would have informed her on each occasion that she was looking very well. This was the second time he had seen her today.

At the outer door he smiled and bowed to the woman who had always addressed him as Mr. Kenny; who never forgot him at Christmas, and not just with a paltry half-sovereign, but with a substantial sum that made all the difference to the comfort of his chilly years. But even without the gift he would have been willing to serve Katie Mulholland.

4

It was on the day before Christmas Eve. Outside the house was a white, hushed world—the snow was packed hard on the ground and the fresh fall was adding to it—but inside

279

there was warmth and brightness, and the comforting smell of Christmas cooking.

Katie, coming from the kitchen, took off a large white apron that covered her blue corded velvet dress and hung it in a cupboard under the stairs; then, looking in the mirror above the gilt and marble hall table, she adjusted her deep lace collar, turned down the cuffs of her voluptuous sleeves and went towards the office.

Seated at her desk, she opened a secret drawer and took from it one of the two letters it held and read it for almost the hundredth time since she had received it ten days ago. It began: "Darling Kaa-tee," And went on;

"I arrived yesterday. Kristin is very ill. I feel bewildered at all I see. My children are grown up and married, all except my son. Everything is very strange, but all are kind and making things as easy as possible for me under the circumstances. I have so much to say, Kaa-tee, that can't write; but you know what is in my heart.

"There is a boat leaving tonight. I will give this to the captain; he will see you get it as soon as possible. Do not worry, Kaa-tee darling. The course is set; no wind can alter it.

I love you,
Andree."

"The course is set; no wind can alter it." What course? A new course that would hold him to his wife and family? Since she had first read them she could not get those words out of her mind. "The course is set." She felt sick to the heart of her—sick, lonely and frightened, and each day the feeling became intensified.

Then there was this other business. This in itself was awful, even horrifying. Mr. Hewitt had received no answer to his first letter to Bernard Rosier; nor yet to his second in which he asked for an appointment to discuss the matter. She knew that Mr. Hewitt saw Bernard Rosier's silence as a refusal to accept such a preposterous situation; furthermore, a refusal to admit that he had ever fathered the child. Mr. Hewitt had not said so openly, but had suggested that as an alternative he should contact the young lady's foster-parents and perhaps the association could be nipped in the bud from that side. . . . It would have to be. Mr. Hewitt had been emphatic about this.

And so she was waiting. Waiting for word from Andy, for word from Mr. Hewitt; and she was also waiting for something else. She would not admit openly to this secret waiting, for it concerned an old, deep longing. It went farther than her association with Andy, this waiting; this desire to look upon her one and only child. There was in her the hope that somehow through this business they would come face to face, and she imagined that once that happened there would be no more secret, lonely corners in her—Joe would not matter then.

She folded the letter and put it back in the drawer; then, getting to her feet, she walked slowly out of the office and into the drawing-room. Everything looked colourful and shining here. She was proud of this room. She had seen few other ladies' drawing-rooms in the town with which to compare it; but, even so, she knew that her drawing-room, with its French gilt furniture and strawberry brocade curtains, its sage-green carpet and fine pictures, was elegant. But without Andy what did it mean to her? Nothing. The room was dead without the great burly sea captain; the man who, although turned fifty, was still handsome and arresting. She could not imagine there would ever come a time when he would not appear handsome to her—this man who could make her love, who could make her forget everything, who was proud of her, and told her so; so much had he praised her she felt that if she hadn't any looks at all she must have developed them from his very insistence. She turned about and walked quickly out of the room and up the stairs to Theresa.

Theresa was sitting, as was usual, on her couch. Her face this morning looked very white; the eyes, dark and bright, lying in deep sockets, were turned towards the door. She, too, was waiting, and almost immediately she asked quietly, "Is there any news?"

Katie shook her head. "No, but there are two boats due in from Norway today. There could be a letter on one of them."

"Yes, yes, of course." Theresa nodded her head. "Don't worry. You know, Katie, I've got an odd feeling you'll hear something today."

"I hope you're right, Theresa." Katie forced a smile to her lips. Then, sitting down, she said, "Shall we read?"

"Oh, Katie." Theresa's hand came out and touched hers gently. "You don't want to read today, now do you?"

"I don't mind, I really don't. Everything's ready downstairs. It'll keep my mind occupied."

"No. We'll give it a rest. . . . Yet wait. There's something I'd like you to hear. It's at the end of one of Chesterfield's letters, I thought it was very amusing. Shall I read it or will you?"

"You read it; you'll do it so much better."

Theresa lifted up a book from her table and glancing towards Katie, said, "It was written in London, November 12th, 1750, over a hundred and thirty years ago. It's hard to imagine there were refinements in those days, but there were . . . Listen, this is what he writes to his son:

" 'My mentioning these particulars arises (I freely own) from some suspicion that the hints are not unnecessary; for when you were a schoolboy you were slovenly and dirty, above your fellows. I must add another caution, which is, that upon no account whatever you put your fingers, as too many people are apt to do, in your nose or ears. It is the most shocking, nasty, vulgar rudeness that can be offered to company; it disgusts one, it turns one's stomach; and, for my own part, I would much rather know that a man's fingers were actually in his breech, than see them in his nose. Wash your ears well every morning, and blow your nose in your handkerchief whenever you have occasion; but, by the way, without looking at it afterwards. There should be in the least as well as in the greatest part of a Gentleman les manières nobles. Sense will teach you some, observation others: attend carefully to the manners, the diction, the motions, of people of the first fashion, and form your own upon them. On the other hand, observe a little those of the vulgar, in order to avoid them; for though the things which they say or do may be the same, the manner is always totally different'."

At this point Theresa looked up and said softly, "You are not listening, Katie," and Katie, with a start, said, "Oh yes, yes, I am. He . . ." She smiled now and said slowly and distinctly, "He was advocating that one uses a handkerchief."

Theresa laughed gently. "Indeed, Katie, indeed." Then, leaning forward, she said, still more gently, "Don't worry." And now, her gaze dropping downwards, she added, "Will you believe me if I say you are not the only one who is missing him?"

Katie's eyes were moist and tender as she looked back at this frail woman who had brought so much disaster into her life, but she remembered, as she often did, that without having been the victim of that disaster she would never have met Andy. And she knew she would go through it all again if at the end she would be sure of meeting him.

Never before had she discussed Andree openly with Theresa. Through time there had evolved between them a mutual understanding with regards to him. It was as if Katie had silently suggested to Theresa that if she accept him she was welcome to stay. But now she said openly, "You like him?"

"More than I can say, Katie. You once said he was a good man, and he is a good man. If I'd had to choose a man for you it would have been a man such as Andree."

"Thank you, Theresa, thank you." Her hand was in the act of moving to touch Theresa when it became transfixed by a yell from downstairs, and they both stared at each other, their mouths and eyes spread wide before clasping hands for a second; then Katie was flying from the room as the voice filled the house, yelling, "Where is that woman? Where is that woman?"

She actually jumped from the third stair and into his arms, crying, "Andy! Oh, Andy!"

Their kiss was long and hard, and when it was finished they gazed at each other, then turned and looked at Betty, who was standing to the side, and they laughed at her and she at them. And then Betty said, "Eeh, Captain, Aa'm glad to see you in. You hungry?"

"As hungry as a shipload of emigrants, Betty. What have you got?"

"Everything, Captain. Everything. All you like. I'll have somethin' for you in a jiffy." She grinned broadly at them before turning and running to the kitchen.

"Oh, Andy. Oh, Andy." Katie was gazing up at him as, with his arms about her, he went to lead her to the drawing-room; but checking his step, and with his head back and turned toward the stairs, he yelled, "Hello there, Theresa. Be up aloft in a minute."

Once behind the closed door Katie said, "Let me take your things," but he, flinging his coat aside, cried, "Never bother with that. Come here." And again they were close.

When, a moment later, they were sitting on the couch she traced his bushy eyebrows with her fingers and, looking into the blue eyes that were as bright as the night on which she first saw them, she said, "I can't believe it. You know . . . I never thought I'd see you again."

"What!" He pressed her a little way from him and drew his beard into his chest. "You actually thought I'd never come back? No, Kaa-tee!"

"Yes." She closed her eyes and nodded her head in small movements. "Yes, I did. I thought that when you got back there, to your own country, and . . . and . . ." Her eyes widened now and became more misty, and when she couldn't go on he said quietly, "You still don't know me, Kaa-tee; after all these years you still don't know me."

"Oh, Andy, I do. But the pull, the pull of a family. I know what that means because I . . . I long for a family." She leaned her head against him now, but she didn't look into his face as she asked, "How did you find everything?"

It was a moment or so before he answered, and as he did so he lifted her hand and stroked each finger towards the nail. "She died a few hours after I wrote to you."

A stillness took possession of Katie's body, but at the centre, deep in the core of her, there was a whirlwind of feeling; hidden emotions, hidden desires were struggling to be free and swamp her with relief, with expectation, with the wonderful knowledge of what this could mean to her.

She clasped the stillness to her, the calm stillness, and let it come over in her voice as she said, "I'm sorry."

When he made no reply but continued to stroke her fingers she asked, "Was she bitter?"

"No, no." His answer came quickly. "That made it worse at the time. No recriminations, nothing like that. If anything she was full of remorse. But it should have been me. Oh yes, Kaa-tee, yes." He now bent his head and looked at her. "I should have been full of remorse, because it was not a good thing I did to her, or my family, but I couldn't help myself. You know I couldn't, could I?" It was a plain statement, not a question asking for support for his weakness.

His face now as he continued showed a deep seriousness. "We talked the day before she went; she wanted to talk. She . . . she wanted to tell me that she was sorry. It was very strange to hear her say she was sorry for all that had happened. She . . ." He swallowed deeply, then went on, "She said she should never have married me, that she wasn't the marrying kind. Some people are not, you know, Kaa-tee.

284

Some women should never marry." He touched her cheek gently and said hastily now, "Oh, don't cry, don't cry; it was not sad at all, not really. She had lived her life as she wanted to; she had her children. . . . You see, some women want children but not the man. Kristin was made like that. She would have been happy with immaculate conceptions." His mouth went into a wry smile now, but Katie's didn't answer it; she just dropped her head against his shoulder, and after a moment asked, "And the children?"

"Ah, yes, the children. You know, I had always thought of them like that . . . the children, forgetting that they were now men and women. . . . Do you know, I am a grandfather many times."

"Really!" There was a dull pain in her chest. "Were they happy to see you?"

"No."

She pulled herself up abruptly and stared at him, her face full of concern now. "But, Andy."

"My daughters were doing what one would have expected their mother to do they were blaming me. Oh! They were very polite, oh yes. 'How do you do, Father?' they said. They looked at this wandering captain who had left his family to live in another country, and they would have been perfectly happy, and felt so righteous into the bargain, if they could have believed I had left my little family starving. The funny thing is that if that had been the case, if they had been poor, I would never have left them, no matter what their attitude towards me."

"And your son? Did you see him?"

"Ah, my son! Yes, I saw him. He, too, was stiff—very, very stiff at the beginning. But you know, Kaa-tee"—he bent to her—"just before I sailed he came to the docks and spoke to me. He asked . . . what do you think he asked me? He wanted to know if, when he was in England, he could come and visit me."

"Oh, Andy, I'm so glad. Does he look like you?"

"Yes. Yes, a bit, but more handsome."

"Never." She patted his cheek and smiled, then asked, "Did you like him?"

He now looked away from her and it was some time before he answered; then he said, "You know, Kaa-tee, it is curious that you should ask, but I'm not sure. Isn't that a funny thing to say, I'm not sure? We were strangers. When I looked at him he didn't seem my son, Nils; he seemed—well, he seemed the son of his grandparents."

"That's understandable, Andy," she said now. "People take after their grandparents. Are they still alive?"

"Oh yes, those two will never die. But they're not so happy as they were. You see, they're not so rich as they were; they lost a great deal of money that they had invested in Sweden. Even at Kristin's funeral . . ." Now his face became straight as he went on, "Even at her funeral her father had to bemoan the fate of his losses. . . . Ah, well, it's over, and I'm back to my Kaa-tee." He stared at her for a moment, his face still straight, then said, "Do you know what this means, Kaa-tee?"

She looked at him without answering, and he shook her gently, saying, "Do you?"

She could not bring herself to say, "We will be married", it had to come from him, and so she remained silent.

Again he was stroking her fingers. "You have never worn rings, Kaa-tee. Was there a reason?"

Her eyes were so misted she could hardly see him now.

"Will you marry me, Kaa-tee?"

"Oh, darling. . . . Oh, my dear, my dear." she was crying as she talked, her face buried in his neck, and as he stroked her hair he said, "It won't make any difference, no law could bind us closer together than we are, but it's a protection I've always wanted to give you. . . . The last protection."

*   *   *

Andree's unexpected return and the joyous fact that she was soon to have a legal claim to the name of Mrs. Fraenkel pushed into the back of her mind, for the moment, "the other distressing business", as Mr. Hewitt called it. All that day it lay buried under the new joy and for part of the next day, which was Christmas Eve, but it was brought startlingly to the fore by the arrival of two visitors in the late afternoon. They were announced by Betty in a whisper. She came into the parlour hastily, closed the door behind her, and, looking to where Katie was standing under the chandelier handing a bunch of mistletoe up to the captain, who was perched on top of a small set of steps, she whispered excitedly, "Two ladies, ma'am. They are asking for you."

"Two ladies?" Katie came forward. "Have you shown them in? Who are they?"

"No, I didn't. They said their name was Miss Chapman, but they are ladies." Betty, smiling at Katie, did not take in the change in her countenance, for she was seeing the visit of the ladies as a breakthrough for Katie—a break through the snotty-nosed lot, as she termed the society of Shields.

At the name of Chapman Katie had turned a quick glance in Andree's direction, and he saw it and the look on her face. Descending from the steps, he came towards her but addressed himself to Betty, saying, "Well, show the ladies in, Betty."

"No, no, I mean . . ." Katie wet her lips rapidly. "I'll see them in the morning-room."

"The morning-room is full of parcels and packages, and my kit's in there; it's no place to show ladies. . . . You know these ladies, Kaa-tee?"

As she looked up into his face she did not know whether he had been making a statement or asking a question; she had only mentioned the Misses Chapman's name to him once on that night long ago. Was it possible that he remembered it? She still didn't know when he turned to Betty and said, "Show the ladies in and apologise for keeping them waiting, Betty. But before you go get rid of these steps." He picked up the set of steps and thrust them at her, and she scampered out of the room. And now he turned to Katie and whispered, "You weren't expecting them?"

"No, no, I wasn't."

"Well, it doesn't matter; you are looking your best."

"Andy." She was walking by his side towards the fireplace. "The Misses Chapman, they are. . . ." He caught her hand and squeezed it and said, "Yes, yes, I know. And if I hadn't I would have soon found out . . . your face gives all your thoughts away, Kaa-tee. . . . Ssh! Here they come."

The door opened and Betty, standing aside, said, "The Miss Chapmans, ma'am."

Katie moved forward towards the two women. She looked first at the taller, at Miss Ann, and saw an old woman, but Miss Rose did not seem to have changed very much since she last saw her; but from their joint expressions she saw that they found a change in herself. They seemed for the moment taken off their guard.

"Miss Chapman," Katie inclined her face first to one and

then to the other, and, half turning, she extended her hand towards Andree, saying, "My husband, Captain Fraenkel."

As Andree bowed slightly the ladies inclined their heads toward him and Katie said, "Will you take a seat?"

Primly the two ladies seated themselves, and immediately Miss Ann spoke. Addressing herself to Katie, she said, "You know why we're here, Mrs. Bun . . . Fraenkel." After a genteel gulp in her throat she added, "We had to come."

When Katie made no reply Miss Rose, with thinly suppressed indignation, said, "It's very very distressing, dreadful." She glanced towards her sister, and Miss Ann nodded in agreement and repeated "Dreadful". Then Miss Rose, inclining her body slightly towards Katie and going on rapidly and with gathering bitterness, said, "And if you had been truthful in the first place this would never have come about. Never. This is what comes of half-truths."

Katie blinked and turned her face towards Andree; then, looking back at Miss Rose, she said, "I don't know what you mean, half-truths."

"Oh, I think you do, Mrs. Bun . . . Fraenkel, for you gave us to understand that the baby was your husband's."

"Oh, no. No." Katie rose sharply to her feet. "I never did."

"Oh yes, yes, you did, Mrs. Fraenkel." It was Miss Ann speaking, stiffly but more gently than her sister. "We have the certificate. Sara was baptised Sarah Bunting."

Again Katie glanced towards Andree, where he was sitting looking hard at the Misses Chapman, then she looked at them again, saying, "Well, yes, yes, she was; I didn't think there was any need to explain further. . . . You wanted her. . . ." She bent now towards Miss Rose, and her own voice held bitterness as she said, "You were crazy for her, you never rested until you got her and got me away from the place, and then you moved in case I might see her. Would it have mattered to you then if you had known who her father was?"

The two ladies glanced at each other; then Miss Ann, in a tone that sounded as prim as her face looked, said, "Yes, I think it would. We would have taken it into consideration, anyway; the Rosiers were known to us. If we had known the father was young Mr. Rosier we certainly would have considered our action very carefully. And even if we had gone ahead with the matter we would have been prepared for eventualities, and the present eventuality would never have arisen; we would have made sure of that."

At the name of Rosier Katie had stiffened instantly. She was still looking towards the two ladies, but she knew now that Andree was looking at her. All these years she had kept that name from him. Now even the mention of it, and in his presence, had overwhelmed her with a sickly fear.

"The situation is a terrible one. We have done our best, but apparently to no avail. Now, we think it is up to you."

"Me!" Katie's voice was very small, but there was an eagerness in it as she asked, "You want me to see my daughter and explain?"

"No, no." Miss Rose was on her feet, her small body bristling. "Never that."

"Why not?" Katie asked the question in a hard, curt tone, and Miss Rose's voice was equally hard as she replied immediately, "Because it would never do. You agreed to her adoption; leave it at that." Miss Rose exchanged another glance with her sister, then their attention was snapped towards Katie as she said, "What if I don't?"

This question nonplussed them for a moment; then Miss Ann, also rising to her feet, said hesitantly, "You . . . you couldn't do that. You wouldn't want to hurt her, would you? And, you see, this knowledge would upset her and cause her great distress, for . . . for she doesn't know that she was adopted from outside."

"From outside?"

"What I mean is . . ." Miss Ann hesitated. "Well, you see, we wanted her to feel absolutely secure, so we told her, when she was old enough, that her mother had been our younger sister, who had died."

Katie had sometimes wondered if her child had ever asked who her mother was, and if she had pictured her mother. But apparently her daughter would have never thought that way; she would have thought of her mother as dead, and these two women as blood relations, her aunts.

For a moment she experienced the feeling of acute aloneness, as she had done on the night she returned from the children's gathering in Jarrow. There was no Andy in her life; she was a woman without prestige; she was a mother who had been deprived of her child; she had a brother who wouldn't own her; she had no family. . . . The feeling passed when she felt Andree standing near her; she hadn't been aware of him moving. She heard him say, "And what do you expect my wife to do now?"

"Oh, well . . ." It was Miss Ann still speaking, her lips pursed, her refined voice picking her words. "We . . . we thought that she might go to Mr. Rosier—Mr. Rosier Senior —and . . . and explain the situation, and he would talk to his . . ."

"No! No! Never. I won't." Katie was standing very straight, her face grim. Her voice, harsh and loud, sounded very unladylike and it startled her visitors. "No matter what happens I won't see him. Get that into your heads right away. I won't. . . ." Andree's hand on her arm checked her, and she drew in a long, shuddering breath as she listened to him saying, "You have heard what my wife has said."

"But . . . but this must be stopped." Miss Rose was looking up at Andree, speaking pointedly to him. "You do understand that they're half-brother and sister, and it cannot go on? It's an offence against God."

"Half-brother and sister," said Andree now, as if explaining something to himself. He said it slowly again, then halted his glance towards Katie and gave his attention to Miss Rose, asking quietly, "She is seeing the son of this man Rosier?"

"Yes, yes. Of course that is the dreadful fact, and we fear it may have been going on unknown to us. We always have kept watch over her, a strict watch, but there were times when she went away to stay with the Spencers, friends of ours, and young Mr. Rosier was a visitor to their house, and we didn't know this, not for some time. She said nothing at all about meeting him until a few months ago."

"Have you spoken to her about her relationship to this young man?" Andree asked.

"No! No." The sisters both spoke together. Then Miss Ann said, "We do not want to shock her. But even before we learnt of the relationship we did not favour her associating with this young man; the Rosiers are not a family we . . . we admire."

"Have you thought of approaching the young man yourselves?"

Now both of the ladies looked somewhat shamefaced for a moment; then Miss Ann said, "Well, I must confess we . . . we called on Mr. Rosier yesterday, but we did not see him, only his father. It . . . it was a most distressing encounter."

"Oh." Andree nodded his head slowly, and the ladies looked away from his gaze, and Miss Ann's voice was merely a whisper as she said, "He will do nothing to stop their association. He is a dreadful man—a dreadful, dreadful man."

Andree now looked at Katie. Her lids were so lowered she could have been standing with her eyes closed. He pressed her arm gently as he said to the ladies, "And you want my wife to go and see this man, this dreadful man?"

There was a long pause before Miss Rose said, her voice stiff again, "We feel it is only right that she should do so. It is her duty."

"Oh, you think it is her duty?" Andree now nodded sharply from one to the other and his beard seemed to bristle. "You have her daughter for how many years?" He slanted his eyes towards the ceiling before saying, "Eighteen years. And now you think that my wife owes her, and you, a duty?"

"The circumstances are not usual, Mr. Fraenkel," said Miss Ann.

"Captain Fraenkel."

"Captain Fraenkel."

"I agree with you, ladies. The circumstances are not usual."

"I would die if anything should happen to her." Miss Rose's voice dropped to a trembling whisper as she added, "I mean, if she had an association with this young man. . . ."

"Well, you just might have to die, ma'am."

The two ladies stiffened visibly as they stared at this big, bearded man, who spoke so callously.

"There are different ways of dying, ladies. My wife here has died many many times over the years through the loss of her daughter. If you want my opinion of the transaction in which you took charge of her child I will give it to you. I think you used more than persuasion, I think you used pressure on a girl who was poor, in trouble, and handicapped by a sick mother and a demented sister."

"Sir!" Again both the ladies spoke together; and to this Andree said "Yes?" as if in enquiry.

"We . . . we have brought her up as a lady. She has had everything her heart desired."

"Except a mother."

The Misses Chapman actually glared at Andree. Then Miss Ann, turning and addressing Katie pointedly, said, "You can't just do nothing."

"What can I do?" Katie spoke dully now. "If you won't allow me to tell my daughter, what would you have me do . . . other than what you have already asked, and I can't do that."

"You could see the young man," put in Miss Rose.

Katie looked down on the pretty, faded-looking little woman and asked, still in a quiet voice, "Why can't you see him?"

"Because I think it would be more . . . well, more authentic coming from you. And in that way Sara would not be involved. I mean, you . . . you could ask him to break off his association with her. In fact, if you told him the position he would do so at once, for, after all, he is a gentleman."

The strange sound like a laugh that Andree made brought the ladies' eyes to him, but his face looked stern and forbidding, and, moving away from Katie's side, he walked slowly past them and, extending his arm towards the door, said, "I regret, ladies, having to ask you to leave. Should my wife come to any decision as to her future action on this matter she will, no doubt, inform you." The words were formal, the tone precise. Miss Ann made a protesting sound of "But, but . . ."; then, glancing toward Katie, she turned and walked down the room. But not Miss Rose. Miss Rose came and stood in front of Katie and cried, "You can't let this go on. It's evil, evil. They're almost brother and sister."

Katie stared at Miss Rose for a moment before saying, "Why don't you tell her this? It's a simple way out, quite simple; just tell her."

"I can't, I can't." Katie watched the face crumple and the lips tremble as Miss Rose whimpered, "She's all I've got. She thinks she's ours, our blood. She's proud of it; I know she is. She's got a feeling for family; she's always delving into our history. The knowledge would break her, change her. She would feel she didn't belong to us. Moreover"—now Miss Rose's head drooped—"we cannot bear to lose her. I . . . I've given my life to her. I look back and I cannot see a time when I didn't have her."

"I haven't had her for eighteen years."

After Katie's words a silence fell on them, until Andree said, quietly, "Ma'am"; and Miss Rose, turning away, joined her sister and went out of the room, and Andree saw them out of the house.

When he returned to the drawing-room he walked slowly

towards Katie, and when he was opposite to her he took her hands in his and asked, "How long have you known this?"

"Just . . . just after you left for Norway." Her whole face was breaking up.

"And you would not have told me?"

"I didn't want you to know . . . his name. I've always been afraid of you knowing his name."

He did not ask why, he knew why. He put his arms about her and drew her to the couch and held her shivering body close to his, and after a time, when she asked "What am I to do, Andy?" he said, "Nothing at present. Wait a day or so and things will likely move of their own accord. Things have a way of doing that. Anyway, it is Christmas Eve; there is very little you can do until after the holidays. Don't worry." He brought his face close to hers. "Nothing or no one can harm you ever again. Just remember that. You are no longer Kaa-tee Mulholland. To me you never have been, you have always been Mrs. Fraenkel, and this time next week you can claim that name. You will, for all to know, be Mrs. Kaa-tee Fraenkel. You have nothing to fear."

5

It was the second week in the New Year and the thaw had set in, otherwise the carriage would never have been able to make the journey from Shields into the country beyond Jarrow. As it was, the horses were often up to their knees in slush, and twice Mr. Weir had to get down from his cab and tug at their heads and use his whip on them to get them out of the mire.

Katie was well wrapped up in a brown fur cloak with a hood attached, which had been Andree's Christmas gift. Underneath she was wearing a cherry-coloured cord suit with the skirt reaching only to the top of her soft leather boots, which covered her ankles. Yet for all the warmth of her apparel she was shivering like a leaf. Not even the presence of the two men, Andree sitting close to her side and Mr. Hewitt sitting opposite, brought her any feeling of security, for it seemed to her, and had done for days, that everything was conspiring to drive her towards "The House".

It was when Mr. Hewitt had paid a social call on Boxing Day that she had told him what had transpired, and it was at his suggestion that they not only write to young Mr. Rosier but send the letter by a special messenger. This was done the following day. The letter requested Mr. Daniel Rosier to get in touch with Mr. Hewitt without delay. The messenger had returned saying that young Mr. Rosier was out for the day; the butler had informed him that the young master was lunching and dining with a family called Charlton and would be home later that evening. He had promised to see that the letter was safely delivered. And so they had waited. They waited long enough for Andree to make a return trip to the Thames; but he hadn't been in the house more than an hour when the reply had come, and not to Mr. Hewitt but to her, asking her to call at the house and Mr. Rosier would be pleased to give her his attention.

Andree had gone with her when she took the letter to Mr. Hewitt, and Mr. Hewitt had been puzzled by it, and after some discussion concerning it he said, "If you decide to go, Mrs. Fraenkel, I will come with you. . . ." He had paused, then added, "With you both. And we will stipulate that our visit is to young Mr. Rosier and no one else."

For the hundredth time she now heard Andree telling her not to be afraid. "Just remember," he was saying, "you are entering this house not as Katie Mulholland but as Mrs. Fraenkel." It was as if he imagined his name, which he had given her by special license last week, had some magic power to protect her. But it hadn't, no more than Bunting's, and she had taken that by special licence too.

Mr. Hewitt was nodding assent to Andree's statement, then quickly he put out his hand to steady himself as the coach gave another lurch, and half smiling he said, "We couldn't have picked a worse day for the journey."

Katie gazed out of the window on to familiar landmarks; it was twenty years since she had travelled this road, and the scene hadn't altered. Jarrow had expanded from its outsize village into a town; it had clawed its way into the surrounding country, but it was still far away from this lonely fell land. When the carriage gave another lurch she knew they were turning the corner round which she had disappeared from her granda's view on Sunday afternoons.

As the journey progressed she thought that some part of her should be proud that she was coming back to this house in a carriage that well might be her own, for she had enough money to buy, and maintain, three carriages if she wanted them. But there was no pride in her, only fear; she was inwardly, as she had been all those years ago, Katie Mulholland, something so low in the hierarchy of the household that only those who worked with her knew she existed.

The carriage was on the drive now, and here she did notice a change. The hedges were no longer trimmed, the yew trees were no longer clipped; their fantastic shapes were now grotesque, birds' tails were sprouting bush, heads were lost in a contortion of branches. She felt Andree's hand groping for hers and she gripped it, and turning to him she said, "Don't come in with me, Andy, please. Wait outside . . . Please." When she felt him stiffen she glanced across at Mr. Hewitt, and he nodded and said, "I think it would be wise, Captain."

Katie watched the beard on Andee's cheek quiver, which indicated the grinding of his jaws, and again she pleaded with one word, "Andy." And in answer he lowered his head a little. And then the carriage stopped.

Before the coachman had time to open the door Andy had alighted and assisted her out, and he looked hard into her face for a moment, then he stood watching her as she mounted the steps to the front door with Mr. Hewitt at her side.

As the bell jangled from Mr. Hewitt's pull Katie's heart began to beat so rapidly she thought she would collapse. Then the door was opened and there stood Mr. Kennard. Twenty years had wrought a great change in him; she was looking not at the spruce, imposing individual she remembered, but at a white-haired, stooped old man.

Kennard looked at the visitor keenly. He recognized her. This was Katie Mulholland; she hadn't changed all that much. He had heard a lot about Katie Mulholland over the years, and not only from the kitchen gossip, for this was the woman who had left her mark on his master, who had obsessed him, who bedevilled him in his drink and made a fiend of him in sober moments. His master had a consuming hate for this woman, a hate almost as big as the hate he himself had for his master. As he looked at Katie Mulholland, the woman, he thought that her infamous life hadn't left much trace on her face; though at present she looked as white as a sheet, she was beautiful. Of a sudden he felt sorry for her. He wondered what the outcome of her visit would be, for that devil in there had been cooking something up for days. He knew the signs. . . . "This way, madam," he said now, while not a muscle of his face moved to show any recognition of her. "This way, sir."

For the first time Katie stepped into the house by way of the vestibule. She kept her eyes straight ahead, yet nothing escaped her. The change inside the house was as great as, if not greater than, outside. Everything looked dull, dusty and dingy. When had the floor of the hall last been polished? The hall that had been the pride of Mrs. Davis and the heartbreak of both the parlour-maid and the chamber-maids who shared the task of making it like a mirror.

They were going towards the library when Mr. Hewitt said, "Mr. Daniel Rosier is expecting us?" It was a question and Kennard answered it with a slight movement of his head. His face was averted from them, and he kept it so as he opened the drawing-room door. Katie walked slowly past him, then Mr. Hewitt, but he announced only one of them. In a low voice he said, "Miss Mulholland, sir."

Quickly now Katie turned to him. Her voice quiet and strangely without a tremor, she said, "I am Mrs. Fraenkel." Kennard now looked at her; then, lowering his head, he turned away and closed the door.

Katie walked slowly forward into the great book-lined room, which on this winter afternoon was so dim she couldn't see to the far end of it. She was turning to Mr. Hewitt when they both started as a thick voice from behind and to the right of them said, "'Mrs. Fraenkel?'"

Katie could not prevent her hand going to her mouth as she looked at the man standing in the far corner of the room where the bookcases met. He was leaning back as if resting in a cleft, his arms stretched out along the shelves. There was nothing about him that she remembered, yet had she met him in hell she would have recognised him.

The man who had peered down at her from behind the curtain on the balcony window had been a young handsome man; the man who had wagged his finger at her demanding her silence in the candle-lit room had been a dark, threatening but still handsome man; the man who had stared silently at her when she had stood in her nightgown with the candlestick in her hand had still been presentable. The man she looked at now had an ugly red flabby face with eyes like chips of black lead, their light coming to her over the distance from between his narrowed lids. She swung round from their gleam and to Mr. Hewitt, whispering between gasping breaths, "Let us go. Let us go."

Mr. Hewitt, with his hand on her arm, was about to lead her forward when the figure moved swiftly from the corner of the room and stood with his back to the door, and the solicitor, drawing himself up with dignity and in a voice that matched his posture, said, "Sir, will you kindly allow us to leave? We came to see your son. . . ."

"You didn't come to see my son, Hewitt, you came to see me. I sent for you and you've come . . . to see me. I've had your letters, Hewitt. They were very interesting. Very interesting." His head, which was leaning against the back of the door, rocked from side to side, and Mr. Hewitt said, "Sir, you are drunk. This lady wishes to leave. Will you kindly allow her to do so?"

"Lady? Oh, my God!" Again the head was moving widely. Then stiffening suddenly, Bernard Rosier, still with his back against the door, brought his shoulders hunching forward as he muttered thickly, "Don't you come that bloody talk with me, Mr. Solicitor; I know all about you. You've been raking off from her brothels for years. It pays you to call her lady, doesn't it? Oh, you can tell me nothing about your little game, or hers."

As Katie closed her eyes and tried to steady her shaking limbs she prayed for only one thing at this precise moment, that he wouldn't raise his voice any louder in case Andy should hear him. The doors and walls were thick, but the library windows faced the front drive. As she felt Mr. Hewitt move away from her she turned to him almost wildly, then saw he was going to the bell-rope that hung by the mantelpiece, and as he tugged on it twice Bernard Rosier cried, "What the hell do you think you're doing! Where do you think you are?"

It was as if Kennard had been waiting for just such a summons, for as Mr. Hewitt took his place by Katie's side again there came a tap on the door, and Bernard Rosier answered it. Without turning round he cried, "I didn't ring for you. Bugger off! Do you hear?"

"Sir! Your language."

"Language. Don't be funny. That's like Sunday-school pap

to what she's used to." He now started to move forward . . . and as he did so Katie backed towards the window, and the light fell on her ánd he saw her as he had imagined her over the years, as he had last seen her standing in her shift illuminated by the light of a candle. His fingers now went up to his brow, where he carried the mark of her aim yet. Once, when she was a stinking scullery-maid, he had taken her; why hadn't he guessed then that she would turn into this? He could have had her, all his life he could have had her on the side. He had had her, but as a curse. This was the creature who had dogged him with ill-luck; this was the creature who had inspired his crazy sister to expound her moral standards until they had brought his life, his future, his very existence toppling round him. Through this creature his wife had made herself almost penniless to spite him, and ruined his chances once and for all of ever getting a footing in Palmer's. Moreover, she had made him the laughing-stock of the county. Through this creature he was now living no better than a tradesman; three servants in the house where once there had been twenty; two men outside where once there had been ten; one horse in the stables.

He thought of the pleasure it would be to get his hands around her neck and slowly strangle her as she had slowly strangled him over the last twenty years, but he'd have to pay for that pleasure, and there were more ways of killing a cat than drowning it. The revenge he was about to take was small compared with that which he would like to vent on her, but nevertheless it was already bringing him some satisfaction.

He would have thought she wouldn't have cared a damn what happened to her brat. Apparently she had let it go when it was a baby, but it seemed that it did matter still. All this fuss about his bastard leering at his son. And those two old dried pumpkins going round like scalded cats. Oh, it was damned funny. Damned funny.

As she moved another step towards the window he stopped and said, "You came to see my son, didn't you? Because he was, to use the phrase of your class, keeping company with our bastard."

"Mr. Rosier!"

"She's used to plain speaking in her business. They are." Bernard Rosier slanted his eyes towards Mr. Hewitt; then, returning his gaze to Katie, he went on, "It would be a sin, wouldn't it, if anything happened between them? Oh my! My! What was the phrase the dear Misses Chapman used, 'A sin before God and man'. I understand from the dear ladies that they didn't want their adopted child to know about her disgraceful birth, so they came here and appealed to me to send my son packing to some far place so their dear child would not be contaminated. . . . Do you know something?" His body was swaying slightly now and he bent towards Katie again. "That was the first I'd heard of my son's association with this Miss Sara Chapman. And what did I do? Forbid my son to associate with his half-sister? Not at all, not at all, I encouraged it. I have never done so much encouraging in my life as I have done this last few weeks."

"Sir, you are a low, low animal. The . . ."

"I've told you to be quiet, haven't I!" Bernard Rosier was now glaring at Mr. Hewitt. "Nobody asked you here, so unless you want to be thrown out keep your mouth shut."

Slowly his eyes returned to Katie's deathly white face, and, his voice low now, he said, "There was something else I learned too, only a few days ago when the dear Misses Chapman were here, and that was you haven't seen your daughter since she was a year old. Dear! Dear! That is a shame. But" —he raised his hand now in a generous gesture towards her —"I can rectify that. I have a great surprise for you. Do you know that your daughter, our dear daughter, Miss Mulholland, is upstairs at this moment?"

This couldn't go on. It couldn't go on. She would do something, as she had done once before. If there was anything to her hand she would pick it up and . . . and beat him with it. She could see herself doing it. . . . But what had he said, just this minute? Sarah, Sarah was upstairs? . . . Her Sarah. Her fingers were pressed tight across her mouth again, and now she watched him turn his head slightly over his shoulder and bellow, "Kennard!" When the door was opened almost immediately, he said, without turning round, "Tell Mr. Daniel to come to the library at once, and to bring . . . his wife with him . . . at once."

Kennard, his countenance still imperturbable, closed the door again, and as Katie swayed and looked wildly about her Mr. Hewitt quickly pushed a chair forward and assisted her to it.

Bernard Rosier, no longer needing to guard the exit in any way, walked to a table on which stood a decanter and glass, and pouring out a full glass of whisky he threw if off in three gulps; then, turning towards the door, he stood waiting, his glance flitting every now and again to where Katie sat with Mr. Hewitt by her side, his hand on her shoulder.

Katie's eyes, too, were on the door and when it opened her heart leapt painfully, but she didn't move. Her eyes were now riveted on the tall, slim young girl coming into the room, and it was as if she was looking down the years to herself, as she was when she first met Andy. Only this young girl had a poise she never possessed. She watched her walking slowly forward, followed by a young man.

He it was who glanced round him, first towards his father, and then to the seated woman, and he stared at her a moment as if puzzled, before turning to his father again and saying, "You wish to see me?"

Bernard Rosier moved forward, and as he did so he picked up a snuff-box from a small table and, snapping it open, lifted a pinch of snuff between his first finger and thumb, dabbed into the hollow between the first finger and thumb of his other hand, then applied it to his nostrils, before saying, "Yes, I do. But not only me; don't you see we have visitors?"

The young man looked towards Katie and Mr. Hewitt again, and he was more perplexed still by the distress he saw in both their faces, especially in the woman's. Turning to his father, his shoulders visibly stiffening, his voice curt, he said, "Would you kindly tell me why you wished to see me, to see us?" There was no deference in his manner as befitted a young man of nineteen speaking to his father, but Bernard Rosier did not seem to notice this. He was smiling widely as he moved forward again and took up his position a few yards from where Katie was seated and from where the young girl was standing, one hand on the back of the couch, and, turning his attention to her, he said, "I want you to look at this person dressed up as a lady." He flapped his hand disdainfully towards Katie. "Does she remind you of anyone?"

Katie and her daughter looked at each other. Katie's hand was now gripping the neck of her cape. She forced herself to sit still, not to move towards this flesh of hers that she longed to touch.

"No." The word sounded precise, definite, and brought a loud laugh from Bernard Rosier.

"You must look in the mirror, my dear. Side by side you

300

must look in the mirror . . . for this"—he bowed to her—"this person is your mother."

Again Katie was holding her daughter's gaze. Their eyes stretched, they looked at each other for what seemed an interminable time, and then nothing Katie had suffered in her life pained her as much as the syllable that the girl now uttered.

"No!" she cried, and it was as if she was casting away something repellent.

"Yes," Bernard Rosier put in. "Look at the eyes. Aren't they proof enough? This person passed you on to the Chapman ladies when you were a year old. I understand you were brought up on the idea that you are the daughter of their sister. You are not. This is your mother." Again he flung his hand out towards Katie, before ending, "And she's a trollop."

"I am not. How dare you! How dare you!" Katie was on her feet, her anger overcoming her fear. Controlling her trembling limbs and lips, she appealed to this girl, this utter, utter stranger, saying, "I am your mother. I am, but . . . but I am not what he said. I am a respectable woman. . . ."

"Huh!" They all looked at Bernard Rosier now, who was standing with his arms flung wide as he cried, "A respectable woman! Owning more than half the brothels in Shields. A respectable woman who lives with a Swede, and he one of many."

"Father!" It was a shouted command, and Bernard Rosier's arms dropped to his side and he turned slowly and looked at his son, and asked in a quiet voice that sounded more terrible than his shouting, "Yes?"

"Stop this! I don't know what devilry you're up to now, but I say stop this. All right. This . . . this lady is Sara's mother. And what does it matter? What do you hope to gain by this exposure?"

"Exposure? Tut-tut!" The voice was still quiet. "You call this reunion between mother and daughter exposure? You have used the word too soon. If you had used it after what I am going to say now it would be in its right context." He moved slowly past his son and went towards the girl, who had her back to the couch now, her hands stretched down on each side of her gripping the upholstery, and when he put his hand out towards her she shrank from him, saying under her breath, "Don't touch me."

His hand in mid-air, he now surveyed her before repeating her words softly. "Don't touch you?" he said. "But I have a right to touch you, my dear. You see, I am your father. I begot you when your mother was a scullery-maid wallowing in slops in the kitchen back there."

The silence that fell on them had no movement in it, no fluttering of an eyelid, no breath escaping from open lips; even the sweat in the pores was checked in its flow. Like a group that had been petrified they stood until, after an endless time, a body moved and there was a great intake of breath, and before it could be exhaled Daniel Rosier had sprung on his father and borne him to the ground.

It was not Katie who screamed but her daughter. She stood with her hands covering her cheeks and letting out one scream after another.

The library door now burst open and Kennard appeared, only to come to a stop just within the room. He stared towards his master struggling in the grasp of his son, but he made no move to interfere, and then he himself was knocked aside as Andree came into the room. After one glance which took in the situation, he grabbed at the man uppermost to him and, gripping the collar of his coat, he wrenched him upwards; then, retaining his hold, he looked down at the other man on the floor, the man who by instinct he recognized, the man he had wanted to see for a long, long time.

"You swine! You filthy, filthy swine!" The young man was struggling to release himself from Andree's hold and his body was shaking as if with sobs; and he was sobbing, he was crying without tears . . . "I'll kill you! I will! I'll kill you for this. I . . . I should have guessed you were up to your devilry with your advice to . . . to go ahead, to get . . . get it over . . . I will. I will. I'll kill you."

Bernard Rosier had pulled himself unaided to his feet, and he now stood swaying as he passed his hand over his face, down to his neck on which his son's hands had left their mark.

Then, looking at him, he said between gasps, "I'll give you the chance any time you like; but just remember, they'll hang you for it. And what will your widow do then, poor thing?"

The young man was again struggling in Andree's grasp, and Andree, still keeping his hold on him, looked at Rosier and said one word in Norwegian. It sounded as if it were issuing from the depths of a cavern and, although not understood by anyone there, the scorn and hatred in it was apparent, and it roused Rosier once again to fury.

"Get out! Get out, the lot of you. Scum! Out of my house." He glared towards Katie now, screaming at her, "You! Get out of my sight, and your whore-master with you."

Katie, Mr. Hewitt, Kennard, and even Daniel Rosier had all to hang on to the great bearded man; the only person who didn't move was the girl who still stood with her back to the couch. Pushing, pulling, pleading, they edged Andree towards the door and into the hall, and no one took any notice of the sallow-faced, dowdily dressed woman who stepped aside and stood against the wall. And when the big, bearded man, shaking off those around him straightened his clothes and, looking back toward the library door, yelled, "I'll be back. Remember I'll be back," she turned and slowly entered the library, and without even looking in the direction of her husband she walked to the couch, where the girl was still standing as if glued to the floor, and taking her gently by the arm she led her out of the room and up the stairs.

6

Sitting at a discreet distance from Katie's bed, Mr. Hewitt dropped his gaze from her strained and painfully sad face. And in answer to her question he said, "I'm sorry, but there is no message—no message at all."

Katie swallowed over the lump in her throat. The wound her daughter's "No" had inflicted was still wide open. That "No!" that had held such rejection, such denial of the relationship, that she wondered how she would be able to live with the pain of it all her days.

"She didn't say anything to . . . to these people, the Charltons, about me?"

"They didn't say so. They . . . It might seem strange to you, but they weren't shocked in the least about the matter, any part of it; they are very modern people. They . . . they apparently had done everything they could to bring the

303

young people together, and they were witnesses at the marriage . . . of course they were unaware of the circumstances then. But now they think it right, even proper, that the marriage should remain as it is. Apparently"—he bowed his head again—"neither of the parties was for an annulment. They are passionately attached to each other, so I understand, and were quite prepared to take the consequences of this union." He raised his head now and, looking at her again, said, "I understand that Mr. Charlton travelled with them and saw them on the cross-Channel steamer."

"Where . . . where are they going?"

"That, the Charltons said, they didn't know, and I believe them. Young Mr. Rosier promised to write to them when they were settled, but I think they intended to travel first. You see, although he's a minor his . . . his father"—again the eyes dropped from Katie's—"his father was agreeable to the marriage. I think his mother, too, although, of course, she was not aware of the circumstances. This, in a way, leaves him free. Apparently there is a clause in the will whereby he can draw a limited yearly sum from his inheritance until he is thirty, when he will come into the whole. The Charltons seem to think that it is the best thing that could have happened—I mean them leaving the country; for the marriage would not have been tolerated here, not in their society. Abroad no one need know. Moreover, they were afraid of what he might be driven to do had he stayed in England. Apparently he has always disliked his father."

Katie now pulled at a piece of down that was sticking out from a stitch hole in the eiderdown, and she rolled it hard between her finger and thumb. There was someone else who might be driven to do something; who, she felt, was just waiting an opportunity to do something. She had been in bed for two days and she had hardly let him out of her sight, but it couldn't go on. If only he was away and had time to cool down. She had never wished him from her since they had first met, but she wouldn't know a minute's peace or ease until he was safely through the piers.

When Mr. Hewitt, after bidding her a sincere goodbye, quietly took his leave she got out of bed and began to dress; and she was in the middle of her dressing when Andree came into the room, saying, "Now, now, what are you up to?"

"I can't stay in bed, Andy, I just can't."

"You know what the doctor said, rest for a few days."

"I'm not sick, Andy, not that kind of sick. I'll be better up and about. It might take my mind off things, but I doubt it. You were talking to Mr. Hewitt?"

He nodded; then, putting his arm about her, he said, "It's for the best that they should go abroad. Try to look at it like that."

She wouldn't have minded them going abroad in the least; she wouldn't have minded them staying together, although it wasn't right—it was, as they said, a sin against nature; but what she did mind was her daughter rejecting her, like Joe had done, only worse. Not a word. Just that "No!"

"Kaa-tee."

"Yes, Andy?"

"I think we must tell Theresa."

Swiftly she pulled herself from him, but, facing him, she cried, "No, you mustn't do that, Andy."

"She knows there is something wrong, Kaa-tee." His voice was patient. "She's worried. She asked me last night what we were holding back from her. She feels cut off, out of it."

"Far better that than her know the truth. Every time that . . . that devil has lifted his hand against me she has done something. And let's face it, Andy, things have got worse, not better. If she had left things as they were in the first place my father would have been alive, even perhaps today. I can't help saying it."

"We have been over all that, Kaa-tee. You have also said that but for her and all that happened as a result of what she did we would never have met, haven't you?"

"I know, I know. But you mustn't tell her."

Andree straightened his back and his voice was firm when he said, "I feel she should know. She is ill, Kaa-tee. Dr. Leonard told me last night that her time is short, it could happen any moment. She might have a few weeks at best, or just a few days, or even a few minutes. It could happen any time."

"Then if you told her it could shorten her life?"

"No, no. I don't see it that way. How I see it is that she is going to die feeling shut out from something that concerns you, something that is upsetting you, that is making you ill. She saw the state you were in when you came back the other day. The tale of the horse bolting didn't carry water with her. She's an astute woman, as you know, Kaa-tee. Apart from the trouble she has caused, there is the other side. She has been good to you, and also you mustn't forget . . . she loves you."

Katie bowed her head, and as he lifted her hand to his bushy cheek he said, "I am going to tell her." And to this she made no reply.

* * *

It was as they finished lunch that Andree said quietly, "I'm going up to the yard for a while," and the simple words brought Katie springing up from her chair, crying, "What are you going to the yard for?"

"What am I going to the yard for? Oh, my dear." He shook his head and gave a little smile. "What do I usually go to the yard for? For my orders."

"You said the other day your boat wouldn't be back until the end of the week."

"Yes, but I've got to go and make arrangements; there's lots of things to be done."

"No, no, don't go, Andy. Don't go."

"Kaa-tee." He turned swiftly from her. "I've got to go to the yard." He was in the hall now, and she followed him, her voice high, crying, "You'll not go the yard, you won't."

"I'm going to the yard, Kaa-tee."

They were standing facing each other at the bottom of the stairs.

"Then I'll come with you."

"To the yard? Don't be silly. What'll they think, a woman coming into the yard to see if her man's got a ship!"

"Andy, I'm coming with you; I can stay outside. I've . . . I've never looked round Jarrow, not for a long time, not the new parts."

"And you want to look round Jarrow on a day like this with the wind cutting you in two? And it's freezing under foot."

"I want to come with you, Andy."

"Kaa-tee, this has got to stop."

"I want to come with you, Andy."

He dropped his head before her. Then, turning slowly away, he said, "Very well, you come." Then, as quickly turning towards her again, he added, "But there's one thing you've got to remember, Kaa-tee; you won't always be able

306

to check my movements. You might know my goings-out, but not my comings-in; tides vary. Let me go alone, Kaa-tee."

"No, no." She flung herself at him now. "No, Andy, I beg you. Haven't I gone through enough? I've known this was going to happen. For years I've felt it coming, dreading me da's pattern repeated. Andy, I can't bear it. Let him be; he'll rot in his own evil juice. It doesn't matter what he said to me, or how he treated me. Anyway, Mr. Hewitt was exaggerating. He was, he was. He shouldn't have gone over it. He had no right to tell you, it's just egging you on. I'm surprised at him. I am. I am. Nothing matters, Andy, only that you don't go back there."

"Who said I was going there, anyway? Calm yourself, calm yourself, and if you're coming get your things on. Wrap up well, because it's going to be a cold business looking around Jarrow. . . ."

The house became strangely quiet, and ten minutes later, when the front door closed on them, Theresa moved from the door and back to her couch and, sitting on the edge of it, stared ahead into the bright fire. After some time she turned and looked around the room, her eyes picking out each piece of furniture, each knick-knack; then, reaching out, she pressed down an enamel handle attached to the bell.

She so very rarely rang for Betty that when she did Betty answered her summons with alacrity, and now she came in without knocking, saying, "Yes, Miss Theresa? You all right?"

"Yes, Betty, I'm all right. Come in. Come here."

When Betty was standing before her, Theresa looked up at her and said, "Will you do something for me, Betty?"

"Aye. Yes, anything you say, miss. Just you say. Do you want a custard made?"

"No, no, nothing like that." Theresa shook her head and smiled weakly. Then, putting out her hand and grasping Betty's, she said, "I want you to go to the livery stables and get me a coach."

"You what, Miss Theresa?"

"A coach, Betty. I want to go for a drive."

"The day! Like this? Freezin'! Eeh no, Miss Theresa." Betty paused. "Ma'am would knock me into the middle of next week if I did any such thing. You go out alone? What's come over you? An' you been real poorly this week."

"Betty. Betty, listen to me. You don't want anything to

happen to separate Katie"—she used the Christian name now, not saying Mrs. Fraenkel as she usually did when speaking to the maid—"from the captain. Do you?"

"Separate? . . . No, miss. Oh no! My God, that would be a tragedy."

"Well then, you must do what I tell you. Go to the stables and ask for a coach to be sent here immediately. I would like Mr. Weir if possible, but it's not important. If he isn't available anyone else will do, but you must hurry."

"But how you goin' to manage a ride on your own? You're in no fit state to get off the couch on your own, never mind go out. And where you goin'?"

"I'll tell you all that later. But now I'm relying on you to help me. And it's for Katie's sake, remember that, and the captain's."

Betty stood upright and looked down on the figure which, as she said to herself, looked like a clothes-prop with clothes on. Miss Theresa was bad, she had a wonky heart, she should never go out by herself. Oh, she wished Katie was back. But she hadn't been gone more than a few minutes. She said now, with what authority she could muster, "I don't think you'd better do it, miss."

"Betty." Theresa's voice sounded stern, different from the one Betty was used to hearing. "If you don't do as I say I'll walk to the stables. Go now. I'll be ready when you come back."

"Yes, miss. All right, miss. But . . . but you'll tell Katie that you sort of insisted, won't you?"

"Don't worry." Theresa nodded at her. "It'll be all right with Katie. Katie will thank you until her dying day."

"Well, I hope so, miss." Betty smiled wryly, then went out of the room, and as she went down the stairs she added to herself, "I doubt it. She'll likely give it me in the neck; but what can I do, 'cos if I don't get her one she'll do as she says an' walk. She means it, she does."

7

It was eight o'clock the same evening and Katie was seated at one side of Theresa's bed, Andree at the other. The hair on Andree's cheeks was wet and the startling blue of his eyes was dimmed. He could only see Theresa's face through a mist, but he held her thin hand firmly between his, and the feeling in his body at this moment was for her alone, and it transcended any other feeling he had experienced in his life, even his love for Katie. "Greater love has no man than this, that a man lay down his life for his friend." And that is what she had done. Dying, she had not wasted her last hours; she had laid down her life for her friend, Kaa-tee, and, yes, for him. Ah, yes, for him. For if she hadn't done it he certainly would. Perhaps he mightn't have gone as far as she had, he might have just used his fists, but he would have left his mark on that man some time or other and to hell with the consequences.

Katie, with Theresa's other hand in hers, was beyond tears. She could not take in what had happened; she knew that if she started to cry she would never stop. There would be a time for crying, but it wasn't now, because Theresa's life was running out fast. Through their long acquaintance her feelings towards Theresa had varied from liking to hate—liking because she was kind, hate because she was a Rosier—and somewhere in between there had been a feeling of revulsion. But strong among her feeling had been compassion. Yet she knew that her compassion for Theresa had never been as great as Andree's, and that was strange. And now Theresa had given her life to save Andree for her, and for that she loved her at last.

There was a movement behind her, and she turned her head and again became concerned at the nearness of the policeman sitting by the door. Why couldn't they let her die in peace? But she was dying in peace. The love in her fading gaze, the calmness of her face, spoke of peace as she waited for her slowing heart-beats to cease. . . .

Down in the kitchen was another policeman. He sat at the table, opposite Betty, who was beating her fist on the board saying for the hundredth time in the last few hours, "If only I hadn't gone and got that cab!"

"But you did," said the policeman flatly, "and if I were you I'd forget about it."

"It's all right you sitting there and sayin' that 'cos it doesn't concern you really, but I went an' got her the cab."

"But you said if you hadn't gone and got it she would have walked down to the stables herself."

"She would have never reached the stables in her condition . . . I should have known."

"She reached Greenwall Manor all right," said the policeman, jerking his chin upwards. "By, I've come across some funny cases in me time, but the day's beats all. What did she want to shoot her brother for? She hadn't seen him for over fourteen years. Gettin' out of bed, where she's been bad for months, an' going shootin' him, it doesn't make sense."

"There she was, sittin' as cool as a cucumber and him lying there, not a couple of yards away from her, swimming in blood, an' his wife standin' in the doorway with the butler next to her, an' a gardener bloke. All like waxworks they were. I don't think one of them had been near to see if he was dead or not. An' when we saw him there didn't seem much doubt about it, the side of his face all mangled, and his hand shattered. God, he looked a mess! She had aimed full belt at his face, that was evident. An', you know, the cook there, she said a funny thing to me on the side when we was waitin' for the maria comin' to bring her down. She said she was crossin' the hall when she saw her coming in." He nodded towards the ceiling. "An', she said, she stood like a stook because it was all of fourteen years since she'd seen her, an' the last time she'd been in the house there'd been fireworks, an' she said she saw her speak to the butler chap, then leave him and walk into the gun-room. And when she came out she had one hand in the breast of her coat, an' she walked straight past him an' he didn't do nowt to stop her. . . . An' another funny thing that cook said—she said her mistress was halfway up the stairs and she turns and looks down on the woman going into the drawing-room but she doesn't do anything either. She doesn't come downstairs and ask her what she's about, she just stands there. And then the cook said she heard this great bang. No raised voices or anything, just a bang. Likely she didn't give him the chance to open his mouth."

Betty was leaning across the table now, her joined hands pressed under her double chin. "They could have taken the pistol off her, couldn't they? Couldn't they? They must have known why she went into the gun-room, mustn't they? The butler would anyway."

"Well, if they had," said the policeman calmly, "it wouldn't have made much difference 'cos she intended to get him. Why else would she have had a gully down her skirt waist with an eight-inch steel blade on it as sharp as a razor? She had taken that from here. Oh, she knew what she was about."

Yes, Theresa had known what she was about—and now she lay looking for the last time at the woman she had loved all her life. Love was a mighty thing, and it was a terrible thing. It had whipped strength into her frail, sick body; it had enabled her to ignore the ties of blood. It had enabled her to kill to save the one she loved. Her life had not been without purpose after all.

8

Bernard Rosier didn't die. Theresa's wavering hand, aiming for his breast, had caused the shot to hit the side of his face, taking off his right ear. Her second shot had hit his left hand as he had raised it to his face, shattering it in such a way that it left him with only his index finger and thumb. The newspapers stated that Mrs. Noble had committed this outrage while the balance of her mind was disturbed.

Although Andree wished from the bottom of his heart that Theresa had accomplished what she had set out to do, he realized that the reason underlying her attack had succeeded, for he felt no longer impelled to meet Rosier. Moreover, now that he was severely maimed, the score, as it were, had become even. And so, three months later, when he was first attacked, he did not connect it in any way with Bernard Rosier.

It was late evening when his ship docked on a particular Thursday night, and darkness had fallen when he left her. He was now carrying a leather case, which replaced his sailor's bag, and he had crossed over a siding and was going in the direction of the gates when from behind a wagon two figures pounced on him. As the burning pain from a blow with something hard pierced his left shoulder he dropped his case and swung up his free fist and rammed it blindly home. Again and again his fist found its target, until another blinding pain on the back of his head brought him toppling down to the ground. The blow didn't knock him out, only dazed him, and after a moment he got to his knees and then to his feet; and, picking up his case, he stumbled back to his ship, where he attended to his bruises and cleaned up before going home.

He had reported the matter to the dock police, stating that he thought his assailants had been after his wallet but that they had gone away empty-handed.

Although he did think that his attackers had simply been after his money, he did not tell Katie he had been set upon, for he gathered that in her state of mind she would jump to conclusions and start worrying all over again. The explanation for his bruised shoulder and the cut on the back of his head he gave as slipping off the iron ladder and falling some distance into the hold, and to this explanation he had added he was lucky he hadn't killed himself, and he was satisfied she believed him.

*　　　*　　　*

It was a month later, and incidentally the first time he had left his ship in the dark since the night he had been attacked, and, on the supposition that lightning never strikes in the same place twice, he took the same road to the gate, and almost at the very spot it happened again, but this time there were more than two assailants.

It seemed at first he was combating a battalion of them and as he opened his mouth to curse a fistful of dirt was rammed deep into it. This outrage brought his stomach heaving, and he reared like an angry giant and tossed the bodies from him, and, his hand coming in contact with another that held an iron pipe, he wrenched it away and flayed wildly left and right with it, all the while spluttering and spitting.

312

And then he was alone, leaning, gasping, against the wagon. At least he thought he was alone, until he heard a moan coming from almost at his feet. Groping over the body until he found the coat collar, he hauled the man upwards, and pushing him forward through the darkness he staggered, like someone paralytic drunk assisting another in the same condition, back to the ship, spitting all the way.

When he was some distance from the quayside he bellowed out, "Mr. Naylor! Ahoy there, Mr. Naylor!" Then, "Cullen! Cullen!"

"Aye, Captain." The voice of the donkeyman who acted as watchman came back to him first, followed by that of the first mate, a Hartlepool man who was sleeping aboard that night. "That you, Captain? What's up?"

"Come down here."

When the two men came to Andree's side he thrust the drooping figure towards them, saying, "Get him aboard."

"God Almighty!" said the mate, peering at Andree. "What's happened to you, sir?"

To this, Andree answered nothing, but, pulling himself up the gangway, said, "Keep a watch on him, Cullen."

"Aye, Captain," said Cullen, then added, "Do you want me to pepper him?"

"No," said Andree. "If there's any peppering to do I'll see to it; just see he doesn't get away."

"Aye, Captain."

In Andree's cabin Mr. Naylor closed the door and, looking close at Andree, said, "That eye, sir; it should have a stitch."

"I'll see to that later." Andree spat a mouthful of water into the sink, then said, "Will you get me a clean rig, Mr. Naylor? I can't touch anything, I'm muck from head to foot."

When he had stripped to the skin he examined his body. His shin-bone was raw and bleeding and a swelling was starting in his groin where a heavy boot had contacted him; also, the mate pointed out, there was a large bruise on his shoulder. "Shall I call the polis, sir?" said Mr. Naylor.

"No, not yet; perhaps later." Andree was now seeing to the cut above his eye.

"How many were there, sir?"

"Well . . ." He paused to consider. "It seemed as if there were a regiment of them, and all dumb, because there wasn't a whimper from one of them. But I should say four or five."

"But why? Have you any idea, sir?"

It was some time before Andree answered. He was pulling on a clean vest when he said, "Yes, Mr. Naylor, I think I've got an idea, but I'll know more in a few minutes."

"Well, whoever they are they're a dirty lot of buggers," said the mate. "To be set upon is one thing, but to ram filth into your mouth is another. I'd like to get me hands on the swine. By God, I would!"

"And so would I, Mr. Naylor," said Andree.

A few minutes later they were down in the engine-room staring at the shivering creature who stood with his back tight against an iron girder, and he looked from the great bearded man to the thick-set man in the blue uniform, then to the burly, aggressive-looking greaser, and his head began to wobble and his mouth open and close, but no words came from him.

"What were you after?"

When Andree spoke the man's head stopped shaking for a moment; then his mouth made a fish-like movement and he muttered, "Nowt. Nowt."

"Money?"

The head was wagging again.

"Answer the captain when he speaks to yer!" The stoker's boot was thrust out and the man jerked sideways and gabbled, "It wasn't money, it wasn't. It was nowt. Nowt."

"How many were there of you?"

The man peered at Andree now and whimpered, "Four. Four blokes."

"Who were they? Their names?"

The head was swinging again, and again the stoker's boot came out, and the man yelped loudly, and, cringing, spluttered. "Honest. Honest, I only knew one, a bloke that I met in a bar. His name is Harry."

"Harry what?"

"Honest, Captain, I don't know."

"The other two?"

"I only knew one was from Wallsend an' the other from Shields. The . . . the Shields bloke seemed the boss."

"What reason had they for setting about me?"

"I don't rightly know. Honest to God, mister . . ."

"Captain!"

"That's enough, Cullen." Andree put his hand out in a checking movement towards the stoker and, nodding to the

314

man, said, "You'd better tell me all you know. If you value your hide, you will start to talk, and fast."

The man began to talk, but incoherently for a moment or so; then, slowly, he said, "But I tell you . . . I tell you I don't know. It sounded all sixes and sevens to us. These blokes, these two, they took Harry and me in and stood us a pint, an' then another, an' they asked us did we want a quid. As I've only worked three months in the year, I said . . ." His head now dropped and he muttered, "I said, laughin' like, I'd murder for a quid. An' that was how it started. I didn't know it was gonna be this. They said they were gonna beat up a sailor fellow who had taken a bloke's sister down, and the bloke would pay well if this fellow . . ." Again his head was wagging. "If this fellow was skinned like."

"The man who was paying well, did they say who he was? Where he was from?"

"No; only that he was a gent an' lived out in the country. That's all I know. Honest, honest, Captain. Them two, they had it all planned. They said they had been over the wall afore; they . . . they had us here last week an' the week afore." The head drooped again. "You got off in the light."

"Dirty bastards!" The donkeyman was making yet another move forward, when again Andree checked him; then, turning to the mate, he said, "Lock him up until the morning, Mr. Naylor; he may remember something more by then."

"Very good, sir."

From the foot of the ladder Andree paused and, looking back along the steel-bedecked engine-room, said, "I'll be sleeping aboard."

"Very good, sir."

He could not now risk going home because Katie would link this attack to his supposed fall down the hold, and she would immediately put a name to the instigator of them, and the name would be the correct one.

He had some thinking to do, and he must know what course he was going to take.

*   *   *

By the following morning Andree had discarded the idea of going to the police; he had no proof against Rosier. His only witness was the man, who could give him no more information other than he had given him last night; and it

315

would take a very good solicitor to connect the gent in the country with Bernard Rosier.

No, the best way, he thought, was to confront this devil, maimed as he was, and warn him what would happen if he attempted any such thing again. He might, he knew, find it difficult to keep his hands off the man, but this he must endeavour to do because, whereas he had no evidence to incriminate Rosier, were he to manhandle him Rosier, he was sure, would use such an action as an excuse to strike back at Katie, for he now saw the previous attacks on himself as Rosier's means of retaliation. He also knew that if he was to meet him it must be before he saw Katie again.

The effects of the second attack seemed worse this morning. His face felt sore, his eye was swollen and discoloured, his groin was stiff and painful, as was his shin, and altogether he was in such a condition that he would rather have lain in his bunk for another couple of hours; but this thing had to be done, and at once.

In ordinary circumstances, he would have walked the four miles to the house, arriving there within an hour, but this morning he was in no fit state for walking, so he made his way to a side street and a ramshackle building that sported the name of livery stables, and there he hired a cab.

It was a clear spring day, promising warmth later on, and as the cab left the outskirts of Jarrow and headed for the country he recalled the last time he had taken this drive, and the outcome of it. In a way he saw his journey now as an extended result of that visit.

The driver took a different road today and they passed a derelict village, all the windows of the cottages gaping wide and the doors hanging off their hinges. It looked so dead it could have belonged to another century; but this, he recognized, was Katie's village, the place where she had been born. The village had died when the pit was closed. All such villages died when the black arteries were cut.

The drive this morning seemed endless, but eventually the cab turned into the dark tree-lined drive and came to a stop before the steps of the Manor.

Andree, getting out, looked up at the driver and said, "Wait for me." Then, mounting the steps, he pulled the long handle that rang the house bell.

It was some minutes before the door opened, and when

Kennard saw who the early visitor was he seemed to lose his imperturbable composure.

"I would like to see your master," said Andree.

"I . . . I am afraid he is out, sir," Kennard's eyes were fixed on Andree's bruised face.

"Tell your master that Captain Fraenkel would like to see him." Andree's voice was low, the words clipped, his foreign accent very defined.

"He is out, sir. It is the truth; he is out riding."

There was a pause before Andree asked, "How long is he likely to be?"

"I don't really know, sir."

"You must have some idea."

"Not this morning."

"Well, I'll wait; I'm in no hurry."

As Kennard made to speak again Andree turned and went down the steps, and, paying the cab driver, he told him not to wait.

As the driver turned the horses round Andree ascended the steps once more and confronted Kennard, who was standing in the doorway. The butler made no move to allow him to pass, but now, joining his hands together and rubbing them as if they were cold, and his voice holding a persuasive note, he said, "If you'd allow me to say so, sir, I think it would be wiser if you didn't wait."

Andree inclined his head towards Kennard before saying, "Wise or not, I mean to wait, either inside or out."

Kennard now took a step forward, pulling the door behind him and, his voice low, he said, "The master is in a very bad way this morning, sir. He's . . . he's been up all night. And I think it only wise to tell you he's already had one . . . one upset this morning." He didn't say fight, but the word indicated such. "He's in a very nasty mood, sir."

"Thank you for warning me. That makes two of us. I also am in a very bad mood." He lifted his finger and touched the cut on his brow, then brought it down to his cheekbone.

"I'm sorry, sir," and Kennard sounded sorry, but he went on. "And I'm sorry I cannot invite you in because the mistress is quite unwell this morning. The doctor says she must be kept quiet and it's very difficult, sir. I trust you understand, sir."

Andree breathed deeply, then asked, "Which road did your master take?"

317

"I think he went in that direction." Kennard pointed a little to the right of him. "By the track that branches off the road over the fells to the quarry and the mine; but I warn you sir . . ." Now Kennard put his hand out towards Andree as if to touch him, then withdrew it before saying, "He's on a horse and he has a whip, and he's very good at handling both—even now."

Andree, looking deep into the eyes of this old man, said quietly, "Thank you, I'll remember." With that he turned about and went down the steps and along the drive to the main road, and after walking up it for a short distance he saw the lane leading off, and it bore evidence of a horse having recently passed that way.

He now walked up the lane, which was long and bordered on each side by a high hedge. When eventually it came to an end he found himself on the open moor, and he stood gazing about him, but nowhere could he see any movement except that of the larks shooting up from the ground. In the distance the land rose slightly and he made for this point, and when he reached it he again paused and looked around. And now he did see something. Not far off a man was walking in a peculiar fashion. He had his back to him and his face to a hedge, and he was going along this crabwise. It it hadn't been for the furtiveness of the figure, he would have taken the man for a ditcher. The man had now moved to where the ground rose into a bank, and he watched him pulling himself cautiously up and peering over, then lying flat against the slope.

To the left of him Andree's eyes were now caught by a gleam of water, and it decided the direction he should take. As he neared it he saw it was the quarry that the butler had mentioned and that Katie had spoken of at times. The water came to within a foot of the top of the rough-edged stone. The expanse looked like a moderate-sized lake. The water was still and clear, and he could see juts of rock sticking out some distance below the surface. Three parts of the place, he saw, was surrounded by rough scrub and stunted bush.

His attention was brought abruptly from the water by the sound of a horse neighing, and after glancing hastily about him he made his way to where he saw a trampled gap in the shrub that indicated a pathway.

He was at the entrance to the gap when he heard the neighing for a second time. Moving into the shelter of the shrub, his face held tight against his shoulder, he glanced up the road. He wanted to see Rosier before Rosier saw him. As the butler had suggested, a man on a horse with a whip had already a big advantage, and put a man of Rosier's calibre in that position and anything could happen. Although Andree did not now look towards the quarry, it was in his mind that he was too near it for comfort, but if he wanted to confront this man there was nothing for it but to make his stand here.

He could hear the horse's hooves now, and when he moved his head forward just the slightest he saw the horse and its rider coming towards him at a walking pace. He saw Rosier's head and shoulders clearly outlined above the bank that hemmed in the lane farther back. The face looked distorted, even terrible. He could not see the ear, or the place where it had been, but he saw the dark patch that was made up of twisted scars covering one side of his face. But what he did see clearly was the thin strip of flesh that was all that remained of his left hand, and as his eyes picked out the solitary finger and thumb curved round the rein there passed through him a fleeting feeling of admiration for this man who could handle the great beast he was riding with practically one hand. Then the feeling was gone, replaced by one of amazement, when from the top of the bank he saw another figure, and his mind registered that this was the man he had seen going furtively down the back of the hedge; and now this man, with a cry that wasn't unlike the roar of a wild animal, jumped from the top of the bank on to the rider, and the next moment the horse, rearing madly, toppled the two figures to the ground and pranced in a terrified fashion before galloping back up the lane.

What was this? What was this? Andree was searching for an explanation. A tramp . . . or someone not unlike himself with a score to settle. He had the urge to rush forward and separate the combatants, but he remained where he was against the hedge, until the two panting figures rolled towards him, then he pressed himself back through the tangle of bush and for a moment they were lost to his sight. He was now almost in the same spot where he had first seen the man, and cautiously he moved up by the shrub wall until, through a small opening in the branches, he found himself looking down on the two gasping and struggling figures, and as the faces turned and twisted away from him, first one uppermost then the other, he realized that there was a similarity between

319

them, for both their faces were scarred. The attacker had a dark blue weal cutting straight across one eye, the lid of which was closed, and another, more fresh-looking, weal across his great loose lips.

He watched the man now deliver a blow into Bernard Rosier's face that seemed to stun him; then, getting to his feet, he swayed a moment before lifting his heavy boot and aiming it at Rosier's middle. But it never reached its target, for Rosier, with the agility of a cat, grabbed the thrust-out leg and in a flash the man was on his back, and he lay still, where he had fallen, his body looking as if he was going into a dance, one knee pulled up and one arm raised in a curved position above his head.

What followed now happened so quickly that Andree could not have prevented it even if he had sprung instantly down into the road. He had watched Bernard Rosier pull himself to his feet and go and stand over the man, then drunkenly stoop to the ground. The next minute he had heaved up a boulder and dropped it with all the force he could muster on to the man's head. The impact caused Andree to screw up his eyes and dig his nails deep into the palms of his hands. It didn't need a second glance to know that the man was now beyond help, and his natural instinct was to spring on this devil and batter him with his fists. Yet he didn't move.

As he watched Rosier tugging the man by his legs towards the quarry he knew exactly what he was going to do with his victim. He also knew what he himself was going to do. This was one time when Rosier would not escape justice.

The plop came sooner than he expected. He could not, from where he stood, see Rosier pushing the body into the quarry, but he saw him a minute later when he staggered into view again, and if ever a devil had a representative on earth Andree saw it in this man. He watched him now lean for support against a stunted tree, then put his hand to his mouth and call. After he had called a second time the horse, stepping gingerly, came down the lane and stopped near him.

Andree watched Rosier making an effort to mount. He had to try a number of times before he succeeded; then, his body drooping forward in the saddle, he muttered something, and the horse turned about and walked slowly up the lane.

Andree now stood gazing into space; then he took off his hat and wiped the moisture from his forehead with his hand,

and when it ran down into his eyes he brought out a handkerchief and dabbed all round his face and beard. Turning slowly, he walked down by the hedge to the quarry and, moving a little way along its edge, he saw the track made by the passage of the body.

The water in the quarry, having been disturbed, was not so clear at this point now, but still clear enough to see, low down, a dark bulk lying against the light brown of the stone. It didn't look like a man; anyone looking down at the shape would not take it for a man. It could be a shadow, or an old sack, or some black earth that had settled on the stone; but it was none of these, it was a man who had just some minutes before been murdered.

His own step was unsteady as he walked up the lane, following in the tracks of the horse, and at one point he knew the need to rest and think, but as yet his thoughts were not clear. The dead man would be missed. They would start searching for him. Or would they? Men walked away from homes every day and never returned. But this particular man had known Bernard Rosier; he had known his movements. Perhaps he was of his household. But whether he was or not he had suffered at Rosier's hands. Of that Andree was sure. The man had been out to wreak personal vengeance on Rosier as he himself had wanted to do.

He must now, he knew, go to the police; but first he must get home and prepare Katie. Although he wasn't personally involved in this matter he was the only one who had witnessed it, and he would be called into court. So she must be told all the circumstances. . . .

But things did not work out as Andree planned, and all because when he stepped from the lane into the rough main road he saw running towards him a lady—to be more exact, a climber. The woman was dressed in a ridiculously short skirt that only reached her calves. This was part of the costume that these mad women adopted when they went climbing the fells. She came panting up to Andree, saying, "Oh, sir, I need your help. We . . . my friend and I have just come across a gentleman who has fallen from his horse; he must have been attacked and is unconscious. Come. Come quickly."

Andree looked down into the thin, pert face and said, "You are running in the wrong direction, madam; his house lies the other way."

"But . . . but"—the lady's eyes widened—"you know him?" Now her hand went to her mouth as she stared at the discoloured eye, then gasped, "It is you! You . . . you have attacked this gentleman. It is you!" She stepped back as if in fear, and he said, "I have not attacked this gentleman, madam; I simply know to whom you refer, and I tell you to go in the opposite direction. Good-day to you." He turned now abruptly on his heel and left her staring after him. It was some seconds later when he heard her running along the road again.

That encounter was very unfortunate, he considered, but then in the final issue it would make no difference.

*　　*　　*

"Kaa-tee"—Andree closed his eyes—"I have told you the truth, every word." When he opened them again and looked into her face he said, "I swear by God all I have told you is exactly as it happened. This"—he tapped his eye, then his shin, and his groin—"this happened last night, not this morning. I did not fight with Rosier; I got these from his thugs."

"Oh, Andy!" Her lips were quivering, her whole body was quivering. This is what she had gone in fear of for years, him and Bernard Rosier meeting. And he had come in like this, his face black and blue, his shin ripped, and a swelling in his groin so painful that he was limping, and he expected her to believe a tale about being set upon by four men. . . .

"You don't believe me even yet. What about the man I saw murdered?"

Yes, what about the man he saw murdered? There was no need for him to make that up. She put her hands out to him and said, "Where is it going to end, Andy? Where?"

"At this point, and finally." He nodded briskly at her. "He's made a rope for his own neck this time. I'm going to the police right now. I would have gone on my way down, but I wanted to prepare you first and not have them come here frightening you."

Frightening her? She was so full of fear now that she could have vomited where she stood. Theresa's great effort had been in vain; she had not saved Andy after all, and Rosier, the maimed Rosier, appeared even more terrible than he had before, more powerful, more vicious.

At this point Betty opened the door, and without even

322

knocking. She looked at the two faces turned towards her. Then, keeping her eyes on the captain, she said, "There's . . . there's two men to see you, Captain."

"Who are they?" Katie had stepped forward, but now Betty closed the door and stood with her back towards it and she repeated, "They want to see the captain. It's all right, they just want to see the captain."

As Andree went towards the door he turned his head to Katie and said firmly, "Stay where you are"; then, looking at Betty, he added, "You, too." And she nodded at him as if he had said, "See that she doesn't come out of the room."

Andree's step halted outside the door immediately after he had closed it, because there, in the centre of the hall, stood two policemen. When Betty had said men he'd had the idea that he would see the man he had released this morning and his pal, who, having got cold feet, had made up their minds to tell him the name of their employer. He walked towards the two officers, one of whom he knew: the sergeant who had sat in Theresa's room until she died. It was this officer who now spoke. Hesitantly, he said, "I'm . . . I'm sorry, Captain, about this."

"About what?" Andree's tone was quiet.

"We . . . we have to ask you to come along to the station, sir."

"Why?" The terse question caused the officer to blink before he said pedantically, "I have to arrest you, sir, on the charge of occasioning grievous bodily harm to one Mr. Bernard Rosier. I must warn you that anything you say will be taken down and used in evidence against you."

"Well! Well!"

The exclamation disconcerted the policemen. They watched the big Swede turn his head towards the door through which he had entered the hall before he said, "I'll come with you; just give me a minute."

"Very good, sir."

Back in the parlour, Andree dismissed Betty; then, taking Katie by the shoulders, he said, "Now listen, darling. Listen attentively. Listen as you have never listened before, because it's very important. Out there are two policemen. I am being charged with causing grievous bodily harm to Rosier . . . exactly what you still believe. At least you have that in common with the policemen."

When her quivering lips moved to say something he shook

323

her gently and said softly, "Listen. What I told you about Rosier murdering that man, I don't want you to say a word . . . not a word about it. Do you hear?"

"But, Andy!"

Again he shook her. "Kaa-tee. I want to do this in my own way. I want this swine of a man to pull the rope so tight around his own neck that he can't get it loose again. Now if you open your mouth a little bit . . . just a little bit"—he now demonstrated with his first finger and thumb, shaking his hand before her face—"you'll spoil everything. What is more, you could quite likely turn the tables and make him prove that I killed that man."

"No! No!"

"Yes! Yes, Kaa-tee! Now you must do as I say. Not a word until I tell you. Promise me. Swear by God you'll not say anything."

She stared at him. In every incident in which she had been involved with Rosier she had kept quiet, and so had suffered. And now she was to do so again. But this would be so much worse than anything that had ever happened before. She found herself nodding her head, for it was impossible to speak, and then she was in his arms and he was kissing her hard. And when he released her he smiled and said, "We'll have tea at the same time; I'll be back."

*   *   *

And they had tea at the same time. Andree had been released on bail in the sum of two hundred pounds. He had also spent the afternoon with Mr. Hewitt. He told Mr. Hewitt of the two attacks on him, of his visit to Greenwall Manor that morning, of his searching for Rosier, and seeing him ride up the lane to the main road, of his meeting with the woman climber. But he made no mention of what he had seen happen near the quarry, knowing full well that, should he do so, Hewitt, as his representative, would be bound by law to divulge his knowledge to the court, if not before.

All through he stressed that he had never met up or spoken with Rosier, and this was true.

The court at Durham was packed, the room so overcrowded that the doors had been closed long before the proceedings had begun. A bill of indictment had brought the case up within a week.

The case of the sea captain who had attacked the owner of Greenwall Manor, and he only recovering from wounds inflicted by his sister four months previously, had aroused not only local interest but had got some people in the county betting on what stretch the captain would get, while others, more discerning, were asking the question why the captain should want to attack Bernard Rosier in the first place. It had never been fully explained in the newspapers what reason his sister had for the attempt she had made on his life.

All eyes were now on the defending counsel. The case seemed to be going against him, for he had as yet come up with nothing in the nature of a defence for his client.

The last two witnesses, one eager to give evidence, one seemingly reluctant, had not helped him. Kennard had muttered his evidence and had been told to speak up by Mr. Justice Gordon. He had then repeated that Captain Fraenkel had called at the Manor the morning of the incident and asked to see his master.

What else had he said, the defending counsel had asked.

There was a pause before Kennard answered that Captain Fraenkel had said he would wait for his master, either inside or outside the house.

"Was his manner ferocious, wild?" asked counsel, and to this Kennard replied briefly, "No, sir."

But the lady climber had been a different kind of witness; she still seemed incensed at the callousness of the man she had met on the road, who had refused to return with her and give help to the poor creature who had fallen from his horse.

Many eyes in the court had turned towards the poor creature. Bernard Rosier was dressed in a snuff-brown suit with wide lapels. His attire was impeccable. His face was such as to arouse pity. The hole where his ear had been was in evidence, as was his maimed hand, which every now and then would grasp the rail in front of him, only to be quickly withdrawn as if its owner did not wish to expose his infirmities. His appearance and demeanour while on the witness stand had brought him the sympathy of the jury and of most of the court, as he related how he had gone out for his morning ride, a pastime of which he had only recently begun to avail himself, and all he was able to recollect after he had entered the lane, leading from the main road, was of someone jumping from a high bank on to his back. In the struggle that ensued he remembered gripping a beard. He also remembered punching at the man's face. What followed was rather hazy; he couldn't really recollect remounting his horse. He did not remember the lady finding him on the road; he knew nothing until he woke up in the hall of his home with his servant attending him.

Now Andree was looking down into the cold piercing gaze of the prosecuting counsel as he finished his cross-examination with the words, "After your evidence it puts a strain on one's imagination as to how you have come to your present position. As a captain of a ship you are supposedly a responsible person, yet you have faced this court and jury and told them such a cock-and-bull story that an idiot would have hesitated to use."

"I object, m'lud."

Defending counsel was waved down, and the prosecuting counsel went on, "You admit going to the Rosier residence and asking to see Mr. Bernard Rosier. The butler has said in evidence that you were determined to wait, either inside or outside the house, until you saw his master. Now you want us to believe that after you left the grounds of Greenwall Manor you took a walk over the fells and the first person you spoke to was Miss Richards, who ran to you on the main road and beseeched you to help the man she and her friend had found unconscious. You admit refusing to come to her aid. You also admit having told her in which direction the unconscious man's house lay. You weren't supposed to have met him, yet you knew that he was the man who was lying unconscious on the road and where he lived . . . Do you seriously expect us to believe that you never met Mr. Rosier that morning, that you did not inflict injuries on him from which he might have died? You are being charged before this court with occasioning grievous bodily harm, but for the good ladies who came across the prostrate man on the road the charge could easily have been one of murder." His voice, from a high dramatic note, dropped to a tone of bewilderment, even sadness, as he repeated, "It is beyond me, sir, how you ever came to be in your present position of responsibility."

There came a little tittering from some quarter of the court, and as Andree stared down into the prosecuting counsel's face he had the urge to thrust his fist into it, but, swallowing deeply, he said, "There is something sir, I have kept until last. When you hear it it may alter your opinion with regards to my mentality."

The words seemed to startle the court, for the tone was like a knife cutting through the proceedings. It was a tone of authority; it was a tone that said, Let us finish with subterfuge, let us have no more shilly-shallying. Let us have the truth.

"I went," said Andree, his words hard and clipped, "to Mr. Rosier's residence to confront him with the evidence of the attack his hired thugs had made on me the previous evening." He put a finger to his eye, which was still discoloured and showed a scar above his eyebrow. "Four hired men had set about me when I left my ship. They not only kicked me and beat me but they filled my mouth and smeared my clothes with filth. I was able to retain hold of one of these men, and from him I got enough information to realize who was paying them. That was the reason for my visit." Andree paused. The attention of the whole court was riveted on him. Then he went on. "As you have heard, Mr. Rosier was not at home. His servant told me the direction he had taken and I followed it until I came to a water-filled quarry. As I stood at its edge I heard the sound of an approaching horse and I guessed the rider was the man I was looking for. Not wanting him to see me first, I stood in the shelter of some brushwood. It was from this point that I saw a man leap from the high bank that bordered this lane and bear that man to the ground." Now Andree thrust out his arm and jerked his first finger like the point of a rapier in the direction of Bernard Rosier, and startled eyes in the courtroom followed it. "I watched them struggling. His assailant managed to get to his feet and was about to kick him when he grabbed his leg and overthrew him. The man did not move after he hit the ground. That could have been enough, but no, that man"—

the finger stabbed twice now—"that man took a boulder and crashed it on to the head of the insensible fellow, and it was over and done so quickly that I was unable to intervene."

A gasp went round the court and there was a turning of bodies towards Bernard Rosier, and Andree went on, "But that was not the end. He took this man by the legs and dragged him to the quarry and dropped him in. The man's name, your honour . . ." Now Andree turned towards Mr. Justice Gordon and, addressing him solely, said, ". . . is William Dennison."

Mr. Justice Gordon now called for order, and when it was restored he said quietly, "Proceed, Captain Fraenkel." And Andree went on, his voice quieter now, "I have learnt, your honour, that William Dennison had worked at the Manor since he was a boy. From being a gardener he had become jack-of-all-trades and bore the brunt of his master's temper. A few years ago his master went as far as to slash his eye out with a whip, and the very night before he died his face was again marked with a whip. What I saw that morning was William Dennison taking his revenge. But instead of being the avenger he became the victim of this man who had ill-treated him over the years. The police were notified that William Dennison was missing, but nobody bothered very much about this William Dennison except his widow. She is in the court today." Again he was pointing, but now with his hand curved, the palm upwards. "When the body is retrieved from the shelf of rock on which it lies in the quarry she will no doubt identify her husband."

Before Mr. Justice Gordon, calling loudly for order, could state that the case was adjourned further uproar broke out, but in it three people remained still, as if transfixed in their hate and fear. Bernard Rosier was no longer the maimed gentleman eliciting sympathy. After gazing at Andree for a space he let out an unintelligible cry, following which his whole attitude became demoniacal; and as he was guided into an anteroom he kept his head turned, with his eyes boring into Andree, then they flicked to where Katie stood, her hand to her throat, and again he made the sound, only louder now, and she bowed her head against it.

10

When the case was opened against Bernard Rosier he was charged with the murder of William Dennison, and he was defended by a leading London barrister. The hearing went on for two days, and again and again the defence counsel brought to the fore the motive of spite behind the chief witness's action in withholding his knowledge of the murder until he had, what he imagined, the most damaging moment in which to reveal it.

The barrister was an eloquent speaker. When at last he addressed the jury he made great play of the fact that when the accused left his house that fatal morning he was still in a very weak state, in fact he shouldn't have been riding at all. The accused's servant, he said, was a stupid man and the previous evening he had annoyed his master, who on this occasion did not remember raising his whip to him. He had frankly admitted that on another occasion, many years ago, he had beaten this man for his neglect of a valuable horse, which neglect had caused the animal to die. This—the barrister now added expression to his words with his outstretched hands—this was understandable to any man who loved a horse. But to return to this particular morning. The accused had been quite candid. He had told the court that he had drunk heavily the night prior to the day on which the incident occurred. He had been in such pain with his facial wound that he had tried to numb his suffering with alcohol. He had, as he said, only a faint recollection of leaving the house. All he had wanted to do that morning was to get on his horse and ride, and ride, and ride, in the hope that it would ease both his mental and physical torment.

The barrister informed the jury that he wasn't merely using a figure of speech when he alluded to mental torment, because the accused had had a great deal of family troubles over the last three years—troubles that could not be brought to light on this occasion but nevertheless were very real, and so . . . The barrister paused long here, and ended, "He goes riding to ease his pain and in the hope of finding peace." Another telling pause. And now with raised voice he goes on, "Yes, yes, he admits to saying on a previous occasion that he thought he had gripped a beard, but"—the barrister swept his eyes over the twelve men—"you find yourself almost battered to death and hear people talking about a bearded sailor who had come to the house demanding to see you, and in an attitude which spoke of vengeance. . . ."

There was a protest at this point from the prosecuting counsel, and a warning from Mr. Justice Gordon, and the barrister, after bowing to the latter, turned once more to the jury and asked them to look at the prisoner, at the extent of his facial wounds, at his maimed hand, and to make a big effort to put themselves in his place, remembering that those wounds had been inflicted only a few weeks prior to the date on which he was brought from his horse and beaten almost insensible. If, when in such a low physical state, they themselves had been attacked, would they remember how they had retaliated? Would they remember picking up a stone and throwing it at their assailant? The barrister did not at this point go on to ask if they would remember taking their assailant by the heels and dropping him in the quarry, but he ended by telling them they were all men of high intelligence, and therefore he felt sure that they would bring in a verdict of "Not guilty". . . .

In answer, the prosecuting counsel picked up practically where the counsel for the defence had left off. "Gentlemen of the jury," he began, "the stone was not thrown at the deceased man as the defending counsel would have you believe. As the one and only witness to the incident has stated, a large boulder was dropped directly on to the upturned face of a prostrate man. A conscious man, seeing a stone coming at him, would instinctively have turned his face away; the deceased was not capable of doing that. We are not to know whether he was already dead when the boulder struck him, but it is most unlikely. I suggest he was but temporarily stunned. Bloodstains were found on the road at a certain point where there was no protrusion whatever that could have caused death. It has been verified by the doctor and the coroner that the deceased must have been lying on his back and quite immobile when the boulder was dropped on to his face. He may or may not have died from the callous, cruel action, but the accused did not wait to find out. The defending counsel would have us believe that the accused dragged his servant to the edge of the quarry and toppled him into the water, then mounted his horse and rode away . . . all unconscious of what he was doing."

Here the prosecuting counsel paused and the court waited. There was not a murmur, a cough, or rustle. Then he began again, "The deceased had been a servant in the accused's house since he was a young boy. He was brought there from an orphanage, and from what you have learnt it would seem that during the whole course of his life he knew nothing but hard work, low wages, and blows. You have heard the widow of the deceased telling how her husband used to sit trembling after his master had stormed at him; that at times he was afraid to go out in the mornings to get his master's horse ready. . . . What was he afraid of? The whip. The whip, gentlemen. The whip that had deprived him of an eye fourteen years ago. You might ask, if he was so badly treated, why he didn't leave this man's service. I myself put this question to the man's widow, and her answer was, 'The master would never give him a reference.' You might go on to say that if the deceased and his wife had been in service all these years —the deceased's wife acted as kitchen-maid at the Manor— they should have saved money enough to enable them to take a chance and leave this terrifying servitude. I, too, thought this until I learnt, as you have done today, that when William Dennison started as a gardener's boy his wage was a shilling a week. He was forty when he died, and he had never been paid more than four shillings a week. His wife was receiving three shillings a week. I think, gentlemen, you have your answer why William Dennison remained to serve the man who treated him so violently that he was driven to seek revenge. It must be evident to you that the deceased was aware that there would be grave consequences to his action, likely imprisonment, but a man who had been treated as he had was past caring."

The prosecuting counsel ended in a sombre tone, "Now, gentlemen, I only ask you to consider the last cruel act of the prisoner to his servant. There is no need for you to recall the many cruel acts that the deceased suffered at the hands of his master. It will be enough to concentrate on his last one, and so doing your verdict will be one of 'Guilty'."

The jury was absent for an hour. When they returned their spokesman, after telling the judge they had come to a decision, said, "We find the prisoner not guilty of murder but guilty of manslaughter."

For the first time in days a lightness came into Bernard Rosier's brooding countenance. He blinked and looked about him as if to say, "There now, what did I tell you? I knew they couldn't do it."

Many eyes were on him. Some faces were smiling slightly, heads were turned to each other, voices whispering, "Well, what do you expect? After all, he's gentry, isn't he?" But there were others, the gentry themselves, who had their attention fixed on Mr. Justice Gordon; and there were Katie and Andree, their joined hands hidden under the folds of her skirt, gripping tight.

As the judge looked about the court, waiting for absolute silence before he spoke, Bernard Rosier kept his eyes fixed on him. He felt so sure of the verdict now that he could almost have cried, "Hurry up with it." His head moved just the slightest when Mr. Justice Gordon began to speak in a flat, emotionless voice. "It could not have been otherwise. It is a fair verdict because there was no doubt that the accused was attacked." Here the judge paused for some seconds, as if weighing carefully what he was about to say next. Then, his manner changing, he leant forward, and, moving his finger stiffly in the direction of the prisoner, his voice, full of condemnation, ran through the court as he said:

"The jury in their mercy have found you guilty only of manslaughter, but I cannot close my eyes to the fact that over the years you treated the deceased man as if he were a mad dog, not a human being, whom together with his wife you kept in underpaid servitude. And by your last and final act, when you crushed this man's skull with a boulder as he lay unconscious, then threw him in the quarry, you have proved yourself to be a vile and vicious individual, and the minimum sentence, in all justice, I can pass on you is one of seven years' imprisonment."

"No! Blast you! No!"

Two officers were restraining the prisoner as he leaned over the box and glared in the direction of Mr. Justice Gordon, who now rose, and the court with him.

There was a general hubbub as the judge left the bench. The great man from London looked enraged. The prisoner was again shouting. Then, suddenly becoming still in the arms of the gaolers, he turned his head to the side and directed his maddened gaze towards two people standing close together, the tall bearded man and the equally tall white-faced woman. His lips opened and froth came into the corners of his mouth and, screaming now, he yelled, "Blast you to hell!" His shouting still penetrated the courtroom as he was taken below.

Putting his arm round Katie, Andree turned her stiff body about and led her away, and as they passed through the crowded hallway a remark came to her. One man was saying to another, "A bit thick, seven years. He'll never be able to stand it, not even if they cut his time, not in his condition." And she found herself praying that the man would be right.

BOOK IV

Catherine
1909

1

Bernard Rosier did not die in prison as Katie hoped. After serving six years of his sentence he was released and, as if making up for lost time, he revelled in drink, riding and debauchery until he had a stroke, following which nothing more was heard of him for some long time.

Between the years 1881 and 1909 Katie's life, to all appearances, ran smoothly. Her image in Shields changed. Perhaps it was the whisper from Mr. Hewitt in the right ear, following Rosier's trial, which incidentally brought her into favour with "the class". Rumours ranged from her being the victim of Rosier's frustrated passion, when she worked for his parents, to the one that said he had set her up in a certain kind of house, and that when it was flourishing she spurned his attentions. The rumour that implied he'd had her wrongfully imprisoned most people thought a bit far-fetched. But everyone saw Rosier's action to try and incriminate Andree as an act of spite against her. But now Katie Mulholland—or Mrs. Fraenkel, as people remembered to call her—was looked upon as a respectable married woman.

Two more people had come into, and deeply affected, Katie's life during these years; one brought joy, the other fear.

The fear erupted one spring day in 1888 when Andree's son, Captain Nils Fraenkel, paid him the promised visit. Nils Fraenkel was thirty-six years old at the time and he looked the very incarnation of his father, as Andree had looked when he and Katie had first met, and right from that spring day peace seeped out of Katie's life, for Andree's son desired her as Andree did. He wanted to touch her as Andree did. He wanted the same things from her as she gave to Andree.

At first she tried to dispel such suppositions by telling herself not to be so vain, for was she not nine years his senior; but finally there had come the time when he asked her to leave his father and go away with him, and from that day real fear entered into her life again.

If Nils Fraenkel had been like his father other than in looks, Katie imagined the situation would have been eased, for then Nils would have drunk deeply, and been able to carry his drink; he would have laughed loudly, talked to all men, and had his women, until he met—the one woman. But Nils drank little, and when he did it made him silly, sometimes nasty. He laughed only on occasions. He did not hob-nob with all men, for was he not a captain of a fine liner. He had a position to uphold, and he upheld it. As for women, all that Katie had gathered regarding his ideas on this subject was that he scorned port women, and this made her question more than once whether Andree had told his son how he had met her, at the very haunt of the "port women", or dock dollies. It was a question she had never put to Andree. Hardly ever did she mention Nils to him. Any talk concerning Nils always came from Andree.

Andree himself welcomed his son warmly to the house. Secretly, Nils's coming eased a pocket in his conscience; he imagined that, seeing Katie, his son would now understand why he had left his family when they were young. But it never dawned on him just to what extent his son understood. Had it done so his wrath would have been greater towards him than it had been towards Rosier, and Katie was aware of this. . . .

The joy that came into her life was brought by Joe's grand-daughter Catherine.

Catherine was Lucy's eldest child, and Katie had first made the acquaintance of them both in 1892 when Lucy, with the two-months-old baby in her arms, had come to the house in Westoe to ask this aunt of hers—this rich aunt—for help.

Only seven months previously Lucy had married Patrick Connolly, the father of the child. And the reason for the hasty union had outraged Joe and he had closed his door on his daughter, but not before telling her she would go head-long to hell like his sister Katie in Shields.

To her great disappointment, Katie found she did not like her niece, and she strongly disliked her brawling husband, but from the first glimpse of the child she had loved her, for she saw Sarah in her, Sarah the baby—not Sara the lady. And with the years the love had grown, until now between Catherine and herself there existed a bond that was as strong as any between mother and daughter.

The embittered Lucy was vitally aware of this bond and would have broken it many years before if it hadn't been that her daughter Catherine was the only bucket she could dip into Katie's well.

Catherine was now eighteen years old, and for the past seven years she had been a day pupil at the convent school, and Katie had had to pay Lucy for the privilege of educating her daughter by allowing her a pound a week. Lucy knew she had a hold over Katie, and frequently she used her power by sending Catherine to "borrow" from her—as today.

Katie was resting on the chaise-longue at the foot of the bed, and Catherine was sitting by her side, her fingers restlessly entwining each other, and Katie, tapping the hands, said gently, "How much does she want, dear?"

Catherine, her eyes cast down, murmured, "A pound. She says she must pay four weeks' rent, but she won't; she'll only pay two and a shilling off the back and spend the rest on . . ." Her voice trailed away, and Katie said, "Has she been at it again?"

Catherine nodded her head once in reply before lifting it quickly, and, her voice now low and rapid, she said, "Oh, Aunt Katie, I feel dreadful, dreadful. I feel wicked because I'm always wishing"—she closed her eyes tightly and shook her head violently before finishing—"that she was dead."

"Oh, child! You mustn't talk like that. She can't help it."

"Oh yes, she can, Aunt Katie. But . . . but because she knows that . . ." She swallowed and did not go on, and Katie ended for her, "Yes, yes, I know. Because she knows that I'll give you anything you ask for that's within my power, she uses you."

Catherine, now holding Katie's hand between her own, stroked it as she said, "There was a terrible row last night, and . . . and she wasn't drunk either. She threatened to take me away from the convent. It was when I lost my temper and threw it in her face—she was on about keeping me at the convent and me getting airy-fairy ways—that I told her she only let me go there in the first place because you said you'd give her the money as long as I stayed. But now I'm terrified, Aunt Katie, that she really might take it into her head to stop

339

me going to college. She could, you know; she gets so bitter."

"She won't, don't worry. I'll see to that. And I'll only give you ten shillings to take back. If she pays the rent—and she'll have to—she won't be able to do much with the change."

Katie touched the soft cheek, the cheek that was of the same texture as her own. But there the likeness between Joe's granddaughter and herself ended, because Lucy Mulholland's daughter resembled in looks her Irish father. She had his dark eyes, his luxuriant black hair, his high cheekbones and large mouth—the mouth which in her father showed weakness but in her portrayed a sensitiveness. But there was nothing of Lucy in Catherine's face, nor yet, apparently, in her character.

Impulsively now Catherine leant forward and, dropping her head on Katie's shoulder, brokenly whispered, "Oh, Aunt Katie, if only I could stay here with you. You know"—she moved her face against the lavender-scented silk of Katie's dress—"when the nuns talk about heaven I don't see angels and great wonderful halls, I see this house and you."

"Oh, my dear." There was both a break and a laugh in Katie's voice. "It won't always go on. Next year you'll be away at college, and once you're a teacher you'll be your own mistress, and then you'll be able to make your home where you like." She raised Catherine's head and looked down into her eyes and whispered, "Where you like, my dear. . . . But now, come on." She patted the cheek sharply. "Cheer up; you're going to stay to tea. . . . And look, go and have a nice hot bath."

As Catherine was going out of the room Betty entered, and, bending her fat body almost double, she said in a loud whisper, "What you think of her dress?"

"Lovely, Betty."

"I'd say it's lovely. She'll be the best-dressed woman . . ."

"Oh, come in and stop your chattering," said Katie impatiently, and Betty, on a laugh, closed the door and came across to the couch. But now, her face taking on a straight prim look, she remained silent for a moment before saying, "He's come back. He's in the smokeroom with the captain."

Katie stared at Betty; then, looking towards the window, she said, "Well, he wasn't sure about sailing. He said so."

"That means I'll have to set for one extra. You didn't want that; it'll be lopsided, spoil the table."

At this point Betty's words were cut off by a sharp rap on

the door, and after exchanging a glance with Katie she opened it and Andree's son entered the room, and she, her lips compressed, left it.

"Oh! You resting?" Nil's English, unlike Andree's, was as a foreigner would speak it.

Katie turned her glance away and, leaning her head against the couch, said with studied calmness, "Yes, Nils, I'm resting."

"You really tired?"

"Yes. That's why I'm resting."

A smile, reminiscent of Andree's, touched Nils's lips. "You want to watch that feeling, it's a sign of old age; it'll have you flat on your back before you know where you are."

"I'm aware it's a sign of old age."

"Don't be ridiculous." The smile had gone from his face, which now looked almost aggressive. "Don't start on that tack again. You don't look a day over forty. You know you don't, I've told you, and told you."

"I know nothing of the kind, Nils. What I do know is that I'm no longer young."

"Stop it!" He was leaning over the foot of the couch, his face thrust towards her, his voice low. "You're young and so am I. You feel young, you know you do. You feel whatever age you want to feel...."

"Shut up, Nils." Katie pulled herself upright on the couch, and now, thrusting her face towards his, she whispered, "Before God, Nils, if you start again I'll tell your father. I swear I will."

He stared into her face, holding her eyes, his own expression changing the while to one of mockery, before saying, "Aw, Katie, don't be stupid. You know you can't shut me up with such threats. If you had been going to tell him you would have done so years ago.... But all right, all right." He straightened up. "Don't get mad at me. I hate it when you look at me like that." He walked away from her now and stood looking at her dress which was lying across the bed. Then he laughed as he said, "I could have tossed my hat in the air when I knew we couldn't go out before the morning, because now I can witness you in rose taffeta and lace conquering the aristocracy of Westoe; the thick cream."

"Don't be silly, Nils."

"Silly! You know I'm not being silly. This is what you've been wanting for years."

"It isn't." Her voice was vehement.

"All right, then say it's what he's been wanting for you for years . . . and rightly so. In his place, I'd have been the same."

They were staring at each other, and Katie was once again seeing Andy in his youth, or as he was in early middle age. But this man was not Andy; he had neither his character nor appeal. For even at eighty there was still only the one Andy, the fascinating, vital man who had taught her to love and live.

Nils was coming towards her again, and she stiffened as he paused by her side and touched her hair gently with his fingers while saying something in his native tongue, as Andy was wont to do when bestowing endearments to her. Then he went quickly from the room.

She remained sitting motionless as she heard his voice calling to Catherine from the landing, "Don't use all the steam, young lady. And get rid of that harem smell; I don't want to be poisoned"; and Catherine's voice, full at the moment of gaiety, coming back at him, "Oh, hello, Uncle Nils. Isn't it lovely? Won't be long." Then another voice, that of Jessie the maid, saying, "Will I run you a bath, Captain, when Miss Catherine's finished?"

Katie did not hear Nils's reply to this, but she knew from Jessie's suppressed titter that it was something risible. Nils joked with Jessie in a somewhat condescending manner at times. It was as Betty said, Jessie needed a strong hand and she had no right at this moment to be upstairs. She had noticed, and not for the first time, that the young hussy was always very much in evidence when Nils was about.

As Katie rose from the couch she thought, and not without some regret, that Jessie was wasting her time, did she but know it.

* * *

The tea over, Catherine was saying her goodbyes when Andree, who was sitting by the drawing-room window, called to her across the room, saying, "I'll bet you'll never guess who's waiting out there for you?"

"Oh, he's not, Uncle, is he?" Catherine moved forward, the colour flooding her face, and Andree mimicked, "Oh, he's not, Uncle, is he? Well, he is, me girl!" Andree held out his hand and drew her towards him, and she laughed self-consciously as she looked over the front garden and between the trees bordered by the white railings to the far side of the road, where stood a tall slim figure with his hands thrust deep in his pockets.

"How did he know I was here?" Catherine was looking at Katie, and Katie, laughing, said, "He likely went home and they told him."

Catherine shook her head, but didn't say, "No, no he'd never go to our house."

"Is it that cousin of yours?" Nils was now at the other side of the window, and Catherine said, "Yes, Uncle Nils. He's got nothing else to do, with the yard being out. I suppose he wants to fill in his time so coming down gives him something . . ."

Andree let out a bellow of a laugh, cutting off her voice, and he squeezed her as he cried, "You're just like your Aunt Katie; you don't know your own worth. Fill in his time indeed! Go on with you and stop the poor fellow pining." He gave her a push. "And tell him from me if he doesn't come in next time I'll go out there and take my boot to him."

"I'll tell him, Uncle Andree. I'll tell him. Bye-bye." She looked slightly embarrassed now and he smiled gently at her, saying, "Goodbye, my dear."

"Bye-bye, Uncle Nils."

"Goodbye, Catherine." Nils's unblinking eyes watched her and Katie leave the room; then, turning to his father, he asked, "Why won't he come in . . . the boy?"

"Oh." Andree tossed his big, white shaggy head. "He's Joe's grandson. You know, the one I told you about. Like father, like son . . . and like grandfather." At this Andree punched his own son in the chest, then added quietly, "Eighteen sixty-five it was when Katie last saw her brother Joe. Four miles dividing them at the most and not running into each other in all these years. Hardly believable, is it? . . . And all through me. Yes, all through me." He shook his head as if the situation at this juncture was slightly incredible to him. "He must have been very fond of her, but then he'd have been a funny man if he wasn't, wouldn't he, Nils?" Andree looked up at his son, and Nils replied in a level tone, "Yes, he would." And this reply brought Andree's hand out to him and with something akin to doting fondness he said, "Ah, you understand. It's always warmed my heart that, always."

Nils stared at his father. It seemed impossible to believe that he wasn't aware of the true situation. But then would he, for his ego was still as big as his old body. Turned eighty, he still saw himself as attractive to her. Nils had the sudden desire, born of deep hidden resentment against this man who had left him fatherless at the time when he needed a father, to bend to him, fix him with his eye and say, "Listen to me, my big fellow, and let it sink in deep. I'm going to take her away. You're going to be alone as you left my mother alone —and me. Yes, and me."

"What are you thinking of, Nils?" Andree looked up at his son whose eyes were on him, yet with his gaze turned inwards.

"A woman," said Nils, turning away.

"Ha! ha!" laughed Andree, punching his fist towards him. "Like father, like son all right."

2

Young Tom Mulholland was tall and sparsely made, with large eyes which he would have seen were like those of his Great-aunt Katie if he had met her. His face was long and his nose straight; he had a clear complexion, and a thin, unsmiling mouth; and at nineteen he was aware of two things he wanted of life. First, he wanted to get out of Palmer's shipyard. What alternative work he would do he didn't know, he just wanted to get away from the noise, dirt, and bustle. The other desire was clear-cut: he wanted to marry his cousin Catherine.

His first desire, although it concerned his livelihood, was simple; the second was fraught with such complications, such obstacles, that he knew he should have strangled it at birth. Had he set his cap at one of the Palmer family, or one of the Redheads' connections in this very village of Westoe, his objective would have been more easily accomplished, because

Catherine was a Catholic and he was Church of England, and you might as well try to plait molten lead with water as to join a Catholic and a Protestant in Jarrow.

As he saw the door of Loreto open he turned and walked slowly down by the row of trees; then he cut through a carriage entrance to the pavement along which Catherine was now walking, and when she came abreast of him he joined his step to hers and after a moment said, "Hello."

"Hello!" Turning her head and looking fully at him, she added quietly, "You shouldn't have come all this way; you'll wear your boots out."

"I can sole them again."

"I'm going back on the tram."

"Well, I'll see you to it."

"You'll not, Tom Mulholland, you'll get on with me."

"I'll do no such thing." Now his voice was harsh and hers equally so as she replied, "Oh, you are a pig-headed individual. For two pins I'd get on the tram and let you walk by yourself."

"That's up to you."

They stopped and stood staring at each other until, her face softening, she shrugged her shoulders and said with a definite air of resignation, "Oh, well, have it your own way. I'll walk, but I'll be dropping when I get there because of your pig-headedness, and likely get it in the neck too for being late."

He smiled at her now, and she smiled back at him before walking on again. Tom, she considered, was good-looking. What was more, he was nice. She liked Tom. She checked her thoughts at this point. Tom was her cousin, but he was more like a brother to her. Yes, she liked Tom; next to her Aunt Katie she liked Tom. But now she turned to him, her voice aggressive again, saying, "Me Uncle Andree says if you don't come in he's going to use his boot on you."

"Oh yes?" The face was straight, the statement a question.

"And he could, you know; he might be eighty-odd but he's like a lintie."

"Well"—his mouth moved up at the corners—"when he lifts his foot up I might cobble his boot for him an' all."

They were both laughing now, and in their rocking they fell hard against each other, only to spring apart quickly as if they had been scorched, and they kept the distance between them all the way through Shields. And it wasn't until they passed the docks and entered the Jarrow Road that their conversation ceased to be monosyllabic and they chattered freely again.

They walked past the Jarrow Slacks and the buildings of East Jarrow and Bogey Hill, and they did not take the forbidden short cut up the tram lines and into Jarrow but went the longer way round by the Quay Corner; and when they reached the corner they paused for a while and sat on a timber and looked at the Don flowing between its black, slimy banks and out on to the mud-flats where the great black posts rotted indiscernibly.

"I hate Jarrow."

He turned his head sharply and stared at her for a moment before saying in a slightly defensive tone, "There could be worse places."

"Where?"

He slanted his eyes towards her. "It's funny, you know, I can't really make it out myself, because I hate the muck and the dirt as much as you do, but I still like Jarrow. I wouldn't want to live any place else. It is funny, isn't it?"

She nodded at him, her face solemn with understanding, but she said, "I loathe it, I loathe living in Jarrow."

"You wouldn't mind living in Shields though?"

"No, I'd like to live in Shields; it's quite different."

"But there are places in Shields that are even worse than those in Jarrow. You go along by Costerfine Town and the dock area."

"Oh, I wouldn't like to live there. . . ."

"No, you'd like to live in Westoe, wouldn't you?" Abruptly he got to his feet; and as he looked down at her she pulled herself upwards and facing him aggressively, said, "And what's wrong with that? What's wrong with wanting to live in Westoe?"

"Nothing, nothing. I was just pointing out to you that every house in Shields hasn't got running water inside, and hot and cold, nor a bathroom and a flush lav. Because your Aunt Katie's got such a place it doesn't make Shields a model town."

"Who's saying it does? And you needn't stress 'my Aunt Katie' because she's as much your Aunt Katie as she is mine, and if you once spoke to her you would . . ."

"Don't start that again. Come on." He gripped her arm and pulled her round; then he released his hold on her and

346

thrust his hands into his pockets, and they walked in silence round by the old church of St. Paul's, where Bede had taught and which was the only claim Jarrow had on history, yet no small claim. They passed the end of the children's park, and cut across the salt grass where once the saltpans had flourished; then, leaving the waste land, they entered the labyrinth of grey dull streets, not one house looking different from its neighbour, front door facing front door, back door facing back door. At the end of Hope Street they stopped and looked down at each other, and nonchalantly he said, "You're going down there again the morrow?"

"I don't know, I might."

"You should know. Are you going anywhere else?"

"No."

"Then you'll be going down?"

"I might."

"Same time?"

"Perhaps." She nodded, and they continued to stare at each other for a moment longer before she turned away, saying, "Ta-ra, Tom." And he answered softly, "Ta-ra, Catherine."

Catherine hurried up the middle of the back lane, being careful to step over the patches of excrement the scavengers had let fall when cleaning out the middens. She turned right at the top, then right again and into her own back lane and then into her backyard, empty for once of any of her six brothers and sisters.

Lucy Connolly was sitting in an old battered armchair in the kitchen. She looked hard at her daughter and said, "Well?"

"She could only manage ten shillings." Catherine did not look at her mother as she gave her this news.

"To hell! You didn't ask her for more?"

"I did, I did." Catherine was shouting back at Lucy now, and becoming aware of this she bit her lip, then put her fingers over her mouth, and Lucy, nodding her head at her, said, "Aye, Aa should think so an' all. You forget your fancy manners when you're home. Keep them for Aunt Katie, don't you? An' I'm tellin' you, if you'd asked her for the pound she'd have given it to you."

"She wouldn't, because she knows where it would go."

Lucy looked up into her daughter's tight face and she surveyed her for a full minute before saying menacingly, "One of these days, me lady, you'll get a surprise—you'll get what you're askin' for. You'll come out of that convent as if you had a hot poker up your arse."

Catherine bowed her head and turned away. Her mother's language could make her sick, actually sick. She sometimes retched after she had listened to her. It was hard to believe what her Aunt Bridget said, that her mother had at one time been nice and jolly and great company. She couldn't really believe it.

"What do you two talk about down there? . . . And come here." She waved Catherine towards her. "Don't you go into that room and start sulking. I said, what do you two talk about when you get together? Sit yourself down and talk to me for a change." She snapped her finger towards a chair.

Catherine sat down. And she looked at the small dark woman and she tried to stop the awful thought coming into her mind again, the awful thought that she wished she would die.

"Well, I'm waitin'. I'm waitin' to hear about your edifying conversation."

"We have no edifying conversation." Catherine's lips hardly moved as she spoke. Her voice was a mutter and she kept her eyes averted from her mother's face.

"No edifying conversation? Well, you must talk about somethin'. Oh! Oh!" She pulled herself up in the chair. "Don't tell me she's instructing you how to make money like she did. Oh, no!" She wagged her finger now in front of her own face. "You mustn't begin by setting up whore shops."

"Mother! Oh, Mother, how could you! You're wicked. And Aunt Katie never did any such thing; you know she didn't."

"Don't tell me what your Aunt Katie did or didn't do. An' don't believe a word I say; just you go down and enquire at the polis station. Ask them if she wasn't put away for keeping a bad house."

Catherine was on her feet bending towards her mother, towards the grinning, leering, half-washed face, as she said bitterly under her breath, "Then why do you take her dirty money? Why do you keep sending me down to borrow from her? Why have you let her support the lot of us for years? Because without her pound a week we would have been in Harton Workhouse long ago. Why? I'll tell you why . . . because you're no good. You blame me da, but he would have

348

been all right if he'd had someone behind him, someone different from you, with your drink and your greed, and your jealousy and dirty tongue, and . . ."

Catherine's voice was cut off by a vicious slap across the mouth. Following this, she received two blows on her bent head, and lastly Lucy's foot came into her back and sent her sprawling through the bedroom door. She came to rest full length on one of the four shake-downs in the small room, and as she covered her sobbing face in her arms Lucy bent over her and whispered fiercely, "An' I'll tell you somethin' else while I'm on. You stop seein' Tom Mulholland else yer da's going to skin you alive. D'yer hear me? Cousin or no cousin, he's comin' too thick with yer for any good. Now those are your da's words, and you remember them."

She took her foot again and pushed it against her daughter's hip, and as she left the room, banging the door behind her, she muttered, "I'll see he deals with you, me girl. By God, if I don't!"

3

Each day, be it rain, hail or fine, Andree took his constitutional. He walked to the fountain at Westoe, took a tramcar to the bottom of Fowler Street, another to the end of Ocean Road, then walked the mile-long pier. This, he claimed, was what kept him fit and well. And undoubtedly it had done, until two months ago when he returned from his walk with a pain in his chest, which he admitted to having experienced before, and which he declared was indigestion due to cook's heavy hand in the meat pudding.

He bellowed when Katie said he must see a doctor, but he did not say no to her suggestion that she should accompany him on his walks.

Katie found the afternoon excursions very tiring, and they disorganised the whole day. Her mornings were usually taken up with business; sometimes she was called upon to visit her solicitor twice a week. She thought of the man who saw to her legal business now as her solicitor. He was the successor to Mr. Hewitt, who had retired ten years ago and was now living in Harrogate. Nor could she any longer call on the guidance and help from Mr. Kenny, who after he had retired had worked for her until he died in 1901.

At the end of the pier Katie watched Andree, seemingly tireless, walking round the lighthouse. She watched him gaze up at the wheeling seagulls, and she felt that always when he reached this point of his walk he was again on the bridge of a ship.

On the return journey he pointed to "the little fellows", as he called the tugs, chugging in front of a liner as they led her towards the gap in the piers, and he said, "How many times have I paddled that road, Kaa-tee?" And she replied, "Times without number, Andy." And he nodded and patted the hand that was resting on his arm, and, his eyes still looking across the water, he said, "It's been a good life, Kaa-tee, a good life." Then, bringing his eyes round to her, he repeated, but in a different tone now, a quiet, deep, personal tone, "A good life, Kaa-tee; and the best of it has been spent with you."

"Oh, Andy." She squeezed his arm, and when he saw the tears in her eyes he said, "There now. There now. But it's true." Then after a moment he added, "We're sad today. I suppose that's because tomorrow we lose Catherine. . . . You know, Kaa-tee, she's not only a daughter to you, but to me also."

"I know, dear, I know. But she'll write often—at least twice a week, she says. And then"—she hugged his arm—"you know that once she leaves college she'll come to us."

"That's two years ahead, Kaa-tee. I wonder if I won't have gone out with the tide before then."

"Andy! Andy!" She stopped in her stride.

"Ah, I'm sorry, my dear, but I'm an old man, Kaa-tee. And lately it has come to me just how old. I . . . I think we should face it, because I worry. I worry about you."

"Well, you have no need to, and don't."

"How can I help it, for at heart you are still the young girl with fear in her eyes."

She turned her head away from him as she said, "That's nonsense. I'm not afraid of anything any more." She made her voice firm, convincing.

Yet he wasn't convinced, for he answered, "It's no use telling me you are no longer afraid, for time and time again I have seen fear in your eyes, and I think to myself the past will never die for her."

What could she say to this?

They walked in silence for a time, then his words checked her breath. "Has Nils ever said anything to you about a woman, Kaa-tee?"

She gulped in her throat, took her hand from his arm and straightened her hat; then, looking into his eyes, which were merely asking a question and not probing anything deeper, she said, "No. A woman? What d'you mean?"

"He's got a woman on his mind."

"What makes you think that?"

"He told me."

Her head was turned from him again, and she was looking over the water to the great stretch of sands as she asked, "What did he say about her?"

"Oh, nothing. Only he had a woman on his mind. And it can't be the one in Hartlepool."

"Hartlepool? He . . . he has someone there?" Her voice ended on a high note.

"He had. He doesn't think I know. A chief engineer's widow. My last mate, Anderson, told me; he knew her. Fine set-up woman, he said, with a house and a bit of money of her own. I thought perhaps Nils would have made a splice with her, but no, it petered out. He's choosey, is Nils. But he's certainly got someone else in his eye, and on his mind too." He laughed softly. "He's thinking of his retirement. The years ahead, without water under their feet, frighten some men, Kaa-tee. I never had that fear, for there was always you to come home to." He pulled her arm tight to his side, and they walked in silence again, until Andree said, "I don't think I'll go to the reunion tonight."

"Why? You've never missed one in years."

"Oh, I'm getting past it. Retelling old yarns, laughing at ones you've heard a thousand times. Even the whisky is losing its taste."

"You're going," she said firmly. "I'm quite old enough to be left alone for one evening. Anyway, I don't want you storming up and down thinking about what you're missing."

They were both laughing; Andree, with his head back, saying, "Aw, you're my Kaa-tee." Then, bringing his bushy face close to hers, he whispered, "Well, promise me you'll hit me

351

on the head with the warming-pan if I raise the roof when I get in."

Looking back at him solemnly, she said, "I promise." And again they were laughing.

* * *

Katie entered the drawing-room and walked to the fire and held her hands out to the blaze. She had felt so cold she'd had the fire lit early in the evening. She hoped she hadn't caught a chill on the pier today; it had been anything but warm.

She had just come downstairs from seeing Betty to bed. She had insisted on her going up early because her legs were so swollen they looked as if they would burst. Betty had the idea that the routine of the house would disintegrate if she were to leave the scene for a day or so.

She glanced down at the almost empty brass coal-scuttle, which condition pointed to it being Nellie's night off—Jessie would never have thought of filling it before she left. She was glad that Jessie was just a daily worker, for it would, in a way, be easier to dismiss her. She had cheeked Betty today. Her hand went out towards the bell-rope—perhaps she hadn't gone yet. It was her late night on and she shouldn't leave till eight, and it wasn't quite eight yet. As she gripped the rope the front-door bell rang and she paused and listened. She heard the kitchen door open and muted footsteps cross the hall, then a voice saying, "Oh, Captain Nils," and ending on Jessie's hick of a laugh.

Katie stared towards the door. Perhaps he'd go straight upstairs and she'd get to her room and to bed; but it was a vain thought, and she knew this.

"Where's everybody?"

"Madam's in the drawing-room, Captain. The master's gone out."

She was sitting on the couch reading when Nils entered the room, and as she turned her head slowly in his direction she saw immediately that he had been drinking.

"Hello, there." He dropped heavily into the armchair to the side of the couch.

"Hello, Nils."

"Where's Father gone?"

"To the reunion dinner."

"Ah-ha! Reunion dinner. And you're all on your own."

She ignored this and said, "I didn't know you were due in. Have you just docked?"

"No. We docked before noon."

She was surprised and it must have shown in her face, for he said in a mocking tone, "Before noon and it's now eight o'clock. Where have you been, Nils?"

She looked away from him, closed her book, laid it to the side of her, then said, "Would you like something to eat?"

"No. No, thank you, Katie. At the moment I am full—replete. Yes, that is the English word, replete. My belly is full of food . . . and drink, and my head is full of knowledge. . . . You'll never guess who I've spent the afternoon with, Katie. An old friend of yours."

She was sitting bolt upright staring at him, her eyes wide.

"At least his father was a friend of yours."

Her mind flew to Bernard Rosier, then off at a tangent to his son . . . and his wife, Sarah! Were they in England?

"Henry Collard. You remember Henry Collard?"

"Collard?" She experienced a sudden feeling of deflation. "I know of no one by that name."

"Oh, come on, Katie. Throw your mind back to the old days. Henry Collard, who was a customer of yours."

Her body was like a ramrod now. The blood was draining from her face. Not only his words but his tone and whole manner as he leaned towards her carried insult.

"Young Collard, his son. But not so young either, 'bout my age. Told me of the night his father went with Rosier—now don't say you don't know Rosier. Well, they went to your house and there was a shindy and you hit old Rosier on the head with a candlestick. . . . Now you remember?"

Her nails were digging into the palms of her hands and her breath hissed through her teeth as she said, "I am not likely to forget that night."

He seemed taken aback for a moment, then said, "Well, we're honest anyway. I didn't expect you to own up to it so quickly."

"What do you mean? I have nothing to own up to. Those men forced themselves into my . . ."

"Oh, stop it. Stop it. You're spoiling it now. One of your whores brought them back with her, to be serviced."

"How dare you!" Her eyes blazed at him.

"Oh, I dare, Katie . . . Now, don't get up." He pushed her

353

back on to the couch none too gently with the flat of his hand, and added in a tone from which all banter had gone, "I dare because I'm mad at myself for being such a bloody fool. You've hoodwinked me all these years, playing the aloof lady, the faithful wife—you, the whore mistress! . . . And he, my dear papa, he gave me a most romantic description of your first meeting; a young girl starving rather than sell her virtue—except, of course, to him. He told me he bought you your first house. That's very funny when you come to think about it. You didn't need him to buy you a house, did you, Katie? . . . Madam Katie. . . . Tell me, how many men have you had altogether? There was Rosier—and Bunting. He married you. Then dear father—and oh, Mr. Hewitt. Oh yes, old Hewitt, and God knows how many half-sovereigns worth on the side."

"When your . . . your father comes in . . ." The words were blocking her throat.

"When my father comes in what will you do? Go on, tell me." He clamped his hand on to her knee, and at his touch an anger boiled in her, swamping her fear for the moment, and she struck at his arm, crying, "Take your hands off me!" and with a jerk of her body she was on her feet. But so was he. And now he bothered with words no more, for, clutching her to him, he pinned her arms to her sides and, forcing her head back with his own, he bit on her neck.

Her body writhing, she kicked at his shins, and when his mouth came on hers, enveloping it, and his teeth dragged at her upper lip, she arched her back so much that she lost her balance and together they fell sidewards on to the couch.

It was at this precise moment that the door opened, and there followed a silence, and in it she dragged her dishevelled body on to the floor, then upwards, to see Jessie standing gaping at them across the room.

"The . . . the scuttle, mam. I . . . I came for the scuttle."

"Get out! It doesn't matter. But . . . but, Jessie . . ." She had one hand hard on her heart to try to ease its racing, and she held the other waveringly out to the girl, saying, "I . . . I must explain to you, in . . . in the morning."

"Yes, mam." The girl looked from Katie to Nils, where he was now going towards the fire adjusting his waistcoat, and again she said, "Yes, mam," but without the slightest deference.

When the door closed on Jessie, Katie turned stiffly and

glared at Nils's back, and there came to her mind the picture of Theresa as she must have appeared when she fired the gun into Rosier's face, and she longed for such a weapon to her hand. The voice that came through her sore and swelling lips was hardly recognizable to her. There was no quiver in it, no fear, as it said, "I won't tell Andree, for I want his days to end peacefully, but I swear before God that if you lay hands on me again I will kill you and take the consequences. One more thing. What you were told today was lies. *Lies.* Do you hear? An incident was misconstrued. The truth was laughed at, as the truth of tonight's incident will be laughed at when that girl takes her tale outside this house." She was standing with her arm flung outwards in the direction of the door, her body leaning sidewards as if she were about to fall.

Nils turned slowly and looked at her with both hate and desire in his eyes, but he said nothing; he just watched her walk unsteadily to the door, and when it had closed behind her he began to swear aloud in his own tongue.

4

It was eight days before Christmas and Andree wasn't well. He hadn't been himself for some weeks now and Katie was worried about him. At odd times she would find him staring at her in a strange way. Sometimes she wondered if he knew about Nils, but then she rejected the idea, for if he suspected his son of having attempted to make love to her he would demand to know why, if she didn't welcome his attention, she hadn't told him about this before. Would he believe it was his happiness she had been thinking of? Perhaps it would be difficult to convince him of this when he looked at his son and saw himself as he had been thirty years ago.

The day following the incident in the drawing-room she had explained to Jessie that Captain Nils had been the worse for drink the previous evening, and had forgotten himself, and the girl had said, "Yes, mam. I understand, mam." But her eyes had been bold as they looked back into Katie's.

She felt sick to her very soul when she thought of what the

girl might say, and after talking the matter over with Betty she thought it wiser to keep Jessie on.

And there was something else troubling Katie. Catherine had been at college a fortnight before a letter had arrived from her, and then it was a disappointing letter. And not once during the term had she taken the opportunity to come home for a week-end. And now the term had ended two days ago and she had not yet come to see her.

When the children came down last week, as they did now every Saturday, en masse, to collect the pound, Mick had said his ma was goin' to knock bloody hell out of their Catherine when she came home 'cos it was weeks since she'd had a scribe of a pen from her. Mick's flowery language always caused Andree great amusement, but Katie could never laugh at the boy.

Yesterday Andree had said, "Wait till tomorrow morning when the children come and you'll know everything then."

But now it was Saturday morning and for once the children hadn't come, and she was definitely worried.

"Why don't you take a walk up to the house?" said Andree.

"No, Andy; I couldn't do that. I've never been asked there; I don't think Lucy would want me to see her place."

"But you can't go on in this state of uncertainty. There must be something amiss or else that girl would have been down here like a shot."

"You know, Andy"—Katie leaned forward and held out her hands to the blaze from the fire—"I'm wondering if going to college could have changed her? I've . . . I've put it to myself time and again and said it's ridiculous. . . ."

"And it is ridiculous. College change Catherine? Nonsense! College would change Catherine as much as it would have changed you, in the way you are inferring. Catherine has character. Look, I think your wisest plan is to take a dander into Jarrow and see Lucy, and tell her you were worried about Catherine and just looked in."

"It's difficult. There's the money question. She'll think because I'm giving her the money each week I'm pressing some claim. It's been a delicate situation for years, as you know."

"Well, I would give her until this afternoon; and if she's not here by then, you take my advice and go up to the house."

And Katie did go up to the house, and not because of An-dree's advice but because of Tom Mulholland.

They had finished their lunch and Andree was settled in the smoke-room with his pipe. Soon, she knew, he would drop off to sleep, and he would sleep until around half-past three, when she would take him in a cup of tea.

She herself had just entered her bedroom with the inten-tion of putting her feet up, when she heard the front-door bell ring, and a few minutes later Betty came into the room and, closing the door behind her, said softly, "It's . . . it's the young fellow to see you, Katie, the one that used to wait for Catherine. Tom Mulholland."

Tom Mulholland. She moved slowly towards Betty. "Some-thing's happened to Catherine?"

"I don't know, lass, but . . . but I think you should pre-pare yourself. The lad looks in an awful mess; he's been knocked about from the looks of him, an' he's got a look on his face like God delivering judgment."

Katie pushed past Betty and went swiftly on to the land-ing, then turned to her and asked softly, "Where did you put him?"

"I took him into the morning-room."

She now ran down the stairs and across the hall and en-tered the room, and then she came to a dead stop as she looked at the tall young man standing stiffly waiting for her. She had never seen him close to before, and if she had she wouldn't have recognized him from the face she was looking at now. One eye was almost closed, and the whole cheek and the brow was a dark bluish hue. His upper lip was protruding and had been split at the side. The face looked as if it had been battered unmercifully. She clasped her hands as she moved slowly towards him, and when she stood a yard from him she shook her head and muttered, "Dear God, who's done this to you?"

She watched his misshapen lips move, and when they parted she saw a gap in the side of his mouth where his teeth were missing. "Catherine's father." The words dripped bitter-ness.

He had not said "Me Uncle Pat" but "Catherine's father".

Again she shook her head, and now she put her fingers to her cheek and asked softly, "But why?"

She watched the whole distorted face tremble. She watched the lips move a number of times before he ground out, "Because Catherine's going to have a baby and he's blaming me."

Katie now pressed her clenched fists into her jaws, and it seemed as if she was squeezing the words out through her stiff lips when she cried, "No! Oh no!"

"Yes! Oh yes!" His words too were forced out, and he bent towards her, muttering brokenly below his breath, "I know nothing about it, nothing. Do you hear! But he didn't give me a chance, he didn't give me a chance to speak. He came to our house and pulled me out of bed and before I knew where I was he was using his fists and boots on me. He would have kicked me to death if it hadn't been for the men next door. I . . . I didn't know why he'd done it, what it was about. When me da came in he said he'd kill him. He went round, but when he came back he would have done for me an' all, except that I was almost unconscious. . . . They all believe it."

Katie was now sitting on the edge of a chair and she made a gesture to him to take a seat, but he said roughly, "No, no, I haven't come here to sit and have light conversation with you. I've come here to tell you who did this thing to Catherine."

"Tell me?" She looked as perplexed as she sounded, and he nodded his head sharply at her, then put his hand up to his neck as if a pain had shot through it. "The night afore she was to go away she was here." He dug his finger downwards. "And I was late in finishing, but I thought I'd take a chance on seeing her and I came down, and just as I was passing the fountain I saw her. I saw her getting on a tram with a man in uniform, the fellow she calls Uncle Nils. Now"—his finger was stabbing towards her—"take it from there. Two days later I saw me Uncle Pat and he tells me that the night before Catherine went to college she had come in in a state and said she had been chased by a man. He said she had come across the salt grass and some fellow had made a grab at her She cried half the night." Again his finger stabbed towards her. "You're with me, I hope? . . . You realise she wasn't chased by any man? That bloke, your son, or stepson or whatever he is, saw her home, at least up to the salt grass. It's pretty dark on the salt grass and there's hollows and places, and nobody's going to take much notice of a lass shouting out there because there's courting going on, and people mind their own business. But that's when it happened. And it was him. . . . It's him I've come to see."

He straightened up as he finished speaking and Katie closed her eyes and eased herself farther on to the chair and leaned against the back of it. Dear God! Oh, dear God! Poor, poor Catherine. Bernard Rosier and the night of the ball; the salt grass and the hollows where the courting couples lay. She would kill him; she would take a knife and she would drive it into him. The dirty, dirty swine! "I can hurt you, Katie. There are many ways I can hurt you without laying a hand on you." That's what he had said the morning after the incident in the drawing-room, and he had seen Catherine to the tram that night; he had said it was on his way to the docks. He had done this deliberately. Oh, the filthy, filthy swine! And Andy. What would happen when Andy knew? And he would have to know. She looked dazedly at the boy and said, "What does Catherine say?"

"She's told them it isn't me, but they won't believe her because she won't name anybody else. And she won't name anybody else because of you. She doesn't want to upset you, and that's what I'm here for. I want you to come back with me and tell them."

Katie got slowly to her feet and, her hands still clasped tightly together, she looked at him and said, "I'll come back with you and see Catherine, but I can't tell them anything. I can't say who has done this. Neither you nor I can say that because we don't really know. It is Catherine who must say who the man is." But as she spoke she saw the old pattern repeated, for Catherine, like herself, wouldn't name the man for fear of causing trouble to those she loved.

"Where is he?"

"I don't know at the moment."

"You wouldn't tell me when he's coming in if you did know, would you?"

"Yes, I would."

He blinked painfully and the water dripped out of the corner of his bruised eye.

She said bitterly, "I'd like you to give him what Catherine's father gave you." Her eyes moved round his bruised features for a moment; then she added, "But . . . but you'd never be able to accomplish that, he's a big strong man. But leave this to me."

She heard the sound of his teeth grinding before he said, "He might be big, but I've so much hate in me this minute that if he was here now I'd have the strength to beat him to a pulp. . . . What you don't know is that I love Catherine, always have done and always will, and I'll tell you something else when I'm on, and you can do what you like about it—she loves me."

She looked levelly at him, pity and understanding in her gaze, before she said quietly, "I'm glad of that, Tom, and I'm on your side."

He seemed taken aback for a moment by her attitude; but still aggressively he said, "You wanted someone fancy for her. Oh, I know. I know. . . ."

"Be quiet," she said sharply, "and listen. . . . If Catherine wants you, then I want you. But we'll talk about that later. Now wait here until I get my things and I'll come with you."

She went out of the room and into the smoke-room and gently shook Andree's shoulder, and when he grunted and answered, "Yes, Kaa-tee? Yes?" she said, "Wake up, Andy. There's something I must tell you."

Blowing the air out through his beard, he pulled himself upwards and smiled at her, saying, "Yes, Kaa-tee?" Then, taking in the look on her face, he asked, "What is it?"

"The boy, Catherine's cousin, he's come to tell me why Catherine hasn't been down." She caught hold of his hand now and paused a while before she said, "She's going to have a baby, Andy."

"Catherine?" He moved his head in slow, wide sweeps.

"Yes . . . Catherine."

"Who? This boy?" His voice was grim.

"No. But the boy loves her deeply, and the father, Catherine's father, has beaten him up unmercifully. The poor lad didn't know why he was being trounced. It's awful. I . . . I think someone attacked her when she was crossing the salt grass. I'm going up now, Andy."

"Yes, yes." He pulled himself to his feet and again he shook his head. "Bring her back with you. Bring her here; we'll look after her."

"I'll try, Andy." As she went from the room he said, as if commenting to himself, "Catherine! Can't believe it. Attacked? Why does this only happen to nice girls?"

Going up the stairs she repeated the question: "Why?"

*   *   *

It was years since Katie had been in this part of Jarrow. When she got off the tram with Tom and walked into the labyrinth of dismal streets, all looking alike and all sprinkled lavishly with running, screaming, playing, fighting children, she was thankful that she had been brought up in the pit village, because, in spite of its drawbacks, it was surrounded by open fells.

Tom stopped opposite a dingy, brown, paint-peeling door and said quietly, "This is it. I'll wait for you at the tram stop."

Katie nodded to him, then paused for a moment before knocking on the door.

Katie had not seen Lucy for years, and she couldn't believe that this was Lucy who had opened the door to her. She knew from Catherine that her mother was going downhill, but the woman confronting her, who was only in her early forties, looked old—older than she herself was; besides which, she didn't look as if she'd had a drop of water on her face for days, nor a comb through her hair.

It was Lucy who spoke first. Her head moving stiffly to the side, she said, "Oh, it's you. Bad news travels fast, don't it?"

"Can I come in, Lucy?"

Lucy pulled the door wider and Katie stepped up into what was the front room of the three-roomed downstairs house. The floor of the room was bare wood and dirty. There was a brass bed in one corner and a cupboard-bed in the other, the doors of which were half open and showed part of a tick mattress oozing out. There was no other sign of furniture in the room, not even a chair. The conditions under which her Catherine, as she always thought of Lucy's daughter, had been brought up appalled her. Then she entered the kitchen and looked to where Catherine was coming into the room from the scullery. They stared at each other for a moment; then Catherine, bowing her head, turned away and made to go into the bedroom, but Lucy's bark stopped her.

"There's no place in there to hide, madam. There's no place for you to hide at all. You should have thought about some place to hide your head afore you got up to your pranks. Sit yourself down, madam; your Aunt Katie's come to see you."

As Catherine, still with her head bowed, lowered herself on to a chair, Lucy, looking at Katie, said, "A waste of good money all you've done for her all these years. She's spit in yer eye, that's what she's done, spit in yer eye."

Lucy now grabbed at a chair near the wall and, dragging it forward, muttered, "Sit yerself down. An' you'll have to excuse the mess; I haven't been able to do anything since this hit me, it's knocked all the gumption out of me. As for her da . . . well!" Lucy closed her eyes, dropped her chin on to her chest, and moved her head as if words had failed her. Then, bringing her chin up sharply, she said, "I'd warned her, Aunt Katie, I'd warned her. I've said to her time and again, your da doesn't want you to see that Tommy Mulholland. At first we didn't know a damn thing about them getting together, 'cos he doesn't darken these doors, but young Mike watched them night after night coming across the salt grass when she'd been down to see you. Night after night he'd meet her. It was all arranged."

Katie was looking at Lucy as she spoke, but out of the corner of her eye she saw Catherine raise her head; she saw the deathly whiteness of her face. She wanted to turn to her, take her in her arms, but she went on listening to Lucy, whose voice was rising now. "Come in here, she did, the night afore she went to college; in a state she was, saying a man had chased her. She must have known then she'd fallen and this was somethin' they'd thought up. He put her up to it. . . ."

Before Lucy had finished speaking Catherine was on her feet and her chair had gone crashing backwards into the wall. Her voice almost a scream, she cried, "It wasn't him! How many more times am I to tell you it wasn't him. I swear by Almighty God it wasn't. . . . I told you it wasn't him."

"You can swear by the archangel and all your bloody saints, girl; you can swear by Father Mackin, King Street Charlie, or who the hell you like; you can swear till you're black and blue in the face and nobody in this house is goin' to believe you."

The mother and daughter glared at each other and their hate was mutual. Then of a sudden the fight seemed to go out of Catherine, and her body slumped as she turned about and stood leaning on the kitchen table, her hand gripping the edge of it.

And now Lucy, sitting down, folded her arms over her dirty pinny and, rocking herself in small movements, looked at Katie and in a voice that was almost a whine she said, "What's goin' to happen when it comes, and no one to father it, and another mouth to feed? I've told her it's Harton for her 'cos we can't do with it, not with a squad of seven we can't. And it isn't likely that after what she's done you'll go on helping us; it isn't to be expected." Lucy's head came forward in wide sweeps now. "Fair's fair, as I've said to Pat. It wouldn't be fair, not after she's spat in yer eye."

"Don't be silly, Lucy." Katie's voice was sharp. It was the first time she had spoken since she had entered the house, and the sound of her voice seemed to hunch Catherine's shoulders even more. Katie watched her head droop downwards until her face was almost lost from sight.

"But the fact is, Aunt Katie, whatever you'd do she's havin' none of it." Lucy brought Katie's attention to her again. "Apart from what you might think about this business, and what your kind heart would let you do for her, she's made up her mind she's going to have none of it. I told her yesterday to come down and see you, but no! No! She wasn't going to her Aunt Katie's, after all you've done for her. If you'd been her own mother you couldn't have done more. I've always said that, Aunt Katie. You can ask Pat. I've always said that if you'd been her own mother you couldn't have done more. And now me fine lady is not going to go to her Aunt Katie's."

Katie got slowly to her feet and, going to Catherine's side, she touched her arm gently, and she said, just as gently, "Come down for a while, Catherine; just for a while so we can talk."

Catherine turned her head as far away as possible from Katie as she muttered, "No, Aunt Katie, I can't."

Katie now went to Lucy and, bending down to her, whispered, "Can you leave us for a minute or so?"

Lucy nodded conspiratorially; then, lifting her forefinger up to her nose, she went into the scullery. A minute later Katie saw her pass the window and go down the yard to the closet.

"Catherine." Katie, taking a firm hold of Catherine's arm, brought her round to face her, but she could only see the top of her head. Nevertheless, she talked to it. Her voice low and rapid, she said, "Listen to me, Catherine. I know all about it. I know who did this to you. You must come down and stay with us. You won't see him; I promise you that, you won't see him. But I must talk to you; we can't talk here."

Slowly Catherine raised her head. Her mouth was agape; her eyes, dry and bright, stared into Katie's and she whispered, "How?"

"I can't tell you now—only this, that I know you have kept quiet because you thought it would hurt me and Uncle. Isn't that so?"

Katie watched the head droop again; and now she said briskly, "Go and get your coat on. Bring what things you want, for if I get my way you'll never darken these doors again."

"Oh, Aunt Katie." Catherine's face began to twitch and her body to tremble, and Katie, gripping her arms, cried, "Not now. Go and get your things, quickly."

Catherine was in the bedroom when Lucy returned to the kitchen and she raised her brows questioningly at Katie, and Katie replied softly, "She'll come"; then added, "But I don't know for how long." At this she turned and picked up her handbag from where she had laid it at the side of the chair, and, looking at it, she said, "As long as she stays you can send the children down on a Saturday."

"Oh, thanks, Auntie. You know, I don't know where I'd be without you. I've said it afore, an' I'll say it again. But I'd better tell you, you'd better not expect thanks for what you're doing for her, because she's turned out a thankless sod if ever there was one. She's me own girl an' I shouldn't say it, but she is. An' what will happen when the bairn comes God knows, an' it being born without a name; 'cos if she did own up to that young scut being the father, Pat wouldn't stand for her marrying him, not for a minute. Not only is he her cousin but there's the religion. He would sooner see her marry an Arab from Costerfine Town than a ranter. Anyway, it isn't right for cousins to marry." She had been looking at Katie when she said this, and now her eyes flicked sideways as she remembered that this woman's daughter had married her half-brother. She had been at the Chapmans when it happened, but she hadn't understood what it was all about until years after. But she didn't wish at this moment to do anything to upset Katie and jeopardise her source of income, so she added quickly, "But it's happenin' all the time. You never know, do you? But it's the religion, you see; it's the religion with Pat. Not that I would mind, 'cos, as you know, me da brought us up in the Church of England, but it's Pat. But, as I say to him, we're all headin' for the same place . . . Yet" —she sighed—"you can't convince him but that the Catholics'll have detached houses in heaven while the rest will be herded into cattle pens."

Lucy stopped her prattle as Catherine came out of the bedroom. She was wearing a navy-blue hat and coat and carried a brown suitcase, and Katie's heart ached as she looked at her. Catherine was only eighteen, but youth had fled from her as it had fled from herself the day she married Bunting. But, please God, there was no such fate awaiting Catherine. Her way would be made as smooth as money and love could achieve.

Catherine did not give any farewell to her mother, and Lucy, preceding them through the front room, said, "You want to go down on your bended knees this night, me girl, and thank God for your Auntie Katie." And at the door she smiled at Katie, saying, "Good-bye, Aunt Katie. And thanks. Pat'll be relieved."

Katie said nothing; she only nodded. Then she joined Catherine and together they walked down the street, past the gaping women at their doors who gave Catherine no word, and through a group of children who followed them shouting: "Got a ha'penny dodger, missus?"

As a hand grabbed at Katie's coat and a voice high above the rest cried, "She's me auntie. Ain't yer me Auntie Katie?" Catherine, with a sudden lift of her hand, struck at her brother Shane and ground out in a ferocious voice, "Get yourself away, you dirty devil, you."

The children stopped dead for a moment, somewhat taken aback by this attack, then Shane shouted after them, "Aa'm glad me da bashed Tom Mulholland's face in. He'll bash yours in an' all, ya stingy bitch, you."

When Catherine caught sight of Tom at the tram stop her step slowed and it was only Katie's hand on her back that urged her forward. But she stood between them until the tram came, and in it she sat between them, and all three were silent. They remained silent while they changed trams at the dock gates and got into another which took them to Westoe. They remained silent as they walked through the village and to the house.

After letting herself in Katie went straight towards the breakfast-room and, making sure there was no one inside, she beckoned Catherine towards her and into the room. Presently she came out and motioned Tom to join Catherine and then she closed the door on them.

She still had her outdoor things on, and as she stood in the hall unpinning her hat she heard Betty's voice coming from upstairs, from the direction of the bedroom, then Andree's voice, shouting, "Fuss, fuss, fuss, that's all you do, woman. Get out of my way." She pulled her coat off quickly and threw it over a chair, and she was hurrying towards the foot of the stairs when the drawing-room door opened and, turning her head, she saw Nils standing there.

She didn't remember how she got from the stairs into the drawing-room, but within a second she was standing with her back to the door, facing him, grinding out between her teeth, "You devil, you."

He stood before her, tall, still handsome, arrogant, and pursing his lips into a long low whistle as he said, "Ooh! Ah-ha! So that's it. That's why the scurry. I watched you mothering them in. So I've given your little duckling a bellyful, have I? Well, well. Now fancy that. Tell me, how does she like it?"

"You evil swine, you!"

He wagged his hand in front of her face now, saying, "I'm not asking your opinion of me, my dear Katie, I'm asking you how she likes it."

"Do you want to know something?" Her body arched forward. "If it wasn't what it would do to Andy I would kill you; before God, I would kill you this minute."

"Huh!" The look in his eyes changed slightly and the lips twisted as he said, "I seem to remember you saying that before."

"You're a filthy, stinking animal. You always have been. . . ."

"Shut up! Don't you dare call me filthy, or stinking. *You! You* to call anybody stinking, the dregs of the waterfront." His face was dark now with fury. "I might have known he would find you in a brothel. You're a pair, like to like. Do you know why my mother wouldn't live with him? Because of his women, any type, any colour. The streets of our town were sprinkled with little blond Fraenkels. Now it's my turn. Your dear Catherine will give him a grandchild—that should please him. . . ."

At this point Katie found herself pushed violently forward as the door was burst open and she turned to see Andree looking past her to his son. As the two men stared at each other she put her hands to her face and whimpered, "Andy, Andy. Don't." But she was powerless to move towards him before, with a roar like that of an angry beast, he leapt on Nils. Like two giants they grappled together, their heavy breathing and curses lost under Katie's screams, and as her arms went round Andree's back in an effort to pull him away she saw Nils's fist upraised to strike, but it never reached his father, for with a sound like air escaping from a balloon, and in much the manner of a deflated balloon, Andree slumped in her arms, and such was his weight that she was borne to the ground with him. And there she remained moaning aloud as she cradled his head, and oblivious to those about her. Oblivious to Nils walking slowly from the room, while Catherine, her face turned from him, pressed herself against Tom as she begged him, "Please. Please. Not here. Not now. Don't. Don't. Not now."

* * *

Andree was dying hard. Such was his inherent stamina and the deep conscious desire not to part from this woman who had been his life for so long, he waged a fight against death that surprised the doctors.

For four days Katie had kept constant watch by his bed. She was sitting close to it now, his limp hand held lovingly in hers. Betty came into the room and went out again, and Catherine came into the room and went out again, and the tick of the grandfather clock on the landing got louder and louder until the pendulum swung in her head, and with each swing it said, "Andy! Andy! Andy! Andy!"

For forty-five years there had been no other name in her mind but that of Andy, no other thought in her mind really but of him. And for forty-five years she had been his Kaa-tee, his beloved Kaa-tee. She doubted if there had ever been a love like theirs. Now it was ending.

The pendulum stopped swinging abruptly in her head as the hand in hers moved; then she saw his lips part, and his voice, as if already coming from another planet, whispered once again, "Kaa-tee."

"Yes, darling, I'm here. I'm here."

"Kaa-tee." The heavily veined lips moved up and the eyes, still surprisingly blue, looked at her with recognition, and for a moment she was so overcome that her tears blurred his face from her view.

"Kaa-tee."

"Yes, darling, what is it?"

"Sorry, Kaa-tee, sorry."

"Oh, Andy!"

"My son . . . Bad. Didn't . . . didn't know, only sometimes puz-puzzled. . . . The look in your . . . eyes."

"Don't worry, darling. Don't talk, just rest."

"No time, Kaa-tee; long rest, long rest."

He was quiet for a time, his eyes closed; then, his lids lifting once again, he whispered, "Lies, lies, Kaa-tee."

"Yes, darling, all lies. Don't worry, I understand. All lies."

"Love you, Kaa-tee."

"And I love you, darling. And I you. Always. Always."

His eyes widened, and as they had done of old they began to move round her face and, his voice taking on a peculiar strength, he said, "She's coming in, Kaa-tee, sails all set. She's coming in."

And his ship came in, sails all set. His hand went limp in hers; his eyes still gazed at her, but fixedly now, and she put her arms around him and gathered him to her. . . .

BOOK V

Daniel The Third
1936

1

The tall, thin, dark young man got out of the train at Jarrow, walked towards the barrier, and put down his tan leather suitcase, handed the porter his ticket and said, "Would you by any chance know of a place called Greenwall Manor?"

The ticket collector pushed his peaked cap farther up on his brow, surveyed the evident American for a moment, then replied, "Greenwall Manor? Aye, well now. I know Greenwall Manor all right, but it's a tidy walk from here; it's right beyond the new estate. A bus goes along the main road that way, but you've got another good mile-and-a-half tramp into the country from there. Old house it is, used to scare the daylights out of me when I was a bairn. Used to go blackberrying there; the place is a wilderness."

"Is it still occupied?"

"Oh, aye, as far as I know. Fred Bateman will take you in his taxi if you like. He's outside."

The taxi was a dilapidated vehicle with a dented body. The young man placed his luggage in the boot and climbed into the back seat.

When the car was in highly vibrating motion Fred Bateman called above the din, "Funny you wantin' Greenwall Manor; two of my friends look after it."

"Oh, that's interesting."

"You goin' to see the old gentleman?"

There was a considerable pause before the American said, "Yes . . . yes."

"He's over a hundred now, you know. Incredible when you think of the condition he's in and all he's lived through. . . . Do they know you're comin'?"

"No, I . . . I didn't inform them. I was rather hazy about my movements."

"Oh. Aye. I see. You a relation, sir?"

"Yes, yes, I suppose you could call me a relation."

"Of the old man or the old lady?"

There was a pause before the American said, "Well, both, I suppose."

"Oh, aye! Aye!" Fred's exclamation was meant to convey that he understood, but at the same time it said that the situation wasn't quite clear to him.

The taxi now turned up a side road and into open country.

"Nice stretch of country this." Fred was nodding out of the window. "Lovely up here on a day like this; you can breathe."

The American, feeling that a complimentary retort was expected of him, said, "Yes, yes. You can see for quite some way."

"There it is, sir." Fred was pointing across to the left now, to a dark blur of trees. "It's in there, the house. Used to be fine gardens there, they said, at one time, but there's nowt but brushwood any more. There was a farmhouse an' all, but that's a complete wreck."

The American was sitting forward in his seat as the taxi turned into a gateless opening and went through a dark tunnel of trees to a grass-covered space, out of which reared a great grey stone house. When the car stopped he got out and stood gazing up at the bleak façade for a moment, then followed Fred into a courtyard where the grass was sprouting a foot high between the flagstones.

It was a very large yard, he saw, surrounded by buildings, and through an archway at the far end came a woman. She had a bucket in her hand and she stopped for a second and stared towards them before walking briskly forward, saying, "Why, Fred!" Then her mouth opened into a gape as she looked at the visitor.

"Hello, Maggie," said Fred. "I've brought this gentleman. . . . He's come to visit."

Maggie, a plump-bodied, round-faced, middle-aged woman looked hard at the taxi-driver and he at her; then she turned her gaze towards the visitor again and quietly asked, "Who do you want to see, sir?"

"Well"—he smiled down on her—"to tell you the truth, I don't rightly know; but . . . but, candidly, I didn't really expect to see anyone. I just came to see the house. I know that my great-grandmother died here two years ago; I didn't expect there to be anyone else alive."

Maggie Robson bent her head well forward before saying, "You're her great-grandson?"

"Well, I'm Daniel Rosier the Third." His smile broadened.

"Well, well!" Maggie straightened up. "What a pity she didn't live to see this day. Will . . . will you come in, sir? My husband's upstairs; I'll go and get him."

She led him into the house, into an enormous stone-flagged room, then left him and returned a moment later, followed by a man not much taller than herself; but whereas she was plump the man was thin and wiry.

"This is my husband, Willie, sir."

"How do you do?"

"How do you do, sir?" The man stared up into Daniel's face. He looked slightly bewildered and gave a nervous laugh as he said, "This is a surprise, sir. My wife"—he nodded towards her—"she tells me you are the old man's—I mean the old gentleman's—great-grandson."

"Yes, I am."

"You're American?"

"Yes, I'm American."

"And you've come all the way from America?"

"Well, not recently; I'm at Cambridge. I arrived back on Monday, and as I have a week to spare I thought I would come along."

"Cambridge?" It was Fred chirping in now. "You going to Cambridge, sir, the university? Oh, you'll like that. I was in Cambridge once. Oh, it's a lovely place, Cambridge."

"Is this your first trip over, sir?"

Daniel looked from Willie to Maggie as he answered, "No, this is my third year at Cambridge, but . . . but, you see, I didn't know I had any relations in England until quite recently when my grandfather died." He paused and his gaze swept over the three of them before he ended. "My father found letters from England—from here, to be exact—among his possessions."

"Oh yes." Maggie nodded at him. Then she dropped her head to one side and said, "She was a lovely lady, your great-grandmother, a lovely lady."

"Yes, yes, I'm sure she was."

Turning from him, she now spread a cloth over the corner

of the long table and on it she placed a new crusty loaf, a platter holding a chunk of cheese, half of a large fruit cake and a large pot of tea.

As Daniel drank the strong sweet tea and ate his third slice of yeasty-tasting bread and butter and finished off with a slice of cake there grew in him a feeling of excitement, a feeling that churned his stomach and made him restless. The feeling wasn't entirely new; it had come into being six weeks ago when his grandfather had died and his grandmother had seemed on the point of following him. It was when she lay in a coma, from which none of the family thought she would recover, that his father began to sort out the pile of letters he had come across in the bureau in the library; letters that had nothing to do with the shipyard, or any of the other businesses in which they had interests, but were private letters revealing an astounding situation—a situation that had upset Daniel Rosier the Second very much. He had been amazed to find that he had a grandparent in England who apparently had been still alive up to two years ago. But when his mother recovered she refused to discuss the subject in any way; and only his fear of causing a relapse prevented him from pressing the point.

Daniel the Second was very interested in the fact that he had forebears in England, for he had always been under the impression that both his parents had been orphans. His mother's refusal to speak of the past pointed to something of a mystery and he wanted it cleared up, and so he had suggested that he, Daniel the Third, should come over a few days earlier and find out what he could about the strange business. And so here he was, and upstairs was his ancient great-grandfather and he was anxious to see him. Yet the couple sitting opposite were making no move to bring about the meeting. It was odd when he came to think of it, but they should have proposed him going upstairs first. Addressing Maggie, he said now, "That was very nice. I've never tasted bread like that before."

"I bake all me own." She smiled at him. "I have to; it's too far out to deliver."

He dusted his fingers against each other; then he took out a handkerchief and wiped his mouth and, looking at Willie, asked, "May I go up now?"

"Oh yes, sir. Yes, sir."

Willie opened the door and stood aside for Daniel to pass,

and led him along a dark corridor, through another door and into a hall.

Just inside the door Daniel stopped and gazed about him in sheer amazement. He saw a huge, high room with a staircase leading out of it. There were a number of dark brown doors around the walls, and in between them hung pictures, the subjects almost indiscernible. The floor was bare and dusty but showed recent signs of having been swept, but the cobwebs hanging from the corners of the ceiling had not apparently been disturbed for many years.

Willie Robson brought Daniel's eyes down to him as he said, "It's an awful sight, sir, but we can't do any more: the old man takes all my time, but every now and again I have a go at the place. But it's like the Swing Bridge; by the time you finish at one end you've got to start at the other. Maggie, she's never done. That kitchen is one body's work besides the meals and the washing, and I'm tellin' you, sir, there's some of that, and with every drop of water to be boiled."

"Please, please, it's all right. Believe me, I'm not finding fault, I'm just amazed at what I'm seeing. God, I just don't know how the two of you live here, let alone keep the place clean."

Willie smiled slightly now, then lowered his head before saying, "You haven't seen anything yet, sir. If it was only the house we could manage and do something with it; it's him—I mean the old gentleman. I . . . I'd better prepare you, sir, for apart from him being very old, over a hundred, he's not a nice sight. He had an accident years back and it took half of his face off, and I think it affected his mind as well. He's . . . he's not very often himself, besides which he's partly paralysed. I just thought I'd better warn you. He hasn't been too bad these last few days, but . . . but he can change as quick as lightning."

Daniel shook his head slightly but said nothing, and when Willie turned and mounted the stairs he followed him, his eyes darting about him the while.

They reached a sort of gallery with long weather-smeared windows through which the sun was trying to shine, then crossed a broad space and along a corridor, and outside the end door Willie paused and glanced up at Daniel. Then he opened the door and went inside, and Daniel slowly followed him.

The first thing he noticed was that the sun was shining

brightly through the two large windows of this room, and that the heavy furniture filling it, although not bright, looked as if it had had some attention. The windows were facing the door, and he had to turn completely round and look to the wall to the left of him, behind the door, before he saw the four-poster bed and the creature sitting in it.

Although he had been prepared, the shock was such that he felt his shoulders coming up as if to protect his head from an onslaught. He was looking at a completely bald head, sickly white in the parts where it wasn't mottled brown. The white parts stood out like scabs and the brown appeared like hollows in the skull. Then there were the eyes, like small black points at the end of two funnels. One side of the face, the side with the ear, presented a wrinkled mass of loose skin; the other side, minus the ear, was drawn together as if it had been stitched with red string; and then there was the white hand, not blue veined but all white, a lifeless thing lying on top of the counterpane. But this wasn't any more horrifying than the other hand that was only part of a hand and had a leather strap around the wrist from which ran a leather lead, like a dog's lead, to the thick post of the bed.

Daniel watched Willie go to the bed and without bending towards the man in it call loudly, "There's someone to see you," and, stepping aside, turn his head to him and say under his breath, "Don't get too close."

Daniel had to force himself to move towards the bed at all, and he stood just beyond the foot of it and after wetting his lips said formally, "Good afternoon, sir."

"Wha'! Wha'! . . . Bloody doctor . . . You won't ge' me out." The voice was thick, blurred, the words disjointed, running into one another; it was as if they had taken their shape from the distorted lips. "Ride . . . ride with the best of 'em." The croak stopped and the two black points at the end of the funnels emerged for a moment and the hand with the strap on it came swiftly forward, only to be checked by the lead. The action seemed to set the left side of the body quivering and the voice, loud now, startlingly loud, cried, "Who the hell . . . are you? Who, eh? Don't stand there! I'm not dead, I'm not dead."

"This is your great-grandson from America; he's come to see you." Willie was shouting again.

The figure in the bed became still for a moment or so; then the face began to move. The skin on the left side twitched, the black spots of the eyes became larger, the jaws worked as if on a mouthful of food; then the single word came sharply, almost without distortion, "Grandson?"

"Great-grandson." Daniel bent his head forward as he spoke and tried to smile.

"Ha-ha! . . . Ha-ha-ha! . . . Oh, ha-ha-ha!"

As the crackled laughter became higher and higher, Daniel felt Willie's hand on his arm, and he stepped backwards as Willie whispered, "It's no use, sir, he's going to start; he's always like this at the beginning. I would come away, sir."

Daniel needed no second bidding, but as he turned towards the door the voice came at him from the bed, jerking his head round, "Bastard!" The figure was leaning towards him, his arm pulling at the strap. "Whore! Mulholland's whore! Jail. The Swede. Mulholland's whore. Jail. No horses. No horses."

"Come away, sir."

When Willie closed the door behind them and they had walked to the end of the corridor they could still hear the voice, at the pitch of a scream now, yelling, "Mulholland. Mulholland."

"I'm sorry, sir, very sorry it had to be like that."

Daniel stood with his hands on the balustrade of the gallery and looked down into the hall. Then, turning to the little man at his side, he said, "Only one thing amazes me: how do you stand looking after him?"

"Use, sir, I suppose. And it's a job. We were glad enough of it years ago, and things weren't so bad when the old lady was alive."

"How long have you been here?"

"Nineteen-twenty we came, sir. I came out of the army in eighteen and couldn't get work, and when this came up we jumped at it. There was a cook then and a maid. My job was to look after the old man and Maggie was to see to the old lady. I said we jumped at the job, but after a couple of weeks, I don't mind telling you, I was for leaving. If things hadn't been so bad all round I would have, an' all because it was sheer hell looking after him. He was bedridden then, and he'd only had one stroke, and you couldn't go in the room unless something came at you. That's . . . that's why I keep his arm tied. He still picks things up from the tray and lets you have them full belt. I have to feed him now, and that's no pleasant job."

377

Daniel shook his head and closed his eyes for a moment, then said, "No pleasant job. . . . That, I should imagine, is putting it mildly. But why can't you have extra help?"

"Oh well, sir; I guess you don't know, but the money went when the old lady died. She was living on an endowment for years. It was quite substantial, I understand, but once she went it was finished. The house has been mortgaged for years, but now we're getting by on the bits and pieces."

"Bits and pieces?" Daniel's brows came together.

"Yes, sir, the plate an' that. There was a lot of silver, but the solicitor had it put in the bank, and other things an' all, bits of jade and jewellery and stuff like that, all valuable, and books—the library's practically empty. Then six months ago they came and took an inventory of the furniture. Every article in the house they've got stock of, and there's some fine pieces here although they might look a bit grubby. All the bills are sent to the solicitor and he pays our wages when he comes once a month. He's always tellin' us to go careful like, and if he lasts very much longer"—he jerked his head backwards—"they'll likely have to foreclose. The doctor can't understand him lasting as he does. He says it's the devil in him, and I agree with him there. There's nobody knows more about his devil than I do."

"This is fantastic, fantastic." Daniel's face was screwed up. Then he asked, "How did he come to have those injuries?"

"Oh well, sir, it's a long story; but, as far as I can gather, his sister shot him."

"No!"

"Aye, sir. She intended to kill him, they say. It's a pity she hadn't, that's what I say. But shortly after she did that he got seven years' imprisonment."

"For what?"

"He killed his servant, sir."

Daniel stared at Willie for a whole minute before he repeated, "Killed his servant?"

"Aye. They say he had treated him worse than a dog, knocked his eye out and used the whip on him nearly every day, and the fellow set about him. But he wasn't any match for him and he killed him and threw him in the quarry."

"God Almighty!" Daniel dropped his chin on to his chest, and Willie said brightly, "Oh, don't let it worry you, sir."

"But my grandfather"—Daniel was shaking his head as he looked at Willie—"my grandfather was such a gentle man

. . . I mean gentle, kind, almost womanlike, he was so gentle. And so is my father."

"Strange, isn't it, sir, but likely they took after the old lady, for, as I said, sir, she was really lovely. Maggie cried for days after she went. There's been many a time in these last few years when I've said I couldn't stick it any longer, but Maggie's kept me here because she didn't want to leave the old lady. Would you like to see her room, sir?"

"Yes, yes." Daniel spoke as if he was in a slight daze, and he turned from the balcony and followed Willie back up the corridor and into a room on the left-hand side. This, too, had a huge four-poster bed, but it was a different room. The woodwork had been painted white, the carpet was a faded green, as were the satin curtains on the long window; it was a woman's room, a gentle woman's room, and had a smell of lavender and orris root about it.

Between the two long windows stood a large escritoire, and Willie, pointing to it, said, "She spent hours and hours at that desk, not writing—only a letter now and again—but just sitting there. You know, she never left this room for the last ten years of her life and she spent most of them in bed."

Daniel's eye came to rest on a painting above the mantelpiece, and when he walked towards it Willie said, "That was her when she was about thirty, I should say. Pretty, wasn't she?"

"Yes, she was very pretty."

"She had an awful life. Right from the word go she had an awful life."

Daniel turned his head now and looked at Willie, and asked quietly, "She told you?"

"Oh no, sir. No sir. She never mentioned the master, not one word. All the years Maggie served her she never mentioned his name. The cook said they hadn't seen each other for thirty years. Can you believe that? Can you imagine that, sir, living in the same house? Of course, it's been understandable this last few years, with him being bedridden in one room and she in another; but afore that they said as soon as she heard him come galloping up that drive she came into this room and locked herself in. Not that he seemed to care, because he was funny from the time he came out of prison. She had gone through something afore with him, but when he started his capers again, bringing women to the house— well . . ."

"How do you know so much about the family history, Willie?" Daniel looked closely at Willie.

"Well, it was the cook, sir, she was as old as Methuselah an' all. She started as parlour-maid here—Fanny Croft, they called her. She knew all the history. Ee, the things she told us he got up to, the old man, and I believe every word she said, I do. I do. Married his only son off to his half-sister, he did. The girl was the Mulholland woman's daughter, the Mulholland woman who he's always on about. He gave her the child when she was in service here and later she got the bairn adopted, and, as fate sometimes does, it played a dirty trick and brought this girl and his son together. Well, the old fellow found out who the girl was and pushed the wedding. There was hell to pay, cook said, and the young pair cleared off abroad. America, I should say, 'cos the old lady used to get letters from . . . Oh, God Almighty, sir. . . ." Willie slowly drew his hand hard down his face and from over his stretched lower lids he gazed apologetically at Daniel.

Daniel had to force himself to say, "It's all right. It's all right. I knew of this."

"You did, sir?"

"Yes."

"Oh well, that's a relief, sir. Oh, I should say it is, springing it like that." He now turned away and, pointing across the gallery to the far wall and to one of four pictures hanging there, said, "That one should interest you, sir." Daniel moved slowly forward and stood in front of it. It was like looking into a mirror, for the face was almost a replica of his own except that his own eyes were darker.

"It was painted, I understand, just afore he was married, sir."

"We are practically alike."

"Aye, sir, it's sort of startling."

"It's no compliment; he's been a terrible man."

"Aye, sir, he has, but I think every now and again most families throw up someone like him. It is as if all the badness is drained out of the rest an' put into one, like. You see what I mean?"

"I hope so, Willie, I hope so." Daniel's face was solemn as he went down the stairs, and it remained solemn as he followed Willie around the rest of the house.

In the kitchen Maggie said, "I'll have a real meal ready for you in just over an hour, sir. Will that be all right?"

"Splendid," said Daniel, "and in the meantime, if you don't mind, I'll take a look round outside. . . . Don't you bother to come, Willie, I'll find my way about."

"Right, sir. But there's not much to see, it's just a 'tangle."

As Daniel walked across the courtyard he took in great draughts of air. That house, it was terrible . . . yet fascinating.

He walked past stables, some with the half-doors hanging drunkenly by one hinge, and the roof of one outhouse had fallen in. He passed through an arch in the high green wall and followed a path, between a tangle of tall bushes, which only allowed the passage of one person, and when he emerged from it he wrinkled his nose against the stench that met him. He guessed that the drainage must be cesspool, and he shook his head as if in disbelief. There was an open space before him now, then a hill rising from it in the distance; and towards this he walked, and when he reached the top he stood and looked about him.

There was the house, looking from this distance like a pre-historic creature, its chimneys like myriad arms clawing their way upwards out of the tangle of overgrown trees. It was difficult to believe that down there in that house his grandfather had grown up; that he had run and played in this garden. But why had he never come back to see his mother? It was understandable why he wouldn't want to see his father, but not his mother, that pretty, gentle-looking creature whose room smelt of lavender and orris root; and why had he thought it necessary to keep her existence secret from them all? It wasn't likely that she would have given away the close relationship between him and his wife.

The letters that his father had found had told him nothing except that his grandmother had been alive up to two years ago. Her letters had been polite letters, letters that enquired after her son's health, letters that told him that she was very well, that his Aunt Gertrude had been to visit her; that his Uncle Leonard had died; that the weather was bitterly cold, or it had been a very nice day; that she had been reading the Brownings, that she did so enjoy the Brownings; but never once had she mentioned her husband or enquired after her son's wife.

Before he had left home his father had taken him aside and said, "Whatever you find out, don't write about it; it'll keep until you return. You understand?" He understood.

He also understood now his grandmother's aloofness and his grandfather's constant care of her. His grandfather always treated her like some precious piece of porcelain to be handled very gently. He could see his grandparents at the family gatherings seated side by side in a place apart, as his brother once said, "Like royalty watching their subjects at play." And all the while, over all the years, they had kept their secret about this house and the man who was their father.

His grandparents had had only one child, his father, but his father had six, four sons and two daughters. He himself was the third son and Victoria followed him. . . . Was Victoria the sins of the fathers being visited upon the children?

When his father had said to him, "Whatever you find out, don't write about it, it'll keep", had he been thinking of Victoria? But people like Victoria could happen to anybody. At least that is what the doctors had persuaded his mother to think; but should she ever find out about the relationship between her husband's father and mother, then, in her own mind, Victoria would be explained and his father would never know peace again.

His mother was a Mason-Crawford; she came from a family of impeccable reputation. No breath of scandal had ever touched them except when Victoria was born, but you couldn't really call Victoria a scandal; she was looked upon as an act of God, although why God should wish to inflict such a family with a child whose mind was not normal would for ever remain a mystery, not only to his mother, Daniel knew, but to all her family. Yet the Mason-Crawfords had one comfort, they knew that Victoria hadn't come from their side. As both Daniel's the First and Sara's parents had presumably been killed in a train crash while travelling together, you couldn't, the Mason-Crawfords agreed, do much by way of research without hurting their feelings, but you could think all the more. . . .

He now walked slowly around the perimeter of the grounds and came by way of the drive to the house again. Maggie had the meal ready and he sat down at the kitchen table, and when she said, "It's no place, sir, to put you down to eat in the kitchen," he answered, "Oh, please don't worry. I'm very grateful to be offered a meal at all. As to eating in the kitchen. I'm perfectly used to that at home."

Daniel had never eaten a meal in a kitchen in his life until earlier on this day. His mother would have been horrified at the bare suggestion, and the servants certainly wouldn't have welcomed his presence in the kitchen. It said a great deal for his charm of manner that both Maggie and Willie believed him. . . .

It was as he sat in the little sitting-room along the passage —the room which had once been Mrs. Davis's—drinking a cup of coffee and listening to Maggie now recounting some of the things Fanny Croft had told him, that the screams came to him. They were muffled, but they startled him, and Maggie said, "Oh, that's nothing, sir. Take no notice. He's not in pain or anything, it's just badness, and because he can't get loose to throw things. He's reached the Mulholland patch again."

"The Mulholland patch?" Daniel's brow gathered into a question and Maggie said, "Every now and again he gets on about her and never stops for hours. It's a wonder, I say to Willie, that she doesn't hear him. Perhaps she does. A hate like his is bound to travel."

"Well, where she is I don't suppose it'll hurt her." Daniel smiled quietly.

"Oh, she's not dead, sir."

"She's not?" Daniel's eyes were wide now and he put his cup down and said again, "She's not? The Mulholland woman—I mean, whatever her name is, she's not dead?"

"Well, she wasn't up till lately, a few months ago, and I've seen nothing in the *Gazette* about her going, and she was so noted that they'd 'ave done a piece on her; but I should imagine her time's running out because she's an age."

"She lives near?"

"In Shields, sir—Westoe way, I think. . . . Yes, it would be Westoe 'cos all the people with money live there."

As a louder scream came to them Maggie rose, saying, "Would you excuse me, sir, he might need help; he's likely changing him."

Daniel got to his feet, and when Maggie had gone from the room he remained staring at the door. The Mulholland patch. Here was the other side of the picture, this Katie Mulholland, and he was related to her. . . . She was his great-grandmother.

Slowly he turned and looked down into the fire. Would it be possible to see her? Would it?

The following morning saw Daniel once more riding along in the broken-down taxi, his mind a confused whirl of gossip and legend. He was learning much from the voluble Fred Bateman about the history and career of Katie Mulholland or, as he had discovered her true name to be, Mrs. Fraenkel.

Fred loved a yarn and he loved an audience, and he knew he had found one in the young American, so he scraped the barrel of his mind for all the tit-bits he could remember about Katie Mulholland.

They came at last to a line of white railings fronting a large house, and Daniel got out of the car and walked slowly across the pavement, through the iron gate and up the long pathway to the front door. As he pressed the button he heard someone laughing inside the house, and a voice calling, "It's all right, I'll go."

There came to him the sound of running steps and then the door was pulled open and standing before him was a young girl. She was of medium height, with dark blue eyes rimmed with short thick lashes. Her mouth was full shaped and wide, and the nose between these two features looked too small in comparison; but what struck him instantly was that she was a silver blonde. He had seen silver blondes back home. His cousin, Renee, had her hair bleached to silver blonde, but this girl's hair had a natural look, and according to the times it was old-fashioned, for it wasn't short cut but piled high on the back of her head in twisted plaits. As his mouth opened to speak, her voice came at him, conveying thinly suppressed laughter. "Look," she said, dropping her head to one side, "it's no use starting, you're just wasting your breath. I have all the books I need, from encyclopaedias downwards. Nor am I interested in the tea-towel you're giving away with the pair of sheets, nor the blanket that will last me a lifetime, so, as I've said, don't waste your breath. I'm sorry, very sorry, but you're the third one already who's been here today; and it's not dinner-time yet. We don't stick 'No circulars, no hawkers' on the gate because we know you've got to live, but there's a limit. Do you . . .?" Her voice had become slower over the last few seconds and now it trailed away and her top lip moved upwards from her teeth as she murmured now in a horrified tone, "Oh Lord, you're not selling anything?"

"No." He shook his head and tried his hardest not to burst out laughing.

"Oh dear, I'm sorry. You wanted to see someone . . . my father?"

"No. At least"—he was still trying not to laugh outright—"I just came to enquire if Mrs. Fraenkel lives here."

"Oh yes, yes, she does."

"Oh, really! Then I wonder if it would be possible for me to see her?"

"Oh yes, yes. Come in."

"Will you excuse me while I tell my taxi-driver not to wait."

"Yes, yes, of course."

When, a minute or so later, he again walked up the path the girl was no longer at the door but he could see her in the hallway talking to another woman, and when he reached the door they both came towards him, and the other woman looked at him hard before she said softly, "You want to see Mrs. Fraenkel?"

"Yes, if that is possible."

"May I ask what your business is?"

"Well . . ." He looked down at his hat in his hands and pulled on the brim as he said, "It's a long, long story, but I think she is my great-grandmother."

"Your great . . .!" The woman and the girl exchanged quick glances. Then the woman, looking at him again, said softly, "Your name is?"

"Daniel Rosier."

"Rosier?"

"Yes, Rosier. I'm Daniel the Third."

Again there was an exchange of glances, and the older woman, her face unsmiling now, said, "Will you come in, please." She turned and walked back into the hall while the girl held the door open and closed it behind him when he entered the house.

The hall was small in comparison to the one he had left such a short while ago, but, with its white paint and rose-coloured carpet mounting up the stairs, it was as different from Greenwall Manor as the top of a skyscraper was from a dungeon, and this impression was carried farther still when, following the woman, he entered a large, beautifully furnished room; and after only a fleeting impression the thought came to him that there were pieces here which would make his mother's mouth water, for she was in the process of "collecting things from the old country".

"Will you take a seat?"

"Thank you." He sat down in an armchair, and the girl and the woman sat to the side of him on a large couch. They sat close together and they stared at him silently until he became embarrassed by their scrutiny, for their faces were unsmiling, and the older woman's expression was a troubled one. It was she who now spoke, saying, "I'm Mrs. Mulholland, Mrs. Fraenkel's great-niece; this is my daughter, Bridget."

He smiled from one to the other, and now the young woman's eyes showed a slight twinkle as she turned towards her mother, saying, "I thought he was a salesman; I was seeing him off."

"Oh dear!" A rippling movement passed over Catherine's face; then, her expression solemn again, she said, "Why have you come now, Mr. Rosier? Have you just found out about the relationship?"

"You could say that. In fact only a matter of hours ago. And it's only a few weeks since we—that is, my father—found out he had any relatives at all in England. My grandfather died and my father found some letters. These had apparently been written by his grandmother, Mrs. Rosier, of Greenwall Manor."

"She is still alive?"

"No, she died about two years ago; but, as I said, we knew nothing about it until just recently."

"And . . . and Mr. Rosier?"

Now Daniel looked down for a second, and when he brought his eyes again to those of the woman sitting opposite he said, "He is still alive. I could add unfortunately, because he is a terrible wreck, both in mind and body."

"Oh!" There was a silence between them for a while. Then Catherine, getting to her feet and joining her hands together, walked to the hearth-rug, and from there she turned and looked at him again, saying, "I don't know how I'm going to put this, Mr. Rosier, but your great-grandfather brought sorrow and shame on to my Aunt Katie in a number of ways. I don't know how she will receive you."

"I understand—I understand perfectly what you mean." He was thinking of the baby who grew up to be his grandmother. "But . . . but that doesn't alter the fact that she is my great-grandmother."

"How did you find out about her?"

"The couple who are looking after my great-grandfather, they told me what they knew." He omitted to mention the man in the four-poster screaming out the name of Mulholland.

"It would likely be a one-sided version," said Catherine stiffly, then went on, "She is ninety-two, Mr. Rosier; and although she has all her faculties and can still get about quite well, the past at times comes flooding over her. If you knew all her history you would know that at intervals during her life she has known great trouble, and she has always been misrepresented, always." She paused; then, shaking her head, added, "I don't really know what to do about this, Mr. Rosier, quite candidly, I don't. Could I ask you to wait until my husband comes in and we could talk it over . . . I mean whether you are to see her or not?"

"Yes. Yes, I'll do that."

"You see . . . It is awful for me to have to say this, but . . . but if your name hadn't been Rosier I am sure she would have been quite over the moon to know she has a great-grandson . . . quite over the moon."

"Let's hope she'll be so yet."

"Would you like a cup of coffee?"

"Yes; thank you. That would be very nice."

"Bridget, perhaps you'd show Mr. Rosier round the garden while I see Nellie."

Daniel was quick to notice that Bridget showed no enthusiasm to act as his escort, but when she opened the french windows and stepped out on to the stone-flagged terrace he followed her.

"It's pretty," he said.

She made no answer to this and continued down the three shallow steps to the path that led between some formal rose-beds.

After he had followed her over a lawn, with a willow tree in the middle, through a privet hedge and round a well-tended kitchen garden, along by a stone wall and back again to where the roses were, he tried once more to open a conversation, for the short tour had been embarrassing, to say the least. He wasn't anything of a chatterer himself, he was mostly content to listen, but this girl's silence made him uneasy; it wasn't a silence created by shyness, but rather it was a condemning silence. He stopped and, lifting a rose head on to his fingers, said, "I'm always amazed how the roses grow in England. Last year I was spending Christmas with some friends in Sussex and they had roses in their garden then."

Looking at him blankly with her dark blue eyes, which now seemed almost black, she said in a flat tone, "How nice for them."

It was a rebuff, an ill-mannered rebuff. He felt himself flush and was annoyed because he did so, and now he returned her look squarely and said, "They wouldn't put you in an electric chair in America before they proved you guilty."

At this moment Catherine called to them from the terrace, saying, "Will we have it outside?" and Bridget, turning hastily towards her, replied, "No, indoors, there's a bit of a wind blowing."

When they were again seated in the drawing-room and the coffee had been handed round Catherine said, "My husband should be back at any minute. I . . . I do hope you understand my attitude."

Daniel nodded gravely towards her. "Yes. Yes, I understand." He looked at the dark slim woman who was, he imagined, somewhere in her early forties, and straight away he decided that he could like this woman.

Not only by way of making conversation, but because he wanted to place her clearly in the picture, he said, "Are you the daughter of Mrs. Fraenkel's brother or sister?"

"Oh!" Catherine smiled now. "It's much more complicated than that. Aunt Katie—that is Mrs. Fraenkel—is my great-aunt. Her brother was my grandfather, if you can work that out."

He dropped his head to the side and repeated, "Mrs. Fraenkel's brother—that is, my great-grandmother's brother —was your grandfather." The smile broadened and he added, "It will come."

Returning his smile, Catherine said, "And Aunt Katie is Bridget's"—she put out her hand in the direction of her daughter—"great-great-aunt, but we all call her simply Aunt Katie. And, you know, she doesn't look anywhere near her age; she's remarkable." She broke off at this point and turned her face towards the door, then rose to her feet, saying, "Excuse me, I think that's my husband," and hurried from the room.

Again they were left alone and the silence was renewed, and Daniel determined that he wasn't going to be the one to break it—he could stand silence; he would like to bet he could resist opening his mouth for a much longer time than she could. And then she said quite simply, "I'm sorry."

He wetted his lips and replied, "Oh, that's all right."

"No, it wasn't . . . it isn't. It was so childish. I've no explanation except that I'm very attached to Aunt Katie and the name of Rosier—well, I've heard so much about it and . . ."

"And nothing to the good."

"Well"—she shook her head—"it's difficult. . . ."

"I understand."

"You don't really. You couldn't."

"Give me time."

She had a soft smile, he noted. "It's a great pity I wasn't selling something," he said now. "I'm sure I could have enlisted your sympathy and made a sale."

"Ah! No, you wouldn't." She shook her head. "If you saw the attic, it's crammed. We've just had to draw the line. You see they tell each other about easy houses, women they can talk over. Mother's hopeless."

"And you are very firm?"

"Yes. Yes, I'm very firm."

They were both laughing when the door opened and Catherine entered, followed by a man.

Daniel rose to his feet and returned the hard scrutiny that was being levelled on him as the man came forward.

"This is my husband, Mr. Rosier."

"How do you do?" Daniel put out his hand, and after the slightest hesitation Tom Mulholland took it. "How do you do?" Another slight pause and Tom said, "Sit down."

When they were seated again Catherine said, "The coffee is still hot. Would you like one?"

"No thanks, dear; I had a cup of tea not long since." Now turning his head towards Daniel, Tom stared at him for a

389

second or two before he began, "Well, this is a strange business, isn't it, Catherine's just told me. You say you're Aunt Katie's great-grandson."

"Well, I'm Daniel Rosier the Third, and as I have told your wife"—he inclined his head towards Catherine—"from what I learned yesterday Miss Mulholland—that is, Mrs. Fraenkel—was my grandmother's mother, and . . ." He paused. ". . . my great-grandfather on both sides was Bernard Rosier."

"You know, then, they were half-brother and sister?"

"Yes. Yes, I just found that out yesterday too."

They held each other's eye, then Tom said, "You know that this will come as a bit of a shock to Aunt Katie?"

"Yes, yes. I can understand that because it came as a shock to me too . . . all of it."

"What . . . what I'm troubled about is that I don't know whether it will be a welcome one or the other way about, not only because of your name, as Catherine has told you, but, you see, Aunt Katie didn't see her daughter from when she was one year old until she was nearly twenty, and then, as far as I can gather, that wasn't a very pleasant meeting. Her daughter sort of rejected her. She had been brought up to think she was somebody and didn't like the fact that she wasn't."

"Oh. I didn't know this. You see, we knew nothing about having any relatives in England at all until my grandfather died, when, as I've explained, we found letters that had passed between him and his mother, my great-grandmother."

"Is your grandmother, Aunt Katie's daughter, still alive?"

"Yes."

"And she's never mentioned having a mother all these years?"

"No. We understood that her parents, together with those of my grandfather, had been killed in a train accident."

"Well." Tom rubbed his hand hard across his chin, then looked at Catherine as he said, "I think he should see her. If we prevent this we'll keep wondering to the end of our days whether we did right or wrong."

"Yes, Tom, yes, I think you're right."

"What do you think, Brid?" Tom was looking towards Bridget, and she, after a pause, said, "You know best, Dad."

"Well, that's settled." Tom nodded towards Daniel. "But the point is now, how is it going to be done? You can't just walk in on her. I . . . I think she should be prepared, don't you?"

"Yes, yes, I agree."

"Catherine." Tom was looking at his wife, and she, getting to her feet, said, "Yes, yes, I'll go up."

When Catherine reached the landing she paused and put her fingers to her mouth and asked herself why this had to happen at this late date. Ten years ago Katie might have been able to withstand the shock, even a pleasant one—if this should turn out to be pleasant—but now she was ninety-two. It would seem she was going to go down to her grave being pestered by the Rosiers. Yet he was such a nice young man, so very nice, it was hard to associate him with the name of Rosier. It would be difficult to dislike him just because of his name.

She went across the landing and opened the door, and on her entry the figure sitting in the armchair by the window turned towards her and said brightly, "Who was that with Bridget in the garden, Catherine? I've never seen that one before. It'll be a good job when Peter is back; that's the third different one I've seen around this week."

"Aunt Katie!" Catherine pulled up a chair to Katie's side and sat down, and taking the old hand in hers she said, "That young man down there, he didn't come to see Bridget, he came to see you."

"Me?" The fine lines on Katie's face converged upwards and gathered around her eyes.

"Yes, dear." Catherine put her free hand out and lifted a strand of white hair from Katie's brow, saying as she did so, "We . . . we didn't know whether to let him see you or not."

"What are you talking about, child?" Katie impatiently brought Catherine's hand from her head, and, patting it sharply, said, "A young man to see me and you didn't know whether to let him see me or not. . . . What do you mean?"

Catherine opened her mouth twice, looked towards the window, then down at the hand she was holding, before saying softly, "How would you like to have a great-grandson, Aunt Katie?"

As Katie lay back slowly on her chair and her jaw slackened Catherine exclaimed, "Oh, Aunt Katie, I shouldn't have put it like that, not so quickly; but, you see, I didn't know. . . ."

"It's all right, it's all right. You mean he's . . . he's Sarah's?"

"Yes, Aunt Katie. Yes, Sarah's grandson. He's from America."

"Oh, Catherine. Catherine." Katie pulled herself upwards, and lifting Catherine's hand she gripped it with surprising strength as she said, "And she sent him to see me? Oh, Catherine!"

Catherine smiled. The shock had been a happy shock; it would do her no harm. She rose to her feet and said eagerly now, "I will bring him up. Now you're not to get excited, do you hear?" She patted Katie's cheek. "Keep yourself calm, now. Do you hear me?"

"Yes, I hear you, Catherine."

Katie squeezed her arm gently, then pushed her away; after which she sat waiting, her eyes on the door. Her heart was beating rapidly and she repeated Catherine's warning to herself, Be calm; don't get excited.

When the door opened and the young man walked past Catherine the beating of her heart turned to a mad gallop and, the old fear returning, she pressed her fingers across her mouth.

Katie knew she had reached a good age, she knew she was a very old woman, but she had never really acknowledged the fact to herself until a few years ago, when she found that things which had happened the previous day, or but a few hours ago, she could not immediately recall. Yet she had only to sit quiet for a minute and she could see herself as a girl again. She had spent many, many hours these last few years going back to the time when she was a girl; when she was a child, sitting picking cinders on the heap, and her mother coming and carrying the buckets away. She could see herself as plainly as if it were yesterday sitting in the kitchen surrounded by Lizzie, and Joe, and her granda, and her mother, while she told them tales. She could see her da at the kitchen table reading, and him saying, "You say it like this." And her thoughts of late had dwelt on the memory of the day before she started up at the house when her mother had washed and ironed her two print frocks and all her underclothes, and she had to sit by the fire in a blanket. And there was an odd thing about that memory, for when she thought of that day she could smell the singeing smell of the hot iron on the print. She could see her mother blowing on the heart of the fire to get it red so it wouldn't smoke the iron, and, when it was hot, lifting it out and rubbing it on a piece of hessian laid on the corner of the mat, then holding it against her cheek, and finally spitting on it. One dobble of spit had bounced off and fallen on her hand and she had taken the Lord's name in vain because of her fright, and then had apologised, saying, "Aw, hinny. Aw, hinny, that slipped out; it was never intended." That day was so clear.

The scene that came often into her mind of late, too, was walking by her granda's side to the top of the rise, and sitting with him, and talking, and learning from him; and she had learned from him, for she knew now that her grandpa had been a wise man; he hadn't been a God-fearing man like her da, but in a way he had been wiser than her da. But never over the last few years had her thoughts touched on one single day she had spent up at "the house". She had, as it were, railed off that part of her life in her mind, because once she stepped over the fence into any memory connected with "the house" it would lead her to the night of the ball.

And now the fences were all down, for here through the door he was walking towards her again. She shrank back in her chair and closed her eyes, and Catherine's voice seemed to come to her from a great distance away, saying, "Oh, Aunt Katie! Aunt Katie!" Then: "I knew this would happen. You'd better go."

"No, no." She held out her hand before she opened her eyes. "I'm all right."

Katie was now looking up at Daniel Rosier, who was Bernard Rosier as she had seen him close to that first time when he looked at her from between the curtains. This was the same shaped face, everything—the same eyes, the same mouth; everything, everything, was the same. But no. No, because he was talking and the other Bernard Rosier had never opened his mouth to her; not on that night, not when he looked like this.

"I'm sorry I startled you. Perhaps . . . perhaps I should call again another time."

The voice belied the looks, the figure, the whole man. It was soft, slow and kindly. Katie put out her hand and motioned him to a chair; then, looking up at Catherine, she said, "I'm all right, Catherine. Don't worry."

"Do you want me to stay, Aunt Katie?"

"No, no, dear. I'll be all right."

393

Catherine turned and gave Daniel a fleeting look, which said as clearly as if she had spoken, "Don't upset her."

When the door closed on Catherine, Katie said, "I'm . . . I'm sorry, but it was a shock seeing you. I . . . I never expected. . . . And then you . . . you reminded me of someone."

"Yes, yes, I know, and I'm very sorry about that. It doesn't make me very happy to know that I look like he did at my age."

"You . . . you know you look like him?"

"I have seen a portrait, only yesterday. It . . . it gave me a shock too. Can you believe me?"

After a moment Katie nodded her head twice, then said, "You've . . . you've come all the way from America?"

"Yes, but it's not my first visit over here. I'm studying at Cambridge. It's my third year there."

Katie looked puzzled for a moment, then said, "And you never came before?"

"I didn't know I had a great-grandmother." He bowed slightly towards her. "I didn't know until about . . ." He lifted his head upwards and looked at the ceiling as he groped to state the right time. ". . . about half-past four yesterday afternoon."

Katie's bewilderment deepened and he smiled at her, then went on to explain about his grandfather dying, and about Willie and Maggie at the Manor. Then came the question that, in a way, he had been expecting, "My daughter . . . did she never tell you, or your father, about me?"

It would have been so simple to say, "No." Simple, but not easy. It was easier to say to this old lady, "Oh yes, she spoke of you—yes, indeed, but . . . but just at odd times. She is a very reticent lady, my grandmother; but when she mentioned you we—that is, my father and the family—were under the impression that you had died. As also," he put in quickly, "had my father's grandparents. We didn't know they were alive either."

At this point he was conscious of the door opening behind him, but he did not take his attention from the new-found great-grandmother because her eyes, like great wells of sadness, were fastened on him and were asking him to alleviate some pain, an old deep pain. He watched the tremor pass over her pale lips, and the fine wrinkles on her cheeks quiver as she said, "Then if my daughter wanted you to think I was dead why have you come today?"

"Because I wanted to see my great-grandmother. And you know something? I feel she wanted me to come—my grandmother I mean."

"What makes you think that?"

The pain was beginning to be eased, and he swallowed hard before he said, "Just . . . just something she said to me one day not very long ago. It . . . it concerned you and . . . and it proved to me that she must have thought of you very often." Looking into the great sunken eyes before him, his lying became easy. "She said that she wished I could have seen her mother. She said that you had only met for a very short time but she remembered that you were beautiful." When he watched the moistness fill her eyes he put out his hand and touched hers, saying, "Oh, please, please, don't upset yourself. I shouldn't have said anything."

"Oh, yes, yes. I've waited a long time. But . . . but you're sure that's what she said?"

"Yes, perfectly."

His sister Amy used to chant to him when they were children, "Tell a lie, fib or story, never, never will you know glory." Given the choice, he would have told these lies even if it meant forgoing all future glory, because she looked so . . . so . . . He couldn't find a word which would describe the look in her eyes.

"You're very alike," he said now. "It's remarkable." This, at least, was the truth.

"How many children had Sarah?"

"Only the one, my father; but he has six. I have three brothers and two sisters."

"Oh, that is nice. Then I have six great-grandchildren altogether?"

"Yes, you have that." They were smiling at each other now, the atmosphere was less tense, and he turned his head to see who had come into the room, and saw Tom standing unobtrusively near the window. Katie, too, looked towards Tom now. "Did you hear all that, Tom? I have six great-grandchildren. Isn't that wonderful?"

"It is indeed, Aunt Katie." He came and stood by her chair, and she pointed to his index finger, which was bandaged, and said, "What on earth have you done to your hand, Tom?"

"Oh!" He lifted it up and wagged it as he looked at it and said, "I put it where a nail should have been when I was fixing the lock on the back gate. Catherine always says I should use a flannel hammer, but, as I've told you afore, Aunt Katie, every time I hit myself with a hammer something nice always happens."

"Oh, Tom!" She put her hand to her cheek and rocked herself while she laughed gently, and Daniel laughed too, but Tom's face hardly showed a smile, and he nodded at Daniel. "It's true, perfectly true. I'm as handy with a hammer as an elephant with a toothpick. I used to work in the shipyards, you know, at one time. I often wonder now how I managed to come out alive, because some of the hammers were a foot across."

Daniel laughed outright now, and as he looked up into the long, solemn face he realized that here was a wag, a natural wag. Here was a smoother of situations, another person in this house he was going to like.

Putting out her hand and catching at Tom's, Katie said, "Tom's been a very good friend to me since my husband died. I just don't know what would have happened to me without him and Catherine. I know one thing, I wouldn't have any business left if it hadn't been for him." She gazed up at Tom, but he looked at Daniel and said, "I rob her right and left, but she won't believe me. I've feathered enough nests to make a rookery out of her but she still keeps me on." He now looked down at Katie and a warm smile spread over his face as he gripped the hand holding his, and, wrinkling his nose at her, he remarked briefly, "You'll do." Again looking at Daniel, he said, "You're going to stay to lunch. The flying squad downstairs are rushing about like mad; it's no use you saying no."

"Oh, well." Daniel's face now assumed a straightness. "If I'm going to be forced to stay, then I can do nothing about it. I was hoping I was going to be asked."

"Good! Good!" Tom grinned at him. "Well, I think you'd better come on down and have an appetizer before the meal. What do you say, Aunt Katie?"

"Yes, yes, go and get yourselves a drink."

"What about coming down and joining us?" Tom was bending over her, and she smiled into his face and said, "No, I won't come down until lunch is ready. Just leave me for a

396

while. I'm fine; don't worry." She patted his hand. "I'm perfectly all right."

When Daniel rose to his feet she looked up at him and murmured softly, "I'm glad I've lived to see this day."

He could find nothing to say to this; he could only give her a little smile before he turned away and walked slowly out of the room, followed by Tom.

At the foot of the stairs Tom turned sharply right, saying, "Come in here for a minute," and led the way into what had been Andree's smoke room and which was now an office, taken up with a desk, a filing cabinet and two leather chairs. "Sit yourself down, I won't be a tick. And, by the way, what's your drink? Sherry, whisky, port?"

"I'll have a whisky, if you don't mind."

"Water or soda?"

"Just neat."

"Good enough."

A few minutes later Tom returned with a tray on which there were two glasses of whisky, and handing one to Daniel he raised his own and, after a pause, said, "Well, here's to a strange meeting."

"For my part, I'm glad it's come about." Daniel raised his glass, then sipped at his whisky, and Tom did the same.

When they were seated, Tom, jerking his chin up out of his collar in a nervous movement that was characteristic of him, said, "Was that the truth you told her, about her daughter, Sarah, talking of her?"

Daniel was utterly nonplussed for a moment. He brought his glass halfway to his lips; then, his hand becoming stationary, he looked down into the amber liquid before his eyes lifted to Tom's waiting gaze and he said quietly, "No."

"She never mentioned Aunt Katie, did she?"

"No. . . . But how did you realize this? If you detected I was lying she is bound to have guessed, too, and that's a pity."

"Oh no, no. She's not bound to have guessed anything. She believed you; she believed you because she wanted to believe you. All these years there's been a great big gaping void in her concerning her daughter and that one brief meeting they had. And, you know, she may be your grandmother—Sarah I mean—but I'm going to say this, I don't think she's much cop. As far as I can gather, it was back in eighteen-eighty

397

when she found out she had a mother, and from that date to this—that's what? Fifty-six years ago—not a penny postcard from her! No, I don't reckon she's much cop."

"There's two sides to it, you must remember that." Daniel nodded towards him. "Under the circumstances, at the time, when the relationship was revealed I think that the shock may have prevented Sarah . . . my grandmother from responding to her natural mother."

"Well, all I can say is it's something of a shock that lasts over fifty years. That's how I see it." Tom jerked his head, then took another sip of his whisky. "What is she really like?" He narrowed his eyes at Daniel, and Daniel replied, "Just a younger edition of her"—he lifted his head upwards—"and not very much younger-looking really. If she's ninety-two she carries her years wonderfully well."

"I didn't mean in looks, I meant—well, what is she like in character and such?"

"Oh!" Daniel now bit on his lip and put his head on one side as if considering before he replied, "Well, everybody's always considered her very aloof, unapproachable, you know, and my grandfather's always worshipped her, and protected her. Nobody, as I remember, had to make a noise when Grandmother had a headache. And for her part she adored him absolutely. They could never bear to be parted from each other even for a day, and Father used to tell me that if my grandfather was going to take a trip to a board meeting, or visit another yard—you see, he was partner in a shipbuilding firm—well, she would always go with him. . . ."

"You're in shipbuilding?" Tom sat forward.

"Yes. It isn't a huge yard, but big enough. My grandfather took a partnership with Simon Quarry, then my father went in, and now my three brothers are in it too. I am the odd man out. It didn't attract me in the least, so when I finished at Yale I came to Cambridge."

"What are you studying?"

"Mathematics."

"Oh, my! Bridget's headache. That was her only weak spot, mathematics. She flew through with everything else—English, Latin, French, the lot—but not maths."

"Oh, that's often the way. I think—I honestly do—that mathematicians are born, not made; it's a kind of deformity in the brain, you know." He smiled, and Tom answered, "Well, it's a deformity a lot of people wish they had. Bridg-

398

et's always saying, 'Oh, if only I'd been good at maths.' She's a teacher, you know."

"Is she?" said Daniel politely.

"Yes, and a good one, although I say it who shouldn't. And it'll be wasted when she gets married."

A voice now came to them from the hall calling, "Dad! Dad! Where are you?" and when the door opened Bridget said, "Oh, there you are. Lunch is ready."

"Just a minute." Tom put out his hand as Bridget turned away, and, going to her, he encircled her shoulders and pressed her to him as he said, "I was just telling our friend here that you are brilliant at maths."

"Oh, you needn't rub it in, Dad. There are worse."

"Not much, dear. Now you've said so yourself." He grinned at her and she turned and dug him playfully in the chest with her fist, saying, "I've told you before that it's to do with the psychological make-up. If you could see the types, of both sexes, that take up maths you would. . . ."

"Ssh! Ssh! Ssh! Don't jump in it with both feet. He's . . ." Tom bent his face towards her and jerked his thumb backwards, saying in a hoarse whisper, "he's up at Cambridge studying maths."

Bridget looked over Tom's shoulder into the dark face. The eyes, like pieces of polished coal, were surveying her with amusement. She bit on her lip and wagged her head before she said, "Here I go again . . . I'm sorry."

"I should think so," he said.

Tom looked from one to the other, then they all laughed. And as they went towards the dining-room Daniel thought, She's rather nice. Doted on by her father, obviously spoiled by her mother, and likely adored by Aunt Katie . . . but still rather nice.

3

It was Friday. Daniel had arrived in Newcastle on Monday afternoon. On Tuesday, after leaving Loreto late in the evening, he told himself that on the morrow he would call and make his goodbyes before returning to Cambridge. But on the Wednesday he went to Newcastle and introduced himself to the solicitor who was dealing with his great-grandfather's affairs, and got a very civil reception.

The solicitor hardly questioned his relationship to Bernard Rosier; anyone was welcome who might be able to straighten out the intricate affairs of that establishment, and from what he learned of this Daniel Rosier the Third he thought it very likely that the mortgage could be cleared.

That business set under way, Daniel decided to stay another day or so and took the train down to Shields. He had arrived in the middle of the afternoon and had spent an hour talking with his new-found great-grandmother, and he had realized that the more he talked to this old lady the more he liked her. Her mind was still alert, and in spite of her great, sad eyes she liked to laugh, and he had made her laugh quite a bit on that second visit as he described to her the eccentricities of his brothers and sisters; that was, until he attempted to describe Victoria. And how he described Victoria was that she was a kind of person who had never grown up, and at twenty-four was still a little girl of seven. At this her face had become sad, and she had said something that set him thinking. This was another thing he would have to tell his father, but on the quiet. "I had a sister, Lizzie, born like that," she had said.

When Catherine and Tom had learned that he wasn't due back in Cambridge until the Saturday they had kindly invited him to come and stay with them. But, strangely, his great-grandmother had not joined her voice to theirs, and this he found a little odd. When Catherine had said, "We can't persuade Daniel to stay, Aunt Katie," she hadn't replied, "Oh, but you must, Daniel"; she had just looked at Catherine and said, "Well, he knows what he wants to do best." Yet she seemed so pleased to see him, and wanted him to keep talking to her.

It was on the Wednesday, after tea, that Catherine suggested that Bridget should show him around the town; he must see Marsden Rock, the mile-long pier, and the grand Town Hall, outside which, Tom had laughingly said, "There stood the only natural women in Shields." Later, he found out that these natural women were outsize nude figures which he considered a brave gesture on someone's part. He enjoyed the evening. They laughed a lot. Bridget had a sense of fun not unlike her father's, he thought.

When he bade good-night to his great-grandmother she asked him to be sure to come down the following day for lunch.

On Thursday he came for lunch, and Katie kept him with her most of the afternoon and he learnt all about Mr. Peter Conway, Bridget's fiancé. Mr. Conway was ten years older than Bridget, but that was nothing. He was a splendid man and serious-minded. He had, when the works were in operation, been well up in the offices of Palmer's. He had been one of the men, too, who had represented the staff when the Duchess of York had come to launch the cruiser *York*. He had been very well thought of by the management and had fought hard, like all the staff, to keep the yard going. Katie had quoted this great Peter as saying that in 1930, when the razor of nationalisation had started at the end of Palmer's throat, and Sir James Lithgow of Port Glasgow, the strong man of steel, had chewed at the other with his plan for a nationalised industry, the blood had flowed so quickly that Palmer's became like an anaemic giant.

This Mr. Peter Conway, Daniel decided, sounded like a stuffed shirt. Had the quoter been any other than his great-grandmother he would have squashed Mr. Peter's simile about the death of the shipyard. He knew of Sir James Lithgow; his father had often spoken of him and the Lithgow firm, which was one of the greatest in Britain. Lithgow came of a shipbuilding family, and the idea of the great steel and shipbuilding industry being taken over by the government was anathema to him as it was to all shipowners. . . . Capitalists, as this Mr. Peter Conway apparently dubbed them.

He was more than a little relieved when, after tea, he once again found himself being escorted on a tour by Bridget.

"I'm going to show you Jarrow," she said. "You won't like it, but I think you should see it."

And he didn't like it. In fact he was appalled. The town looked dead, it even smelt dead to him. The district around the station had appeared dreary enough, but these dejected grey streets with groups of men leaning against the end walls, all attired in similar uniform, cap, muffler, and greasy-looking oddments of suits, were depressing to say the least. Men who smiled thinly, and chatted, and said at intervals, "Watcher there," yet who looked bewildered and numb, and at the same time aggressive. He knew this country was suffering under a slump; he wasn't unused to it in his own country, but here in this town the poverty was so stark, so raw, it was like looking on a body from which the skin had been ripped.

As they walked up the long road towards the dismembered shipyard that was once the proud Palmer's, she said, "Did Aunt Katie tell you Peter was away helping to organise the march to London?"

"Yes, she did say something about it."

They were silent until they came to the shipyard itself where the great gates had stood, and she stopped and, pointing to the vast jumble of contorted iron that the oxy-acetylene burners had made of the steel girders and cranes, and the great heaps of bricks where the blast-furnaces and their chimneys had once stood, said quietly, "I never come into Jarrow but I am drawn here to watch this. I suppose it's because this whole business—I mean the closing of the yard—hit me personally." She slanted her eyes at him, and there was a shyness in her look as she said, "You see, it stopped my wedding. Peter losing his savings, all twelve hundred pounds of it, and being responsible for his mother and the house; his father's dead. Then the fact that if we married I would lose my job. . . ."

"How's that?"

"Oh, they don't allow you to teach after you are married, not the women. We, too, are dead if we marry. But I suppose it's to be expected. There aren't enough jobs for the male teachers. We know a friend of ours who put in for a post down South; he's a maths master. Do you know how many applicants there were for the job? Two hundred and fifty."

"You don't say!" His brows were drawn together. Then he said "Your fiancé—he . . . he didn't get any of his money back from the firm?"

"No, but he was just like hundreds of others in the town. There were families who had saved and saved for years and put it into Palmer's; perhaps it was only a couple of hundred pounds or so, but to them it was a fortune, and they lost every penny, and now they're on the dole and stunned by the hopelessness of it all."

He looked hard at her as she looked at the gigantic wreck, and he had the strange disturbing urge to grab her by the hand and run pell-mell from this place. He had a picture of them tearing down the main street never stopping until they reached an open space where they could see nothing of tangled iron, dreary grey streets and hopeless-looking men and women.

"Come," he said, his voice brisk-sounding. "Let's get out of this."

"What?" She turned and looked up at him; then, her head drooping to one side, she exclaimed, "Oh, I'm sorry." Then, laughing, she added, "There I go again! I never stop saying 'I'm sorry' to you, do I. But I know I shouldn't have brought you here, it's so dismal; only I thought . . ."

"I know what you thought. It was for my education. An American should see these things. Life as it really is. Well, I've seen it, and now, marm, we are going to see life in a different way. . . . Which is your best theatre?"

"Oh, but we can't; it's too late now."

"Oh! . . . Well, what about tomorrow night?"

She hesitated, looking at him the while. Then, on a little laugh, she said, "All right."

"Good. Now come on." He grabbed her hand and hurried her away down the road, and for a time they did not speak; then, quite suddenly, she began to talk—gabble would be a better term—and he listened, his face turned towards her, looking at her intently.

When they reached Dee Street a bus rattled past them, and he broke in on her, saying, "It said Shields. We've missed it."

"Oh yes." She blinked quickly; then, lowering her eyes, she said, "All this can be boring to an outsider. . . . Well, you know what I mean."

"Yes, I do, Miss Mulholland." He was laughing down on her. "And for this evening at least I've had enough of social science, Ellen Wilkinson, Mr. Walter Runciman, that big grand Irish Councillor David Riley, the Mayor, Bishop Gordon and Uncle Tom Cobleigh and all."

"Oh, I'm . . ."

"Now. Now. Now."

They were laughing together again, and after a moment she said, "You know, it's funny how I feel about Jarrow. I like it, in spite of how it looks. Perhaps I should say I like the people—well, most of them. I was born in Westoe, and whether you know it or not, sir"—she moved her head gravely—"Westoe is the place to live in Shields. But I have always liked Jarrow best. My mother is just the opposite. She can't stand Jarrow. You see, she was born here. . . . Oh, here's a bus coming. This one will take us as far as Tyne Dock."

When they were seated in the bus she said, "It's a pity I haven't got the car, but it's so useful for Peter to get around in."

"I didn't know you had a car."

She turned her head slightly towards him and whispered, "My answer to that should be: the Americans aren't the only ones who have cars."

He brought his lips to her ear and whispered back, "And then you would have to say again you were sorry." They smiled at each other with slanted glance, then they laughed as he asked, "Do you drive?"

"Yes, it's my car. Aunt Katie gave it to me for my twenty-first birthday. It's a bit battered now, but it's given me a great deal of pleasure."

"A bit battered? You make it sound as if your twenty-first birthday was twenty years past. How old are you, may I ask? I'll give a guess. Twenty-three?"

"Twenty-six."

"M-mm!" He pressed his lips together. "You wear well."

"Thank you."

"You know, as I said last night, you're not a bit like your parents. They're so dark and you're . . . well, slightly more than fair, aren't you?" As his eyes rested on her head, which was without a hat, she turned her face from him and looked out of the window, and when she made no comment whatever on his statement he asked, quietly, "What is it? Have I said the wrong thing?"

"We're getting off here."

"Oh!" He got hastily to his feet and led the way out of the bus, and when they were walking side by side again he picked up where he had left off, saying, haltingly now, "I feel I've put my foot in it somewhere and for the second time. I . . . I remember now that my remark to your father last night about the contrast between you brought on a sudden silence. I'm sorry; I wasn't meaning to probe or anything of that nature. Believe me. For a moment I had forgotten that I had touched on the subject before. You do believe me, don't you?"

"It's all right. Don't worry; you weren't to know."

She was looking straight ahead as she said, "I'm not Dad's: my father was Aunt Katie's stepson. He was a Norwegian."

"I'm sorry. Indeed I am. I wouldn't for a moment . . ."

"It's all right. Please don't worry." She was shaking her head and smiling at him now. "It's perfectly all right. I used to remark on the contrast too, and it must have become so embarrassing for them that my mother told me all about it when I was sixteen."

Hesitantly, she repeated the story that, now, she accepted for granted—the story of Nils and her mother and Tom Mulholland. At the end she turned her face towards him. "Now you know. That's the family skeleton."

He looked at her, his eyes moving over her face. She had a beautiful skin, like deep thick cream. He shrugged his shoulders. "Not much of a skeleton as skeletons go," he said casually.

She smiled gently. "Have you a better one?"

"What do you think? My great-grandfather causing me to have only one great, male, grandparent." He dropped his head back on to his shoulder and gave an amused chuckle as he said, "If my mother and her side of the family ever got to know about that. . . . Oh, boy!"

They were laughing loudly when they entered the house, and Katie, who was sitting in the drawing-room, turned her head sharply in the direction of the door at the sound, then looked at Catherine who sat sewing by the window.

Catherine, too, turned her head towards the door, and when it didn't open and she heard the muted footsteps going across the hall she looked at Katie and said, "They're going into the study."

"Catherine!"

"Yes, Aunt Katie?"

"Come here."

"What is it?"

Catherine was bending over her now.

"I . . . I thought you said she didn't like him?"

"Well, now, I didn't say that, Aunt Katie. I told you she thinks he's a bit snooty, sort of high-hat, top-drawer American."

"But they were laughing?"

"Yes." Catherine straightened up and looked towards the door again. "Yes, they were laughing; but you know she likes to laugh, and he's amusing. . . . You said so yourself."

"Go and see what they are doing."

"Oh, Aunt Katie! Now look, don't worry. Oh, my dear." She put out her hand and stroked the thick white hair. "Look, you mustn't get such ideas into your head. That's the last thing in the world that could happen."

"Catherine." Katie now closed her eyes and bowed her head. "I can't get over the fact that he's a Rosier."

"But you said you liked him."

"I do, I do." She looked up at Catherine. "I want to like him more and more, but I'm afraid. It's the old fear all over again. It's just as if I were back seventy years. I told you, I told you yesterday, I'm as fearful for her as I was for myself then. He's a Rosier, Catherine."

"All right, all right. There now. Don't get agitated." Catherine was holding the hand that was clutching at hers. "He's leaving tomorrow. Peter will be home any time now and everything will be as it was. And you know, Aunt Katie, she thinks the world of Peter; the sun shines out of Peter for her. Look at all of them who were after her, but she wouldn't look at one until Peter came on the scene. She not only loves him, she admires and respects him."

"I know, I know, Catherine, I know; and if only he wasn't so stubborn they could have been married months ago and settled in here."

Catherine gave a small sigh and closed her eyes for a moment before she said, "There's his mother. He's explained it all to us, and I admire him for his honesty. He's not going to live on Bridget, and he's certainly not going to live on you. He'll get a post soon, I'm sure. Miss Wilkinson's looking out for him. . . . Ssh! Ssh! Here they come. Now don't worry, dear. Don't worry. You'll see. This is all imagination."

The door opened and Bridget entered. Her face was lit with laughter, her blue eyes were shining. She looked very young and beautiful, but Katie saw something more, something that she had never seen in Bridget's face. It was a glow, a joyous glow. And the man coming in behind her, tall, thin, dark, he too looked different. His eyes were bright and glistening, his red lips were wet. They, too, were glistening, as were his big white teeth. And when Bridget, who was looking at her mother and was about to say something, tripped over the pouffe and the three books she was carrying dropped from her hands, Daniel Rosier's arms went out to catch her.

406

And they did catch her, and they held her, and as their laughter mingled Katie gave a low cry and slumped in her chair.

4

"Mother, she must be going into her dotage. I hate saying that about Aunt Katie because . . . because I love her. You know that. But I ask you! Him and me! Why, it's fantastic. He only came on the scene on Tuesday, and today's only Saturday. What's put it into her head?"

Catherine drew in a long, deep breath. "It's the past, it's always with her, and she tells me he looks the spitting image of the first one. And his name too, the very name upsets her."

"But he can't help his name. And as for him being like the first one, I wouldn't believe it for a minute."

Catherine turned her attention to the dining-table again. She straightened the cloth and proceeded to lay out the mats; then after a moment she asked quietly, "Did you say definitely you would meet him at the village near the house?"

"Yes, yes, I told you. He said he wanted to show me over. And . . . and something else."

"What else?" Catherine straightened up and stared towards Bridget.

"Oh, he just wanted to convince me, I think, that, as he said, it wasn't only the poor that suffered. We . . . we were talking about Jarrow. I think he wants me to see his great-grandmother's room where she mostly lived for the last thirty years of her life. And . . . and to see him—I mean old Rosier. . . . And I can tell you, Mother, I feel awful not keeping the appointment. Just to leave him waiting there . . . Well!"

"He'll realize something is wrong and call in."

"He's going back to Cambridge this afternoon; there won't be time for him to come all the way down here."

Catherine's eyes narrowed just the slightest as she stared at her daughter. Aunt Katie was a very discerning woman. She might be ninety-two, but there was nothing the matter with her mind. Sometimes she imagined she had second sight. . . . But, oh no, dear God, she prayed she hadn't second sight on this occasion. Anyway, as Bridget had said, he had only come on the scene on Tuesday, and this was Saturday. Of course it was fantastic, ridiculous.

When the door bell rang she gave a start, and Bridget, turning her head towards her, said, "Oh Lord! I bet that's him. And now for more explanations."

"Well, just tell him the truth. Or leave it to me and I'll tell him. I'll tell him that Aunt Katie was in such a state that she couldn't be left; at least, she didn't want you to leave her."

Bridget went hastily out of the room and said to Nellie as she came from the kitchen, "I'll see to it, Nellie." She went to the front door and opened it; then, her face stretching in surprise and her voice high, she cried, "Why, Peter!" The next moment she had her arms around the big man's neck and he was holding her tightly and kissing her hard.

"Peter!" Catherine's voice, too, was high and expressed her relief as she came forward with outstretched hands. "You weren't expected until Monday."

"I couldn't stick it any longer." He looked at Bridget, then hugged her to him once more as he laughed.

"Oh, I am glad to see you, Peter," said Catherine again, and he, putting his arm around her shoulders, answered, "No more than I am glad to see you."

"How are things going, the arrangements and everything?"

They were all close linked as they went towards the drawing-room and, looking down on Bridget, he said, "Splendid! Fine! People are tickled, you know, at Suddick and Stoddart, two opposition agents, working together and arranging the route; but as far as I can gather, they are doing fine. Mayors, all kinds of societies, all kinds of people, seem to be putting out their hands."

"You look tired." Bridget gazed up into the rather square face of the man she was going to marry. It was a reliable-looking face; the eyes were grey and kindly, the nose was blunt, the mouth straight and wide, but it was the chin that gave the square look to the face. It was a blunt chin, not aggressively thrust out but wide, and gave an indication of his nature—honest, thoughtful, and loyal but rather unimaginative. He touched her cheek now as he said, "It's only for lack of sleep. I worked through most of the last two nights to make it back home today; I couldn't stand another week-end in Doncaster."

"Miss Wilkinson. How is she?" asked Catherine now.

"Oh, she's fine, Catherine, fine. By, she's a girl. If only we had some more like her. But still, they're coming on. . . ." He now took Bridget's face between his palms. "Would you like to take a bet, Catherine, that in ten years' time Mrs. Bridget Conway will be standing for Shields?"

"Huh! That will be the day." Bridget gave a high laugh as she pushed at him. "You're as bad as Aunt Katie. She says she's not going to die until she sees me a headmistress. You'll both lose your money."

"By the way, how is she?" He turned to Catherine.

"Not very well, I'm afraid. I'll go up and tell her you've come; that'll please her." She cast a swift glance over her shoulder at Bridget as she finished speaking, then left them together and went up the stairs to Katie. Immediately on opening the bedroom door she said, "Our worries are over, dear. Guess who's home?"

"Peter? No!"

"Yes, he's just come in. He'll be up in a tick to see you."

Katie was sitting propped up in bed, and she held out her hands to Catherine, and Catherine grasped them and said, "There now. And she's over the moon, like a fourteen-year-old."

"Really?"

"Yes, yes, I'm telling you." Catherine disengaged one hand and patted Katie's cheek.

"Oh, thank God, thank God. . . . Catherine, listen to me. They must be married as soon as possible."

"Now, now, don't start and worry about that. You know what the big obstacle is, his mother, and what would you think of him if he left her high and dry, and her over seventy?"

"Bridget will just have to make up her mind to go and live there."

"Oh, Aunt Katie, you know for a fact she wouldn't do that. You know that she doesn't care very much for Mrs. Conway. Moreover, you've always been against it."

"Well, I can change my mind, can't I? I'm not too old for that." Katie smiled at Catherine, and in the distance the front-door bell rang, and this sound brought Catherine upwards from the bed, saying, "Peter will be coming up in a minute. Now don't excite yourself. I'm laying the table. Be good now." She slapped Katie's hand gently, then hurried from the room, and as she went down the stairs Nellie was letting Daniel in through the front door.

He put his case down in the hall, then looked up and saw her, and when she came towards him he said, "Is . . . is anything wrong?"

"No, no, Daniel, only Aunt Katie. Well, after that turn last night, we kept her in bed and . . . and she won't let Bridget out of her sight. She's like that, you know." Catherine nodded at him and smiled. "I'm sorry Bridget couldn't come."

"Oh, that's all right; but I thought I'd just pop in to say goodbye before leaving."

"Of course, of course, Daniel. We would have been very vexed if you hadn't." She was walking towards the drawing-room now, her back towards him, and she stopped suddenly and said, "We got a nice surprise just a short while ago. Peter came back. He wasn't expected until Monday." She turned quickly from him again, and as she opened the drawing-room door she called loudly, "Bridget! Here's Daniel."

Entering the room behind Catherine, Daniel looked towards the two figures standing near the french windows. They were standing apart, but he knew that a second before they had been close together. He looked at the man first, tall, rather heavily built, not unpleasant to look at, but much older than himself, much older than Bridget.

"Hello, Daniel. I'm sorry about this morning." She came towards him.

"Oh, that's all right." He smiled at her, and when she turned from him and, pushing her arm backwards, said, "This is Peter," the man came forward with his hand extended, and Daniel took it.

"I'm very pleased to meet you." Peter shook Daniel's hand vigorously. "Bridget was just telling me about you. Oh, I wish I'd been here when you first came, I do indeed; I would have shown you around."

"Palmer's." Daniel said the one word without a smile on his face, and Peter threw his head back and laughed loudly. "Oh, Palmer's! Did she take you to Palmer's?" He reached out and pulled Bridget towards him and, circling her with his arm, he said, "Oh, she's a great girl for Palmer's, or what was Palmer's. But there are other places besides Palmer's." He nodded at Daniel. "I am so sorry I wasn't here."

"You'll be staying for lunch, won't you, Daniel?"

"No, no, Catherine. I've got a longish journey before me; I'm getting the half-past-one train from Newcastle."

"Oh, but that leaves you no time at all."

"Well, just enough time to say goodbye to Great-grand-mother and get the taxi to the station."

"You're not getting any taxi," Peter said now; "I'll run you to the station. I'll run you to Newcastle."

"Thank you, but I ordered the taxi to come here"—he glanced at his watch—"in exactly twenty minutes' time."

"Oh, what a pity!" said Catherine; then added, "Well, Daniel, if that's all the time you have you'd better go upstairs, hadn't you?"

"Yes, Catherine, yes." He inclined his head towards her, then at the two standing close together, and Peter smiled broadly at him, saying, "It's a pity, it's a pity. It's just hail and farewell." But Bridget neither spoke nor smiled; she looked straight at Daniel, and he at her for a second before he turned away and left the room and went upstairs.

Catherine had preceded him, and again she was announcing his presence, louder this time. "Here's Daniel, Aunt Katie! He's only got a minute or two and then he's off. Isn't it a shame?"

Katie, her head leaning back in the pillows, looked up at Daniel, and at this moment her feelings were mixed. She couldn't understand them herself. She wouldn't know a minute's peace until this young man was gone from this house, gone from the town, and soon, she hoped, gone from the country; yet, although he was the spitting image of the other one, there was something about him that she liked. If there hadn't been Bridget to consider she would have now gripped his hand and said, "Come back soon, Daniel," because he was, after all, flesh of her flesh; he belonged to her, more than Catherine or Tom; more than Bridget, which was hard to believe, but Bridget, after all, was only the offspring of her brother's grand-daughter and a man from another country, whereas this boy's grandfather had been Bernard Rosier's son, and his grandmother had been Bernard Rosier's daughter and her daughter. The link here was intertwined, plaited strong. He was more hers than any of them, yet the only thought in her mind at the moment was for him to go away and never return; and the thought brought a strange sharp pain with it.

He was talking to her, but the words were going over her head because she was trying to resist the desire to put out her arms and gather him to her.

"I won't be going home at Christmas. I generally stay with some friends in Kent, but I'd like to pop down and see you."

She noted his last remark about Christmas. Well, if she had her way Bridget would be safe by then. She smiled and put out her hand, saying, "Yes, Daniel, I would like to see you at Christmas."

He was bending towards her now, and when his firm warm lips touched her brow her stomach muscles tensed. She was being kissed by a Rosier. For the first time she was being kissed by a Rosier. "Goodbye, Daniel," she said.

"Goodbye, Great-grandmother." His hand softly stroked her shoulder twice; then he left her.

A few minutes later he was at the front door and Peter was putting his case in the boot of the taxi.

"Tom will be so sorry to have missed you, Daniel."

"Give him my regards, Catherine. I'll be popping down at Christmas; I've told Great-grandmother."

"At Christmas?" said Catherine. "Oh, that'll be nice."

"Goodbye, Catherine. And thank you for being so kind to me."

"Goodbye, Daniel. It's been a pleasure."

They shook hands.

"Goodbye, Bridget."

"Goodbye, Daniel."

They shook hands formally. He looked into her face. Her blue eyes had no shine in them; there was no smile on her lips; she looked tired, and at the moment not at all beautiful. "I'll never have another guide like you." He smiled at her, and, her face still unsmiling, she said, "I shouldn't think you'd ever want one."

"I enjoyed every minute of it. Jarrow, Palmer's an' all. Goodbye, Bridget."

"Goodbye, Daniel."

Peter was shaking his hand through the taxi window, and then the car started and turned in the broad roadway and he looked round over his shoulder and waved, and the last he saw of them was Bridget standing in between her mother and Peter. Peter had his arm around her, as had Catherine, and they were all waving.

As he settled in his seat he became enveloped by a deep

sense of loneliness. In his mind he saw himself, his great-grandfather, and that stark mansion on one side of the picture; on the other there was that house, bright and beautiful, a home, and in it four closely-knit people—and soon to join the unity was this new acquaintance, Peter. He made up his mind when he had first heard Peter's name mentioned that he would dislike him, but now he felt it was impossible to dislike him. Yet somehow he wished he could. But what did it matter? He had no intention of returning at Christmas. Making the acquaintance of his great-grandmother and of her relations had been a pleasant interlude. He must look upon it as that; it was over.

The only thing that would bring him north again would be the death of his great-grandfather, and he need not even come for that. Why should he? The purchase of the property and the transference of the best pieces of furniture and silver back home could be arranged by letter. And there were Willie and Maggie to see to things for as long as he cared to employ them.

As he boarded the train at Newcastle he thought they were right at Cambridge, the North was a most depressing place. He couldn't remember feeling so low for years. Well, this state of affairs was easily remedied. All he had to do was to keep away from it.

5

"Easter? It's a long time away," Katie said. "Why couldn't they do it before Christmas?"

"Well, first of all she wants to be married during Easter week," said Catherine; "and then Peter will feel better when he has a bit by him, and if this job lasts he'll have a nice little bit saved by Easter. And then there's his mother; she's very poorly at present and in no fit state to think about weddings."

"It strikes me," said Katie tartly, "that Mrs. Conway always has a turn when the wedding is in the offing." They both slanted their eyes towards each other, and Catherine laughed, saying, "Oh, Aunt Katie! You've got a bad mind."

"I know I have, and I maintain if she had her way Peter would never get married."

"Well, it's all settled now and Easter it is, bad turns or no bad turns." Catherine nodded her head quickly at Katie, and Katie, with a twist to her lips, said, "What do you bet she doesn't go and pop herself off the day before?"

Now they were both laughing heartily, and Katie gripped her waist, saying, "Oh, don't, don't! It pains me when I laugh like that." She dried her streaming eyes; then, looking towards the window, she said, "It's a frightful day; she'll get drenched. She should take the car."

"Well, you know what she says about taking the car to school; it looks so pretentious."

"Oh, bunkum! Fiddlesticks!"

Catherine smiled into her book, then glanced over the top of it to where Katie sat in her chair to the side of the roaring fire. She was in good form these days. She was now in her ninety-third year and didn't need glasses, or a hearing aid, and could still do the stairs, slowly, but nevertheless she made them, and resented help. She was wonderful, wonderful. In all ways Aunt Katie was wonderful. And she wanted her to stay wonderful, her days untroubled, and that was why for the past three days she had been praying he wouldn't come. When Bernard Rosier's death appeared on the front page of Saturday's paper she had said to Tom, "We won't let her see it; there's no need. It'll only take her mind back again." But she knew she wasn't so much afraid of Aunt Katie's mind taking her back into the past as of it taking her into the future. Daniel's appearance would set her worrying again.

About ten minutes later, when the front-door bell rang, Catherine, looking up from her book, said, "She must have forgotten her key; but if she had she would go round the back." She put the book down, and said to Katie under her breath, "I do hope it isn't visitors." Her heart was beating just a little faster now.

"It's likely someone selling things again."

"Not at the front door; not since Tom put the notice on the back gate." She laughed now as she added, "Bridget says we are betraying the Labour Party—'Tradesmen's entrance. No hawkers'."

Katie was smiling too, but rather sadly as, her head nodding, she said, "Don't times change. No circulars, no hawkers . . ." She was still talking when the door opened and Nellie announced, "Mr. Rosier, ma'am."

Daniel came into the room. He had taken off his greatcoat and hat and he was stroking his black hair back with his hand. His face bright and smiling, he now held out his hands, one to Katie, and one to Catherine, and they took them, and their silence went unnoticed because he was talking rapidly, explaining his unexpected visit. "He died four days ago. I suppose you saw it in the papers. The funeral is tomorrow. I came down yesterday morning; I felt I must come and see you all."

As Catherine disengaged her hand from his, saying, "This is a surprise, Daniel," he bent over Katie, and for a second time during their acquaintance he put his lips to her face. Then standing back from her, he said, "I declare you look younger —ten years younger than the last time I saw you."

Katie looked up at him. He had said Bernard Rosier was dead. At last, at last he was dead. She had lived to see it. . . . "Oh yes, yes Daniel, I'm very well, and how are you?" Her eyes were moving tenderly over his face. Then she looked at the hands that clasped hers. They were brown, thin, strong hands. If only she weren't afraid they would clutch at her Bridget, as the other one's hands had clutched at her. "Sit down, sit down," she said to him now, and when he was seated by her side she asked, "How long are you staying?"

"My time's my own until the middle of January. I've promised to spend at least a week with my friend in Kent, but during the rest of the time I'm here I want to get the business of the house settled . . . the renovations I mean. You did know I bought the manor?"

"No! No, I didn't." Katie shook her head slowly as her eyes widened . . . Bernard Rosier was dead, but this other Rosier had bought the house. It would go on.

"You've bought Greenwall Manor, Daniel?"

"Yes, Catherine. Why I don't know, so don't ask me." He was laughing, brightly, happily. "But I'm glad I have. And Father is too. He seems tickled with the idea of an English manor house. And mother . . ." He flapped his hand at her. "Oh, she's a frightful snob." He turned his face towards Katie now and found her eyes tight on him, and he continued, "She is, you know, Great-grandmother, a frightful snob, but if I'd sent her your Crown Jewels she couldn't have been more delighted than she has been with the furniture."

"You've sent the furniture from the house across to America?" Catherine's voice was high.

"Only a few of the nice pieces."

Katie said nothing. A few of the nice pieces, he had said. She could see the nice pieces. She was peeping through the green baize door on the landing; she was peeping through the door that led into the hall. And she knew each piece of furniture in the drawing-room and dining-room, and the rest of the ground floor, because she could hear Fanny Croft and Daisy Studd describing them. And from Florrie Green and Mary Ann Hopkins she knew all about the bedroom furniture. It was strange, but she couldn't picture anything she had seen on the one time she had crossed the hall and stood in the drawing-room. And now the nice pieces were going to America. The Rosiers' furniture would be in the house of her grandson, her own daughter's son. Rosier's furniture, the articles that had furnished that fairy palace of her brief childhood, was now in the possession of Katie Mulholland's offspring. Katie Mulholland who for a time had been known by the name of Mrs. Bunting, then Mrs. Fraenkel. But those names, even that of Mrs. Fraenkel, had not altered Katie Mulholland, the girl inside. Bernard Rosier's raping, Bunting's belt, Andree's love and kindness, they had really not touched Katie Mulholland.

Katie Mulholland was a name that was known far and wide on the Tyne; it had been given notoriety by one man, and now he was dead. She was not elated by his death, not even relieved, it was too late for that; but what she did feel was surprise that his great-grandson, and her great-grandson, should be here at this moment looking handsome and happy, and talking, even gaily, when tomorrow he was to bury him.

"Are you sorry he's gone?" The question surprised herself much more than it surprised him.

"Sorry he's dead? My great-grandfather Rosier? No! No! Not in the least. Nor am I going to pretend I'm sorry. It would have been better, don't you think, for most people if he had died years ago?"

"Yes, yes." She was nodding her head in small movements.

"It's merely a matter of formality, me going to the funeral. There'll only be Maggie and Willie Robson—they are the couple who've looked after the house and him for years, you know—and the solicitor, and he'll only be there because of the legal business to be attended to afterwards."

Katie lay back in her chair. Only four people attending him, and these all apparently under compulsion. She had the weird idea that the going-out of this man, who had caused so much havoc in her life, should be attended by some big burst of ceremony, like fireworks and bonfires such as they had at the end of the war—something, anyway, to proclaim to the world that Bernard Rosier was no more; yet tomorrow he would go into his grave with only four people standing by.

She was wondering in which part of hell they would accommodate him when her mind was brought back to the room and her great-grandson, for the door had opened and Bridget was standing just within it, and Daniel was going forward holding out his hand; and as Katie watched Bridget's face light up, her eyes shine and her lips part widely as Daniel bent above her, she spoke sternly to her heart to stop its rapid beating. There must be no more fainting attacks. She must be calm, and think, and act; or, what was more to the point, get Peter to act, even if it meant telling him outright what he stood to lose. Some men needed prodding. . . . Some men, but not men like her great-grandson, the descendant of Bernard Rosier; these men needed no prodding, they took what they wanted.

6

Daniel discovered, over the Christmas holidays, that Peter Conway bored him. He was a good man, a kind man, yet with all that he lacked the mercurial spark that was needed to match Bridget. Daniel, sitting with Peter waiting to accompany Bridget to a party, wondered, not for the first time, how she bore with his rather heavy discourse.

When the phone rang Catherine rose from the couch, where she had been sitting quietly listening to Peter, and it seemed to Daniel that she, too, was thankful for the intrusion. He watched her going into the hall, and a minute or so later he turned his attention away from Peter as she re-entered the room, saying, "It's for you, Peter."

"Me?" Peter got to his feet.

"It's Mrs. Clay."

"Oh my Lord!" Peter screwed up his face and hurried into the hall, and Catherine walked to the fire, saying, "It's his mother. She's had a turn. That was the woman who comes in."

"No!" said Tom, who had been silent for a long while. Most people were silent when Peter was talking.

"It's just like the thing, isn't it?" Catherine moved her head impatiently.

"I'll lay ten to one she does it on purpose." Tom nodded towards Daniel. "She won't let him out of her sight if she can help it. Oh, some mothers have got a lot to answer for, Daniel."

Before Daniel could reply, Bridget came into the room. She was looking over her shoulder as she did so; then she said to Catherine, "What is it?"

"His mother, dear; she's had a turn."

"Oh no!"

"Yes."

Bridget patted her knuckles against her closed lips and looked from Catherine to Tom; then to Daniel.

Daniel was already looking at her. He had never seen her dressed like this. She was wearing a pale-blue chiffon dress. It was three-quarter length and had a number of skirts that seemed to float around her slim legs, the motion being caused by the slight draught that came from the open door. The skin of her neck and breast looked the same as that of her face; her arms too; all her skin seemed of a piece, warm, creamy. And her hair, not plaited and twisted on the back of her head but taken upwards in a soft pile like a crown, a silver crown. And then her eyes, the same colour as the dress, but not merry now, not laughing, as they had been earlier.

They all turned towards the door as Peter entered the room. He had been talking practically non-stop for the last hour, but now he seemed to have to search for words. He looked at Bridget as he came slowly forward, and it was to her he spoke. "I'll . . . I'll have to go home," he said; "she's asking for me. Mrs. Clay says she's sent for the doctor, so . . . so she must be bad."

No one spoke when, with bowed head, he made great play of buttoning up his coat, until Bridget, going towards him, said flatly, "I'll run you there."

"Oh no; no, you won't." He wagged his head vigorously

418

now. "It's no use spoiling everybody else's fun. No, Bridget. You go along with Daniel. It'll likely be nothing, anyway. I'll see what the doctor says, and if I can leave Mrs. Clay with her I'll do so and slip along."

"But I could drop you there."

"No, no, you'll do no such thing. It's right out of the way, and you'll want the car to go to Ivy's."

"I won't." Bridget's voice was firm. "Ivy's is no distance. Now look, you take the car, and then if you can come on you'll be with us all the sooner."

"She's right, Peter." Tom spoke quietly. "You take the car. It isn't fifteen minutes' walk to Ivy's, and it's a dry night. Go on now."

"I'm sorry." Again Peter was looking at and speaking only to Bridget, and she, looking back at him, her face soft and her eyes holding a tender light, said under her breath, "It's all right, Peter. Don't worry, it's all right."

They left the room together, but Bridget wasn't away for more than a few minutes, and when she returned Catherine went to the fire and poked it vigorously, and as she did so she said, "Why don't you hang on a while. He might phone back."

Bridget looked at Catherine's back as she replied flatly, "He'll not be coming to the party, Mother. You know that as well as I do. Mrs. Conway is the best timer in the world; she's had a lot of practice by now."

As Catherine straightened up and looked towards Bridget, Tom said, "I shouldn't say it, I know, but I hope it's the real thing this time and she kicks the bucket."

"Oh, Tom! Fancy saying that." There was a strong reprimand in Catherine's voice, and he replied, "I mean it, I mean every word of it. You know, Daniel"—he nodded towards Daniel—"some women shouldn't have sons; they should be taken away from them at birth, they should. I'm telling you. The way that some of them hang on to daughters is bad enough, but when it's a son, God alive! It's awful. That poor fellow, I'm sorry to the heart for him, always have been."

"We'll go then," put in Bridget now, and Tom answered, "Yes, you go on, honey. And enjoy yourself. Show Daniel here what a North-country party is like. It's a pity you're not going to be here at the New Year, Daniel; you'd see something then. Wouldn't he, girl? But go on now . . . The only thing is, mind"—he wagged his finger from one to the other

419

—"if you come back drunk take your shoes off outside, and keep quiet."

"I'll remember that." Daniel laughed, then turned and followed Bridget into the hall, and as he helped her into her coat and donned his own coat and picked up his hat Catherine stood within the framework of the door watching them. When he turned and said, "Be seeing you then, Catherine," she said, "Yes, Daniel."

Bridget didn't say goodbye to her mother, nor did Catherine give her any word; but this unusual procedure was overlooked because Tom was seeing them out, and Tom, as usual, was being amusing.

*　　*　　*

Altogether Daniel was finding the whole proceedings childish in the extreme. If he had been invited to a party such as this when he was sixteen he would have termed it a wow. But now, just a few days off his twenty-fifth birthday, there was more than a touch of condescension in his attitude towards the whole affair, but he managed to conceal this effectively.

He was not unaware that he was a popular figure with the young ladies present. Was he not American? As one had said, while exaggerating his slow drawl, she got quite a kick out of hearing him talk.

There were twenty guests present, but the noise and commotion they made suggested there might be at least a hundred in the house. And he imagined that the hostess must have expected a hundred from the amount of food that was prepared.

The house was a large, rambling one on three floors, with a warren of attics above. It was well and expensively furnished, but somewhat lacking in taste, he decided, as he moved from one room to another as the evening wore on. His entry into the rooms was in the course of the many games in which he took part; self-consciously at first, then, soon losing this feeling, with the kind of mad abandon that seemed to possess all those present, even to the parents of the hostess who ran up and down stairs in treasure-hunts and joined in the game of murders.

And now they were to play sardines. Lots were being drawn as to who was to be the first sardine in the game, and this questionable privilege fell to Bridget. There was laughter and shouted cries of "Put all the lights out!"

"You must give me two minutes' start, two full minutes," Bridget was calling as she held two fingers up to them, and somebody cried, "All right, teacher; two full minutes from . . . now!"

Daniel watched Bridget running from the room, and some-one rushed to the door and shouted after her, "Put out the lights as you go." And her voice came back crying, "Right."

The timekeeper was counting now; a hundred and sixteen, a hundred and seventeen, a hundred and eighteen, a hundred and nineteen; then on a loud yell, "Two minutes! Away! Away!"

Like a pack of hounds after a fox they rushed from the room into the darkness of the hall. There were squeals and shouts and yells, and a voice above the rest crying, "Once you get into the 'tin' no talking, mind. Don't give it away; make it last."

Everybody seemed to be making for the stairs, and Daniel himself was groping towards them when he felt a hand clutch his, and he recognised the owner of the hand by the feel of a large dress ring, an outsize ring. It was a pert little miss who had been after him all evening. He disengaged himself tact-fully from the hand and made for the passage near the stairs. There was a large cloakroom to the left, where the gentlemen had left their coats, and opposite to it a door in the stair pan-elling. This had been open when he arrived and a light was on in some sort of room behind it. His host, too, had noticed it and had put out the light and shut the door, which fitted into the panelling and became part of the wall.

It was a place she might make for. He moved noiselessly on the thick carpet until he touched the end wall; then, his head close to the panelling, he listened. But he heard no sound of smothered giggles, but what did come to him was a recognised scent. As a Christmas gift he had bought her a bottle of perfume; it was of an exclusive make and had a dis-tinctive smell. When she had come downstairs into the draw-ing-room earlier this evening he had been pleased she was wearing it. This house was full of the smell of perfume. All the girls were using perfume, but not this particular kind. This was a perfume well known to him; it was his mother's favourite scent. He could have picked this perfume out of a hundred others.

A frantic urgency filled him now as his hand groped over the panelling trying to trace a knob, or a catch. When his prodding fingers came in contact with a raise in the wood he pressed it, and as he felt the door open his excitement mounted.

Gripping the edge of the door with his hand, he stepped tentatively forward into the blackness, but before he closed it behind him he put out his other hand and moved it in a wide half circle. It did not come in contact with anything until it was stretched straight out to the right of him, and then his fingers touched a face. He now pulled the door gently closed and, easing forward, raised his hand upwards above the face to the hair; then, sweeping his other arm into space to make sure that no one else had got into the 'tin' before him, he whispered, "Bridget."

There was no giggle, no laughter, no response whatsoever except the trembling of her body. He had both hands on her shoulders now, and again he whispered, "Bridget." But the only reply he got came through his hands: her whole body was shivering.

When he put his arms about her and pressed her to him the shiver passed into his body and they stood in trembling awareness until he whispered, "You know, don't you?" and to this her cheek made answer against his, and when his mouth found hers she answered its fierceness and they clung and swayed together in the blackness.

Not until there was the rapid sound of muffled feet above their heads did their lips part, and then Bridget, gasping for breath as if at the end of a race, buried her mouth against his neck, and he turned his face into her hair and moved it back and forward as if intent on losing himself in its depths.

"Oh, Bridget, Bridget!" His mouth was moving over her ear now, murmuring her name. While outside the door there were giggles and laughter and high squeals as bodies bumped in the blackness. When the door clicked open and a hand came groping around them they were standing apart, but when the huddle of bodies pressed them into the corner she was once more held tightly to him.

The game came to an end with more squeals and yells and the lights going on, and everybody describing where they had searched; most of them saying they had been sure Bridget had made for the attic.

"Fancy you going under the stairs, Bridget," someone said.

"I thought of under the stairs when I was up in the attic," said Ivy. "I thought to myself: she would never come up here, this is the obvious place; Bridget would choose something so simple that nobody else would think of."

On and on the chatter went, while Bridget sat at one side of the room and Daniel at the other, and when their searching eyes met it was as if they had been newly born and nothing had ever happened to them before tonight, when they had come alive in the dark.

7

The stranger came and stood by his side and, pointing down the hill to where row after row of new houses could be seen and the foundations of many more laid, he said, "That's a different scene from what it used to be, lad. I remember that place when it was a ghost town, or a ghost village. Pit village it was. Stood empty and gaping for years, the houses did, and then after the war they got going. Brave new world and all that. Afore your time, I suppose. They were goin' to break eggs with a big stick, but then came the slump. Well, I suppose it's no use puttin' houses up when there's no one to pay the rent. But things are lookin' up; oh aye, things are lookin' up." The stranger nodded at him, then went casually on his way as if they would meet again and continue this one-sided conversation.

They were strange, these northern people, Daniel decided. Harsh, argumentative, bumptious, loquacious, narrow-minded, yet kindly, all-embracing, like that old man walking away there . . . coming up and speaking to him as if he had known him all his life, then walking away without saying goodbye. Yes, they were strange. . . . And beautiful, and wonderful, and exciting. . . . Would she never come?

For three-quarters of an hour he had stood here and the wind was finding its way through his fleecy-lined overcoat, through his suit, and his fine woollen shirt and vest. For three days now he had stood at this same spot waiting for her, and if she didn't come today he would phone and tell her he was coming to the house. That should bring her out.

He was feeling desperate, ready to do anything. He had been playing with the idea all day of going and confronting Peter, telling him that he loved Bridget and she him. . . . And she him? She had never said she loved him. But what need was there for words? Hadn't she told him all he wanted to know in that cupboard in the dark? But he had been unable to get near her since.

Peter had turned up at the party at the last minute, and they had all gone home together, and on the journey they had been quiet. Peter, too, had been quiet. Their quietness had been the outcome of guilt, and love, and worry about the future, while Peter's quietness had presumably been because his mother had again spoiled another evening for him.

For three days following the party he had not had one minute alone with her. Always there was Catherine or Aunt Katie near her. And in the evenings there was always Peter. He hadn't been able to stand it; and so he had taken his leave of them, presumably to visit his friend Carruthers in Kent. But he couldn't go. He couldn't put so much distance between them.

The following day he had phoned the house, and by luck it was Bridget who answered the phone, and he told her that he was still at the Manor and that he must see her alone. He told her he would wait for her at the end of the Manor road around two o'clock each day until she came, and to this she had said softly, "Don't, Daniel; it's no use," and had added quickly, "And a Happy New Year to you too." From this he guessed there was someone in the hall. She had then said good-bye and rung off. And this was the third day of waiting.

He looked at his watch, which said a quarter to three. He would give her another fifteen minutes, then he'd go to the phone. They weren't to know where he was ringing from. He could enquire after his great-grandmother; and he would tell them he had business to do with regards to the house and was coming back north tomorrow and would look them up.

When the car came towards him and he saw her through the windscreen he didn't believe it was true, and so he stood perfectly still until she drew up opposite him. Then, as if he had been shot from the grass verge, he sprang across the road and opened the door and took the seat beside her. She did not look at him but kept her eyes fixed on her two hands, which were on the wheel, until he put his hand over one of hers, when she turned her face towards him, her blue eyes strange to him because they were full of deep sadness, and she said softly, "Oh, Daniel, we mustn't; it's wrong."

"No, Bridget. No. It can't be. Look, drive to the house along here."

"I can't stay; they expect me back for tea."

"Well, that isn't until nearly five. I want you to see the house. Really I do. Come on."

She put in the clutch and set the car in motion and within five minutes they were going up the tree-covered drive and on to the grass-covered shingle in front of the house.

When she stopped the car she bent forward and gazed up at the huge stone pile; she still looked upwards as Daniel opened the door and helped her to alight.

"It's so big," she said. "I never thought of it like this."

"Come on round the back and meet the Robsons."

"Oh no! No, Daniel; I don't want to see them."

"They're nice, you'll like them. Come on. I told them I may be bringing a friend."

In the kitchen he introduced her to Willie and Maggie and they shook hands with her, both saying the same thing, "We're very pleased to meet you, miss." And they sounded pleased. And she smiled at them, and after a moment said haltingly, "I know all about this house. My . . . my Great-aunt Katie used to work here—in . . . in this very kitchen, I suppose."

"Yes, indeed. Indeed." Maggie nodded at her. "But it would be more comfortable in those days, miss. At that time, I understand, they had twenty or more servants in the house. Just fancy, twenty or more."

"And Aunt Katie was the lowest of them all," she said, "being the scullery-maid."

"Well, we all have to start somewhere, miss, and she didn't stay a scullery-maid for long, did she?" Willie asked and answered his own question, which was followed by an awkward silence until Maggie said, "Well, sir, I suppose you want to show the young lady the house, and by that time I'll have a cup of tea ready for you and a bite to eat along in the sitting-room. Will that be all right?"

"Fine, thanks, Maggie."

When Daniel led Bridget along the dim corridor she whis-

425

pered to him, "I won't be able to stay that long; I mustn't be too late," and he whispered back, "You just need to take a cup of tea, just to please them." Then he opened the door and she was in the hall, and, as he himself had done when he first saw this place, she stopped and gazed about her. After a while she brought her eyes to him, saying under her breath, "I've always seen this hall as a place of brightness; even when Aunt Katie's told me it was dingy, dirty even, when she last saw it, I still had a particular kind of picture in my mind of dark wood and shining glass and silver."

"It could be bright again," he said; "it just needs cleaning and redecorating."

He led her into the drawing-room, and then into the dining-room and the library; he showed her the little parlour, the gun-room, and all the small offices that seemed necessary to an establishment of this kind; then slowly, side by side, they mounted the stairs and when they reached the gallery he stopped.

Again Bridget gazed around her. This was the place, she was sure, from where her Aunt Katie had watched the dancers on the night of the ball, and it would be behind those faded curtains that she hid and went to sleep; and it would be behind there that he found her. Her eyes moved from the windows to the other side of the gallery and to a row of heavy-framed portraits, and slowly she walked towards the end one and gazed at it for a moment before turning to Daniel and saying, on a high surprised note, "It's you!"

"I hope not. But there's no getting away from the fact I'm remarkably like him. But, as I've said before, I don't take it as a compliment."

"But it's so striking, the likeness. I can see now why Aunt Katie was troubled the first time she saw you, and why she's afr . . ." She stopped, and turned to face the picture again, and he caught at her arm, saying, "What? Why she's what?"

"Nothing."

"But you were going to say something. You were going to say 'why she's afraid', weren't you?"

"No, Daniel."

"But you were. And I've sensed something too."

"Daniel, don't talk about it, please. Come along, show me the rest. I can't stay long, I've told you."

He looked at her hard before turning away and saying,

426

"All the rooms are very much the same on this floor, except two. I'll show you his first. I meant to show you him himself if you had been able to come that morning, you remember? But now I'm glad you didn't see him."

He pushed open the door and entered the room first; then, turning, he looked towards the four-poster bed, the coverlet neat, the pillows lying flat, no sign of the terrible grotesque figure that had lain there for years, except the end of the leather strap that was still attached to the bed post, its length hidden by the back of the bed. He moved towards the bed-head and picked up the strap and looked at it as he said, "He was bedridden for twenty years and paralysed all down one side, and for part of that time his one good arm was held by this strap in case he did someone an injury. He looked the most terrible sight I've ever seen, or ever likely to see. He was a bad man, yet since his funeral I've been wondering if his sentence didn't outdo his misdeeds. I hadn't a scrap of sympathy for him, not even when I saw him dropped into the grave, but since I haven't been able to get him out of my mind. Each day I see him clearly—not as I saw him lying in this bed, but as a young man, like I am, looking like I do, and I am wondering more and more how it all began, this twist in him. You know, it's odd, Bridget—" he looked into her face, "but these last few days when I've been wandering round the house, killing time, I've felt him near me. Every time I mounted to the gallery I felt that picture speaking to me, as if he were trying to tell me he had another side to him, and yet I have only to go into my great-grandmother's room and I see him as an evil man. He acted evilly towards her; he acted evilly towards . . . Aunt Katie. When I look at him through their eyes I see him as wholly bad; but even so, I ask myself, did he deserve this and for so long?" He weighed the strap in his hand, then let it fall back into place behind the bed, and when Bridget shivered he said, "You're cold; take my coat."

"No, no; I'm not that kind of cold." She put out her hand protestingly. "Don't take it off, Daniel, because I won't wear it."

He did not press her, but led the way out of the room and down the wide corridor and into another room. "This," he said, "was her room. His wife's."

"Oh, this is different. This has been a nice room."

"She made it nice. She, too, lived alone here for years. From what I can gather, it used to be his room when he was a young man, and theirs when they were first married."

She walked towards the bed and, bending over it, touched the faded silk coverlet, and as she did so he said, "Can you imagine them living year after year in this house, in these two rooms, and never seeing each other? Do you know, they never saw each other's faces for over thirty years, and he had hurt her so much that I think she must have prayed daily that he would die. You know, that's what I meant when I said to you it isn't only the working-class that suffer."

She looked into his eyes for a moment; then her lids dropped as she murmured, "You wouldn't have to argue that point very long for me to agree with you."

"Bridget." With a swift movement his arms were about her, and when she tried to press him away he held her closer and, his face hovering over hers, he said, "When did you know?"

She closed her eyes tightly and moved her head from side to side, but she did not answer him.

"Bridget, tell me. I want to know. From our first meeting? I know I did. Bridget, you love me. Say you love me."

When she still did not answer, his lips sought hers; but her hand came between them, and now, her eyes wide, she pleaded, "Please, please, Daniel, don't. It's no use; it can lead nowhere."

"What do you mean, it can lead nowhere? It's got to; it must, it must. You don't know how I feel about you, Bridget. I'm . . . I'm all burned up inside, racing. I've never felt like this before in my life, but I know now this is what I've been waiting for. This is the answer to everything; it's given meaning to living, the lot. Oh, how can I explain. I want to say so much. . . ."

"Daniel! Daniel!" Again she closed her eyes. "Please don't go on. Look, let me sit down." She turned her head from him and looked towards the edge of the bed, and still with his arms about her they sat down, and she tried to disengage herself, saying, "Hold my hand, Daniel. Just hold my hand and let me talk."

Their hands linked tight, she looked down on them and, keeping her gaze on them, she began to talk. "It . . . it doesn't matter what I feel, Daniel, I'm going to marry Peter. . . . Now . . . now listen." She shook her hands within his grip. "Listen to me. Listen to me. . . . The other night was a moment of madness. It . . . it was the party; everyone being silly, and the wine and . . . and the darkness. . . ."

"It was no such thing, Bridget. You know it and I know it." His voice came flat and sounded strangely unemotional at this moment.

She lifted her face up to his and looked deep into his eyes, and her mouth opened and shut as if she were gasping for air. Then, swallowing hard, she went on, "We're a happy family, Daniel. At least we were. We are all very close, so close that what happens to one affects us all. It's always been like that. Aunt Katie adores Mother, and Mother adores Aunt Katie; and Dad adores Mother; and they all adore me." Her chin dropped on to her breast now as she ended, "That, I suppose, is the trouble, the way they feel about me. So I couldn't do anything to hurt them, not if it meant me being unhappy all my days. . . ."

"Adore! Adore! Adore!" Daniel's voice was no longer calm. He moved his body restlessly on the bed. "That's the feeling you reserve for gods. It's love that has happened to us, Bridget . . . love and that's what we've got to talk about. You love me, I know you do. You could go on denying it to your last breath and it would make no difference; I know right here." He pulled her hands to his chest and thumped them against himself. "You couldn't marry Peter feeling like you do."

"I could, Daniel, I could. What's more, I've got to marry Peter."

"Got to?" He screwed up his eyes.

"Yes, got to. You don't understand; it would be hard for you to because you don't know Peter. He's never known any real happiness in his life. He's been persecuted by his mother; his father was an invalid and he worked for him for years, then he was saddled with her. What money he saved he lost. He lost his job. He talks very brightly about politics and all the rest, but at bottom he is sad, and hurt, and frightened. Yes, frightened of life. If I did this to Peter, I would never know any real happiness—apart from what I would feel about Dad, and Mother, and Aunt Katie. There's four people, Daniel, balanced against the two of us."

He stared at her, holding her eyes. She didn't look beautiful to him at this moment. It was an odd thing about her face; sometimes it looked beautiful, at others almost plain.

429

But he had never loved her, or wanted her, as much as now. His voice quiet again, he said, "Will you answer me one question truthfully? That's all I ask, give me a truthful answer. Now this is the question. . . . Do you love me?"

He would not allow her eyes to move from his, and when she did not speak he whispered, "A truthful answer, Bridget." He watched her lips tremble and her teeth bite into them; then her eyes closed tight, and when the tears pressed from between the lids she was in his arms, and when his mouth found hers she returned his kiss as she had done on the night of the party, but as she did so her tears swamped his face. And now he kissed her eyes until his mouth was salt. Then the moan that started deep within her forced its way upwards, and when it reached her throat she gave a stifled cry and buried her face on his shoulder.

"Bridget, darling, don't. It'll be all right, you'll see. You must leave it to me. Just leave it to me. I'll break it gently, let it creep up on them as it were."

He was moving his mouth in her hair, talking to her, soothing her. His words were muffled, but not so muffled that she did not hear him when he ended, "One thing I'm certain of, you're mine and they're going to know you're mine. You're not going to sacrifice yourself for any of them. After all, Great-grandmother is due to die any day; ninety-three, she can't last much longer, and what price sacrifices for her then. And your father and mother; they have each other. As you said, they adore each other, so in that case you don't mean the whole of life to them. And that leaves Peter—and, as I look at it, Peter, like myself, is on the outside, so let the best man win. . . ."

She struggled up from his grasp and stood with her head back, wiping the tears from her eyes with her fingers. Then, groping in an inside pocket of her coat for a handkerchief, she passed it roughly around her face before saying brokenly, "Daniel, it's no use, I won't do it. Even if you went and told them, it would still be no use; I wouldn't do it. You haven't the faintest idea of our family life."

"Damn and blast your family life and the whole lot of them!"

The tears slowly ceased their flowing. She blinked away the moisture on her lids to see him more clearly, and she saw him, not as the Daniel she knew, as the Daniel she had fallen unreasonably in love with, but as the man in the picture on the gallery wall, the man who had taken Aunt Katie down, the man who had persecuted her. The face was dark, stiff, the eyes coal-black and glistening. But as she gazed at him the resemblance to the picture faded; she watched him bow his head and hold his brow in his hand as he said, "I'm sorry, I didn't mean it. I . . . I just wanted to say that you cannot put the family before me, before us. It's our life. They've lived theirs, the joyous years anyway. We must have our chance of happiness, and I know now that I'll never find happiness without you."

The look in his eyes weighed down her head, and there was anguish in her voice as she whispered, "And I could never find it with you, Daniel, because they'd always be between us. I . . . I'm not made like . . . that, I couldn't be ruthless."

He gazed at her dumbly. He could have ridden rough-shod over any feeling she had for the man she was going to marry; for all her talk about him he knew this. It was her family who were the obstacle between them; her mother, not so much her father, and above all her Aunt Katie.

Aunt Katie, his great-grandmother. When he was with Katie and looked into those great eyes of hers he felt he loved her, that in some way he belonged to her; but now he knew that she, more than any of the others, stood between him and Bridget, and he hated her for it, and would go on hating her—that is, if he didn't win her over to his side. He meant to try; he wasn't finished yet.

When, her head still bowed, she said, "I must go back," he took her firmly by the hand and led her downstairs. If it meant fighting them collectively or singly, he would fight, clean or dirty, but he was going to have Bridget. . . .

Half an hour later, when he got out of the car on the rise of the hill overlooking the village, he said to her, "No matter what you say, Bridget, I'm coming back. Now listen to me and don't forget what I say. I'll send a postcard—a picture one, you know. I'll send it to Great-grandmother enquiring about her health. No one will suspect anything then, will they? But when she gets it you'll know that I'll be at the house"—he lifted his head—"that following week-end. I'll get down on the Friday night until the Sunday night; and if you don't come to me on the Saturday, then you can expect me at Loreto on the Sunday. . . . Now, you hear?"

"Daniel. Daniel." She was beseeching him, and in answer

to this he put his hands through the window and pulled her face roughly to him and kissed her—a short, hard kiss; then, looking into her eyes, he said, "I'm a fool; I should take no notice of you. I should go straight down now and tell them how things stand. That's what I should do."

Silently she looked up at him and he withdrew his head and stood stiffly, watching her while she drove away.

* * *

Before leaving the garage Bridget opened her handbag, took out her mirror and dabbed at her face with a powder-puff; then, wetting the sides of her forefinger with her tongue, she pushed back her lashes and, finally, nipped her lips and cheeks hard to bring colour into them. Then of a sudden she leant against the garage wall and muttered into her hands, "Oh my God! Oh my God! What am I going to do?"

And the answer was given to her as soon as she entered the hall, for Catherine came hurrying down the stairs. She came towards her with outstretched hands. Her face bright yet un-smiling, she said, "I know this is no time to be exultant, but I can't feel sorry. Peter's just phoned to say his mother passed away half an hour ago."

8

A week later the card came for Katie. It arrived on the Wednesday and bore the Kent postmark. It was very brief. It said, "My Dear Great-grandmother. I do hope you're keeping well. I return to Cambridge a week on Friday. If it is at all possible I will look in on you before then; if not, perhaps I may come down some time during the term. My love to all at home, Daniel."

After Katie had read the card she looked at Catherine and said, "He'll come. This is just a way of telling us he is going to come."

"He may not, Aunt Katie; it may be quite innocent. . . ."

"Oh, Catherine, don't be silly. You know yourself there is something going on, you said so."

"Yes, I know." Catherine shaded her eyes for a moment. "I just don't want to believe it, that's all."

"She hasn't been herself since he was here at Christmas, not a laugh in her. There's something going on between them. I feel it, Catherine."

"No, Aunt Katie, I wouldn't think that. Bridget would never do anything underhand; she's as straight as a die. She'd tell me, she tells me everything. You know she always has."

"Yes, yes, she always has, until she met a Rosier. . . ."

"Oh, Aunt Katie! It's just because of the name. It puts all kinds of ideas into your head. I understand . . . I understand perfectly."

Katie let her head rest against the high chair and her gaze turned inwards as she said, "It isn't only the name, Catherine; there's something about him I can't explain. It's just a feeling. But there's a determination there; behind that smiling manner of his he's got iron in him, like the other one had. Oh! Oh!" She shook her head. "I don't mean he's like him, God forbid. But there's something there that disturbs me. Yet, you know, Catherine, I like him. I could say I love him, and not just because he's Sarah's grandson; just for himself. . . . But he's not for Bridget, is he?"

Catherine looked down tenderly at Katie as she said, "No, Aunt Katie, he's not for Bridget. Peter's for Bridget. Always has been. She's admired and loved him since she was fifteen. And he understands her. What's more, they both speak the same language, whereas Daniel . . . well, he could be a foreigner, he's so different in his ways and outlook. No, you're right, Aunt Katie, he's not for Bridget." She sighed and turned away, and as she went to leave the room Katie gazed after her; then called to her, "Catherine!" And when Catherine turned round she said, "I'm going to speak to Peter."

"Oh no, Aunt Katie! Not yet. Just let things be. We could be making a mistake, an awful mistake, and if Peter was to speak to Daniel what then? Bridget would never forgive us. No; let things be for the time being. Please, Aunt Katie."

* * *

At eleven o'clock on the Sunday morning, when Catherine, answering a ring on the door-bell, saw Daniel standing there

433

smiling warmly at her, she put her hand to her throat and before she spoke to him she said to herself, "She was right. She was right."

"Hello, Catherine."

"Hello, Daniel. Come in, come in."

"No doubt you're surprised to see me."

"No, no."

"I felt a bit bored and I came down yesterday to see how they are getting on with the house. I've got men in, you know, now, and I couldn't be so near and not pop down."

As Catherine looked up into Daniel's face she saw that behind the smile he was flustered. In the ordinary way there should have been no need for an excuse for his visit—he was coming to see his geat-grandmother. "Give me your coat," she said. "I'll hang it up."

"That's all right. I'm big enough to wait on myself, and I should know where it goes by now." His voice was higher than usual. He quickly took off his coat and went across the hall and into the cloakroom. And when he had gone from her sight Catherine stood nibbling at her nails until he appeared again, and then she said, "Aunt Katie has just come downstairs; she's in the drawing-room." She went forward, adding, "Tom had to go out, but he won't be long." She entered the drawing-room without mentioning Bridget and, her own voice high now, she said, "I've got a surprise for you, Aunt Katie. Daniel's popped in."

Katie was sitting to the right of the fire, and she would have had to turn her head to see who was entering the room. But she didn't turn her head, she waited for him to approach; and when, having first stood facing her, he bent down and put his lips to her cheek, saying, "Hello there. Surprised to see me?" she looked up into the dark, shining eyes and said, "No, Daniel; I was expecting you. I said . . . I said as much to Catherine. I said I wouldn't be surprised but Daniel will pop in."

"Oh well, that's all right." He smiled broadly from her to Catherine; and Catherine, wetting her lips, said, "Would you like a hot drink, coffee or something, Daniel?"

"I would. Yes, I would, Catherine. It was cold coming down. . . . Where's Bridget, by the way?"

"Oh! Oh, she's gone with Peter to some friends at yon side of Hexham. He's in the antique business—I mean Peter's friend. They're seeing about some furniture."

434

She watched the smile seep from his face and the dark-red glow come up under his skin. She watched the eyes flash as if in response to some angry impulse from within him. She watched him turn and look down on to Aunt Katie for a moment, but Aunt Katie was looking towards the fire and she was saying, "Sit yourself down, Daniel. Sit yourself down."

"Will she be away all day?" He was looking at Catherine again, and she replied quietly, "Yes, I'm afraid so, Daniel."

"She . . . they won't be home until this evening then?" His voice was lighter now, and to his enquiry she said, "You can never tell what time they'll be back after a day at Hexham."

Daniel sat down and Catherine went out of the room, and Katie, still looking at the fire, said, "Peter's been given a new lease of life since his mother died. And not before time, for if ever a man deserved a break it's him."

There was a pause before he said, "His mother died after all?"

"Yes, she died after all." Katie looked at Daniel now. "She was buried just a few days ago, and at long last he can think about living his own life. They've got the house—there's no trouble that way; I could have given him a house years ago, but he wouldn't hear of it, he's that kind of a man—but the furniture that his mother had gathered about her I wouldn't have offered to the bairns for a bonfire, if you know what I mean, and Bridget could never have lived with it; so they are clearing it all out and starting from scratch. Don't you think that's sensible, Daniel?"

Daniel stared into the wrinkled face before him, into the brown eyes lying in the deep hollows, and he wondered just how much she knew and how far she would use her strength against him, the strength that lay in her age, the strength that was fed by the gratitude of all those in this household. As he continued to stare at her he felt that she wasn't real, she was something from the past; even her dress bore out this illusion, for she was attired as a woman of fashion would have been thirty years earlier. She was wearing a brown velvet gown with a high neck trimmed with a lace collar. The dress reached her ankles, and her feet, resting on the footstool, looked narrow and neat. Her hair was dressed in what his mother would call farmhouse-loaf style, all gathered up to form a rise in the middle. Her hands, which were big and capable-looking—rather outsize hands, he thought—lay one on top of the other in her lap. . . . But she was real, and she

was formidable; and, what was more, she was determined
that he wouldn't have Bridget. Of that he was certain now.
He could see himself talking his way round Catherine and
Tom, but not around this old woman. He would never talk
his way around her; he would, as he knew all along, have to
fight her.

When the door opened and Tom came breezily into the
room Daniel felt a sense of relief, and as they greeted each
other warmly he thought, Tom isn't in on this. He knows
nothing about it, suspects nothing either way. And this was
borne out when he said, "Oh, Bridget'll kick herself for missing you. . . . What do you think about the news of his
mother going? They've told you?"

"Yes, it was very sad."

"Sad my eye!" Tom jerked his head and went towards the
fire. "She played wolf for so long, that one, that I bet when
she found herself dead there was no one got a bigger surprise." He laughed and bent over Katie, pushing her gently
by the shoulder, and she laughed back at him and caught at
his hand and slapped it, saying, "You're a wicked man, Tom,
a wicked man."

Tom now turned to Daniel and said, "I was just thinking
yesterday that your time's running short at Cambridge. Will
you be sorry when you're finished?"

"In a way, Tom, but I'm seriously considering staying on
in a teaching capacity. I think I would like that."

"Won't you miss your folks?"

"Oh, I don't think I'll have time to miss them, for once the
manor is habitable they'll come storming over in droves just to
sleep in an English mansion." He laughed as he ended,
"We're frightful snobs about such things, we Americans."

"Oh yes, so I've heard." Tom shook his head solemnly for
a moment, then grinned, saying, "but that'll be grand, Daniel,
to have you around, simply grand."

As Catherine entered the room carrying a tray Tom went
towards her and, taking it from her, said, "Do you hear the
latest? Daniel may take up teaching at the college and live at
the manor. What do you think of that?"

"Oh, there's nothing settled," Daniel put in quickly. "It's
just a sort of an idea. It all depends. . . ."

As his voice trailed off Katie asked quietly, "On what does
it depend, Daniel?" She was looking at him, and he stared

back into her eyes as he replied, "On many things, Great-grandmother, such as my relatives wanting me to stay—and Tom here assures me they do." He glanced at Tom. "And . . . and settling down, you know, getting married."

"Oh, you thinking of getting married, Daniel?"

"It's a natural thought, Tom."

"Oh, I'll say, I'll say it's a natural thought all right. Is it somebody back home?"

"No, nobody back home, Tom."

"Oh, then, you've got your eyes on somebody this side of the water?"

"You could say that, Tom."

"Well, I never. Would you believe that, Catherine! And there were all the lassies at Ivy's party pinning their hopes on you. I heard you were a wow. Ivy hasn't stopped talking about you since. . . ."

As Tom chaffed, Katie and Catherine exchanged glances, and the look in Katie's eye said, "What did I tell you?" And Catherine thought, Men are stupid, even men like Tom; they can't see things right under their very noses. Yet would she have seen things so clearly if it hadn't been for Aunt Katie? No, it would never have dawned on her. Now Tom must be told. That would be another one who would be unhappy. If only Daniel hadn't come into their lives, or, having come, he had borne any other name in the world but Rosier.

*   *   *

It was half-past ten the same evening and Catherine and Tom were alone in the drawing-room. They were standing facing each other in front of the couch, and Tom, his face stern now, where it had been broad with laughter and jokes all day, said, "I just don't believe it. I won't believe it."

"Why do you think he's stuck out all day? Not because of us, or Aunt Katie; he was waiting for her coming back. He sat there making conversation all night just waiting, waiting."

"But Bridget . . . does she know?"

"Yes, she knows. Haven't you noticed how she's changed since Christmas? And even before that she was all tensed up, high wires, laughing too much, singing too loudly. She was never like that before, and never with Peter; she's always been serious-minded."

"Well, I'll be damned!" Tom rubbed his hand over his face. Then, after a moment of consideration, he exclaimed, "But he said he had a girl somewhere, didn't he?"

"Yes, of course. Don't be so stupid, Tom. She was the girl he was meaning. I fully expected him to tell you her name at any minute. I felt he was just waiting for a lead in. You know Aunt Katie has always said that old Rosier was an utterly ruthless man. Well, now I'm thinking that he might have passed some of it down, because as the day's worn on I've had the feeling that Daniel will stop at nothing to get her. It got stronger with each hour he sat there."

Tom dropped heavily down on to the couch and, putting his elbows in his knees, he stared towards the fire, and after a short silence he asked, "Would you mind him if Peter wasn't on the scene?"

"I don't know, Tom. I've asked myself that question already. One thing is I couldn't bear the thought of her going to America."

"But would you mind him having her?"

Catherine closed her eyes. "I don't dislike him, Tom—you can't dislike him, he's so attractive and kindly; yet underneath I'm seeing him all the time as Aunt Katie sees him now, as a chip off the old block. Anyway there's Peter, and Peter's gone through enough, God knows, without this hitting him. . . . And she loves Peter, I know she does, Tom. I think what she feels for Daniel is a sort of . . . . of fascination. No girl could help but feel otherwise if she was with him for long, because he's got everything in his favour—looks, manner, voice, the lot. But she loves Peter."

"Well, if she loves Peter she'll marry him." Tom's voice was flat now.

"She mightn't get the chance."

"What do you mean?" He jerked his head round to her as she walked behind the couch towards the door, and she replied, "I just don't know what I mean, Tom." She had paused and was looking over her shoulder. "Only I've got the feeling, as Aunt Katie has had since shortly after he came here, that if something isn't done there's going to be trouble. I think you should give Peter the tip."

"What!" Tom got to his feet. "Tell Peter that Daniel's after her? Oh, lass, have sense. Do you want to cause ructions?"

"Well, there'll be more ructions, I'm warning you, if he doesn't get cracking, and soon. And I mean soon."

"You mean, them get married right away?"

"As soon as ever possible."

"But . . . but his mother isn't cold yet."

"That's nothing but old-fashioned twaddle. You talk to him, tell him plainly what's happened. You could tell him that she's not really aware of it. That's a lie, but it'll ease his mind. And advise him to go ahead and suggest a special licence. Now look, Tom. . . ." She turned right round now and walked a few steps towards him again. "If you don't want Peter to be left on the rocks and broken up, because that's how he'll be, and if you don't want us to lose her altogether, because all this talk of him staying teaching here is, to my mind, a lot of eyewash, and if you don't want Aunt Katie to die before her time, then you'll do what I say. This way there's only going to be one hurt, and that's him; the other way there are all of us, and our whole family life will be broken up, because what would we be like, dear . . ." Her voice dropped now, "just imagine what we'd be like with her and Aunt Katie gone. They are such a part of us that nothing would ever be the same again."

Tom stared at her; then he watched her turn slowly away and walk out of the room, and when the door closed on her he still stood looking at it. She had said "part of us" when she meant "part of me". He loved Bridget, but he was always aware that she wasn't his. He was very, very fond of Aunt Katie, but, he faced it, not to the extent that Catherine was. Catherine and Aunt Katie were like mother and daughter. If both Bridget and Aunt Katie were gone he would survive because he would have Catherine; and, after all, Catherine was all he wanted from life. But with her it was different; she needed them both to complete her happiness. The hurt, that over the years he had covered with a joke and a laugh, brought his head down to his chest and his teeth clamping on his lower lip.

9

The letter came on Wednesday morning. Nellie had brought the mail into the breakfast-room, as usual and left it on the sideboard. Catherine, sorting through it, held the particular letter in her hand. It was addressed to "Miss Bridget Mulholland, Loreto, 18 Tree Drive, Westoe, South Shields". She recognised the writing. The letter was still in her hand when she heard Bridget's voice calling from the stairway, saying, "Mother, have you seen a blue notebook?"

She paused only a second before thrusting the letter into the pocket of her flowered overall and going to the door. "What sort of a note-book dear?" Her voice cracked on the words and she put her hand over her mouth and cleared her throat.

"A school book, you know."

"Was it a particular one?"

"Yes, I was checking it last night when Peter came round. I don't know where I've put it."

"Oh well, look in the office; I cleared up a number of papers and things and pushed them in there."

As Bridget went into the office Catherine put her hand in her pocket again. What had she done? Oh, what had she done? Well, she could give it to her at lunchtime, saying that it came by the second post. But first she must talk it over with Aunt Katie. But oh, dear God, she felt awful, awful. . . .

A few minutes after Bridget had left for school Catherine went upstairs and taking the letter from her pocket she held it out towards Katie, who was sitting propped up in bed finishing her breakfast, and said quietly, "There's a letter for her from him. I've . . . I've held it back. I feel awful, terrible."

Katie took the letter from Catherine's hand and gazed at it. She gazed at it a long while before she said quietly, "Steam it open, and we'll know then if we've been right or wrong."

"Oh, Aunt Katie!"

"It's the only way, Catherine. Do it carefully so that if we're wrong it can be stuck back. If we're right, then you must burn it."

Catherine bowed her head deeply on to her chest as she said, "This is awful. I feel terrible about it . . . terrible."

"I know, dear, I know. I feel dreadful myself. . . . Do . . . do you think Peter spoke to her last night?"

"Yes, yes, I'm sure he did, but she's said nothing so far. But then there was no time this morning as she was late getting up. I . . . I think"—her head bowed again—"I think she had been crying last night; her face was swollen."

"Well, far better she cry now, Catherine, than cry for the remainder of her life."

"Yes, yes, I suppose so. But, you know, I'm finding that I can't look her in the face. Since Sunday I've felt that I'm deceiving her in not letting on he was here."

"Open the letter, Catherine," said Katie, quietly now, "and find out if she's been deceiving you. . . ."

Catherine steamed open the letter in the kitchen while Nellie was working upstairs, and on taking out the single sheet of paper she screwed her eyes up and closed them immediately she read the heading, "Darling, darling, Bridget." Then, looking at it again, she read, "You'll know now I waited until late on Sunday evening for you. I was determined to see you if only for a moment. Talk about a day in hell. There they sat willing me miles away. I felt it every moment, but I stuck it out. And you didn't come. Can you guess how I felt? On the way back I made up my mind to come down on Monday and tell them the truth—the truth that I can't live without you and I don't intend doing so; but in the cold light of Monday morning the fact that any such action of mine might finish Great-grandmother prevented me, because I know if anything happened to her through me you would never forgive me.

"Still thinking along these lines, darling, I am quite willing to wait until she goes, if you'll only make the situation clear to Peter. Don't think I'm not sorry for him, I am; he's a nice fellow. But I love you so, Bridget, and were he a thousand times nicer I'd willingly see you dead before he'd have you."

Catherine turned the sheet of paper over and continued reading.

"I have so much I want to say to you, I am full of plans. Do you know what I'm thinking? The Manor would make a first-rate private school. What about that? It's a great idea, isn't it? You and me running it. . . . Yes, marm. No, marm. I'd be your most willing pupil, dearest Bridget.

"Bridget, Bridget, come to me. Please, I beseech you, don't make me do anything silly. I don't want to hurt anyone, believe me. I'm considering them as much as you are, and I can stand anything as long as I see you. As you know, I'm due

441

back in Cambridge on Friday. I'll be at the house on Thursday, and I'll wait for you as before. I know you can't get along until after school, but come then, please, please.

"You remember my tirade about adoring—well, I have succumbed and joined the rest. I adore you, Bridget, adore you, adore you. Your Daniel."

"Oh, dear God! Dear, dear God!"

When she took the letter upstairs and Aunt Katie had read it they both looked at each other but did not speak. They had no words with which to condemn their beloved Bridget or to condone their action, but in Catherine's heart she was saying now, "Oh, I wish, I wish it could be possible," and something like a faint echo of it was in Katie's also; but it was only faint because she was remembering the saying about the rotten apple contaminating the rest of the barrel. And it wasn't to be imagined that Daniel the Third had escaped the taint of the Rosiers.

* * *

Three more letters were to be steamed open. The first arrived the following week, and it did not begin "Darling, darling Bridget", but started abruptly, "How can you do this, Bridget? I could never imagine your being hard or callous, but you are being both. I'm in hell. Don't do this to us. I waited until ten o'clock on that road. I was for coming down the next morning and shaking the life out of you, but where would I do it? At your school, or in the street? If I hadn't had to return here on Friday I would surely have come to the house and blown the whole thing up. I am still angry at you for being so stubborn. I only asked you meet me, to see me, so that we could talk; that was all. I promised you faithfully I wouldn't do anything rash, I just asked to see you.

"I'll take back what I demanded in my last letter, that you explain the situation to Peter. You can have it all your own way, but I must see you, or at least hear from you. I feel utterly frustrated because I cannot get away for the next two week-ends. Write to me, Bridget. I beseech you, write to me. . . ."

Catherine could read no more. She crushed the letter up in her fists and thrust it into the fire; then gave a great start as the door opened and Tom entered the room.

Looking at her face, Tom came to her quickly, saying, "What is it? What's the matter?"

Catherine shook her head and wetted her lips again and again before she could say, "Nothing; I just felt faint."

"It's all this damned business. I wish it was over. I always looked forward to her wedding, I could see it as a great day; but this hurry-scurry. . . . What's puzzling me now is she seems eager to hurry it up, almost as much as Peter is."

Making no comment on this, Catherine turned and looked towards the fire, to the black twisted blob resting near the top bar. . . . God forgive her for what she was doing, for she could never forgive herself. And should Tom ever find out about this particular side of the business . . . well!

*　*　*

There were no letters from Cambridge during the next week, but the following week the other two arrived; and then on the Saturday morning Daniel himself came to the house.

Nellie opened the door, her face one broad beam until she saw who was standing there, and after letting out a long-drawn "O-oh!" her mouth dropped into a gape.

"Hello, Nellie."

"Hello, Mr. Rosier."

"Well, aren't you going to let me in?"

"Oh yes, sir. Yes, sir." She stood aside and pulled the door wide, and when he entered the hall and he heard no movement, either upstairs or down, he turned to her and said, "Where is everybody?"

Nellie looked up at Mr. Rosier. His face looked pinched with the cold, he looked thinner somehow. Eeh, this was awful; she wished the missus was back. There was going to be high jinks, if she knew anything. There was something fishy going on, the missus telling her not to let on to Miss Bridget about him being here that Sunday. . . . Funny, that was. "They're all out, sir," she said. "That is, except m'am— Mrs. Fraenkel."

"Oh well, I don't suppose they'll be long. Is Mrs. Fraenkel upstairs?"

"Yes, she's upstairs." Nellie raised her hand to the stairs, at the same time stepping back in the direction of the kitchen, and before he had taken his coat off she had scurried through the door. He looked towards it. What was the matter with Nellie? She was acting strangely. She knew something —most servants did. Had Bridget had the courage to speak out? His face lightened and he made for the stairs and took them two at a time, and when he reached Katie's door he paused only a moment before knocking. But there was a longer pause before her voice came to him, saying, "Come in."

Immediately he opened the door he saw the shock registered on her face, and when he walked quickly to the window, where she was sitting propped up in a chair, her agitation increased.

"Aren't you well, Great-grandmother?"

Her lips moved in a pathetic fashion, denoting her age, before she said, "I'm . . . I'm all right, Daniel. I . . . I haven't been too well lately, but . . . but I'm all right now."

He pulled up a seat to her side and, after looking at her closely for a moment, said, "You look very beautiful today. That is a lovely gown you're wearing."

Katie looked down towards her lap where her fingers were twitching one against the other, and her hands began to smooth the folds in the blue woollen dress; the dress that she hadn't worn for many a long day, the dress that she knew was much too young for her. "I . . . I used to fill this dress at one time"—she nodded down at her hands—"but it hangs on me like a sack now."

"Nonsense. Nonsense."

He felt that they were both parrying, but about what he wasn't sure.

"They're all out," he said now. "The house is very quiet and empty downstairs."

"Yes, yes, they're all out." She drew in a long breath and leant her head back against the cushion on the top of the chair, and now, as she looked at him, her gaze was steady and her voice firm as she said, "I wish you hadn't come today, Daniel."

He didn't answer her for a time, and then, in a low tone, he asked, "Why do you wish that?"

"What time is it?" She turned her head slightly towards the mantelpiece as he looked at his watch and said, "Two minutes after half-past eleven to be correct." When he lifted his gaze to her she was staring fixedly at her hands and she kept her attention on them for a time before she said, "They should all be back shortly. Bridget was married at eleven o'clock, Daniel."

Katie did not raise her eyes to his face. From under her lowered lids she could see his legs and his body up to his waist, and no part of him had moved. He had not jumped up and upset his chair. He was not screaming abuse at her, but even so her heart was thumping as if it would leap from her breast. When the silence became unbearable she slowly lifted her head, and there was his face staring at her like the face of his great-grandfather the night she had thrown the candlestick at him. His dark complexion was grey and white, his eyes were pieces of shining pitch, there was a great silence about him; it was a force pressing against her, pushing her down the years to that room at the top of No. 14 Crane Street. It was a silence that only a Rosier could maintain. She put her two hands underneath her breast to try to still the thumping against her ribs. If . . . if he didn't speak she would die, she would have a heart attack, and she didn't want to die at this moment, not before she saw Bridget again. . . . Bridget married.

When at last he spoke it was not of Bridget, nor was his voice harsh, yet it held a quality that pierced her through more than any recrimination could have done. "You hate me, don't you?" he said.

"Oh no, Daniel; no! No! I don't hate you."

"You hate me. You have manœuvred all this because you hate me."

"I don't, I don't, Daniel." Her breath was coming in small gasps.

"You planned all this." His voice had a painful level tone to it. "You knew I loved her and you planned this for revenge because of him. You made me pay for what he did."

"No! No, Daniel."

"Yes! And you've made her pay too, because she loves me; with every fibre of her being she loves me. I know that. But she didn't want to hurt you, or Catherine, or Tom. I didn't want to hurt you either because you are old; but you're not old inside, are you, Great-grandmother? You're still young and suffering under the hands of my great-grandfather. That's how you feel, isn't it? And so you did this to pay him out."

"No, Daniel! No! It wasn't like that."

"You rushed her, flung her into this. You must have kept on and on at her. She was afraid to answer my letters because she knew that if we met just once again she would have to hurt you." He was on his feet now and his face was no longer distinguishable to her, for the tears were raining from her eyes; but even so she knew that the face before her now was not that of Bernard Rosier, it was the face of a nice young man, an upright young man, the face of her great-grandson whom she loved. She put out her hand and whimpered, "Oh, Daniel. Daniel." But he was no longer there. She bowed her head and the tears rained on to her hands, and when she heard the front door close she roughly dried her eyes and, leaning forward, peered through the window and saw him walking down the path. When he reached the pavement her vision was blurred again, and again she wiped her eyes and followed his slow step across the road to the far line of trees. And there she saw him stop almost in the same place where Tom used to wait for Catherine in years gone by.

A few minutes later, when the car drew up to the door, she did not wave from the window down on her Bridget and her husband Peter. They had set her up near the window so that she could wave to them, but she did not even look in their direction, for her eyes were fixed on the figure standing under the trees across the road.

For the first time in her life Katie felt guilt. So many things had happened to her, she had suffered so many injustices, yet none had pained her as the guilt of her own action was doing now. He had been right, Daniel had been right. She had made him suffer for something that had happened years ago, something that the other one had done; somewhere in the back of her mind had been the hard persistent thought that a Rosier wasn't going to get the better of her again, not at this stage in her life. She had had, during the past three weeks, the strange idea that she was fighting a Rosier with his own weapons, which were deceit and subterfuge, and that at last she was winning. Well, she had won, and the victory was like gall pervading her whole body.

There came the sound of laughter from downstairs; the steps and the voices were mounting nearer to her, but she did not take her eyes from the window. The two cars down below moved away, and when they turned in the broad road she saw the tall figure look after them; then, his step, still slow, she watched him walk into the distance.

When Bridget and Peter came into the room, followed by

Catherine and Tom, she turned a tear-drenched face towards them, and they stopped their forced chattering, and all became concerned because their Aunt Katie couldn't stop crying.

Later in the day they decided that it had been too much for her. Well, she was a ripe age now, wasn't she? But her reactions had been somewhat disappointing because she had been so bright when they had left her to go to the church.

Only Catherine knew why Aunt Katie cried and cried. A quick word from Nellie behind the kitchen door had put her in the picture, and she, too, felt she wanted to cry and cry. But that was a relief she knew she must at all costs postpone until she was in bed, and there Tom would comfort her, thinking she was crying because she had lost her daughter.

BOOK VI

Bridget
1944

1

"You know, dear, I used to love to go to the Theatre Royal.
Andy used to take me to the Theatre Royal." The words
came slowly, tired-sounding. "And Dick Thornton used to
come here to dinner. Do you know that, Bridget? Dick
Thornton used to come here to dinner. He started playing his
fiddle to the holiday crowds up at Frenchman's Bay. Oh, he
could play the fiddle. From a lad he played the fiddle. And
then he started the Empire. I saw Vesta Tilley and Little Tich
there. Oh, I liked Little Tich. And Charlie Chaplin, he was
on at the Empire. Now, would you believe that, Bridget?
Charlie Chaplin was on at the Empire."

"Yes, Aunt Katie."

"And the Queens, the poor Queens. They bombed the
Queens. Is the fire out yet, Bridget?"

"Yes, Aunt Katie, it's out." Bridget rose from her chair by
the bed that was placed to the side of the fireplace in the
drawing-room, and she arranged the pillows behind Katie's
head, saying, "There now. Go to sleep. That's a dear, go to
sleep."

"Will they come back tonight, Bridget?"

"I don't think so, dear. Go to sleep."

"If they do, you and Catherine must go into the cellar."

"Yes, Aunt Katie, we'll go into the cellar. Don't worry."

Bridget resumed her seat and took up her pen and continued to mark exercise books. After a while she raised her eyes
and looked towards the bed. Aunt Katie was asleep. Her
mind was wandering a lot these days. The Queens Theatre
had been destroyed in an air raid in April 1941, it was now
June 1944. She gazed at the shrunken face lying deep among

451

the pillows. If Aunt Katie lived until October she'd be a hundred.

Bridget rested her head on her hand and moved it slightly. She hoped she didn't live to be a hundred. She felt tired and weary, old herself. She was thirty-four. The years were rolling on, and what had come out of them? She turned her gaze from the bed to the window. The long twilight was deepening and she would soon have to draw the black-outs; she hated the black-outs. She rose heavily to her feet and walked to the window and looked out into the garden. There were no roses in it now, no flower-beds, no shrubs. One side of it, down to the privet hedge, was completely taken up with potatoes and cabbage; the other side showed a mixture of lettuce, radishes, carrot tops, parsnips and other vegetables. In the greenhouses beyond the hedge the tomatoes were ripening. But Bridget didn't notice the garden. She was looking inwards, seeing Peter hooded against the cold of the night, standing near a gun, waiting. This was the fourth convoy he had sailed in, without so much as a scratch; many other boats had been sunk, but his had always got off scot free. It seemed, he had said to her, that God was with him. She had not questioned this with the cynicism it deserved: God had apparently left the other boats to fend for themselves while protecting his. You couldn't be cynical with man like Peter, with a face and heart as kind as his. He had been gone two days now. She did not know his destination. He didn't know it himself; he only guessed that it would be weeks before he returned.

Her mother had said to her yesterday, "It's a good job you didn't have any children after all; you would have been worried to death. You worry enough about them at school." Her mother very rarely said stupid things like that, and she had wanted to round on her and say just that, "Don't be stupid!" The ache in her for a child was like a canker inside her stomach, growing with the years. Instead of something swelling her womb, this ache swelled her whole body. At times part of it erupted and pushed itself up through her chest and struggled out through her throat and brought the tears gushing from her eyes and mouth; it opened her pores and made her sweat; and part of it pressed up into her mind and yelled "Why? Why?" and "If only". When this happened she hated her mother and father . . . and her Aunt Katie. She hated Peter. Most of all, she hated Peter. And Peter was so kind, no one should hate Peter. She was wicked, inside she was wicked. She didn't go to confession any more because of the things she thought. At times she thought she wasn't married, that she was still a virgin, an old maid even. This kind of thinking frightened her, but the fact was she didn't feel married, she had never felt married.

She turned from the window. Poor Peter out there on the sea. She hoped he'd get safely through. She wished her mother was in, but Catherine would be another two hours at the post, and her father would be on duty until nine-thirty or ten o'clock. She stood by the little table and looked down at the exercise books. She should finish them, but she couldn't be bothered. She caught a glimpse of herself in the mirror above the mantelpiece. She looked tired. She smoothed her hair back and ran her fingers up through the short ends. She must go and have a trim tomorrow, she looked awful. But what did it matter? She'd make a hot drink while Aunt Katie was dozing, then put the black-outs up, and when her mother came back she would have a bath—she couldn't risk having one when there was no one downstairs with Aunt Katie. And if the warning should go while she was in the bath? Well, it would be too bad; she might as well die in the bath as anywhere else.

"Snap out of it!" She spoke half aloud to herself as she crossed the hall towards the kitchen.

There was no maid in the kitchen now. Nellie, at fifty-five, was working in munitions and married to a soldier. She made herself a cup of cocoa and carefully measured a small spoonful of sugar into it.

It was as she was crossing the hall again towards the drawing-room, the cup in her hand, that the front-door bell rang. She put the cup on a side-table and walked to the door, and when she opened it there stood an airman, an American airman. He was leaning on a stick. He had a brown face and very dark eyes. He took off his cap and a strand of straight black hair fell down over his temple. "Why, hello, Bridget," he said.

She just stood staring at him, the door in one hand, the other, with fingers spread, placed flat on the bare flesh of her neck above the square-topped print dress.

"I'm not a ghost and you are Bridget, aren't you?"

The small movements of her head became wider, then the smile broke over her face, but when she said "Daniel!" she couldn't hear her own voice.

"Daniel!" It was louder now, and she pulled the door wide and watched him as he lifted a stiff leg over the step, then, with the aid of his stick, walk into the hall.

"How are you, Bridget?"

"Oh. Oh, I'm all right, Daniel." She was looking up into his face. "I . . . I just can't get over it, the surprise. You are the last person on earth I expected to see."

They stood staring at each other. And then they laughed, and he turned to look for some place to put his cap.

"Here, let me have it." She took it from him and placed it on a sidetable, then said, "Come along and sit down. No, not that way. . . ." She smiled again as she pointed across the hall towards the dining-room. "The whole house is upside down. We brought Aunt Katie down into the drawing-room; it's safer there."

"She's still alive?" He had stopped, and she turned to him and said, "Yes, but . . . but she's very frail and lives mostly in the past now."

The smile had gone from his face and he nodded his head, then followed with his limping gait into the dining-room, and there he let himself down into a chair with a jerky sidewards movement and his left leg stuck out straight across the hearth-rug.

Bridget looked at the leg, then pulled a chair forward and sat on the edge of it with her hands clasped before her in an attitude very much like that of a nervous child. "You've been wounded?" she said. Then, jerking her head upwards and closing her eyes for a second, she muttered, "That's a silly question. I mean, where did it happen?"

"Oh, somewhere in the North Sea."

She waited for more, but he didn't go on, and again they were looking at each other. He was older, she thought—much more than eight years older. He wasn't as thin as he used to be. He had put on weight, especially about the shoulders, and there were two deep lines on his face, running from his nose to the corner of his mouth; deep lines that hadn't been there before. The one thing that hadn't altered about him were his eyes. They were still black and shining as she remembered them.

Daniel, looking at her, thought, She's older. Then, Of course I knew she would be, but she's different. And then he saw where the difference lay, and he was amazed that he hadn't recognized it the moment he had set eyes on her; be-

454

cause of all the things that he remembered about her, her hair, coiled up on the back of her head, was the clearest. He said quickly, "You've had your hair off!"

"Oh yes." She ran her fingers up from the back of her neck to the crown of her head. "It was too much trouble, and there wasn't time to see to it. When the raids were bad I seemed to be always running down into the cellar, pinning my hair up as I went."

"It suits you." He could still lie convincingly.

Again she pushed her hand up to the back of her head, saying, as a young girl might, "Oh, it's an awful sight. I haven't bothered with it; there doesn't seem time."

"Are you still teaching?"

"Yes, I went back when war broke out."

"How . . . how is Peter doing?"

"Oh, he's in the Merchant Navy. He's away on convoy at present." She nodded her head and smiled as she spoke.

"Merchant Navy." He pursed his lips, and the action was a compliment.

"How are your mother and father?"

"Oh, not too bad, considering. Mother's on duty three nights a week. . . . She's on tonight and won't be back until nine o'clock. And Dad's a warden. . . . But tell me." She unclasped her hands, then turned them over and clasped them the other way. "How have you come here? Are you stationed near?"

"I've been in hospital near Newcastle for some time."

"For some time?" She brought her head forward.

"Well"—he slanted his eyes to the side—"let me see. Three months."

"And you didn't let us know you were here?"

He stared at her without answering. Women were the limit. Lord, but they were the limit. When he did answer her he said, "Well, you know how it is."

The silence between them now screamed aloud and brought her to her feet, saying, "Can I get you something to drink? There's a drop of whisky somewhere."

"No, no, thank you."

"Something hot then, Daniel? A cup of tea or cocoa? We haven't any coffee."

"I wouldn't mind a cup of tea."

"All right, I won't be a minute."

She was five minutes, and he sat staring straight ahead of

him until she returned, and he noticed that she had combed her hair and put on fresh lipstick on, and he didn't smile to himself because she had done this. When she handed him the cup she said, "Is it still two lumps?" and he laughed as he replied, "It's one now. It's my war effort."

When she had seated herself again, still on the edge of the chair, she stirred her tea vigorously before she said, "Tell me what's happened to you all this long while."

"Oh, well now." His chin went up and he rested his head on the back of his shoulders and he seemed to consider. Then he said, "Well, I joined the Air Force."

"This is evident." She nodded at him.

He brought his head forward and sipped at his tea before saying, "And I got married."

She stared unblinking at him, but he was looking down into his cup. "Have . . . you been married long?" The questin sounded polite, ordinary.

"Oh, since the beginning of thirty-seven."

Now they were looking at each other again.

"Have you any children?"

"Have you?"

"No."

"Well, we're both in the same boat." His lips twisted slightly.

"Your . . . your wife . . . is she doing war work?"

His brows went up and again he looked down into his cup before he said in a very quiet voice, "I wouldn't know what she is doing, Bridget. I was divorced in thirty-nine."

"Divorced!" The word came over on a high note.

"Don't sound so shocked." He was smiling.

"Oh, no! No! No. I'm not shocked. I'm only sorry, Daniel."

"Oh, there's no need to waste any sympathy on us; it was mutual, a mutual agreement."

As another silence fell on them and they looked at each other she began to search madly in her mind for something with which to break it. "The house," she said. "Have . . . have you seen it lately?"

"The house? Oh yes, yes. I've just come from there."

"You have? I thought it was taken over by the Army?"

"Yes, it was; but one lot moved out and the other lot hasn't moved in yet, and I don't know when they will. Anyway, I have an arrangement whereby three rooms were set aside for the storing of the furniture, and I have access to them. Did you know that a bomb dropped quite near it a month ago?"

"No! No, I didn't hear that."

"Most of the glass is shattered and the outhouses are a complete write-off. Two or three soldiers were killed in there, I understand. I thought at the time it was just as well it hadn't been turned into a school after all. Although a lot of the children have been evacuated from around here, it being some way out from the town they might have used it to house a few—you never know."

"Oh, did you think of turning it into a school?" Her head was tilted at an enquiring angle.

He stared back at her, his eyes slightly narrowed now, and after a considerable pause he said, "Perhaps you've forgotten, Bridget. I did mention it once to you."

"That . . . that you were going to turn the Manor into a school? No, Daniel. If you had ever mentioned that to me I would surely have remembered, because I have always thought how marvellous it would be to have a private school."

His face looked completely blank as he stared at her. It couldn't be possible, could it, that she hadn't got his letters? At times during the years he had wondered about this. The repeated ignoring of his letters and the subsequent final act of hers had, for some time, made him see her as someone self-righteous, bent on doing good and be damned. Bitterness had stamped out his first reaction, that she had acted under pressure, but then he would remember how she had responded when he held her in his arms—the pain on her face at the thought of their parting, the tears she had shed—and then he would be puzzled. But now, now, he was coming to something.

He moved his right hip on the chair and his stiff leg jerked a few inches on the carpet. "I did talk about turning the house into a school, Bridget." His voice was low. "I particularly remember mentioning it in one of my letters to you."

He watched her eyes crinkle at the corners and her mouth open just the slightest. He saw her put her cup down on to the table where it almost overbalanced, and after she had righted it her fingers clutched at each other in her lap again and she stared towards him, but she didn't speak.

He was leaning farther forward now, his face straight, his voice low. "I sent you a number of letters, Bridget."

Still she didn't speak; she was at the moment quite incapable of uttering a sound. She stared into the dark bright eyes and gathered each word he spoke to her and held it close while her heart cried, "Oh, Daniel! Daniel!"

"I sent the card to Aunt Katie. You remember, I said I would. It was to tell you that I would be at the house that week-end. You didn't come, so I kept my word and came down on the Sunday. I waited all day." He was smiling slightly now. "I remember I nearly drove them mad with my presence, and I ran out of things to talk about. Did they tell you I waited all day, Bridget?" She made no movement, gave no sign, and he went on, "And then I wrote to you. I wrote four times. Then one Saturday morning I came, determined to tell them how things stood, to relieve you of the painful duty. The house was empty that morning, except for Nellie and Aunt Katie. I went upstairs—I remember it so plainly— and she told me in her own inimitable way that you had been married at eleven o'clock, and that she was expecting you back. I saw you when you came back, Bridget. I stood across the road and watched you. . . ."

There was something swelling inside her. It wasn't the canker erupting again, but an anger, and it wasn't only anger. There was hate swelling in her too, and threading her emotions was a feeling of astonishment that they could have done this to her. They all must have been in it; her mother, father, and Aunt Katie—even Nellie. . . . And what about Peter? Had Peter been in this too? His sudden idea of them getting married by special licence? She had been willing to marry Peter rather than hurt him. Even if she had received the letters and had known Daniel had come she still might have married Peter. . . . But would she? Wasn't it a fact that she had fallen in with the idea of a special licence because she thought that Daniel had taken her at her word? Hadn't she waited for some sign from him and it hadn't come? Yet all the time they had been getting her letters. Who? Who? Her mother? Yes, it could have only been her mother . . . unless Aunt Katie had got them through Nellie.

When he stood up and limped the three steps towards her she sat gazing up at him, with her hand gripping her throat. She saw his face as she had seen it in the bedroom of the house that day, warm, tender; she did not look for the other emotion it held, eight years had gone by.

"Oh, Bridget! You never got them, did you?"

She made a small movement with her head, then brought her hand up to her mouth and pressed it tightly across her lips.

He took up the hand that was still lying in her lap and gently undid the clenched fingers, then he brought it to his face and laid her palm against his cheek.

The touch of his face was like a lock key releasing a dam that had been building up for years, and when it burst he braced himself and pulled her upwards to him. And he held her gently, and she lay against him and cried and cried as she had never been able to do for years, and the ache within her melted somewhat.

Holding her with one arm now, he dried her face, and when at last she spoke she muttered under her breath, "It was cruel, cruel."

"Yes, Bridget, it was cruel. It's amazing to what lengths people will go because they think they have right on their side. The familiar excuse is they do it for your good, or because they love you."

Swiftly now she disengaged herself from him, but when he overbalanced she grabbed at him to steady him. "Sit down . . ." she said. She had almost added "darling".

He bent sideways, and, picking up his stick, said, "I'd . . . I'd rather walk about; I'm all at sea at the moment." He leant on the stick and put one hand out to her, and she hesitated a moment before placing hers in it. As he gripped it he said, "It's going to be damned awkward meeting them."

She nodded at him, saying, "Yes, and for me too, Daniel. I . . . I just can't believe they could have done this to me. But . . . but they did, didn't they?"

He looked deep into her eyes as he answered, "Yes, they did, Bridget. But there's another side to it for me. I'd rather know that they fixed this than continue under the impression that you received the letters and didn't bother to answer them. . . . They didn't tell you that I came that Sunday?"

"No, Daniel."

"Nor the morning you were married?"

"No. But I remember that when we came back Aunt Katie was in a bit of a state."

"She would be."

A bell tinkled in the distance and her hand jerked in his. "That's her now. She must have woken up. I don't think you had better see her right away."

459

"I have no particular wish to see her at all, Bridget."

"No, I can understand that, but . . . but she's very old; she'll be a hundred this year and she's fading fast."

"She was very old eight years ago, but she could still scheme."

"Yes, Daniel." Bridget looked down, then said, "I won't be a minute. Do sit down."

"I'd rather trot round if you don't mind."

"If she's all right—what I mean is, she sometimes wanders just a little, but most of the time her mind is quite clear. But . . . but if she's all right, as I said, would you come in?"

"I'll leave it to you, Bridget. Call me if you think I should, because I really have no feelings about it one way or the other now."

She looked at him for a moment longer, then turned slowly away and went out of the room.

As she entered the drawing-room Katie turned her face towards her and said, "I've had a funny dream, dear. Do you know I thought Betty was back, but Betty has been dead for years, hasn't she?"

"Yes, Aunt Katie, Betty's been dead for years." Bridget stood by the bed and looked down into the hollowed eyes. The hate she had felt against this old old woman had gone, only a sadness remained. As Daniel had said, the things people did in the name of love.

"What's the matter, dear? You look tired."

"I am a bit tired, Aunt Katie."

"It's that siren. If it only didn't go at night-time."

"Yes." Bridget now bent and straightened the coverlet. "It would be nice if we could arrange it just for the daytime."

"Oh, Bridget, you sounded just like your father then."

"Aunt Katie . . . do you remember Daniel?"

"Daniel?"

"Yes, Daniel. Daniel who came from America, your great-grandson."

It was many years since Katie had heard the name of Daniel spoken aloud. The name churned over in her mind incessantly at times, and now Bridget was saying it. "Yes, yes, dear, I remember Daniel."

"Well, he's in the Air Force now, and he's been wounded, and he's in a hospital near Newcastle. He's"—she paused—"he's called down to see you."

There was a deep quietness in the room as Katie stared up into Bridget's face.

"Would you like to see him? You needn't if you don't want to."

"He's been wounded?"

"Yes, dear, in the leg. Would you like to see him?"

"Is . . . is he different, changed?"

"Oh, he looks much older. But of course it's eight years since he was here; we're all very much older."

"Did he really come to see me?"

There was a pause before Bridget said, "Yes, dear, he came to see you."

"I'm very tired, Bridget."

"All right, dear, we can leave it until another time."

"Yes. Tomorrow perhaps, or the next day. Is Catherine in?"

"Not yet, dear."

"Will she be long?"

"She's not due in until nine o'clock."

"I wish she was back."

"You just rest quietly. Would you like a drink?"

"No thanks, dear."

When Katie closed her eyes Bridget moved from the bed and went to the window and drew the heavy curtains; then, leaving the room, she crossed the hall and went into the dining-room again, and looking at Daniel, where he was standing by the empty fireplace with his elbows leaning on the mantelshelf, she said, "She's too tired tonight; perhaps . . . perhaps some other time. Will you excuse me a minute? I'll have to do the black-outs."

He made no reference to her remark on Katie but said, "Can I help you?" He hobbled towards her.

"No, thanks. It'll only take two or three minutes. I generally do them early in case I should switch on a light and forget, you know."

As she turned from him he said, "Bridget!" and she turned to him again. "I've, I've got to leave shortly. There's a friend picking me up about twenty-to-nine." He glanced at his watch. "It's nearly half-past eight now. He got hold of a jeep and came down to see some friends. We must be back by half-past nine . . . hospital orders, you know."

She came towards him now. "Well, in that case the black-outs can wait."

461

When they were standing opposite each other again he gazed at her for a time, then asked quietly, "Have you been happy, Bridget?"

To keep things normal, to assist things to move along as they had moved during the last eight years, she should have answered, "Yes," but what she said was, "No, Daniel."

"Oh, Bridget."

As she heard herself talking now it was as if she was listening to the secret part of her that became alive only in the night, when Peter was fast asleep and she lay staring up through the blackness; but the thoughts that came alive in the blackness were formulating into words and pouring out of her now. "He's good," she was saying, "very good—so kind and thoughtful; but . . . but it hasn't been enough. Never was enough." And now she gasped as she added to her spoken thoughts, "Oh, it's dreadful me saying this, and so soon. We haven't met but an hour and here I am talking like this. I'm sorry, Daniel, I'm sorry. . . ."

"Sorry!" He clutched at her hand and held it to him. "What have you got to be sorry about? It's them that should be sorry . . . old people. Even he was older than you, so much older, like a second father. He talked like that, I remember. For months and months afterwards I used to hear him talking, never stopping, imagining you listening to him, the good stolid man talking. Good stolid men can drive you mad, simply because they are good and stolid and so right—so very, very right. But he wasn't right in taking you, Bridget. He was in on this with all of them." He drew her closer and went to put his arms around her, and as she stiffened slightly she said, "Wait, Daniel. Wait, I'm . . . I'm all at sea." The term made her think of Peter and she bowed her head. But it would be easier to think of Peter if he had really been in on this, as Daniel said. She looked up into his face now and asked simply, "Will you be coming back, Daniel?"

"Will I be coming back, Bridget? What do you think? I'll be here tomorrow."

"But how . . . how will you get here? Can you manage the bus?"

"Don't you worry about that, I'll get here. What time are you finished school?"

"Four o'clock. But I don't get in until about a quarter to five."

"I'll be here shortly after."

He glanced at his watch again; then, moving forward, still gripping her hand, he said, "There's a lot of talking to be done, Bridget, and some rearranging."

She did not answer or look at him, but picked up his cap as they passed the side-table; and then they were at the door, and as she went to open it he checked her and, bending his face down until it almost touched hers, he gazed at her and waited. When she closed her eyes his mouth fell on hers and they clung and rocked drunkenly together, and he, losing his balance for a moment, fell against the door and she with him, and there they rested, their bodies, their mouths hungry.

When their lips parted she lay against him for a time in silence, then gently pressed herself from him and picked up his cap that had fallen on the doormat and handed it to him. He put it on, adjusting it slightly to the side, then touched her cheek and whispered, "Tomorrow, Bridget, and all the tomorrows."

They exchanged one long look before she opened the door. Then she watched him limp down the drive to the gate, and as he went through and closed it after him he looked up towards her and smiled, and she smiled back and raised her hand to him. When he had limped from her sight she went in and closed the door and, leaning against it again, she bit hard on the ball of her thumb.

* * *

When Bridget heard Catherine come in she took up her position with her back to the fireplace. Her hands once more clasped tightly in front of her, her eyes on the door, she waited. She heard Catherine go to the drawing-room, then come out almost immediately, which meant that Aunt Katie was still asleep, or pretending to be—she was a good pretender, was Aunt Katie. Then she heard her mother go into the kitchen and a minute or so later come out. And now she was coming across the hall to the dining-room.

When Catherine entered the room and saw Bridget standing stiffly in front of the fire, her hands joined tightly in front of her, which always spelt agitation, she asked quietly, "What is it, dear? Something happened? I've . . . I've just been in; she's asleep."

She came forward, smoothing her grey hair back behind her ears, and she paused when she reached the back of the couch and, looking across it to Bridget, again she asked, "What's the matter?"

Bridget jerked her chin upwards as if it was being restricted in some way, then very quietly she said, "Daniel's been."

"Dan . . . Daniel?"

"Yes, Daniel Rosier. You may remember him."

Catherine stared at her beloved daughter. She had often wondered over the past eight years what the outcome would be if ever Bridget and Daniel met; but she consoled herself by thinking that the meeting was hardly possible. Even when America came into the war she saw no reason why Daniel's silence should be broken. If he came to England it wasn't likely that he would visit them now. Catherine's nerves had troubled her a lot during the past eight years—she had been attending the doctor for nervous debility for a long, long time —but the doctor couldn't give her medicine for her conscience, nor could she get comfort from the priest in confession, because she had withheld this sin of hers. At times it seemed too trivial to mention, at others too enormous to voice; but, after all, what she had done she had done for the best. But what had she achieved? Just the secret misery of five people, and that wasn't counting Daniel. She gripped the back of the couch as Bridget said, "What made you do it, Mother?"

"Made me do . . . what?"

"Don't fence; you know what I'm talking about. The letters."

Oh, my God! She would die. She couldn't bear this. She would drop through the earth with shame in having to admit to doing such a vile thing.

"Four letters you owe me. Did you read them all?"

Catherine was moving her head slowly from side to side now, its action begging understanding.

"You must have been hard put not to give the show away that he had been here all day on the Sunday when you packed me off to Hexham, remember?"

"Oh, Bridget! Bridget!"

"And . . . and he was here on my wedding day, that very morning. He was just an hour late. You must have been very thankful for that, because if he had come before I left the house I might never have left it, at least not with Peter, because I knew then—I'd known for weeks—that I didn't love

464

Peter; that the feeling I had for him was tenderness, and pity, but not love. . . . But I may be wrong there, at least about not marrying him, because I had already told Daniel that I intended to marry Peter because I couldn't hurt you all. That was my main concern, not hurting anybody, particularly Aunt Katie. Oh, Aunt Katie mustn't be hurt. Yet you all put your heads together to hurt me, by getting me married off as quickly as possible. . . . Tell me one thing; was Peter in on this?"

Bridget watched Catherine leave the support of the couch and grope towards a chair. She watched her drop her elbows on to a small table and bury her face in her hands, but she felt no pity towards her for the moment, and she repeated her question, "Was he? I'm asking you, was Peter in on this? I want to know."

"Partly, partly." The words were smothered. "Your . . . your father told him how . . . how things stood."

"Dad! Dad told him? No! No!" Bridget's tone was bitter. "I wouldn't have believed he'd do that, not him."

Catherine raised her face from her hands. Her eyes were bright and dry and her voice held a flat, hopeless sound as she said, "He . . . he was against it. He didn't realize there was anything between . . . between you and Daniel until I told him. He wasn't for it at all, for no part of it. Believe me on that."

There came to them the sound of the front door opening and they both turned their eyes in the direction of the room door. Then Catherine, once more putting her elbows on the table, buried her face in her hands; and she was like this when Tom came in.

He stood just within the doorway and asked sharply, "What is it? Aunt Katie?"

Catherine made a movement with her head but did not lift it, and Tom, going to her side, looked down at her for a moment, then towards Bridget, her face stiff-looking, her eyes hard, and he asked, "What's all this about? You two . . .?"

He did not end, "You two had a row?" He had never known Catherine and Bridget to have cross words in their lives, so he dismissed the idea, and on a rising note he demanded, "Well! What is it?"

"Daniel's been."

"Daniel!" Slowly Tom lifted his eyes from Catherine's bent head to Bridget, and after what seemed a long time he said,

"I knew this would happen some day. I'm sorry, lass. I'm to blame for a lot of things. I shouldn't have listened to your mother, I should have told you he had been here waiting for you."

"Oh—oh, that! That's nothing, that's nothing." Catherine had sprung to her feet and was confronting Tom, her voice hysterical now. "If it was only that it wouldn't matter. Anyway, you've got to know now; I've been wanting it off my chest for years. . . . I . . . I opened his letters to her, and . . . and kept them." Her chin was thrust out as if in defiance, but her face was twisted with pain, and Tom looked from her to Bridget and back to her again before he said, "What's this? You . . . you opened his letters?"

"Yes, yes; you heard me. He wrote her four letters from that Sunday, and I opened them and burnt them."

"No! No, lass." It had a sorrowful sound, pitying and sorrowful.

"I became as frightened of him as Aunt Katie was." Catherine was now holding her hands over her ears as if unable to bear her own voice. "And then there was the thought of her going away, to America perhaps, and . . . and not knowing what would happen to her, and always . . . always remembering his name and what he had come from. But anyway, no matter, that's just an excuse. I shouldn't have done what I did. I know that. Oh God, how I know it! . . . And I'm not blaming Aunt Katie, mind; I should have put my foot down, but, as I said, I was as frightened as she was of him. . . . So there! And now you know."

She brought her hands down from her face, and, leaning them on the little table for support, she bent over it, and Tom, coming to her and putting his arm about her, said, "Whatever you did, lass, you did with good intentions. Of that I am sure. Come on now, come on. What has to be will be." He was talking to her as if Bridget wasn't there, and Bridget realized that her father wasn't so concerned about Daniel coming to the house and his reaction on herself, but he was deeply concerned about Daniel's reaction on her mother. His love for her would shield and shelter her from any censure, even her own. But Bridget knew it wasn't her husband's condemnation that Catherine feared but her daughter's, and when she remembered all the love and kindness she had received from her over the years the hardness inside her melted. She remembered that, in a way, she herself had been thrust upon Catherine; there had been no real love in her begetting. But Catherine had loved her devotedly from the beginning, as had her father. No, not her father; he was just Tom Mulholland, but he had been to her as no ordinary father could have been. His love for her mother could have made him jealous of this child that was not his, but never once had he shown the slightest jealousy of her. He had made her feel wanted, protected.

She moved towards them both, and they turned and looked at her; and when she put her arms about Catherine and Catherine began to cry piteously, Tom put his arms about both of them, and together they stood united once more, at least outwardly, for they all knew in some measure, that the chain between them was broken. For good or bad, the last eight years was about to be wiped out, and as yet there were only two people not aware of it; Peter and Aunt Katie.

2

"It's all right, Aunt Katie. Now, it's all right. You needn't see him if you don't want to."

"I don't want to, Catherine."

"Well, then, there's nobody going to force you."

"Will he think it very funny, me not wanting to see him?"

"No, no, of course not. He knows you are not well and very tired."

"Are you sure he doesn't know, Catherine?"

Catherine turned away to a side-table and carefully measured out a dose from the medicine bottle before saying, "Now, Aunt Katie, I've told you a dozen times already he knows nothing about it. Everything is all right."

"What if Bridget should find out?"

"She won't."

"She didn't come and kiss me good-night last night, Catherine."

"She was very tired, Aunt Katie. And she came in this morning, didn't she?"

467

"Yes, yes, she came in this morning. Catherine. Catherine."

"Yes, dear?"

"If . . . if I saw him I'd have to tell him, because it's been on my mind for many a long day."

"Don't worry about it, dear."

"But I do, Catherine, I do. And don't . . . don't"—she smacked Catherine's hand away—"don't treat me as if I was in my dotage. I'm old, I know, and my mind gets clouded at times, but at others I can still think clearly."

"I know you can, Aunt Katie."

"Catherine."

"Yes, Aunt Katie?"

"Look at me, Catherine."

Catherine turned from the table and, taking the big bony hand in hers, she said, "What is it?"

"It's just this, Catherine. Do you know that Bridget has never been happy?"

"Oh, Aunt Katie. Aunt Katie." There were tears in Catherine's voice and she buried her chin on her chest. "Don't say that, please, not at this stage."

"It's the only stage left to me, Catherine, the only stage, and I've got to say it. I could say to you an' all that I'm frightened because he's come back and of what might happen to her, but I won't; it's all in God's hands. But she's not happy, she's never been happy. I did her a great wrong, Catherine."

"No, no, Aunt Katie, you didn't. It was me."

"Oh. Oh." Again Katie slapped Catherine's hand.

"You wouldn't have dreamed about it but for me and my fear of the Rosiers. I did it because of my fear of the Rosiers. And it's funny, Catherine, but I don't fear him any more. I saw him last night as plain as a pike-staff. He was crossing the yard on the way to the stables dusting down his boots, and I had fallen with some buckets of slops and it had splashed his clothes and he helped me to my feet and said it was all right; and then I watched him going to the stables. That happened a long time ago, and he didn't help me to my feet, it wasn't him, but last night he did. And I wasn't afraid of him any more."

"Lie quiet now, dear, and don't talk."

"Catherine. Catherine, don't treat me like a child."

Catherine drew in a long, deep sigh; then, picking up a

dirty glass and spoon from the table, she went towards the open door, and as she did so Katie said to her, "Will you close the door, Catherine?"

The door was nearly always left open so that Katie could see into the hall, and now Catherine closed it and stood with her back to it and bit on her lip before going into the kitchen. . . .

Daniel arrived at half-past four. Catherine opened the door to him and he looked straight into her face and said quietly, "Hello, Catherine." And she looked back at him and, her voice also quiet, she said, "Hello, Daniel."

As he brought his stiff leg over the step she looked down at it. Bridget hadn't told her it was his leg. In fact, she had hardly spoken to her since last night. She may have forgiven her, but there was a barrier between them which she felt could never be torn down. And now she had to face this man, for Daniel was no longer a boy. And she had looked upon him as a boy, although he was twenty-five when they had first met. The Daniel before her now was a man, very much of a man. She took his cap and walked towards the dining-room, and he followed, and they both seated themselves without speaking.

When he did speak it was the polite enquiry of, "How are you, Catherine?"

But her answer wasn't the formal reply, for she said, "I'm feeling dreadful, Daniel, so low that I could crawl under a stone."

He did not come back immediately with the soothing comment, "Oh, don't take it like that, it's all over and done with, there are graver issues to be thought about, and worried over. There's a war on, remember." What he did say was, "I find it hard to fit you in the picture, Catherine. Do you know what I think? I think you were led by Aunt Katie."

"Oh, no! No, Daniel. No."

"Yes, yes, Catherine. You didn't hate the Rosiers as Great-grandmother does. You had no cause to hate as she did. You were fearful, yes, that I might turn out like my great-grandfather, but I think that, left to yourself, you would have given me the benefit of the doubt. But not Great-grandmother; she had gone through all the mill at the hands of a Rosier, so there were no good Rosiers. I loved Bridget deeply then, Catherine. I'd never loved before, and I've never loved since. I've been married and am now divorced, but I've never loved anyone but Bridget. I hated her for a time when I thought she had coldly ignored my every move towards her, but hate is so akin to love that I don't know where one stopped and the other started. You know, over the years, whoever I've met—women, I mean—I've always compared them with Bridget; and that's strange, because we knew so little about each other really. But deep down there's been the knowledge that she's the only one I wanted . . . ever."

"Oh, Daniel, Daniel. I'm sorry."

"I believe you, Catherine, so don't worry any more about it."

"But she's married now, Daniel, it's done. There's no divorce for her."

His eyes darkened for a moment and his eyebrows moved upwards, but his voice was quiet as he said, "We'll see about that, Catherine."

She moved her hand slowly up to her throat, and as she whimpered "Oh, Daniel!" Tom came into the room. He came in hurrying, and then stopped abruptly just over the threshold; and he pushed the door closed without turning round, and as Daniel edged himself to his feet he came forward unhurriedly now and said, "Hello, there, Daniel. Don't . . . don't get up."

But Daniel was up. Supporting himself with one hand on the back of the chair, he held out the other, and Tom took it. Gravely they shook hands.

"How are you, Daniel?"

"Oh, pretty well."

Tom now pulled a chair forward, and as he sat down Catherine rose to her feet and quietly left the room; and after Tom had glanced in the direction of the door for a moment he turned and, looking at Daniel's leg, said, "How did you come by that, Daniel?"

"Oh, the plane came down in the sea, and me with it."

"You're lucky to be alive."

"Very lucky, Tom, very lucky."

"Did they pick you up right away?"

"No, no, five days later."

"Good God! And you had that all the time?"

"Oh, I didn't know much about it, that was one good thing."

"You didn't lose it?"

"No, no, it's still mine." He patted his thigh. "But there's a pin up here and another in the middle. Someday, when they bring out a contraption of hinges, I might be able to bend it in both places."

"I should say again you're lucky to be alive."

"Yes, Tom, you could say that."

"Are you going to be long in hospital?"

"I think I'll be there another fortnight, or three weeks; then, as far as I can gather, I'll be attached to a training station. It was touch and go when I first joined whether I would take a backroom job or train as a pilot; now it looks as if I'm going to get experience in both fields."

Tom now walked to the mantelpiece, and after a moment said, "I'd better get this off my chest, Daniel, for it's lying on me like a hundredweight of coal. We've all done you dirty and we're not very happy about it. I might as well tell you I've never been very happy about it, but it was owing to the circumstances. You see, Daniel, it was the circumstances." He turned and looked down on Daniel. "Peter's a good fellow, honest as the day's long, steady and reliable, and he thought—and still thinks—the world of her. What's more, they were of the same religion; there was no trouble that way —not that I care a tinker's cuss about what religion anybody is. It wouldn't have mattered to me if he had been a Salvation Army wallah, but it matters to other people, if you see what I mean. Well, what I'm trying to say, Daniel, is that at the time it seemed the right thing to do to help it forward, but since . . . Well, I don't mind admitting to you now I've had me doubts, but mind you"—he wagged his finger at Daniel—"I still think Peter's a good chap, he hasn't altered a scrap. He'd cut off his right hand for her. But she doesn't want anybody to cut off their right hand for her, if you see what I mean."

"I see what you mean, Tom. And it's all right, don't worry. The matter's closed, and let it rest there."

"Oh! It's not going to be as easy as that, Daniel. From the way I see it . . . it's just opened, not closed."

"Well, it's all the way you look at it, Tom."

"Aye, Daniel, it's all the way you look at it. But there's one thing I know—there'll be no more interfering with her life if I can help it. The saying that life is short was never so

471

true as it is the day. My mother used to say 'You're here the day and gone the morrow', but now you can whittle that down to 'You're here one second and gone the next'."

As Daniel said, "That's true enough. Yes, it's only too true today," Tom put his head on one side and cocked his ear. "That's her coming now," he said. "I'll leave you for a time . . . you'll be staying to tea?"

"If it's convenient, Tom."

"Oh, it's convenient, Daniel. Any time, any time."

He went out of the room and Daniel heard the murmur of his voice in the hall; then a minute or so later Bridget came in. She was wearing a pale-grey print dress with a pattern of small flowers on it. Her eyes looked deep blue, her mouth was soft, and her hair danced with each step she took, like a child's when newly washed. She walked slowly towards him, each step tentative, and when they were within touching distance their hands clasped.

"You all right?" His voice was just above a whisper.

"Yes, yes, I'm all right." Her voice, too, was low.

They gazed at each other before he said, "Was it very bad last night?"

"Yes, very bad."

"It's been awful just now. First Catherine and then Tom. I wanted to say to her, 'Don't talk about it. Forget it, forget it.' But I think we both felt relief at being able to voice it."

"Dad knew nothing about the letters, Daniel. I feel I must tell you that."

"He didn't?"

"No. He'd never have stood for that. That business was between Mother and Aunt Katie, and on looking back I think that Aunt Katie was the prime mover in it all."

"I just don't think that, I know it."

"Yet I still love her."

"Go on loving her."

Her head drooped forward and her voice broke as she said, "Oh, Daniel! You're kind, so kind."

"You don't know me." His voice, too, was unsteady. "I'm anything but kind. I'm selfish and ruthless, and I've no intention of changing. I'm going to get what I want this time, Bridget. You could say that I'm . . . I'm like him in that respect. Aunt Katie's fears will be justified all right this time."

She lifted her eyes to his and said, "Oh, Daniel!" Then, wetting her lips and shaking her head, she added, "I don't know where I've been all day. I haven't known what I've been teaching. Yesterday life was just a matter of routine, trying to keep the children happy, waiting for the sirens going, hurrying home, taking my turn with Aunt Katie, going to bed, jumping up and rushing downstairs—the same routine over and over again. That was yesterday, but . . . but not today." She gathered his hand impulsively between her own and brought it to her mouth and pressed her lips against it; and he pressed his face against her head for a moment and murmured an endearment under his breath, then whispered softly, "Will you come out to the house with me? We can get a bus to within fifteen minutes walk of it. I have a late pass; I needn't get the train from Jarrow until after ten."

"Yes, Daniel." There was no hesitation to her answer. She looked up into his face and watched his bottom jaw moving backwards and forwards. She watched him drag his lower lip deep into his mouth with his teeth, and when he gripped her chin the force behind it shook them both, and quickly he said, "I'm sorry, I'm sorry. Did I hurt you?"

She moved her head now and whispered quickly, "They're coming."

Daniel was in the act of sitting down when Catherine and Tom came into the room, but Bridget did not move. She stood within an arm's length of his chair, and the action spoke to Catherine as clearly as if Bridget had yelled her intentions, and in the turmoil of her mind she cried silently to her daughter, "But you can't do this, Bridget, you can't! You're married to Peter. There's no such thing as divorce for you. You'd be living in sin. And he's not a Catholic either, which makes it worse. You can't . . . you can't do it."

Catherine did not consider her way of thinking ludicrous in any degree. She had been educated in a convent, she had been brought up by one Catholic parent, and even if she despised his bigotry she believed in the doctrine whereby he lived and for which, in his ignorance, he would have died.

* * *

When they got off the bus at the top of the hill, where the land rolled down into the valley, she said, "Oh, it's too far for you to walk from here."

"No, it's only about a mile, and they tell me I should walk." He reached out and drew her arm through his and

473

pressed it to his side, and as they walked down the rough road they were silent for a time. They both knew why they were making for the house. They must be alone together; after eight years they were craving to be alone together. They could never be alone in Loreto; nor, like an ordinary couple, could they walk the streets. Mrs. Conway, the school-teacher was too well known in Shields. With his uneven gait, his body rubbed against her with each step he took, but had she been naked and he clothed in sandpaper she wouldn't have flinched from his side.

She felt strangely elated. That was the only way she could describe the racing, churning feeling that had consumed her since last night. She was like a girl who had just fallen in love. And wasn't she a girl who had just fallen in love? Because the feeling she had for Daniel, which had its birth eight years ago, had been the first love she had experienced.

When he said to her, "Did they try to prevent you coming?" she shook her head, then said, "No."

"Did they know you were coming to the house?"

"I didn't say where I was going; I just said I was going out."

Again they were walking in silence. Then, some distance farther on, as if he was continuing the conversation, he said, "I just can't believe this is true."

"Nor me," she said.

When at last they came to the place where the gates had been they stopped for a moment and she exclaimed, "They've cleared the trees away!"

"Yes; that's one good thing the Army has done. They've cleared the drive and all round the house, but left a good border edging the land. They've also kicked the panelling to shreds inside, and carved their names all the way down the balustrade. Boys will be boys."

When they came on to the broad drive fronting the house, which was churned up now by heavy vehicles, she looked up at the grey gaunt structure. Most of the windows were broken, and to the side, as Daniel had said, all that remained of the outbuildings was a heap of rubble. She said softly, "What a shame!"

"They can be rebuilt."

She turned her eyes towards him as she asked, "Why . . . why did you keep it, Daniel?"

"Oh, for a number of reasons. My mother liked the idea of

an English manor house; I knew she would." He nodded at her. "She thought how nice it would be to have a real English manor house as a sort of—well, holiday home where all the family, and in-laws, and the children could come. She saw herself entertaining on a grand scale. I wanted to sell it, but she wouldn't hear of it unless she could buy it from me. . . . You see, I had paid for it myself. I had money of my own— my grandfather divided the yard shares among us many years ago. Anyway, I kept the house on, and the Robsons. You remember Willie and Maggie? They were here until the military moved in. They did a lot of work. Willie saw to the engaging of the decorators and to the panelling being renewed in the hall. It rather vexed me when I saw what had happened to that."

"You . . . you came back before the war then?" She was gazing up at him in surprise.

"Yes, after my divorce, in June 'thirty-nine."

"Why . . ." She paused. "Why didn't you come then, Daniel?"

"That's a question, Bridget. Why didn't I come then? The truth isn't very pleasant, even to myself. I . . . I was drinking hard at the time. I had just been divorced, after making myself and an innocent person very unhappy for two years. Anyway, I only stayed here for four days—that was all, four days—and I was high most of the time. But every day I was coming down to see you. Yet I knew if I did they would say, 'She's had a lucky escape. What did I tell you! There are no good Rosiers.' And there was just something, some spark of pride, that kept me away. I didn't want them, and you, to be proved right; so back home I went, took a pull at myself, said to hell with all women and wished a special hell for Bridget Mulholland." He put his arm round her shoulders and smiled softly. "It sounds very ordinary and everyday, doesn't it? The disappointed suitor marries, on the rebound, a girl he had known all his life—a beautiful girl, mind you." He nodded at her and hugged her closer. "But nobody should marry on the rebound, nobody. . . . Come on." He ended abruptly, "We'll have to go through the kitchen. I haven't a key for the front door."

In the kitchen she exclaimed, "The old stove's gone!" She pointed. "And you've put electricity in. Oh, Daniel!"

He led the way along the corridor, and when they entered the hall she stopped, as she had done before, and looked around her and said softly, "Even as bare as it is, it looks so different, lighter."

"It could look marvellous. It was beginning to, and the Robsons were so pleased with it all."

"Where are they now?"

"Oh, they've got a little house in a place called Low Fell. They're both in munitions, but when it's all over they say they're coming back. We must go and see them."

He limped across the hall and pushed open the drawing-room door. "They made a mess of this," he said. "It was all done in blue, gold and cinnamon. My mother sent over the colour scheme, right to the particular shades. But there's not much colour left now, except up towards the ceiling."

As they gazed upwards she said, "Oh, it is a shame. Pure vandalism."

"Still, we're the same—I mean our fellows. Put them in an empty house and it's a licence to go mad; and the better the house the worse they seem to treat it. But wait until you see the bathrooms. I'll swear to you that the whole company got into those baths with their boots on."

"Oh, Daniel!" She smiled at him and dropped her head for a moment against his shoulder. Then, laughing softly, they slowly mounted the stairs.

All the walls in the gallery were bare; and as she looked to where the picture of Bernard Rosier used to hang, he said, "They're all packed away."

He moved across the gallery and down the corridor, and inserting a key in the lock of a door he opened it. It was stacked to the ceiling with furniture, the only space left being a narrow passage that led from the door to the window. Going first, he edged his way between the stacked chairs and wardrobes, dressing-tables and bureaux, and when he came to the window he glanced at her over his shoulder and said, "You remember this room?"

Looking at the high posts of the bed, she nodded.

The bed was stacked with pillows, curtains and household linen. He pulled the covers aside and flung the things high up on top of others until there was enough room for them to sit down. And when they were seated they leant against each other, quiet and shy for a moment, knowing that they had reached the end of their destination . . . for the time being.

His cheek rubbing gently against hers, he said, "Do you know what I expected when I knocked on the door?"

"No."

"Well, I thought I'd be met by a very much older edition of the school-marm with almost a school of her own—at least six."

"Oh, Daniel!" She brought her face from his and looked into his eyes.

"Honest I did. At least, I think I was hoping to find that, but . . . but it never, never, never dawned on me that within an hour of seeing you I'd be holding you in my arms. Can you believe that?"

She nodded slowly. "Yes. Yes, I can believe that, Daniel. Yet I can't believe it's happened. I just can't. Anyway, not in such a short space of time. I feel I'm dreaming. I often imagined meeting you again and wondered how I would react, but I never thought I'd fall into your arms straight away . . . almost throw myself into them. Oh, Daniel!" She put up her hand and touched his hair. "I'm in a maze. I can't think clearly about anything, yet at the back of my mind there's a big question-mark: what's going to come of this?"

"You don't know?" His brows shot up towards his dark hair-line. "Well, I do. We're not going to be separated again, that's all. You know, and I know, for good or ill we're together. You'll get a divorce and we'll get married. . . ."

"No! Daniel, no! That's what I mean." Her head was moving in wide desperate sweeps now.

"*What!* Now, Bridget. *Now! Now!*" He thrust his hand beneath her chin and brought her face to a stop and forced her to look at him. "You're going to get a divorce and we're going to be married!" His voice sounded thin, tight, steel-edged.

"Yes, Daniel, yes. That's what I would say if I was speaking for myself, but I know that Peter will never divorce me."

He gazed fixedly at her. His lips were apart and he closed them twice before he asked from way down in his throat, "Then what, Bridget? You can't intend to . . .?"

"No, no, Daniel," she put in quickly, "I can't intend, and I don't intend, to stay with him. I'll go with you wherever you want me to." She was looking deep into his eyes. "As long as I'm with you nothing matters, married or not married."

"Oh, Bridget! Bridget!" Her name was smothered as his mouth moved around her face, and in their passage his lips broke into endearments. "Oh, darling, darling, Bridget, I love you. Do you hear me? I adore you. Remember adore, adore?

477

Well, I adore you. We'll live together and work together. We'll build that school together. It was a great idea, the school. We'll build it here in this house. . . ."

She did not stop him at this point and say, "No, not here, Daniel! It would be too near Peter, too near them. We mustn't hurt them more than we can help." Moreover, in this moment he didn't seem to realise that very few parents would send their children to a school where the proprietor was living in sin with a woman, and that's how their association would be looked upon. But it didn't matter, that was all in the future. The main thing at present was he knew that she would go with him; wherever he went, if it was possible she would be there also. She felt one arm leave her and knew that he was thrusting back the bedding, making a space for them to lie down. They could not fall naturally on to the bed because his leg didn't permit it, but, releasing her, his eyes never leaving hers, he stood up and gently pressed her backwards. Then, sitting on the edge of the bed again, he gave a swinging motion with his body and he was lying beside her. His eyes still holding hers, his hands caressing her, they came together for the first time and in the bed where his great-grandfather had slept in his early youth and young manhood, where he had taken Katie Mulholland on the night of the ball and had implanted in her the seed that was eventually to bring forth himself, Daniel Rosier the Third.

3

"I've been seeing a lot of Joe lately, Catherine."

"Have you, Aunt Katie."

"He was talking to me last night; he said he had been thinking about me just the night before he died and was sorry for being so stubborn. . . . Are you listening to me, Catherine?"

"Yes, Aunt Katie. Yes."

"I'm not wandering, Catherine, I'm wide awake."

"Yes, yes. I know you are, Aunt Katie."

"And I wasn't wandering last night when Joe was talking to me. I wasn't asleep either; he was as plain as plain, standing there where you are now. He said we always leave things too late, 'cos he was killed in that raid. You remember, Catherine?"

"Yes, yes. I remember, Aunt Katie, when the bomb from the Zeppelin hit Palmer's."

"But it didn't only hit Palmer's, it hit that row of houses. He had worked hard to buy that house, Catherine."

"Yes, yes, I know, Aunt Katie."

"It's a nice day outside; the sun is shining."

"Yes, and it's very warm for October."

"I'm a hundred, Catherine."

"Oh, you're a hundred and a bit, Aunt Katie. You've got to look forward to being a hundred and one."

"Catherine!"

"Yes, Aunt Katie."

"Don't you think it odd that I never see Andy?"

Catherine didn't answer but went on dusting the room.

"You know, I've seen all the others, talked with them all, right down as far back as I can remember, and yet isn't it funny, Catherine, that Andy was the only one that ever mattered to me and I never see him. Andy never comes and talks to me."

"Well, I suppose you were so close, Aunt Katie. I should think it's because he's . . . he's sort of inside you, he can't get any closer."

"I've never thought of that, Catherine. It's a nice thought. But still I'd like to see him. Andy was a wonderful man, Catherine."

"I know that. I know that, Aunt Katie. Now don't talk any more, just rest."

"Oh, don't say that, Catherine; I want to talk." The voice from the bed was several tones stronger and had a note of irritation in it. "I've always talked, Catherine. I was a great talker when I was young. Don't stop me talking, Catherine."

"Oh no, Aunt Katie." Catherine was bending over the bed now, stroking Katie's hair from her brow. "I wouldn't stop you talking for the world, but I thought it might tire you."

"What do I do to get tired? Lie here all day, waited on hand and foot. The way you look after me I could live until I'm a hundred and ten."

"You could indeed, Aunt Katie, you could indeed."

Katie was holding Catherine's hand now. "When is Peter coming home, Catherine?"

"Oh, Aunt Katie, we can't tell that, but it shouldn't be long. It's nearly fourteen weeks now. It's the longest he's been away yet. He could come walking in at any minute, or we could get a phone call if he has docked some place else, but we've just got to wait patiently."

"Catherine."

"Yes, Aunt Katie."

"Does . . . does he ask why I don't want to see him?"

Catherine bowed her head. "You mean Daniel?"

"You know who I mean, Catherine."

"No. No, he doesn't ask, Aunt Katie. He knows that you don't want to be bothered."

"It's funny him being in the house and me not seeing him, isn't it, Catherine?"

"But he so seldom comes here."

"But he was here yesterday."

"No, no, dear. He hasn't been near the house for weeks. Five weeks, I should say."

"I thought I smelt his pipe yesterday."

"He doesn't smoke a pipe, dear, he smokes cigarettes."

"He was here, I was sure, Catherine."

"You're mistaken, dear."

"What's going to happen to Bridget, Catherine?"

"Now don't you worry, dear; everything's going to be all right."

"No, it isn't, Catherine; not all right for Peter. I know. It doesn't matter about me or you or Tom, it's only Peter; and when he comes back there'll be nothing for him. I can see it in Bridget's face, she's happy."

Catherine turned from the bed now, saying under her breath, "Well, I thought that's what you wanted for her, to be happy."

"Yes, yes, I do."

"Well then."

Catherine now picked up a vase with some fading flowers in it and went out of the room, and as she crossed the hall to the kitchen Bridget came running down the stairs, Bridget the girl again. Dear, dear God! What was going to happen to her now with this new turn of events which she had foreseen right from the beginning?

480

Bridget stopped at the bottom of the stairs and said, "Mother, may I have a word with you?"

Catherine turned towards her, the vase held in both hands, and, looking over the flowers, she said, "When have you had to ask to have a word with me?"

Bridget lowered her eyes, then walked slowly forward and together they went into the kitchen, and there Bridget, standing near the table, brought her joined hands up into her neck as she said quietly, "I don't know how you're going to take this, but . . . but I'm going to have a baby."

"I know that."

They stared at each other across the table.

"How could you? I didn't know myself until yesterday."

"Your face told me, child. It's been full of hope for weeks now."

"Oh, Mother!"

"It's his, isn't it?"

"If you mean Daniel's, yes."

"My God!"

Catherine turned from the table and Bridget said sharply, "Why need you be so shocked? I've been open with you right from the beginning. I only stayed here because you asked me to, for Aunt Katie's sake, but once Peter comes back I'll go. I've told you, Mother. I'll have to go. We couldn't live in the same house, could we? And he has no other home now."

"It isn't fair to him, it isn't fair." Catherine was facing Bridget.

"Was he fair to me? Were any of you fair to me?"

"We've been all through that. I thought it was ended."

"Yes, it's ended. But when you talk of fairness to Peter I'm not just going to stand here and feel guilty. I don't feel guilty, nor do I feel sorry for anything Daniel and I have done. What we've done now we should have done eight years ago."

"Have . . . have you imagined what it will be like when Peter comes in and you've got to tell him?"

"Yes, yes, I've imagined that. Every day for the last three months and more I've imagined it, but that's not going to stop me from telling him." Again they were staring at each other, silent now, hostility rising between them.

"What if anything happens to him . . . to Daniel, and you're left with a child? Because what you seem to forget is that the war is still on. Your rosy dawn is only affecting you two. If anything happens to him, what's going to happen to the child if you insist on being on your own?"

Bridget's brows went up and her eyes stretched. "Good gracious, what do you take me for? I can always work, Mother. And listen. Whatever happens, I'm not going to let someone else take the responsibility. I was thinking about that yesterday. All that's happening now goes back to the time when Aunt Katie relinquished the responsibility for her daughter, and you . . ." Bridget checked the natural sequence to this; she could not face her mother and say, "And you in a way let someone else take the responsibility for me." But Catherine said it for her. Her voice bitter, she spoke under her breath, saying, "Go on, tell me I'm another Aunt Katie; that I married your father just to save my face. Well, it isn't true, it isn't true. I loved your father from when we were children."

"I'm not saying anything about my father and you," said Bridget softly. "I'm only answering your question, if anything should happen to Daniel what would I do? Well, there's one thing I wouldn't do. I wouldn't let Peter shoulder the responsibility. The child will be mine and Daniel's, no one else's— not by proxy or by any other way. Of that you can rest assured. He'll be a Rosier, and, one way or another, he or she will be brought up a Rosier. There's been enough hate and fear connected with that name, and it's going to end. It's only the fact that I still don't want to hurt any of you more than I can help that the child won't be brought up in the house that by rights will be his. . . . But you never know, he may be yet; things can happen."

Catherine stared long and hard at her daughter, and then she said, "Yes, things can happen. You're born, lass, but you're not buried yet; there's a lot can happen in between."

* * *

Bridget was standing at her bedroom window looking down on to the trees in the broad roadway. There were more people about than usual, likely because it was warm and a Saturday afternoon. She glanced down at her watch for almost the twentieth time in the last hour. It was a quarter past three. Daniel had said he would phone around half-past two. He must have been held up. She heard someone coming upstairs, and then her mother's voice from outside the bedroom door, saying, "Bridget?"

When she went to open it, Catherine, her face tired-looking and sad, said, "I've just had a message from Mrs. Pope. She wants to know if I'll do a few hours this evening because two of them have gone down sick. Would you mind staying in? It will only be from six until eight or half-past."

Bridget didn't answer for a moment, she just stared at Catherine. On Wednesday Daniel and she had planned to go up to the house today as usual, but last night he had phoned to say that things were a bit uncertain and that he might not be able to get down on time, but he would ring her and she had to stay put until she heard from him. What if he were to ring any minute and say he was waiting there for her? But here was her mother asking her to do this simple thing. "All right," she said, "go ahead. But . . . but I'll ask Daniel to come here when he phones."

Catherine said nothing to this, she just turned blankly away, and as Bridget went to close the door the phone rang, and she had to stop herself from running across the landing and down the stairs; but when she picked up the phone she was gasping a little as if she had been running. "Hello," she said.

"Bridget?"

"Yes."

The conversation from her end was always terse.

"Listen, darling, I'll be at the top of the road somewhere around seven. I can't make it before. All right?"

"Daniel, I've got to stay in until half-past eight or nine; Mother's got to go out. Can you come here?"

There was a pause before he said, "Yes; yes, of course. But, Bridget, listen. I . . . I want you to come back to the house tonight, to spend the night there."

"At the house?" She was screwing her face up at the phone.

"Yes. I can't explain it here, you understand? But, you see, I'm due to be moved. Monday, I should say. I thought we would have the week-end there. I can bring plenty to eat."

"Yes, yes, Daniel."

"You'll do that?"

"Yes, yes, of course." Her voice sounded ordinary, formal, but at the back of her mind she was picturing telling her

483

mother that she was going to spend the week-end with Daniel in the empty house.

"Daniel."

"Yes, darling."

"You don't know where, do you—where you're being sent?"

"I'll explain when we meet. But don't worry; it isn't all that far away. No water, you understand?"

She drew in a long breath before she said, "Yes, Daniel. Yes, I understand." And she was smiling a little now. "Daniel."

"Yes, my love."

Her voice dropped to a low whisper. "I've got news for you too. What we were talking about on Wednesday, you remember?"

There was a long silence and she said, "Daniel, are you there?"

"Yes, I'm here. Oh, Bridget, my Bridget."

"I've got to go now."

"Darling. Darling. I can't wait to see you. I'll be there as soon after seven as possible. Till then . . . my Bridget."

"Goodbye, Daniel."

She turned from the phone and put her fingers across her mouth. She was going to spend the night with Daniel, all night. They could lie in each other's arms and not have to say "We'd better be going now."

Now she did run upstairs. She had the silly notion that she must pack some clothes; but there was no need to pack anything, not a thing.

*   *   *

Catherine left the house at six o'clock. She just said, "I'm going now," and Bridget answered, "All right, Mother." She hadn't told her she'd be staying out all night; that was better said at the last minute so there'd be no time for argument, persuasion, or recrimination. But the recrimination, no doubt, would come later.

She went into the drawing-room and seated herself near the window. Katie had her eyes closed, and Bridget didn't know whether she was asleep or not until, after a while, she spoke, saying quietly, "Catherine."

"It's me, Aunt Katie."

"Oh, Bridget!" Katie opened her eyes. "Where's Catherine? I want to see her for a minute."

"She's had to go out for a while—to the post, you know. They're short-handed. She told you."

"Did she? Yes, perhaps; I've likely forgotten. I've been sleepy all afternoon, I wish I didn't want to sleep so much. You know, I've had a very nice dream, Bridget."

"Have you, Aunt Katie."

"It was about a sailing ship. I was on it, and yet I wasn't on it. Yet I could see its name as plain as plain. It was called the *Mercur*. Do you remember the *Mercur*, Bridget?"

"No, Aunt Katie, I don't remember it."

"Oh, you must have seen a picture of it in the *Gazette*. You remember I cut it out. It said it was sailing to Norway with coke. Don't you remember? And that isn't so very long ago either. Andy used always to speak of the *Mercur;* that's how I know her so well. She was a Danish ship, you know, Bridget."

"Was she, Aunt Katie?"

"I like to dream about ships. Andy was always dreaming about ships."

Katie went on talking, mostly to herself now, her words unintelligible, and Bridget sat looking out of the window, counting the minutes to when Daniel would come.

Towards seven o'clock she went quietly out of the room and into the kitchen, and having heated some milk and put it on a tray, together with some biscuits, she went back into the drawing-room, and said softly, "Are you awake, Aunt Katie? Would you like your milk now?"

"Yes, yes, I'm awake, Bridget. Yes, dear. Thank you, I feel like a hot drink. . . . Do you think there'll be a raid to-night?"

"Oh no, I don't suppose so. We haven't had anything for some time now; there won't be any raid tonight."

"I had a funny feeling a little while ago. I thought I heard the warning, but I must have been dreaming, mustn't I, Bridget?"

"Yes, Aunt Katie. There hasn't been any warning, and it's such a nice evening there won't be anything tonight."

"I hope not, I hope not. I get a little frightened when the warning goes; and that's silly, because it doesn't matter, does it?"

"Drink your milk up, Aunt Katie."

"Yes, dear. Yes, dear." With a hand that was remarkably steady Katie held the saucer on which stood the glass of milk, and slowly she sipped it; and after a while, when Bridget was seated near the window again, she said quickly, "Peter should soon be home, shouldn't he, Bridget?"

There was a short pause before Bridget answered, "It's very uncertain when he will be here, Aunt Katie."

There was nothing further said, and after a while Bridget rose and took the tray from off the bed-table and went out of the room. As she did so the bell rang and, putting the tray down, she hurried to the door. And there stood Daniel.

When she had closed the door behind him they enfolded each other tightly, and they stood like this for some seconds. Then, their faces apart, he looked down at her and said, "It's true then?"

"Yes, darling. Yes . . . Ssh!" She stilled his exclamation and, taking his hand, led him towards the dining-room; but once inside, their arms about each other again, he said, "Oh, Bridget! Bridget! This is the happiest moment of my life. . . . Are you happy?"

"So happy I feel drunk. I do, I do. Oh, Daniel! If you only knew how I've longed and longed for this to happen over the years."

"You were waiting for me. Oh, my dear. My dear." He was pressing her head into his neck and running his fingers through her hair, when, suddenly jerking her body back from him, she said, "What is this about moving? I'd forgotten for the moment." Her face was straight now and full of concern.

"Oh, it's not as bad as it might be. I'm being sent to a place called Creydon Hill in Herefordshire."

"Herefordshire? Oh, that's miles away."

"Yes, it is, but it's still in England. I had the jitters yesterday when I was sent for; I thought I was going to be packed off home."

"Oh no, Daniel! That would have been awful."

"I'll say. But look; you . . . you can come down there. I understand it's all countryside and there are cottages and farmsteads where you could be put up. I was talking to one of the fellows in the office this morning. He's an English fellow. He used to be at Madley; that's an R.A.F. station not far off. He said it would be a piece of cake getting digs. He had his wife staying there for nearly two years."

"Oh, Daniel!" She released herself and moved just the slightest way back from him. "I couldn't come right away."

"Why not?"

"Well . . . well, there is my teaching. If I don't do it they could drop me into something else. I could always ask for a transfer, but it might take time. And then, Daniel, I'll . . . I'll have to face Peter before I come. It'll have to be a clean cut."

"Yes, yes, I know, dear. I know." He dropped his head slowly. "But . . . but as soon as he gets in you'll tell him; you won't put it off, will you?"

"As soon as ever he comes in I'll tell him. I promise you, Daniel."

He brought the palm of her hand up to his mouth and whispered against it, "You won't let them talk you round? I mean because of . . . Aunt Katie. I can hear Catherine saying, 'Wait until she goes'."

"She's already said that, dear, and she's had her answer. The only one I'm waiting for is Peter. When that's over, I'll be ready to leave the house, and the town, if it's all right with the school, as I said."

"Oh, we'll fix that in some way." He tossed his head now as if that was a minor issue and pulled her towards the couch, and when they were seated he put his hand into his inside pocket and brought out a long envelope. Then, placing it in her hand, he put his over the top of it, saying, "This is for you. I had the idea of doing it eight years ago. It's late in coming, but there it is, all signed and sealed. And what better day to give it to you than on the day on which Daniel the Fourth is announced; because he will be a Daniel, I feel it in here." He dug his thumb into his chest. Then, smiling tenderly at her, he said, "Well, aren't you going to open it or even ask what it is?"

The envelope wasn't sealed and she extracted from it a thick folded document, and when she opened it her eyes flicked over the closely written legal terms, then came back to the top and read, "The free-hold property known as Greenwall Manor, situated in the outskirts of Jarrow in the County of Durham. The property stands in thirty acres of land. It is built of quarried stone and has twenty main rooms comprising . . ." She lifted her eyes and glanced up at Daniel; his expression was slightly amused—pleased, but slightly

487

amused. "Turn over the page," he said. "Better still, turn to the last page."

Slowly she did as he had bade her, and there she read, "I hereby make as deed of gift to Bridget Conway the house known as Greenwall Manor in the County of Durham, together with all furniture and effects therein. . . ."

She lifted her face again to his. Her mouth wide, her eyes stretched, she gaped at him, then whispered, "But why? Why, Daniel?"

"Why! Because I wanted you to have it. Yours. Somehow I've always wanted you to have it. It's a strange feeling, but there it is. That day when you first entered the house—you remember?—I said to myself, 'One day I'll give her this'."

"Oh, Daniel! Daniel, I can't."

"You can't what?"

"Well, I mean, a manor house—take a manor house."

His face was solemn now as he said, "If I were your husband, Bridget, you would take a gift from me. I look upon you as my wife. I have done from that evening back in the house. I always shall. It's a gift from a husband to a wife. What should surprise you about that?"

She drooped her head and held her brow for a moment, saying, "It's so colossal, Daniel." Then, with a cry, she fell against him, her arms about him, hugging him to the limit of her strength, whispering the while, "Oh, Daniel! Daniel."

When he looked at her again the tears were running from her eyes and she said brokenly on a laugh, "What if I threw you out?"

"You just try it, madam." Again they were close, and after a while she said, "I . . . I just can't take it in."

"Well, you'd better try, because that's where our boy is going to be brought up. Likely with dozens of other squalling brats. . . . Oh, oh, not yours, ma'am!" They fell against each other, laughing now somewhat unrestrainedly, until Bridget, coming to herself, put her hand over her mouth and glanced towards the door. Then, gazing up at Daniel, she said softly, "I wouldn't mind having dozens of your children, Mr. Rosier."

"Thank you, Bridget Mulholland. . . . I think of you by that name, you know." There was a pause while their glances held the love in each other's eyes, then in a mock stern voice he stated, "Eleven, that's all I'm going to give you. Not another one over eleven." Again they were leaning against each other, their bodies shaking, and after a moment he said, "It's all right about tonight?"

She nodded at him and he squeezed her chin in his hands. "I've left a parcel of foodstuff at a little shop on the main road. You know, near where we branch off. I said I'd collect it later; I didn't want to lug it all this way."

"How will we make a fire?" she asked.

"There's plenty of wood; we'll play Boy Scouts in the kitchen."

"Oh, Daniel!" She rubbed her cheek against his, then said, "It's getting dusk; I'd better put the black-outs up." As she rose from the couch he put his arm around her waist and pressed his face into her breasts. "Don't be long," he said.

In the drawing-room, Katie, her eyes wide, greeted her with, "Who was that called, Bridget?"

"Someone from the school, Aunt Katie." She switched on the shaded bedside light before going towards the window and pulling down the dark blind; then she drew the curtains.

"Have they gone now?"

"No, not yet, Aunt Katie."

"Is it Ivy, Bridget?"

"No, you wouldn't know them, Aunt Katie." She went out of the room without looking towards the bed again.

She had just finished completing all the black-outs when the menacing wail of the siren blew over the town and brought her head snapping back on to her shoulders as she looked upwards. "Oh no! Not tonight."

As she reached the dining-room door Daniel was there, and they looked at each other, and after a moment he said, "It may not be for long; it may just be a hit-and-run."

She nodded at him, then said, "Aunt Katie's always nervous of the raids, I think I'd better look in."

"Yes, all right. . . . Look, about this. You'd better put it in a safe place." He handed her the envelope. "I must take you up to Barretts in Newcastle and introduce you. I should have done it before. They handle my business."

"Yes, darling. Yes, I'll put it into a safe place." She reached up swiftly and kissed him, and as she did so a thin voice came from the drawing-room, calling, "Catherine! Catherine!" and Bridget started and said, "I'll have to go in with her. She'll get agitated."

She glanced down at the envelope in her hand, then towards the stairs, then back to Daniel, and, thrusting it into his hand, said, "Keep it for me for a minute." And she turned and hurried towards the drawing-room.

As she opened the door Katie was again calling, "Catherine! Catherine!" and she said quickly, "It's all right, Aunt Katie. Don't worry."

"Where's your mother?"

"She's still at the post, Aunt Katie; but it's all right, she won't be long. She should be back any minute."

"The warning's gone, Bridget."

"Yes, I know, Aunt Katie, but it may be nothing. They're likely miles out to sea."

"I wish Catherine was back."

"Now don't worry." Bridget was bending over the bed.

"I can't help worrying. She should be in the shelter. You go down to the shelter."

"I'll do no such thing."

"Do this to please me, Bridget. Go down to the shelter. I don't mind being left alone."

"Don't tell fibs, Aunt Katie."

"I don't want you to get hurt, Bridget."

"There's no one going to get hurt, Aunt Katie. Now don't worry. I'm going to sit here." Her voice was cut off by the sound of the phone ringing, and she ended, "I'll just go and answer the phone. Now don't worry."

As she went across the hall she looked towards the dining-room door where Daniel was still standing, then she lifted the phone and said, "Hello."

"Is that you, Mrs. Conway?"

"Yes. Who's speaking?"

"It's Mrs. Faulks. I'm at the post. Your mother has had a bad turn. She fainted right away, but she's come round now. I'm rather worried; there's no one to see her home. There's only Mrs. Bailey and me in the post, and we can't leave. She says . . . your mother says she'll be quite all right, but I don't think she should go back on her own. It's no use trying to contact your father; he'll be around the dock and will have to stay there until the all-clear. Do you think you could slip along?"

Bridget looked over her shoulder and beckoned Daniel towards her, then said, "Yes, Mrs. Faulks, I'll be along as soon as I can. It'll take me about ten minutes to get there. Keep her there until I come, anyway."

"Yes, I'll do that, Mrs. Conway. Goodbye."

490

"Goodbye."

Bridget turned and looked up at Daniel, saying, flatly, "The fates seem against us. Mother's unwell. They've phoned through for me to bring her home."

"Where is she?"

"At a post near the Chichester. It won't take me long to get there. I can do it in ten minutes if I hurry, and I'll try to get some kind of a lift back." She paused for a moment and, putting her hand up to his face, said, "But if she's not well I won't be able to leave her until father comes, and that could be any time with the warning on. I'm sorry, Daniel."

He smiled at her. "Don't let it worry you. We'll have tomorrow, and all the tomorrows. Go on, get your coat on. Be quick."

After he had helped her on with her coat he put his hands on her shoulders and said, "I should be worrying with you going out and the warning on, but I'm not; for, you know, I've got a feeling on me tonight that we're going to live forever, you and I, and Daniel the Fourth." He dropped his hands to her stomach, and she put both of hers on top of his for a moment, then swiftly she flung her arms around his neck and kissed him hard.

At the door she paused and, pointing towards the drawing-room, said softly, "If she gets agitated and calls out, do you . . . do you think you could go in to her?"

"Leave her to me," he said. "Go on now and get back quickly, quickly, for I can't bear you out of my sight."

He watched her running down the path; at the gate she turned and waved to him. He watched her until her figure was lost in the deep dusk between the trees, then he closed the door and walked towards the dining-room again, and as he entered it he heard the thin voice coming once more from the drawing-room, calling this time, "Bridget! Bridget!"

He put his head on one side and listened for a moment, considering; then slowly he limped across the hall and, after tapping on the door, he entered the room.

Katie was in the act of ringing the bell and she exclaimed, "Oh, Bridget, I'm so . . ." Her thin voice trailed away and she peered through the subdued lighting of the room and said, "Who's that?"

"Just me, Great-grandmother. Daniel."

When he reached the bed her eyes were wide and unblinking, staring up at him.

491

"How are you?"

When she didn't answer he pulled the seat forward and eased himself down and, looking at her, he saw she was agitated. Her old face was quivering, the lips chewing on one another. He put out his hand and taking hers patted it gently, saying, "Don't worry. It will all be over soon. The all-clear will go any minute now."

Katie made a movement with her head, and then spoke his name softly. "Daniel," she said.

"Yes, Great-grandmother?" He waited until her munching lips became steadier, patting her hand the while; then she asked in a whisper, "Where's Bridget, Daniel?"

"She's . . . she's had to go out for a moment."

"Where to?"

"Catherine wanted her. She called her from the post."

"Something's happened to Catherine?"

"No, nothing has happened to Catherine. She called her from the post."

"Tom?"

"No, nothing has happened to Tom either. They're all right."

"Why did Bridget have to go?"

He again patted the hand in his, saying, "I think Catherine had some things to carry back and they were too heavy for her."

The explanation seemed to satisfy her, and she sank farther into the pillows and lay quiet for a moment. Then, without looking at him, she said again, "Daniel." And again he said, "Yes, Great-grandmother?"

"I'm a wicked woman, Daniel."

"You wicked, Great-grandmother! What makes you think that?"

"I'm a wicked woman, Daniel. You know why I'm a wicked woman, Daniel?"

"Don't talk any more."

"I've got to talk, Daniel. Bridget has turned against me, Daniel."

"Nonsense. Nonsense." He shook his head.

"She has, because I sent you away. It was me who sent you away. It was me, Daniel."

He made no reply to this, and she was quiet for a moment. And then she said, "I missed you, Daniel."

"Did you, Great-grandmother?"

"Yes, very much. I didn't tell Catherine that because of what I'd done to Bridget, you see, but I did miss you I . . . I wanted to see you again—even . . . even if you were like him I wanted to see you again."

There came a dull crunching sound from the distance, and her thin jerky voice stopped and she gripped at his hand before saying, "They're dropping."

"No, that was just an anti-aircraft gun. Don't worry."

"It was a bomb."

"No. No."

"I'm . . . I'm always afraid when they're out they'll get killed."

"Don't worry. Don't worry." He glanced at his watch. She should be nearly there now. Ten minutes, she had said. Hurry, Bridget, my love. Hurry. Hurry.

"You love Bridget, Daniel?"

He looked down into the eyes that were looking up into his now, and he said from deep in his throat, "Very much, Great-grandmother. Very much."

"You're going to take her away, aren't you, Daniel?"

"Yes. Yes. I'm going to take her away, but not far. After the war we're going to live in the house."

The hand trembled in his and she whispered, "The house?"

"Yes. Look." He put his hand into his inside pocket and drew out the long envelope. "I gave this to Bridget tonight. It's the deeds of the Manor. I've made a gift of it to her."

Katie's body made a movement in the bed. Her elbow dug into the mattress and she tried to raise herself. Her head flopping back, her mouth open, she remained like this for a while. There was a light on her face, a brightness in her eyes. Her chin moved up and down before she said, in a voice that seemed to hold a touch of laughter, "Andy bought me a house. Mr. Kenny gave it to me, and when I opened it I had a house . . . three houses. Andy did that for me."

"Isn't that strange, Great-grandmother. Isn't that strange, now." He was smiling broadly at her. "Your Andy bought you a house and I've bought my Bridget one. Don't you think that augurs well for the future? When did your Andy buy you the house, Great-gran?"

"What?" Her attention had gone from him, and she brought it back to him, saying, "What did you say, Daniel? What did you say?"

"When did your Andy buy you a house?"

"Oh, a long, long time ago. I was very young, just turned twenty or so. But that would be . . ." Her eyes screwed up in an effort to remember the year, and he, doing some quick arithmetic, said, "It must have been 1865 or 66."

"Yes, Daniel. You're right. That's it, 1866." Her voice quivered. "My Andy was a wonderful man, Daniel."

"I'm sure he was, Great-grandmother."

"You know, I was saying to Catherine that I never see Andy. I've seen all the others, they've all been here, but not Andy. Isn't that funny, Daniel?"

"You'll see him one of these days, Great . . ." His voice was cut off by another crunch—this time one that shuddered the house; and when it passed he was on his feet holding both Katie's hands, saying, "There now. There now. Don't worry; it's over."

When her grip loosened on his hands and she lay back she smiled weakly, saying, "I get frightened, Daniel. It's silly, but I get frightened. But you know, Daniel, I feel I will know when I'm going to die because at the last minute I'll see Andy. I know he'll come for me then."

"Well, you're not going to see him tonight, dear."

"I've wondered, Daniel, how I'll tell Andy about you, and you a Rosier, because he knew that a Rosier had been an enemy to me all my life. Do you think he'll understand me being able to love a Rosier, Daniel?"

"Yes, Great-grandmother." His voice was soft and deep. "I think he'll understand all right."

He took his hands from hers and was about to assist himself into the chair again when the earth erupted beneath his feet and the heavens split open above his head. As her arms came out to him he flung himself into them, and over her, and together they went down, and Katie died in the arms of a Rosier.

*   *   *

It was dawn the following morning when, after carefully moving the wreckage brick by brick and timber by timber, they exposed the top rail of the bed. Across it, in a crazy pattern, lay beams, splintered floorboards, and part of a window-frame. The chief warden, after holding up his hand for silence, listened, then called sharply and waited, after which he nodded and the group of men started once more to hand pieces of debris one to the other.

On the outskirts of the rubble Catherine stood holding on to Bridget, and her voice sounded raw and cracked as she said, "Stay where you are, they've told you; you'll do more harm than good."

Tom, stumbling over the rubble, came towards them; covered from head to foot in dust and dirt, he was almost as unrecognizable as they were. It was at Bridget he looked and to her he spoke. "Go to the rest centre, lass . . . please," he said. "I'll come for you the minute they get through."

For answer Bridget shook her head slowly, and Tom exchanged a look with Catherine, then asked softly, "You all right?"

Catherine nodded. All right, he'd asked. She'd never be all right in her life again, not after this night; and what it would do to her Bridget, God only knew.

There came an exchange of excited voices from the manmade crater that had once been the cellar of the house, and Bridget, with a twist of her body, broke Catherine's hold and in a second she was scrambling over the rubble.

Tom caught hold of her as they reached the rim of the hole and his eyes followed hers to where, under a trelliswork of two big beams and a layer of grey laths, was the back of a man's head and shoulders.

"Daniel. Daniel."

"Steady, lass, steady. Listen a minute."

"Can you get through, Fred?" The man's voice was soft as if he were afraid to shout.

"Aye." The answer came just as softly.

"Steady now. That one looks as if it's just hanging by a thread."

"Daniel. Daniel."

Some of the men glanced upwards.

"What d'ya think, Fred? Can the Doc get down? Any use him trying?"

"Shut up a minute, will you." The voice came from the hole, and the command was followed by silence. Then the voice again. "Can't tell one way or t'other. Both legs pinned. Drop that rope an' I'll try a sling on this beam. . . ."

Daniel. Daniel.

She cried soundlessly now. The world was opening beneath her feet. Daniel, oh Daniel, don't be dead unless you take me

495

with you. The ground was heaving; it lifted her up and threw her down into the hole, and she cried to the head covered with grey plaster, "It's me, Daniel. It's Bridget. Wake up, darling. Wake up. . . ."

"Come on, dear. Wake up, wake up. Come on now, drink this. You're all right. Listen. Do you hear me, Bridget—he's alive. Daniel's alive."

"Daniel?" She blinked up into Tom's face.

"Yes, dear."

"Alive?"

"Yes, dear. His leg's crushed, but I think it's his bad one, and . . . and one arm."

Daniel alive. He was alive.

"There now. There now. Steady. They'll have them up in a minute."

Them! She had clean forgotten about Aunt Katie. "Is . . . is she dead?"

"Yes. Yes," said Tom softly. "It's to be expected."

At the sound of a broken sob Bridget turned her head and looked at Catherine sitting on the rubble by her side and she caught at her hand and held it for a moment.

As Tom assisted Bridget to her feet they brought Daniel over the rim of the hole and laid him on a stretcher. When she reached it she called out his name once more and his heavy, grey-powdered eyelids fluttered, then lifted, and there was clear recognition in his eyes as he muttered thickly, "Told you. Told you. Live for ever, Bridget."

When the ambulance door closed on the stretcher and Bridget, Catherine turned her weary gaze to the crumpled figure they were now lifting out of the hole, and she cried to herself that it wasn't right. It wasn't right that Aunt Katie should die like this. There was no dignity in this kind of death. And she had always been dignified, had Aunt Katie. She made her way to her and knelt down by her side and looked at her face. It hadn't a mark on it. It did not look dead and it did not look old. A powdering of dust that resembled a thick face powder lay on it. It looked at peace; in fact it had the look that it had worn when it was going to burst into laughter.

A voice coming from somewhere above Catherine said, "Well, that's the end of the old girl. A legend she was in her day, Katie Mulholland."

FENWICK HOUSES

Catherine Cookson

A FAMILY AFFAIR

'You can't move a step without them lads,' said one of Christine Winter's chums, and she was right. In and around the street of pitmen's cottages they called Fenwick Houses, Christine could never venture far without Ronnie, or Sam, or Don.

Even when Christine reached the age when she started to turn men's heads, their lives were inextricably bound up by custom and the close-knit ties of family circumstance. To Ronnie and Sam she was joined by a thread of harmony, but Don was the needle through which the thread was drawn, and its point was sharp and deadly. Sooner rather than later, the needle would slip, and it would draw blood . . .

FUTURA PUBLICATIONS
FICTION
0 7088 4423 5

ROONEY

Catherine Cookson

JACK THE LAD

Rooney was the only one of the dustbin gang who wasn't yet married. He was too cute to get caught, his mates would chafe him. They knew it took skill and determination to have evaded four widows and two spinsters in the past ten years.

Rooney liked his life to follow a pattern. A pint at the Anchor at dinner time; the pictures every Monday; betting on the dogs up at Horesly Hill and then Saturday rounded off back at the Anchor again. That and his independence was what made Rooney tick.

But it all went flying through the window when he moved into Ma Howlett's place. And once the rug of his comfortable old habits had been yanked out from under him, Rooney came down on the lino with an almighty bump . . .

FUTURA PUBLICATIONS
FICTION
0 7088 4429 4

MAGGIE ROWAN

Catherine Cookson

SETTING HER SIGHTS

There were plenty around Fellburn who said she was as plain as a pikestaff, but Maggie Rowan more than made up for Nature's omissions by her dogged will to succeed. They reckoned that once a miner's daughter like her tasted power, she'd be like a beggar on horseback – and ride straight to hell.

There were only two things Maggie thought she wanted from life. One was a child she could love, and the other was what was in her eyes when she asked Christopher Taggart to marry her – one of those big houses on Brampton Hill. And she meant to have them both, despite the scorn of folk who thought they knew better than she did herself what Maggie Rowan did and did not deserve . . .

FUTURA PUBLICATIONS
FICTION
0 7088 4428 6

THE BLIND MILLER

Catherine Cookson

A CUT ABOVE THE REST

Though the social gulf between their families was as wide as the Tyne, it did not stop Sarah Bradley loving David. He'd been sweet on her for years, and she thought he was the nicest man in the world.

But marrying into the Hetheringtons wasn't just a matter of forsaking a poky terrace and a bitter, bullying stepfather for a bright new home at the top end of town, where folks kept marble clocks – not Woodbines – on the mantelpiece, and ate fruit with a knife and fork.

For Mary Hetherington was a mother who dominated her menfolk, and quickly took against the girl who brought life and laughter into her dustless world. And Sarah, for her part, found that even the best people had their quarrels, and secrets they were anxious to hide.

FUTURA PUBLICATIONS
FICTION
0 7088 4384 0

All Futura Books are available at your bookshop or newsagent, or can be ordered from the following address: Futura Books, Cash Sales Department, P.O. Box 11, Falmouth, Cornwall TR10 9EN.

Please send cheque or postal order (no currency), and allow 60p for postage and packing for the first book plus 25p for the second book and 15p for each additional book ordered up to a maximum charge of £1.90 in U.K.

B.F.P.O. customers please allow 60p for the first book, 25p for the second book plus 15p per copy for the next 7 books, thereafter 9p per book.

Overseas customers including Eire please allow £1.25 for postage and packing for the first book, 75p for the second book and 28p for each subsequent title ordered.